THE
SLUMBER
PARTY

BOOKS BY SHANNON HOLLINGER

Best Friends Forever

THE SLUMBER PARTY

SHANNON HOLLINGER

bookouture

Published by Bookouture in 2023

An imprint of Storyfire Ltd.
Carmelite House
50 Victoria Embankment
London EC4Y 0DZ

www.bookouture.com

ISBN: 978-1-80314-892-2
eBook ISBN: 978-1-80314-891-5

To my parents, for giving me their unconditional love and support in all things, always.

PROLOGUE

It was supposed to be the best night of our lives.

Just moments before, we had crossed the backyard and entered the woods. The trees had held hands overhead, creating a cathedral. Moon beams filtered through the leaves, pine needles carpeted the land beneath our feet; everything was cast in a magical glow. I had looked around at all my friends and laughed, lifted my face to the stars above and screamed into the night, "We're eighteen! Whoo!"

I had closed my eyes, the gentle lull of my friends' voices a background noise that blended into the night, becoming a part of it, like the damp smell of earth and the chill that carried on the breeze. If I could have chosen one moment in my life to hit pause on and live in forever, it would have been that one. It had been perfect.

But now, just minutes later, I sit here watching one of my closest friends in the world bleed out on the ground before me, I don't want to believe it. I keep telling myself that it has to be some kind of elaborate hoax, but I know that I'm telling myself a lie. Because as I stand here, looking down at her limp body, I know she's gone.

But I can't stop staring at her, watching for some movement, some sign that I'm mistaken. I have to be wrong. This can't be happening.

I have no idea how long we stand there, frozen in shock, surrounded by the darkness. Thinking my thoughts while the scent of blood and gun powder invade my nose. The cool night air chilling my skin until I'm as cold on the outside as the inside.

Then suddenly, I realize that there's a persistent tugging on my arm, a voice saying, "We need to call someone. We need help."

Help sounds nice. But it could also be dangerous, bringing with it questions that are too hard and painful and shameful to answer. Help will want to know what happened. Help will want to know where the gun came from.

"We can't," I whisper.

And all I can think is, how did everything go so wrong? And how will I ever keep what happened here tonight a secret?

ONE

LIZ NOW

2014

I know what it means. I keep the smile frozen on my face, a mask of deceit, doing my best not to betray the fear flowing into my stomach in poisonous waves of acid. Looking through the glass windows of the sunroom to the pool beyond, I watch my daughter, Olivia, laugh with her friends.

Enjoy it while it lasts. The thought comes from an unwelcomed corner of my mind, a dark little recess where I've erected a barricade of barbed wire and electricity between the secrets kept there and my daughter. I feel my smile falter, break for just one second, then it's back, as strong and bright, as fake as before.

"Wow, Liz, I would have thought you'd have known already. I mean, you two were so close in school."

"Honestly, I had no idea. I haven't heard from her in years."

"That's just so weird. I mean, you guys were close. Like, close, close. All four of you were, but I thought you and her especially." Francine has found a scab and she can't resist picking at it.

I turn to her, making sure the smile is in my eyes, too,

because that's how you properly fake it. *Francine, you over-weight, troublemaking busybody. You always wanted to be one of us, but you never stood a chance. You were too annoying, and you and I both know that the only reason we're in the same room right now is because our daughters are friends.* It's probably not the best thing to say, so I give a little laugh instead.

"You're right. We were close. It's funny, you know? When you're their age," I nod toward the girls, "you think that's the way it's always going to be. Best friends forever. But then you grow up and you're out of school, getting married, having kids, and it just gets harder and harder to keep in touch. Before you know it, suddenly your BFF is a stranger, and you hear she's back in town from someone else."

This explanation seems to satisfy our third companion. Barb is an older mom. She's sitting to my right, having a cocktail while watching her change-of-life baby splash around with my daughter.

Barb already had kids when Francine and I were in high school. She doesn't care about the details of our teen years. The only thing the old prune cares about right now is pickling herself with the mommy juice in her glass. I give a wistful little shrug and hope Francine takes the hint.

"Nah, I don't buy that." Francine leans forward, staring at me with beady little eyes placed too closely together on her puffy, pink face. "I mean, the four of you were inseparable from, like, the first grade. Something must have happened. So, what was it?"

I turn toward her, eyebrows raised, my nose slightly wrinkled like she's a rotten piece of meat, and stare at this woman who seems so sure she knows about my past. Until two years ago, when I suffered the misfortune of having her move in next door, with a daughter in the same grade as my own, we had barely spoken a word. Waverly, Massachusetts, isn't a tiny town, we're too close to Boston for that, but with its neatly planned neighborhoods, a community so close-knit because no one ever leaves, it has a distinctive small-world feel at times. Sometimes too small.

"Nothing happened, Francine. We grew up and we went in different directions. That's all."

"Hmph. Well, I guess. If you say so."

Raising my margarita to my lips, I take my time, filling my mouth with tart lime juice and tequila. Setting the drink down, I watch the condensation bead up where I touched the glass, until my finger marks are erased. Then I fix the fake smile back on my face and answer.

"I do."

"Do you ever hear from the other one? The one who moved to L.A. to be a star?"

"She sends postcards from time to time."

"Oh, yeah? Where'd she end up?"

I lick my lips, thinking carefully before I say, "The last one was sent from Taiwan."

Laughter carries over from the pool, light, airy peals from fairy bells. I look at the girls, high school freshmen just reaching the age in life when everything starts to become real. My daughter, Olivia, pushes herself up onto the edge, her golden hair catching the light, white teeth flashing like silver fish scales in the sun. Her smile is real. That, I tell myself, is all that matters.

Turning to Barb, I ask, "How's your drink holding out?"

She gives me a wink, raises her glass and chugs until the contents are gone, then hands me the empty cup. "I could use a refill, if you don't mind."

"Not at all." Standing, I pointedly ignore Francine. "If you'll excuse me, ladies, I'll go make us another round." I carry the empty glasses into the kitchen and set them on the counter. Then I check to make sure I haven't been followed before walking down the hall. Entering my bedroom, I lock the door behind me. I leave the lights off, let myself crumple to the floor, my back leaning against the side of the bed.

I close my eyes, and, right there, directly behind my eyelids, the memory is waiting, an image of the four of us. We were the girls that everyone knew as a unit. An inseparable foursome of friendship. Amy, Mo, Sami, and me.

As Sami used to say, our friendship was of that magical ilk found in fairy tales and storybooks. Francine was right. We'd had that *friends-'til-the-end* relationship. But that end had come. Some things are best left in the past. Some secrets are meant to be forgotten.

I reach up to the nightstand and grab the phone off its base. Sami has lived in the same split-level ranch house just a few miles away since she moved back after college a decade ago. I haven't talked to her since she left five years before that. But I know her number. I looked it up once, after I heard she had returned.

I dial it now by memory, my fingers pushing the buttons like they're following a pattern they've pressed every single day, because in my heart, they have. The phone rings, once, twice, then the ringing stops and I hear the vibrant tones of violins in the background, the teasing, sweet, cheery notes of Vivaldi.

"Hello?"

After all this time, after all these years, I should probably tell her who the voice on the other end of the line is, but I know I don't have to. What I say will tell her everything she needs to know. Taking a deep breath, I find my voice and say the two words I'd hoped I'd never have to say.

"She's back."

Sami and I met on the playground when we were four years old. My mom, as the mother of five, of which I was the youngest and the only girl, used her parental experience to sway Sami's mom, mother of an only child, to relax her hawk's eye and, "Let the girls play," while they chatted.

Sami's mom would talk about her college days and career and what it was like having her first child at thirty-five. My mom would talk about marrying her high school sweetheart at eighteen, the wild hijinks of raising a bunch of rowdy children born over a span of twelve years, and how much easier it was now that she was older and had a little girl. While they talked, Sami and I would work on the hole we were digging to China.

Our moms became friends, so we became friends. I'd like to think that we still would have found and chosen each other somehow, but it's one of those *what ifs* that I'll never know the answer to. Some of my earliest memories are of Sami. Some of my best memories are of her, too.

I listen to the sounds on Sami's end of the line. Her earring brushes against the phone. The music shuts off. She swallows hard.

"Did you see her?"

"No. Not yet. Someone told me."

"Okay. Well... thanks."

There's so much I want to say. So many things I want to tell her. I have no idea where to begin, what words to use to break the silence that clots so thickly between us like spoiled milk.

"Listen, Sami."

But it's too late. I've waited too long, and my words are spoken to a dial tone. Pulling myself to my feet, I put the phone back on its base and take a deep breath. The fake smile back on my face, I unlock the door and head back to the kitchen to see to my guests.

TWO

SAMI NOW

2014

I stare at the phone, wishing I hadn't answered it. It's not like I didn't know better. When it rang, I knew it had to be bad news. Nobody calls me on my landline anymore besides telemarketers. Actually, no one calls me anymore, period.

But, at the same time, answering that call was exactly what I needed. Because hearing Liz's voice just now? It turned on the tap, and now an endless stream of memories flow through me, making me remember what it was like when my phone did ring. A time when I was blanketed by laughter and companionship, instead of solitude and loneliness.

There's something about the friendships you develop when you're younger, something that's impossible to replicate as an adult. Maybe it's the lack of responsibilities as a child that free you up to focus on your friends and make them your priority. Or maybe it has to do with how easy it is to trust when you're a kid, before life has beaten you down and reality has shown you how foolish that is.

Either way, I can't deny that the years I was friends with Liz and Mo and Amy were the best of my life. I would do anything to go back. To have them be a part of my life again. To have our friendship the way it was.

Only, they weren't just friends, were they? They were part of me, and their loss has left me reeling all these years, like I've been missing pieces of myself. Their presence feels like the itch of a phantom limb.

We would have done anything for each other. We *did* do anything for each other. Even when we shouldn't have. Even when the consequences were deadly.

THREE

SAMI THEN

1995

It's the first day of high school. My mom woke me up super early because she was nervous and wanted to make sure I had plenty of time to get ready. I should probably be nervous too, but I'm not. Instead, I'm sitting on my bed, reading. Perfectly relaxed.

The house is silent in the way that only single-kid households can be. Add another kid to the mix, and things get shaken up. Subtract the kid and the adults will talk to each other in the intimate, open way of the unobserved.

But just one kid in the equation and you get utter, complete silence. Not always, of course, and especially not when my friends come over, but in the early morning hours before school, when most homes are in a state of chaos trying to get the kids out the door, all is peaceful here.

Which is why I can hear my mom's footsteps as she paces in the hall outside my bedroom. Finally, she works up the nerve to disturb the peace, tapping against the door before sticking her head into my room. "Hi, honey. All set?"

I look up from my book. "Mm-hmm."

"First day of high school. It's kind of a big deal."

"I guess."

"Are you nervous?"

"No."

"Really?"

"Yeah, why?"

"I was terrified my first day of high school." My mom was an only child, too. She was a shy, quiet bookworm like me, an introvert who didn't easily open up and make friends. But I don't have to worry about that. I already have friends—best friends.

She sits on the edge of my bed and takes my hand, the one not holding the book. "I'm not trying to worry you. But it's okay if you're a little scared."

I smile. "I'm not, Mom. I've got Liz and Mo and Amy. Everything is going to be fine."

She gives my fingers a squeeze. "You're right. I never had friends like that when I was growing up. You're lucky."

"I know."

She stands. "Well, we should probably get going."

I look at my watch. If we leave now, I'll be almost a half hour early. If I don't leave now, the remnants of my mom's nervous tension from her own adolescence will eat us both alive. Slipping the novel into my backpack, I heave the bag over my shoulder and join her at the door. "Let's go then."

"Oh, gosh." My mom looks at the time. "Do you want to stop anywhere on the way? Dunkin's, maybe?"

"No, that's okay."

"But you'll be so early!"

"Mom." I smile, doing my best to let her know that everything is all right. "It's okay. Let's go. It'll be fine if I'm early."

I can literally see the *but* on her lips, the wonder and amazement. How can her daughter, so like her, be spared the agony and dread of the first day of high school? I let her keep holding my hand as we walk to the car. I wish I could tell her what it's like, how it feels, but I don't have the words. The closest I can come is untouchable.

The other kids don't have to like me. They don't have to be nice to me. But they can't be cruel to me, either, not without consequences, because of my friends. Because I am a member of a group with such a tight bond that our allegiance to each other is unquestionable. And everyone else is disposable.

I have gym class first period, which is a most unfortunate thing. Who wants to get all dirty and sweaty at the beginning of the day, and then have to spend the next six periods like that? Yeah, there are a few showers in the locker room, but no one uses them.

I don't think girls have taken showers after gym classes since, like, the 1970s, when that movie *Carrie* came out. There isn't enough time, anyway, even if you wanted to try. The three minutes coach gives us to change from our gym clothes before the bell rings results in a mad dash that produces more sweat than the class itself did.

As if this wasn't a bad enough way to start freshman year, all the other girls in the class are part of the *It* clique. The group that somehow, despite their slightly different hair colors and features, manages to look like clones of each other in their stylish clothes and overdone makeup. I'm sure that as soon as tryouts are open, they'll all become cheerleaders with notes excusing them from participating in gym class, leaving me the only girl in a gym full of freshman boys.

Then again, that may be a good thing. Not that I want to be alone with the boys. There are no *It* boys in the class, just gamers and Trekkies and booger eaters, but the way those girls are all clustered together, watching me like I'm a dying cockroach limping across the floor, well, I'm not looking forward to a year of their audience. Tugging my gym shirt over my head, I fold it and place it on the shelf for tomorrow.

"Hey, Sam. You're in the wrong locker room, you know that, right?"

It takes me a couple of seconds to realize that they're talking to me. I manage to choke out a "Huh?" and then feel my cheeks burn.

"You're supposed to be in the other locker room. The one next door."

"The boys' locker room?"

"Well, yeah." Tami Potter is advancing on me, her coven of minions at her heels. "*Sam.*"

"It's Sami."

"*It's Sami,*" she mimics in a falsetto. "Yeah, and it's obviously a boy. I mean, there's not even anything for that little play bra to train."

Her friends titter in the background. I glance down at my chest, or lack thereof.

"That is, like, the flattest chest I've ever seen. There's no way that you're possibly a girl. So why don't you go back to the right locker room, pervert. We're not going to change in front of you. We're, like, girls, with like, boobs, and I, for one, am not interested in putting on a show for some weirdo."

Pulling my shirt on, I grab my book bag and run from the locker room before the tears in my eyes well over. Laughter stalks behind me, chasing me down the hall as I hurry toward the English wing for my next class. A sob escapes my lips as the bell rings.

Suddenly, I'm adrift in a sea of bodies, carried along the current. Fighting my way to the edge, I fling myself from the throng and through the classroom door. Amy is already there, saving a seat for me. The sight of her friendly face, her warm smile, is enough to break me. Tossing myself into the desk behind her, I hang my head low and wipe my tears.

"She did what?"

I hear Mo's voice before I see her. Rounding the corner, I find my friends clustered by the door to the cafeteria. The guilt on Amy's face gives her away. She's told the others, even though she promised not to.

But Mo hasn't noticed me yet. She's too busy scanning the faces among the rows of tables in the room. "Do you know if she has this lunch period?"

"Hi, Sami." Liz gives me the smile she always wears to awkward situations.

Mo spins, searches my face for a moment, and then says, "That bitch is going down."

"Mo, don't. Please. It's the first day of school. I don't want any trouble."

"And I'm gonna make damned sure that you aren't given any."

"I can fight my own battles."

"Can you?"

Her words sting me, sharp, hot pokers burning from all sides, like I'm in a hornet's nest.

"Sami, I'm sorry." Mo reaches for my hand, squeezing it in her own. "It just pisses me off. I mean, it's not fair. I know that you can take care of yourself, but it's not a fair fight when it's ten on one. Someone needs to teach that witch and her gaggle of flying monkeys a lesson."

Amy giggles. I snort. Liz asks, "Gaggle?"

"It's a word."

"I know. It's a pretty funny word."

"Yeah, well it's going to look even funnier when it's stamped across Tami Potter's forehead."

———

It's seventh period. The day is almost over. I've been doing my best to keep a low profile. I duck into the world civilizations classroom and take a seat in the corner, under an antique-looking map. I'm turned in my seat, studying the chart behind me, fascinated by the Viking ship and the kraken drawn in the Atlantic, when I hear:

"Oh my God, no way."

"For real."

"Really? On purpose?"

"Well, she didn't act like she was sorry about it. Lisa, did you hear?"

"Hear what?"

"Morgana Ripley turned on one of the gas burners in the chemistry lab and lit Tami Potter's boob on fire."

"What?"

"Yeah. Tami's lucky her bra had so much padding."

"So what happened to her?"

"Well, so, Mr. Patterson started writing Morgana up, to send her to the principal's office and she's, like, standing next to his desk at the front of the room and she tells Tami, like, in front of the whole class, that she just did her a huge favor because now Tami could sue her parents and use the money to buy herself a pair of tits, which would, like, definitely improve her future career as a stripper, which, like, everyone knows she's gonna be."

"No way!"

"Uh-uh."

"Well, Tami should have expected something like that to happen. Did you hear what she did to Sami in first period?"

"Oh, I know, Tami totally deserved it after that."

"You're just saying that because you feel Sami's pain."

"Are you calling me flat?"

"No, I'm just saying your bra would have left even more ashes behind than Tami's."

"Bitch!"

"Well, I don't feel bad for Tami at all. It was her own stupidity. I mean, everyone knows better than to mess with one of them. They get, like, crazy. Completely insane. Or has everyone forgotten about Timmy Mitchell's original nose?"

"Oh, God. Who could forget that honker? If you ask me, that was the real favor. He looks *so* much better with the nose he has now."

I feel myself sink lower in my seat, trying to disappear behind the book bag on my desk. Timmy Mitchell was my fault. Tami suffered at Mo's hands. How many other kids have been hurt over the years because they had messed with one of us, and was avenged by another?

It doesn't seem healthy. Correction. Setting someone on fire is just plain psycho. How did Mo even know Tami's bra was padded? Although, now that it's done already, and no one got hurt, I have to admit that I would've loved to see the look on Tami's face as her boobs went up in smoke.

FOUR

LIZ NOW

2014

When I step outside in the morning, and see the piece of paper slipped under my wiper blade, a tremor of unease ripples through me, though I'm not sure why. I linger on the doorstep and scan the street, searching my neighbors' cars, but their windshields are empty. Whatever this is, it's intended for me only. And that worries me.

I cross the yard reluctantly, stop beside my car, and stare down at the folded white letter. I don't want to touch it, but I can't very well drive with it still there. Reaching forward with two fingers, I try to minimize my contact with it as I tug it free by a corner, like it's a piece of toilet paper stuck to the bottom of my shoe.

Snapping my wrist, the page unfurls. My hand trembles as I read the handwritten note.

I'm back.

XXO ∞

A wave of dizziness crashes over me. I lean against the car and look around, checking to see if anyone's around. I don't see a soul, but I know she's out there, watching. She must be. She's the only one I've ever known to sign a note like that.

It's too much of a coincidence.

Yesterday, Francine told me that Mo was back in town. Today, I get a note.

A lump lodges in my throat. My breath catches in my chest. The grief hits just as hard as it did fifteen years ago, the memory just as raw and tender and painful as it ever was. And so is the fear.

Sami and I met Amy and Mo at the same park that we met each other. It had become a regular thing, our moms coordinating visits to the park for playdates. They'd meet each other there several times a week. By the time Sami and I started preschool, we were joined at the hip.

It happened maybe a week after our kindergarten class started. Sami and I were playing at the park. We had abandoned the hole to China, and were now obsessed with guarding our fort, a little wooden platform on stilts, with a ladder on one side and a slide on the other.

I had my arms stretched across the opening above the ladder, refusing entrance to a little boy with a green slug of snot oozing out his nose, when the shouting started. My mom was the first one on her feet, the first to reach the commotion, although I think every other adult and child at the park was crowding around behind her within thirty seconds.

"No! I don't know you. Let. Me. Go!"

My mom put one hand on the adult, a woman with skin so fair she appeared almost translucent, and another on the little girl's shoulder. I recognized her from school. A quiet kid who sat in the back corner of the classroom, under the happy thought board. Looking down at my classmate, my mom asked, "Honey, do you need help?"

"I'm sorry, ma'am." The woman's accent was thick, foreign. "I am the girl's nanny. I don't think she likes me."

"Is that true, honey?"

"No!"

Sami gripped my arm, her hand clammy against my skin. I sensed her interest in our classmate and I felt an instant rush of jealousy. I was overcome with possessiveness. She was my Sami. She was even called Sami because I couldn't say Samantha when we met.

"Morgan, please. Come with me."

And then there were two. An almost exact replica of the first girl appeared at the side of the nanny. Although, as I stared at them both, studying them as they stood so close to each other, I could see small variations. One had fuller cheeks, the other a sharper nose. One wore her hair longer, the other had bangs. But besides a few minor differences, they were practically a mirror image of each other.

The new girl tugged at the woman's coat, stamping her little foot up and down as she said, "It's *Morg-ah-nah*. Say it right!"

I sensed that the adults were shocked, but at the time I thought it was because of the sassy little girl who dared stomp her foot and yell at a grown-up. I felt drawn to her immediately, this naughty child with attitude, and I distinctly remember thinking, *Good, there's two of them, one for me and one for Sami*, like they would be our pets or something.

I don't remember how the situation was sorted out. I've been told that Amy's dad's girlfriend of the moment, who had brought her to the park but forgot to watch her, finally realized what was happening and came forward. That Mo's nanny was replaced soon after. And that the two nearly identical cousins, who previously knew nothing of each other, were introduced.

What I do remember is thinking that it was completely unfair that Sami's girl went to school with us, and mine did not. But by the end of that school year, after enough foot stomping and wheedling, Mo's parents took her out of the fancy private school she was in and let her start the first grade with us.

If I knew then what I do now, would I still have pursued that little girl and made her my friend? Or would I have avoided her like the plague, pretended she didn't exist? My head answers one way, my heart another.

I ball up the note in my hand, shove it into my pocket as my daughter barrels out of the house toward the car. I pin a smile on my face and pretend that nothing's wrong as I climb behind the wheel. I'm going to have to deal with this. I'm going to have to figure out what to do. What she wants. But I'm not sure I'm going to be able to give it to her.

Because everything's changed. I'm a mother now, and that trumps everything. Sorrow. Regret. Fear. Even friendship. Even one you thought would last forever.

FIVE

LIZ THEN

1996

"Did you see what Rachel Patton was wearing today?" Mo leads the way into the kitchen, tossing her book bag onto the quartz-topped island. "I mean, what the hell *was* that?" She shakes her onyx hair loose from its ponytail and pulls the refrigerator open.

"I think it was some kind of onesie," I say, dropping my bag next to Mo's.

Sami snorts.

"Ha. You're right. It was a onesie." Mo's muffled voice comes from inside the refrigerator. "Jeez, my stupid parents spend fifty grand on a remodel for a kitchen that never has any food in it. I'm ordering pizza."

Turning, she bounces off Amy, who reaches past her to pull out a carton of juice, and for an instant the two cousins reflect each other, a near mirror image. The resemblance never fails to shock me.

"I think it's called a romper. Or a jumpsuit." Amy's voice is softer than her cousin's, more lyrical.

"Well, whatever it's called, she ought to be arrested, because I'm pretty sure it was criminal to make us look at it."

"Please." Amy rolls her eyes. "You just wish you'd worn it first, so you'd have gotten all the attention." The softness of her tone does little to curb the edge of its bite.

"Excuse me? I don't have to commit fashion crimes against humanity for that."

Sami squeezes between them and grabs four crystal glasses from behind a dark wood cabinet and passes them to me. I put them on the counter for Amy. The conversation ceases for a moment, Mo flashing Amy a dirty look before calling to order the pizza. It's our new weekend ritual, flocking to Mo's empty, oversized house where everything is extravagant and overdone.

Not one of us would ever mention how it would be easier to go to Sami's house, where her mother fusses over us, or my house, which is overflowing with food and boys. It seems cruel, somehow, the imbalance of things. Amy fills the glasses and puts the juice back in the fridge. Mo hangs up the phone.

"Fifty minutes." Her eyes narrow and she huffs out a sigh. "I forgot it was Friday."

She catches my expression. None of us forgets when it's Friday. Ever. We spend all week looking forward to the weekend. Mo spends the entire week looking forward to the company.

"Okay, so I forgot about how impossible it is to get a pizza on a Friday." Mo grins. "Well, what are we waiting for? Let's get this party started."

We head into the living room, leaving a trail of teenage girl debris in our wake, an extravagant mess of sweatshirts, socks, and shoes. Sami and I sprawl across the ivory leather couches while Mo grabs a remote and turns on some music.

Amy perches on the end of a cushion, stiff and self-conscious, like she's sitting on top of an egg she's trying not to crush. She always looks so out of place here, nowhere else *but* here. Watching her, I can't help but wonder what I always wonder—if she's bitter at being dealt the worst hand out of all of us. Amy is a member of the Van Cline lineage, like Mo. A family of super-rich romantics that give their daughters names like Charamy and Morgana, or Vivienne, like Amy's mom.

Only, Vivienne's romantic notions extended beyond names to actual love. She turned her back on her family and fortune to marry the quintessential forbidden poor guy from the wrong side of the tracks. Then she died and left Amy alone with a man who was both broke and broken. A wealth like this could have been Amy's. Instead, the only things she really has in common with her cousin are a solitary home life and her stunning features.

Still... even though we'd never say it in front of Amy, none of us could blame her mom. Her dad is gorgeous. His name is Sonny. You can't get much less Van Cline than that. But he's tall and has broad shoulders and muscled arms with veins popping out, dark, dark hair and eyes the most incredible shade of green, so green that they seem inhuman, like a cat. You look at him and you think, *only a cat could have eyes that green.*

A pillow bounces off my head, knocking me out of my thoughts. I retrieve it from the floor before I stick my tongue out at Mo, because the damn thing probably costs a few hundred dollars. As soon as she blinks, I launch it back at her. The atmosphere is festive, like a holiday, which for us it kind of is. Not just because it's the weekend, though. It's because of what we do during the weekend.

———

We first discovered the little stone hut in the woods behind Mo's house when we were eight. It was completely round, like an igloo, with rocks layered in rings to form a corbeled dome roof. It would be years before we'd have a name to put to the structure, but we were eight, we didn't need anyone to tell us what to call it.

To us, it was our castle, our lair, our clubhouse, our magical fortress where we were safe from harm and the disapproval of adults. Over the years, we've never tired of the place, seeming instead to grow even more enchanted by it.

Last year, Mo's parents decided that, since she was finally in high school, she didn't need them to pay for a nanny to watch her anymore. She hadn't really needed the supervision for years. It was the company she craved.

Left on her own in the huge house with its cold corridors, she wasn't our Mo anymore. She changed, became withdrawn and sullen, and we knew it wasn't just a mood swing. It was depression.

Not that any of us could blame her. Sure, as teenagers we think about how great it would be to not have an adult peering over our shoulders all the time, that it would be nice to be left alone, but not like that. Not the total isolation that Mo was faced with. That's when we started spending the weekends at her place.

Until then, we had always had slumber parties at either my house or Sami's. None of us ever liked sleeping over at Mo's. Hanging out and parties, yes, but something about the hollowness of the halls, the chills and drafts and noises, made it an impossible place to sleep. It was like a creepy Victorian mansion from a horror story, where the ghosts would come to collect your soul if they found you there after dark.

But Mo needed us. She needed our warmth to cheer the place and give the empty corners life. She needed the memories of our weekend shenanigans to keep her company during the long, lonely week. So, we compromised. We spent our weekends at Mo's. And we sleep in our little stone igloo hidden in the woods out back.

That night, it isn't the moonlight that wakes me, though it filters in through the cracks in the stone, a light so strong and white and pure that the entire room is cast in its glow. The forms of my sleeping friends are lit with this ghostly luminescence. I listen to the sounds outside, the soft scratching of a tree branch against the outer wall, the wind rushing through the leaves, the hoot of an owl, soft and hesitant through the bright night air. It isn't a noise that has woken me, either.

Sitting up, hugging my knees to my chest, I look at my friends around me. To my right, Mo is sprawled on her back, mouth open and slack, dark hair pooled in a crown over her head. Next to her, Amy is curled into a ball, her teal sleeping bag pulled up tight under her chin. On my left, Sami is on her stomach, face hidden under mounds of auburn hair.

This is my favorite part of the weekend stretch, these early morning hours when the others are sleeping. It gives me time to reflect, to enjoy the feeling of togetherness without being distracted by words or actions. I take one last look around, tune into the soft, sleeping sighs, and take a deep breath of the sweetened air before I scoot down and settle in to go back to sleep. I know that one day, this is what I'm going to miss the most.

SIX

LIZ NOW

2014

Although it's after eleven when my husband comes home, he's earlier than usual. I'm in the living room, sitting on the couch in the dark, thinking. David comes in and flicks the lights on.

"Jesus Christ, Liz. You scared me half to death."

He stares at me with his bright, cerulean blue eyes from across the room, making no attempt to close the distance between us. It's been years since he's considered me worthy of that much effort.

"What are you doing?"

There is no concern in his tone. It's a question of annoyance. *What are you doing, sitting in the dark like some kind of weirdo? What if the neighbors see you? What would they think? Is this another one of your desperate cries for attention? Jesus, Liz, what the hell is wrong with you?*

I know he doesn't want an answer. He just wants me to move, to leave and go to bed so he can tinker around the house until I'm asleep and it's safe for him to join me. So I give him what he wants.

Wordlessly, I stand and cross the room. When I pause across from him in the doorway, he flattens himself back against the wall. I am a contagious disease, and even after fifteen years of marriage, he fears infection.

I shake my head as I continue past him. Walking down the hall, I enter the room we share, the last vestige of normalcy we maintain solely for Olivia's sake. I hear the relief in his sigh as I'm closing the door.

The sheets are hot beneath me, damp with sweat. My mind has been in overdrive all day. My gears are spinning so fast that I'm producing heat like a furnace. I flip my pillow over, trying to find a bit of coolness.

The sounds David makes in the kitchen fill the darkness around me. A cabinet thudding shut, the high-suction pull of the refrigerator as it opens, a piece of stoneware clanging as it's set on the counter. Even though I'm roasting alive, I pull the covers over my ears to help drown the sounds out.

Olivia was already born by the time I realized that I was a million times lonelier with David right beside me than when he was away. My husband is like a vacuum. He sucks the air right out of me. Drains the oxygen right out of the room and lets the wind out of my sails. He makes my world uninhabitable. It's a horrible feeling, knowing that you made a mistake, that you're responsible for your own unhappiness.

I'd like to think that there was a time when I loved David, and when he loved me, but the truth is, I'm not too sure there ever was. We were teenagers. It was easy to get caught up in each other, and I needed someone so badly after what happened, needed love and companionship and someone to chase the shadows away when the lights got turned off at night. David was there, so I clung onto him like a life preserver, which is exactly what he was, and I'll always be grateful to him for that.

But really, it was the baby. That's why he's here. That's why we're married. The only reason. Despite two years of dating in high school, I'm sure we would have gone our separate ways if it hadn't been for one careless, drunken mistake.

We'd been together two years and had always played it safe. If it hadn't been for prom night... well, everything would have turned out differently if prom night hadn't happened. Everything.

I might not have my husband, but I would have my friends, instead. All of them.

But prom night did happen, and now here I am, in a marriage where both parties are miserable, and even though I know I should just call it quits—and if I'm honest, I knew that even before Olivia was born—I'm still too scared to do it alone. Terrified, really.

Especially now that she's back.

Although, I probably would have found the strength to brave life as a single mother if I'd had to. The courage to step out of the comfort of my home, to face the menial jobs that I imagine would be available to me, a high school graduate with no work experience. But I've never been forced to make that decision. David's always been there for me and Olivia, and I'm grateful that he's in our lives—even if it means making certain sacrifices.

My daughter is my everything—my heart, my soul, my reason to wake up and breathe every morning. I would do anything for her. Even sleep beside a man who doesn't want me.

I've often wondered how Olivia would feel if I left her father. A part of me thinks that I would be setting a better example for her if I did. That I would be showing her how to be a strong, independent woman.

The problem with that is, I'm not strong. Or independent. I never have been. I've always needed someone to lean on, to hold my hand during the scary parts. And now that she's back, the scary parts are back, too.

SEVEN

FRANCINE NOW

2014

"Mo?" She hurries to catch up with the other woman, her flip-flops sliding noisily across the sidewalk as she shuffles. "Morgana Ripley, is that you? Hey, Mo, wait up!"

The woman turns toward her with an irritated expression, her lip rising in a sneer as she looks Francine up and down. Francine doesn't notice, is too excited to have spotted the elusive socialite. "I thought it was you," she pants, struggling to catch her breath.

"I'm sorry. Do we know each other?"

"It's me. Francine. You know? From high school?"

Her ice blue eyes narrow as she gives Francine a closer inspection. "We went to school together?"

"Well, yeah. You, and me, and your cousin, Amy, and Sami and Liz. You're going to think this is hilarious, but I actually live right next door to Liz now. Our daughters are besties, just like you two used to be."

"Is that so?" Her expression softens as she takes a step

closer. "I think I do remember you now. We had that class together, didn't we?"

"English? We had that together sophomore and junior year. Or did you mean algebra? Or Spanish?"

"That's right! Wow, I haven't seen you in forever." Cupping a hand around Francine's elbow, she says, "We should definitely catch up. Are you busy right now? Let me buy you a cup of coffee."

Francine grins so widely her eyes almost disappear behind her cheeks. "Really?"

"Well, of course. It's not every day I get a chance to catch up with an old friend."

"That would be awesome. Just wait until I tell Liz."

"Actually, I'd rather you didn't."

Francine frowns, her lower lip jutting out with disappointment.

"It's just that I've been so busy, I haven't had a chance to give her a call yet. You know how it is, I'm sure."

"Oh, yeah. Sure."

"I wouldn't want her to get her feelings hurt. And it's been so long since we've seen each other. I want to plan something special. Like, truly memorable. And you know what? I actually just had the best idea. Maybe you could help me plan something? A surprise for Liz?"

"Oh my God. I'd love too!"

She stifles a wince as Francine squeals. "Fantastic! Come on then. Let's grab that coffee. I can't wait to hear about what you've been up to all these years."

Francine chatters happily as they walk toward the shop on the corner, not noticing as her companion glances around them, making sure that they're not being watched.

EIGHT

SAMI THEN

1997

Outside, the night is cold, an arctic chill making the leaves that still cling to their branches heavy and still. You'd never know that it wasn't summer from inside the clochán, though. The stones seem to hold the warmth of our bodies as we lounge on top of our sleeping bags, eating potato chips and cookies.

"Daryl Halwell tried to kiss me today." Amy makes the statement in the same nonchalant tone she would use if she were telling us about what she had for lunch.

"What? Ew. Isn't he the one who smells like he's taken a bath in a vat of egg salad?" Mo asks, even though this is a fact she knows is true. "How?"

Amy nods. "Yep. We were working on painting the same scrim today, and I guess he thought I was breathless from lust and not lack of fresh air. He walked up and stood next to me, and just stared until I looked at him and when I did, he leaned in and made this duck face and tried to peck me with his beak."

"Ha, are you jealous, Liz?" I can't resist.

"What do you mean?"

"Wasn't he your first kiss? You thought you had ruined him for the rest of womankind and now his heart belongs to another."

"Oh, you're just gross. That *so* doesn't count as my first kiss."

"Doesn't it?"

"No. For one, it was kindergarten, and two, it was nap time. I was sleeping and I woke up to his duckbill in my face. Only consensual smooches count toward a first kiss. *And*, if you want to talk about *smell*, could you please put your socks back on?"

I look down guiltily at my feet. "What? They don't really?"

"Yeah, they do." Mo waves her hand in front of her face.

"But it's hot in here."

Liz grabs her throat and makes choking noises. I roll my eyes but pull my socks back on anyway. "You better watch out, make sure Daryl isn't around. That sounds like a duck's mating call to me. Or are you *trying* to recapture his heart?"

Liz throws her pillow at me. It bounces off my head. I catch it and, grinning, use it to prop up my feet.

"Ugh. Now I'm going to have to burn it." She tugs it back into her possession and gives it a tentative sniff. "Who was your first kiss?"

"Who? Mine?"

"Yeah." She looks around to see if Amy or Mo will answer. "Why don't I know this?"

"Well, maybe I never told you. Who was yours? The real one, I mean?"

"How can we possibly not know this about each other?" Liz asks. "I know Amy's was Doug Kirkland, but you and Mo's?"

"No it wasn't," Amy says. "Doug was my second kiss."

"Then who was your first?" I ask.

"You first."

"Fine," I say, pulling myself forward onto my knees. "We'll all take turns, but if we're doing this, we're doing it right. Name, place, and how old you were. Mine was that kid Joe we met at the pool the summer we were thirteen, behind the snack stand. Remember the one who was visiting his grandmother and had that crappy little homemade tattoo he'd done with pen ink or something?"

We all nod.

"Oh, yeah. I remember him. What was that thing of, anyway? Wasn't it a cross?" Amy asks.

"It was supposed to be a J. For his name."

"Who would have guessed that you'd go for the bad boy," she teases.

"Okay, then. Who was yours, Amy?"

"Eddie Montenegro. We were waiting for the bus, in like, sixth grade, only it was the day that old lady ran the stop sign and hit it and they had to send another one out, so it was like an hour late. Well, he got bored, I guess, so he kissed me."

"He was cute. Whatever happened to him?"

"His parents got divorced and he moved to another state. What about you, Liz? Who was yours?"

Her cheeks redden. She stares down at her hands, spinning the bracelet around her wrist.

"Come on, Liz," I prod.

She raises her eyes slowly, reluctantly, to meet my mine. Her voice is soft as she says, "Mine was that guy Joe, too."

"What?" I hope they can't tell the genuine upset behind my shriek. "Was it the day that little kid crapped in the pool, and we had to wait three hours until the chemical shock wore off so we could go back in?"

"Yeah, how'd you know?"

"Because when he kissed me he tasted like that vanilla lip gloss you always used to wear, and I remember wondering if he had put on some kind of ChapStick or something."

"So he kissed me first, then." She smirks. "I guess that made me his first choice."

"Or his practice," I say.

Amy and Mo are snickering.

I round on them, half snarling. "Who was yours, Mo?"

The smile drops from her face. "It doesn't matter."

"Come on, Mo. It's only fair. Spill." Liz leans toward her like she's preparing to hear something juicy. Mo remains stone-faced.

"Wasn't it Danny Tremont?" Amy asks.

"Yes."

"No it wasn't." Liz shakes her head, trying to clear the confusion. "Danny kissed you, you didn't kiss him back, and that wasn't until eighth grade. By then Gil Tuckerman and Ron Smith had thrown kisses at you already. So who was it? What are you hiding?"

Mo looks like she's been burned by Liz's words. The color is gone from her face. "I'm not hiding anything. I just don't want to do this. It's private." She stands and walks out of the hut leaving us staring, open-mouthed, behind her.

NINE

LIZ NOW

2014

I gape in horror at the TV. A moment ago, I'd been passing through the living room with a hamper of dirty laundry, wondering how I was going to get the marinara sauce stain out of Olivia's favorite wool sweater, when I happened to glance at the screen on my way by. What I saw froze me in place, the clothes slipping from my grasp and tumbling to the floor.

I'd caught the broadcast in the middle, missing the news-caster's lead-in to the story, but I didn't need her to tell me the details to know what was going on. I'd recognize those ornate iron gates anywhere, penning in the small-scale replica of the Fountain of Trevi in front of the towering house. Ripley Manor.

And the uniformed police officers milling about with people in white disposable suits behind a line of crime scene tape can only mean one thing. They've found the body.

Is this why she's back?

I sink onto the couch, legs suddenly weak and numb. Raising my fist to my mouth, I bite my knuckles to keep from screaming. I always knew there was a chance this could happen. But I never believed it would.

We were the only ones who knew where our secret was buried. She was never supposed to let the house be sold. So what changed?

The note I found under my windshield wiper flashes to mind. It had to have been from her. But why? What's she up to? Maybe she's lost it.

But maybe I'm wrong. Maybe the body was discovered by accident. She has just as much to lose as the rest of us. But as an image of my daughter's face pops into my mind, I realize she doesn't, not really. I have the most to lose. And I'll be damned if I'm going to give it up.

The story ends and I grab the remote, intending to see if I can't use the rewind function, watch it from the start to see if I'd missed anything important, when I notice the time. Olivia's just about to get out of school. If I hurry, I can make it in time to pick her up.

I have a ton of chores left to do, errands to run, and though I'd usually just let her take the bus instead of dragging her along with me, I can't stomach the thought of it, my daughter coming home to an empty house. Being left alone for hours. Not today. Not while *she's* out there, somewhere, up to God knows what.

My mind is made in an instant. I hop up, run to the kitchen to grab my phone and my purse, fire off a quick text to Olivia to let her know I'll be picking her up. I know I won't be able to keep an eye on her indefinitely, but I'll worry about that later. Right now, I need to see my daughter. I need to keep her close.

Olivia is late. I push the cart across the parking lot, load the groceries into the back of the Subaru, return the cart, and she still isn't here. It's always a shock, how I can roam the aisles of the grocery store, and conquer the checkout line, in less time than it takes her to pick out a new nail polish at the adjacent beauty store.

Don't get me wrong, it's not that I don't remember the agony of finding just the right shade to paint fourteen-year-old fingernails, because I do. It's just that it never fails to amaze me how long the process actually takes.

I'd been reluctant to let her out of my sight, wanting to keep her beside me while I did the shopping, but when she'd begged off, asking to go next door instead, I couldn't think of a valid reason why she couldn't. I don't want her to know that anything's wrong. I can't give her cause to worry, and she was already suspicious when I picked her up from school. Besides, what's going to happen in broad daylight in a busy shopping center?

I slide behind the wheel, turn the key halfway so the radio plays, searching until I find a decent station, trying to distract myself. I need to stay calm. Relax. Closing my eyes, I lean my head back and focus on my breathing, letting the deep in and out release some of the tension from my muscles.

The song stops and a series of ads begins. Listening to commercials for investment products and pharmaceuticals makes me antsy. Even worse is when the DJ comes on and reminds me that I'm listening to an oldies station. Since when is *Green Day* an oldie? Switching the radio off, I send a text to my daughter.

Where are you?

I press my back deep into the leather seat, absorbing the warmth that's left. The heat feels good. Summer is a luxury in Massachusetts, and I'm always happy when our shortest season lingers, pushing fall back. But while I love the summer sun, that sun is currently frying my groceries. I think of the chicken I bought for dinner turning fetid. *Come on, Olivia, hurry it up or your stomach will face the wrath of mamma's chicken surprise.*

It's funny, but it's not. I'm tired of waiting. She hasn't replied to my text yet and I'm starting to do the mom thing and worry, only this time it's a normal mom reaction, not a helicopter-mom-with-dirty-dark-secrets-that-may-be-exposed-any-minute irrational fear.

I stare out the windshield, debating. A greasy-looking man walks by, scanning the parking lot with hungry eyes before he gets into his vehicle. Everything about him is suspicious, from his appearance, to the way he seems to be casing the area, to his sketchy old van with the tin-foiled windows.

As I watch him drive off, I wonder how much a blonde, American teen goes for on the black market now. My feet are out of the car and on the pavement before I have the chance to think of an answer.

I've worked myself up into a snit. I know I'm blowing this out of proportion, but it doesn't matter because I need to find my daughter. Now. I need to see her and make sure she's all right.

Storming across the parking lot, I try to calm myself, so I don't come down too hard on her. She doesn't really deserve it. It's not her fault I'm so on edge.

It's that damn letter.

And all that it entails. Being forced to play a dangerous game I have no interest in, with a playmate I'd rather avoid.

I'm halfway across the lot when I spot Olivia standing outside of the beauty supply store, talking to a woman who has her back to me. *See,* I think. *It would be rude of her to be looking at her phone while in the middle of a conversation with an adult. You raised her right.*

Then my feet plant to the ground so suddenly that I almost lose my balance, my upper-half lurching forward. It takes me a moment to recover. It takes me another for my thoughts to catch up to my brain. Something about the way the lady just tossed her hair. The manner in which she holds herself, the way her weight is balanced on her feet. I'd recognize the body language anywhere.

It's her.

Of course she would recognize Olivia as my daughter. She looks like a taller version of me, from the blonde hair to the smile, the shape of the face to the set of her shoulders. And, yet, I suspect it wasn't Olivia's similarities to *me* that caught her attention and made her take notice.

I'm overcome with the urge to run forward, to defend my cub with all the wrath that a momma tiger can muster. But as I watch my daughter smile and nod, raising her hand in the half wave thing she does whenever she says goodbye to someone, I realize I shouldn't play my hand. Not yet. Olivia's safe, for now.

She steps off the curb, heading toward me. Turning, I rush back to the car, get in the driver's seat, my sweaty hands clutching the steering wheel. I can't think about what this means right now. I can't question my daughter too much or she'll get suspicious. All I can do is focus on getting us home safely. And then on keeping us safe.

I have been too comfortable for too long, which is funny, because I haven't been comfortable at all. I live my life feeling like I'm stuck in a damp bathing suit, sandy and crusty, with seams digging too deep into flesh that's a little too clammy and cold and soft, afraid to sit on the furniture and get things wet. Maybe I should have surrounded myself with searing hot sand to burn my feet every time I stepped off the towel, too.

Because now I feel blindsided. I've been caught off guard. She was alone with my child.

When I asked Olivia what kept her so long, she told me

she'd been stopped by a nice lady who asked if I was her mother. Someone who said she was my friend growing up. Someone whose name she failed to get, but who now knows my daughter's name and the street that we live on.

Although, judging from the letter, she already knew where I lived. And it's dumb denial to think she doesn't know whatever else she wants to about me and my life. She has enough money, she could easily hire a team of private investigators to dig up all the dirt in my life.

But still, I feel that as a parent, in general, I have failed. My daughter flunked the stranger-danger test.

Later, after dinner, when Olivia's tucked safely away in her room trying out her new nail polish, I google the name. Morgana Ripley. It's odd how easy it is. To think, all these years, all the questions that skulked over my shoulder like an angry storm cloud, and I could have been keeping tabs on her the whole time.

I still have no idea why she's back. Or what her intentions are. But it can't be good. That whole family was trouble.

TEN

LIZ THEN

1997

I race across the front yard and around the side, knowing I must be the last one to arrive. Pausing on the step, I catch my breath. Wipe the sweat from my upper lip, run a hand over my hair, and straighten my shirt before yanking the door open and flinging myself inside the kitchen.

All eyes are on me as I drop my backpack on the floor and punch both fists in the air. "I got an A!"

I round the table, throw my arms around Sami and give her a big kiss on the cheek, popping my lips with a noisy smack. "I didn't think I stood a chance on that stupid, boring history test. Thank you, thank you, thank you for all your help!"

Sami ducks away, pulls her sleeve down over her fist and uses it to wipe her face. "Gross. Do you kiss David with all that gunk on your lips?"

Heat flares in my cheeks as I sneak a peek at Amy's dad, Sonny, to see if he's listening as he pulls a tray of pizza rolls from the oven.

Mo snorts, laughing as she says, "Nah. His mommy hasn't signed the permission slip for that yet."

Sonny plates the snack and brings it over. Sets it on the table, then pauses beside me, gives me a wink and a grin as he says, "Well, it's his loss."

Amy scowls at him, trying to banish him from the kitchen, but he doesn't take the hint, instead pulling a chair out to sit with us. "Dad. Don't you have something else you could be doing right now?"

"Yeah, but why would I choose housework over such gorgeous company? The laundry can wait."

She huffs and rolls her eyes.

Mo grabs a pizza roll from the plate, squeezes some of the filling out the top and blows on it. "Hey, Sonny. Did you see last night's episode of *Madness and Mayhem*?"

Sometimes she's such a show-off. Just because the rest of us aren't allowed to stay up late enough to see it—and probably wouldn't be allowed to watch the raunchy sketch comedy show even if we were—she has to rub it in and make the rest of us look like little kids.

"Nope. Had a hot date and I missed it. Was it any good?"

Mo launches into a recap. Usually I'm on the edge of my seat because the skits sound hilarious, especially the way Mo tells them, but this time I'm not even listening. Because Amy's face is starting to turn strange colors, first pink, then fuchsia, then red. It's obvious she's super pissed and getting ready to blow.

I don't know why Amy hates having her dad around so much. Or why she doesn't realize how lucky she is that he's so cool. He's so much more laid back than the rest of our parents. It's almost like he's one of us.

"That sounds like it was a riot, I'm sorry I missed that one." He smiles around the table. When his gaze reaches Amy, it falters. "Well," he claps his hands together and stands. "I'm going to stop distracting you ladies and let you get to it. I'll be in the dungeon doing laundry if anyone needs me."

As soon as the sound of his boots clomping down the basement stairs fades, Amy releases an epic sigh. "I wish you guys wouldn't encourage him so much."

"What do you mean?" Mo asks. "What'd we do wrong? We were just talking."

"Just because you're desperate for attention doesn't mean you have to chat up my dad to try and get him to hang around. It's pathetic."

Mo falls instantly silent. Her eyes narrow and her jaw hardens.

I exchange looks with Sami. She reaches for my hand under the table and holds it tightly. In my head, I'm yelling for Sonny, shouting for him to return.

"Why would you say that?" Mo asks.

"Because it's true." Amy blinks. Any anger in her expression has vanished. She leans her head against Mo's, gathers her in a one-armed hug. "Don't be so sensitive. I'm only trying to help. We're family. You know I love you."

Beside me, Sami breathes a sigh of relief. Whatever storm was gathering has already passed, if it was ever actually there at all. Mo was probably just overreacting, anyways. As Amy always reminds us, she has a habit of doing that. And we'd never actually do anything to hurt each other. Not ever.

ELEVEN

LIZ NOW

2014

I walk around the house, turning off lights, checking doors to make sure they're locked, carrying stray dishes to the sink—making the mom rounds, my nightly bedtime routine. Turning off the hall light, I stare down the darkened corridor for several seconds, and then sit at the desk in the corner of the living room.

Moonlight filters through the blinds, casting stripes across me. I bask in the glow for a moment, imagining my skin absorbing something vital, like vitamin D from the sun. Opening my laptop, I wake it from its sleep and click the icon in the corner of the screen, my other nightly ritual. The site loads quickly. My eyes scan for the dot on the webpage. It isn't there.

I fight to swallow, my mouth dry, my throat tight, my heart pounding against the walls of my chest. My gallbladder gurgles as it spits bile. I know I shouldn't panic, not yet, not when the answer is so close at hand.

Clicking the image to zoom out on the map, I watch, but the results don't change. The worst possible scenarios race through my head as I stand. My legs feel weak, my feet heavy, my head light. Walking down the hallway, I stand before the door to my daughter's bedroom, hand resting on the knob. Taking a deep breath, I brace myself for what I may or may not find and push the door open.

A bundled cocoon lays in the bed. I release the breath I had unknowingly held hostage, my veins filled with equal parts blood and relief. My daughter is here, asleep. Spotting the black rectangle on her pillow, I creep across the room. I'm reaching for it when her eyes open.

"Mom?"

"Hey, sweetie. Go back to sleep."

"What are you doing?"

"Putting your phone on the charger."

"What evs."

She lets me lift the phone from her pillow, watches as I connect it to the charging cord that lays draped across her nightstand, then rolls over to go back to sleep. I fight the urge to kiss the top of her head, which would earn me another demerit in the clingy mom book, so I imagine it instead.

Shutting my laptop down, I retreat to my bedroom feeling both relieved and cross. *What evs.* I hate the way kids shorten everything these days, as if even one extra syllable is too much effort. I want to blame texting, but the truth is, it probably started with my generation, when pagers found their way into every teenager's hand.

It was amazing how a device could have such a drastic makeover in terms of use, no longer just for doctors and drug dealers, but morphing into a way in which parents could keep tabs on their kids and teens could send each other abbreviated messages. If you were where you were supposed to be, you could return you parents' call when they paged you within five minutes. Caller ID would confirm you were calling from the right house.

My own parents had bought me a beeper but rarely used

the ploy to keep tabs on me. Then again, I was always where I was supposed to be when they knew I was gone. It was when I was supposed to be in bed, asleep, that my parents had lost control of their daughter.

I wasn't going to make the same mistake. I would use every technological advance available to help me keep watch over my kid, even if it meant stalking her using the GPS locator on her phone. Perhaps if my parents had done the same... but I know that it's no use dwelling on *what ifs*.

Even if I had the opportunity to go back in time and change things, I wouldn't. Because despite all the difficulties that surrounded what happened to me, I got something amazing out of it.

The real surprise is that my parents made the effort to buy me a pager in the first place. I was the youngest of five, the only girl. The only one not in constant need of new cleats or new skates or new gear for whatever sport was in season. The only one who didn't just hear the mumbled voices of our parents late at night, when we were supposed to be sleeping, discussing the dire situation of their finances, but who actually listened, who heard every word and knew what it meant and did my best not to add to the problem.

When Mo and Sami started horseback riding lessons in the third grade, I pretended not to like horses and made stuff with Amy out of glue and glitter instead. Billabong jackets, Ugg boots, CDs—there was an endless list of items I pretended not to like to spare my parents the worry of trying to find a way to afford buying them for me. I didn't really mind, not really, and it made me feel good to know that Amy wasn't the only one going without.

It wasn't until I was grown that I discovered the resentment that had built up from all that sacrifice. That my self-imposed martyrdom had decimated my sense of self-worth. Of course, by that time I was in a loveless marriage, caring for a baby, so I didn't have much need for it anyway. Except that maybe, if I had a little more confidence in myself, I would have spoken up and talked to David about his infidelities before the situation became what it currently is. But then again, maybe not.

Who knows? I've never liked confrontation. I've always chosen to take the easy way out. Always opted for the path of least resistance.

Pulling the blankets back, I get into bed. I lean across David's side and tap on the light that sits on his nightstand, so he'll be able to see when he finally gets home. It's the last thing I do every night. Snuggling down under the covers, my day is finally over.

I wonder if my mom had any hopes and dreams for me. I suppose she must have, most moms do, to some extent, but mine never shared hers with me. Maybe she somehow knew that I'd blow my future at a young age. But it didn't have to be that way. One bad decision doesn't have to ruin your life, as long as you learn from it and stop making terrible choices.

My hope for my daughter is that she lives her life free. That she isn't forced to plan every step of every day in advance to make sure she makes it through. That she doesn't have to constantly look over her shoulder, checking to make sure that she's staying ahead of the dark cloud that follows at her heels.

Actually, my dream for her is that she never has a secret so big and bad that it follows her around through the years of her life, an albatross she has no choice but to wear around her neck. I fall asleep wondering what it would feel like not to know the burden of that weight. Or even just to have it removed.

TWELVE

LIZ THEN

1997

Forcing myself forward, one step and then another, I focus on my breathing. Watching my friends' backs as they skip ahead of me with barely contained excitement helps a little, but not much. There's more adrenaline throbbing through my veins than blood. I'm already damp with sweat. Drawing a shaky breath, I try to distract myself.

Sometimes, when Mo walks, there's the tinniest little hitch to her step. Just the hint of a limp, a whisper left from when she broke her leg skiing years ago. I don't think anyone else would ever pick up on it, but I do.

When I notice it, like I do now, I can't help but wonder if it still causes her any pain. She never says anything about it, but I'm not so sure she would. Mo's not the type to display any weakness, even among her best friends. On occasions like tonight, I wish I had that luxury.

They've reached the first line already and are beckoning for me to catch up. I break into a jog, running past a vampire and a ghoul wearing a *Scream* mask. A chainsaw jumps to life right behind me, the sound ripping through air that quickly becomes thick with the stench of gasoline.

My stop isn't as coordinated as I'd like. I jostle into my friends, bumping them into the crowd ahead of them. A witch my mom's age turns and gives us a disapproving stink eye, which sets the others giggling. I try to join them, but my heart isn't in it. My fake laugh is too loud.

October is here, bringing with it jewel-toned leaves, shorter days, and all of the Halloween festivities I'd rather not attend. Yes, it's true. It's impossible to keep secret, so why not embrace it? I am a coward.

I'm not the girl you hear screaming for attention or to be cute. I'm the one drenched in sweat trying to catch her breath between scares so that I don't pass out. Looking down, I realize that I've got Amy's arm clenched in the death grip of my fist. I release her and she rubs the spot like I've caused a bruise.

"It's not going to be that scary," she tells me, a small smile nearly hidden by her zombie makeup.

"It better be. We didn't drive all the way the hell out here for nothing." Mo adjusts the drape of her *Little Red Riding Hood* outfit, looking around to see if anyone has noticed her yet. "It better be frickin' terrifying."

This year, instead of the local haunted hayrides and corn mazes we usually go to, we've driven an hour and a half to attend a huge Halloween Night of Horror. I had known it was coming. This and traffic circles are the only two things that made me dread getting a driver's license.

"Maybe I'll just sit this one out." Looking around, I locate the closest food booth. "I'm going to grab some fries. I'll meet you over there when you get out."

"What? No." Mo crosses her arms across her chest, accentuating what's revealed by the low neckline for the group of guys in line behind us.

"Yeah, if I have to go, you do, too." Amy hooks her arm through mine.

Only Sami seems to get it. "You guys can't make her go. If she doesn't want to, she doesn't have to."

Mo looks at me, and I know she's judging the Joan of Arc costume I have on instead of the sexy *Alice in Wonderland* dress she wanted me to wear. "I don't understand why you're acting like such a baby. It's just a haunted house."

"Not everyone is fearless like you, Mo. Some people get scared, and if Liz is one of them, you shouldn't try to make her go. I'll stay out here with her." Sami tosses one long auburn braid over the shoulders of her *Anne of Green Gables* smock.

"I'm not fearless," Mo whispers.

I can't think of a single time when Mo was afraid of anything. I remember in the fourth grade when we had chorus, and the teacher wanted to hear everyone sing on their own. Amy is shy, but she's always loved to sing. Even standing at the front of the room, all by herself, she managed to croon the melody in a voice that made the teacher swoon.

I went up there and carried a tune. When it was Sami's turn, she started sweating. I could feel the heat radiating off her as she turned a deep shade of tomato red with all those eyes staring at her. She didn't even go to the front, just stayed where she was on the carpeted semicircle of stairs and mouthed the words to the song. The teacher threw her hands up, and then turned to Mo.

"I'd rather not."

"Morgana, that's why you're here. It's part of the class."

"I can't sing," Mo said.

"Just try your best," the teacher prodded.

"Okay, but you won't like it."

Mo belted out the song as loud as she could, off-key and out of tune. When she was finished, she looked at the teacher, waiting for a response.

"Well, I guess the resemblance between you and Amy ends at appearances, dear."

Mo spent the rest of the semester shouting whatever song we were given, making sure the monstrosity of her singing drowned out everyone else. You'd have to be fearless to do something like that.

"Yeah, right, you're totally fearless."

"I'm not fearless," Mo says again, her face pale beneath its many layers of makeup. "I'm just not afraid of any of this silly pretend crap that's supposed to be scary."

"Then what *are* you afraid of?"

"Life."

It's one of those moments that changes the way you look at someone. I don't know how to respond. None of us do. The way she said the word, the look in her eyes, her serious expression, I can feel it searing into my memory like a cattle brand.

Sami is the one to break the tension. "Ugh, I know. I hate that game. I'm afraid that if I have to sit around that stupid board one more time, I'll puke all over those little pink peg kids."

It isn't funny, but we all laugh anyways as we moved forward, closer to the gaping black clown's mouth that gives entrance to the haunted house before us. It's our turn. An evil joker hands us 3D glasses to put on. Stepping through, over the jagged plywood teeth into the dark beyond, I feel a hand close over my own, enveloping it in a tight grip. It's Mo's.

Seven haunted houses, one hundred scare actors roaming the lanes of the midway trying to give spooks, and two servings of greasy fair food later, we stumble across the rutted grass field that served as a parking lot back to the car. I survived it all. Do I feel stronger?

Not really. Just more worn down and tired, like I've lost the battle and become more compliant.

Driving home, my hands clench the wheel and I hunch forward, staring through the darkness for unseen hazards. When I check my rearview mirror, I can't help but let my glance linger over Mo and Sami, their heads leaning against each other as they sleep in the back seat.

"That was kind of fun, right?"

My eyes dart beside me to Amy, then back to the road.

"I guess."

"Didn't you enjoy it at all?"

"I did when you screamed in the doll house and decked that guy for scaring you."

"I didn't mean... I wouldn't have... It was just a gut reaction, an accident. I couldn't help it."

I take another peek at Amy, her cheeks now pink, eyes shining. "I'm just teasing you. I know you wouldn't. Not like..." I swallow the name and let the sentence fade, unfinished, into the surrounding night. Several minutes pass as we both battle our own thoughts.

"Sometimes, I worry." Amy's confession rips through the silence that drapes between us.

"Yeah." I shift my weight, trying to get comfortable behind the wheel. "Me too."

THIRTEEN

LIZ NOW

2014

The words snag my attention as I'm driving Olivia home from volleyball practice. After seeing the news report yesterday, I was waiting for this to happen. The other shoe to drop. I just never expected it to happen so quickly.

I pull into our driveway and put the car in park, my body working on autopilot. Olivia hops out and grabs her bag out of the car. I hit the button clipped to my visor, watch the garage door rise to let her into the house, then turn the radio up and listen.

It's started. It won't be long now. This careful existence I've created is at risk of crashing down.

Pulling myself out of the car, I find that my legs are weak. They wobble when I try to use them. I take a moment, balancing myself against the door, ordering my steps. Fix dinner, help with homework, watch some TV with my daughter, send her to bed, then large quantities of alcohol and some deep thinking for me.

I can still salvage this. It's not too late. I just need to come up with a plan. Fast.

Feeling slightly calmer, I slam the door shut and turn. Right into Francine's trap. She's watering the hedge of shrubs that runs along the property line between our two houses. I wish the damned things would hurry up and grow taller. I put my fake smile on and wave, trying to portray the image of a rushed mom with no time to stop and chat, just go, go, go. She doesn't buy it.

"So, Liz, did you hear?" Her voice is low and secretive, like she's got some juicy gossip.

"Hear what?"

"Your old friend, Morgana Ripley? The one we were talking about the other day?"

I nod, smile stretched tight. "Actually, Francine, I'm super short on time right now. Would you mind if we talked later?" Or, given that she obviously still hasn't gotten over the obsession she had over Mo when we were younger, never. She's one person I have no desire to discuss.

"Well, sure. I guess. I just thought you should know that she sold that gaudy old mansion she grew up in. And the new owners decided to have some work done." Francine stops, looking at me. It appears that she's waiting for me to comment.

"I'm not surprised. It's been empty for a long time."

She grins and continues. "Well, apparently they were doing some construction, something in the woods out back, and..." She looks from side to side, making sure no one else is within earshot. "And they found a body!"

"A body!" I do my best to sound surprised. "Like, a dead person?"

"Yep. Bones."

"Oh." Now I try to sound disappointed. "Those woods were full of ruins, old houses and stuff. They probably just dug up some poor pilgrim."

"Nope. My friend CeCe says they've got forensics people

over there right now. She says they've been there for days already."

"That's probably just routine. I bet they have to do that anytime they find human remains."

"Nope. It was definitely murder."

I bite my tongue to stop from saying that the report I just heard on the radio said investigators believed it was a homicide. *Believed.* They don't know for sure. Not yet.

"And whatever they found, it's recent enough that the killer is probably still out there, like, still alive. They have specialists that can tell things like that. They have specialists for all of it now. It's gotta be near impossible to get away with something like that today, once the cops find out it's been done."

Her words echo in my head.

"Well, that makes me feel safer. Thanks, Francine. I've got to go start dinner. I'll catch up with you later."

She keeps squawking like a crow as I walk away. I can still hear her faintly after I've shut the door. But the only words in my head are the ones she's already said.

———

That night, I'm still awake, pacing, stalking the halls as quietly as I can while Olivia sleeps, when David gets home. He looks surprised when he sees me, surprised and guilty. I know he can tell something is wrong by my expression. I see the fear flicker behind his clear blue eyes.

"Liz. Honey."

The word sounds weird to both of us, so uncomfortable coming out of his mouth and so foreign to my ears that we both stop for a minute and just stare at each other. Then I shake my head, clearing my thoughts and getting myself back on track.

"David, I need you to stay here and take care of Olivia tonight." It seems ridiculous to say this. I know she's old enough to be left alone, but I really don't want her to be, especially not now.

"Why? Where are you going?"

"Out."

"Out where?"

"Just out."

"Liz, you seem upset. You probably shouldn't be driving." He raises a hand toward my shoulder. His fingertips hover mere inches from my body as he realizes what he's almost done. His palm smacks against his thigh as it drops.

"I'll be fine."

"Why don't you let me drive you?"

I give him a look, eyebrows raised, lips quirked in a snarky smile, and hope it says what I'm thinking. *What? You want to stand up and be my husband now? You've suddenly decided you want to take care of me?*

"That's not necessary." I squeeze past him in the hallway.

"Liz, what's the big deal? Let me take you."

But I don't want to be in a car with him right now. I don't want him to know where I'm going. Maybe things aren't great between us, but we've been together a long time. The more time we spend in each other's company, the more likely it is that he'll know that something isn't just wrong. It's catastrophic.

I don't respond, simply slip out the front door, closing it softly behind me.

———

The windows fog as I drive. I'm so hot and flushed with tension that I feel a fine vapor rising off my skin. Between that and the electrical pulses of energy from my nerves, it's a wonder that I haven't short circuited or electrocuted myself.

My nerves jangle as I pull into the driveway and park

behind a dark sedan. A single light is on in the house before me. It's strange. All these years and I've never been here before.

Opening the door, I step out onto the cracked drive, weeds squeezing through the fractures etched in the pale concrete, collecting dew in the dark. Grass grows over the edges. There's no landscaping besides a lonely sapling in the middle of the yard and a pot by the front steps, a withered plant skeleton peaking over the top.

My fist shakes as I knock on the door. I imagine her inside, her head tilting as she hears the sound, shuffling to the door in her socks. That used to drive her mom crazy. She would always wear her socks. No slippers, no bare feet, just socks, ingraining permanent dirt stains on the bottoms that her mom could never bleach out.

What if she's expecting someone? What if she's not alone? What if she takes one look at me, and slams the door in my face?

But then there she is, standing before me. Sami. She looks surprised to see me, but also a little relieved, like maybe she was hoping I'd come. Before I can stop myself, I throw my arms around her. We stand, embracing, in the open doorway, light from inside casting our mingled shadows across the hood of her car.

Pulling back, I keep a firm grip on her upper arm with one hand. I tuck a strand of her hair behind her ear with the other, the light catching on a few fine silver filaments woven among the auburn. I've always loved her hair.

"What the hell is she doing?" Sami asks, her voice barely above a whisper.

"I wish I knew."

She takes my hand and leads me inside, closing the door behind us. The décor is everything I would expect it to be. Oriental dragons, Mayan calendars, Viking ships, ancient Egyptian ornaments, an amalgam of cultures and ethnicities.

Sami's always loved history, always been fascinated by ancient cultures.

She shows me to the living room, where the couch is deep, soft-cushioned, black leather. I sink in and it instantly conforms to my body, like it has always been my spot. We sit facing each other, knees touching.

"Do you think this is it, then? The beginning of the end?" I ask her.

She shakes her head, slowly at first, but it gains speed as her conviction grows. "No. I don't."

"But how? What can we do?"

She looks hard into my eyes, making sure that we're on the same page. "We stick together. You and me. No matter what happens. We go on living our lives as normal, we pretend that nothing's wrong, because nothing *is* wrong. Yet. Maybe nothing will ever come of it. But if something does happen, we don't know anything. If it comes down to it, it's our word against hers."

Then she smiles and leans against my shoulder. I lean against hers. We hold hands, drawing strength from the other. If only it were really that easy.

I wake to the sound of my phone buzzing. Rolling over, I prop myself up and spread my hand over the sheets, searching for the cell. Sami yawns and flops onto her stomach. My fingers close around the phone, and I swipe the screen to answer, padding into the kitchen to see if I can't figure out where things are to start some coffee. Sami and I got drunk and caught up on fifteen years last night. It's going to be a rough morning.

"Hello?" The sound of my voice sounds foreign. It's raspy from the drinking, but it also sounds younger, more girlish.

"Uh, hi. You didn't come home last night."

Peeking through a slat in the blinds I can see the gray light of early dawn. "I guess I didn't."

"Listen, Liz..."

"Everything's fine, David. Tell Olivia that I forgot that I had to take your mother to an early doctor's appointment this morning. Set out some cereal, give her a few dollars to buy lunch, and I'll be home before she gets back from school this afternoon."

"Okay. So, you are coming home? That's good."

"Uh-huh. If you can, try to make it home for dinner tonight."

"Why?"

"I'm having an old friend over."

"Why do I have to be there if it's your friend?"

"Because it's Sami, David. She used to be your friend, too. Or do you not remember?"

The silence on the other end of the line stretches so long that I'm sure the call has dropped. I'm getting ready to hang up by the time he responds.

"Sami? You mean, like, from high school?"

"That's exactly who I mean. So, will you be there or not?"

I hear the gulp of air he always takes when he's preparing himself to say something I don't want to hear. I wonder what kind of lame excuse he's going to offer. But instead, he surprises me.

"Yeah." He sounds reluctant, subdued. Swallowing loudly, he says, "I'll be there."

"Good. We still eat dinner at six thirty. Just in case you forgot. I know it's been a while."

I hang up because I have nothing more to say. I feel powerful, like I'm taking life by the wheel and steering it where I want it to go. I feel confident, like I'm finally in control. I feel terrified, like I have absolutely no idea what I'm doing. Probably because I don't.

FOURTEEN

SAMI THEN

1997

It's Friday, and everyone has something to do except me. Amy has a drama club meeting. She keeps trying to get me to join, saying that I could add authenticity to their set designs, but the idea of being stuck in a room full of big personalities competing with each other sounds like a nightmare to me.

Not that Amy is like that. People can't help but notice her. She's just so striking. But still, totally not my thing.

Liz has to stop by her house to meet the girl one of her brothers brought home from college. She's basically providing moral support for her mom, who thinks the girl may be *the one*, even though the last two weren't, and for her brother, who needs Liz to help take their mom's focus off the girl. It's the kind of intricate dance around feelings and boundaries that makes me thankful to be an only child.

Mo has a workout scheduled with a personal trainer, at a gym she joined after seeing the trainer through the glass while walking by. It's the kind of brazen thing that's classic Mo. She sees a hot guy, wants an excuse to spend time with him, so she hires him for his services, thus creating an awkward situation in which said guy would have to cross the lines of professionalism *and* ignore the fact that she's jailbait, therefore getting whatever attention she's after while ensuring nothing actually happens. It's the kind of confusing stunt that stems from her personal brand of issues.

So I have a short window of time in which to occupy myself. It's like a gift from the heavens above. Don't get me wrong. I love my friends. I cherish the time we spend together. But I'm right at the end of this awesome novel that I can't wait to finish, and now I have the perfect opportunity to read the end without interruption before we all meet up later.

I carry my night bag around the back of Mo's house and into the woods, following the winding path our feet have worn over the years to the stone hut nestled under the pine trees. We were eight the day we found it, four ballsy little girls expanding their boundaries into the dark of the forest during a game of hide and seek. From the second we saw it, we fell in love with it. There was never a moment's doubt that it was our place.

I was on a big Irish kick in seventh grade when I discovered what it was. A clochán. A drystone hut with a corbeled roof that looks like an igloo. We went on a mission that year to discover how a piece of Irish architecture found its way to the middle of the Massachusetts woods. We became obsessed with the mystery, spending hours at the local library, the land use office, public records hall, anywhere we thought there might be information that revealed the source of its existence.

We daydreamed a million different romantic scenarios that only twelve-year-old girls would imagine. We'd sleep in our clochán, lulled to sleep by the stories we'd tell each other. I'd love to say that we found out something amazing, a heart-rending story of sorrow, a magical tale of romance, even something lurid, but it was much simpler than that.

The land that Ripley Manor was built on used to belong to

an Irish immigrant who erected the hut for his kids to play in. But the lack of a spicy backstory didn't lessen our love for it. It's still our favorite place to be, and my number one reading spot in the entire world.

For a short snippet of time, I'll leave reality behind. I'll be someone else. Someone better. Happier. Less confused. Rolling my sleeping bag out on the floor, I lay on my back, book propped against my raised knees, and enter the story world of my novel.

I must have fallen asleep. I wake, eyes tired and burning from a good cry. My nose feels crusty, and my cheeks are stiff with dried tears. There's nothing like a book with an ending so tragic that it cripples you with a gut-wrenching sorrow.

The late afternoon light filtering through the gaps in the stones makes my eyes ache. Reaching to rub them, I realize that someone has tucked their sleeping bag over me as a blanket. I take a deep breath, breathing in the scent lingering on the fabric. Mo.

I spot her sitting by the door, staring blankly outside, chin propped on top of knees that are hugged to her chest. She jumps a little when she catches me watching her. Her lips twitch into a small smile. A sad smile. She crawls across the floor to me, cradles my head in her lap and strokes my hair.

"Another good book?"

Mo isn't much of a reader herself. Besides schoolwork she mostly just thumbs through magazines, but she likes to hear about the books I read.

"Brutal."

"I guess so. It looks like you had a good cry." She flashes me that sad smile again, then breaks eye contact, her gaze going back out the door. "How does it feel?" Her voice is a whisper. Even with our bodies so close I can barely hear her.

My head and my heart fill in the words I can't hear, like somehow I just know what she's asking. "To have a good, hard cry fueled by something other than what's happening in your own life?"

I study the curves of her face, all highlights and shadows in the fading light.

"It feels, well, I know it sounds kind of weird, but it feels great. It's cathartic. To turn into a complete emotional wreck over something that's simply going to disappear when you're done. It's, like, power, control that you don't have when you're crying for other reasons. Real reasons."

Her lips purse together. She swallows hard. I see her neck muscles bulge as she gulps down the lump in her throat. I can hear the sound of it. "Maybe I should give it a try sometime."

"Just let me know when you're ready. I'll hook you up with some books that will absolutely destroy you."

She makes a strange noise, one I've never heard before. Probably disbelief. Or amusement. We both know that even the most gut-wrenching book wouldn't affect her like it does me. She's impervious to things like that.

Sitting up, I lean my cheek on her shoulder and drape my arms loosely around her. "How did your workout go?"

"Ha." A single laugh, harsh but unemotional. "As soon as I saw the trainer up close? Ugh. He was, like, almost forty or something. I can't believe I made myself suffer through the whole thing."

"So, no love connection?" I sense that the trainer fiasco is not what's bothering her; it's safe to tease.

She pulls her shoulder from under me, distancing our faces enough so I can see her expression, her eyebrows raised, her nose wrinkled, one side of her mouth raised in a sneer. "Ew, no. The only reason to date a guy that old is if you need his money, and I have plenty of my own, thank you." She gets that faraway look again, staring into space, and says, "Money is the one thing that I do have."

A part of me knows that I should speak up, that I should remind her of the other things she has, the friends who love her, but the rest of me wants her to hurt, even if I know it isn't the right thing, my feelings stinging from the blow she doesn't know she landed.

FIFTEEN

FRANCINE NOW

2014

Francine's mouth drops open and her eyes grow wide when she sees the number that's calling. Her heart pounds in her chest, hands shaking so badly that she fumbles the phone when she goes to answer it. "Mo! Oh my God, hi! I can't believe you actually called."

She winces, pausing momentarily as she realizes how desperate she must sound. She quickly segues on, hoping Mo didn't notice. "So, have you given any thought to how you want to surprise Liz?"

She laughs over the line, the same throaty, confident chuckle that she'd had in high school. "Oh, I have a few ideas. Too many. I feel like I've been planning this for years already."

"Well, I'd be happy to hear them all out, help you choose the best ones."

"Thanks, Francine. I really appreciate that."

Francine can feel herself glowing. It's finally happening. Morgana Ripley is finally becoming her friend.

She'd tried so hard when they were teenagers, but for some

reason she'd never made any headway. It was probably the other girls' faults. Liz and Sami and Amy—they'd always seemed kind of cliquish. Liz still is, if she's being honest. She knows the snooty bitch doesn't like her, only puts up with her because their daughters are friends.

It's a shame that the time she and Mo spend together will be wasted planning something nice for her. It's not like she deserves it. But still... she's talking to Morgana Ripley on the phone! And *she* was the one to call Francine! She squeals inside her head, trying to feign nonchalance.

"Actually, I was hoping you could tell me more about Liz's daughter."

"Olivia?"

"Yes."

"Um." It seems a little strange, but who's she to judge. Mo probably just wants to include Olivia in whatever she's planning. It's kind of sweet, in a way. "Okay. Sure. What do you want to know?"

"Everything."

"Like?"

"How old she is. What she's like. What her interests are."

It's odd that Mo doesn't know anything about Liz's daughter, given how close they used to be. They must have had some kind of falling out. Especially since Liz must have been pregnant while they were still in school.

Francine knows. She's done the math. Repeatedly. Reminds herself with no small amount of superiority and glee every time Liz takes a jab at her that her own daughter is six months younger than Liz's. At least she'd graduated before becoming pregnant.

"Olivia's almost fifteen," she says, trying to temper the judgment in her tone.

"Fifteen," Mo repeats.

Francine knows Mo's doing the math for herself. Figuring

out what it means. That maybe she and Liz weren't as close as she had thought.

"Mm-hmm. She's a very nice girl." A lot nicer than her mother ever was. "My Gina is her very best friend. She says that Olivia is a natural at volleyball. Made the varsity team even though she's only a freshman."

She racks her brain for something more to say, but the truth is, she doesn't know much about Olivia.

"Liz must be so proud." Mo sounds strange, almost choked up.

"Oh, she is. That girl means the world to her." It's the only thing Francine can't find fault with—the way Liz loves her daughter.

"I need to go."

"Huh?"

"I'm sorry, Francine. I just remembered an appointment. I've been so overwhelmed with coming back to town, wrapping up the sale on my parents' old house, catching up with old friends like you, it just slipped my mind. I hope it'll be all right if we talk later?"

"Of course, yeah, I totally understand—"

But the call has already ended. Francine hopes she didn't say anything wrong. More likely, Mo was just upset when she realized Liz had been keeping secrets. Guess their friendship wasn't as good as everyone thought.

SIXTEEN

LIZ THEN

1998

You'd think with as many brothers as I have, that I would have learned to like sports, but I don't. At all. As far as I can see, there's only one positive thing about football season, and that's the homecoming dance. True, it's not as exciting or formal as the prom we've been fantasizing about since we were little, but it's good practice. By the time we're seniors, we'll have enough experience to make sure our prom is perfect.

The four of us are squished in Sami's tiny bathroom, vying for space in front of the mirror. I duck low, squeezing in beside Mo. Pull my eyelid taut as I uncap my new liquid eyeliner.

"No, not like that." Mo sighs as she snatches the pen from me. The truth is, I'd been hoping she would. I'm hopeless with the stuff, but Mo? She's an artist. "Look up."

Her mouth twists into a knot as she draws a series of short, dashed lines around my eye. "Now the other one."

I stare up at the ceiling, trying not to blink, waiting for the soft pressure of her hand, but it doesn't come. "Um, Mo?"

When she doesn't answer, I chance a peek in her direction. And instantly know that something is very, very wrong.

"Where did you get that?" Her voice shakes. Her expression is absolutely stricken. I follow her gaze to Sami, who's fingering the choker around her throat protectively.

"Amy gave it to me."

Mo turns on her cousin like a rabid animal ready to attack. Amy shrugs, unconcerned.

"It was a long time ago, when we were little," Sami explains.

"Second grade," Mo whispers.

"Huh?"

"I said, in the second grade." Mo's voice grows louder with each word. "At least, that's when it went missing. It was my mother's."

A vein pops out from the middle of her forehead. She looks like she can't decide whether to cry or wage war. Her breathing becomes harder, more labored. Just when I think she's going to explode, she shoves her way out of the bathroom.

"Mo, wait." Sami fumbles with the clasp, removes the necklace and holds it out to her. "I'm sorry?"

Mo stares at the choker like it's a rat carrying bubonic plague. Her face crumples, head shaking from side to side as she refuses to touch it. "No, keep it. It's way too late for that."

"For what?" I ask, touching her shoulder gently.

"To convince my mom that I wasn't the one who stole it." She swipes angrily at the lone tear that dares to trickle down her cheek. "She insisted she saw me with it. Ransacked my room looking for it. Called me a wicked child when I wouldn't tell her where it was. All these years... it never even occurred to me."

Her face hardens as she looks at Amy. "Why?"

"It was my mom's first. I saw her wearing it in a picture."

"Not that. Why didn't you tell me you took it? Why did you let her think it was me?" And then softer, "Is that why you wanted to dress like my doll?"

A memory surfaces of a playdate at Mo's, four little girls gathered excitedly around a doll that had been made to look exactly like her, down to the identical outfits they both wore. Of Amy, begging for Mo to swap clothes with her so that she could mirror the doll for a while. Of the three of us braiding Amy's hair into plaits until she was an exact match.

And suddenly, I'm sure. That had to be the day it happened, the one Mo's talking about. Because things were different after that. She seemed harder, colder. Sadder. I'd thought that it was because her parents were around a lot less, that she was just lonely because they were away so much, but maybe it was something else. Something more.

"It was my mom's necklace," Amy says again.

"Do you have any idea how much trouble that caused me? My mom never trusted me again after that."

Amy's eyes look drawn and sad as she says, "I'm sorry, Mo. Really, I am. But it's not fair for you to blame me for your poor relationship with your parents. There were issues long before I took the necklace. Your mom didn't even realize that I wasn't you."

Mo looks like Amy just spit in her face.

"Hey." I step between them, wincing as I do because I'm sure I'm going to get hit. "You guys. It happened a long time ago. There's no use getting upset over it now."

Mo stares at me for a long minute, then grabs her overnight bag and starts shoving her stuff back inside. "Screw this. I'm out. I didn't want to go to some lame ass dance anyways."

She stomps down the stairs. I rush after her, knowing I shouldn't let her be by herself right now. Knowing I should go with her. But when she storms out the front door, I stand frozen on the threshold, just gaping after her. I can't seem to make myself follow.

Because I saw something behind Mo's eyes just a moment ago, something I can't quite name. But whatever it was, it's big and dark and scary. And somehow, I know it has the potential to change all of our lives forever.

SEVENTEEN

LIZ NOW

2014

When I got home from the grocery store today, I found another note. This one was tucked under the handle of my front door. She's gotten bolder. She's coming closer. I have to find a way to put an end to this.

The single sheet of paper caught in the wind, fluttering in my hand almost as violently as my heart in my chest as I read it.

The time has come. You need to tell them what you did.

XXO ∞

But it makes no sense. It wasn't just me. We all played a part in what happened that night. So then, what is it, exactly, that she wants?

I feel like I'm walking on glass—just one wrong step and the floor beneath me will shatter, plunging me into the fathomless depths below. I can't let that happen. I have too much to lose.

I'm in the kitchen chopping ingredients for dinner when Olivia comes home. She sits on a stool at the end of the island and watches. I go through the roster of mom questions, inquiring about her day, school, homework, and extracurricular activities. Her answers are short, with none of the details and embellishments she usually includes.

"Are you feeling all right, honey?"

"Yeah."

Laying down the knife, I walk over and give her a kiss on the forehead for a surreptitious temperature check. It may be my imagination, I may be oversensitive, but I swear my daughter just flinched away from my kiss. I tell myself it's nothing. I go back to the chopping board at the other end of the island, cut the end off an onion.

Peeling the onion, I slice it, first one direction and then the other before I start cutting slivers off the end. My eyes sting, tears welling to extinguish the burn. I peek at Olivia. Even through my blurred vision I can see her watching me, staring intensely at my face, her nose slightly wrinkled.

"Olivia? Darling?"

"Hmm?"

"Why are you staring at me like that?"

"No reason."

Her eyes dart away. I can see the gears turning inside her head. Ever since she was a little girl she's worn her heart on her sleeve. Something is bothering her.

I bite my tongue. Teenage Olivia is skittish. When she was younger, I could keep asking questions until she spilled her problems, dropping them into my lap one by one like a handful of jellybeans, but now those questions set off the teenage alarm for prying and the forcefield will drop, shutting all communication down.

The key is to stay quiet and wait out her silence until she tells me on her own. It may sound easy, but it's impossibly hard.

"We're doing a section on genetics in biology class." She throws the statement out into the space between us. "Punnett squares and stuff. You know anything about it?"

My heart rate returns to its normal speed. She must need help with her homework and be worried that I won't be able to assist. The tops of my ears burn with shame.

I'd been accepted into a good university. I never would have been a rocket scientist, but I could have been something, found some kind of success. It's never been okay with me that I didn't go. I always meant to enroll in some classes at the local community college once Olivia was in school, but I never got around to it. I'm setting a horrible example and my own child thinks I'm an uneducated idiot.

"Sure, honey. Mendel and the pea plants, right?"

"Uh-huh. The laws of genetic inheritance."

Whatever relief I felt has vanished. I see where this is going. I really am an idiot. My daughter, however, is not. "Oh."

"Yeah. Oh."

I lay the knife down and face her. Her eyes are watery. She's too far from the onion for that to be the cause. I sit on the stool next to her and cover her hand with mine. She snatches it away like I've burned her. I deserve this.

"I have several genetic traits that can only be inherited if one of my parents has the dominant expression for the gene. Like my cleft chin. And I can roll my tongue. Neither you or dad have a cleft chin or can roll your tongue."

All these years, I told myself there was no way to know for sure, not without a paternity test, but it turns out the answer was so simple that my fourteen-year-old figured it out for herself. Have I just been lying to myself this whole time? I look into her eyes, and know that I have.

"I'm guessing you have questions."

"Yeah, I do."

"I'll do my best to answer them for you."

I stare at the countertop, at the random sparkly spots in the granite. You can polish a piece of stone, you can make it shine, but you can't make it sparkle unless that special inclusion is already there. I wonder if there's any way that I can turn that thought into something that will make Olivia feel better right now. Probably not.

"Does dad know?"

"We've never discussed it."

Her eyes harden against me.

"I was never actually sure. If, you know..." If your father was your real father. Or if *he* was. I had hoped and prayed she was David's. Even if a part of me had always suspected she wasn't.

Olivia looks at me like I just drank out of the toilet.

"I don't think he does," I whisper.

She nods, satisfied. She looks over her shoulder, making sure no one is behind her. "I'm not going to say anything about this just yet."

"Thank you."

"Don't thank me. It's only because I realized you'd get full custody, and I don't want to be alone with you right now."

It feels like someone ran my heart through a paper shredder. Every facet of my life has chosen the same moment to implode, but this—my daughter looking at me with eyes full of shame and contempt? It easily tops the list as the worst. And it's not even the part that could land me in jail.

"Do you even know who my real dad is?"

"Yes."

"Were you ever going to tell me about him? Give me the chance to meet him?"

"Oh, honey." Just thinking about him makes hot tears run down my cheeks. "I wish you could."

This is a lie. Even if it were possible, I would never let that man in the same room with my child. I might not have realized it at the time, but he was a monster.

"Well, why can't I?"

"Olivia." It's hard enough to have a conversation with your daughter about how the man who raised her for the last fourteen years is not her real father. What I have to say now is even harder, but I have to do it. Because I need to squash any interest my daughter has in him. Taking a deep breath, I lie again. "Olivia, your dad, your biological dad, wants nothing to do with either of us."

Her head snaps back like I've slapped her.

"I was young, just a few years older than you. And I was stupid. And some men... they're only out for themselves. They don't care about anyone else. But your dad, David, I mean, he was there for me. For both of us. And we both love you so very, very much. Do you hate me now?"

"No." Her head turns slowly from side to side. "I don't. But I don't want to talk to you anymore right now, either."

I've always known this day might happen, and that if it did, it would be my cross to bear. I've spent the last fifteen years looking down at the wooden crossbeam at my feet just waiting for the day I'd have to pick it up and put it on. Now that its weight is across my shoulders, though, it's not that bad.

Olivia stands, looking at the stool like she never wants to sit there again. She slowly pulls her eyes away from it and heads toward her room. In the doorway she stops and turns. "By the way, who's coming to dinner?"

"One of my best friends from high school."

"High school? So she probably knew my real father, then?"

I gulp hard, remembering the shock of discovering just how well Sami knew him. I can't tell her the truth. I ignore it, instead. "I really think you're going to like her."

She rolls her eyes. "Sure I will." Her head shakes as she retreats to her room, shoulders high and hunched beneath her ears.

I know that I've gotten off easy. I have no idea how I'm going to tell her the rest of the story, or even how much of it I should tell. But I don't have the time to figure it out right now. I have more pressing issues to deal with first. I put the thought on the back burner to stew and go back to preparing dinner.

Sami arrives right on time, six thirty on the dot, and she comes bearing gifts. I'm so happy when I first see her standing there, but as I relieve her of the bottles of wine, a white and a red, and she comes inside, I feel a momentary surge of unease.

I know I'm being silly, but I can't help my nerves. Because as weird as it might seem given the circumstances, it's important to me to impress Sami now that we've reconnected after so long. I'm worried that she'll pick up on the tension between me and my family.

"Liz?" Sami puts her free hand on my shoulder.

I manage a weak smile and shake my head. "It's nothing. I'm fine."

"I keep having those moments too."

I know what she's referring to. I don't know how to explain that I'm juggling that with this, my daughter finding out that my husband is not her father, jeopardizing my perilous grasp on an already strained marriage. Then the oddest thing happens. I just let it go. At least I know Sami. And after last night, I've discovered that I still kind of trust her.

"I'm glad you're here." This time my smile is genuine.

"I am, too."

We head into the kitchen where David's head is lost in the fridge, his voice muffled as he asks Olivia questions about her day. He withdraws a moment later with a beer in hand. When he sees me and Sami standing together, a flush creeps from his collar, washing up his neck and into his face like watercolor paint spreading on damp paper. Even his ears turn pink.

"Olivia, this is Sami, one of my very best friends from child-hood. Sami, this is my daughter, Olivia."

Olivia is immediately smitten. She latches on to Sami's arm, insisting that Sami tell her about all the bad things I did while I was growing up, interrogating her as she leads the way to the dining room. After they've left, David turns to me. He reaches a hand tentatively toward my arm and rests his fingertips lightly on my skin. It feels like the memory of a touch that took place long ago. "Are we okay?"

"Yeah, why wouldn't we be?"

There's a rather long list of reasons that answer my question, but nothing's changed. It's an odd time for him to decide to check on my feelings. But his confused expression is mixed with relief, and for the first time in a long while, I'm touched. Maybe I was wrong. Maybe he does care. I give his hand a soft pat. It's awkward and strange, the ghost of an intimacy that's long passed away.

"Will you please set the table?"

He nods, a sad smile settling on his lips. He grabs the silver-ware and follows Olivia and Sami into the other room. I relish this moment. This fleeting sense of calmness just might be the closest thing I'll know to peace in a very long time to come.

EIGHTEEN

LIZ THEN

1998

Things have been so tense with my friends lately that I spend most of my time walking on eggshells, barely able to breathe. But right now I'm tiptoeing for a different reason. An incredible, amazing, fantastic one.

My heart thumps inside my chest. It's from the thrill of the risk, the excitement of waiting for that perfect opportunity to slip out unnoticed between my brothers' late-night arrivals and departures, but, mainly, it's the anticipation of seeing him. The only times I've ever snuck out have been to see him.

I loop my fingers through the back straps of my sandals. The floor is cold and gritty beneath my bare feet. Bathed in the moonlight filtering through the window, the dark wood and red nail polish accentuate my pale skin. My back presses hard against the wall.

I lean forward, risking another peek outside. My second oldest brother, Bert, is finally in his friend's ratty old Wrangler, the torn topper hanging from the roll bar in stalactite formations. The car idles at the end of the driveway. *Get a move on already.*

Finally, with a dirty gray cloud puffing from the exhaust pipe, they're in motion. I watch the taillights fade down the street and disappear around the corner, before I slide along the wall, the fingers of my outstretched hand closing around the doorknob. Then it's open and I'm through, darting across the lawn, sprinting until I'm in the shadows of the empty lot across the street. I pause to catch my breath, slipping my sandals over feet damp with dew, plucking a blade of grass from between my toes.

In case you didn't know, the world is completely different at night. Things you'd never notice under the light of the sun take center stage after nightfall, spotlighted by moonbeams, skulking in shadows. It's both ominous and innocent, restrictive and freeing. Even the scents and sounds are different.

I keep to the side, walking along the tall hedge that outlines the boundaries of the lot until I'm through, the soles of my shoes slapping against the sidewalk as I hurry down the street. My arms cross over my body, rubbing at the rising goosebumps. The night is balmy, the heat from the summer day lingering, hovering over the ground. I'm not cold. It's thinking of him that makes me shiver.

I see our meeting spot up ahead and my steps quicken, my breath catching in my chest. Just the thought of him makes my pulse race. He makes me feel alive in a way I've never felt before.

Not like when I'm lost in the shuffle at home, the youngest, the only girl, the good one who behaves and can be trusted to do things on her own, without being told. Not like at school, where I'm a good student who can be counted on to make good grades, who isn't a disruption or an active participant and therefore is not a pupil the teachers need to pay attention to. Not even like my group of friends, where it seems more and more like everyone has an important role to play in the group except me. I'm just there, fading into the background.

But it's not like that with him. He sees me for me, sees me despite the others, and makes time for only me, just the two of us, one on one. To him, I'm special. It's obvious, or he wouldn't be waiting for me right now. I run the last few steps because I can't wait to have him all to myself.

NINETEEN

SAMI NOW

2014

I smile and laugh and make polite conversation, but on the inside I'm dying. This is so uncomfortable. It's clear that Liz and David are miserable together. They can barely even look at each other. I can't help but feel like it's my fault, even though I know it isn't.

I'm always doing that. Blaming myself.

Liz was my best friend for so long. My ride or die. When we severed ties, it was hard to breathe—like I had lost a lung as well as a friend.

But as much as I loved her, I could still see her faults. And this is one of them. She's always been good at sticking her head in the sand. Ignoring the things she'd rather not face, no matter how obvious they are.

Growing up, the four of us always had each other's backs. No one else could touch us. We'd defend each other 'til the end, sometimes crazy or violent in our loyalty. But we never hesitated to call each other out on our shit. And Liz needs to be called out, loud and clear. Because it's obvious this situation is making everyone miserable—unnecessarily so.

Real love might be hard and messy, but it's even more so when you try to force it. It's clear that her marriage has run its course. She's looking for love in the wrong place, and she's going to get hurt.

But there will be time to deal with that later. In the grand scheme of things, she's not the one I have to worry about right now. But when this is all over? I'm going to fix this and make sure everything is as it should be.

TWENTY

AMY THEN

1998

That first time I only did it because I wanted to know what all the fuss was about. Sex. It was something talked about in whispers, accompanied by giggles and the exchange of knowing looks. Only, I didn't know, so I couldn't be in on any of the looks, could I? And I couldn't understand what all the fuss was about. What it was about that three-letter word that was such a big deal? Even my friends and I didn't talk about it. Not *really*.

But then they kind of did. Only, not so much in words, but in those giggles and knowing glances that I didn't understand anything about. Liz and Sami would make vague references to let us know they'd joined the club, and Mo, well, we all assumed Mo, being so much more worldly and sophisticated than us, was already a member and just didn't talk about it, because she was so much more worldly and sophisticated. I couldn't stand thinking that there was something between us, an unspoken wedge that would divide us into them and me.

There was no one special, and frankly I had no interest in finding that special someone. I just wanted to know once and for all what all the fuss was about. Like a science experiment, only without the careful attention to detail, performed more like pulling off a Band-Aid—just do it fast and get it over with.

I had never really planned to go down to the place where the good girls don't go, my feet just sort of brought me there one night and suddenly there I was, strolling down the sidewalk by the minimart where the guys from the football team hung out after dark, smoking and drinking and trolling for girls.

I still hadn't quite made up my mind, not until one of them whistled at me as I walked by. It was Johnny Donovan, a senior with a reputation that made me confident that he'd know what he was doing. So, I played the role I'd cast for myself. I hooked my eyes to his, held them for a long moment, and then gestured with my head for him to come over to me. The other boys hooted and hollered as he sauntered over with his best cool-guy strut.

"Hey. Whatcha doing?" Not the best pick-up line, but lucky for him my expectations were low.

"Looking for someplace better to go."

"And where's that?"

"I don't know. Where do you want to take me?"

He slung an arm around my neck, tossed a glance over his shoulder to his cheering friends, and led me down the path. We walked side by side in silence, every nerve in my body on edge. He took me to a park. I followed him past the picnic tables and playground equipment, through a narrow break in the brush to a small knoll surrounded by trees. Then he answered all my questions.

I wasn't really impressed. I still didn't see what all the fuss was about, but at least now I knew. Now I could be in on the looks and innuendos and not be left behind in the cold, while my friends went on lightyears down the road ahead of me. But then the next day, at school, I overheard the rumor while using the restroom between classes.

"Oh my God, did you hear, Morgana Ripley did it with Johnny Donovan in the park last night."

"Oh my God, she's *such* a slut!"

I should have said something right then, should have burst out of the stall and defended Mo's honor, should have taken credit for my own sins. But I didn't. I was frozen, rooted to the spot on that grimy floor, surrounded by graffiti on walls the color of aged parmesan cheese, breathing that dirty-water-mingled-with-cigarette-smoke stench school bathrooms always have.

It had never occurred to me that I would be mistaken for Mo, that the dark would conceal the differences in our appearance, that such brazenness would be considered so out of character for the Amy people thought they knew, that they would assume it was her instead of me. I know that I should do something to squash the rumor, but I can't. What if Johnny only went with me because he thought I was her? What if all the guys felt that way?

Because as much as I didn't see what all the fuss was about, I did want to do it again. Something about the intimacy, the closeness, filled a hole inside me that I hadn't known existed. Only, now I did know, and I could feel it inside me, a huge, gaping emptiness surrounded by loneliness and hurt.

There are already dozens of rumors swirling around about Mo. People love to hate her, they always have, and she never lets it bother her. So what's a few more?

TWENTY-ONE

LIZ NOW

2014

The house is empty when I wake. It's like the apocalypse came overnight and swept everyone else away. The effect is eerie, the sounds of my steps echoing down the hall, seeming louder than they ever have before.

I pour coffee grounds into a filter, add water, and hit the brew button. Then I walk around the house, pulling curtains shut and drawing blinds. I have a headache that demands darkness. I feel hungover, which is strange—I didn't have much to drink last night, just a single glass of the white wine Sami brought over.

Maybe I'm just dehydrated. Or it's all the drinking Sami and I did the night before last finally catching up with me. Whatever the cause, the very roots of my eyes ache and even though I just woke up, all I can think about is crawling back in bed. Maybe I should have had some of the red wine instead. Sami and David finished the entire bottle last night, and I bet they're both feeling fine.

At the side window in the living room, I catch sight of

Francine. She waves at me. I wave back, mine a goodbye instead of a hello, and yank the thick drapery over the glass.

I'm hyper aware of my senses, the feeling as my feet leave the thick, plush carpet and slap against the rough hardwood floors. Then the tiles, cold and hard as I head back to the kitchen because the aroma of coffee has permeated the air.

Filling a mug, I carry it to the couch and sit, curling my feet up beside me. The coffee tastes better than usual. Maybe there's hope that today will be a good day after all.

But then a knock against the door carries from the front of the house and infiltrates the room around me, and I know I was mistaken. I felt relief too soon.

As I'm on my way to answer it, my first thought is that it might be Francine, but it's not. I know it's not. There was something authoritative about the knock, a demanding quality. I take one more sip before I set my mug down, the coffee coating my tongue with a thick layer of sludge, and suddenly it doesn't taste too good after all.

I sneak a look through the peephole and then dart away like the man on the other side of the door can see me. I have to remind myself that he can't. I glance down at the worn pair of jeans and booster shirt for the high school volleyball team that I'm wearing. I have no makeup on. My wedding ring is still on the soap dish next to the sink in the bathroom. None of that bothers me that much. What upsets me are my bare feet.

If I could change one thing about the image I'm going to present when I open the door, that would be it. I'd be wearing shoes. Something about bare feet has always struck me as kind of intimate. It makes me feel vulnerable and exposed.

It would take too long to run to my room in the back and slip a pair on. I consider not opening the door at all, but then I remember that Francine was lurking about outside. She knows I'm in the house and would no doubt revel in the opportunity to share that information with this stranger. I take a deep breath, tell myself that it's fortifying, and pull the door open.

The man is tall and good looking, his brown eyes the same color as his smooth, unlined skin. A tidy mustache highlights his full lips. His suit is impeccable. And he holds himself with an air of distinguished confidence.

All this disturbs me in a way I can't quite describe. It's clear that this man has been around the block, that he's seasoned, that he has it together. Why couldn't it have been some slob or a kid?

"May I help you?"

"Are you Mrs. Elizabeth Bentley? Formerly Williams?"

"May I ask who wants to know?"

A badge appears with ridiculous speed and is opened with practiced efficiency.

"Detective Everett Johnson, from the Waverly Police Department."

"I'm Liz Bentley."

"May I come inside, ma'am?"

I ignore the curious look on Francine's face as she gawks opened-mouthed from her yard, and stand back, letting the detective inside. I wish she hadn't been here to see this. I know that, as soon as I close the door, she's going to hop on her phone and tell anyone who will answer her call that there's a police officer at my house questioning me. It wouldn't surprise me if she gathers a little crowd in her yard while the cop and I are talking. I show him to the living room, where he chooses an armchair in the corner, the only seat with its back to the wall.

"Can I get you something to drink? Coffee?"

"No, thank you. Ma'am, I'm here today to ask you some questions about someone I believe you used to be acquainted with. A Charamy Russo. Does that ring any bells?"

"Of course. Amy was one of my best friends growing up. Has something happened? Is she all right?"

"You said was. Why not is?"

"I haven't seen Amy since high school."

"Is there any particular reason for that? Did you two have a falling out of some sorts?"

"No, not at all. Has something happened to Amy, Detective?"

"That's what I'm trying to figure out. Please, just humor me, if you would. Tell me about how the two of you fell out of contact."

"Well, we aren't. Not exactly."

"I'm afraid I don't understand."

"It's simple, really. Just because you haven't seen someone doesn't mean you aren't in touch." I think about the notes I've received. The ones *she* sent. But I can't tell him about that. So I tell him about the postcards instead. "I might not have seen her in a long while, but I do receive postcards from time to time."

"Postcards."

"Yes."

"And is that the only communication you have? Do you two ever talk on the phone? Text?"

"Well, no."

"And why is that?"

"No reason in particular. Just busy, I guess."

He pulls a notepad and pen from his pocket, flips to a clean page. "What can you tell me about Ms. Russo?"

"Well, let's see. Amy was a singer. She had incredible talent, I mean, really, she wasn't just one of those girls who thinks she can be a star because she can hold a tune. Amy was the real deal. She got an offer for a music deal when we were still in high school. She left to follow her dreams."

"You used the past tense. Was, had... is there a reason for that?"

I feel like an idiot. I curl my feet, trying to hide my toes under the couch. "No. I guess that it's just been so long since I've talked to her that I don't really feel like I know her now."

"And where was it you said that she went?"

I didn't. I think of the stack of postcards in the bottom drawer of my nightstand. "Well, when she first left, it was for Los Angeles. But I don't think she's been in the States for a while now. The last I heard from her, she was in Asia. Taiwan, I believe."

"And how long ago was that?"

"I'm not sure. I'd have to check, but probably three, maybe four months ago." The nail of my forefinger digs at a cuticle on my thumb. I notice him watching and force myself to stop, sliding my thumb under my thigh.

"You didn't happen to save them, did you? The postcards she sent?"

"Well, yeah. I've saved them all, actually. Living vicariously and all that. Why?"

"Would you mind if I look at them?"

"Listen, Detective... I'm sorry, what was it?"

"Johnson."

"Detective Johnson. I realize you're just doing your job, but I have no idea what's going on and I really don't feel comfortable answering any more questions until I know why you're here. Has something happened to Amy?"

"We're not sure yet, Mrs. Bentley, but we are looking into the possibility that she may have met with some harm."

I press a palm to my chest, trying to calm my heartbeat. "Is she all right?"

"We're investigating a set of remains that have been discovered."

My hand flies to my open mouth, a reflex reaction even though I knew what was coming. "Oh my God. And you think that it's Amy?"

"The information we've obtained is leading us in that direction, yes."

"I always worried about her traveling so much on her own."

"Actually, ma'am, the remains are here. In town."

"What? When did she get back?"

"If the remains in question do indeed turn out to be your friend's, it's possible that she never left."

I can barely make myself choke out a whisper. "So she never even made it to L.A.?"

"I can't say anything for sure yet, ma'am."

"But then who's been sending me postcards all these years?"

"That's a very good question. And one that I would like an answer to as well. Mrs. Bentley—"

"Liz. Call me Liz, please."

"Okay, Liz. Can you tell me about when Amy supposedly left town?"

"It was the Monday after prom. She'd gotten an offer from a record company out in L.A. She'd turned eighteen over the weekend, so she was finally free to accept it and fly out there. We had a slumber party that weekend to celebrate."

"Did she say goodbye?"

"Of course. She went to school that day to say goodbye to everyone."

"Did you see her get on the plane?"

"No."

"Then why did you assume that she had left for Los Angeles?"

"Because she said she was."

"But did anyone actually go with her to the airport?"

"I'm not sure. But why would that matter?"

He ignores my question, instead asking another of his own. "So, to your knowledge, was there anything—or anyone—to keep Amy from leaving?"

"No." I shake my head, sure about this answer. "Her father

had just passed away. Her mom had died right after she was born. She was an only child."

"Any other relatives?"

"Mo was her cousin. I guess Mo's parents would have been her aunt and uncle, but they were never around. They traveled a lot."

Detective Johnson sits forward, resting his elbows on his knees. "Sounds like that must have been rough on their daughter."

"It was."

He looks down, inspecting the nails of his right hand as he asks, "How did all that time alone affect her? Any behavioral problems? Anger issues? Maybe a sense of over-entitlement?" His eyes shoot right back to my face, watching while I answer.

"Who, Mo? No. I mean, out of all of us, Mo had the most attitude, she could be a bitch sometimes, but she wasn't like that to be spiteful. She just spoke her mind and didn't take shit from anyone. We all wanted to be a bit more like her."

"Was there any bad blood between Amy and her cousin?"

"No, never. They were like sisters."

"Even sisters fight."

"Yeah, but... why are you asking this? You honestly don't suspect that Mo had something to do with...?"

"When was the last time you spoke with Ms. Ripley?"

"Graduation, I guess." I take a sip of my coffee, wince as I force down a cold swallow.

"And when was that, in relation to the prom and her birthday?"

"About two weeks later."

"So, if Amy left town, she did it only two weeks before she would have had her diploma?"

"I guess."

"And Mo? That's what you called her? Are you two still in touch?"

I shake my head. "She left right after we graduated to travel. To do the whole world tour thing. As far as I know, she's never been back."

"Surely she could have picked up a phone, sent a letter from time to time, something. Can you think of any reason why she didn't?"

"I don't know. Maybe she was having too much fun?"

"For a group of friends as close as it sounds like you were, and I have spoken to outside sources about this, it sure does seem like your friendship unraveled pretty suddenly. And easily. That never bothered you?"

I wonder who he's been talking to. Francine, knowing my luck. She probably filled his head with all her inane little theories. But regardless of who it was, I need to discredit them and put an end to this line of questioning, fast.

"Detective Johnson, if you've been talking to other people about what was going on at that time, then surely you know that by the end of the summer I'd gotten married and was expecting a baby at eighteen years old. I loved my friends, I still do, but I had a full plate of my own. I had a lot to worry about back then. So if it seems to you that I failed my friends by not being more aggressive in maintaining our friendship, well, I would apologize, but quite honestly I really don't give a damn what you think."

"Fair enough."

"I mean, seriously. Things change. Take my neighbor, Francine, for instance. Not to be mean, but she was a real pest in high school. She practically stalked me and my friends. Like, total creeper. But now we have daughters the same age, so we end up together all the time. Do you think that makes me happy? Don't you think I'd rather choose who I spend what little free time I have with? But it doesn't always work that way, especially after you have kids. Sometimes you have to make sacrifices."

"I can respect that."

"Can you respect that enough to tell me why you're jumping to all these horrible conclusions about my friends?"

"The story has been on the news, so I guess there's no harm in telling you. The remains were found on property formerly owned by the Ripley family."

"What?"

"Ripley Manor, I believe it was called. The new owners were having some construction work done when the bones were discovered. We still have a team out there working on recovering all of the remains, but we've found enough so far that both the pathologist and forensic anthropologist feel comfortable in their determination that the bones in our possession are those of a girl in her late teens to early twenties."

My voice breaks, turning the word into several syllables as I ask, "Where?" Clearing my throat, I try again. "Where was she found?"

"Under a big heap of rocks, just within the edge of the woods. It looks like it might have been a structure at one time. Are you familiar with it?"

"The clochán."

"Excuse me?"

"It was an Irish clochán. It was our favorite place when we were little, kind of like our clubhouse, where we spent most of our time. It's where we used to sleep when we spent the night at Mo's. Why would... the new owners, they were having it torn down?"

"No, it was already down. They were sourcing the stones for another project, building a retaining wall in the back garden when a worker discovered the skull. Was that clochán where the four of you spent that last night together? Your slumber party?"

"It was."

"So, the structure was still standing at that time?"

I nod.

"And obviously there wasn't a dead body in there with you that night, was there?"

I don't even know how to respond to that. I hope the look I give him lets Detective Johnson know what I think about his question.

"Hey." He holds his hands out in front of himself like he's warding off an attack. "I had to ask."

"None of this makes any sense. It sounds like you suspect Mo, but she loved Amy, the only family they ever really had was each other. Mo's not really a suspect, is she?"

"Well, ma'am, I have to be honest with you." The look he gives me sends a chill down my spine. It takes all my willpower not to shiver. "At this time, she is."

"I'm sorry, Detective, but that's impossible. She would have never hurt Amy."

"Well, that's just one theory."

"What's another?"

"As far as I've been able to tell, only a handful of people knew about that, what did you call it, a clochán? And one of them is dead."

"Are you saying that I'm a suspect?"

"No. No, ma'am, I'm not. But I am suggesting that you don't try to leave town while the investigation is under way."

I sit still for a moment, stunned. When I find my voice, it has the sharp edge of anger. "Then I'm going to suggest, Detective, that this conversation is over."

Detective Johnson rises to his feet like he's been expecting me to ask him to leave for some time already. He nods. "Very well. If I could get those postcards..."

I hurry down the hall and into my room, not wanting to leave him unsupervised for too long in my home. Yanking open my nightstand drawer, I grab the shoebox containing the postcards and rush back, handing them over without a word as I usher him toward the door.

Halfway through, he stops. "Like I said—"

"I have no reason to leave and nowhere to go," I say, interrupting him.

He nods, satisfied, and finally leaves. I lock the bolt behind him, press my back against the door and breathe a sigh of relief to have him gone. I need to warn Sami. Now.

But self-preservation is a funny thing. Just as quickly as I make the decision to call her, I question it. As a parent I have a duty to put my daughter, and by proxy, as her caregiver, myself, first. I wonder if Sami would do the same for me if the situation was reversed. Then a strange part of me I've never met before decides that it doesn't matter.

That whole all-for-one and one-for-all thing? We tried it. If it had worked, there wouldn't have been a detective on my doorstep in the first place.

TWENTY-TWO

SAMI THEN

1998

I'm supposed to be studying, but I can't focus. I slam my textbook closed with a huff, earning a raised eyebrow from Mo, sitting across the table from me. I hold her gaze, challenging her to make a comment. Wanting to get in an argument. But not with her.

A small smile plays about her lips as if she knows this. Closing the magazine she was thumbing through and placing it on the table, she says, "It's all their fault. They're being super annoying out there, all happy and cheerful, aren't they?"

I look out the window, toward the bench in my backyard where Liz is helping Amy run through her lines for the school play. They look cold even though they're bundled in blankets. They shouldn't be disturbing me, but they are.

Liz glances up, catching me staring at them, and smiles. I try to return it, but it's tough. Everything seems so easy for everyone else. Everyone else but me. It's just not fair.

Singing comes naturally to Amy. Confidence comes naturally to Mo. Liz barely studies, but her grades are better than mine in every subject but history. I have to work so hard all the time just to be mediocre, and it's exhausting.

The doorbell rings, disturbing my thoughts, and I shoot a scowl toward the front of the house. The last thing I need is another interruption.

"I'll get it," Mo says, pushing her chair back from the table and standing.

I roll my eyes as she leaves the room because it's probably for her, anyways. Even the visitors who come to my own house aren't for me. I just wish I didn't feel so invisible all the time.

But all my friends are so perfect and gorgeous. It's hard not to want what they have sometimes. Even if I know it's wrong. Even though I know I shouldn't.

Turning my attention back out the window, I debate whether or not to go outside. It's nice and warm in here. I have a ton more work to get done. But maybe I could regain my focus after a short break.

Before I can decide, though, Mo returns. Two sets of shoes slap against the tile floor, letting me know she isn't alone. I round on the visitor, cross and needing a victim, but I freeze mid-snarl. All the static chaos jumbling around my head stills. I feel my face relax into a genuine smile.

"Sonny."

"Hey, Sami. Always great to see you." I feel myself blush. I know he's just being polite, but still. It's nice that he thinks I'm worth the effort.

He knocks on the window, then taps at an imaginary watch on his wrist, obviously a sign to Amy. "I was on my way home and figured I'd stop and pick up Amy. She's always complaining about walking home when it's cold."

"We were just getting ready to order a couple of pizzas if you want to stick around," I offer.

"Nah. I've got a lot to do tonight so I've got to get a move on, but thanks."

"Oh," I say, unable to hide my disappointment that he won't be staying longer. Wondering what it is that he plans on doing instead. "Well, maybe another time."

"Yeah, maybe."

"Aw, come on." Mo flashes an evil grin my way. Flicks her eyes toward the window where we can see Amy and Liz approaching the house. I stifle a smile of my own as I realize what she's thinking. "Don't be like that. Please? Sami's mom is at her book club tonight. We're here all alone. And it's scary."

She sticks out her lower lip. Sonny laughs, but whether it's at Mo's fake pout or the idea of her being scared, I couldn't say. What I can say is that it will drive Amy absolutely crazy if her dad sticks around and hangs out with us, and, for some reason, the idea of seeing someone else as miserable as I've been feeling seems like the very thing to cheer me up—even if it is at my friend's expense.

"I'll help you do whatever it is you need done if you stay and eat dinner with us. Promise." It's a brazen offer, something much more out of Mo's playbook than mine, but right now, I don't care. Sonny's always heavy-handed with the compliments, and I could use that right now.

The French door rattles open, and Liz and Amy shuffle inside, cheeks pink and eyes bright from the cold. The wind has artfully styled Liz's topknot, pulling strands free to sexily frame her pretty face. I watch helplessly as Sonny gives her an appreciative once-over while I stand there beside him, forgotten and invisible once more. Then he glances back over at me and gives me a wink.

"I'm all set," Amy says.

But Sonny's big rush has been forgotten. "Change of plans, kid."

"What do you mean?"

He tosses an arm around my shoulder. "We're staying for dinner. I believe I was promised some pizza?"

He gives me a gentle squeeze as he looks at me, waiting for my answer. But I can't look back. And I can't speak. His face is too close to mine. What if my breath stinks?

"Ha, ha," Amy says, but from her expression you can tell she doesn't think it's funny at all. "We should get going."

"And garlic knots," Mo says, waggling her eyebrows. "And... chicken wings?"

Amy glares at her as Sonny grabs at his chest. "How can I resist all that?"

Mo gives her a smirk as she asks Sonny, "Blue cheese or ranch?"

"Surprise me."

"Dad?"

"Relax, Amy."

She huffs. "But—"

"Is it your car?" he asks.

Her eyes fall to the floor as she shakes her head.

"Are you paying for the gas?"

Another head shake.

"Then it's not your decision, is it?"

It's not. It's his. And he's choosing to stay a little longer. I really hope it's because of me.

TWENTY-THREE

SAMI NOW

2014

It's funny how life turns out. You can make all the plans you want, but reality doesn't follow any set blueprint. It doesn't even take suggestions. It's like an animal, an entity unto itself that reacts and evolves and changes and adapts and isn't even aware of rules or guidelines. What reality really is—and I know I've both seen and heard this dozens of times, but I don't think I really got how true it was before—is a bitch.

I have always prided myself on being one of those people who does the right thing. What a load of shit. I mean, how deluded would I have to be to believe that's true?

Sure, I obey traffic laws and try my best to be environmentally responsible and have several charities draw a small pittance every month from my checking account, but have I really allowed myself to be fooled into believing that I'm a good person when my moral compass is so completely screwed? And if I'm really honest with myself, which I haven't been, obviously, for far too long, it's been that way for most of my life.

Have I always been a fraud? I think maybe so.

I'm just going to come right out and say this. I have never had a relationship with a man who was available. They haven't all been married, but none were in the position to establish a healthy adult relationship. This was the way I liked it, the way I wanted it, because I wasn't an available woman.

My heart died with the first guy I ever loved. His death was such a shock, such a horrible, tragic blow that I didn't think I had it in me to try to love again. It wasn't until now, with the insight of what I've recently discovered, that it even occurred to me that I could ever be happy again. But I think that I can. I think I deserve it. And more.

I wasn't the most outgoing girl. I was the studious one, the one most often found with my nose buried in the pages of a book. That's not a huge turn-on for teenage boys, especially when your friends are all traffic-stopping gorgeous. Next to them I was invisible.

Liz was the cute, petite blonde, the girl next door type that was easy to approach. With all her brothers, she was naturally comfortable with the opposite sex. She was relaxed, unintimidating, and she knew when to laugh at their jokes and when to call them out and give them shit.

Mo was the ice queen, who, by making herself unattainable, made the boys want her even more. In college, there was a girl with the same kind of attitude. She wasn't even pretty, she was actually extraordinarily plain, but she had to practically beat the boys off with a stick. So, you can imagine the reaction Mo got, with her jet-black waves and her iceberg blue eyes and her flawless skin and perfect features.

And Amy, she was a near carbon copy of Mo, only soft-spoken and seemingly sweet. She was the one that made all those girl-crazy, pubescent boys think about the woman they would marry one day.

Then there was me, who usually couldn't even manage to stutter out my name. So when a guy finally came along who made me feel whole and complete and wanted and loved and deserving and special, how could I not give him my heart?

I still remember how it began, our shoulders bumping, his hand brushing against mine, our eyes locking. Everything else in the room shrinking into the background, sucked back into oblivion. If it wasn't one of the two of us, it didn't exist.

Accidentally-on-purpose touches and stolen glances changed with the seasons. As the ice melted and the warmth of spring crept forward, our encounters heated up. But we had to keep our feelings secret.

And then something horrible happened. I lost him. He was gone.

I would never want to make someone feel the way that I felt. Not even the person who hurt me. Not one of my best friends or my worst enemy. Even if they were one and the same.

TWENTY-FOUR

AMY THEN

1999

Mo is throwing a party. You'd think, during all these years she's had that huge mansion all to herself with no real adult supervision, that this would have happened before, but it hasn't. And that's because it's a very bad idea.

I don't know what she's thinking, inviting a bunch of strangers into her house. Sure, we've gone to school with most of them for over a decade, but we don't really know these people. They'd only be coming to say they were there, to satisfy their curiosity, like it's some kind of freak show at the circus.

We just started the last semester of senior year. I wish she would let us finish out the high school jail term in peace. I want to pitch a fit and get her to change her mind, but she's been acting kind of odd lately, and I can't help but feel guilty and wonder how much of it I'm responsible for. Probably more than I'd like to admit.

So of course I have to be supportive and invite anyone I can think of who will actually show up, because the only thing worse than an out-of-control teenage party is a party that had all the ingredients to be epic and still failed. This seems to be really important to her, so the rest of us are making it a priority to do everything we can to make this fiasco into the party of Mo's dreams.

That's why, instead of finishing my biology homework and watching my favorite TV show, the way I should on a Tuesday night, I'm putting makeup on and getting dressed to go out. At least *Buffy* is a rerun. I grab my jacket and wander the house, looking for my dad.

His car is in the driveway, but he's not home. Worse, he's taken the car keys with him, so I can't even borrow the raggedy old truck that's as old as I am. My legs are more reliable, but the truck is slightly quicker, and tonight I'd prefer to make a fast in and out. I can't say I'm pleased.

The night air is thick with the scent of the neighbor's prized night-blooming jasmine as I step outside. Locking the door, I wrap my arms around myself to ward off the chill, and start down the sidewalk toward town. A bunch of the theater kids are getting together, to brainstorm a list of fundraisers that might entice the school to support a musical for our spring performance.

I'm kind of excited by the idea, even if it does mean leaving my comfort zone to socialize with kids who are acquaintances at best. And sometime during the night I have to find a way to work in an invitation to Mo's party. Ugh.

I blow my breath out heavily and feel my bangs lift off my forehead. Rolling my eyes up, I watch the wisps of hair settle back over my eyebrows, just within the upper realm of my vision. They're getting too long. I should have trimmed them already, but Mo is growing hers out. I don't want to do it just because she is, but if I don't, there'll be a surefire way for people who don't know us well to tell us apart.

It could be just what I need to put an end to my late-night alter ego. But I'm not sure I'm ready to do that just yet.

Rounding the corner, I'm lost in thought, until something snags my attention. A man is walking ahead of me. He has the familiar, swaggering stride of my father.

I jog a few feet, intent on catching up with him, but something stops me; a need, a desire to be a larger part of my dad's life, to know him better. Or so I tell myself. I suspect, though, that I really just want to see what it is that he does with his time while I'm being neglected.

My subconscious has already made the decision. Slowly the message relays to my body, and then to my mind. It's time to find out where my dad goes at night.

I quicken my steps as he nears the next corner, afraid of losing sight of him. The tempo of my heart speeds up. A surge of adrenaline heightens my senses.

I can hear his shoes scuffing dully against the concrete sidewalk. The faint scent of his cologne carries on the wind. The change in his pocket jingles. Suddenly, he turns to his right, takes three steps, and then disappears into the shadows of the park.

He's gone by the time I catch up. Standing still, I listen to the night. Dry leaves scratch against each other in the breeze. Something scurries in a bush beside me. Then, very faintly, I hear the soft whisper of grass crushing underfoot.

Following the sound, I catch a whiff of his cologne and know I'm on the right track. Parting branches, I creep along as quickly as I can without making too much noise. Then, in a clearing up ahead, I see him.

When I see who he's with, my heart leaps, sure that my dad has asked my friends for help with a surprise for me. Maybe this year he'll remember my birthday. Or he'll send me somewhere to celebrate graduation. My cheeks warm with a flush of happiness.

But then I'm not quite sure what it is that I'm seeing. Because my brain refuses to process it.

I feel dizzy. I try to swallow, but my throat is squeezed shut, the muscles refusing passage in either direction. It traps my cries of protest, preventing them from reaching the outside world. My ribs are too tight. I rub at the center of my chest, pull my bra away from my skin, but I can't get any relief. It feels like a snake has wrapped around my body and is squeezing, constricting my airway. I can't breathe.

Tearing my eyes off the scene before me, I stumble away, branches scratching my arms and legs, thorns snagging at my clothes as I fight my way through the brush, making my own path to escape on. Then I'm running blindly through the park, not caring where I'm going as long as my feet carry me away.

Muscle memory gets me home. My hands are shaking too bad to unlock the door—I keep dropping the keys. I decide to leave them, abandoning them in a heap on the doorstep as I wander around the side of the house.

I trip over a rock, the same rock my dad cusses about every time he mows the yard. Bending, I pick it up, feel the weight of it in my palm, its surface both rough and smooth. It flings from my hand like a dart, straight through the living room window.

I follow after it, breaking the rest of the glass with my bare fist. The cuts weep, crying blood, leaving a trail of dark teardrops across the carpet as I head toward the kitchen. Wrapping a dishtowel around my fist, I sit down at the table and wait.

The front door slams, drawing me away from the safe place I've created in my mind, back to the world of the living. After a few blinks I'm able to focus my vision. My gaze lands on the towel still tightly wrapped around my hand. The bright red splotches have morphed into hard, rust-colored patches.

"Amy?"

I remain silent.

"Amy?"

There is no worry in the tone, only irritation.

"Jesus, Amy, you could have answered me. You left your keys on the front stoop."

The keys land on the table next to the fingertips of my injured hand. Sonny whistles as he opens the refrigerator door, vanishing from view as he leans in to grab a beer. Straightening, he pops the top on the can and takes a long swig before shutting the door. He leaves the kitchen. I hear his feet crunch across the broken glass in the living room.

"What the hell?"

His head pops around the wall, into the kitchen.

"What happened to the window?"

For the first time, he notices the blood-soaked towel on my hand.

"You need stitches?" When I don't respond, he takes that as a no. "Well, then, clean it up. It's not like we've got a maid service around here."

I snort. His eyes fly to mine, flashing with anger. Something he sees in my face quells it.

"What the hell has gotten under your skin? Has some boy done something to you?" He enters the kitchen and slams his beer down on the table, liquid splashing over the aluminum mouth onto the cheap faux-wood laminate. "Well, what is it? Can't you speak?"

I try to set him on fire with my glare. When that doesn't work, I let the words spill out of my mouth in slow syllables. "I. Saw. You." I rise from the table so suddenly that my chair falls over backward, bouncing across the floor behind me. "With. Her."

I narrow my eyes to match his. Tighten my jaw to the same taut-muscled tension. Curl my fingers into fists, the skin over my wounds pulling tight. Square my feet until I'm mirroring his pugilistic stance.

"So. What's it to you? It's none of your business."

"She's my friend."

"Well, I guess she's my friend, now, too."

"She's a minor."

"I haven't heard her complaining."

"You're using her. You used me to get to her."

"Maybe she used you to get to me, did you ever think of that?"

"You're a pedophile. A pervert. Stop it or I'll tell. I'm serious."

"Shut your fucking mouth before I shut it for you. And give me the respect I deserve. I'm the one that puts food on this table and keeps a roof over your head."

I roll my eyes. "Barely."

"Goddamn it." Sonny flings his beer against the wall. It hits the China clock, the Portmeirion piece falling to the floor, shattering. It was one of the few things in this place that was my mom's. One of the only things I had to remember her by.

I look from the ruined clock to Sonny. His chest heaves with each breath. I can practically see steam curling from his nose like a cartoon bull. He's never been violent before. Quick to anger, bad tempered, but he's never thrown something before. He's never hit me.

But I always knew the potential was there, lurking like a hungry crocodile just below the surface. There's a dark, hidden part of me that has always wanted to chum those waters.

"Is that why you kept me around all these years? Because you knew that one day I'd be of some use to you? That once I got old enough I'd bring some fresh victims around for you to prey on?"

"Ha. Don't fool yourself, Amy. You've never been any use to me. I don't know why the hell I kept you around. Sentimental, I guess. Maybe I thought you'd grow up to be like your momma, but I knew years ago you'd never be a thing like her. Not a piece of trash like you. She was a real lady."

The wad of spit hits his cheek before I realize I did it. That it came from me.

His open hand strikes my face. I stumble back a couple of steps before catching my balance. My slapped cheek burns, but not nearly as much as his words.

"I should have sold you to the Ripleys with your sister. The money would have done me a world more good than having some cheap memento hanging around." His hand moves toward me again. I resist the urge to flinch. His palm cradles my chin. For a moment I think this small bit of tenderness is his way of apologizing. Then he spits, a gob of saliva gluing my eye shut. "Now make yourself useful for once and clean this shit up."

My one open eye stares at the scuffed toes of my worn sneakers. I stay motionless, waiting for him to leave. Once I hear the front door slam, the grumble of his old truck choke to life, I grab the towel from the table and use a clean corner to wipe my eye before I flush it with water at the sink.

My mind is churning, my course of action plotting across an imaginary map. Most of all, though, my brain is turning one word over and over inside my head, like a globe spinning on its axis.

Sister. He said I had a sister, that he *sold* my sister. Mo.

There's no other explanation. We look so much alike. We even have the same birthday.

Why the hell didn't he sell us together? Everything would have turned out different, better. Maybe she and I wouldn't be so damned screwed up if our whole lives hadn't been spent denying something that every cell in our body knew. A part of us was missing. A vital part. A twin.

TWENTY-FIVE

FRANCINE NOW

2014

Francine snakes a finger between two slats in the blinds and gives the top one a gentle lift, ducking her head down low so she can peek through the gap. The car is still there, parked at the curb. She lets the shade fall back in place, blowing out a deep breath as she backs away from the window.

The man who went inside Liz's house was obviously a cop. A detective.

She wipes her sweaty palms absent-mindedly across the thighs of her jeans. Eyes her phone on the coffee table. Normally she would have already called half her contacts to dish that she'd seen a detective go into her neighbor's house, but not this time.

When she'd seen the suited man and realized what he was and what his presence most likely meant, her throat had grown tight, and her stomach had clenched into knots. Because he had to be questioning Liz about the body discovered at the old Ripley Manor, didn't he? What else could it be?

Swallowing hard, she makes a decision. Francine grabs the

phone, but instead of dialing she shoves it into her purse and palms her keys. She needs to get out of here. She needs to think.

Slinging the strap over her shoulder, she hurries through the house and flings the door open. Stumbles back several steps, knocking her hip painfully against the corner of the console table, which she'd thought would look classy but just makes the front entrance feel cramped. "Oh."

"Sorry if I took you by surprise, ma'am. I'm Detective Everett Johnson, from the Waverly Police Department."

Francine stares blankly at the man, a sour taste coating her tongue.

"Are you Francine Blakely?"

She nods.

"I was wondering if I could come in and speak with you for a moment."

Her voice sounds high and shaky, strange to her own ears as she replies. "I'm afraid now's not a good time. I'm on my way out."

"It will only take a moment."

She tries to think of a good excuse, but her brain fails her. She steps back to open the door wider, again bumping into the table. She swears she's going to throw the thing out first chance she gets as the detective squeezes past her into the house.

Showing him to the living room, she perches on the end of the sofa as he settles onto the couch across from her. He takes his time, slowing withdrawing a notebook and pen from his jacket pocket as Francine squirms. It feels like the silence is threatening to suffocate her, pushing down on her with the force of an elephant.

"What's this all about?" she finally asks.

"You may have heard on the news about some remains that were recently recovered locally."

"What's that got to do with me?"

"It's come to our attention that you may have known some of the people surrounding the case."

Francine's lips feel dryer than they've ever felt before. She pushes them together, drawing them inside her mouth. Digs her fingernails into the palms of her hands, regretting her decision to chase Morgana Ripley down the other day when she saw her. She should have known better, kept her distance. Drawing a noisy breath through her nose, she says, "Someone told you that? Who?"

"Your neighbor mentioned that you all went to high school together."

"Liz?" That bitch. But how had she known? Had she spotted Francine with Mo, decided to tell the detective about their friendship out of bitter jealousy? "Well, yes, we did go to school together, but we were hardly friends back then, Detective. We're only civil now because of our daughters."

"Yes, she mentioned that, too."

Of course she would. "So I really don't see how I could be of any help. I'd hardly be the one she'd ask to help her bury a body at her old friend's house."

She was trying to lighten the mood, but she can tell, immediately, that it was the wrong thing to say. Detective Johnson straightens on the couch across from her. Scribbles something down in his notebook.

"You said that you weren't friends with your neighbor back in high school. What about the other girls in her group? Were you friends with them?"

"Well, no, I wouldn't say that exactly."

"Did you want to be?"

She opens her mouth to answer, but can't manage the lie. She nods slowly, finally manages to say, "I did think it would be nice. Yes."

"Did you ever feel frustrated that you weren't welcomed into their group?"

Francine feels a hot flush creeping up her neck, into her cheeks. She clears her throat, trying to curb her temper. "Well, of course I did, but that's life, isn't it? I certainly wouldn't have helped them commit a crime or cover one up just to get them to like me."

He arches an eyebrow at her. "I never said you would. Tell me. What do you remember about Charamy Russo?"

One memory in particular burns brighter than the rest. She quickly removes the scowl from her face, trying for a neutral expression. But she can't help the anger that seeps into her response. "Amy? Oh, I don't know. Probably the same thing everyone else remembers about her. That she was gorgeous and talented and was probably just about as perfect as she thought she was. Why? Did she say something about me?"

"She didn't say anything, Ms. Blakely."

Francine snorts. "She wouldn't, would she?"

"I suspect it's more of a case that she couldn't."

She sucks in a sharp breath at the implication.

Detective Johnson stands, giving her an unreadable look as he stares down at her. "Well, this has been enlightening. Thank you for your time, Ms. Blakely. And please." He draws a card from his pocket, sets it on the table in front of her when she fails to reach for it. "Give us a call and let us know if you plan to leave town anytime soon. I'll be in touch."

She's speechless as she watches him leave. But on the inside, she's screaming.

TWENTY-SIX

LIZ THEN

1999

I'm sitting in the back row of the auditorium, slouched down so no one will see me. On stage, scenes are shifting, changing, a jumble of chaos that the crew will work out by opening night. I have my physics book open to kill the time, balanced on top of my book bag on my lap.

"Did I miss it?"

I look toward the stage as Sami slips into the seat next to mine. Her whisper is louder and carries farther than her normal voice. Shaking my head, I close the textbook and slip it back into my bag.

"No, not yet. Where's Mo?"

"Right here."

Mo drops heavily into the seat behind me. Leaning forward, she props her chin on my shoulder, leaning her head against mine. I wasn't sure she would come.

She and Amy have been arguing more and more lately, the battles getting nastier, more personal. Seeing my friends squaring off, out to draw blood from each other—it's made me look at our friendship in a new light. The horrible, unflattering kind that they use in dressing rooms.

I'd thought that what we had between us was special, but now I'm not so sure. And if I was wrong about that, what else am I fooling myself about? But then there are times, like this, when I can't help but wonder if I'm not just being dramatic, because it all still feels so right.

A crash up front draws our attention. The lights change from bright to dim. A spotlight appears center stage. Amy steps out from one of the wings, eyes wide, shoulders hunched, casting wary glances around the auditorium as she makes her way toward the circle of light.

"There she is!" Sami grabs my arm.

"Own it, Amy. Walk like you own the stage." The command booms from the front row, where the drama teacher sits, flanked by a pair of pale-faced lackeys dressed in black.

Amy lifts her head, tilting her chin up. She tosses her hair, pushes her shoulders down and back. The transformation is immediate. It makes her look like Mo.

The music starts low, barely audible over the background noise. The notes build, gaining strength and speed. When Amy starts singing, all other sounds in the room cease. The hair on my arms rises. Sami's fingers tighten their grip, digging into my flesh, but I don't say anything. Like everyone else in the room, I'm enchanted.

I don't process another thought until the song is over. Then I reach over and pry Sami's fingers open. They latch onto my hand instead of my arm, our fingers threading together the way they have thousands of times over the years.

"Wow." This time her whisper counts as a whisper. "She's incredible."

"I know, right?" Mo sits back in her seat, bouncing up and down excitedly. She gives my shoulders a squeeze.

On stage, Amy retreats to the wings. It's been years since

our school has put on a musical. This year they're doing *The Phantom of the Opera*. Amy will star. We've always known that Amy would be famous. Now the rest of the school will, too.

———

Amy comes home with me after school. I invited her over under the pretense of needing her to help me study for a test, but really, I just want to make sure she eats a good dinner. She keeps skipping lunch because she's dieting. She's been looking a little skinnier every week, and I'm starting to worry.

I know it's a lot of pressure, being up on stage in front of the entire school. And wanting to be a famous singer and actress, both professions where many of the people who aspire to succeed crash and burn. She wouldn't be the first teenage girl to deny herself food thinking it would help her achieve her goals. I need to see her consume a full meal with my own eyes, for my peace of mind.

Once we're settled in my room, she turns an expectant look on me. "Well?"

"Well, what?"

"Your test. Did you want me to quiz you, or help you run through flashcards, or what?"

The truth is that there is no test. I don't even have any homework tonight. But I don't want to tell her that.

"Actually, I was doing the practice questions from the back of the book during seventh period, and it finally clicked." I give her an embarrassed smile.

"Oh. Well, if you don't have anything else to do, do you want to help me run lines?"

"Sure." I study her profile as she rummages around in her book bag for her copy of the play. "Amy?"

"Yeah?"

"You know that you're gorgeous and uber talented and that you're going to be a huge success, don't you? Just as you are?"

She cocks an eyebrow at me. "What brought all this on?"

I can't tell her that I've noticed how much weight she's lost. So, instead, I say, "Well, I mean, you're perfect, and I was just wondering?"

"I can't marry you, Liz. We're too young."

I snort, then she snorts.

"Seriously, though. Why do I feel like you're buttering me up? What gives?" she asks.

"I guess I kind of just wanted to ask about acting. I mean, you're so good at it. And I feel like everything I think, or feel, is, like, completely obvious all the time."

"Well, it is. But that's one of the things everyone loves about you."

"Yeah, but. What if I didn't want to be so obvious? I want you to give me some pointers about acting."

"Okay." Her eyes roll up in her head like she's searching for some piece of profound thespian wisdom to impart on me. "The most important thing I can tell you about acting is to pretend." Catching my expression, she says, "Seriously."

"But, there's, like, a butt ton of bad actors out there."

"Yeah, but that's because they're trying to act."

"You lost me."

"The thing about acting is that you don't just do it when you're on stage. You've got to fake it all the time. Like, in everyday life. Everyone else is. And if you learn to do it well enough, they'll never know that you are, too."

It makes a certain kind of sense. It's almost genius in its simplicity. But at the same time, I can't help wondering—what exactly is it that she's faking? And how much of the girl I know is pretend?

TWENTY-SEVEN
SAMI NOW

2014

I stare wistfully at the door to my cage, the tiny wood-paneled box where I grade papers and hold my office hours at the local community college, wishing I could escape. Or at the very least, leave early. But knowing my luck, if I did, one of the students failing one of my classes would choose to stop by, then lodge a complaint against me when I wasn't there, use it to get their grade raised. No, I better just suck it up and stay here. God, I hate my job.

Other than teaching, I also sell my soul by working for the local government as a Cultural Resource Consultant, determining whether any archaeological sites uncovered in the area should be conserved and studied or bulldozed over for whatever road or strip mall some contractor wants to build over it. If it paid more, I wouldn't be sitting here right now. But with an ounce of luck, one day soon they'll uncover an important site in a primo location, and I'll be able to leverage my decision for a nice payday.

I wasn't always like this. There was a time when I thought

old things were worth saving. That's why I returned to my hometown after graduating college, despite knowing that doing so would have a detrimental impact on my career options. But I couldn't stop myself, I had to come back. Besides, it wasn't like I could escape the memories of what happened by living somewhere else. They were always there, lurking in my mind, haunting me.

So, I did it. I came home. And as a heavy fist bangs against my office door, and a man who is most definitely a cop enters the tiny room without waiting for an invitation, I regret, not for the first time, that decision. I should have stayed as far away as I could have and never come home.

Detective Johnson sits across from me in the threadbare, green corduroy armchair that I keep for students. He's fingering a worn spot on the arm, making it worse. His foot is tapping a rapid staccato against the floor. He's driving me absolutely crazy. Every ounce of willpower I have is focused on not asking him to stop. My body is literally vibrating with the urge to grab his hand and his knee and make him hold still.

I catch him looking out the window and I'm even more irritated that he's wasting my time. Then I realize that he's watching my reflection. He's trying to annoy me. He's trying to throw me off my game. And now I'm hot and panicked and paranoid because he obviously has a plan, and I have no idea what it is.

"Tell me about the group. Your friendship."

He's already questioned me about the circumstances under which Amy left. I've told him about how talented she was, how she left for L.A. to pursue her singing career, leaving as soon as she'd turned eighteen. How I'd been hurt that she hadn't tried to keep in touch besides sending a random postcard here and there, but that I understood she was busy fulfilling her dreams. But it's not what he wants to hear, and now he's punishing me, grating on my nerves because I'm not giving him what he thinks I should.

"What would you like to know?"

"What kind of friends were you?"

I stare out the window, watching a hawk soar across the sky. "We were the kind of friends that most people think only happen in books." I know my voice has a faraway sound. I hear it. My words sound like they were spoken by some stoned hippie.

"Books?"

I stop watching the bird and meet Detectives Johnson's eyes. "TV? Movies?"

"So, pretend?"

"No. Like good, lifelong friends who love each other and would do anything for each other."

"So, unrealistic?"

"Yes. I think that for most people it would be."

"And why's that?"

"Most people don't even put their children or their spouses' needs before their own anymore. To put three other people before yourself, as little girls and teenagers... I just don't think most people are capable of being that selfless."

"Selfless?"

"Yes."

"And you would have done anything for each other?"

"Yes."

"Then what happened?"

"What do you mean?"

"Well, you just spoke of being lifelong friends. But the four of you aren't friends now. It's been fifteen years since either you or your friend Liz have heard the sound of the other two's voices."

"How do you know that?"

"You told me."

"You've talked to Liz?" I can't believe her! She had to have known he'd be coming to see me next. The least she could have done was give me some warning.

"I have. And as far as I can tell, all four of you fell out of contact very suddenly. There wasn't a long, drawn-out period where you get together a little less often, the phone calls made farther apart. There was no weaning process. So that tells me that something bad happened. Something bad enough to rip your little fairy-tale friendship to shreds."

"It wasn't like that. You make it sound so... calculated. So final."

"And it's not?"

"No. It's not. Put any of us in a room together and it will be like no time at all has passed. Like we've never been apart."

"But you have."

"Yes, but not for any specific reason. Because we grew up and went different directions. Our friendship didn't end. It just went into stasis."

"Stasis?"

I nod.

"I hear what you're saying, Ms. Warner, honestly, I do. But I have to tell you the truth. I don't believe one word of it."

I try to adjust my face, try to conceal my shock, but I know I've already given myself away. "I'm sorry you feel that way."

"Yeah, me too. But picture things from my point of view." Detective Johnson sits forward in the chair, leaning over my desk. "You see, on the one hand, I have you sitting here telling me how close you all were, how much you loved each other. On the other hand, I have a set of remains with a bullet hole in the skull."

I feel myself flinch as he says the word bullet.

"So far, all signs point to these remains belonging to one of these friends of yours, a friend who supposedly left right around the time you all coincidentally stopped talking. You see, to me, that's more than suspicious. Add to that the fact it never struck you as odd that you never even received a call or a text from—"

"She sent postcards."

"Anyone can send a postcard. I can mail you one as soon as I leave here, sign it Justin Bieber, but that doesn't mean that the Beebs sent you something. No offense, but if you really expect me to believe that you cared about that girl at all, you're crazy."

He had me until then. Detective Johnson could have gotten anything he wanted out of me, up until the moment when he questioned my love for my friends. Hatred flows through my veins, hardening them like ice, fortifying me.

"You're welcome to your opinion, Detective, as wrong as it may be. But since the truth isn't going to change, and you've decided not to believe it, I don't think there's anything left to say."

He stands, using his height advantage to stare down at me, like I'm an ant under a microscope. I glare right back at him until he breaks eye contact and heads for the door. His hand on the knob, he pauses and looks back at me.

"I will find out what happened that night, Ms. Warner. I promise you that."

With those words he leaves, the door closing behind him with a small click. I bite my tongue to keep from yelling, to try and control my temper. I bite it harder as the tears come, teeth gripping into the flesh with a firm pressure, not hard enough to justify the pain I'm in.

The man is a bully. How dare he question the strength of our bond just because he doesn't understand it? Everything we did that night was done out of love. Even if it wasn't the right thing.

TWENTY-EIGHT

AMY THEN

1999

Even though it's mid-April it's a bitterly cold day, winter hanging on with a vengeance that suggests spring will never come. I pull my thin sweater tighter, scowling at the gray sky, as I continue the lonely climb up the steep hill. Lonely, and dangerous. There's no sidewalk, and the cars take the winding road too fast, tires squealing as they veer around the curves, drifting over the line.

I know the drivers see me, but no one stops. Why would they? I don't belong here, and they know it.

Still, I dare to hope. There's a blister on my baby toe that makes each step painful. My skin is chapped from the icy wind, my runny nose stinging the raw flesh of my upper lip. The strap of my purse cuts deep into my shoulder. My burden felt too heavy to carry even before I started this journey.

But it's too late to turn back. I'm almost there.

I stop outside the fence and stare through the bars. A fountain depicting a scene from Greek mythology sits before a towering brick house, surrounded by lush perennial gardens coaxed into bloom despite the season. It seems like another world. But is it a better one? I wish I knew.

Punching in the code, I stand back, waiting for the iron gate to swing open. Squeezing through as soon as the gap is large enough, I hurry up the drive, looking forward to getting out of the cold and off my feet. I still haven't thought of a good story, and I can't tell the truth. But I've always been good at winging it. Hopefully, this time will be no different.

My ankles complain as I haul myself up the front steps, my calves threatening to go into spasm. I wouldn't consider myself out of shape. I suspect the long hike, up what is practically a mountain in near-freezing conditions, would have sapped even an athlete's strength. Or maybe that's just a lie I'm telling myself; obviously I'm not that fit. There's no time to think about it as I ring the doorbell.

I can't remember ever ringing the bell before, or even using the front door, but the side entrance doesn't have a ringer and she isn't expecting me. Maybe I should have called first. I probably should have. But she might have asked too many questions, she might have tried to talk me out of it, and I couldn't allow that to happen.

Wrapping my arms tight around myself, I shift from foot to foot, wondering if maybe she's out, if this was all for nothing, if I'd be able to get up my nerve and my strength to do this again. I conclude that I wouldn't, that if this falls through I'll use it as a sign to abandon the plan completely, and strangely, there's an odd kind of relief that comes with the decision. Then the door opens.

"Amy." Mo frowns at me, then leans forward, peering to look down the drive, obviously searching for the others. When she realizes it's just me, that I'm alone, her expression turns to one of concern. "Jesus. Did you walk all the way here?"

I nod and try to say yes, but my teeth are chattering too hard to get the word out. She pulls me inside and ushers me into the living room.

"Your sweater feels damp, we should get you out of it." She tugs on one of my cuffs, pulling the sleeve down my arm and over my wrist, and gasps. "What's that?"

I jerk the sweater back up, covering the bruises.

"What the hell was that?"

I study the floor as I say, "It's nothing." But we both know it's not. There's no disguising the purple fingerprints still darkening my skin hours after the hand released me.

Mo growls in disapproval and gathers a plush blanket off the back of the couch, draping it over my shoulders. "Is that nothing, too?" she asks, running a fingertip lightly over my cheekbone where the concealer I applied obviously isn't doing its job.

"Mo—"

"Don't," she cuts me off. "Don't try to tell me it's not a big deal. Don't tell me not to worry."

"I wasn't going to." Looking up, I catch her by the hand and hold it in my own. "Not this time."

"We should call the cops."

I shake my head sadly. "That'll only make it worse."

"But—"

"I only have to hold on a little bit longer." I'll be eighteen, we both will, in less than six weeks. The end is on the horizon.

"I don't understand how this happened. It wasn't always like this, was it?"

It wasn't. But I can't tell her why things changed, how bad they've been since I found out about what Sonny's done. I can't tell her that she's my sister. Not quite yet.

Because as much as I've resented Mo, as many times as I've done horrible things that I let other people blame on her, she loves me. And she always has. I need to show that I deserve to be her twin. I need to earn it.

If she knew exactly how difficult my life had become, or why, she'd go over there right now and kill him. And I can't let her do that. This is my mess to take care of.

I owe her this. To solve this problem for both of us. Then we'll both be free.

"I need you to hold on to something for me."

Reaching into my purse, I pull out the weapon, still wrapped in its oilcloth, and hand it to her. Her eyes widen when she feels the weight of it, nostrils flaring as the acrid odor hits her nose. "What is it?" A second later she answers her own question. "A gun! Jesus, Amy, what the hell are you doing with this?"

She stares down at the firearm in her hand, seemingly unable to take her eyes off it. "I don't want this. I can't have it around."

"Mo, please. Just for a little while."

Just so I'm not tempted to use it on him. Just so he can't use it on me.

She looks at me, really looks, and sees the desperation on my face. "Is it loaded?"

"I don't know. I'm not sure how to check."

"Does it... do I have to keep it in the house?"

I shake my head. "I was thinking we could keep it out back." Even though I don't say it, she knows what I mean. *In the clochán.* That way I could still get to it if I needed it. If I could manage to make my way back up here, that is.

"And it's... just for a little while?"

"Yes. I promise. Just until we graduate, and I can leave his house."

Her lips blanch into a thin white line as she presses them together, thinking. "All right then," she agrees. Just like I knew she would.

TWENTY-NINE

SAMI NOW

2014

That cop really did a number on my head. I've called in sick the last three days, unable to be surrounded by the naïve faces of my students, or jail myself in that tiny little box of an office. But I can't make myself stay at home, either.

The truth is, I know this is far from over, and I don't want to be anywhere that detective can find me when it's time for round two. So I have no destination in mind as I get behind the wheel of my car this morning, no goal other than to put some space between me and anyone who might want to ask me any questions.

I head out of town, needing a change of scenery. Seeking complete isolation. I take a random exit off the highway and, after a series of unfamiliar turns, find myself coasting down a two-lane stretch of asphalt, no break in the trees lining the road within sight. Perfect.

The white trunks of birch and maple blur as I increase the pressure on the accelerator. A few maples have already taken the fall plunge, bursts of red, orange, and yellow splattered like paintballs among the green leaves. I turn the radio off, my thoughts wandering to the soundtrack of tires grinding over the road.

Somehow, I end up thinking about fathers.

Liz's dad was a big, bald, bear of a man with a jolly smile and a rock-hard beer gut, who never passed up the opportunity to tease us. He'd call us heartbreakers and fairy princesses and tell us how much better it was to raise a little girl after so many boys, because girls were just all around better.

He put a Band-Aid on my elbow once when I was seven, after I'd slid down the tree in their backyard. I didn't really need it, it was just a tiny little scrape that wasn't even bleeding, but he made a huge fuss over what a brave girl I was, swooping me up in his arms, making siren noises as he carried me to the bathroom and sat me on the counter and then, when I couldn't choose between a *Barbie* and a *My Little Pony* bandage, he put them both on me, one on each arm.

To be loved like that.

Even Mo's dad made an effort when he was around. He never failed to gush over what beautiful ladies we all were, while Mo's mom stood off to the side, smiling stiffly in an outfit she didn't want to risk getting mussed by the children.

Then there was Sonny. Amy's mom died shortly after giving birth to her. Amy never really knew anything about her, only what she could glean from a few old letters and a stack of dog-eared pictures she stole from her dad's dresser. Sonny couldn't talk about her mom without shutting down, could never fight his way through his emotions to tell Amy what her mom's favorite color was, or favorite song.

But of all the dads, he was around the most. That was probably because he had to be, as a single parent, but I think we were all jealous of the face time Amy got with her dad. I know I was.

The truth is, I can barely remember my father. No matter

how hard I try, his face is a blur, like when they try to protect a witness' identity on TV, which is strange, because I was twenty-eight when he died. I've seen pictures, I know what he's supposed to have looked like, but to me he was never the smiling man from the photographs.

At his funeral, someone came up and told me how much they were going to miss Carl. I stopped myself just before asking, "Who's Carl?", making the connection and answering my own question at the last second. Carl is the man in the casket. It didn't even seem strange to me that I didn't recognize my own father's name.

In my memories, his voice is like thunder, a loud, angry crack. "Why isn't she in bed, Lorraine?" "What's she still doing up?" "Why is she here?" Never addressing me, always asking my mom why I hadn't been removed from the room before he entered it.

He was a good provider, though, I know that much. After I was born, my mom didn't have to go back to work. Once I was in school she dabbled at the law firm where they had met, taking a case here and there, but it was clear that her main job was me. Mainly, making sure that my father never had to come in contact with me. No matter how good I tried to be, how sweet, how quiet, how smart, it never mattered. I wasn't wanted.

My mom made endless excuses for him. She always had a lie ready for why he wasn't at my birthday party, why he couldn't make it to my recital, why his voice was so different when he talked to her at night after he came home from work, laughing and joking but only appearing once I was removed for the night, in bed. Why he couldn't be bothered to attend my high school or college graduations.

It wasn't until I gained the wisdom that comes with age that I realized that my father was one of those people who had no need for people he couldn't use. And that way of life seemed to work out for him just fine, which seems, perhaps, the most important lesson he taught me in life—seek out those who can serve a purpose.

So maybe he never told me I was smart, or pretty, or even a worthwhile human being. Never gave me a kiss or a hug. I know that there are a lot of worse things to experience than a parent's indifference, that I was fortunate to never know hunger or what it was like to be beaten. But I've also never known what it's like to have a normal, healthy relationship with a man.

But now, for only the second time in my life, I feel like maybe I could. Like I actually want to. It took a long time for my heart to heal after losing my first love, and I'll never forget the man who made me feel so alive, but maybe it's time to finally move on.

The more I think about it, the more excited I get. The man I've been seeing lately is actually kind of perfect for me. I'd never considered taking the next step and getting truly serious with him because of his family, but they're not a problem anymore. So what's stopping us?

Absolutely nothing.

I pull a U-turn in the middle of the road, eager to get back to town. To start my new life. Because suddenly, I have a destination in mind after all. Happiness.

THIRTY

LIZ THEN

1999

It happened the same week Amy was to make her debut in the Longfellow High School performance of *The Phantom of the Opera*. Her dad was at work, driving a forklift like he had done for the past seventeen years, when his heart stopped beating. It was the day of his thirty-ninth birthday. He was dead on the spot.

I just can't believe it. I'm still in shock. I'd been over there that very morning, helping Amy make him a special breakfast for his birthday, and he'd looked fine.

Now he's gone, and I can't stop wondering—if Amy had known what was going to happen, would she still have asked me to come over? Does she resent that the final moments she got to spend with her dad were shared with me? Could a part of her hate me for that?

My mom can't stop talking about the devastating tragedy. It's thrown her into a downward spiral of worrying about my dad's health, and her own since they're both older than Sonny was, every sniff or sneeze or random body pain sending her into a panic. And then there's her concern for Amy.

Yesterday, I stopped by the house to grab some more clothes to take over to Sami's, where we've all been staying since it happened. Catching Amy's name as I passed by my parents' bedroom, I backtracked and pushed my ear against the door so I could hear their whispered words.

They were discussing Amy's situation. Our high school graduation is in five weeks. Amy will be eighteen in three, her birthday, by some strange twist of fate, falling on the exact same day as Mo's. The rent on the house she lives in is already past due.

I held my breath as they debated whether they could swing feeding another mouth with one son in college, another in grad school, and me heading off in the fall. I crushed my tears with clenched fists as I listened to them to reach their decision—maybe Sami's parents could continue to keep her.

Now I'm standing beside a hole in the earth, a violent gash in the soil of reality, one link in a chain of teenaged girls dressed in black. With one arm hooked through Amy's and the other through Mo's. I feel the shudder that runs through Amy as the casket starts its journey into the ground. Can feel her weight sag against my shoulder as we prop each other up as it disappears from view.

When the service is over, Sami, Mo, and I stand off to the side, waiting for Amy while people offer her their condolences on their way out. My parents are talking to Sami's over by the cars. I turn my back, not wanting to watch.

"Ugh. How much longer do you think this is gonna take?"

Sami and I both look at Mo in disbelief.

"What? I've got other things I'd like to do besides waste my whole day out here."

I stare at her a moment while I find my voice. "Jesus, Mo,

Amy's dad just died. Can you maybe muster up a little sympathy?"

"Why? Because her dad died? So what, it happens. It's not like he was dad of the year or anything. She didn't even like him."

"Mo!"

"Seriously. I'm lucky if I see my parents once a year. You don't see me crying, do you?"

"Your parents are still alive," Sami says.

"No, Mo, you don't cry. We spend every single weekend of our lives babying you at your house just to keep that from happening." I regret the words as soon as they escape, but it's too late to rein them back in.

"You know what? Fuck you, Liz. Seriously. Like you're so perfect."

Sami and I stand side by side, watching Mo stomp off across the cemetery. The back of her hand brushes mine, and I know that she wants me to hold it, but I can't. I'm empty. I've nothing left to give.

"What should we do?" Sami knows, but she wants me to say it. So I do.

"What can we do? We let her go."

That night, we squish together in Sami's bed. We used to do this all the time, playing how many ways can four little girls fit in one bed, but it's been years since the last time. It's a much tighter fit now, and there's only three of us tonight. Mo isn't here.

My heart feels like a hole has been punched through the middle. I can't handle anymore grief right now. I wish she were here beside me, holding my hand. But she's not. And I feel paralyzed by loss as I lay shoulder to shoulder with Sami and Amy.

The lights are off, the room pitch black, but I know my friends are still awake. I can feel it in the air, an electric energy of nerves, the static crackle of tension and words left unsaid. I answer the question that's on everyone's lips.

"You're going to be okay, Amy." It might be a lie.

"Am I?" She knows I may be lying. I can hear it in her voice.

"Yes. You are."

"I don't feel like I am."

"It takes time," Sami says.

Silence blankets over us once again.

"He was seeing someone, you know." Amy's voice cracks the quiet like an egg. "I don't know who, but I wish I did. I'd like to tell her, make sure that she knows what happened."

"I'm sure she does," Sami says.

I hear Sami's words, the uncharacteristic strength in her voice when she spoke, and feel a sickening lurch in my gut. I hadn't realized before, but now I think I do. I think I know exactly what it means. And nothing good can come of it.

THIRTY-ONE

FRANCINE NOW

2014

Francine frowns down at the cold cup of coffee on the table before her, lost in thought. Wishing she had told the detective that Liz was secretive. That Sami was easily manipulated. Even that Mo, finally, at last her friend after all these years, had always had a wicked temper.

That any of them could have been a killer. But instead, she'd taken the light of suspicion and shined it on herself. Stupid.

One of them is probably talking to him right now. Telling him about that night.

It's not fair.

A part of her had known better than to go to the party. Even her own mother had suggested that she not. She hadn't been invited. But who had?

Besides. It was senior year. And as she'd parked along the road, joining the throng of fellow classmates as they climbed the hill and flooded through the gates of Ripley Manor, she knew she had made the right decision.

Opulence surrounded her as she stepped through the double front doors, thrown wide to the crowd, and into a foyer the likes of which she'd never seen. A crystal chandelier caught the light and sparkled overhead. A set of stairs curved along the sides of the room, meeting in the middle. And though streamers had been zigzagged across the top along with a sign saying "off limits", it was that forbidden space that Francine knew she had to go.

She had to find Morgana Ripley's inner sanctum. She had to see it, just once. Just so she could picture herself there and imagine what it would be like, hanging out with the girls she so desperately wanted to be friends with.

Clusters of teenagers huddled on the stairs, trying to avoid the mob below. And though she didn't know any of them, she climbed up to join them, lingering on the edge of one group, then the next, and finally the one closest to the top. If the kids thought she was being weird, she couldn't tell. Then again, they probably didn't even notice her. She was good at flying under the radar. At lurking like a ghost, unnoticed and unwanted.

She waited several minutes, working up her nerve, before casually stepping closer to the crepe-paper barricade, creeping nearer and nearer until the streamers moved with her breath. Then she sat, pretending to tie her shoe. Looked around to make sure no one was watching. And entered the prohibited territory.

She still remembers the way her heart had hammered against her ribs as she pressed herself into the shadows. The feel of the walls as she trailed her fingers along them. The strange heat of the doorknob, as if there were a fire on the far side, as she wrapped her palm around it and turned.

She'd gasped when she saw them. The couple parted in surprise. The boy had laughed. Whether at her embarrassment or his partner's, she couldn't say. She'd felt herself wilting under

Mo's gaze as she struggled to find her voice and apologize, but then she'd noticed.

The bangs were wrong. They weren't quite long enough to tuck behind her ear, but as their owner tried, she revealed a small birthmark on her neck. "Amy?"

The boy had laughed harder until he caught the girl's expression. "Huh?" He'd squinted at her. Scratched his head. Taken a step away, toward the door. "I think I'm gonna go get a drink."

And then he was gone.

Francine had glanced nervously at the room around her, still, despite her faux pas, trying to claim her prize, to take it all in, but she couldn't absorb the details she'd been after because the girl standing across from her was seething. Anger burned bright in her eyes and, for a second, Francine had thought she'd gotten it wrong. That it was Mo she had walked in on. But it couldn't be.

"Amy, I'm so sorry. Really."

"Who the hell are you?"

It was the first time the girl had spoken, and though she sounded like Mo, there was something off. Something wrong. And that's when she realized—Amy was trying to impersonate her cousin.

"It's—I'm Francine. We've gone to school together for years. Listen, Amy, I won't tell anyone, I promise."

"There's nothing to tell. Now get out of my room."

Feeling suddenly emboldened, she'd said, "Oh, so you live here now, too?"

Hands fisted on her hips, Amy tried one of Mo's signature hair tosses. "What the hell is wrong with you?"

"Nothing. But you're speaking just a little too fast if you want to pull it off. And when Mo tosses her hair, she shrugs her shoulder just a little bit afterwards. And you should probably cover that birthmark on your neck, because that's a dead giveaway."

"Oh. My. God. You're a stalker."

"No, I'm not. I just—"

"Then what? You're in love with my cousin?"

It should have been a victory, getting Amy to admit that she'd been right, but it didn't feel like anything to celebrate. "No, I—"

"You're pathetic, is what you are."

She had thought Amy was nice. Sweet, even if she failed to notice Francine just as much as the others did. And so maybe she felt embarrassed, and ashamed, and backed into a corner, but it was clear now that her claws were just as sharp as her friends' were.

"I'm sorry. I'll go now."

"Good. Go all the way home, little piggie. Because you do *not* want to be around when I tell Mo about this."

And so she'd run out of the room, ducked under the streamers, but not far enough, ripping some as she raced down the stairs and out of the house. When she'd gotten home, her eyes swollen and puffy, skin sticky with dried tears and snot, she'd found a piece of crepe paper trailing from the bottom of one of her shoes.

She still has it, pressed between the pages of her yearbook. Marking Amy Russo's page.

And now, if that detective can be believed, Amy's dead. And she's sure that he's been told all about Francine's motive.

THIRTY-TWO
LIZ THEN

1999

Everything feels out of control. Nothing is as it should be. Life has just gotten so... real. It's flinging one thing after the next at me like an angry monkey and there's no way I can escape, nowhere to hide.

It's been two weeks since Sonny died. Mo still isn't speaking to me. And the wound still feels so raw.

I don't know what I expected, maybe it should have been this, but it wasn't. Broken, yes, but not completely shattered. How can I force myself to move on when each breath is such a struggle? I need my best friend.

I thought everything would be okay, eventually. I knew it would take a while, but I thought that, one day, things would get back to normal. But I'm starting to worry that will never happen. That this is the new normal. I don't think I could live with that, because this, the way things are now, is horrible.

Every night, Sami, Amy, and I pack into in Sami's full-sized bed, but I haven't been sleeping. My body feels heavy and sluggish. When I move, it's with a weariness I'm unaccustomed to, like an injured person dragging their body against its will. I'm just so tired.

Last night, I heard Sami whisper in the dark, when she thought Amy and I were sleeping. She said, "What if things are never the same again?" So I know I'm not alone. I know that we're both trying to push our worry and grief aside for Amy's sake. I just wish we could go back in time and have things back the way they used to be.

This is the end of our senior year. We're supposed to be focused on the prom we've spent years dreaming about and Mo and Amy's eighteenth birthday bash next week, on our graduation at the end of the month. We're supposed to be having the best time of our lives, not the worst.

Another surge of nausea rolls over me. I can feel it building. I feel it rising, curling, cresting. Running to the bathroom, I throw my arms around the cool porcelain rim of the toilet just in time as the wave breaks.

THIRTY-THREE

LIZ NOW

2014

I sit on the couch, staring at the TV, but the TV isn't on. I wouldn't be able to focus on watching anything even if it were. There are too many other, more important things that I need to watch. What I say. What I do. How I act.

It feels like I'm walking a tightrope, and one end is on fire. Trying to keep my balance and stay ahead of the flames is exhausting. I'm not sure how much longer I'll be able to do it. How did everything turn into such a mess?

"Hey, Mom?"

I turn toward my daughter, elated to hear the sound of her voice, thrilled at her use of the M-word. There's no denying that things have been tense between us since she found out the truth about her father. I'd meant to sit her down, have another talk with her, a better talk, but my mind's been such a mess since that detective stopped by a few days ago that I haven't been able to think straight.

"Yeah, baby?"

Her brows are creased low over a frown, forehead wrinkled

with confusion. She crosses the room toward me, holding a piece of paper out in front of her. My vision tunnels as I see it. A high-pitched ringing fills my ears.

"What's this?"

She holds the page out to me. I feel myself shirk back involuntarily, like she's brandishing a snake. I know I should take it from her, but I can't make myself move yet, my limbs paralyzed by dread.

The shadow of the words are visible through the paper. It's another one of those notes. From *her*.

"Where'd you find that?"

"It was on the table out back. Pinned under a rock. Why? Weren't you the one who put it there? Was someone in our yard?"

I didn't put it there. Which means that someone *was* trespassing in our yard, *she* was, but I don't want Olivia to worry. So I lie.

It feels like I'm cracking ice cubes out of a tray as I push my mouth into a smile, the skin and muscles of my face hard and rigid and moving in stages. I force myself to reach out and grab the paper. "Of course it was me, honey."

"But why? Who's it for?"

"Well, I'm not quite sure. I found it blowing around in the yard earlier. It must have come over from a neighbor's house. I meant to bring it inside and throw it away, but I got distracted. I guess I forgot all about it and left it out there."

"Geez. I wonder which of them it was meant for. It seems kind of sinister, don't you think?"

I stare down at the open page.

Confess now. While you still can.

XXO ∞

Alarm bells go off inside my head because Olivia's right. There is something distinctly threatening about the letter. But what is it that she's trying to accomplish? She can't possibly want me to tell the truth. We all took a part in what happened that night. If I tell the police what I know, we'll all go down for it.

Then it hits me, the realization striking so hard that it takes my breath away. I fold the paper so I can't see the words anymore and focus on not betraying the shock that I feel. She wants me to take the blame. For everything.

"It's probably nothing," I say, hoping my daughter doesn't notice the tremor in my voice. "Most likely something silly, like who took the last cookie, or something."

Olivia smiles, liking the idea. "Bet you're right. Hey. Is it okay if I go over to Gina's?"

"Is your homework done?"

"Yep."

"That's fine then." Her blonde ponytail swings from side to side as she skips out of the room. "Oh, but Olivia?"

She stops at the threshold, turns reluctantly to face me, her expression tense, obviously expecting me to assign her a chore before she leaves.

"Do me a favor and don't say anything about the note to her, okay? You don't want to embarrass her if this is Francine's way of dealing with a cookie thief."

A wide grin spreads across my daughter's face. Her eyes roll toward the ceiling, her head shaking from side to side as she chuckles. "Yeah, right. You and I both know that would never happen." She spins on her heel, calling over her shoulder, "We'd hear the firing squad all the way over here if they ever ran out of cookies in that house."

The second the front door slams behind her, the smile vanishes from my face like water down a drain. I wipe at the sweat that's gathered at my hairline, then snatch up the note and tear it into tiny shreds, squeezing the scraps inside my damp fist. I should never have had to lie to my daughter like that. Thank God she believed me.

But then again, you're supposed to be able to trust adults—that's what makes it so easy to get kids to believe what you want them to. Like Santa Claus. Or the Easter bunny. Or that what you're doing is okay, even when it's clearly not.

As I watched my daughter grow, as I saw the innocent way she viewed the world, how she looked at the adults around her for guidance, I realized how much I'd been wronged. How I just blindly believed what I was told. Like Olivia had so easily accepted my explanation just now.

But I'm not manipulating her for my own selfish agenda. I'm just trying to keep my daughter safe.

And no part of that includes taking the sole blame for a crime that is not my own. She's made a very bad mistake if she thinks I'm going to let that happen. I'm not the girl I used to be. I'm not the girl she used to know.

I carry the letter to the bathroom and dump the pieces in the toilet. Watch as they circle the bowl before finally being sucked away. I've been scared plenty of times before. But it's been a long time since I let that stop me.

THIRTY-FOUR

LIZ THEN

1999

I skip seventh period so I can wait for her outside of her class. Lingering just to the side of the classroom door, I keep my eyes peeled for any teachers or administrators roaming the hallways, a pilfered bathroom pass crumpled in my pocket. But no one comes, the corridor deathly silent, making me think of those movies Sami likes where people wake up and find out that they're one of the last ones left on earth.

I don't like those films, never have. There's something too eerie about them, too depressing and lonely. I'm not sure I'd want to struggle and fight to stay alive if everyone else was gone. What would be the point?

But the solitude gives me plenty of time to think. There has to be a way to patch things up. I have to make things better. This is the first time there's been a rift in our friendship like this, and we're all suffering from it.

The bell rings, and the door slams open. I take a step back, watching, waiting, falling into step beside Mo as she exits the classroom. She glances over at me, and for a brief second, I see it

—she's as hopeful as I am. Then it passes, her face hardening into a stony expression.

"What do you want?" she asks, quickening her pace like she's trying to lose me.

I jog a couple of steps to keep up. "World peace. But I'd settle for having my best friend back."

Her throat stretches as she swallows hard. She keeps her gaze focused straight ahead.

"Mo, I am so, so sorry that I upset you. You have to believe me."

"Fine."

"And forgive me?"

She ignores me as we reach her locker. Her tapered fingers deftly spin the lock. She jerks the door open, narrowly missing my face. I watch her through the vents as she shoves her books inside. Her porcelain skin has turned a soft shade of pink. Her usually full, naturally rose-colored lips are pressed into a thin white line.

Slamming the metal slab shut, she finally looks at me. "You really hurt my feelings."

"I know."

"You were way harsh. I didn't deserve that."

"I know that, too."

I wish there was a way to make her understand. But I can't. Because I've vowed to take that deep, dark secret with me to the grave.

Her mouth screws up into a knot as she studies my face. Then her granite façade crumbles. Her lower lip quivers and her eyes turn shiny. "You made me feel like I was all alone. No matter how bad things have ever gotten before, I've never felt like that. Abandoned by you."

"Oh, Mo." I wrap my arms around her. Her body is rigid against mine. "I would never abandon you. Not ever. Even when we're old and gray and senile, I'll be the stranger sitting beside you, holding your hand. You'll never be rid of me."

"Promise?"

I tighten my hug. Try to ignore the weird girl standing by the lockers directly across from us, watching. "I swear it."

Mo relaxes in my embrace. Returns it. Sniffs loudly in my ear. "I'm going to wipe my snotty nose on you, okay?"

I can't help smiling. "It would be an honor."

Then I feel the pressure on my shoulder, the dampness on my shirt, and I jump back, squealing. "I didn't think you were actually going to do it!"

She grins. "Well then, I guess the honor is all mine."

We giggle in the way we always have, with abandon, completely unconcerned with being cool or mature, or even how goofy we appear to others. Though judging from the way that girl is still staring at us... I'm pretty sure her name is Francine. I've seen her hanging around us before, on the fringe, but she's never been so obvious about it. It's kind of creepy.

Our eyes meet, and she takes a step forward, toward us. "Uh-oh. I think we have a fan club," I mutter to Mo under my breath.

"Huh? Who?" She turns just as Francine reaches us. Eyeing her with a haughty look and using her bitchiest tone, she says, "Uh, hello. May we help you?"

Francine's face turns an unflattering shade of red, accentuating the puffiness of her cheeks. Her small, beady eyes appear black, like they're all pupil. Her tongue darts nervously out of her mouth, giving her a reptilian quality.

But I have to give her credit. Her voice is bright and perky as she says, "Hey, guys. I was just wondering if you wanted to go grab a coffee? Or we could get milkshakes, that would be fun. My treat."

I put a hand on Mo's arm, signaling her to be nice. Or, at least, not to completely annihilate the poor girl. I don't know why, but she has a tendency to get downright hostile to other people who want to be our friend, as if they pose some kind of threat. It's almost like she's defending her territory.

"With you?" Mo asks.

"Well, yeah."

"Why?"

"Well, uh..."

"I tell you what. You think about it."

Mo loops her arm through mine and pulls me off down the hall, muttering loud enough for Francine to hear us, "God, some people. Stalker much?"

A microsecond later, Mo's moved on, the other girl completely forgotten. As she happily chatters about how far behind we are on prom preparations, and all the ideas she has, I glance over my shoulder and spot Francine still standing where we left her, watching us with an anguished expression on her face.

And I feel bad. I really do. But guilt is something that I've already become accustomed to.

THIRTY-FIVE

SAMI NOW

2014

I watch him get dressed, his back to me as he pulls on his pants, buttons his shirt. I wish he could stay. I don't want to be alone right now.

"Are you sure you have to go?" I ask. "We could order some takeout. Watch a movie?"

David turns to face me, a sad smile on his lips. "I should really get back."

He rounds the bed, leans down to give me a kiss. It's brief, just a peck, with none of the lingering, bittersweet goodbye that I've become used to. It's not just my imagination. Something has changed between us.

"Well, tomorrow, maybe."

"Actually, Olivia has a volleyball game tomorrow."

I don't see what that has to do with anything. Olivia's had plenty of volleyball games. The season's almost over and, as far as I know, he hasn't bothered going to a single one of them.

"Oh."

He's pulling away.

I knew accepting Liz's dinner invitation was a mistake. But I couldn't resist. Going into their home, seeing the way they interacted together—or didn't.

All my life, she's been there right in front of me, just a step ahead. Always beating me out. Always reaching the finish line first.

I wonder if he'd still want to go to Olivia's game if he knew the truth. It's right on the tip of my tongue. I'm dying to say it. Five little words that carry such weight that they could change everything.

But I can't be the bad guy here.

"I'll walk you out."

I reach for my robe. He puts his hand on my wrist to stop me. Draws my hand up to his lips, kisses my palm.

"You should stay." He gives my fingers a gentle squeeze before releasing them.

I chew the inside of my cheek, debating. Trying to keep my mouth shut. But I can't do it. He's halfway through the door when my resolve crumbles. "I didn't say anything about us. To Liz, I mean. I wouldn't."

He stops, but he doesn't turn to look at me. He sounds regretful as he says, "I know. I blame myself for that."

And then he's gone. I strain my ears, listening to the soft click of the front door behind him, the tumbling of the bolt as he uses his key to lock it. And then I cry.

Liz had always been my closest friend. And, growing up, I thought it would be that way forever. It's just that keeping in touch would have been too painful, a constant reminder of what had happened.

But even after all that time had passed—fifteen years, five months, and six days—without a word spoken between us, all it took was us meeting face to face for everything to feel normal, for us to pick up right where we left off, like it had been minutes and not years between us.

But here's the thing. I had made my choice already. I chose him over her, and all it took was an instant.

When my eyes met David's across the crowded bar and I decided to approach him, it was with one thing in mind.

Though our conversation started with Liz and high school and how everyone was doing, I saw that he was open to more. I was the one who changed topics. I'm the one who flirted first. I wanted to make him mine.

And now I want to keep him.

David and I had never been big fans of each other back in school. I resented the time Liz spent with him. Didn't think he deserved her. Never understood what she saw in him.

But once she was removed from the equation, and we reconnected that night, there's no denying that sparks flew. He breached the barbed-wire barrier around my heart, the one other men had caught on, like it wasn't even there.

And for the first time in years, I felt hope. Maybe I *could* have my happily ever after. It seemed fitting, though, so fitting, that it would be with David.

Liz and I, we have that childhood bond that knows no bounds. And growing up, we always swore that no man could ever come between us. But the truth is, that's all that ever has.

THIRTY-SIX

AMY THEN

1999

I wait in the wings for my cue. On stage, the lights are dim. The scene is colorless and simple, an auctioneer standing on a platform auctioning off a musical monkey doll. In a minute the chandelier will crash from above and we'll all spring into motion, bringing new sets and colors and life to the performance.

No one thinks I should be here, not with my father so freshly dead and buried. The timing is horrible, I'll admit, but I'm not going to let it stop me. I'm not going to let anything stop me, not now. I'm hoping most people will think it's just my way of grieving, to stay busy and keep my mind off what happened, to throw myself into my performance, and if I seem different, if I seem happier now, that it's just an act.

But the truth is, I *am* happier now. I've never felt so liberated. Everything, every little thing in life, is sweeter. Better. Colors are more vibrant, foods are more flavorful, even each breath I take is deeper, the air cleaner. And it's all because he's gone.

And her. My sister. I gaze out into the crowd, blinking against the lights, almost blinded, but still I find her. Mo, here to see me, watch me perform, to provide me with support in my time of need.

I wonder what she'll say, how she'll feel about mourning Sonny when she finds out the truth. I wonder how she'll feel about me, too. We've both heard the rumors over the years, of course, but I don't think either one of us ever dared to believe them. But they were true, and now that hole inside me, that drafty, lonely spot I felt when I was little that ballooned into a vast, huge, frozen emptiness over the years, that missing piece that's left me feeling cored out and hollow, is sitting right out there in the audience.

I've found myself finding reasons to spend more time with her, stand closer to her, look at her more deeply these last few days. Every moment it gets more physically painful not to scream it from the rooftops, *Morgana Ripley, you are my twin sister.* The words are burning on my lips. I have to say them, and I'm afraid that if I don't tell her soon, I'll let it slip to someone else. I have to tell Mo first.

The chandelier crashes against the floor. The lights go out on stage. The fixture reverses its fall, drawn high into the rafters until later in the show. Stagehands scurry to change the sets, actors rush to their spots. I join them.

The time has come. I'm telling her tonight, after the show.

The streetlights in the school parking lot seem dim after spending so much time under the harsh glare onstage. Teenagers cluster here and there in tiny groups, clinging to the dark spaces. I take the final step through the side door of the auditorium and let it shut behind me, abandoning myself to the night.

Sami and Liz come rushing over, Mo trailing behind them. Sami places a bouquet of flowers into my arms, roses mixed with peonies, my favorites. "You were fantastic!"

Liz sets a tiara on my head. It's one of the fake little kid ones from an accessories store, but the oversized rhinestones still catch what little light there is and sparkle. She kisses me on each cheek, European style, and then gives me a wide grin. "Seriously, Amy, your singing was amazing."

I look to Mo, still hanging back a few feet, head hanging. As if she senses my eyes on her, she looks up at me with a small smile. "Good job."

I close the space between us and hook my arm through hers. "Hey, would you guys mind if we caught up with you later?" I can feel Mo tense next to me. Sami and Liz exchange confused looks. Me and Liz have been staying at Sami's since my dad died. It's late, it's a school night, and we've only got one car with us. "Mo and I will walk."

"Okay." Sami smiles, but I can tell by the way her forehead crinkles that her feelings are hurt. I'll tell her later that Mo and I were talking over birthday ideas. She'll be fine. "You two be safe."

"We will."

Mo and I stand side by side, watching as they get in the car and pull away. The taillights become smaller, until they're two cigarettes burning in the distance, finally winking out to nothing at all. Then Mo pulls her arm from mine.

"What the hell was that about?"

"What?"

"Brushing them off like that? Volunteering me for a two-mile walk back in the dark? Any of it? We were supposed to finalize our plans for prom."

I feel my lips tremble. I push them firmly together, folding them into my mouth to stop it. Mo's face softens.

"I'm sorry. I know you're upset. Is this about your dad?"

"Yes and no."

"Liz and Sami would want to be here for you too, you know. But I know what it's like. Not wanting to discuss family with people who actually have one." She draws me into a side hug and starts pulling me down the street beside her.

"But that's just it, Mo. You're my family."

"We're all your family. You know that."

"Yeah, I know what you're saying, but this is different. You're my blood family. Not just my cousin. My sister."

Mo freezes next to me, mid-step. She lowers her raised foot back to the ground and turns to face me. There's something feral in her face, a wildness threatening to break free. I rush to finish.

"Sonny told me. I don't think he meant to, but he did."

"What did he say?"

"He was yelling at me, and he said, 'I should have gotten rid of you and sold you to the Ripleys like your sister.'"

"Sold?"

Her voice is so fragile it brings to mind a snowflake. So delicate, so beautiful that you want to touch it, you have to, if only to better admire it, but you ruin it in the process. I watch as something breaks behind her eyes. Then she blinks and it's gone, any emotion that was there vanished, replaced with an expressionless mask.

"That doesn't matter, Mo. That's just what some asshole did."

"That's easy for you to say. You're the one he kept. The chosen one." She starts moving, marching ahead of me down the road. I run to catch up. Grabbing her arm, I make her stop.

"Mo, that's ridiculous. I'm not the chosen one. The one chosen for what? To be his maid and his cook and his punching bag? Listen, you're missing the point. The point is that you're my sister. My twin. The blood that flows through our veins? It's the same, yours and mine. I've always felt that something was wrong, was missing, and now I know why. Haven't you felt that way, too?"

Sadness flashes over her face and is gone in an instant, like a lightning strike. "I have."

"Don't you realize what a good thing this is? Believe me, Mo, you didn't miss out on anything by not growing up in that house. Really. We don't need him. We're better off without him, both of us."

I know she wants to believe me. I can feel her heart reaching out, tugging on mine. I can feel her sadness. I want nothing more than to take it from her, make it my own, and replace it with love and happiness and warmth.

"I mean, doesn't it strike you as just a little bit odd that I grew up with the man and I'm not the least bit saddened by his death?"

Her head cocks to the side, her arms crossing over her chest. The muscles in her neck stand out like cords. Her jaw is slung forward, tense. "You know? I thought you were different. I thought you were like me. But you're just like everyone else out there in fairy-tale land who thinks they have it so rough. But you know what's really rough? Not having anyone want you. Ever."

"But that's not true. Mo, the man was evil. He took us from each other. He was more concerned with getting laid than with either of us."

Mo laughs, an empty, hollow noise. "So the bastard wanted everyone *except* me. I get it."

"No, that's not it at all."

"But don't you see? It is. That's exactly it, Amy. That's always it, the story of my damn godforsaken life. If he'd sold you and not me, my parents would probably have stuck around and raised you. Because it's not you. It wasn't him. It's not any of them. It's me. I'm the one with something wrong with me. I'm the one who's filthy inside, the bad apple with the rotten core.

He got rid of me because he could sense it, like everyone else does."

"That's not true."

She gives me a pitying look. "But it is."

"But—"

"No, Amy. Here's the simple truth. I'm like a hot potato. Getting tossed around because no one wants to keep me. Because they don't want to get burned. So what does that say about who I am? About *what* I am?"

"Mo. There's one person who would do anything for you. Who already has. Me." I lean forward and whisper in her ear, telling her the one thing that should make everything right.

But it doesn't.

She moves away, mouth twisted in a knot of disgust. "And you're still the good one."

Then she turns her back on me and takes off, running down the street. I want to go after her, but my feet are rooted to the spot. I watch her leave, my mouth hanging open, muscles slack, not sure what just happened. I thought I'd be my sister's salvation. I might just be her ruin instead.

THIRTY-SEVEN
LIZ NOW

2014

I startle awake, the oven timer stirring me from a dreamless sleep. I scramble dazedly to my feet only to discover that my left leg is numb. I stumble when I try to put weight on it, gasping as the movement pulls a stiff muscle in my neck. I rub at the crick, pins and needles stabbing my foot, as I limp through the dark house toward the kitchen to silence the buzzer.

I turn the oven off, and with it, the incessant beeping. Wrinkle my nose against the odor of burning cheese. Curse and grab a hot pad and pull the slightly singed lasagna out. How long had the timer been going off before I woke? My eyes land guiltily on the empty wine glass on the counter.

Taking a seat on one of the stools, I cradle my head in my hands. My brain is absolutely throbbing. Every inch of my body aches. I feel like I'm coming down with something, the flu, maybe. But I've got to pull it together. I can't afford to fall apart now. And I can't let my daughter see me like this.

Where is Olivia, anyways? I remember telling her she could go visit Gina at Francine's house, but that was hours ago. She knows to be home in time for dinner. I hunt my phone down, find it on the window ledge over the kitchen sink. There's no message letting me know she's eating elsewhere tonight. She must have lost track of time.

I type out a quick text reminding her to come home to eat, then root around in the refrigerator. Pulling out a head of lettuce and some random veggies I get to work washing and chopping. Next, I dig out several half-empty containers of salad dressing. Set the table. Eye the bottle of wine, debating whether to pour myself another glass or not.

I'm still alone.

It should take Olivia less than two minutes to get from Francine's door to ours. I check the timestamp on the message I sent. It's been ten. I draw a deep breath—telling myself it's calming—and dial. My call goes straight to voicemail.

I know that my daughter's at the age when kids start pulling away from their parents. And that our relationship is especially fraught right now since she discovered that David is not her biological father. *And* that I've been too distracted by other things to have properly handled the situation, but still.

She's only fourteen. This behavior is unacceptable. She doesn't get to disrespect me like this.

Scrolling through the contacts in my phone, I find Francine's number. My jaw tenses. Anger heats my skin. I can't believe that I'm having to do this. Olivia's going to be grounded for a week. Two if Francine gloats too much.

The line rings four times before it's answered. Plenty of time for me to sweat it out as my humiliation grows. I'm seriously considering hanging up, right up to the second where it becomes too late.

"Liz?" Francine asks timidly. "Is everything all right?"

"Yeah, Francine, everything's fine. I was just wondering if you could send Olivia home for me. Dinner's ready." There's a long stretch of silence. I grab the wine, struggle to uncork it one handed. "Francine?"

"Um, Liz? Olivia's not here."

The bottle slips from my grasp, shattering across the kitchen floor.

"What?" I whisper.

"I don't know what to tell you. Are you sure she told you she was coming over here?"

I nod, then realize she can't hear me. "Yes, I'm sure. Positive."

"Hold on for a second." I hear her calling for Gina. Can hear their muffled conversation in the background.

Hey, was Olivia supposed to come over today?

She said she'd ask if she could. I never heard back, so I figured her mom said no.

Do you have any idea where she could be?

No.

Gina Marie, I'm serious.

God, Mom, so am I. No.

Has she been hanging around anyone new at school lately?

Uh-uh.

Has she been talking to any boys?

Not like that.

Do me a favor, honey. Call your friends and see when the last time someone heard from her was, okay?

Suddenly, I'm very grateful to this woman I've been so hostile toward. She comes back on the line a moment later, her voice calm and soothing. "Liz? Gina hasn't heard from her, but I have her calling around. Don't worry, I'm sure this is all just a misunderstanding. Do you want me to come over?"

I'm already heading toward the front door. Yes—I want her to come over. I want her to take charge. I want any help she can give me because I'm lost, and I'm panicking, and I don't know what to do. The word is on my lips. And dies there.

I stare at the folded slip of paper that's been shoved through my mail slot, not wanting to touch it. Knowing that I have to, even though I can feel the evil radiating off of it. The heat of her hatred is so strong that my fingers feel blistered as I open the note.

I've got something precious of yours. If you want it back, you know what you have to do. Tell the cops anything but your confession, and I'll keep it forever.

XXO ∞

I can't breathe. I shove my fist into my mouth, biting down until I feel the skin split and the copper tang of blood taints my tongue, but I can still feel the scream building, wanting to erupt.

"Liz?"

Squeezing my eyes shut, I knock the back of my head against the wall, one, two, three times. Draw a deep breath. Clear my throat. Steady my voice.

"You know what? Francine, I'm so sorry. I feel ridiculous."

"You do? Why?"

"I do. David just texted. I forgot that Olivia was staying with her grandparents this weekend."

"Oh. Okay." But I can tell by her tone that it's not. That I've just become the type of person who doesn't know where their fourteen-year-old daughter is. That whatever she might have thought of me before, from now on, in her eyes, I'll always be a bad mother.

Which is fine. Let her think whatever she wants. I don't care. The only thing that matters is that I remain a mother. Which means doing whatever it is I have to do to bring my daughter home safely.

THIRTY-EIGHT

SAMI NOW

2014

I'm carrying a pizza box out for recycling when my cell rings. I wrestle the cardboard in half and shove it in the bin before pulling my phone out of my pocket. Check the screen to see who's calling before I answer.

"Hey, Liz. What's up?"

"Sami, she took her."

"What? Who?"

"My daughter. That psycho bitch took my daughter." She sounds crazed, manic, her words firing too fast from between her lips.

"Liz, calm down."

"Don't tell me to calm down!"

I glance around, checking to see if anyone's close enough to overhear my end of the conversation, but I'm alone. I lean against the side of the house and take a deep breath. I keep my tone low as I say, "I know you're upset, but just slow down for a minute. Are you sure?"

"Yes, I'm sure."

"But why would she do that? It doesn't make sense."

"Why has she done any of this? What part of anything that she's done has ever made sense? She's crazy, plain and simple. And now she has my daughter." Her voice shakes. She must be crying, not that I blame her. "I have to get Olivia back. She has to be okay."

"She will be, I'm sure of it. But, Liz... maybe you're jumping to conclusions. I mean, Olivia's a teenager. Sometimes they—"

"She left another note. A threatening one."

"Wait, what? What do you mean, *another*?"

"It's not the first. Haven't you gotten any?"

"I would have told you if I had." The implication of my statement is clear—what else has she chosen to keep from me? "Have you called the police?"

"I can't."

"But if she has—"

"She'll hurt Olivia if I tell the cops she took her. I can't risk it."

"Then what are you going to do?"

Her voice is a whisper as she says, "I have to give her what she wants. I'll confess. What choice do I have?"

"Liz, you can't, I mean—"

"Not the truth, obviously. I doubt she's doing this because she wants to share a cell with me. I'll tell them it was me. That I was the only one."

I swallow hard, wet my lips. "Where are you now?"

"Home."

"Where's David?"

"I don't know."

"Do you... do you want me to come over?"

"No. I don't think so."

"Then what can I do?" There's a long stretch of silence that leaves me wondering if she's hung up. "Liz?"

"I don't think there's anything any of us can do."

"Well, are you going now?"

"Where?"

I try to keep the impatience out of my tone as I say, "To the police? To confess."

"There's something I need to do first."

"But if she has Olivia—"

"Sami, I'll take care of it. Trust me, I'm not going to risk giving her a reason to hurt my daughter. I just, I wanted to ask you for a favor. For after..."

She doesn't need to finish the sentence. I know she means for after she confesses. When she's locked up behind bars.

"Of course. Whatever I can do."

"I need you to promise me that you'll take care of Olivia. And David. Try to keep them together, if you can. Please."

"Yeah, of course." We both know why she's asking. There's only one reason she'd suspect David might possibly abandon their daughter. There's no telling what most men would do if they found out a secret like hers.

I imagine most would react badly, to say the least. Maybe even violently. But could you really blame them? It's a nasty shock, for a man to find out that the child he's been raising is not his own.

Then I realize that even though I've agreed, she hasn't hung up yet. And I know why. I know that there's only one explanation for why she's still on the line. I need to hear it and she needs to say it. I check around, again making sure no one can listen in before dropping my voice and asking, "Olivia. She's Sonny's, isn't she?"

"Yes."

THIRTY-NINE

SAMI THEN

1999

I can't concentrate. Usually, history is my favorite subject, but right now, I only have energy for the present. Even if it sucks. Closing my textbook, I blink back tears, wondering how things got to be such a mess.

I know that we're all hurting. That we're all struggling. That we need each other now more than ever. And yet I still feel the bonds between us loosening as we all start to pull away in different directions.

We've always been there for each other before this. Always had each other's backs. Always managed to band together against our problems, no matter what it took. Even if we had to do things we weren't proud of. Including resorting to violence.

And it hasn't always been Mo who's done the dirty work.

My thoughts stray back in time to the furthest corner of my mind, and I think of Timmy Mitchell. I've been thinking about him a lot lately. Mainly because I can't help wondering if it was the last time I was the one to solve a problem.

It happened the year we were in kindergarten. We had just

come in from recess. I was looking for Amy because I had let her borrow my *Strawberry Shortcake* coloring book and I was ready to have it back, but as the kids filed in and sat down, her seat remained empty.

I looked over at Liz, but she was already busy coloring in the turkey we'd made by tracing our hands before the break, the tip of her tongue sticking out from the corner of her mouth as she concentrated on staying within the orange crayoned lines. Mrs. Finlay, our teacher, was standing at the back of the room by the hamster's cage, talking to the teacher's aide. They were laughing. Neither of them had noticed Amy's absence, either.

I'm sure it was probably only a minute, but I got tired of waiting and marched right out the door unnoticed, back outside to the playground to find Amy and my coloring book. I caught sight of her black hair shining through the metal bars of the jungle gym, near the back fence. It wasn't until I got closer that I noticed she wasn't alone.

Amy's face was purple and screwed up like she was sucking on a sour candy and the howl of her pained cries made me move a little faster.

"Owww, Timmy, stop. You're hurting me." Then I saw him, Timmy Mitchell, with Amy's arm grasped between his hands as he twisted her skin, which shone bright red and angry. "Stop, Timmy."

I felt anger like I had never felt before, my body pulsing with rage and indignation. That was *my* friend he was hurting. *My* friend he was making cry.

"Stop."

I was a shy kid, a quiet only child, but I shouted the word with the force my mom had made me practice using in case a stranger ever tried to take me. I shouted so loud that the sound of my own voice echoed in my ears. Timmy Mitchell looked at me, held my eyes for a long minute, then smiled before his grubby hands went back to work on Amy's tender flesh, and her cries rose like a winter wind.

I didn't even think. Couldn't even see, if I'm honest. The next thing I knew, my fist smashed into Timmy's nose. Blood burst from his nostrils like a popped water balloon, tiny splats covering us all. Then Amy was beside me and together we watched Timmy wail, backing away from us as he held his nose, crying and stumbling as he ran inside to tell the teacher.

"Thanks." Amy smiled at me, tears still swimming in her reddened eyes. "I kept your book safe." The arm without red welts came out from behind her back, *Strawberry Shortcake's* freckled face grinning from the shiny cover of the coloring book.

"Hey, thanks."

"Do you think you'll get in trouble?"

I looked down at Amy's thin arm, a dark shade of maroon speckled with red dots and shrugged. "It doesn't matter. I'd do it again." Moving to my other side, she laced her good arm through mine, and we went inside to face whatever punishment lay ahead together.

Because that's what friends *should* do. Stick together. Share the consequences. Good or bad.

FORTY

LIZ NOW

2014

If I'm going to do this, if I'm going to sacrifice everything, I need to make sure that my daughter's okay. And that she remains that way. I'll do anything as long as that's true, and she must know it.

After all—isn't that why she chose me? She wasn't sending letters to Sami. No, it was me and me alone who was her target. I'm the one who's vulnerable. The one who's weak because my heart lives outside my body, walking around on her own two legs.

And while motherhood hasn't been all tea parties and rainbows and kisses, I wouldn't give up a single second of it. Not the sleepless nights or the tummy aches, the dirty diapers or the projectile vomit. Not even when she threw fits or called me names or got old enough to be embarrassed by me. My daughter single-handedly took the biggest mistake of my life and made it into the best thing I've ever done.

But that doesn't mean I want her to follow in my footsteps. I want more for her, so much more than falling in love with a sexual predator, a man who knew me from the time I was a small child, who groomed me for the day I'd be useful to him.

And I know that he hurt her, too, maybe even more than he hurt me. But that still doesn't excuse what she's done.

There was a time when I would have trusted her with my life. Now I wouldn't even trust her to take out my trash. There is no honor among thieves. Or coconspirators, as the case may be.

I can't think of that night, of all the mistakes leading up to it, of the many more that came after, without blaming myself. There was so much I missed. So many times where I could have tried harder, done more.

Maybe if I had, things would have gone differently. Maybe we'd all still be friends. Maybe we'd all still be alive. So I guess it seems fitting that I'm the one who's going to take responsibility for what happened. It kind of was my fault, in a way.

But I have one last hope, one final straw left to grasp at. I wake my computer from its sleep, holding my breath as I bring up the browser window and search for Olivia's phone. Nothing. It's as if she never even existed.

So it's true. I'm going to lose everything. The fragile ice castle I've managed to build is about to come crashing down, shattering into a million jagged pieces that I won't be able to escape. I'll be left alone, bleeding out, cold and alone and dying. And I deserve it. Every last cut.

I feel sick and queasy, slick with nervous sweat. I get up and grab my keys and purse. I can't put this off any longer. Not when my daughter's waiting. Especially since this is something that I should have done a long time ago.

FORTY-ONE

LIZ THEN

1999

I watch the limo pull up through my bedroom window. The long, sleek body is silver. Gunmetal with metallic flake, to be exact. Mo's favorite. A chauffeur in a gray suit with matching cap emerges from the front, circles the vehicle, and opens the door to the back. I turn before I can see who steps out first.

"It's here. Liz, the limo's here."

My mom is so excited that her voice sounds ten years younger than usual. It's as if she's been looking forward to this night more than I have. She's stocked up on enough rolls of film for an entire year of pictures, leaving no doubt that tonight will be immortalized for eternity. But what if it turns out to be a night I'd rather forget?

I pause to check myself in the mirror. Passing a hand over my hair, I run a fingertip over the edge of my mouth to check for stray lipstick and try to steady my nerves before heading down the stairs.

Mo had the driver pick up our dates first, then her. Now

she's holding court in the center of the living room. She looks gorgeous.

Her dress is exquisite. The ivory silk flows over her skin like milk. The neckline plunges almost to her navel, iridescent sequins lining the dip, drawing your attention to the luminous skin of her chest. The gown is full length, slit high up her thigh on each side. She has one leg jutting out, her tiny foot arched in a super high stiletto with beadwork matching the dress, her toes a pale shade of pink.

My mom circles her like a professional photographer, capturing her from all angles. The guys have gathered in the corner where my father is showing off his new semiautomatic handgun. It's meant to be a subtle warning, but the intention is lost, instead resulting in him being Mr. Cool Dad.

I linger in the shadows on the stairs, watching, until David glances up and notices me. Something's different. Something's changed, but I couldn't for the life of me say what.

As he watches me descend the last few steps, his smile transforms his face, and I can see exactly what he must have looked like as a grinning little boy on Christmas morning. The way he's looking at me makes me feel like I'm in a fairy tale, floating down the remaining steps like Cinderella on a magic cloud.

We can't take our eyes off each other as we pose for pictures. I feel enchanted. It usually feels like David's just going through the motions of being a boyfriend. His sudden interest has taken me by such surprise that I barely register anything else, but I do catch the look on Mo's face as her date leans in and whispers in her ear. I see the anger flash in her pale eyes, her teeth, frozen in a smile, suddenly looking sharp and dangerous. Then I'm turned away for one last picture before we pile into the car and head for Sami's house.

David holds my hand on the drive. He tells me how beautiful I look. I tell him how handsome he is in his tux. I'm trying to enjoy it, to be in the moment, but I keep prying my eyes off him to sneak glances at Mo, who is staring out the window, arms crossed over her chest.

She looks so sad, so utterly unhappy, that a part of my heart breaks. I can't imagine what her date must have said. Right now he has his back turned to her while he jokes with the other guys. I don't recognize him, have never met him before, know only what Mo said when she told us she had found a date—that he'd look great in the photos, which is true, but still.

We arrive at Sami's and the driver opens the door for us to spill out and begin our next photo shoot. I catch Mo by the hand as we walk to the door and give it a squeeze. She gives mine a half-hearted pinch back and releases it before fixing the movie siren smirk back on her face.

Sami's mom opens the door, camera in hand, and immediately starts taking candid shots. Sami and Amy are waiting for us in the living room. I can tell by their strained expressions that, like us, they've already had to endure a barrage of photos. We're already tired of smiling and the night has barely begun.

Sami greets her date with a kiss to the cheek, and then her mom does the same. Her cousin blushes until his freckles disappear against his stained cheeks, and then he holds out the corsage that his mother no doubt picked out. The lavender orchid perfectly matches the color of Sami's retro party dress, mid-length with a sweetheart neckline and flared skirt. Her auburn hair is piled high atop her head. She looks radiant.

Amy's date is her super shy biology lab partner, who turns out to be a secret hottie in a suit, his blond hair brushing the collar, his glasses suddenly more Clark Kent than Millhouse from *The Simpsons*. She looks like Mo's opposite in a simple dress with a modest cut, the material an exact match to her glossy black hair, which hangs in curls collected in a loose ponytail down her back.

Sami's mom poses us for half an hour, group shots, singles,

couples, all girls, all boys, until every possible combination has been exhausted. Then, with only a few tears and kisses, she sets us free. We bound down the steps and jumble into the limo like a bunch of kids going trick-or-treating. Only, instead of candy, there's alcohol.

Mo's date has a flask out before we've left the curb. She rolls her eyes and wedges herself between Amy and the door on the opposite side, occupying herself with Amy's hair. Seeing them side by side, so different yet so similar, always stirs something deep within me. I've never been sure exactly what it is, but as I watch the care with which Mo wraps Amy's curls around her fingers, the love in her movements, I realize, for the first time, that it's jealousy.

No matter how close Mo and I are, we'll never be blood family like she and Amy. And it hurts. To know that I'll never be her number one. But that doesn't mean that I can't be somebody's.

David shifts beside me and I'm surprised when he accepts the flask, taking a long draw. He doesn't usually drink. This, I realize, must be why he's acting so different. But if that's the case, who am I to argue? I like this new version of my boyfriend. Maybe this night won't be so bad after all. And while a part of me can't wait for this night to be over, the other part can't wait for it to really begin.

FORTY-TWO

LIZ NOW

2014

The hallway is sterile and void of color. White walls, white marble tiles, white furniture. Some designer was probably paid a butt-load of money to come up with this idea. It's some kind of statement about something, I'm sure, but whatever it is, the statement is lost on me.

I knock on the door of the penthouse apartment before I can change my mind and think about my husband's undershirts, the crusty yellow armpits that form despite large quantities of bleach. Maybe the statement is that rich people are neater and cleaner than the rest of us. Or maybe it's just that their staff are aware of secret ways to keep their whites whiter.

Whatever the significance, the white on white on white theme creates a cold, uninviting atmosphere. It's like being in a sci-fi movie right before it turns to horror. God, I hope nothing jumps out at me. I don't think I could take it. Just the thought of seeing her face to face is terrifying enough.

My heartbeat feels jerky and irregular. My mouth has gone dry, leaving me unable to swallow the taste of bile that's climbed up the back of my tongue. I feel light-headed and frail. I wish I was anywhere but here.

The door opens, enveloping me in a wave of sandalwood scented air, and I'm relieved to see that the interior is more welcoming, done in shades of tan and sea foam green that gives the place a beachy feel. A woman in her early twenties stands before me, a heavy, dark gray sweater falling off one shoulder, shiny mahogany hair gathered over the other. She's wearing jeans and ballet slippers. I step back to check the number on the wall next to the door.

"May I help you?"

The girl is dressed too casually to be a maid, too old to be a daughter. I pray that I have the wrong place, that I can retreat back home and work on gathering my nerve. "I, uh, I'm here to see Ms. Ripley."

"Is she expecting you?"

I open my mouth to respond, but the words don't come out. My jaw drops as she enters the room. Our eyes meet.

"It's okay, Anna, let her in."

The girl steps back, allowing me entrance. My steps are faltering, my legs shaking. It feels like I'm trying to balance my feet on top of a floor made of Jell-O.

"Would you mind running those errands alone?"

"Not at all, Ms. Ripley."

Anna slips past me, closing the door softly behind her, and I realize I'm still staring with my mouth wide open. It takes all of my effort to shut it. While I do, she crosses the room and stands before me. I fight the urge to flee.

Her arms fly out, and for a second I think she might hit me, that maybe I should brace myself for an attack, but then those arms are wrapped tight around me. I can feel her tears through my hair, against my neck. I make myself breathe, fighting the tightness in my chest, and the familiar scent of her triggers connection after connection in my memory. It's too late now.

Finally, she releases me, stepping back a step to take me in, a soft smile bending her lips. "Liz. It's so great to see you."

My voice shakes. My entire body trembles. "I'm going to the police. I'll confess to everything."

"Huh?"

"I just wanted to make sure my daughter was okay, first." I stare hard into those ice blue eyes of hers. "And I want you to promise me that you won't hurt her. That you'll let her go."

"Liz, what are you talking about?"

She's an even better actress than she used to be. She really looks confused.

"Cut the shit. You've already won."

"Are you feeling okay? Why don't you sit down?"

"I don't want to sit," I snap. "I want to see my daughter."

She backs away several steps. Her eyes flit around the room like she's looking for an escape. If I didn't know her so well, know firsthand what she was capable of, I'd think she was scared. But I'm the one who has cause to be afraid. "Liz, I don't..."

I snatch the note from my purse and wave it in her face. "What? Did you forget about your little love letters?"

"What letters?" She grabs me by the wrist, holds my hand steady, her eyes narrowing as she reads it. "What the hell, Liz. I didn't send this."

"Then who did?"

"I don't know, but it wasn't me."

I wrench free from her grasp, shoving the letter back in my purse. She no longer looks scared, just hurt and confused. "Did you really think I would? I mean, granted, we've done some messed up things. And we've seen each other at our worst. But did you really think I'd take your daughter?"

Up until this moment, I had. I'd been sure of it. But her reaction seems so genuine, her shock so real.

I stumble over to a chair and drop into it. Run my hands

through my hair, tugging fistfuls as I try to make sense of what's going on. I don't know what to think anymore. Is there any way I could have possibly gotten this wrong?

The notes started right after she got back to town. It makes too much sense to be a coincidence.

The problem is, I want to believe her. And, honestly, I almost do.

But there's another explanation that fits. A way that this could all still make sense. And that's if she's even crazier, even sicker, even more evil, than I could have ever imagined. I have to remember—this woman has killed in cold blood before.

FORTY-THREE

LIZ THEN

1999

The music spills out of the community center as we pull up, the thrum of the base pulsing around us like we're in the womb of the limo. Then the door opens, and we're birthed from the safety of our dark sanctuary out into the light, surrounded by chaos and confusion. No wonder babies cry when they're born.

Inside, the music is even louder, too loud, and it's too dark, with lights flashing violently. I want to run, but I'm pulled onto the dance floor by Mo. I keep my hand clenched around David's, bringing him with me.

The air is humid, poisoned with the odor of too many scents, perfumes and colognes and hairsprays and deodorants, combining together with fatal intensity. My lungs constrict. Sights and sounds and smells meld together into some kind of acid-induced nightmare. I want out.

The second Mo releases me I'm running off the dance floor, ankles wobbling in my high heels, the straps biting deep into my flesh. David's arm encircles my waist, helping me along. I bury my face in his shoulder and let him lead me back through the double doors, out into the night.

A cool breeze raises goosebumps on my skin. I take in deep breaths of air, gasping like I've been rescued from a near drowning, while David stares down at me, brows furrowed. I tell him I'm fine, but I can't put distance between myself and the mayhem fast enough in these stupid shoes. So he scoops me up into his arms and carries me down the sidewalk. It's a wonderful feeling.

But I can smell the booze on his breath. Can tell by his off-balance gait that he's sampled too much from Mo's date's flask. He's drunk.

Still, I like this version of David. He's romantic and chivalrous and all the things I never knew he could be. Things I never knew I wanted. And as our lips meet, his kisses are deeper than they've ever been before, almost needy. The truth is, I need his too, if only for one night. I'm so desperate to feel something other than loss and grief and pain that I'll take whatever he's willing to give me.

He takes me to the park down the street, empty of people, full of shadows, but I feel safe in his embrace. He sets me down on top of the picnic table, takes his jacket off, and drapes it around my shoulders. I slip my fingers under the straps of my shoes and slide them off, my bare feet glowing in the moonlight. Then I stand, take David by the hand, and lead him deeper into the park.

David is heavy on top of me, his weight unevenly distributed. A hip bone carves his name into my thigh. His breath is hot and humid, filling my ear in short pants, making it feel like it's filling with fluid, tender, infected. I stretch my neck, trying to get my

chin to reach over his shoulder so I don't smother. Our movements are awkward, bumbling.

When it's over, he lays beside me, our shoulders touching. I
stare up at the stars in the sky, wondering if anyone is up there,
looking down on me. I try not to be ashamed, but I feel my
cheeks burning with disgrace.

Because I'm pretty sure I just took advantage of him. Two
years of dating and we've never once crossed the line before.
He's always made his beliefs clear. I've always respected them
until now. And I'm positive that he never would have made this
decision if he hadn't been drinking. But what's my excuse?

Is sex always like this? One person using the other?

I listen to the sound of his breathing growing slower,
wondering if he's fallen asleep. Knowing that my friends must
have noticed I'm gone by now. I'm sure they've figured out
what's going on. They'll think that it's romantic. Two years of
abstaining only to give it up on prom night, like some kind of
lame teen movie. My shame burns hotter.

Remembering Mo's irritation with her date, I realize she
was probably ready to leave prom as soon as they got their
portrait taken. They're probably all waiting for me to come back
so we can go. I nudge David's shoulder with mine. He tilts his
head to face me, strokes my cheek gently with his fingertips.

"We should probably start thinking about heading back."

"Is that what you want?"

I take his hand in mine, kiss the back of his knuckles. "No.
But, remember, it's Mo and Amy's birthday."

"Yeah." He looks sad. I'm not sure why. "What am I
supposed to do the rest of the night?"

I think for a moment, searching my memory for a good
movie line, but I can't find one to fit. "Have sweet dreams."
Leaning forward, I brush my lips against his. "About next time."

David grins and gives me another kiss, a longer one, his lips lingering against mine. Heat spreads through me. This time it isn't from shame. My friends can wait a little longer.

FORTY-FOUR

SAMI NOW

2014

My eyes are immediately drawn to the maroon Subaru in the parking lot. Liz is here. I suspected she would be, but I'm not sure if what I'm feeling is jealousy or annoyance. It's a lifelong theme. Liz is always doing things first, me following behind, trying to mimic her footsteps.

The building is cold, goosebumps rising on my arms the second I step inside. That must be why I'm shivering as I cross the lobby to the far wall and push the elevator button. But why is it that, as the metal doors slide open, I find myself feeling queasy?

It makes me realize that I'm not ready yet. I don't want to do this after all. But time is running out. So I force myself forward, anyways.

I can't stop fidgeting in the elevator on the way up. It seems to being taking too long. I suppose I *am* going to the penthouse apartment, but the longer I'm stuck in this tiny little box, the longer my nerves have to jangle.

My stomach feels all flip-floppy and sour. I wonder if my

ulcer is back, and if it can really happen that fast or if it was lying dormant just below the surface, like a volcano waiting for the right time to erupt. It seems a fitting metaphor for this entire situation, actually. I imagine the thick black clouds curling up from the mouth of an ancient crater, clearing its throat after waiting years to blow up, like the dark secret that rots my insides.

But it wasn't always this way. Somewhere, deep inside, I also remember all the times that were good. Slumber parties where hysterical giggles lasted late into the night. The comfort of knowing that I wasn't alone, that there was someone who would always have my back. The memory of what it felt like to fit comfortably inside my own skin.

I have so many regrets, but maybe it's not too late. Maybe I can still make things right.

Bursting from the elevator, I jog down the hall. Hesitate for only a second before I raise my fist and knock, suddenly antsy to get inside and join my old friends. "You guys? It's me."

The door opens, and there she is. I fall into her arms, holding her tight. Breathing in the familiar scent of her, hundreds of memories come flooding back, things I haven't thought of in years. When she pulls away, she has tears in her eyes. "Sami."

I give a happy sigh. I've always loved the way she says my name. And the way she has my hand in hers, cradled like something precious? It melts away the years of hard feelings and regret. I allow her to pull me into the living room, where Liz is already waiting. Here we all are. Those of us that remain, at least.

"Liz's daughter is missing."

I avoid both of their eyes. "I know. We need to do something. That's why I'm here." Only, that's not true. I'm here for my own selfish reasons. "We owe it to him. Sonny. To bring his daughter home safely."

I watch her eyes closely for any sign of surprise, but there's none. She already knew. Like always, I was the last one to catch on.

"We're doing it for Liz," she corrects. "Not Sonny. Why would any of us want to do anything for him?"

I don't understand. At all. I look between both their faces, but all I see is a hard edge to their expressions.

"Why wouldn't we?" I ask.

She grunts. "Are you kidding me? He was a predator. He used us, all of us. Some of us in worse ways than others." She reaches out to me, softens her voice as she gives my shoulder a gentle squeeze. "And I am so very, very sorry for that. You guys deserved better."

The words hurt, shredding my heart like a cheese grater. "It wasn't like that."

"It was, Sami. What Sonny did was wrong. Very wrong. He took your trust and used it."

"But."

"Sami." Liz's voice is hushed but stern. It's the voice of a parent. A mother. I gape at her in confusion as she says, "She's right."

I shake my head from side to side. "No. That's not true."

"We were kids, Sami. Children. He'd known us since we were practically babies." Liz reaches out to take my hand, but I snatch it away.

"He wasn't... it wasn't like that. He wasn't a predator. He didn't force me. I wanted to. He loved me." My voice has risen higher, the words coming quicker, piling on top of each other, a panicked streak running thick through the middle.

"It doesn't matter what we thought we felt, or even if it was real, Sami. He was the adult, and he never should have let what happened happen in the first place. Don't you get that?"

"You're wrong, Liz. It wasn't like he was some kind of child abuser."

"That's exactly what he was. He used both of us, Sami."

"But how can you say that? That can't be what you really think. You wouldn't have your daughter if—"

"Sami." Liz reaches out her hand to me again tentatively. This time, I let it land on mine. "I love my daughter. I love her more than I ever believed would be possible, more than life itself. But it was wrong, Sami. If a grown man touched my baby girl like that, I don't care how much love they thought was involved. I would kill him."

They exchange a tense look over my head. I feel like there's something I'm missing, something they're keeping from me. Once again, I'm on the outside, looking in.

Liz shudders, eyes suddenly drawn and haunted. Her voice wavers as she whispers, "I'm glad he's dead. He was a sick, sick man."

"What are you talking about?" I ask, clutching Liz's arm, my nails making little half-moon indents, blanched skin radiating from my grip. "How can you say all of these horrible things about him? What's wrong with the two of you?"

"Sami—"

"No! I'm not listening to any more of this!"

I have to get out of here. I have to get far, far away from these people. And that's just what I do.

FORTY-FIVE

SAMI THEN

1999

This has got to be the worst prom night in the history of prom nights, ever. I mean, seriously. First, the whole lame photo shoot that my mom insisted upon.

She must have taken a hundred pictures of me and my date, which is my cousin, for God's sake, my cousin! And not even the cute one, either, but his pimpled, owlish younger brother, who couldn't even manage a mint or some mouthwash after eating what could only be tuna by the stink of it.

Then she turned to the others, making a particularly huge fuss over Mo and Amy, posing them and their dates, trying to take just as many crappy, unwanted photos of them so they wouldn't feel like some outcast orphans with no mother hen to chase them with a camera.

And all of it made me miss him so much. I couldn't help but wonder how much different things would be if Sonny were still alive. If I'd even be going to prom tonight, or if we'd be doing something else, together, just me and him.

I couldn't get out of that house soon enough.

Not that the limo ride to prom is any better, with all the guys getting drunk and all us girls just sitting there in silence, watching them. And we still have to get through this dumbass prom before we can take off and go back to Mo's and celebrate her and Amy's birthday, which, come on, it's their eighteenth so we have to do something special to salvage the night from being so lame.

But I seem to be the only one interested in any of that. We're drifting apart. I have to have a way to hold us together.

It seems too soon that we're pulling up in front of the rec center and getting out of the car. I do my best to keep my eye on everyone, but one minute we're all on the dance floor, and the next Liz and David have snuck off. I know I've allowed my first big failure of the night. Then Mo pulls away, yanks her date away from the girl he's talking to, drags him off to have their portrait taken before she gets too hot and sweaty.

Mo has taken extreme effort to make sure that her life is documented by a series of perfect portraits. If a stranger were to look at them, at her yearbook photos and the pictures taken at school dances and other events, each with a different but equally gorgeous boy on her arm, they'd think that she led a perfect life. I think that's why she does it—so one day she can look back and tell herself that things were better than they really were. That she led a normal life instead of the lonely, sad existence of a girl basically abandoned by her parents, whose only true family is her friends.

Suddenly, I realize that I'm standing by myself on the dance floor like a doofus. My cousin has found his way over to the corner where the video gamers are discussing the merits of some controller over another. Drawn like a magnet to nerd metal.

At least Amy looks like she's having fun over by the refreshment table. Her date hands her a glass of punch, leaning in to say something close to her ear, and she laughs, her whole face lighting up. She didn't mention anything about liking her date, just said something about going with her biology lab partner, but I can tell by the way he's looking at her that there's more to it than that.

My gut shifts, a strange movement, like someone kicked me from the inside, moving my internal clutter out of the way to make room for more hurt. Why would Amy feel like she couldn't tell me? We've shared the same bed every night since her dad died. Every night we've fallen asleep whispering our fears and hopes and dreams to each other, but she never said a word about this.

Or maybe she did, just not outright. Maybe she gave me a clue, maybe I was supposed to catch it and ask for more details, unravel the mystery, but I was too preoccupied with keeping tabs on the other two, and Amy's crush got lost in the chaos. Whatever the reason, I feel like a piss-poor friend.

But at least she looks happy, which is more than I can say for Mo, who's drinking off by herself in the corner, glaring at her date while he flirts with every girl he sees, and I can tell by the way she's tipping the glass back that there's booze in it. But that, I can handle. I look at Amy as I head over to Mo, just one last glance to reassure myself that she's okay.

But when I turn back, Mo is gone. Vanished. The feeling in my gut creeps up, sharp-clawed hands squeezing my esophagus in a daggered fist as it climbs higher. Shit. I promised myself that I'd be the strong one tonight, the one to keep us together. And I think that I've blown it already.

FORTY-SIX

LIZ NOW

2014

I watch Sami run from the apartment, wishing I could join her, but I feel too weak, too imbalanced. And now I'm here alone again. With *her*. And I'm terrified. But I have no choice. Not while Olivia is still missing.

She denies kidnapping my daughter, but she can't be trusted. I know this better than anyone—at least anyone who's still living. And I don't know what game she's playing, but I have to play along, keep her on my side.

"I'm sorry," I say. Sorry my daughter is missing, sorry I'm here, sorry this is happening. And yeah, maybe even a little sorry that we were ever friends. "I should go too. I need to find my daughter."

"I met her, you know. Last week." Her tone is soft, wistful. "I knew the second I saw her. She has Sonny's eyes. Why didn't you ever say anything?"

"I wasn't sure."

Her expression lets me know she doesn't believe that.

"I didn't want it to be true."

This she believes. She nods, taking my hand as she settles onto the arm of my chair. "I don't blame you. But I'm glad it is. She's my family, too. My only family."

Is this why she took my daughter? Does it matter?

No, it does not. All that matters is Olivia's safety. I want so badly to believe that this connection between them will keep my daughter safe, but she's never let blood ties stop her from hurting someone before. I need to keep her thinking I'm her friend. So I say it again, with feeling. "I'm sorry."

"Does she know?"

"Olivia? Not everything." Not about you. Or her. Or the ugly truth about her biological father. "She only found out recently. She figured it out herself. Olivia's so smart like that."

She laughs. "Well, the brains, obviously, came from you."

But that's not entirely true. The Van Clines have always been crafty. Crafty enough to mastermind this whole thing without getting caught, back when she was still just a teenager. I don't dare say it, but my eyes must betray what I'm thinking. She looks away, stands. Walks over to the window and stares outside.

"Why'd you sell the house?" I ask, unable to help myself. Because that's what put this whole thing in motion, the move that took the finger off the pause button from fifteen years ago, starting the final countdown.

"I didn't."

I shift in my seat so I can see her reflection.

"The Ripley Manor never passed directly to me. It was held in trust with some of their business holdings. There was some legal trouble, and the lawyers sold it to pay the settlement. There was nothing I could have done to stop it."

She turns to face me. "But I came back for you and Sami. Because I knew they'd find the body eventually."

We stare at each other, her words and their implications lingering in the air between us, and once again I think of the latest note. She wants to make sure that someone else takes the fall. That she gets off scot-free. Again.

My skin crawls. I fight the urge to shudder. I have to get out of here. Away from this woman and the death and destruction that surrounds her. And yet I can't manage to move. It's like I've fallen under her spell and lost my free will.

A knock breaks the silence, and I gasp in a startled breath, sucking in air like I'd been suffocating. She looks toward the door with dread, like she somehow thinks it's the body wanting to join us. The thought freaks me out, makes my toes curl inside my shoes.

"Do you think Sami came back?" I ask hopefully.

She pulls nervously on her lower lip. "Maybe. I guess I should go see."

I stay where I am, listening as she crosses to the front of the penthouse. Unlocks the bolt. Opens the door. Asks, "May I help you?"

"Are you Morgana Ripley?" It's Detective Johnson, I recognize his voice. I push back farther in my chair, as if trying to make myself invisible.

"I am."

"Ma'am, I'm afraid you're under arrest."

"What? That's ridiculous." I imagine the indignant look on her face, the haughtiness that's served her so well. Until now. Oh, God, I didn't expect this. Things are about to get worse than I ever imagined they could, so much worse.

"Actually, ma'am, I assure you it's not."

I hear her protests, the snap of the handcuffs, the words of the Miranda warning, outlining her rights. I feel a second of relief that's quickly followed by terror. Jumping to my feet, I run to the door, sheer panic flowing through my veins.

"Wait! You can't take her."

But she's already down the hall. I watch as she steps into the elevator, led by Detective Johnson. I stare in horror as she vanishes behind the metal doors as they slide closed. A uniformed officer steps in front of me, blocking my way, but I push past him, hurrying to the stairwell, feet pounding desperately as I race down the steps.

Bursting through the door into the lobby, I startle an elderly woman and her small dog. The dog yips at my heels as I dodge around them, out into the fading daylight. I have to catch up. I can't lose her now. Not until she tells me where I can find my daughter.

FORTY-SEVEN

LIZ THEN

1999

When I get back to the prom, Sami's in a panic. She can't find Mo anywhere within the dark corners of the rec center, and from what she's told me, she's sure that something is wrong.

If something bad happens, it's going to be all my fault. We'd be gone already if I hadn't gotten sidetracked with David.

My head swivels left and right, eyes searching as I thread my way through the crowd of dancing bodies, but I don't see her anywhere. It's like she vanished into thin air, was beamed up into the sky by aliens. But that can't be true. She must be here somewhere.

Light spills from a hall, catching my attention—the bathrooms. It's the only place I haven't looked, and I need to pee anyways, so I duck inside.

A quick check for feet under the stall doors reveals that I'm alone. I choose the cubicle on the end and slide the lock, making sure my dress doesn't touch anything. The silence is heavenly; a needed reprieve that's shattered all too soon as a group of girls flood inside.

The throb of the music thuds off the tiled walls, filling the small space until the door shuts again, a barrier fending off the chaos. Through the gap along the edge of the stall, I see the blurred movement of bodies swarming in front of the mirror.

"Oh my God, can you even believe it? I mean, she just totally freaked out."

"Seriously, right? You'd have thought the poor guy was raping her or something, not trying to make her feel better about her date trying to pick up every girl here except her."

"I mean, obviously she's messed up, but being filthy rich and living in a fancy house up on the hill can't be that hard, can it?"

That's when I realize they're talking about Mo.

"Oh, please. She's just embarrassed because it was Kevin Lewiston."

"What's that got to do with it? Kevin's hot."

"Yeah, but his dad is, like, a college professor. A guy whose dad doesn't even make six figures is slumming it for someone like Morgana. Or, like, who she thinks she is, at least."

I slide the lock and throw the stall door open. Every eye that lands on me darts away as quickly as possible once they see who I am. I take my time looking around the room, daring one of the gossipy skanks to make eye contact. They move away like liquid mercury, giving me a wide berth as I make my way to the sink to wash my hands.

It's so quiet that I can hear the water dripping from my fingers against the tile floor as I reach for a paper towel. I take my time drying my skin, drawing the process out. I walk to the door and can palpably feel the collective sigh of relief gathering behind me. Instead of leaving, I turn to face them.

"What? You couldn't stop your fat mouths from talking shit a second ago. What's changed? Go on, I want to hear it."

"Liz, we don't have anything against you."

"But you do against Mo? Why? What's she ever done to you?"

No one answers. I watch their eyes roll back in their heads as they search their memories for something, some slight or crushed toe, but no one can remember any reason for their dislike.

"Well? I'm waiting."

"It's just, I mean, she's kind of weird, you know. She just had a complete meltdown because a cute guy put the moves on her. I mean, who does that? It's not like it's anything she's not used to."

"What do you mean by that?"

"Oh, come on, Liz. Everyone knows she's a bit of a slut."

"Excuse me? Who's everyone?"

"Well... just, everyone. We've all heard about the things she's done."

"What the hell are you talking about?"

"She's, like, slept with half the guys in school."

"No she hasn't."

"Yeah, she has."

"According to who? Some guy who decided to lie? Or the guy after him who decided to give it a try after you stupid bitches were so quick to believe the first one? And all because why? Because she's gorgeous and rich and you're jealous so she's easy to hate? Because you'd much rather laugh at some dumb loser's lie and hope it makes him like you, even though he's dumb and a loser? Because you're so miserable and insecure that you'll hate on anyone as long as it makes you feel better about yourselves?"

"Whoa..."

"Oh, shut up. You make me sick. You should be ashamed of yourselves. Seriously. It's girls like you that make it so easy for guys to play us off each other. You see in the movies how rumors snowball into fake reputations that aren't deserved, and when it really happens every single one of you just jumps on board with your claws out, ready to draw blood. Go to hell."

Spinning, I slam my way out the door, back into the pulsing throngs of bodies dancing to the deafening music. Fighting through the crowd, I make my way toward the front, needing to escape the strobing lights and suffocating thick smog of comingled perfume products. Falling through the front doors, I stumble across the paved walk, trying to catch my balance.

My heels sink deep into the grassy lawn as I'm pulled, as if by invisible strings, around the side of the building. As I approach the gazebo nestled among the trees at the back of the rec center, I know what I was drawn here by. My heart.

Mo looks up as I approach, her tear-streaked face graffitied with running makeup. She looks back down at her hands in her lap as I sit next to her. I wait for a moment to see if she'll break the silence, staring at her discarded shoes lying on their sides by her feet. When she doesn't talk, I do.

"Hi."

"Hey."

"What happened?"

"Nothing."

"If you don't tell me, I'm probably going to think that it's something worse than it was. I won't be able to eat, I won't be able to sleep, I'll just imagine one horrible scenario after another until I drive myself insane and then I'll cover you in bubble wrap to keep you safe."

"Shut up."

I can hear the smile in her voice. Leaning over, I slip my shoes off and try hers on. I lift my legs straight out and twist my ankles from side to side, so we both can see them sparkle as they catch the light.

"They look good on you," she says.

"Better on you."

"No, you should have them. I want you to."

"That would just be a waste. I'd never have the guts to wear them. You should keep them."

Mo lifts her face to me. I watch as it crumples all over again. "Why are people always saying that? I don't have guts. I'm not brave. I'm not anything. I'm just a pathetic mess that's afraid of getting out of bed in the morning."

"Mo, that's not true."

"It is. Everyone thinks that I'm all fearless and gutsy, but it's all just an act. A lie."

I think about what Amy told me once. "Don't you think we all have to do that? Lie to ourselves, pretend to be something we're not sometimes, just to make it through the day."

"You know what I mean."

"Tell me."

"Kevin Lewiston is a dick."

"Tell me something I don't know. Like why you think so."

"It's nothing." She turns her head, looking off into the distance. "It's just, I thought, never mind."

"Mo? Please."

"I came out here to be alone because my date, well, you know."

"I saw."

"It didn't bother me too much, you know I don't really like him, but that doesn't mean I don't feel disrespected and kind of, well, embarrassed. I mean, I didn't have to sit there and watch him hit on everything in a skirt, so I came out here. And then Kevin came out. And we were just talking, you know. It was kind of nice. It felt like he was actually interested in what I had to say, and so when he kissed me, I kissed him back."

Mo's voice trails off. Her profile is limned by the moonlight, the ethereal glow of an angel. I watch the outline of her throat stretch as she swallows.

"And then?"

"And then he tried to go for the whole nine yards. So I stopped him, told him I wanted to go slow. And then he got really nasty, started talking about what a slut I was, that I shouldn't pretend to be better than I am because everyone knows the truth." Fresh tears roll down her face. "Liz, why do they all think I'm a slut? How did that happen?"

"I have no idea."

"I'm not, you know."

"I know." I wrap my arm around her shoulder. A cricket waxes poetic to his lover behind us.

"I've never even done, I mean, I don't understand..." Mo's voice breaks. "I'm not even sure that I like men, Liz. Or women, for that matter. I've never really felt attracted to anyone. I just feel empty inside, all the time. What the hell is wrong with me?"

My cheeks are damp with my own tears. It breaks my heart to see my friend like this. I have to try to help her.

She turns to me, her liquid eyes filled with more sadness than they should be able to contain. Sniffing deeply through her congested nose, a weak smile bends the corners of her lips. She wipes her eyes with her fists. "Do you ever hear things?" she asks.

We've all heard the rumors about her. But admitting it seems like some kind of betrayal. I study her, sitting beside me with her head tilted like she's listening, hearing the answer I refuse to say.

"Mo," I start. "Maybe you should talk to—" But she interrupts me before I can say it. A professional. Someone besides us, her friends. Someone who knows how to help, because obviously nothing we've tried is working.

"Not tonight. Tomorrow. We'll talk about it tomorrow."

"Promise?"

"Yes. But we have to try to salvage tonight and have some fun." Mo inspects the dark makeup smudges transferred to the backs of her hands. "Ugh, I must look like such a mess. Help me get cleaned up so we can go find Amy and Sami and blow this joint. We've got some birthday celebrating to do."

I grin and run my thumbs under Mo's eyes, trying to fix her makeup. But there's no happiness behind my smile, or even relief. And I don't buy her sudden change of mood, either. There's a strange feeling churning through my body, one I've never experienced before, but if I had to guess, well, I don't think it means anything good.

FORTY-EIGHT

AMY THEN

1999

It's prom night. When we were younger, like twelve or thirteen, we used to talk about what this night would be like—the perfect date, the perfect dress, the perfect night. If only we had known then what it would really be like, we could have saved ourselves a lot of time and trouble. Maybe I wouldn't have built the occasion up so much in my mind.

My date is my biology lab partner, Will, who isn't perfect, but he's cute, and I've never slept with him before, which is a bonus. I couldn't stomach the idea of going with someone who'd had sex with me, thinking I was Mo.

My dress is a simple black satin number, also not perfect, but it fits well, and I feel like I look good in it. And the night... well, it just might have potential.

Will whispers another funny comment in my ear. This time it's about Ms. Vernon and Ms. Baxley, the gym teacher and the librarian, who are two of the faculty chaperones. His suggestion that they're here at prom together, as a couple, doesn't seem too far off the mark. I feel Will searching my face, looking for how far he should take this tale, whether I'll find it inappropriate if he continues or keep laughing at his jokes.

I force out another laugh, past the fuzz in my head. The humming drone in my ears is getting louder. I paste a smile on my face while I focus on my heartbeat, as I concentrate on each breath, waiting to see if the feeling will pass or if I'm dying.

I know I'm probably not actually dying, but the pills I took, pilfered from the bottle in Sami's mom's medicine cabinet, are doing a bit more than I had hoped for. I just wanted to take the edge off, lower my expectations of what was supposed to be a perfect night. I just wanted to have a good time.

I feel the sweat pop out of the pores along my hairline. My heart beats faster, louder, until the rush of my blood overtakes the hum in my ears. I feel my vision fading in and out, and although I focus all my efforts on keeping my legs straight, I feel them buckling beneath me.

"Sit... down..."

I'm not sure if Will hears me, I can't see his face through the gray haze cloaking my vision, but I feel his arm wrap tightly around my waist. He leads me to a chair and guides me down. His hand brushes along my temple, and as bad as I feel, I'm acutely aware that he's just got his hand wet with sweat and makeup. He must think I'm disgusting.

I try to fan myself, but my arms feel like they're made of lead. My coordination is off. I feel like I'm overheating, like my blood is boiling just beneath my skin, and any second now I'm going to burst into flames. I think my brain is cooking. An image of that commercial with the egg sizzling in the frying pan comes to mind. *This is your brain on drugs.*

Then a cool rush of air soothes my burning skin. I feel Will lift my ponytail up and blow across the back of my neck. Goosebumps sprout on my arms.

"... punch is spiked. Guess you're not used to drinking, huh. But you'll be all right."

Will's words rise above the rush of my pulse. Or maybe my pulse is subsiding.

"As soon as you're up to it, let me know and I'll help you outside. Some fresh air will help you feel better."

A light spot breaks through my cloudy vision. Will's face blooms in the middle, brows furrowed in concern. My pulse has slowed, and gravity has lessened its pull.

"I'm starting to feel better. Thanks."

The worried look on Will's face cracks into a smile. "That a girl. You're not much of a drinker, are you?"

I shake my head. A series of excuses run through my brain, the alcohol reacting with medication that I'm on, not eating enough today, but I decide to just keep my mouth shut. Why do I always feel the need to provide an explanation? Why do I constantly feel like I need to make excuses for myself?

"I think I'm okay now."

"Yeah?"

"Yeah." But there's still a deep furrow between his eyebrows. And it's obviously my fault. "I'm sorry."

"For what?"

"For ruining prom night for you. I bet you wish you hadn't agreed to come with me, huh?"

"Are you kidding? Don't be ridiculous. I'm having a great time."

"Uh-huh, sure."

"I am, Amy. Honestly." He takes my hands in his, the skin of his palms rough and dry. "I had actually wanted to ask you to come with me."

"Then why didn't you?"

"Because I didn't think that there was a chance in hell that you'd say yes."

"Really? Why not?"

"Well, look at you. You're beautiful and talented and gorgeous, and I'm just some science nerd who paid Sarah

Kinsley twenty bucks to switch with me when we drew names for lab partners."

"No you didn't."

"I did. Really."

He's leaning toward me, his face nearing mine, and I realize he's going to kiss me. I push off the chair and struggle to my feet. "I think I'm ready to walk now."

"Then let's get you that air."

I let Will lead me through the crowd, an arm still around my waist. Will is such a sweet guy. I wish I had met him a few years ago. Maybe things would have turned out differently.

There's really no way to tell a guy who's treating you with kindness and respect that there's something vitally wrong with you; something that makes his caring behavior a real turnoff. I really don't want to hurt the guy, but I suddenly can't stand to be near him.

The crisp night air soothes me with a welcomed touch. Leaning against the brick exterior of the rec center, I feel the throbbing bass vibrating through the wall from inside. White lights adorn the trees around the building. They twinkle every time the wind blows. Will shifts from foot to foot in front of me, unsure of what to do next.

"We could walk down the street and get you something to eat, if you want. Or some coffee. Or you can stay here, and I can go get it for you."

"Thanks, Will, but I'm fine."

I'm starting to get an itchy feeling under my skin.

"I don't mind. Really."

My jaw clenches, teeth grinding together to keep the words inside my mouth. I want to scream and yell, but mostly I just want to get the hell out of here. And I think I'm going crazy. I swear I hear Liz and Mo's voices, but how can that be possible?

I survey my surroundings, desperate to find a way to escape. My eyes land on the person exiting the rec center right now. Salvation is coming. I just wish she was walking a little faster.

"Actually, I should probably just go home and lie down."

"What? I thought you were feeling better."

"I am. But I'm still not feeling good. I'm sorry, Will. I hope you'll stay and try to have some fun."

"But—"

"There's Sami," I interrupt, pointing. "She'll take me home."

Will's face falls, and I can see an objection rising on his lips, so I hurry up and put an end to any hopes he might have. Laying my palm flat against his chest, I give him a gentle push away. "Really. Go."

"But—"

"No offense, Will. You seem like a really nice guy, but you come on a little strong, you know what I mean?"

Hurt flashes across his face, replaced a moment later by anger. "Are you serious right now?"

"See. This is what I'm talking about."

His expression scrunches up with contempt. "I should have known better. You're just as crazy as your cousin."

I call him a dick as he storms off, because taking a jab at Mo was uncalled for. I'm the one rejecting him, not her. And now I'm glad that I did.

"What was that about?" Sami asks, standing beside me as we watch him walk away.

"Don't worry about it. Let's find the others and take off. This whole thing is giving me a headache."

As if by magic, Liz and Mo round the corner. My voice fails me when I see Mo's face. Our eyes meet and like an electric zap I feel all the pain and emotion weighing so heavily on her heart.

Despite whatever has happened to make her feel this way, I can see her pick up on my emotion, too.

"Guess it wasn't such a magical night after all," I mutter.

"Maybe not yet," Sami says, giving my arm a squeeze. "But the night is still young, and we've got two birthday girls to celebrate."

I grit my teeth together so I don't make a nasty reply to Sami's suggestion. Try my best not to glare as Mo and Liz approach. But I can't help it. Because as far as birthdays go, this one's a bust. And why'd Mo turn to Liz if she needed a shoulder to cry on? Why not me? I'm her sister, after all. Not that she was thrilled when she found that out. So, yeah. I have a feeling that neither of us feels like celebrating right now. Personally, I'd rather curl up in a hole and die.

FORTY-NINE

LIZ NOW

2014

I've got an iron grip on the steering wheel the entire drive to the police department. My fingers cramp and my palms sweat as I blow through my second red light, horns blaring in my wake, but I still don't slow down. I can't.

I can't shake the image from my mind of Olivia cold and alone and scared, locked in a room somewhere. A room she can't escape. A room where she could become sick and weak and dehydrated, and if her captor remains in police custody long enough, potentially something worse. I need to save my daughter.

My tires squeal as I pull into the parking lot, drawing several curious stares from the uniformed officers loitering outside. I have their full attention as I park in a handicapped spot at such a severe slant that I'm over the lines on both sides. I barely remember to turn the engine off, grabbing my keys only because the car dings at me when I open the door. One of the officers, a short woman with her hair gathered in a tidy bun, starts to approach, but I rush past her on my way inside before she can stop me.

"I need to see Detective Johnson," I tell the lady sitting behind the plexiglass window. I lean against the counter, using it to hold myself up. "Immediately."

Her eyebrows raise as she looks at me over the tops of her glasses. "I believe Detective Johnson is busy at the moment, but I can find someone else to assist you if you'll tell me about the nature of your visit today. Are you here to file a report?"

"No, it needs to be Detective Johnson." I smack the worn Formica under my hand, adding, "It's an emergency."

"It's okay, Cheryl, I'll handle this. Ma'am." The female officer from outside is now standing at my elbow. "I'll take you back to speak with the detective."

"Thank you." I almost collapse with relief. I give her a grateful smile, allowing her to take me by the arm and steer me through a door leading to the back. She shows me into a plain room, empty other than a table surrounded by four chairs.

"Wait here, it'll only be a moment."

She gestures toward one of the chairs and I sit compliantly. It's not until the door closes behind her and I'm alone that I notice the seat is bolted to the floor. And that there's a camera mounted high in the corner of the ceiling. I'm in an interrogation room.

I fight the urge to jump up and try the door handle, positive that I'm locked inside. A prisoner. Just like Olivia is, being held somewhere against her will. They could keep me in here for hours, wasting time that should be used to find my daughter.

A sob rises in my throat. I've screwed up everything. Again. And an innocent person will pay the consequences. Again. I'm toxic, filled with poison and self-loathing, so much so that I feel like my body can barely contain it all. Just when I think I'm going to explode, the door opens, and Detective Johnson appears.

"Mrs. Bentley. To what do I owe the pleasure?"

He strokes the ends of his mustache, probably to hide the smirk he must be wearing. But none of that matters. I need his help.

"You arrested Morgana Ripley."

He takes a seat across from me. "Actually, I haven't."

"But." There's no use hiding it. Several officers saw me. "I was there. Just a little while ago, when it happened."

He cocks an eyebrow at me, rounds the table and takes a seat. Pins me with a pointed look and asks, "Then maybe you can tell me who it was I just arrested."

"I just told you. Morgana Ripley."

"I assure you, ma'am, that was not Ms. Ripley."

"What do you mean?"

"I mean, we already have Ms. Ripley in custody."

"What?" It's impossible. I know because—

"Or, at least, her remains. The bones we recovered from Ripley Manor? They were hers. She was positively identified this morning by the serial number on a surgical pin, used to repair a broken femur she sustained during a skiing accident when she was eleven. Dental records confirmed the identification. So, you see, ma'am, your friend? There's no way she is who she says she is."

I can't breathe. It feels like all the oxygen has been sucked out of the room. The smug satisfaction in his expression changes as he watches me gasp for air. And then his hand is on my back, his voice in my ear, but he sounds far away, like we're separated by a great distance.

We were so careful. We were sure we'd thought of everything. But we were wrong.

FIFTY

AMY NOW

2014

Life is a series of memories, of hopes and dreams and wishes, of chances seized and opportunities missed, of decisions made, both right and wrong. The director's cut, a montage of clips cut and edited together to tell the story that hurts the least. Or the most. It depends on the individual personality, I guess, whether they view themselves as a victim or a villain, or maybe even a bit of both.

But where does the true art of it lie? In a life lived to the fullest, fading to black while surrounded by loved ones at a ripe old age? Or in choosing the ending, choreographing the dance, and going out with a bang?

When I was little and my friends and I played make-believe games, sometimes the lines of reality would blur, and the place where the game ended, and real life began, would become confused. You expect that from children. But what about adult Amy? What's my excuse now? Because the truth is, I never stopped playing the game.

It was a dream role, being in a play where you've been cast in the part of a beautiful young rich woman with the entire world at her fingertips. Someone who would never have to swish water around in a milk jug to wet her cereal in the morning, sometimes long after the remnants have been washed from the sides of the container, when you can't even get a whitish tinge to the water, but you keep doing it because to stop would be a form of giving up.

Same thing with the days I used to pretend to be on a diet, so my friends didn't know that I didn't have lunch money and insist on buying me something. A girl has her pride, you know. Sometimes it's all that she has.

It's not that my dad didn't try. It's just that he didn't try very hard. He was more concerned with his libido, with being a womanizer than a provider, and occasionally that called for the grocery money. I like to tell myself that he wasn't like that before my mom died, that her death pulverized his heart in such a way that he was left desperately searching for someone who could piece it back together. So I guess I've always been good at swallowing my own lies.

It's a skill that's really come in handy. For years I've played the part, capturing the role of Morgana Ripley in a stunning performance. There were even days where she wasn't constantly on my mind, mornings that didn't start with a vision of her lifeless face as I left the dream world of sleep where we still play together.

I sit on the hard metal chair at the hard metal table, knowing there's a lot more hard discomfort in my future. But maybe there's still a way to work this to my advantage. An angle I can leverage. I just have to figure out what role I need to play.

We were young, sure, but we were old enough to know better. And I'm the one who maintained the lie for so long, keeping up the dual existence. Living it up, appearing in the society pages and traveling as Mo, sending postcards as myself. Only, the girl I once was never *really* was. Does that make any sense?

I spent my whole childhood playing a part. I was the sweet one, the shy one, the patient one. But really, I was none of those things. I longed for the spotlight, to be the center of attention, to be admired and desired. But the world had cast Mo in that role. Nobody even noticed me failing to thrive, like a plant growing pale and spindly as it strains toward the sun but never quite makes it. And I resented the hell out of that.

All the things I wanted just fell into her lap. And she didn't even want them. Sometimes you have to take what's yours.

FIFTY-ONE
LIZ THEN

1999

I cast a glance over at Mo as we walk back toward the front of the rec center and catch a glimpse of an expression as tense as my own must be. Tightening my grip on her hand, I offer her strength. She squeezes back, taking it. Yet at the corner, she pauses.

I'm worried that she's changed her mind. That she wants to retreat. But instead of trying to run, she tosses her hair back over her shoulders and raises her chin high. She gives a curt nod, letting me know she's ready, then, together, we step around the end of the building.

Sami and Amy are standing out front, waiting for us. They hurry over, Sami wringing her hands, looking like she might cry. But instead of concern, Amy's scowling. She's never looked more like her cousin than at this moment, tossing her hair over her shoulder, her tone and inflection the exact same as Mo's as she says, "Where were you guys? We were worried."

Beside me, Mo flinches like she's been stung. A strange noise sounds from the back of her throat as she studies her cousin's face, head cocked to the side. Finally, she says, "I think I get it. It all makes sense now. That's why you love acting. Because it's freeing to pretend to be someone else, isn't it?"

Amy pulls back, covering her open mouth with her hand. Her eyes widen as she stares at Mo's face. I feel like something's happening that I'm missing, like a joke I'm not in on, only this is obviously no joke.

A tear spills over, slipping down Amy's cheek. "Mo, I'm so sorry. I—"

Mo wipes Amy's cheek dry and smiles. She's showing too many teeth. "I guess it's worth it if it gets you what you want."

Sami and I exchange confused glances.

"Let's go," Mo says. "I don't want to be here anymore. I'm over it."

I fall into step beside her, relieved. Prom night's been a bust. To think that we'd looked forward to it for so long.

For three and a half years I didn't really mind being in high school, but this last semester has been brutal. The next two weeks until graduation can't go fast enough. Looking at the others, I wonder if I'm the only one who feels this way. There was a time when we would have talked about it. Shared our feelings.

But lately it seems like we've all been lost in our own secrets, our private worlds. Maybe that's what growing up is. Internalizing your hopes and fears instead of discussing them. And intimacy is confiding your inner thoughts. That's probably why my mom is always telling my dad he needs to communicate more.

Mo hooks one arm through Amy's, her other through mine. I link elbows with Sami. At least, for now, our chain remains unbroken. But for how long?

I cast a glance over my shoulder at the rec center, sensing that somehow, in this moment, we're leaving our childhood behind. It feels like it should be bittersweet, but honestly, I'm ready to let it go. Let it burn, for all I care.

Just as I'm turning away, a movement in the shadows draws my attention. There's someone standing there, up against the side of the building, watching us. A girl from our class. Francine.

I've seen her more and more often lately, lurking around the periphery of one group or another, including our own. Always overlooked, never included.

Our eyes meet, and something unreadable flashes across her face. I'm not sure what it is, but it makes me shudder. I turn away, goosebumps spreading from the back of my neck, where I can still feel her gaze boring into me.

But I don't have time to dwell on what's going through the mind of some strange girl right now. I have more important things to worry about. Because I'm still really concerned about Mo. Something strange is going on with her. And I'm starting to suspect it has something to do with Amy.

FIFTY-TWO

AMY NOW

2014

Unlike the interrogation rooms I've seen on TV, there's no one-way mirror in here. There *is* a camera mounted in the corner, up on the ceiling, but I can't tell if it's on or not. I figure it must be. No way would they leave me in here so long on my own, completely unsupervised. I get up to take a closer look and read some of the writing on the walls.

I wonder if they know yet.

I'm sure they think they do. But they can't possibly, not unless someone told them. I don't think Liz would, especially since she still seems to think that I have her daughter hidden away somewhere, even though I told her I didn't.

It hurts that she doesn't believe me, like I'm some kind of criminal and not one of her best friends. Although I do have to admit—that letter she showed me did look exactly like my hand-writing. And it is the way I always used to sign my notes when we were in school.

But that's only strange, not damning. Circumstantial

evidence at best. And, believe me, I've done a lot of research about evidence over the years.

No, Liz wouldn't tell. You don't poke the bear that has your kid, even if it's just a suspicion. But Sami? Something's changed about her. And not in a good way.

It's funny. Out of all of us, I would have thought she'd end up being the most stable, not the least. But it's like she never grew up. Like she's spent all these years in denial, not understanding how screwed up our childhood was. Not realizing that all those little fairy tales we told ourselves about how special we were and how great everything was were just lies.

There was nothing special about us. We were just average little girls at the mercy of society and the world around us, like all the rest. Sweet until we learned better. Innocent until we weren't. Dumb until we wised up.

But Sami never wised up, did she?

Obviously not if she still hasn't realized that Sonny was a monster. Sure, he was good looking. Funny. Smart. Charming when he wanted to be. I can't deny any of that. But all those things just made it even worse when he let the mask slip and his dark side was revealed.

And believe me, that dark side was as pitch black as it could possibly be. Why else would I have done what I did? It's not like I wanted to do it. I didn't have a choice. But the truth is, I'd do it all over again. It's that bastard's fault that Mo is dead.

FIFTY-THREE

LIZ THEN

1999

The sound of our high heels clicking against the pavement is loud against the still background of the night. It gives our position away. And our gender. Our vulnerability, because I doubt any of us could run in these ridiculous shoes if we needed to, except maybe Mo, who always makes everything look so effortless. But that doesn't really help the rest of us, does it?

I search the darkness nervously as we walk. This doesn't feel safe. It feels like a really bad idea. No. Not just feels like. Is. And suddenly, unexpectedly, I find myself wishing I was back at prom with David. Or just about anywhere else, really.

But it's too late for that now and, besides, the lights for the shopping center where Mo told the limo to wait are just up ahead. We're almost there. There's no turning back now.

Not that I actually would if I could, not really. And it's more than just a loyalty thing. The truth is, I've never been good at making tough decisions. Even if I know it's something I should do. Have to do. Like end an inappropriate relationship with an older man.

But I was too weak, wasn't I?

He said that he loved me, but if that was true, why wouldn't he have waited for me instead of pressuring me into showing my love for him? All those sayings about hindsight—they're true. I don't know what I was thinking. I've come to realize that like most secrets that you have to keep, it was wrong. I just didn't want to see it at the time.

The limo appears up ahead and we trip over the parking lot toward it. Sami giggles as she stumbles and catches herself against me. I look over at her and can't help smiling. I know she'd hate me for saying it, but she looks so young tonight, so innocent, like a little kid playing dress-up. It reminds me of the girl I once shared everything with, before the secrets between us grew and spread us apart.

I turn to my other side, toward Mo and Amy. The resemblance between them has grown stronger with age. They look so much alike right now, except that Amy's face lacks the stress that creases Mo's. Not for the first time tonight, a ripple of unease pulsates beneath my skin.

I wish I knew what was going on with her.

Tomorrow I'm going to talk to Sami and Amy and see if they're willing to help me hold an intervention. Mo will hate me for it, but it doesn't matter. She's my best friend and I love her. And sometimes, love means making tough decisions, no matter how painful you know they'll be.

FIFTY-FOUR

LIZ NOW

2014

I meet Detective Johnson's concerned eyes over the top of the paper bag that I'm breathing into. Though my nerves remain strung tight like piano wire, I've finally managed to catch my breath. The layer of sweat coating my body is starting to dry, and my head has stopped spinning.

"Mrs. Bentley? Are you feeling better now?"

Besides feeling exhausted and humiliated, I am, so I nod.

"Good. Do you think you're able to resume our conversation? Maybe tell me about what got you so upset?"

I made it here within minutes of his arrival with Amy. Surely that wasn't enough time for her to tell him much. It will be my word against hers, and I have the opportunity to be the first on record. Only... my daughter is still missing. The note was clear—I can't tell Detective Johnson about Olivia being kidnapped. But how can I not?

It doesn't matter what happens to me, what consequences I'll face. All that matters is that my daughter is returned safely.

I nod again, still breathing slow and deep into the bag,

buying myself more time to make up my mind. Because Amy as Mo said she hadn't written the letters or taken my daughter. And for some strange reason, I believe her. But what if she doesn't realize she was lying?

I mean, obviously she has some severe mental issues. She's a murderer, for God's sake. If you weren't already living in crazy town, wouldn't doing something like that drive you there?

I think of all the sensationalized TV talk shows I've watched over the years. Split personalities, dissociative identity disorder, call it what you will, but it's a thing. A rare thing, but still a thing.

What if, after so many years of pretending to be both women, her psyche cracked, and she actually became both women? And one of them knows where my daughter is?

I can't do this alone.

It's out of my hands. There's no way that Amy is leaving here. I might not be, either. It's too late for self-preservation. There's only one thing I can do. I have to trust this man across from me. I have to come clean. About everything. No matter how bad it hurts.

"Detective? I'm ready to talk. I'm ready to tell you everything you want to know."

FIFTY-FIVE

AMY NOW

2014

Fear is a powerful emotion. It can make you do stupid things. Crazy things. And even though you realize what you're doing is stupid and crazy, you do them anyway, because you're scared.

But panic? Panic is a state of mind. And it doesn't matter how smart you are, how rational, how sane, when panic has wrapped its dirty tendrils around your brain, you're at its mercy, like when those tiny parasitical bugs infect wasps and turn them into zombies.

You might think you'll be good under pressure, but you never really know until it happens. You could screw everything up. You could make things worse. Especially when you're desperate.

You see, desperation is like those parasites. It can take over your brain and make you do things you wouldn't normally do. Things that you would never do. Not if you weren't desperate. But when you are, and you see a solution to all of your problems? You get tunnel vision, and that way out becomes all that you can see.

You can't see the consequences, or how they'll affect your future. You can't see any better options or alternative solutions. All you can see is that tiny little speck of hope that promises you an escape from the bottom of a very deep hole.

So you take it.

You snatch it up inside your sweaty palm and ball your hand tight into a fist and keep hold of it no matter what. And maybe it lasts a day or a week or a year. Maybe it works for you indefinitely. But sometimes, life requires both hands. And when that happens, you have no choice other than to let go, or risk crashing onto the cliffs far below.

FIFTY-SIX

LIZ THEN

1999

I keep up a steady stream of chatter in the limo, almost like I'm trying to create a diversion from how miserable we all are. Sami makes a feeble attempt to engage, and Amy chimes in every once in a while, but you can tell our hearts aren't in it. But still, I try, because what else can I do?

"I thought they did a good job decorating the rec center. It looked a lot better than when we went to that Beanie Baby convention thingie in middle school," I say.

Sami chuckles. "You mean the one where those two old ladies got in a tug of war over that green beanie and ended up tearing it in half?"

"Have we ever been to another Beanie Baby convention that I'm forgetting about?"

She snorts. "Nope. I'm pretty sure one was enough to last a lifetime. What was that thing, anyways? A cucumber?"

"I think it was a dragon."

"It was an iguana," Amy says. Her eyes are glassy, and her

words come too fast, her voice bordering on shrill. "And his name was Iggy."

I forgot that she was the one who liked those things in the first place. I had wondered how we had ended up there. "Oh, that's right. And there was that fat guy with the ponytail who had, like, the best collection there and you were so jealous that you were ready to get in his murder van and go home with him until Mo told him he was a greasy old perv and said she'd tell the cops unless he gave you the beanie of your choice."

Elbowing Mo in the side, I say, "Isn't that right, Mo?"

She stares out the window like she hasn't heard me. Sami and I exchange frowns.

"I really liked the backdrop they used for the portraits. I bet your prom photos are going to look amazing, Mo," Sami says.

Mo continues to blankly watch the scenery passing by without acknowledging us, like a kid who's got the TV up too high and can't hear their mother. I wonder what it is that she's listening to, what thoughts are going through her head so loudly.

Outside the limo, fancy metal gates and extravagant land-scaping lets me know that we've reached Ripley Manor. Hope-fully, she'll perk up once we're out of the car.

Sami hops out and punches in the gate code for the driver. We're all silent as we travel up the long driveway. And then, like an evil spell has been cast aside, the fog lifts and she's back with us.

I have to bite my tongue when I see the tip she gives the chauffeur, but she seems, if not happy, satisfied, so I keep my mouth shut. Then the limo is gone and we're all alone. At last.

We traipse around the house to the clochán out back, and just like I'd hoped, once those stone walls come into view, the atmosphere changes. The night becomes the way it was supposed to be. We return to a simpler time, when we were princesses and fairies and everything was magic, the night air full of laughter and glee. A time when we were happy. We become us again.

These are the moments I live for.

When we talked about what our prom night would be like when we were little girls, we had such big ideas. The gorgeous dresses, the handsome dates, the fancy limo. From the outside, it looks like we're living our dream.

But then I see the gun.

FIFTY-SEVEN

AMY NOW

2014

Everyone loves a victim. And that's what we were. Victims. Each and every one of us. Of men. Of society. Of each other.

And my father was the worst perpetrator. He preyed on my friends. But the second worst? That was me, because I did, too.

I tried to deny it for years, but I'm not a good person. I've always put myself first. My wants and needs. My ambitions and pride and desires. Even my own safety.

I knew more than I ever let on. I always told my friends that Sonny never talked about my mom, but that's not quite true. He just couldn't do it when he was sober. But with a fifth of whiskey in his belly, he'd tell me everything I wanted to know. And plenty that I didn't.

Because the truth is, my mother didn't die after childbirth. She died before it. A slow, miserable death. When her heart stopped beating and her brain ceased to function? That was her release.

I didn't want to end up like my mother.

When I left Waverly, I hopped a plane to France. I'd always dreamed of seeing a show at a theater in Paris, of seeing the Eiffel Tower and visiting the Louvre. I thought it would be a great place to start, a way to clear my mind of the shock of what had happened, to get my bearings and plan my next step, but mostly I chose France because it's the one place I'd always hoped to visit.

I'd never traveled before that, not farther than the six flags a couple of states over, and certainly not by myself. I'd never been on a plane before. Hell, I'd never even used a credit card before I stood at the counter with Mo's passport in hand and bought the plane ticket.

It's funny, the number of potential obstacles that never even occurred to me. Like not speaking French or even knowing what currency they used. There I was, a high school graduate— but only because I'd finished out Mo's semester—supposed to be ready to take the world by storm, and I couldn't even find my way from the airport. The only time I'd ever been so scared in my life was that night.

After an hour of wandering, a lady traveling in a Jackie-O-type skirt-suit and hat named Adora Struthers took pity on me. When she heard the name Morgana Ripley, she attached herself to my hip like a barnacle to a ship's hull and didn't leave until five months and three countries later, when her sister had a bad reaction to her liposuction surgery and needed companionship. That was when I learned the power of the name Ripley, the way that people literally scurried to do whatever it took just to be around me when they thought I was her.

But there was also a darker side to being Mo. The side attached to the Van Cline name. The secrets about our mother.

After a couple of years of traveling, of living as Morgana Ripley, I started listening to the rumors whispered in my shadow. Only then I came to realize that they weren't rumors. That what I was hearing was the vestige of the truth, myth based on fact, like the kraken. That the story Sonny spun for me was a spider's web of lies.

Vivienne Van Cline, my mother, Mo's mother, was not a hopeless romantic madly in love with a man from the wrong side of the tracks. Her family didn't write her off. They didn't abandon her for choosing love.

Vivienne Van Cline was a young, mentally ill woman who was preyed upon by my father. The whole romantic, forbidden love story Sonny used to tell was a whitewashed version of the truth. He seduced my mother, talked her into going off her meds, got her pregnant, and fed her delusions to estrange her from her family, friends, and physicians.

I've been in contact with some of the doctors who treated her. I've read their notes and listened to their diagnoses. I've delved into my mother's illness, her battle with reality, and come to accept that her sickness is in my blood.

Maybe that knowledge has made me a little too aware of my own behavior, a little too sensitive to things another person wouldn't even notice, maybe even a little too introspective. I was not a nice person. I was especially horrible to Mo. My own sister. I tore her down to build myself up because I thought she had everything.

The pangs of poverty were so great that I equated money with happiness. But that's not the way it works, I realize that now. Even at the time I should have noticed that Mo, despite all her riches, was miserable. But I guess I was too busy being miserable myself.

For years I've driven myself crazy wondering—if I had been a better sister to Mo, a better friend, would she still be here? If I had shown her more kindness, if I hadn't contributed fodder to the rumor mill for her antagonists to use against her, if I had been supportive and caring and careful with her heart, would it have made a difference?

I suppose I'll never really know.

But now I have a glimmer of hope. Another chance. Another sister.

FIFTY-EIGHT

SAMI NOW

2014

I get up, walk to the kitchen, and immediately forget what I went there for. Return to the living room, remember, then forget again. I can't keep my train of thought. All I can think of are all the hateful, disgusting things they said about Sonny. The man I loved. It's unforgivable.

Am I really just supposed to go on with my life pretending everything is all right?

I don't think that I can.

The movie playing too loudly on the TV is almost over. I'll have to come up with something else to watch, and soon, because I can't risk catching another glimpse of the news. I need the distraction, need to buy some more time to think.

But my thoughts keep circling back around to the news report. They've arrested her. They must know who's dead. And it's only a matter of time before the house of cards we so carefully constructed comes tumbling down around us. Only a matter of time before they come for me, too. Maybe I should just take off before that can happen.

Then what? I leave behind everything and get left with nothing? I glance at the living room. Or maybe not.

The idea starts out as just the tiniest little flame, but within minutes it's turned into a raging wildfire. Because I can do this. It's not too late.

So she's in jail already. And for all I know Liz is, too. They could both be behind bars. They could even be sharing a cell.

Good. They deserve it. I'm sure if they had their choice, they'd bring me down with them.

But that's not going to happen.

Because I don't deserve that. All I've done is lost the people I loved most.

Not this time. I still have options. Leverage. I still have a way to get my happily ever after.

FIFTY-NINE

AMY NOW

2014

I've been here a while now, in this stuffy interrogation room, left to sweat it out on my own. I wonder if they're doing it on purpose, if this is some kind of tactic they use—leaving someone alone with their thoughts. Because let me tell you, I think it's working. It's enough to drive you crazy—even if you don't have a family history of it.

The thing about having a mother who suffered from mental illness is that you always wonder about yourself. Did I imagine the conversation about pickles that I had with the lady at the deli counter? Was the man with the mullet who stared at me too long in the parking lot a delusion? When I misplaced my purse, was that just an oversight? Or was there something more sinister going on with my brain?

The big question is, am I sick too? And if I'm not, then why not? Obviously, the gene is in my blood. Is there some switch inside me just waiting to be turned on? Is it just a matter of time?

Sometimes, I feel like a bomb, just waiting to explode.

Sometimes, I wish it would just happen already. Then they can lock me up in a room with padded walls and I can stop trying to balance on that fishing-line bridge between sanity and psychosis.

After what happened on prom night, I spent two weeks holed up alone in that giant house on the hill, becoming my sister while her body was rotting out back. Do you know what that does to a person? How it makes them feel? The things it makes them think?

I couldn't even leave because I couldn't risk being seen. Not if I wanted the story to work. So I spent two weeks trapped in that place under the pretense of being sick with mono, finishing up the schoolwork for Mo's senior year.

Then I was free. To spread my wings, to travel, to do all the things I'd always dreamed about doing. And if I had to send a postcard every now and then, sign the name I'd grown to hate, well, it was a small price to pay for the luxury I was enjoying. Flying first class, high-end shopping sprees, appearing in the society pages of magazines—it never grew old. In fact, with each passing year, it got even more addictive.

No one ever questioned that I wasn't who I said I was. All I had to do was wear my hair a certain way, talk in the clipped, upper crust voice I'd practiced so much, dress and behave the way I was expected—there was no way I could mess up acting the part. I'd been doing it most of my life, after all.

Even Mo's parents believed me. Once a year we'd meet up for the holidays, someplace like Paris or Geneva or whatever the hit "it" spot was at the moment. We'd exchange pleasantries, exchange gifts, and then exchange empty promises to keep in touch and get together more often.

Then they went and died, a one-two punch, her of cancer, him in a car crash only months after. I mourned those strangers far more than the loss of my own parent.

The truth is, over the years, I've lost track of where the fake

me ends and the real me begins. I'm not so sure that the real me
even exists anymore.

I think I kind of hoped that coming back might spark a little
flame of recognition. *Oh yeah, the girl who likes that place right
there, that's me. Not her.*

But it didn't. Or maybe it just wasn't enough.

Because when it comes to being satisfied, I have no idea
where to start. I've been miserable for so long. The thing about
unhappiness is that it's like a drug. Once it's in your system too
long, you require more and more of it, and then, before you
know it, you get stuck in a cycle you can't break.

But then I saw her. Olivia.

And in an instant I knew that this was what I'd been
waiting for.

SIXTY

LIZ NOW

2014

"I'll tell you everything you want to know, but first you have to help me. My daughter's missing. She's been kidnapped."

Detective Johnson leans back in his seat, studying me as I fumble in my purse for the note. Finding it, I spread it on the table between us.

"Why am I just hearing about this now?"

"Because look." I jab at the letter. "She told me not to tell the police. She threatened my daughter's safety. But now you have her in custody, and wherever my daughter is, she's all alone. You need to get her to tell you where my daughter is."

"Who is *she*?" He falls silent, crossing his arms. Leveling me with a steady gaze. Making it clear that he's the one in charge here. "And what is it that she wants you to confess to?"

"She's Amy. Charamy Russo."

He nods like he expected this answer all along. "Ms. Ripley's cousin."

"No." There's no use lying anymore. They're going to find it all out anyway. "Amy and Morgana were sisters. Twins. When their mother, Vivienne, died after giving birth, their father, Sonny." The name tastes so bitter on my tongue that it takes me a moment to recover. "He sold one of them to Vivienne's sister. Apparently she couldn't have children of her own, so she offered to raise one of her sister's."

"And you know this how?"

"Amy told me."

"The same Amy we have in custody. Who's lived under an assumed identity for the last fifteen years?"

When he puts it that way, it's obvious she's not trustworthy, but she wouldn't have lied, not about this. "Listen, none of this matters. What matters is my daughter, Olivia."

"Who you think was kidnapped by Ms. Russo?"

"Yes."

"Who wants you to confess?"

"To something that's not my fault. I'll tell you all about it, I promise, but first we need to find my daughter."

"When did she go missing?"

"Today. Earlier."

"And you really believe she's been kidnapped? There's no way she could be at a friend's house? That maybe this note was just left to scare you?"

I hesitate for only a second before saying, "No."

His lips form a grim line under his mustache. "Mrs. Bentley." His voice is too gentle, too soft. "Is there anyone else who may have taken your daughter?"

"What? No. It had to have been her."

"Are you sure."

I bulge my eyes, my frustration mounting. "Yes, I'm sure."

"I only asked because we've actually had Ms. Russo under surveillance for the last several days."

"What?"

"If she was behind your daughter's kidnapping, she didn't do it herself."

The room spins. I think I'm having another panic attack.

"But your friend is definitely a very dangerous woman. I'm going to suggest that we place a call to the FBI requesting their assistance with this. First, though, I want you to be sure about what you're saying. Making false accusations of this nature carries very serious consequences. So are you sure?"

"Please. Make the call."

"I'll get right on that."

As he gets up to leave the room, I put my hand on his arm to stop him.

"We're going to find your daughter, Mrs. Bentley. Don't worry."

"Can you please also call my husband? I haven't told him, and he... he should know."

He looks at me like he's not surprised, that this just underpins what he's suspected about me, then gives a terse nod before leaving the room. I wait for the door to close behind him before allowing myself to implode. Sweat coats my body as I sob. I'm overheating. I feel like I might burst into flames, my fear for my daughter like a furnace that won't turn off.

They've been watching Amy. They think she's dangerous. And they're not mistaken.

SIXTY-ONE

AMY THEN

1999

I'm still buzzing pretty hard when we get back to Mo's. I feel sloppy and uncoordinated but also happy and free. I'm not used to breathing easy. Usually I'm so tied up in knots. But this? Filling my lungs deep with fresh air, a smile on my face, a song in my heart, not worrying about tomorrow, or the next day, or the next—I could get used to this.

I look at Mo, so relieved that she knows—and that she's forgiven me—for all the random guys I slept with and let think I was her. I throw my arms around her neck and whisper in her ear. "Happy Birthday." I know what gift I want from her. I want to be able to tell. Not just Liz and Sami, but the whole world. I test the word, saying it out loud. "Twin."

It fills me with such elation that I feel like I could fly. I give Mo a kiss on the cheek, grab her by the hands and lean back. She pulls against me and a second later we're spinning in circles, just like we used to do when we were little. Before I got bitter and resentful and tried to hurt her. Before she got damaged by me and the rest of the world.

We fall apart, but we're two halves that make a whole. It won't be for long. I know we'll be one again soon.

I laugh, lifting my face to the stars above and screaming into the night, "We're eighteen! Whoo!"

Then, just like I expected, she's back, her face lowering close to mine. She takes my head in her hands, looking me in the eyes. It makes me giggle. I can't stop.

When she releases me, I flop back onto the ground and stare up at the sky, sighing happily. I don't think I've ever felt this peaceful before.

I close my eyes, the gentle lull of my friends' voices a background noise that blends into the night, becoming a part of it, like the damp smell of earth and the chill that carries on the breeze. If I could choose one moment in my life to hit pause on and live in forever, it would be this one right here. It's perfect.

And then it's not.

"Mo, are you okay?"

Liz sounds concerned. I roll onto my belly, locking gazes with my sister. And I can immediately tell that something's wrong.

A dangerous expression flashes behind her eyes, the eyes of a stranger. But that's not right. It can't be. I blink, but it's still true. I don't recognize this girl standing before me.

But I do recognize the gun. Because the gun—it's mine.

SIXTY-TWO

AMY NOW

2014

It's funny. For the longest time when I thought about that night, I'd think about what happened as "the accident". But it wasn't an accident, not in the least bit, and now, for some reason, thinking about it that way seems like an insult.

Now, in my thoughts I refer to it as "the life changing event" that happened that night. That's exactly what it was, right? A life changing event? Mo was alive before, she was dead after, and all of our lives changed forever. In an instant.

I think of Liz's daughter, my half-sister, again. It was just by chance that I looked up from my phone at the very moment I walked by her the other day, as we were passing each other on the sidewalk outside a store, and I knew immediately who she was—and that my life was about to change again.

She looked exactly like Liz had at her age, only she was taller and had the brightest green eyes. Sonny's eyes. There was no mistaking that unreal shade of sea-glass green. It was the only thing I ever used to wish that I'd inherited from him.

I want a chance to know her. I want her to know about me. I

want to tell her all about Mo, and secrets about her mother, and the friendship we had when we were younger. I need her to understand. Then maybe I can, too.

It seems like it's been hours by the time the detective comes into the room. I've read every inch of graffiti on the walls by then, plenty of it about him, and know that I'm facing off with a formidable opponent. I'm going to have to play this just right.

I settle back in the uncomfortable metal chair, straight, high back, no arms, and no padding, waiting patiently as Detective Johnson tells me he'll be recording the conversation, then gives me my Miranda warning again before he states his name, the date, and the time for the video.

"Detective, my friend's daughter, Olivia—"

"We're aware of the situation."

"But—"

"We've received a call from her giving us her location."

"So, she's safe?"

"A rescue team is en route now."

I feel like a thousand-pound boulder has been removed from my back. The tightness in my chest that I'd been struggling to breathe against is gone. Like flicking a light switch, there's a night-and-day difference between the way the world felt thirty seconds ago and how it feels now. It's been a long time since I cared about anyone other than myself. It's a wonder I haven't forgotten how.

"Now then, ma'am. There's the little matter of who you are."

"My name is Charamy Russo." I draw a deep breath. "And on May 22, 1999, my twin sister, Morgana Ripley, from whom I was separated shortly after birth, died. I have been living under her identity since that date."

SIXTY-THREE

MO

1999

I listen to the click of our heels against the sidewalk as we walk to the car, and I swear with each pair of steps I hear *no more, no more, no more*. That's the way I feel. I really can't take any more. All this... ridiculousness needs to come to an end. Someone needs to stop this. Someone needs to save us.

Luckily, there's no one lingering in the parking lot. No witnesses to what I can only imagine is an eyeful, four girls in prom dresses tripping across a grocery store parking lot in our fancy shoes, looking like we just weathered a raging storm. But the squall isn't done yet. It's still brewing, gathering strength. I can feel it. Right below the surface of my skin.

We reach the limo and I knock on one of the windows. There's a click as the locks disengage. Pulling the door open, I watch my friends pile inside. I pull a dead twig out of Liz's hair as she passes. When did we all become such a mess? What happened to us?

What hasn't happened to us?

I suppose I know the answers to my questions. I know more than I ever wanted to. So much darkness, so many secrets, where did the innocent little girls we once were disappear to? Where did we go?

I, for one, have lost myself.

Part of me is dead now. The part of me that yearned for salvation.

My breath catches in my throat as the dark thoughts fill my head. I squeeze my eyes shut, telling myself not to listen. That it isn't true.

Then the car comes to a stop, and when I open my eyes, I see that we've arrived. I wouldn't say that we're home, but we're here. The driver lowers the partition separating him from the passenger compartment and passes me a clipboard with a credit card receipt and pen on it. I add an obscene tip, total the charge, sign, and pass it back.

His eyebrows practically fly off his forehead when he sees the amount. I watch him jump out of his seat and scramble around to open the door for us. As we exit, he nods and bows respectfully before retreating.

I am a Ripley, hear me roar. Only I'm not. Not really, not according to Amy.

I don't doubt what she's said, it makes perfect sense, and it's not like I haven't wondered over the years. And if I had found out five years ago, hell, maybe even two, it might have made a difference. It may have been the answer to everything.

But not now. It's too late. Now I don't even have my crappy little mantra. Now, the fortune I've hid behind, the money that I believed would always protect me in the end, isn't even right-fully mine. So now what do I have?

I know, I know, friends who love me. But that's all, that's absolutely it, because there's nothing left inside this empty shell that I carry around like a hermit crab. I'm just a dry, brittle husk with nothing underneath. I have no life skills. I haven't needed them. I haven't been living a real life.

Everyone always thinks I'm so strong and so brave, but I'm not. They only see those things because they want to, because they look at me and they have to see something, so they make it up, see what isn't really there because it's easier than admitting I'm not even really here.

Because I'm not. I'm just a ghost, a memory that they carry with them. I died long ago. It's time for them to put their imaginary friend away and let me rest. I'm tired.

I tug my shoes off, abandoning them on the ground as I trail my friends around the side of the house to the clochán out back. My feet sink into the spongy earth, grass painting my ankles with beads of dew. Their faces, their laughs, are distorted, like the fun house at the fair. Like a dream. Because that's what this is, isn't it?

It isn't real. It's all pretend.

We cross the backyard and then enter the woods. The trees hold hands overhead, creating a cathedral. Ahead, in a small clearing, is the clochán. Moon beams filter through the leaves, pine needles carpet the land beneath our feet; everything is cast in a magical glow.

This is where we held court as princesses and danced as fairies. A place without judgment, a place where we could be ourselves. Here was a place to be free.

I look around, at my friends. All smiling. All so calm, so relieved to be here, in our place. The one place where no one can hurt us.

And then I know. I know what I must do, what I've always needed to do, the reason that I'm still here. I've wondered for so long, but now the answer is clear. I can feel it in every atom of every cell of my body. My entire being thrums with the realization.

Over the years we've decorated and redecorated the clochán

dozens of times. We've hung streamers and draped fabric and laid rugs. There's not much room for furniture, but we keep a folding table and chairs out there, and a single dresser that we all share. It's behind this dresser that I found a perfect spot for the gift my sister brought me.

I hadn't thought it was a gift at first. I'd been scared of it. The power of it. But now I see the truth. It was always meant for me. It was always supposed to be mine.

My power. My fate. My gift to give.

The stone walls of the clochán aren't perfect. There are spots where rocks curve in, areas where they bow out. It's in front of one of these recessed areas that the dresser sits. You can't see the gap from the sides or top, but if you slide your hand behind it, you'll find the gap. And filling part of this hollow, taped to the wooden back, is the gift.

Amy throws her arms around my neck, startling me. "Happy Birthday," she whispers into my ear, and then adds, "Twin."

Her weight is heavy against me, simultaneously dragging me down and buoying me up. I know she never meant to hurt me. But her cut was one of the deepest.

Her lips brush my cheek, her hands slide down my arms. Taking me by the wrists, she leans back. Locking my hands around hers, I pull, and then we're spinning in circles, heads back, laughing like we used to do when we were little.

Liz and Sami's faces are blurs as we turn, faster and faster, gravity pulling stronger, harder, and then I lose my grip, or maybe she loses hers, and we're falling apart, stumbling backward. I land on my back, panting. I catch a glimpse of a single star staring down at me through the branches high above. Amy's laughter pops in the air like bubbles.

"We're eighteen!" she howls into the night. "Whoo!"

Amy is the quiet one, the reserved one. This isn't right. Maybe this isn't Amy. Or maybe I'm just not used to this Amy, the one in this dream, this reality. I push myself to my feet. I have to look into this Amy's eyes and see.

I walk unsteadily over to where she lays. I'm still reeling, dizzy, my head cloaked in puffy indigo clouds. Reaching her, I kneel down and take her head in my hands, sticking my face close to hers. Her pupils look funny. She lets loose another peel of laughter, bells tinkling. Then I realize that she's high.

I hate this world, this place where the innocent are abused, drugged, led to damnation like lambs to slaughter. This world that hurts and maims and ruins. There's a better place. There has to be.

Releasing Amy's head, I look away and sit back, dropping hard to the ground. Sami sits beside me. Liz lowers herself to my other side.

"You never told us what you wanted for your birthday this year," Sami says, only it's not her. Sami's mouth is moving, but it's Liz's voice that comes out. I try to pretend that I don't notice, that I'm not aware that the fabric of this reality is torn, that the edges are curling up, allowing another world to flow in as this one ebbs.

My eyes are closed. I hear the words inside my head, echoing within the dark recesses. What I really want. I know what I really want. I want what we need. What we all need. A release from this madness. To be free. Untouchable. Never to be hurt again.

"Mo? Where are you going?"

If I'm quick, I can do it. No one will stop me. Running into the clochán, I head for the dresser. I slip my fingers behind it, my palm running down the rough wood, cold, smooth stone glancing against the back of my hand. Everything is all mixed up, all rough and smooth and wrong, wrong, wrong. I have to stop it before it happens.

My fingers find the gift, curl around it. Ripping away its

tape tethers, I bring it to me, holding it against my chest. A part of me always knew.

He wanted everyone. Everyone but me.

He needed all of them. He did not need me.

I was his daughter. But I was not his.

But this was. It was his before, and now it's mine.

He must have known that I was the one. That it would be up to me to save us, to protect us, to deliver us from the evils of this life. That must be the reason he didn't want me. My power was too great.

Peering around the doorway, I look out at my friends, spotlighted by a moonbeam, an angel's light painting the way. Amy is laying on her back. Sami and Liz are a few feet away, their backs to me, huddled together. I decide the order. I want Amy to go last, with me, like we came into this world.

I walk up behind Sami and Liz, my bare feet silent across the pine needles. They've lost their color, painted in shades of gray. I let my heart swell with the love I feel for them. I suck in all their pain, taking it for my own. When I release them, they will be spotless, clean.

But then something stops me. This is not my Liz. Her face is too full. She has a hand draped across her belly, no longer flat, but starting to round. And I realize I'm too late. This is something that I cannot draw from her, a poison I cannot take for my own. Liz startles and looks over her shoulder at me. I have lost my power. She can see me.

"Mo, are you okay?"

Amy rolls onto her belly, our identical eyes locking. It's too late for them all. It's all my fault and now I'll have to pay the price. I'll have to go alone.

I raise the gift to my head. It's found its home. The place it's belonged this whole time. My finger tightens on the trigger. I give one last tug with my heart, pulling out all the bad, all the hurt and harm and agony. Mo is going to make the ache go away. She's going to make it all better.

I feel the smile on my face. It feels like the most beautiful smile. I see it reflected in their eyes. It is beautiful.

My being is flooded with serenity. I take a deep breath, making sure I've collected everything I need to take with me. I have. It's time to go.

SIXTY-FOUR

SAMI THEN

1999

As I sit here watching one of my closest friends in the world bleed out on the ground before me, I think about my hair. I've always hated the color. It isn't light enough for me to be a true redhead, not dark enough for me to be a brunette.

I've always wanted to dye it, but my friends made me promise I wouldn't. Liz in particular was adamant that I not. She always promised that it was a gorgeous color, and that one day, I'd think so too.

I don't know if I'd ever say gorgeous, but for the first time in my life I decide that it *is* pretty. It's very close in shade to the blood that's spattered across the fabric of Mo's dress. Not quite a rust, not quite a ruby, but some hue in-between.

Liz is sobbing. I wish she'd shut up. It's not going to do any good. That old adage about crying over spilled milk comes to mind and I have to stifle a giggle, because laughter probably isn't appropriate right now.

And Amy. Just staring, eyes wider than I've ever seen

before. She looks like she's seen a ghost. Then again, maybe she has. Maybe I should look around, and I'd be able to see it, too. But I can't take my eyes off the pretty color staining Mo's dress. Pretty like my hair.

Sonny's gone. He's never coming back. Now Mo's gone, too.

SIXTY-FIVE

AMY THEN

1999

"Mo!" I can still feel the force of my scream tearing through my lungs, drowned out by the ringing in my ears. I can still see the chain reaction caused by that bullet—flesh, blood, bone, hair—all reacting to the projectile in excruciatingly slow motion. I can still feel the immediate void left inside me as my twin sister left this world. And I thought I felt empty before.

I don't want to believe it. I keep telling myself that it has to be some kind of elaborate hoax, some special effects joke that Mo spent way too much money on, but I know that I'm telling myself a lie. Because as I stand here, looking down at her limp body, I know I'm looking at an empty shell. My sister is gone.

But I can't stop staring at her, watching for some movement, some sign that I'm mistaken. I have to be wrong. This can't be happening. Even if I knew.

I knew that Mo was unhappy. I knew about her growing depression. I knew that sometimes she made off the wall comments that should have been cause for worry. I saw all the signs, and I chose to ignore them. In fact, I made them worse. This is my fault. The blame is mine.

It doesn't matter that I've been treading water in a pool of my own troubles. I've been entirely too self-absorbed. I should have made time. I should have tried to help her more. But I didn't, and there's no excuse for that. Because now my sister, my other half, is gone. And she used the gun that I gave her, the one I asked her to hold for me because I was concerned more about my own safety than hers.

People are going to hate me when they find out. This is going to follow me around forever, my future squashed before it even got started.

I have no idea how long I stand there, frozen in shock, surrounded by the darkness. Thinking my thoughts while the scent of blood and gun powder invade my nose. The cool night air chilling my skin until I'm as cold on the outside as the inside.

Then suddenly, I realize that the persistent tugging on my arm is Liz. I turn to look at her with surprise. I'd forgotten she was here. That I'm not alone in this hellish abyss. But of course it's her. Why couldn't it be Sami?

Her face is red and puffy and tear streaked, her voice choked with hiccups and emotion as she says, "We need to call someone. We need help."

Help sounds nice. But it could also be dangerous, bringing with it questions that are too hard and painful and shameful to answer. Help will want to know what happened. Help will want to know where the gun came from.

"We can't," I whisper.

But she doesn't hear me.

"Something's wrong with Sami," she says.

I glance toward my friend, see her gazing off into space with empty eyes and a partial smile and I wonder exactly where it is that she's at right now, and why I can't be there, too.

Liz pulls on my arm again. "I'm going to go up to the house to use the phone. Come with me."

I turn to face her with stilted movements. "No." It's not just that I can't leave Mo yet.

"But we have—"

"No," I say, more forcefully this time, shaking her hand off me. "No one can know."

"This isn't something that we can keep hidden, Amy. Mo's dead. People are going to find out."

And then those people will know what a horrible sister I've been. That can't happen. There has to be another way.

"No, they aren't. Please, Liz. I have nothing left. I need this. Will you at least just hear me out?"

She looks at Sami, then deflates, defeated, as she realizes there's no one to back her up right now. It's just me and her and, of the two of us, we both know who's stronger.

"Here's what we're going to do," I say slowly. "We'll tell everyone that Mo is sick. Something that takes a couple of weeks to get over."

Liz shakes her head. "That won't work. Remember that time I had mono, and I was out sick for a month? The school still called my house every single day, even though my mom went in to talk to them."

I stand up straighter. Lift my chin. Pull my hair out of its ponytail and flip it over my shoulder. When I speak next, it's in a carefully modulated tone. Mo's tone. "Then I'll stay here and answer the calls."

"But then what do we tell people about you?"

"Yeah." The light is back on behind Sami's eyes, signaling that she's returned from wherever she went to. "You've been staying at my house. My mom's going to notice if you're not there."

"Tell them." I think about all of my hopes and dreams, all

the things I wanted to get out of life. It's obvious that none of it is going to happen now. But maybe, on some level... "We'll tell everyone that I got offered a music deal, and I'm going to L.A. We'll tell your mom and I'll pack up and leave tomorrow. I'll go to school on Monday, late, after I call in sick as Mo. I'll announce it to the drama club. That way, everyone will have heard by the end of the day."

"That's only a temporary fix. Eventually, people are going to notice that you're missing when they don't hear from you. Or about you. And then they're going to ask questions."

"Who? Who is there in my life who's going to notice I'm missing, besides you guys?"

Liz knows I've got her there. Because the answer is no one. There's not one person who would really give a damn whether I was alive or dead that isn't standing here right this moment. She holds her hand out to me, begging me with her eyes to take it. But I can't.

"There's only two weeks left until graduation. I'll stay here and talk to the school when they call. And I'll do Mo's assignments. After graduation, I'll leave. I'll take Mo's passport, travel as her, and I'll mail postcards to you guys as me. No one ever has to know."

"But what about..." Her eyes flick toward Mo's body.

"We'll pull the clochán down," Sami says. "Bury her under the rubble. It's only fitting, don't you think?"

I do. Even Liz gives a reluctant nod. It's settled. We have a plan. Approaching the clochán, I squint at it, trying to decide the best way to knock it down.

"Ooh. Hold on. I'll be right back."

"What? Sami, no, we don't have time—"

"Mo's journal," she says, voice thick with emotion. "She'd want it with her. I know where she keeps it. It'll only take a sec. Please."

She spins on her heels and hurries off without giving me a chance to answer. I draw a deep breath as I watch her go. I still can't believe that Mo is gone. That I'm officially alone in this world now. But I can do this. If there's one thing my life has taught me, it's how to make the most of a bad situation. And there's a chance my situation just got much better.

SIXTY-SIX

LIZ NOW

2014

When I was little, I was afraid of strangers. Not just shy or standoffish or wary, like some kids are, but full-fledged, heart-pounding, cold-sweating, hiding-behind-my-mother's-legs terri-fied of them. I'm not sure when I grew out of it. Maybe a part of me never did.

Because people are scary. Unpredictable. Dangerous.

But here's the thing—it's not the people we don't know that we have the most to fear from. It's the people we do.

Because people are scary. Unpredictable. Dangerous.

You can know someone practically your whole life, only to realize that you don't really know them at all. You only know what they let you. And sometimes, that's a lie.

SIXTY-SEVEN

AMY THEN

1999

I can do this. I can pull this off. I just need to be careful. Methodical. Control the situation.

"This is... It's wrong, Amy. We're making a mistake. We need to call the cops."

Trust Liz to ruin everything. But I can't have that. I need her to stay silent. Whatever it takes.

Even if what it takes is the truth.

"No. We're doing this my way." I straighten my spine and push my shoulders back, lift my chin, already assuming my Mo posture. Use my height advantage to stare down at Liz. I don't see what everyone sees in her. Why she's always everyone's favorite. Mo's. Sami's. Even my father's. "Mo was my sister. My father sold her to the Ripley's because they couldn't have any children of their own."

Her gaze widens, but she holds her ground. "Just because she was your sister doesn't mean—"

"Trust me on this, Liz. You don't want to cross me. I'd tell you to ask Sonny, but you can't. Because I killed him."

She gasps, stumbling backward away from me until her back is up against the trunk of a tree. I stalk forward, closing the distance between us. "Don't be so surprised, Liz. You helped."

"What?" Her whisper is so soft I can barely hear it. But I can feel it, her shock, her surprise. That she knows I'm telling the truth. It gives me the confidence I need to go on.

"Remember that quiche I asked you to help me bake for his birthday?"

She whimpers.

"Remember how he died later that same day?"

"It was a heart attack."

But she doesn't sound so sure. I grin as I say, "Was it?"

I watch her throat stretch as she swallows hard. The fear that flashes in her eyes. "How?"

"You know that play I was in sophomore year? The one based on the Agatha Christie book, where the evil stepmother gets killed by her own heart medication?"

She makes no sign that she's heard me, but I continue anyway.

"Well, Mr. Fergus, the drama teacher, took the same stuff. Digitalis. Made from the foxglove plant. Medicinal in small doses, but lethal in large, as he was foolish enough to tell us. So when I saw the vial on the desk in his office one day, I couldn't resist stealing a few. You know. Just in case. I never thought I'd actually use it, but Sonny left me no choice."

I glance toward the house, but there's no sign of Sami.

"It was easier than I thought it would be. To grind it up, bake it into a special birthday treat for my dear old dad. And I had you help me feed it to him because he would have suspected something was up if it was just me trying to do something nice for him."

"But... why?"

"Why? Because someone had to punish him, and that someone was me. He deserved to die."

"But—"

"Why you?"

She nods.

"Because you had so much going for you. A loving family. A caring boyfriend. Good grades and a bright future. And yet you did it anyways. You had sex with my father. Why, Liz?"

Her mouth opens but no sound comes out.

"Did you know that he was sleeping with Sami, too? My dad was a predator, and, Sami, she's so naïve and desperate for attention. The perfect prey. He abused her, Liz. Took advantage of her trust. And you're the one who paved the way for that."

"No." She shakes her head, eyes squeezed shut, tears running down her cheeks.

"But it is. I saw it with my own eyes. And after that, I started following him to see what else he was up to. Imagine my surprise when I found out that Sami wasn't the only one. That he was hooking up with you, too. Only, it was different with you, wasn't it, Liz? Because you didn't have daddy issues. You weren't trying to fill some void inside because you felt empty. You did it because you wanted to. Because it was fun."

"That's not true," she whispers.

"Isn't it?"

"I was only fifteen when it started. Just a kid. When he told me that what we were doing was okay, I believed him. Because he said he loved me. But even if that was true, it was wrong. I know that now, but still. I feel so dirty and ashamed. I wish it had never happened. And oh God. Poor Sami." Her voice breaks as she hides her face in her hands, shaking her head.

I look away, disgusted. How did we all end up so broken like this? Victims of the same man. How could it be that there was no one who saw what was happening, no one to intervene, to protect us? How can society fail its girls so much and still hold its head so high?

Spotting Sami jogging down the path from the house, Mo's journal in her hand, I force myself to take a step away, to release my hands from the fists they've balled into. I can't let myself get sidetracked. There's only one thing that matters now.

I lay a hand gently on Liz's shoulder. Give it a soft, reassuring squeeze when her eyes meet mine. Because like it or not, we're in this together. "We need to start working the stones loose," I say. "We've got a long night ahead of us."

SIXTY-EIGHT

AMY NOW

2014

I listen to the dust settle in the room around us while the detective finds his voice. His eyes flick to the camera over my head. He clears his throat, strokes his mustache.

"Can you tell me the details surrounding the event? What type of weapon was used?"

I nod.

"She used a gun. It was... our father's. It was prom night. Our birthday. Everything was weird that night. Mo, well, if I'm honest, she hadn't been right for a while. Mental illness runs in our family. I knew she was depressed, but I didn't have any idea that she was so... none of us did, or we would have tried to help. She didn't say anything. We never even suspected."

If only Sonny had been honest with me. With us. Or even the Ripleys. As her sister, Mo's "mother" must have known how serious Vivienne's issues had been. But I guess it's easier to bury dirty laundry than to air it. Only, I would give anything to tell the world my twin was sick if it meant she was still here with me.

So I say it now, out loud for the first time. "Our mother was mentally ill. Bipolar. Maybe even borderline schizophrenic. I suspect that Mo was, too." I swear that I feel her beside me right now, taking my hand in hers, imbuing me with the strength that I need to get through this.

I take a deep breath and continue. "Mo came out of the clochán."

I pause to see if he needs an explanation on what that is, but he nods for me to go on.

"We were in the woods in a little clearing just outside of it. She went inside, and when she came back out, she had the gun. I... when I first saw it, I thought she was going to shoot all of us."

I fall silent, thinking about the emotions that had flashed across Mo's face like a slideshow.

"Do you think that was her original intention, but then, for some reason, she changed her plan?" His voice is low. There's no judgment in his tone. I appreciate that.

"Yes," I whisper.

"Can you think of any reason in particular why Morgana would have felt that killing her friends would be the right thing to do?" He asks the very question I've been trying to answer for years.

"I think that... maybe... she thought that she was saving us."

"Did that play into some kind of delusion that she was suffering from? That you needed saving?"

"No. Well. I'm not sure. I don't know if she was having delusions or not."

"Then why would you think that she was trying to save you?"

A cynical sniff of laughter comes from my nose. I close my eyes, trapping my tears, refusing to let them escape. My lips are pressed hard together. It takes all my willpower to part them to speak.

"Because we needed saving."

I'm surprised by the sound of my voice. It sounds so young. Like a lost little girl's whisper for help. The detective stares at me from across the table. I silently beg him not to ask.

"From who?"

Drawing a shaky breath, I tell him. "From life. From my father. From ourselves." And though I don't say it out loud, from each other. Because I was the one who hurt her the most, wasn't I? "Take your pick."

I'm quiet for a moment, stunned as the one thing I forgot comes back to mind. Mo's diary.

We had dragged Mo into the clochán after the life-changing event. We were going to pull the hut down and bury her under the rubble. But Sami had gone and got Mo's journal. Wrapped it in plastic. Insisted on burying it by her head. Like a headstone. That random act might be my downfall.

I thought it would be safe to confess. We hadn't done anything heinously wrong, after all. We hadn't killed Mo. But I had killed someone.

What if Mo wrote about me poisoning Sonny?

I'd told her, after all. Whispered it in her ear the same night I told her we were sisters. I had thought she'd be happy that I'd punished the man who kept us apart. But she wasn't. It was just one more injury between us.

A sob bursts like a bubble in my throat.

"I don't think Mo was ever quite right after our father died. It was so sudden. So unexpected. She had just found out he'd separated us, and she never got the chance to confront him. To find closure."

It's amazing how easy this is, how the words and emotions just supply themselves, like it's a role that was scripted just for me.

"And then we found out he'd abused our friends."

Detective Johnson clears his throat, shifting in his seat. "I don't suppose there's any evidence to prove that the abuse is more than just an allegation?"

"Liz's daughter."

"What about her?"

"If you test her DNA against mine, you'll find that we're half-sisters."

He sits back in his chair like my words have shoved him. The word sisters forms silently on his lips. He shakes his head, recovering himself.

"What makes you say that she—" he makes air quotes "—'wasn't right' after your father's death?"

"Because she wanted me to take credit for it."

"To confess to killing him?"

I tilt my head to the side and frown like I'm confused. "Well, not exactly. It's just that after he died, she thought that I should tell myself that I had done it. Like, taken a stand and killed the man who hurt me. She thought it would make me feel like I had taken my power back. The power he had taken from me."

"How did you feel about that?"

"I don't know. It seemed strange."

He clears his throat. Twists a pen between his fingers as he studies my face. "Ms. Russo. You should probably know that a judge has already approved the exhumation order we requested for your father's remains."

When will it end? Here I am, once again trying to twist the events of my life into a tale that makes me appear innocent. And suddenly, as much as it sickens me, I realize that I truly am my father's daughter.

I open my mouth to speak, but I have nothing to say. Luckily, I don't have to. Because the universe realizes it owes me. And it chooses that moment to repay its debt, sending someone to interrupt by knocking on the door.

SIXTY-NINE

SAMI NOW

2014

I'm almost through packing when there's a knock on the door. I jump, startled, a worm of panic starting in my stomach and spreading its way through my body, threading through my limbs, making them twitch and jerk. I can't believe this is happening.

I'm too late. It's the police, it must be. But maybe there's still a way out of this.

Inching toward the window, I hook a finger around the curtain and tug it back an inch. Peek outside. And feel an overwhelming surge of relief.

David's SUV is parked in the driveway behind my sedan. This could be a good thing. I can use this to my advantage. I hurry through the house and unbolt the lock, opening the door just enough to slip my head through.

"David."

"Sami, I need your help."

"Now's not a good—" I hadn't meant to let him in, I had

intended to keep him outside, but when he closed the distance between us I thought he wanted a hug and my body responded before my brain could. But instead of embracing me he brushed right by me, pushing his way into the house.

I rush to get in front of him, stopping him in his tracks. "Baby, what's the matter?"

But I already know. His wife is in jail for murder.

His eyes are red and bloodshot. His hair sticks out at random angles from his head. He's falling apart, and I have to admit, I'm kind of pissed. All this time he's let me be under the impression that he didn't care about her anymore. But this is not the face of indifference. This looks more like devastation.

"It's Olivia. Someone's taken her."

"What?"

He nods like a bobblehead, like he's still trying to convince himself that it's true. "Liz is at the police station now. They've called the FBI in. I have to look for her. I need your help."

I can't believe it. I should have known. All she's ever done is mess things up.

I hook my arm through his, guide him back toward the door. "Of course. Anything I can do to help. Do they have any idea who took her?"

"Dad?"

This is the proverbial moment when the shit hits the fan. I have to salvage this. I have to make him understand.

"Olivia, go back to the living room. Your dad and I need to talk."

But it's too late. David's seen her and now everything, the whole plan, is ruined. He rushes over and throws his arms around her, enveloping her in the hug that should have been mine. "Olivia, honey, what are you doing here?"

Her voice is muffled against his chest. "What do you mean?"

He spins toward me, tucking Olivia behind him like I'm some kind of threat. He hisses through bared teeth, barely controlling his anger. "What. Is. She. Doing. Here."

"Dad." Olivia grabs his arm, tries to make him face her, but he won't take his eyes off me. Guess he's smarter than I thought. "Dad, what's the matter? You're scaring me."

His eyes search my face for an answer. "Sami?" When I don't respond, he glances over his shoulder and asks, "Did she hurt you?"

"What? No. I don't understand. Sami said she spoke to mom. That mom thought we both needed a little space to think after, well... she said it was okay if I stayed here for a while."

"This is our chance, David, don't you see? This is our opportunity to be together."

Olivia's eyes narrow at me, her head tilting with confusion. "Dad?"

I can't help it. I have to speak the words that have been running through my mind for days now in an endless loop, ever since I laid eyes on Olivia and realized the truth. "He's not your dad."

"Don't you say that. Don't you dare ever say that," he roars.

"But. It's the truth." I hold my hands up in supplication. "I'm sorry that Liz tricked you, but that's just all the more reason why we should be together. She doesn't deserve you. I can make you happy. I can give you a real family. Of your own."

"Liz didn't trick me."

This is going very wrong. I take a step backward, down the hall, toward my bedroom. He takes a step forward, not allowing me to retreat.

"Olivia, here." He pulls his keys and phone out of his pocket. "Go lock yourself in the car and call 911. Tell them where we are. And that Samantha Warner was the one who kidnapped you."

"Kidnapped? No, this is all just a misunderstanding, it has to be."

"This isn't a misunderstanding. It isn't a joke. Your mom received a note threatening your safety. She's at the police station talking with the FBI right now. There are people out there looking for you, trying to find who took you. This woman is a criminal."

Olivia's eyes widen with understanding. She snatches the keys and the phone.

"Your mom is too," I call after her as she scurries from the house. Once the sound of her hurried steps is gone, I try to convince him again. "David, it's not too late. We can fix this." I chance turning my back on him even though he looks like he wants to throttle me and continue down the hall to my bedroom.

"For the record..." his voice is cold and detached.

And I know I've lost this particular battle. But I haven't yet lost the war.

"I knew Liz was pregnant. I don't think she even knew yet, but I did, I suspected. And I chose to be with her. To raise the baby as my own."

"But you don't love her."

"I do. I've always loved her."

I laugh. "Please. You have a funny way of showing it."

"I didn't cheat because I wasn't in love with my wife. I cheated because I was hurt. Because something happened and she wouldn't let me in. She kept me at a distance. You and me? Well, I guess part of the allure was that you made me feel closer to her. And a part of me hoped that maybe one day you'd say something that would let it all make sense. I'm sorry if you thought otherwise, Sami."

I tug open the drawer in my nightstand and shove my hand inside, rifling around. "You really love her?"

"I really do."

"And you're choosing her?"

"I am."

They always do.

"Then I hope she's worth dying for."

I pull the gun out. I aim. And I pull the trigger.

SEVENTY

LIZ NOW

2014

I stare at the watch strapped to the FBI agent's wrist, watching the second hand pass the time in jerky little movements. I swear I can hear the small *tick-tick* in the otherwise silent room, each one of them making it a little harder to breathe—each one marking another moment my daughter is gone.

I've got to get out of here. There's got to be something I can do to help. Something other than just sitting here in this tiny room with its stale air, nibbling at the raw mess I've made of my thumb. I haven't chewed on my nails since grade school, but now they're bitten down to the quick, the ends of my fingers tender and bloodied.

They need to let me go. I've said all I have to say. I fulfilled my end of the bargain, told Detective Johnson every horrible detail that I remember from that night. And then I had to do it all again, so one of the agents from the local FBI field office could determine whether there's a possible connection between that night and my daughter's kidnapping.

How could there not be?

But reliving that night over and over again is a small price to pay as long as it remains the worst of my life. I pray to God that it doesn't get replaced by a new one. I pray every single second that I sit here in this room, listening to the soundtrack of the agent's watch, while all the horrible things that could be happening to my daughter right now run through my head in an endless loop.

Someone taps twice on the door. The agent's eyes meet mine as she rises to answer it. She gives me a nod as if to tell me, *be strong, you've got this.* But I'm not so sure I do.

I haven't been a good friend. Or a good wife. I'm not even sure I've been a good mother. But I've tried. And if I'm lucky enough to get the opportunity, I'm going to do better. It's a promise I make to myself and whoever is out there listening in the world.

The agent steps outside, closing the door behind her. I scratch nervously at my arm, managing to raise angry welts from the ragged edges of my gnawed-up nails. I imagine the relief I'll feel when she comes back into the room smiling and tells me that they've found Olivia. That she's all right. I start a list in my mind, all the ways I'm going to be a better person.

But the agent's been out there too long now. She'd be back already if the news was good.

A sob rises in my chest. My eyes water. The back of my throat feels tight and burns. I stare at the door until it opens again, and Detective Johnson enters the room.

I draw a deep breath. Hold it. Curl my fingers around the metal edge of the chair seat, knuckles straining painfully as I squeeze tight, bracing myself.

"Mrs. Bentley. I'm very sorry."

"Oh, God." I shove a fist into my mouth, yet still manage to somehow wail my daughter's name around it.

Detective Johnson's hand settles gently on my shoulder. He

looks down at me with sorrow. "Your daughter is fine. She's been rescued and is on her way to the station now."

My grief turns to laughter. Olivia is okay. My prayers have been answered.

"But I'm afraid I have to inform you that your husband was shot by the kidnapper."

"What?" It feels like a hole opens up in the floor and that I drop through, deep into the bowels of the earth. I don't understand. David wasn't a part of this. He was supposed to be safe. "But, how?"

"He's the one who found your daughter, ma'am. A true hero."

I thought I didn't love my husband anymore. I thought I'd be just fine without him. But now I think I was wrong.

SEVENTY-ONE

SIX MONTHS LATER

2015

I watch Olivia wade into the surf, waves breaking against her legs. The sun shines bright overhead, the salty wind catching her hair, sweeping it out behind her like a golden flag. I cherish each moment like this. Every one of them takes my breath away.

She moves deeper into the water, and I fidget on my blanket, fighting the urge to call her back. I want to keep her safe. I want to protect her. But I also want her to live her life free from the constant fear that's haunted mine. So I keep my mouth shut and just sit here, on the beach, surrounded by worry.

Because I'm a mother. And the world really is a dangerous place.

After Detective Johnson told me the details of what happened, I felt shattered into a million pieces, the shards melted into shapes that would never fit back together. I knew a part of me would be broken forever. But Olivia didn't have to be.

I work every day to make that true.

David and I raised such an amazing daughter together.

She's so brave and strong. I don't think I would have made it through this if it hadn't been for her. She's given me more than she'll ever realize.

After David arrived at Sami's asking for her help, after he discovered that she was the one who had kidnapped our daughter, he gave his keys and phone to Olivia and told her to lock herself in the car and call 911. She called the police, but never went to his car. Instead, she crept back into the house, overhearing everything David told Sami.

That he had known I was pregnant by another man, yet chose to spend his life with me and raise the baby as his own. Because he loved me. Loved us. Because even though I thought any affection we had felt for each other was gone, I was wrong. His love for me never wavered, even when I pushed him away. And I did. He was right about that.

I just felt so guilty when I started having suspicions about who might have really fathered Olivia. I didn't know what else to do. I didn't feel like I deserved him. So I sabotaged us.

I wish I had just talked to him instead. Trusted him. Been honest. Surely the worst that could have happened would have been better than what did happen. And I'll never forgive myself for that.

But for my daughter, our daughter, I have to keep trying. I owe it to him, to her, to us all. Even if each breath is still a battle for me, I try not to let her know it. But staying there, in Waverly, where memories haunted the shadows and ghosts waited around every corner wasn't an option, so we sold the house in Massachusetts.

We haven't bought a new one yet. We haven't decided where we want to live. For now, I'm homeschooling Olivia while we chase the sun south.

The forensic pathologist who conducted the postmortem on Sonny's exhumed remains found traces of the drug Amy had used in gastric tissues they sampled. Unfortunately, with the amount of time that had passed, it wasn't enough for the police to bring charges against her.

Luckily, Mo had written extensively about Amy's confession to Sonny's murder in the journal Sami had buried with her, exonerating the rest of us. When confronted by her sister's own words, she broke down and confessed. Now Amy's in jail awaiting prosecution. And to be honest, that's probably the best place she can be.

What she did to her own father, and making me a part of it? It's clear that she needs help. That she should be kept away from the rest of society, especially my daughter. Even if they are sisters.

Despite the way I feel, though, I've allowed Olivia to have weekly Zoom chats with her. She's old enough to make her own decision about this. It's not my place to stand in the way of their relationship. But I think—I hope, I pray—that on some level, Olivia knows not to trust her. And even if she doesn't yet, she will by the time Amy is released. If she ever is. At the very least, she's going to be in prison for a long while.

Sami is in a medical rehab facility. After she shot David, Olivia ran out of the house, straight into the arms of the local SWAT team. When they surrounded the building, Sami turned the gun on herself. She took a chunk of her brain and a portion of her skull, but not her life.

Her mother told me that she'll never be able to function on her own again. That she can't walk or talk or even feed herself. But I don't want to hear about it. I don't care to know any of the details about her dismal future.

The police say that she was the one who sent me the letters, but that pales in comparison to the fact that she kidnapped my daughter. Who knows what her intentions were, what she would have done if David hadn't intervened.

What is it that drives us to such desperate measures? Friendship? Secrets? Betrayal? I don't think there's just one answer. But I suspect that maybe honesty is the solution. Because that's when things started falling apart, when we started hiding things from each other. When we hid the truth even from ourselves.

So that's how I'm breaking the cycle. I've owned up to my mistakes. Confronted the shadiest parts of my past. Allowed Olivia to ask me anything she wants to, and responded with the facts, no matter how painful they may be. But forcing yourself to face the harsh glare of reality has its perks.

Yes, the world is a dangerous place, and I'll always be concerned about Olivia's welfare, but for the first time in the longest time, I feel safe. A small part of me is even remembering what it feels like to be happy. And those are the things that I want, more than anything, for me and my daughter. I aim to lead by example.

A shadow falls across me, and I squint up at the figure blocking the sun. Return my watchful gaze to Olivia as I shift to make room on the blanket next to me, leaving my hand splayed wide in the middle. Feel a smile spread softly across my lips as his pinky finger brushes against mine.

It hasn't been easy. Or quick. There's a lot of hurt on both sides. But in those first few moments, when I thought I'd lost David forever, I realized how much I truly loved him. Sighing happily, I lay my head on his shoulder.

He fought for me. Our daughter. His life, after Sami shot him, leaving him bleeding out on the floor with a collapsed lung. Now, I'm fighting for our marriage.

SEVENTY-TWO

FRANCINE

2015

She peers through the windows, watching the new neighbors move in. The daughter looks nice enough. Probably right around her Gina's age. But the mother looks like the nasty sort, the kind that wouldn't have given her the time of day in high school. Just like Liz and her friends had been.

It's fitting, what happened to them. Amy rotting away in jail. Sami practically a vegetable. And Liz... well, once again, Liz seems to have come out the other side basically unscathed. Lucky bitch.

Francine pulls back, away from the window as the new mother next door scowls in her direction. She might have been spotted, but it doesn't really matter. The woman won't have a choice but to be nice to her if their daughters become friends. What won't a mother do for her child?

And girls are so impressionable at that age. So easily malleable. She remembers what she said to Mo on prom night, the way the words had felt as they'd flung off her tongue like darts, sharp and barbed. The expression on Mo's face as she sank her fangs in deep and tore chunks away.

She doesn't understand why nobody noticed how weak Mo was. How easy it would be to pulverize her fragile ego with just a few accurate statements. Then again, all these years and no one seemed to notice that Amy's birthmark had somehow transferred to Mo's neck. People see what they want to see.

But not her. No, she sees everything. And she's patient. Willing to play the long game.

Although she has to admit, she's disappointed that Liz took her daughter away. All the effort of getting knocked up so young as soon as she found out Liz was pregnant. Of planning and maneuvering, her outrageous luck when her mother died just in time for her to purchase the house next door when it came on the market. But the girls will keep in touch. She and Gina will see Olivia again—she'll make sure of it. In the meantime, she needs to stay sharp.

She'll send Gina over in the morning, have her invite the new girl over for a slumber party.

A LETTER FROM SHANNON

Readers!!!!! Decades ago, when I was a little girl writing stories, I dared to hope that one day I'd write something that someone other than my parents would want to read. Thank you so much for making that dream come true! I have more things dark and twisty on the way – if you want to know about my latest releases, please sign up at the following link. Your email address will never be shared, and you can unsubscribe at any time.

www.bookouture.com/shannon-hollinger

I hope you were able to find something to love about this book, and that you enjoyed the time you spent with it. If you did, I'd be forever grateful if you left a review. All of you wonderful reviewers out there are how I find the books that keep me up late every night reading, and it would be amazing if you helped other readers find this one!

Happy Reading!

Shannon

KEEP IN TOUCH WITH SHANNON

shannonhollinger.com

 facebook.com/thiswritersays

twitter.com/thiswritersays

ACKNOWLEDGMENTS

A huge thanks to Susannah Hamilton and the rest of the team at Bookouture for giving me the opportunity to join the ranks of some of my favorite authors!

Also, endless gratitude to my family:

My mom, who didn't just teach me to read at a young age, but also fostered my love of reading, took me regularly to the library to check out huge stacks of books, made me summer reading lists (without which I probably would have ignored many great and classic books), and who taught me how to write stories of my own. I couldn't have done any of this without her.

My dad, who always believed I could do anything I put my mind to. I wish you were here to celebrate this achievement.

My grandmother, Marvis, who fostered my book addiction in the most wonderful ways. It's because of her that I never have to worry about being homeless – I could literally build a house out of books!

My husband, who doesn't read fiction – even mine – but is absolutely certain that anyone who doesn't like my writing has something wrong with them. That's blind love right there, and there's no one I'd rather get lost with on our adventures.

My furred assistants who sat (sometimes impatiently) by my side for hours during the crafting of this book.

And finally, to all you readers who took a chance on a new author. There are so many fantastic books out there and not nearly enough time to read them all, so thank you so much for choosing to spend some of your precious reading time with one of mine! It means so much to me, and I hope you loved reading this book as much as I loved writing it!

Printed in Great Britain
by Amazon

21629870R00171

VELOCITY 2.O

PAINT, PIXELS & PROFITABILITY

DALE POLLAK

NEW YEAR PUBLISHING LLC

DANVILLE, CALIFORNIA

VELOCITY 2.O
PAINT, PIXELS & PROFITABILITY

by Dale Pollak

© 2010, 2013 by New Year Publishing, LLC
144 Diablo Ranch Ct.
Danville, CA 94506 USA
http://www.newyearpublishing.com

ISBN 978-1-935547-39-6
Library of Congress Control Number: 2009937598

Contents

ACKNOWLEDGEMENTS

Many people don't have the opportunity to author one book, much less two. It is with profound wonderment that I find myself once again in the enviable position of thanking people for helping bring a book to life, this time, *Velocity 2.0: Paint, Pixels, & Profitability.*

When I wrote my first book, *Velocity: From the Front Line to the Bottom Line,* many things were very different from how they are today. My youngest son Samson is now old enough to help me select the title for my book. My older sons, Austin and Alex, are both off to college. My company, vAuto, Inc., which had only a handful of employees and several hundred customers, is now the leading provider of used vehicle software in the United States with well over 2,500 customers. Perhaps the most profound change is within the automobile industry itself, having undergone transformations that are beyond simple definition.

However, the more things change, the more things stay the same. Once again I owe tremendous thanks to Lance Helgeson, my ears, eyes, and sounding board. I again want to thank my family for their support and love with a special thanks to my father, Len Pollak, for his guidance during these challenging times.

I would also like to thank all my friends at vAuto, notably Keith Jezek, President and CEO, Michael Chiovari, Chief Technology Officer, John Griffin, Vice President of Performance Management, David Hawkins, Vice President of R&D, Jill Tyson, Vice President of Finance, Morrie Eisenberg, Vice President of Corporate Development, and my incredibly hard-working and ever-smiling assistant Susan Taft. The passion, creativity, and dedication of this team is truly remarkable.

I would like to thank all of our customers and industry associates, many of whom I am fortunate to count as friends, and many of whom were essential to the writing of these pages. It is a testament to our industry that so many of us are still committed despite the enormous challenges we have faced and will continue to face.

Finally, it is with the greatest love and devotion that I acknowledge and thank my wife Nancy, who has pored over these pages for countless hours, doing what no other person could or would, for me.

Introduction: A New Day Requires a New Way

This book was written to help dealers and used vehicle managers who aspire to do a better job managing their used vehicle operations. I hope it will provide a window to examine why today's marketplace is far more challenging than ever, and highlight the new tools, technology, and best practices that a growing number of dealers and used vehicle managers are deploying to achieve success.

The name "Velocity 2.0: Paint, Pixels, & Profitability" was chosen to address the "one foot in the past, one foot in the future" nature of today's used vehicle marketplace.

"Paint" accounts for the spot-on instincts that have traditionally defined a good used vehicle manager. Every dealership needs someone who can tell which vehicles are right for their store and ensure that they stand tall. But, as you'll read in the book, I believe the instincts and skills that we've rewarded handsomely in the past need to evolve to meet the needs of a changed marketplace. This evolution requires going beyond instincts and relying on new metrics and data to manage the "paint" part of our business. Without this evolution, used vehicle managers and their dealers will achieve only sub-par success.

"Pixels," meanwhile, represents the new set of skills that dealers and used vehicle managers must understand, develop, and deploy to have a realistic shot at capturing today's Internet-enabled buyers. Today's customers start their used vehicle shopping online and what they find there defines and drives where they'll take their business. In some ways, this ever-increasing online buying dynamic has made dealers' online inventory presentation more important than their physical front line. The book will examine how some dealers and used vehicle managers have successfully embraced this trend and navigated the myriad of third-party players to craft a recipe for success. You'll also see how these efforts have transformed many of their in-store processes for managing both used vehicle inventory and customers.

"Profitability" remains the essential objective of dealership operations. In light of the dramatic changes in the environment, and the new, more varied and complex tasks that are required, dealerships must reconsider how best to structure their organizations to achieve optimal results. This subject is carefully discussed in the later chapters.

There are key themes in this book that are well known in the financial industry, but provide a new way of looking at the used car industry. These themes provide the foundation for this new way forward:

> **Volatility:** Economists call a marketplace volatile when there are significant swings up and down in the value of a given product or commodity. This definition fits our used vehicle business like a glove. With our uncertain economy, factory financial difficulties, and a greater degree of competition among franchised and independent dealers for used vehicle buyers, the valuation of used vehicles can seem like a crapshoot. It's this volatility that has spurred the leading wholesale value publishers like Kelley Blue Book and Black Book to begin publishing their benchmarks more frequently. NADA is also finalizing plans to launch weekly auction value updates in early 2010. Upshot: Pretty much everyone recognizes that wholesale values are fluctuating faster than ever before. They recognize that wholesale values are changing faster than monthly or even

weekly. Volatility is also the reason why leasing has lost its luster. The smart money people recognize the inherent risk of trying to predict the future value of vehicles in this more volatile market. The book will detail how a new approach to managing used vehicle operations helps to mitigate some of the volatility-driven risks.

Efficiency: Financial types use this term to describe a marketplace in which buyers and sellers have roughly equal knowledge. In these markets (think of metals, grain, oil, etc.), the price of a product or commodity is largely governed by supply, demand, and price sensitivity. I believe our new vehicle business has long been an efficient market. The same is now true for used vehicles, thanks in large part to the Internet. Customers can easily find vehicles and make quick comparisons on price, features, trim packages, and financing options. The old "you can't find another vehicle like this one" line rings increasingly hollow for today's buyers. These new realities, in turn, require that dealers and used vehicle managers be more efficient and sophisticated about how they purchase, price, and present their vehicles. This book will examine the critical, often painful, steps a growing number of stores are taking to become more efficient and profitable used vehicle retailers.

Metrics-based management: The realities of a volatile, efficient market require that dealers and used vehicle managers take utmost advantage of the tools and technology available to improve the proficiency and profitability of their used vehicle operations. This book will delve into what I believe are the most critical, data-based management benchmarks to guide used vehicle decision-making and reduce the risks inherent in today's used vehicle market. I'll share first-hand examples of how dealers and used vehicle managers use these metrics to light a pathway for success.

Used vehicle primacy: You may have picked up this book because you're looking for fresh ideas and perspectives to help you manage your used vehicle operations more effectively. Make no mistake: The road ahead is not easy, especially if you consider yourself "a new car store." The success you seek will not come without making your used vehicle department a primary focus of your time and energy. The good news: This book reveals how to get there and reap the rewards of increased volumes, growth in net profits, and improved cash flow. The bad news: It takes tremendous fortitude and committed, hands-on leadership to make this important cultural transition happen. Anything less than this level of commitment invites failure.

As with my first book, *Velocity,* I will not pull any punches in the pages that follow. If I come across as too forceful at times, I ask that you pardon my passion for our business and for what I truly believe is a fresh path that will help our industry.

Our industry is at a critical crossroads. We all need to rethink and retool the processes and approaches we have long relied on to manage used vehicle operations at dealerships. It's not that these processes and approaches are bad in and of themselves. Rather, I believe today's marketplace has rendered them largely obsolete and ineffective. As a growing number of dealerships focus on used vehicles for sustenance and, in some cases, salvation, the time is right to suggest a new way forward for our industry.

Thank you for the opportunity to share this important and transformative story.

Enjoy the read.

A New Way Forward for a Changed Business

John Chalfant has a secret.

John is the architect behind a fast-paced turn-around in used vehicle sales at Edmark Superstore, Nampa, Idaho. In five short months, he's cranked volume to 300-plus units per month. He's turning his 400-car inventory 17 times a year. I'm paying him a visit to find out how he does it.

"So what's your secret?" I ask.

"I'm happy to talk broadly about what we do," Chalfant says. "But I don't really want to create more competition for myself."

"Come on, John," I insist. "Your success is an inspiration for every dealer and used vehicle manager at a very tough time in our business. What's your secret?"

"Dale, I can't do it."

"Now I know why you thought you'd make a good lawyer," I say. He laughs.

"Let's just say we've done away with the 'golden gut,'" offers Chalfant, who had considered becoming a lawyer before joining the family business. "We make our decisions—purchasing, pricing, and wholesaling—based on data, not instinct. We have taken the emotion out of the deal. That's the moral of our story."

Ahhhh. Now we're getting somewhere, I think.

I ask a softer question: "How is it that you wound up managing the used vehicle department?"

"My uncle, my dad, and our GM thought I'd be good at it," Chalfant says. "We'd been having trouble dealing with the wild fluctuations in used car prices. We were taking massive wholesale hits. We were having a hard time acquiring product at local auctions, and we didn't have trade-ins to back us up because new sales volumes had dropped dramatically."

"That's a familiar story these days," I say. "So, the crimp on inventory was causing trouble. What did you do to address that?"

"We thought we had a problem acquiring vehicles," he says. "But when I started, I spent two weeks looking at Manheim and other auctions online and thought, good gracious. There are thousands of vehicles out there every day. Our problem was that we'd only been buying at our local auction where 50 dealers are picking over 300 vehicles. That's just not a broad enough selection."

Chalfant describes the three computer screens on his desk. One shows his inventory and market metrics, which he uses for pricing and setting appraisal and wholesale values. Another serves as his window on wholesale auction run lists and other data across a five-state region. The third screen checks email and monitors live auction feeds. "At any time, I've got 120 vehicles in transit," he says. "Over the last three months I have only bought cars online."

We chat more about his velocity-based used management philosophy and how it has changed the store's operations and the traditional role of used car manager. John spends most of his time doing what can only be described as "inventory engineering," and overseeing the online merchandising of the store's inventory.

It's quickly apparent that Chalfant thinks and
works differently than many dealers and used
vehicle managers. For example:

> *Take gross profits.* Chalfant doesn't obsess over
> gross profits on every deal. In fact, he thinks it's
> an irrelevant metric for determining whether a
> used vehicle department is humming or not. "I
> refuse to have a conversation about gross profit
> per unit (GPU) or per vehicle retail (PVR). I
> think it neglects the whole story of revenue
> generation of a car deal," he says. Instead, he
> focuses on a new breed of metrics—Cost to
> Market, Price to Market, and Market Days
> Supply—to guide his inventory decisions.

> *Take his inventory engineering.* Chalfant isn't
> managing inventory age; he's managing the
> seven-figure investment his inventory represents.
> In practical terms, this means age is a secondary
> factor. Chalfant makes pricing changes much
> more frequently than traditional dealers and
> used vehicle managers. He bases these pricing
> changes on market metrics, not educated
> guesswork. He'll also dispose of a vehicle much
> faster than other stores—irrespective of its time
> in inventory—if the metrics indicate it'll be a
> drag on ROI.

> *Take his view of today's customers.* "They are
> more educated," he says. "They understand
> what's out there and what it's going for." As a

result, Chalfant views sales as a process where transparency, shared knowledge, and limited negotiation are the new orders of the day. He doesn't resent the fact that his customers are better armed; he embraces it.

Take his reconditioning process. Here, Chalfant definitely doesn't want to go into "huge detail" about the system he's built to ensure efficient throughputs of vehicles for reconditioning. He knows this is a make-or-break aspect of a velocity-based management process. "The service department knows what vehicles have been bought and when they're arriving," he explains. "They're ready for them. I'm pretty popular over there."

Take his online presence. Chalfant knows today's online ROI flows from monitoring metrics like "detailed page views" and conversions to identify potential turnoffs for online customers: inconsistent prices, poor/ missing photos, and dull vehicle descriptions. He's an articulate student of this pixel data, unlike other dealers and used vehicle managers who offer blank stares when I ask about their own online metrics.

As we close our conversation, I'm amazed.

At 25 years old and with only three years of experience in our business, Chalfant impresses me as

more knowledgeable about how to guide a used
vehicle operation toward success in today's more
challenging market than many more seasoned dealers and used vehicle managers—guys who continue
to struggle with the same problems he tackled in
a short five months. I begin to wonder if his inex-
perience is actually an asset, given our industry's
reluctance to change.

As I think about what Chalfant has accomplished,
I realize that his story is one of the more profound
examples of the kinds of performance improvement
in used vehicles that I'm seeing with increasing
frequency as I travel the country to discuss today's
business and the challenges it poses. It is fair to say
the people who are driving these success stories are
either guys like Chalfant, who don't have to undo
years of traditional used vehicle management experience to embrace a new way forward, or they're
more seasoned dealers and used vehicle managers
who, out of necessity or sheer will, have the courage to change processes they've relied on for years.

As Chalfant so aptly puts it, good instincts, guesswork, and an unflinching reliance on familiar
processes won't cut it anymore. Success today
requires better use of data, technology, tools, computer skills, and a conviction to achieve it.

Chalfant's story also foreshadows the problems that
will inevitably develop as dealers and used vehicle
managers recognize that what they don't know

about today's more challenging used vehicle marketplace is hurting them, and what they do know isn't helping very much.

The conflicts include the inevitable clash when technology-driven efficiencies meet people-driven inefficiencies, and the struggle between change agents and those who, either by fear, disbelief, or lack of skill/interest, resist change.

Chalfant is a shining example of someone whose success highlights what occurs when dealerships adopt the new thinking and processes necessary to drive improved profitability.

I congratulate Chalfant on his success and appreciate his willingness to share that success—if not his secret—to help other dealers chart their own course for success in a more challenging used vehicle marketplace.

A Look Back at "The Old Ways"

Across the country, dealers and used vehicle managers are facing the kind of wholesale losses and diminished sales problems that John Chalfant tidied up in a hurry.

These problems appear to be indiscriminate. They are happening at stores that our industry has long regarded as top-shelf success stories, at dealer groups in metro markets as well as at single-point stores in small towns. What's worse, they are happening despite the best efforts of dealers and used vehicle managers to address them.

Dealer Clay Close of Atchison (Kansas) Automotive knows this frustrating scenario all too well. He bought his four-point GM store in 2007 and gave his "I'm the new boss" speech on the day the Dow Jones average hit 14,000 and national unemployment was about 4 percent.

"It was downhill from there," says Close, a 30-year auto retailing veteran.

In late 2008, he carried an 80-unit inventory in a truck- and SUV-friendly market, and saw wholesale losses and reduced floor traffic that almost put him out of business. "There was nobody coming in here to lay down for $3,000 on a car," Close says. "I realized that I was either going to have to start sending out applications to work for someone else or do something different."

The something different came with Close's decision to adopt the velocity-based principles that Chalfant successfully utilizes. He's trimmed his inventory to about 50 vehicles and focuses on turning them quickly to avoid the risk of costly drops in market values. He uses live market-based tools to set online pricing that attracts buyers from a wider geographic range than he'd previously targeted. He's making rather than losing money, averaging about 50 used deals a month.

"I can live forever doing this," he says. "Once we get out of the recession, we'll start looking at building this up and making some real do re mi."

Close's turnaround highlights the underlying dilemma for dealerships today: Our industry is struggling to adapt to a used vehicle marketplace that's faster and more risk-prone than it has ever been. Meanwhile, the prevailing "what to do wisdom" hasn't kept up with the market's pace of change. Sure, we've got "45 is the new 60," vehicle "sets," and other changes on the traditional used vehicle management theme.

But I view these as signs of "tradition" under strain rather than a solution to achieve sustainable success. A fast-moving market requires fast-moving management metrics, tools, and techniques—the fundamental elements of the velocity-based approach that Close and Chalfant use to succeed.

It's no wonder many dealers and used vehicle managers complain that while they're putting more time and attention into their used vehicle operations, they are not gaining any ground.

I'm in a unique position to observe this historical convergence between our industry's traditional used vehicle management practices and the new marketplace. I was a student/disciple of the traditional management practices at our Cadillac store in Elmhurst, Ill., in the mid-1980s. I understand how they work, and recognize their obvious appeal: They're familiar and they made us good money for a very, very long time.

I've since taken what I learned from my time as a dealer and built a company, vAuto, Inc. Our whole purpose is to help dealers and managers understand and capitalize on today's Internet-driven used vehicle market.

So I think there's value in a short trip down memory lane to examine our industry's best practices and why they are less effective than they used to be.

A CONFESSION: WHAT ELMER AND I MISSED

Elmer was the quintessential used car guy. He'd worked for years in the business and he'd gained a special understanding of the Cadillac brand. He was my right-hand man as the two of us managed used vehicle operations at my family's Cadillac store.

As I think back, there were two underlying beliefs that Elmer and I applied to our used vehicle operations—beliefs that many dealers and used vehicle managers still cling to today:

1. There's an "ass for every seat," and it's just a matter of time before we find the right one for a vehicle.

2. We should always price our vehicles based
    on what we paid for them, whether a unit
    came through a trade-in or at auction.

Taken together, these beliefs touched every aspect of
how we managed the used vehicle department.

Perhaps the most telling example of how these
beliefs affected our management decisions arrived
every week, when our controller, Mike Chiovari,
showed up in our used vehicle office with the general ledger. Mike Chiovari was there at my request.
Our weekly meeting was to review how much negative equity or water we had in our inventory.

The three of us would sit together and dutifully go
through each vehicle, comparing what we'd paid
for the unit and its wholesale value.

The problem? At least 50 percent of the time, Elmer
and I could not agree on what a vehicle was worth
at wholesale. Inevitably, I'd defer to Elmer because
he was our in-house expert who'd spent time at
auctions and knew what a vehicle would bring.

Because Elmer and I often couldn't agree, we rarely
made decisions about getting rid of any inventory
before our 90-day clock had expired. It was only at
or near that time when we'd tweak our pricing and
try to retail out of a vehicle. If a unit hit 90 days
in our inventory it went to auction because I was a

stickler about adhering to our inventory age/turn policy.

In hindsight, I realize that while Elmer and I were following industry best practices for managing our used vehicle operations, our efforts were largely empty gestures.

Our weekly standoff on used vehicle values, and our inability to make a decision to dispose of a vehicle that might pose a problem, meant that Elmer had more time to retail it and earn a hefty gross profit. It's only now that I recognize that Elmer got the better end of the deal—his pay plan emphasized gross profit per vehicle and the more opportunities he had to achieve a hefty gross, the better off he'd be.

From a store perspective, however, I wonder how much better we'd have done if we had dumped those vehicles that appeared questionable during our weekly exercise and found a new unit that might not have been as problematic. Back then, I wasn't aware of what's called an "opportunity cost," or the "benefits you could have received by taking an alternative action.[1]"

But even if I had known or understood the concept of opportunity cost, I'm not sure it would have made a big difference. Both Elmer and I were emo-

---

[1] Forbes' Investopedia, http://www.investopedia.com/terms/o/opportunitycost.asp.

tionally tied to each vehicle and to our own belief that we'd find an ass for every seat and retail our way out of what might be a problem.

I have come to understand that there was a second problem with our weekly exercise and our standoff on wholesale values. I believe we were focused on the wrong number. Instead of trying to determine how much water a vehicle held, we should have been evaluating its likelihood to sell in order to meet an investment return objective. In essence, our weekly exercise should have been spent trying to get the firmest read possible on whether our "ass for every seat" belief would prove true and how tall our vehicle stood in the marketplace.

That's the crux of a velocity-based approach to used vehicle management. It's based on what I could never figure out when I was a dealer.

Of course, back in the mid-'80s, the necessary market-based information that's available today didn't exist. The closest barometer I had was Elmer's head. He was the guy who knew the market. I now recognize that I had no empirical way of knowing if his instincts were correct or not.

A FORGIVING BUSINESS
FORGIVES NO MORE

Ah, the good old days. We were happy, flush with hefty profits and the customers kept coming. Today's dealers and used vehicle managers don't have it so easy.

Today's customers know as much, if not more, about specific vehicle values as Elmer and I did when we ran our department. The one-sided nature of our deal-making, which gave us as dealers a distinct advantage, is long gone.

At the same time, Elmer and I faced less competition. For the most part, competition came just from other Cadillac dealers. Dealers with other franchises stuck close to their own brands, as we did ours, when it came to buying and selling used vehicles. In turn, that meant the competitive playing field was smaller. We didn't have to face the encroachment from independents, other franchise dealers, or velocity-minded stores that put additional pressure on most markets today.

Elmer and I had another advantage: We were Cadillac dealers and our customers were largely loyal to the brand. In addition, the "aspirational" aspects of the Cadillac brand meant that our used inventory appealed to buyers who wanted to "step up" to the luxury tier. It was a segment leader that had cache across all household income levels.

Today, the landscape is completely different. Brand loyalties aren't what they used to be. To make the situation worse, today's customers have easy access to websites where they can compare vehicles in any segment against others with similar price points and equipment configurations. Similarly, these websites also allow comparisons between dealers. The idea that any given used vehicle is one of a kind and unique isn't as true as it used to be when you account for how easy it is for customers today to find alternatives.

I'd like to believe that if Elmer and I were still running our used vehicle department, we'd be successful. But there's no way we could keep up with guys like John Chalfant or Clay Close, who use all of today's market data and tools to determine how to acquire, price, merchandise, wholesale, and retail their inventories.

Thankfully, Elmer and I operated in a marketplace that masked and forgave our mistakes. Buyers had little knowledge about whether we were trying to sell at a price that was out of line for the market. And, if they had a clue, we'd use our negotiation skills and Elmer's charm to make them feel good about paying it.

As I listen to the struggles many dealers and used vehicle managers are having today, I'm struck by the degree to which many still follow the same beliefs and operational practices that Elmer and I used over 20 years ago.

But I understand why they remain. It's difficult for anyone to change from something that has worked successfully for so long.

Perhaps the first step toward making this change to a more market-attuned, velocity-based approach to managing used vehicle operations is to understand exactly the kind of market forces we are all up against.

THE GREAT EQUALIZER
ARRIVES—AND THRIVES

It's 10 a.m. in Peoria, Illinois and dealer Bill Pearson's running late.

It's not his fault.

Mechanical difficulties had grounded his flight home the night before, forcing an overnight stay in Chicago. He was back on track this morning, driving from a nearby airport to meet me at his store, Finish Line Ford.

No matter. The delay offers a chance to get a feel for his operation. It's got buzz ... more so than many other Ford stores these days. Salespeople here actually have customers with them—at their desks, on the phone, on the lot and, on their computer screens via the Internet.

The showroom has an air of purpose, a crispness of pace. I hear the sound of a belly laugh from a nearby office, a sign of levity, if not job satisfaction. It's readily apparent, when Pearson arrives, flashes a smile, and apologizes for the lag, where the vibe at Finish Line comes from.

"I'm a sunshine type of person," he says. "It's easy to work for me if you do your job well."

Judging from the results Pearson's achieved in the past two years, he and his entire team are doing their jobs well. He's taken a store that did about 50 used vehicles a month and turned it into a 300-unit-per-month machine. On average, most used vehicles get sold before they hit the 25-day mark in his inventory. He's turning his inventory of 400 vehicles roughly 15 times a year.

I've come to visit Pearson and tour his store to get an insider's view of his operation. Right off the bat, it's apparent that he and the store are attuned to the Internet and velocity-based used vehicle management processes. In fact, they've harnessed both to create a double-barreled, net-profit generating powerhouse.

"I really believe we're an Internet store," Pearson says. "Some dealers think it's not fair that the customer has the Internet and often shops there first. We take the opposite view and go the other way."

I find his statement to be both powerful and painfully true for our industry. There's no question that the Internet has changed our business, and it is dealers like Pearson and John Chalfant who are proving that embracing the Internet's role in the used car-buying process is a key ingredient for a dealership's success. All too often, though, dealers and used vehicle managers bemoan or resent the fact that the Internet is now forcing them to run their stores in a more transparent, customer-friendly and price-conscious manner.

WHY THE INTERNET IS SO POWERFUL AND DISRUPTIVE

It's pretty amazing to think, in 2009, that a 10-year-old company, *Google*, and a roughly 15-year-old phenomenon, the Internet, have become such powerful forces in a business that, for the most part, hasn't changed much in nearly 100 years.

The reason the Internet has become such a transformative force in our business is because it has leveled the playing fields between dealers and consumers. It has also opened the door to a wealth of new opportunity.

"The Internet is the same everywhere," says Pearson. For him, this means his competition is not the dealer down the street. He sets his mark on other online used vehicle retailers such as Texas Direct, Missouri City, Tex. He estimates nearly half of the 300 units he sells a month go to customers outside of a 75-mile circle from his dealership.

I like to say the Internet has dealt dealers and managers two hands:

> **The bad hand:** This is the one that forces dealers and managers to adopt new ways of pricing and presenting their vehicles that they've not had to consider before. It's the same hand that means a re-set in your sales processes to acknowledge the fact that today's online customers may often know more about an individual vehicle, and comparable alternatives at other stores, than your salespeople.

> **The good hand:** This is the hand Pearson has chosen to play. The Internet provides a steady stream of customers who gather on websites like *AutoTrader.com, Cars.com,* and to some extent, dealers' own websites, looking for vehicles. As Pearson and other dealers have learned, if your price, vehicle, and process are "right" for these customers, getting them to buy is almost a foregone conclusion.

"We don't get people looking to shop for cars online," Pearson says. "They are online to buy a particular car." And when they get to the store, "there's very little or no negotiation. We've already shown them our value online."

This is a striking change for retailing veterans like Clay Close at Atchison Automotive. He came up in the business as a gifted "closer." Now, much of the "closing" happens online. "I sold a guy a Yukon XL the other day. He didn't want a phone call. He wanted to handle the deal while he was at work through email and be done with it. This story happens over and over," Close says.

Given these dynamics, demonstrating online value for today's Internet consumers is absolutely critical to gaining their attention. The Internet is the gateway that determines whether a customer will choose to contact your store or just show up to inquire about a used vehicle.

To make matters more challenging, all this shopping occurs without you knowing it, aside from after-the-fact indicator metrics like detailed page views and search results placements (assuming one knows what those mean and pays attention to them). In this environment, transparency is the order of the day, as is a customer-focused transaction process.

"A lot of dealers think if they're on the Internet, they're in the game," says Chip Perry at *AutoTrader. com.* "That's simply not true."

So what are the factors that drive interest in your store and put new pressures on traditional used vehicle management practices?

Here's a broad, quick look at three critical factors that address why the Internet has been a disruptive force for many traditional dealerships. We'll address these and other factors in more detail in the upcoming chapters:

> **Factor 1: Your Vehicles:** Just as it's always been, the "right" vehicle will find a customer. But there are two key differences in today's Internet-driven marketplace that make stocking the correct inventory a more challenging arena for dealers and used vehicle managers.

First, what you've long considered "right" for your store is not always "right" for your market. When Elmer and I ran our family's used vehicle department, roughly 80 percent of our vehicles were Cadillacs. We believed customers would intuitively shop us for used Cadillacs given the strong appeal of our franchise brand.

While that's still true, it's far less of a motivator for today's buyers. Their loyalties to specific brands have eroded, while their loyalties to finding a vehicle that fits their budget and lifestyle have cemented.

In response, dealers like Pearson are using live market data to show them what vehicles may be "right" for their stores and potential customers—and have the best shot at selling quickly.

At Finish Line, Pearson studied market data that showed untapped demand for luxury vehicles, including Mercedes-Benz, Lexus, and even Lamborghini. "We're supplying pent-up demand in Peoria," he says. "In the past, these buyers would have looked to Chicago or other areas to find these vehicles."

Make no mistake, Pearson still sells plenty of Fords amongst the 300 sales he achieves every month; but his understanding of consumer interests led him to a segment he likely would not have considered in the past.

"I never dreamed I'd sell a $30,000 Corvette," says dealer Jon Whitman of Whitman Ford, Temperance, Mich. "But I did the other day. The data told me it would sell and I was brave enough to believe it."

Based on the data I see from reviewing live market metrics, I can confidently suggest that today's Internet-enabled marketplace requires a roughly 50/50 mix of franchise to off-brand vehicles in your used vehicle inventory to gain maximum attention and traction with today's less brand-loyal customers.

If you're still in doubt about the need for a more varied mix of inventory, here's a question: Which vehicle brand today has a lock on the used car market?

The answer is none really does. There are definitely some vehicles that are hotter than the next, but no single brand commands every market corner and vehicle segment. Yet, many dealers and used vehicle managers continue to stock their used vehicle inventories as if their franchise brands actually *do* own the market.

Years ago, this made sense. But today it doesn't— not with access to market data to guide inventory stocking decisions. Think about new vehicles, for a moment. Every dealer would jump at the chance to sell as many new Toyota Prius or BMW 3 series units that they could get their hands on. But only dealers with the Toyota and BMW franchises have this opportunity and blessing. Every other dealer is locked out of the action. Except on *used* Toyotas and BMWs. There's nothing stopping any dealer or used vehicle manager from stocking these brands, or any other brand, that the market deems a hot seller.

I believe it is far better for dealerships to position their used vehicle inventories to maximize their ability to attract all customers, irrespective of brand. The key is paying attention to the available market data and adjusting used vehicle inventories to reflect market demand for specific makes and models.

That's been an eye-opening change for dealers like Pearson and Whitman. Because they had the courage to make this shift, they are now enjoying the benefits of additional sales volumes and profits at the expense of their more franchise-focused competitors.

Factor 2: Your Pricing: Before we discuss online pricing dynamics, I need to clear up a misconception that I still hear among dealers and used vehicle managers—a perspective that owes more to yesterday's philosophy for setting used vehicle prices than the realities of today's buyers.

You do not have to be the lowest-priced dealer on every unit to attract customers and achieve your profit expectations.

There it is. I've said it. For dealers and used vehicle managers who believe the Internet is simply a game of low-price leaders and too-low gross profits, I must implore you to "take the road to Damascus and have a Saul-like moment." [2]

---

[2] *The Holy Bible,* "The Book of Acts," Chapter 9, v. 3-9

The idea that the Internet is solely a place for low-price vehicles misses the fact that *all buyers* use the Web to shop. These buyers care about price, and there is a correlation between the price you set and the attention you'll get from online buyers.

But these dynamics do not mean a race to the bottom to find the lowest-price vehicles. The key in an Internet-driven marketplace is to make sure your pricing is competitive and, if it's above market averages, to ensure your vehicles tell a story that merits your asking price.

One of the key problems here is that many dealers and used vehicle managers still use the "mark up from cost" approach to pricing their used vehicle inventory that Elmer and I followed at my family's Cadillac store.

In today's marketplace, this is a pricing strategy that's problematic. Let's examine why.

First, when consumers search for vehicles, they're typically using a third-party site like *AutoTrader.com* or *Cars.com* to view a broad selection of units and prices. Each of these platforms allows customers to sort from lowest to highest to create a price pecking order.

Guess what this means if your vehicle has the highest price as a result of your reflexive, mark-up-from-cost approach to pricing? I can't emphatically predict you'll be out of the running as the consumer shops and selects, but it's fair to say you'll get far less attention than that vehicle may well deserve.

Second, and perhaps most important, is the fact that a mark-up-from-cost pricing approach is based on a faulty presumption that how much you paid for a vehicle has any bearing on what a customer should pay. The fact is, consumers don't care, nor should they, how much you paid for a vehicle. What they care about is how much it will cost them to own it.

"What you paid for a vehicle is important, but with the Internet, it's more important to know potential selling price and the vehicle's likelihood to sell at that price," Pearson says. "From there, you can figure out what kind of gross profit and time in inventory you can expect."

I recognize this is a 180-degree shift in thinking for many dealers and used vehicle managers. So let's drill into why our industry's traditional mark-up-from-cost approach is a problem for today's Internet-driven marketplace.

For example, in the summer of 2009, the wholesale marketplace was on fire. More dealers than ever were in the used vehicle game and the collective demand was pushing up wholesale values.

Let's say a used vehicle manager acquired a three-year-old Honda Accord for $10,000 at auction. The price, the manager knows, is inflated because he and other buyers were bidding strong to own it. (I call this type of "irrational exuberance"[3] a herd mentality—a dangerous auction dynamic.)

The manager brings the vehicle to the store and adds a $3,500 mark-up to set a $13,500 asking price. The goal here is a gross profit of $3,500 if the store can get it, or something around $2,000 after negotiation.

So far, so good—except that all the other similar model year Honda Accords are listed in this used vehicle manager's marketplace for $11,500.

In this scenario, the Accord at $13,500 probably won't get much online attention because it's priced at 117 percent of market—in other words, it is listed at a 17% premium to the average price of identically equipped vehicles in the market. What's more, the store's used vehicle manager probably knew he'd paid too much at auction, but had no choice: The store needs inventory to keep sales moving.

The problem, however, is that the $3,500 mark-up from cost means the store is effectively asking a potential buyer to cover the cost of an acquisition

---

[3] *Irrational Exuberance*, Robert Shiller, http://www.irrationalexuberance.com/definition.htm

mistake. (In the old days, that might have worked, but today's customers know a whole lot more about the going rate for vehicles.) I would suggest that this vehicle is destined to become a problem and, potentially, a wholesale loss for this store.

Now, let's flip the exercise. Say the used vehicle manager got really lucky and stole a three-year-old Honda Accord on a trade-in for $7,500. What are the chances the manager would add a $3,500 mark-up-from-cost and price the vehicle at $11,000?

Pretty minimal, I would suggest.

Instead, I'll bet the manager would have an instinctive feel that an asking price of $11,000 is better than the market and set an asking price of $12,500. Why? Because the manager is aiming for a hefty "four-pounder" gross profit and expecting it might end up around $3,000. Here again, a perfectly good vehicle may end up becoming an aged unit because the mark-up did not reflect the market's average asking price.

By contrast, here's what I believe velocity-minded dealers like Pearson, Close, and Chalfant would do: They'd take the vehicle they "stole," and set an asking price at or near the $11,500 average for similar Accords. They might even beat the market average because they're in the vehicle so "right" to begin with.

Either way, I'd bet these dealers would sell the unit much faster than the used vehicle manager who set a too-high asking price and they'd then be able to put another used Accord in their inventory and repeat the cycle. At Pearson's store, where the average days in inventory runs about 25 days, he'd likely sell two used Accords while the traditional used vehicle manager is still trying to sell the one unit he acquired for a song.

Now, don't get me wrong. I'm not suggesting dealers and used vehicle managers should not exercise their right to achieve maximum gross profits. I'm simply trying to point out that the "old school way" of marking up vehicles from cost carries a greater risk for your store than a more market-attuned approach to pricing.

As Pearson says, "you've got to pick your spots to play."

> **Factor 3: Your Presentation:** I noted above that much of the online action for used vehicle buyers occurs on third-party listing sites like *AutoTrader.com* and *Cars.com*.

So, if a consumer searches for a 2007 Honda Accord, each site will list those units from dealers who've got them. We've noted how, if a dealer's asking price is out of line with market expectations, consumers will likely scroll right past a listing, unless a dealer or used vehicle manager makes it abundantly clear why the vehicle should command bigger dollars.

Similarly, the dealers and used vehicle managers who offer '07 Accords at competitive prices also must make sure that their presentation of this vehicle online—from photos to detailed descriptions—offers a compelling reason for an online shopper to take a closer look.

The key: The challenge for today's used vehicle retailers becomes how to present vehicles online in a manner that distinguishes and differentiates them from competitors when these units appear as one of many on a shopper's computer screen.

"Dealers have their physical showroom and their virtual showroom," says Perry at *AutoTrader.com*. **"Pictures and vehicle descriptions are critically** important. We still see dealers taking shortcuts."

Pearson goes a step further. "You can't miss on anything—whether it's price, pictures, mileage, video, equipment," he says. "I pay extremely close attention to how our vehicles look online. We're always trying to improve our online presentation."

Pearson and other velocity dealers recognize that effective online presentation and merchandising of vehicles requires a great deal of time and special skills. Each of them has tapped support from others at their store to get the job done right.

At many stores, however, the used vehicle manager ends up with the responsibility for handling the online presentation—on top of other responsibilities like managing inventory, taking TOs, and desking deals. I would submit that this amounts to an overload of responsibility on one person, making everything this individual does less effective overall.

"Everyone's pressed for time," says *Cars.com* president Mitch Golub, who acknowledges compelling presentation is essential for online used vehicle retailing success. "The question is how to reinvent how the work gets allocated and investing the time and energy into doing it right."

Two Key Internet Blessings

If nothing else, I hope this chapter's review of the Internet's role in used vehicle retailing success gets dealers and managers thinking hard about how they should adjust their inventory management, pricing, and merchandising approaches to better fit the expectations and needs of today's consumers.

Before we move into discussing another disruptive factor for today's dealers and used vehicle managers in the next chapter, I'd like to share a little more on the "good hand" the Internet has dealt our industry.

I mentioned above that the Internet makes it much more cost-effective and easy for dealers and used vehicle managers to connect with customers. They are, after all, using the Internet to find and make choices for the used vehicles they intend to purchase.

Beyond that, however, the Internet has also provided a window that makes possible the kind of velocity-based management metrics that dealers like Pearson, Chalfant, and Close use.

For example, my company, vAuto, Inc., uses proprietary technology to search the Internet for data on vehicle sales rates, retail asking prices, and other data that help dealers manage their online presentation and inventory decisions more effectively. This is competitive market intelligence that would not exist without the Internet.

Likewise, activity on the Internet is infinitely measurable. That means dealers who use vendors like *AutoTrader.com* and *Cars.com* have ready access to metrics that detail their online merchandising effectiveness. I've added another layer to these metrics, using the experiences of vAuto's clients to develop benchmarks for what success means in terms of the amount of time and attention consumers give to an individual dealer's online inventory.

For a dealer like Pearson, the blessings the Internet offers in terms of access to customers and measurable results, plus his adoption of velocity-based used vehicle management practices, have given him a renewed lease on his auto retailing career.

"I was truly debating getting out of the business," says Pearson, who had purchased Finish Line with respected Peoria dealer Jeff Green in 2006. For two years, he struggled. "It was brain damage," he says. "We weren't having any fun and we weren't making any money."

Now, Pearson has a different management dilemma: how to feed and manage what has become a net-profit generating machine. For him, it means weekly trips traversing the country to source vehicles to maintain his inventory supply and turn rates.

"The question is how far we can take this?" he says. "It definitely takes intestinal fortitude to jump in."

HELLO,
MR. EFFICIENT MARKET

In the fall of 2008, like many dealers, Dan Sunderland realized he had a problem with used vehicles.

He had opened a new Mercedes-Benz store the past June for his four-franchise dealership Sun Motor Cars in Mechanicsburg, Pa. By autumn, following big spikes in gas prices and the grip of a recession, Sunderland and his used vehicle manager, Steve Barnes, realized they were losing ground.

"We were having trouble turning our cars," Sunderland says. "We began to have problems with aging vehicles and wholesale losses."

Barnes estimates the store's inventory water neared $200,000 with gross profits on the units they sold only averaging about $2,400—much less than the $3,500 PVR they'd been accustomed to in prior years.

A few states west, dealer Keith Kocourek faced similar problems at his Wausau, Wis. store. "September 2008 through December 2008 were the worst four sales months we've had in our history," Kocourek says. "Our wholesale losses were north of $200,000." As he evaluated his inventory, he found nearly half of his vehicles were older than 60 days—a symptom of holding out for buyers who just were there.

Germain Motor Company in Columbus, Ohio tells a similar story. Six-figure wholesale losses combined with slowing sales spurred the dealer group to look for a new process to help address their persistent used vehicle problems, according to John Malishenko, director of operations for the nine-store dealer group.

"There was an urgent need to change the way we were doing things," Malishenko says. "What we had done historically wasn't working anymore.

"We had a static strategy in an erratic marketplace," he explains. "With a velocity mindset, we now have a dynamic strategy that changes with the market— whether it's the vehicles we buy, the reconditioning we do, or the prices we set."

Wow. Thank you, John! He hit the nail on the head.

The reason used vehicle management troubles persist is because there are dealers that continue to operate with a match-up that doesn't work. They are fighting a volatile market without the philosophy, technology, and processes that enable them to respond to rapid change. It's like "rope-a-dope" with an opponent who never tires.[4] No wonder dealers and used vehicle managers are frustrated by a lack of results.

I believe that a velocity-based approach to managing used vehicles offers a solution that, as Malishenko says, moves with market conditions. If the market goes suddenly south, dealers and used vehicle managers who follow velocity metrics and principles will inevitably see the signs of trouble sooner and be able to respond more quickly than those who continue to rely on traditional management best practices.

"It's working for us," says Malishenko, who notes wholesale losses have been cut by $340,000

---

[4] Muhammad Ali,
http://en.wikipedia.org/wiki/Rope-a-dope

and volumes are surpassing store records set in 2007. "In the middle of a recession and the worst economy in years, we're selling a record number of used vehicles."

I also believe that the volatile market conditions that emerged in 2008 and 2009 are the final signs of a transformation of the used vehicle marketplace from one that's traditionally been highly inefficient to one that grows more efficient with each passing day. The Internet plays a starring role in this transformation, with supporting roles going to the sagging economy, gas price swings, factory closures, and lender belt-tightening.

AN EFFICIENT MARKET MEETS INEFFICIENT PROCESSES

Economists describe a market as "efficient" when there is roughly equal knowledge between buyers and sellers of choices and alternatives and, as a result, the prices are governed largely by supply, demand, and price sensitivity.

Let's break this down a bit.

> *Is there equal knowledge between buyers and sellers in today's used vehicle marketplace?* In the last chapter, we discussed how the Internet is the "great equalizer" that arms consumers with more information about vehicle

prices, equipment/trim levels, owner histories, wholesale values, and dealers' reputations than they've ever had before. It's not uncommon for customers to bring printouts of competing vehicles when they come to stores—just to let dealers and used vehicle managers know they've got a bead on the market. So, to answer the question, while the knowledge may not be 100 percent equal, it's enough to alter the dynamics of traditional deal-making. Likewise, whatever knowledge gap may exist is shrinking on a daily basis.

Are used vehicles commodities? I get this question a lot when I talk about efficient markets with dealers and used vehicle managers. In their view, it's impossible for a vehicle to be a commodity since "every vehicle is unique." My view is more nuanced: Every vehicle definitely has an individual value story. But there's little that's unique about an '07 Honda Accord when a consumer can readily find dozens of comparable vehicles with similar colors and equipment/trim packages at the click of a mouse. In this sense, used vehicles are commodities, and I believe they should be managed and retailed with the same mindset as those who work in a commodities market—that is, with a key understanding of market data and dynamics so as to effectively and efficiently mitigate risks to investment returns.

Is the price of today's used vehicles determined by supply, demand, and price sensitivity? The answer to this question, in my view, is an unequivocal "yes." What happened to dealers Sunderland, Kocourek, and Malishenko in late 2008? Their problems in used vehicles were a direct result of higher gas prices and less interest among financially troubled consumers to purchase vehicles. In turn, these more circumspect consumers were less likely to buy vehicles that bore traditional mark-ups to achieve gross profit expectations at dealerships. The end result was widespread difficulty at dealerships with aging vehicles and wholesale losses.

"We'd spend $1,500 on a car to recondition it, put it on the lot and price it to make $4,000," Malishenko says. "We'd sit there and wait for someone to come in. The car would get 90 days old and, because we'd spent money on reconditioning and knew we'd get killed at the auction block, we kept it another 30 days."

This traditional approach to managing used vehicles is out of step with today's efficient market. By definition, "waiting for a buyer" is an inefficient way to retail a vehicle. It's a far more dangerous and speculative bet than using a velocity-based approach that ties acquisition, pricing, retailing, and wholesaling decisions to real market data.

"We run our department now based on a calculation of where each vehicle stands in our market," Kocourek says. "It's just logic. There's no guesses, hope, or wishful thinking."

As a result of this more efficient velocity-based approach, Malishenko and his team have achieved their own efficiencies: They invest $6 million less in inventory; turn their vehicles two to three times faster; experience far fewer wholesale losses; and enjoy increasing sales volumes.

"Between the reduction in wholesale losses, the efficiencies of cash we've freed up, our improved sales volumes, and the positive impact on service and F&I, it's a no-brainer," he says.

As I talk with dealers and managers about efficient markets and why I believe today's used vehicle marketplace is increasingly efficient, I note that the concept of an efficient market should not be unfamiliar.

In fact, as I make the case for a velocity-minded approach to managing used vehicle inventories, I'm in many ways suggesting that dealers apply some of the same principles to managing their used inventories as they do with their new vehicle inventories.

On any given day, dealerships follow principles of supply, demand, and price sensitivity when they order new vehicles from factories. To varying degrees, dealers recognize their new vehicles are essentially commodities sold by themselves and competitors.

Dealers base new vehicle ordering decisions on market data from factories and other sources that provide a read on supply and demand projections for sales volumes. It's also true that dealers say "no" to factory reps every day when they get pressure to take additional inventory that, instinctively or empirically, they know will not sell well in their market.

For the most part, these inventory decisions are unemotional. They are calculations based on using the best available data and marketplace dynamics of supply and demand.

Likewise, pricing decisions on new vehicles typically follow market realities. If a new vehicle is "hot," dealers are more likely to sell at or near MSRP, particularly if the supply of these vehicles is scarce. The converse is also true for vehicles with high supply and less demand. These units are far less likely to command MSRP.

Part of the reason for more market-attuned pricing on new vehicles flows from dealers understanding that prospective buyers have equal knowledge about invoice pricing and retail asking prices, as well as incentives. Today's consumers can easily access this data and shop to find the dealership that offers what they believe is the best deal.

It's fair to say that most dealerships at least initially organized their Internet departments and business development centers around prospective new vehicle buyers in recognition of the more efficient nature of this marketplace.

To me, it's ironic that while new vehicle departments operate with an understanding of marketplace efficiencies, this thinking has been largely absent in used vehicle departments. The signs of this dichotomy are readily apparent:

- Used vehicle inventories typically skew toward a franchised brand, rather than account for supply and demand for off-brand vehicles that could prove to be good sellers. In essence, used vehicle managers continue to "go with what they know."

- Pricing decisions reflect what a store paid for a vehicle rather than an assessment of the going market rate for a vehicle.

- Acquisition and wholesale decisions often reflect the biases and emotions of the used vehicle manager who's in charge of making them. Given that it is assumed that a "good used vehicle manager" typically represents someone who "knows" used vehicles, there's deference given to this knowledge, whether it's warranted or not. A decision to "retail out of a problem" owes more to this up-front emotional investment than any firm gauge on whether the market will reward that decision.

When I highlight the contrast in management philosophies between new and used vehicles, many dealers and used vehicle managers start to see why they continue to struggle. They recognize that they're battling an efficient market with inefficient management practices. Some take this realization further, and commit themselves to operating in a way that's more agile and attuned to today's faster-moving and more efficient used vehicle marketplace.

STANDSTILL SPECULATION VERSUS ROI-MINDED RETAILING

For much of the past three years, I've had the privilege of working with one of our country's finest dealer groups, a group that has been an industry innovator, sales leader, and household name for years.

On a recent visit to the group's main store, I sat with the used vehicle manager and other top executives to examine why the store's used vehicle volumes have dropped by about 50 percent and why, after months of effort, they still hadn't been able to move the sales needle.

On the surface, the dynamics at this store are the same as many dealerships across the country—even with the store's enviable West Coast location and reputation: New sales had dropped for the store's domestic franchise brand, sapping trade-ins that normally fueled the used vehicle department. Likewise, the store had trouble finding vehicles it could purchase at auction, given an upward swing in wholesale values due to greater competition among buyers in the auction lanes.

But a deeper examination revealed other problems that, when taken together, amounted to a standstill in their used vehicle department.

- The store still emphasized its franchise brand, with 80 percent of its used inventory reflecting the nameplate. As we reviewed marketplace dynamics, the store had virtually none of the off-brand highline models that were selling like hotcakes, nor did it stock enough off-brand, "plain Jane" units that, while not as exciting as sports cars and other snazzy units the store preferred to stock, were selling at faster rates.

- The store's average days in inventory ran well above 100 days. Its retail asking prices were, on average, 10 percent above the market if not more. Both of these, I learned, were symptomatic of a dealership goal of generating $3,000 gross profit per unit.

- The store did not show any wholesale losses on the books. I was mystified, although a deeper discussion revealed that "packs" and "moving money around" likely masked the true wholesale loss picture.

- The store had not taken any steps to acquire inventory beyond a local auction or two— despite acknowledging that more aggressive sourcing was likely needed.

As I discussed these dynamics, it became clear that the dealership's desire to achieve its gross profit goal on every vehicle was undermining its ability to become a more efficient and market-attuned used vehicle retailer. In addition, the management practices that masked the true costs of their inefficient processes also inhibited the store's ability to transform to a new used vehicle management model.

So while this store stands still, here's what's happening in the fast-moving, more efficient marketplace that surrounds it:

Wholesale Value Volatility: At the time of writing, the wholesale values of used vehicles are increasing, not falling as they had been the previous year. Manheim Consulting says the reversal is the result of a drop-off in new vehicle

sales, diminished supplies of used vehicles
at auctions, and greater demand for vehicles
from wholesale buyers (essentially the dealers
and used vehicle managers who've made used
vehicles a priority in the past 12 months).[5]

*"I used to look at inventory age reports
once a month and now I look at them daily,"
says Steve Barnes at Sun Motor Cars. "In
the past, I didn't re-price some vehicles from
the day I bought them until I sold them.
Now I evaluate where a car stands in the
marketplace and re-price at day 10, day
15 or wherever I need to. This stuff didn't
happen before. Now we focus on it daily."*

Lender Volatility: The rise in wholesale vehicle
values is contributing to a pincer-like effect on
deal-making at dealerships. Lenders, who are
retrenching from losses and recalculating risk,
are less likely to pay as much advance on deals,
and they're far less likely to absorb any negative
equity than they did in deals just a few years
ago. This dynamic, which I view as another sign
of marketplace volatility, means dealers and
used vehicle managers must be attuned to the
vehicles and customer credit profiles that can
and will get the ultimate OK from lenders.

---

[5] Manheim Consulting, http://www.manheimconsulting.com/
Used_Vehicle_Value_Index/Current_Monthly_Index.html

"We have our list of vehicles that we know will give us the best shot with lenders and F&I product penetration," says the GM for a South Carolina store that's adopted velocity management principles. "It's typically fast-moving stuff like '08 Impalas and Ford 500s."

> **Consumer Volatility:** As noted above, today's consumers are more circumspect than in the past about spending money on big purchases like used vehicles. What's more, their interest in buying is more erratic: If gas prices are going up, they move toward fuel-efficient vehicles. If gas prices stabilize, the market for SUVs and trucks picks up.

These market nuances are lost on traditional dealers and used vehicle managers like my West Coast dealer friend who effectively stocks and sells what he knows instead of determining the vehicle segments where demand bubbles are building and breaking.

"With a static strategy in a dynamic market, you might get lucky and find that your strategy meshes with the market," Malishenko says. "More often than not, though, you're missing opportunities."

The key take-away: An efficient market, with its innate volatility, creates risk for dealers and used vehicle managers. The longer a vehicle stays in a store's inventory, the greater the chance that wholesale value changes, shifts in consumer preferences, and other factors will impede a vehicle's ability to sell and produce an acceptable ROI. Likewise, the longer a vehicle remains in inventory, the longer a dealer's investment is tied up in a unit that may be a less effective retailing proposition than another.

Meanwhile, a velocity-based approach to managing used vehicle operations by its "from money to metal, money to metal" nature, reduces risk by enabling dealers and used vehicle managers to efficiently track marketplace dynamics and sell vehicles in a shorter time to minimize exposure to the market's volatility.

"There's no going back to the way we used to do things," says Sunderland at Sun Motor Cars.

AN INTRODUCTION TO VELOCITY METRICS

As the guy who oversees used vehicle operations at Irwin Motors in Laconia, New Hampshire, Chris Irwin isn't what you might consider a typical used car guy.

He's 25, with only minimal experience in a dealership, much less a used vehicle department. He doesn't go to auctions. He doesn't appraise vehicles. He's not on the front line.

Yet Irwin has managed to achieve results in his used vehicle department that guys twice his age, with 15 times more experience, have not been able to accomplish.

Irwin's store is cranking through its inventory. The store sells about 70 units a month out of a 60-vehicle inventory. He's on a trajectory to turn this nearly $800,000 inventory investment 15 times this year, generating an estimated $200,000 return every time it flips. He's freed up cash for the store. He's making his F&I and service teams happy. He has plans to grow his sales volume and inventory investment.

"We've got a first-class problem now," says Irwin, the store's vice president who also oversees F&I, service, and parts departments. "We're selling our vehicles faster than we can replace them."

So goes the power of a live market, velocity-minded approach to managing used vehicle operations. It can help someone like Irwin who, by traditional standards, lacks the experience necessary for success in used vehicles.

The key to his success is his commitment to a velocity-based management philosophy and a near-religious devotion to the market-based metrics that make it hum. These metrics give Irwin the real-time market information he needs to make informed decisions about what to stock, what to pay, how to price, and how to adjust his inventory to meet market conditions.

To be sure, Irwin's not in it alone, nor are the metrics the sole reason for his success. He leads a team of players who possess the traditional paint expertise and the skills to complement his knack for understanding metrics-based data. This group handles the tasks of acquiring, merchandising, and reconditioning vehicles. Collectively, they've created and maintained a velocity-focused process that has the results to prove it's working.

"We had the same mentality that's typical of most stores—we were trying to hit a home run by getting lucky by having somebody stumble into a vehicle on our lot," he says.

With the market turmoil of late 2008 and 2009, Irwin took it on the chin as they retailed their way out of a watered-down inventory. He knew there was a better way. He launched the velocity-based approach to address the persistent issues they encountered with traditional management practices and went after the huge opportunity Irwin believed the store could achieve in used vehicles.

Now, Irwin's team has sourcing and stocking issues—and less concern about any damage caused by fast-moving swings in the market.

"When you take into account market supply and demand, and price yourself aggressively to the market, you're essentially hedging yourself against gasoline and vehicle price fluctuations," he says. "You're able to react very quickly. You're nimble. You don't get stuck with something that you don't own right and can't get out from under. Even when you have market volatility, you can remain very profitable."

The turnaround success Irwin has achieved is a story that's similar to the experiences of other stores where leaders and managers have adopted a velocity-based approach to managing used vehicle operations.

The foundation for this approach lies in three key paint-oriented metrics that effectively replace, but do not eliminate, the traditional barometers dealers and used vehicle managers have relied on to manage their used vehicle departments. The metrics offer a more reliable gauge for the dynamism and volatility of today's efficient used vehicle marketplace, and they do a better job of helping dealers and used vehicle managers like Irwin mitigate the risks this new marketplace poses for their inventory investments.

Jack Anderson, the director of used vehicle operations for Buffalo, N.Y.- based West Herr Automotive Group credits velocity-based metrics for helping his stores achieve 20 percent growth in used vehicle volumes (about 1,000 units/month) in the past year.

So far in 2009, Anderson's stores have sold more than 400 Dodge Avengers, based on his read of market supply and demand and pricing metrics for the units that showed them as financing-favorable "switch" cars other dealers might overlook. He started with a mass buy of 150 units, and has since kept them rolling through his inventory.

"Other dealers call me to get them," he says. "We're not afraid to take a chance if we know we can absorb the risk."

As dealerships adopt market-attuned metrics, the time-honored measures, such as PVR, a vehicle's average time in inventory, negative equity, 45- or 60-day turn policy performance and the like, remain important. But I would submit the new metrics should take priority[6].

In the next three chapters, we'll discuss these new, velocity-style metrics that address the paint side of our business in great detail—Market Days Supply, Price to Market, and Cost to Market. We'll define how they came about, what they mean, and how they play out in day-to-day used vehicle management decisions for guys like Irwin and others who use them to drive success.

---

[6] A disclosure: I've developed these metrics in tandem with my team at vAuto. So, I have a vested interest. But I believe the success of velocity-focused dealers is a testament to the efficacy of these metrics as operational benchmarks for any dealer or used vehicle manager.

After we've established these new benchmarks for the paint side of used vehicle management, we'll address another set of essential metrics. These metrics give dealers and used vehicle managers the management insights and intelligence they need to be efficient, competitive, and profitable players with their online merchandising, or the "pixel" side of today's business.

"PAINT" METRIC 1: MARKET DAYS SUPPLY

Chris Irwin pays close attention to the Market Days Supply of his inventory for a couple of reasons.

It gives him a key read on the vehicles that will sell well in his market. And it works. He's selling vehicles as fast as he can find them.

The Market Days Supply metric will also be Irwin's guide to take his used vehicle operations to the next level.

"We want to crank this up," he says. "We can stock more of the right units that are selling in our market and ultimately sell more of them."

The definition of Market Days Supply is straight-forward. It is the current available supply of a given vehicle in a market divided by the average retail sales rate for the vehicle over the past 45 days.

So, if there were 10 vehicles of the same year, make, model, trim, and identical equipment in a market-place, and they had sold at the retail rate of one per day during the past 45 days, the car would have a market days supply of 10.

The Market Days Supply metric flows from track-ing used vehicle supplies and sales rates across the country and in each market through the use of sophisticated technology. This data-driven market intelligence allows managers to compare the units they might buy or own against the identically equipped, competing vehicles in their market areas.

When dealerships know the Market Days Supply when appraising or trading for a '07 Volkswagen Jetta, they will know exactly how many other identical '07 Jettas they will compete against in their market if they acquire the vehicle. The Market Days Supply metric also gives them insight as to how fast they are likely to sell the car.

This is a powerful metric to aid stocking decisions at any dealership. It enables dealership personnel to fine tune their inventory by stocking a greater share of vehicles that have high demand and low supply in their markets—*i.e.*, those units with a low Market Days Supply.

Conversely, it helps them avoid going too heavy with high supply and low demand inventory—*i.e*, vehicles with a high Market Days Supply.

Market Days Supply provides a window into what used vehicle shoppers want in any given market. It takes the gut and guesswork out of stocking decisions. Dealers and used vehicle managers no longer have to base their inventory decisions on what they *think* will sell or what they are accustomed to selling. The Market Days Supply tells them exactly what is selling in their market.

Understanding and using this metric is a critical first step for dealers who want to adopt a more market-attuned, velocity-based approach to managing their used vehicle operations.

A LOOK AT HOW MARKET
DAYS SUPPLY WORKS

The following composite offers a snapshot view of the Market Days Supply for the used vehicle inventories at three different dealerships in the same market.

The first is a velocity dealer that uses the Market Days Supply to aid in stocking decisions. The two other stores represent traditional dealers, who use prevailing industry best practices to manage their inventories.

The composite tells an interesting tale.

At first glance, which store appears best positioned, before the dealership doors open and the lights go on in the morning, to have a better day? Which store will attract more customers and potentially sell its vehicles more quickly?

The answer should be obvious: The velocity dealer has an average Market Days Supply for its inventory that's less than half that of its closest traditional competitor, regardless of how long those vehicles have been in each dealer's inventory.

This take-away raises several questions. What does the velocity dealer know that the other stores don't? Why does the velocity dealer's inventory possess the winning product characteristics any retailer would

Days in Inventory	Key Metric	Velocity Dealer	Traditional Dealer #1	Traditional Dealer #2
1-30	Market Days Supply	32	67	114
31-60	Market Days Supply	34	73	104
61-90	Market Days Supply	–	76	87

want—high demand and low supply—while the traditional stores seem to have a knack for stocking vehicles that are perhaps more familiar, but that the market is less interested in buying? Why is the concept of a used car Market Days Supply seldom utilized?

Let's address these one at a time:

Question 1: What does the velocity dealer know that the other stores don't?

For starters, he or she knows the Market Days Supply metric exists and uses it.

The metric would not have been possible without the advent and advancement of the Internet and related technology that allows real-time reads of vehicles available in a market, and the aggregation and normalization of sales data down to specific trim and equipment levels and factory certifications on individual vehicles in any market.

The upshot here is that no dealer or used vehicle manager should feel they've been asleep at the switch. This is new stuff. Market Days Supply and other critical "paint" metrics strike me as the guideposts for a better way to go about making used vehicle management decisions than the methods our industry has used for years.

Question 2: Why does the velocity dealer's inventory posses the winning product characteristics any retailer would want—high demand and low supply—while the traditional stores seem to have a knack for stocking vehicles that are perhaps more familiar, but that the market is less interested in buying?

The answer to this question has several facets—all of which largely owe to the way dealers and used vehicle managers have traditionally thought about what used vehicles to stock at their stores.

John Malishenko understands what it's like to see an inventory with Market Days Supply metrics like those of the traditional dealers in the composite. It's a snapshot that isn't much different than how inventories looked at Germain stores before they switched over to a velocity-based approach to management.

"The vehicles we typically bought were, in most cases, the make of our new car franchise," Malishenko says. "That's what we thought we should sell. That's what everybody did."

This skew toward franchise brands is a key reason the Market Days Supply at these traditional stores is out of line. In essence, dealers have long gone with what they know, rather than what has the best shot of selling in a marketplace.

I did a study of used vehicle inventory make-ups at different dealerships across the country. On average, most franchised dealerships stock 70 percent of their used vehicle inventory with units that represent their franchised brand.

Based on what I've seen from studying market dynamics across the country, I suggest the optimal inventory mix should be 50/50 between franchise and off-brand vehicles. There are some exceptions, particularly for select brands with strong factory certified programs.

Now, there are good reasons why decision makers have developed this bias toward stocking franchise brands in used vehicle inventories. It flows from a natural desire to avoid costly mistakes. This risk aversion flows from what I call "gotcha!" moments.

Every dealer and used vehicle manager has at least one "gotcha!" moment. It happens most often with off-brand vehicles. A used vehicle manager or buyer acquires a unit that, for all intents and purposes, should be a winner. Then it tanks. Big time.

The problem? The buyer bought the right make/model but with the wrong trim and/or equipment options—a sunroof, entertainment system, navigation, or another feature that would have made the vehicle more desirable to the marketplace.

These gotcha! moments are completely understandable. They occur when a used vehicle manager or buyer steps outside what's familiar and dabbles in off-brand vehicles.

The immediate consequence of such gotcha! moments is also understandable; the used vehicle manager and buyer don't want to make another costly mistake and, in turn, they shy away from purchasing off-brand vehicles. This mentality contributes to the average franchised dealership's used vehicle inventory skewing 70 to 80 percent toward franchised brands. And it means far too many dealerships are not exploiting opportunities outside their franchised brands.

For dealerships that believe they should stock their used vehicle inventories with their franchise brand more heavily than off-brand vehicles I would offer the following observations that I've gleaned from studying the dynamics of dealership market areas across the country:

Observation 1: <u>No franchise brand has a monopoly on all the hot used vehicle sellers in a market.</u> Ever walk an independent used vehicle dealer's lot? If the operator is successful, it's likely the inventory includes a wide array of makes and models, and it isn't likely to lean too heavily toward any particular brand. This mix is the independent dealership's best guess at what's likely to sell. It may not be the right mix for the market, but there's a fairly strong chance that the mix is better positioned, given its variety, to appeal to a wider array of buyers than a franchised store that sticks mainly to its franchised brand in used vehicles.

Why this difference between independent and franchised dealer inventories? It's because the independent lacks the blessings and the baggage of a franchised brand. This dealer isn't beholden to factory certified pre-owned programs nor a trade-in supply that might not reflect the best-selling vehicles for a market. Likewise, the concepts of "core inventory" that have sprouted alongside the franchise brand stocking bias do not burden these independent dealers.

Observation 2: <u>Today's buyers are less brand loyal.</u> As we've noted earlier, the Internet is a powerful equalizing force. It allows consumers the opportunity to compare similar used vehicles as they shop. They may have a preference for a given brand, but the ubiquity and availability of all buying options online works to erode any degree of brand loyalty across most vehicle segments. The consequence of this marketplace reality is that customers don't consider a Ford or Infiniti store as the sole place where they can buy used vehicles that carry those brands. For dealership personnel who cling to this old belief, and stock their inventories accordingly, the outcome is often a Market Days Supply that is higher than it should be.

So what's the good news in all this?

First, managers no longer need to fear the gotcha! moments. The technology, tools, and the Market Days Supply are now available to minimize the risks of any gotcha! moments. Dealers and used vehicle managers can now identify the myriad of trim and equipment configurations that can make a difference between a winning vehicle and a loser—no matter the brand. They can make "same-same" comparisons on any vehicle.

Another "good news" item is that the Internet makes it a whole lot easier for dealers and used vehicle managers to find buyers when they model their inventory to market demand. When a store stocks the vehicles that the market craves, and

The "Core Inventory" Myth

Most dealers and used vehicle managers have heard the term "core inventory." By definition, this is the inventory that's ostensibly the "right" inventory for a given store, given its past sales history.

This concept is problematic and has a corrosive effect on a dealership's ability to build sales volume and profits in their used vehicle departments.

Why? For starters, most dealers and used vehicle managers have built their used vehicle departments around selling the makes/models that match their franchise. It's this inventory and past selling history that defines the core products they should sell.

The problem is that the store's franchised brand bias doesn't offer a true picture of what is selling in the dealership's market area. What if it's a Ford store that's historically stocked 80 percent of its lot with Blue Opal models? Would its core inventory reflect the fast-moving pre-owned Camrys that the Toyota dealer up the street is selling?

It's far better for dealers and used vehicle managers to tune their inventories to supply and demand dynamics of the market, not past performance.

Metrics like Market Days Supply can guide such market-based stocking decisions and help dealers and used vehicle managers engineer an inventory that's better suited to attract buyers and meet today's more dynamic and fluid market demand.

prices and presents them in a way that's competitive and effective, buyers will seek them out.

This provides a natural advantage for velocity-
minded dealers who use the Market Days Supply
metric to stock their inventories. They don't have to
spend as much on advertising to find buyers—the
buyers will come to them. What's more, because
these stores have the vehicles the market wants,
there's less friction and pressure in the buying process. Customers have self-selected and landed on a
dealership's vehicle because it's the one they want—
not the one a used vehicle manager or salesperson
needs to convince them to purchase.

If all this sounds almost magical, it's not. It's actually natural in an efficient market. Efficient markets
reward the retailers who are the most proficient at
identifying and taking advantage of opportunities.
It also punishes the retailers who fail to dial into
their respective markets.

Question 3: Why is the concept of a used car Market Days Supply seldom utilized?

There's an irony in the answer to this question. The
fact is, dealerships are extremely familiar with the
principles behind the Market Days Supply metric. In fact, their new vehicle inventory managers
follow them every day when they order from their
factories.

These managers use a variety of data sources, including their specialized knowledge of their own particular brand market as well as factory partners, to know what's hot and what's not. It's this knowledge that gives them negotiation strength when a factory rep pushes them to take additional orders that they know won't fare well.

Likewise, these market-informed new vehicle inventory managers know when to take everything they can get when there's high demand and low supply for a particular model. Those are the units that command MSRP and above, and allow salespeople to politely smile when a customer asks about a discount.

Now comes the twist: Dealers and used vehicle managers typically don't follow these same supply and demand insights when they manage used vehicle inventories. And who can blame them? The old ways have worked for so long.

The difference now, of course, is that today's more volatile and efficient used vehicle marketplace makes the traditional, less market-attuned approach to inventory management more problematic. The composite we just reviewed shows the advantage for stores that deploy velocity-based metrics like Market Days Supply and those that don't.

The contrast is striking. It should also serve as a wake-up call to every dealership that still follows traditional inventory management practices. Why would anyone who's invested millions in facilities and used vehicle inventory want to compete in a marketplace that punishes mistakes with anything less than the most up-to-date market information, such as Market Days Supply, to guide their decisions?

To me, the answer's a no-brainer. It's metrics like Market Days Supply that allow dealers to leverage the give-and-take power of today's more volatile and efficient used vehicle marketplace to their advantage.

It should be clear from this review of the Market Days Supply metric that becoming more attuned to the used vehicle marketplace, for any dealer or used vehicle manager, offers a better way to drive used vehicle inventory stocking decisions than the guesswork and historical brand-reflexive approaches our industry has relied on in the past.

Let's take another look at our three-store composite and ponder the question: Which store would you rather be—the one that benefits from a steady stream of customers because you've done the up-front, metric-enhanced homework to acquire vehicles your market wants, or the store that relies on traditional practices and wonders why Dealer Joe up the street is doing so well?

"PAINT" METRIC 2: PRICE TO MARKET

In writing this chapter, I was torn between being brief versus really getting into the nuts and bolts of velocity pricing. Feel free to take a quick read and come back later. As we all know, pricing is not something that we can or should take lightly.

When it comes to pricing vehicles, there are two key features of today's more efficient and volatile marketplace that many traditional dealers and used vehicle managers often misunderstand.

The first is that they are most likely underestimating the borders of their market.

For Cary Donovan, who heads used vehicle operations for the Sam Swope Auto Group, the recognition of a new market area for his dealership group arrived in unlikely places—the local car wash and Starbucks coffee shop.

"The eye-opener for me came a few years ago when I would see vehicles with temporary tags from out of state," Donovan recalls.

At a Starbucks, he saw a black Lexus GX with an Illinois tag. "I complimented the guy for having a sharp-looking vehicle and asked if he lived in Illinois. 'No,' he says. 'My wife and I live in Louisville.' Oh, I'd say and ask if he'd looked for vehicles at Louisville dealers and visit any stores? 'No,' he says. 'We went online and found what we wanted on *Chicagocarsdirect.com*.'

"The next day I was at the car wash and saw a black BMW convertible with a Georgia tag. The guy lives in Louisville and found the car he wanted from a dealer in Atlanta. He bought the car and spent the weekend with friends before driving it home," Donovan says.

"It was like an out-of-body experience for me. I thought, 'Cary, what the heck have you been thinking? These are our customers telling you that they know what they want and will go find it outside Louisville if we don't have it priced competitively.'"

Donovan's wake-up call underscores one of the key misconceptions that linger at traditional dealerships. With today's Internet-enabled buyers, the market area for a dealership is a lot bigger than the 10-square mile radius that's detailed in most factory franchise agreements. Therefore, when it comes to pricing vehicles, the competition is more regional, and sometimes national, for most franchised stores.

A second misconception held by many traditional dealers and used vehicle managers is that they can continue to use the time-honored practice of pricing vehicles by marking them up from their cost.

With today's Internet-driven used vehicle buyers, this traditional pricing practice is often dangerous. What if a used vehicle manager or buyer paid too much to acquire a vehicle? Would today's price-conscience buyers give that vehicle a look as they're clicking through online listings?

The answer is that they might eyeball the traditional dealership's higher-priced unit, but they'd likely skip past it to find a vehicle that's more competitively priced.

It seems ironic that dealers price their used inventories in this way, because they would never allow themselves to use the pricing practices of placing a standard transaction mark-up on their new vehicle inventories. If they purchased a hot new vehicle from the factory that would command a premium asking price, they would price it above the standard mark-up.

The converse is also true: If new vehicles were selling for less than invoice pricing, dealers would not mark up the unit from invoice and advertise it to the world at or near MSRP.

But this, in effect, is how dealers and used vehicle managers have long established their retail asking prices for their used vehicles.

How the Price to Market Metric Works

The Price to Market metric offers our industry's first-ever, real-time strategy to help dealers and used vehicle managers set competitive, profit-minded retail asking prices for their used vehicles.

> **Price to Market**
>
> DEFINITION:
> **How your vehicles are priced relative to other identically equipped vehicles in your market**

The Price to Market metric provides this market intelligence by comparing the average retail asking prices for identically equipped, competing vehicles in a dealer's marketplace.

Example: If a dealership has a vehicle priced at $10,000, and the average retail asking price for identically equipped, competing units is $9,500, the Price to Market is 105%. Likewise, if the price on this same vehicle is $9,000, its Price to Market is 95%.

I recognize, out of the gate, that the Price to Market metric may seem like a stretch for traditional dealers and used vehicle managers that are accustomed to marking up from cost and not considering these values.

Additionally, in the past, it's been impossible to assess how one vehicle compares against another in a market, due to the vast matrix of available trim and equipment configurations on a given make/model. Traditional dealers and used vehicle managers have also long believed that every vehicle is unique, a mindset that raises suspicion when anyone like me claims that there's a way to show detailed same-same comparisons between vehicles.

But this is where advances in technology allow more market-attuned and vehicle-specific price-setting strategies.

Today's leading technology allows the gathering of pricing information on every used vehicle in a given market area and enables a series of cross-checks against, not just VINs, but also detailed equipment descriptions to assure dealers and used vehicle managers are comparing vehicles that are, in fact, same-same. It's simply not enough to perform-apple-to-apple comparisons. Today's market requires a Granny Smith-to-Granny Smith comparison. Dealers can now see exactly what vehicles compete for consumer attention in their markets in a manner that's much more efficient than scanning newspaper ads or driving a competitor's physical or virtual lot late at night.

The Price to Market metric is another powerful part of the toolkit that velocity dealers and used vehicle managers use to increase sales volumes and profitable through-put of their used vehicle inventories—particularly when coupled with the knowledge of hot-selling vehicles that comes following the Market Days Supply metric.

So what is the right way to use the Price to Market approach to maximize both volume and profitability? The answer is not to price all vehicles high for the first 30 days nor is it to price all vehicles low out of the gate. Rather, the answer is to *know* which vehicles can and should be priced high and to be reduced slowly, and which vehicles should be priced low and reduced rapidly. In order to *know,* consider the following two tactics.

First, it's critical to know the physical qualities and appeal of the vehicle. There is still a merchandising and emotional aspect to used vehicles. This simply must be considered when determining an optimal price strategy. Second, after you know the physical qualities and appeal of the vehicle, the only relevant remaining consideration is the Market Day Supply of the vehicle at that moment.

The key advantages for velocity stores that use the Price to Market and Market Days Supply metrics in tandem include:

- The ability to know when they can price above market averages, because their vehicle stands taller than the competition and merits a higher asking price;

- The knowledge of when to re-price their unit to meet shifts in market demand and supply;

- Up-to-the-minute awareness of their vehicle's competitive positioning in the market-place—an impressive nugget that dramatically changes the nature of their sales processes and corresponding customer behaviors;

- The insights needed to adjust pricing and manage profit expectations on individual units as they age to avoid wholesale losses.

None of these advantages are available to dealers and used vehicle managers who follow traditional best practices for two reasons:

Reason 1: Yesterday's inefficient used vehicle marketplace never required this level of pricing sophistication. Decision makers would mark up vehicles from what they paid and call it good. Buyers, meanwhile, had a harder time comparing one dealership's used vehicle asking price against another. So, even if a dealer set prices above the market, customers often didn't know it. And, if they did, the dealers and used vehicle managers had negotiation-savvy salespeople to convince customers to pay the higher price.

This entire pricing dynamic falls apart in today's more efficient, volatile, and Internet-driven used vehicle marketplace. Today's online-shopping customers *know* what constitutes a competitive price and they'll pay less attention to vehicles that strike them as too high for the market.

"Nobody knew whether a car was worth $10,000, $11,000 or $12,000 unless they absolutely shopped around," says dealer Clay Close. "Now it's altogether different. All the information is out there online."

> **Reason 2:** Because traditional dealers and used vehicle managers have not had to pay much attention to pricing, thanks to yesterday's inefficient market, they simply don't.

At most stores, the initial asking price that gets placed on a vehicle typically remains the same for 30 or 45 days, sometimes longer. Meanwhile, astute velocity dealers like Chris Irwin and Cary Donovan

are making multiple prices changes every week—
sometimes daily—on the same vehicles.

Donovan says he gained an appreciation for the
necessity of these more market-attuned and frequent price changes from keeping his ear to the
ground with customers and friends in Louisville.

"It dawned on me that the Price to Market and
Market Days Supply metrics made a lot of sense
when I realized how the calls I would get from
friends who were buying vehicles had changed," he
says. "In the past, they'd call me and ask what they
should buy and pay.

"Now, when they call me, they say they're looking
at a G35, white with a tan interior and X number of miles and they think the price should be
$18,000," Donovan continues. "They're not asking
me to tell them what the market is for the vehicle,
they know the market because they've done their
homework."

I like to say the Price to Market and Market Days
Supply metrics give managers the ability to set used
vehicle prices that are reflective of their respective
markets, rather than reflexive to their acquisition
costs.

The following composite shows how powerful the
Price to Market metric, when combined with the
Market Days Supply metric, can be for a velocity

dealer in comparison to more traditional dealerships in the same market area.

Days in Inventory	Key Metric	Velocity Dealer	Traditional Dealer #1	Traditional Dealer #2
1-30	Market Days Supply	32	67	14
	Price to Market	90%	108%	105%
31-60	Market Days Supply	34	73	104
	Price to Market	85%	105%	107%
61-90	Market Days Supply	–	76	87
	Price to Market	–	105%	110%

Let's take a closer look at what's happening at each
store as their respective vehicles age:

The 1- to 30-day Bucket: As we established in
the earlier section on Market Days Supply, the
velocity dealer is more effective at stocking the
vehicles that the marketplace craves. When
combined with the Price to Market metric, this
dealership is producing the equivalent of a double whammy: It not only has more in-demand
vehicles, it's pricing them more competitively.
The 90% Price to Market ratio for the velocity
dealer means that, on average, the store is pricing a vehicle with an average retail asking price
of $10,000 at $9,000.

This is similar to the dynamic we noted in our Market Days Supply discussion wherein today's more efficient marketplace rewards velocity dealers with the blessing of more buyers seeking out their inventory and the profits that come from selling more vehicles faster. When the velocity dealer adds competitive prices to its in-demand vehicles, it's almost like it can't lose.

Meanwhile, the traditional stores are pricing their vehicles at $10,800 and $10,500. They are also creating their own double whammy, but theirs has a less-positive outcome than their velocity competition. The traditional stores are far less likely to attract buyers given they stock vehicles with less market demand, and price them higher than the marketplace's retail asking price average.

In this critical first 30 days of a used vehicle's lifecycle, when units are at their freshest and dealers and used vehicle managers stand to gain the most return on their investment, which of the three stores is best positioned to sell more vehicles and do so more quickly?

The answer once again should be obvious—the velocity dealer offers the most compelling value proposition for potential buyers in the marketplace these three stores share.

The dynamics highlighted during the first 30 days in this composite square up precisely with the kind of pricing approaches that Chris Irwin deploys at his store.

When a vehicle's hot and fresh in his inventory, he wants to be positioned in a way that makes his vehicles more competitive and compelling than his competition's vehicles. "We want to be in the top 50 percent" with our initial pricing, Irwin says. "If I want or need to, I can get more aggressive with my pricing strategy."

> **The 31- to 60-day Bucket:** This inventory age tier is a critical one for any dealership. It's in this window that vehicles will typically reach their win or lose threshold. During this stage, dealers and used vehicle managers intuitively understand that holding costs have mounted, and the potential for profit on these vehicles has diminished.

It's this intuitive understanding that leads more astute dealers and used vehicle managers to typically begin to make pricing adjustments. These pricing tweaks are intended to drum up buyer interest and remove aging units more quickly from their inventories.

The composite shows that two of the three stores understand the confluence of rising costs and diminished profit potential that occurs in this bucket. The velocity dealer has adjusted the initial Price to Market (90%) downward to 85%. Traditional Dealer #1 has also made an adjustment, from 108% to 105%.

Meanwhile, the Price to Market for Traditional Dealer #2 is heading the other direction. Why? There are two likely causes—both of which belie managers who are either less attuned to their market or flat-out asleep at the switch:

1. The dealer and used vehicle manager at Traditional Store #2 have not made any pricing adjustments from the initial, mark-up from cost approach they used. In this instance, I would bet the dealer regards his operation as a new car store and, consequently, not even the used vehicle manager is truly worried about stocking and pricing used vehicles to sell quickly.

2. Management has made some pricing adjustments but the tweaks were not significant enough to change the downward direction of the Price to Market metric for their overall inventory. For example, they may have several big-dollar vehicles that they believe will command a high price if/when they find a buyer. They haven't touched the pricing on these units, given they hold fast to the "ass for every seat" axiom.

But as they sit on these units, the efficient marketplace moves like water finding a low point. The consequence is an inventory that's even more out of line in this crucial 31- to 60-day bucket, competitively speaking, than the other competing stores and their shared market.

It's also worth examining the size of the pricing adjustment the velocity dealer makes during this make-or-break 31- to 60-day bucket.

Given the 34-day Market Days Supply metric for the velocity dealer, it's fair to say the store still has "in demand" vehicles. Ostensibly, it doesn't need to beat the market price any further than the 90% Price to Market it set during the initial 30-day bucket.

But the dealer and used vehicle manager dial in an 85% Price to Market during the 31- to 60-day bucket—a full 5 percent price drop.

Why? The dealer and used vehicle manager recognize the importance of a consistent application of velocity-based principles. That is, the vehicles in this 31- to 60-day bucket are older and their ability to deliver a return on investment has diminished.

So, the pricing adjustments reflect a belief that the store needs to rid itself of these vehicles even more quickly to make room for other units that offer a greater likelihood of selling faster and delivering a better return on investment. The result of this thinking process is a downward pricing adjustment that's almost twice as deep than its closest competitor (5 % versus 3%).

Did this velocity dealer lose some money on these units that it cleared out in the 31- to 60-day window? I would suspect that it did, but these losses will be significantly less than the losses the competing stores will take as a result of stocking vehicles that are less in demand in the market and pricing them above the competition, even as they grow longer in tooth in inventory.

"When vehicles start to age, we take the mentality like the stock market. Our first loss is our best loss," Irwin says.

Tom Kelley, CEO of Kelley Automotive, a seven-store dealer group based in Fort Wayne, Ind., who follows velocity principles to sell 400 used vehicles a month, takes a similar view. "If I'm not losing a little bit here and there, I'm not doing my job," he says. "That's the nature of an efficient market."

Some velocity dealers like Jack Anderson question whether the price reduction to move vehicles at the 60-day mark is truly a loss.

At the 60-day mark, his managers re-price inventory to rank No. 1 in their market—a move that Anderson says virtually guarantees calls and buyer interest. "You may lose money at retail, but I'm still ahead when you add in the $750 average for

F&I, the service and parts, and the opportunity for repeat/referral business. I'll retail these vehicles unless a 'loss' is thousands of dollars."

> **The 61- to 90-day Bucket:** The story here's similar to what we've already seen in the preceding inventory age buckets—with a key exception for the velocity dealer. It has no vehicles in its inventory because it priced them aggressively and got rid of them by the 60-day mark.

Contrast this move-the-iron mentality with the two traditional stores. Traditional Store #1 has made no additional pricing adjustments in this bucket. It's a "hold our ground" decision that owes, I suspect, to the earlier decision to adjust prices when vehicles were in the 31- to 60-day bucket.

The dealer and used vehicle manager at Traditional Store #2, meanwhile, still appear to be missing the boat. Maybe they're both tied up on the phone trying to arrange pick-ups from their wholesale buyers and don't have time to make pricing adjustments that might give them an increasingly diminished shot at turning a profit on their used vehicles. Whatever the case, Traditional Dealership #2 is poised to lose out even more than either of its competitors.

As we look at the composite with the Market Days Supply and Price to Market comparisons between these three stores, let's again ask: Which of these

stores is best positioned to attract customers and
sell more vehicles at a faster rate?

Fine-Tuning the Price to Market Metric

Today's technology allows dealership personnel to
massage and manage the Price to Market metric to
meet the needs of their respective businesses[7].

Chris Irwin at Irwin Motors can set his Price to
Market to achieve retail asking prices that place his
vehicles in the top 50% of his marketplace. He says
this is a starting point for most vehicles—middle
ground that balances his interest in achieving an
inventory turn and retaining a profit margin on
each unit.

For example, if there are 12 vehicles competing
against the one he owns, Irwin can set his Price to
Market metric to position the vehicle, price-wise, at
6 out of 12. Likewise, if Irwin's appraisers or buyers stretched to own a unit, he might set the metric
to position the vehicle at 4 out of 12. He does this
to account for a higher acquisition price and the

---

[7] The vAuto system allows this flexibility by rendering the
Price to Market metric through a Price Rank, which shows
how a vehicle's price stacks up against identically equipped,
competing vehicles in a dealership's self-selected market area.
Example: If a vehicle has 10 competing units, a Price Rank of
6 would mean the unit's pricing ranks sixth among the competitive set; a Price Rank of 1 would make it a price leader.

unit's reduced potential to achieve his target profit margin.

The decision effectively positions the vehicle to sell more quickly, and allows Irwin to replace it with another unit that may bring a better return on investment. "It's a piece of metal and it's money. You've got to keep them moving," he says. "We can't be emotionally attached to our merchandise."

But velocity dealers like Irwin may not always make that price-lowering adjustment, particularly if a vehicle's Market Days Supply metric is low and it still stands tall, even with a bit of inventory age.

In some ways, the Price to Market metric allows dealers to "eat their cake and have it too" if they are running a velocity used vehicle department.

"We can also choose when we want to make a bit more money because we own the right vehicle better," Irwin says. "The converse is also true. We can price vehicles with higher days supplies more aggressively to move them more quickly."

Enter the "art" of fine-tuning the Price to Market metric.

As with any metric, the Price to Market metric serves as a numeric, market data-based barometer of how a used vehicle compares price-wise against competing vehicles in a given market area. Within this metric, however, there's flexibility for decision makers to let their own market and paint expertise carry the day.

Here are two examples of this fine-tuning in action:

> **Recalibrating a dealer's market area.** It's not uncommon for velocity dealers and used vehicle managers to review comparative vehicle prices at radii that run up to 250 miles from their stores. Today's technology allows this "pick your market reach" flexibility. These dealers will adjust this market area, depending on supply and demand dynamics. If a vehicle's hot, they might opt to sell it close to home while it's fresh in inventory, and then expand the radius to match prices in other markets to move the vehicle quickly as it ages.

"If we've got a small comparative sample size, we'll go out 100 miles to get our comparisons," Irwin says.

Likewise, dealers may go even further if a vehicle's a rare bird.

John Creran, general sales manager for Ramsey Nissan in Upper Saddle River, N.J., notes how he couldn't find a unit comparable to the '02 Land Rover Discovery he took in on a recent trade, and therefore expanded his search for comparable units to scan the U.S.

"There wasn't anything like it out there. This vehicle was loaded. I put it on *eBay National* and it sold," he says.

> **Adjusting pricing buckets.** The composite of three stores with the Market Days Supply and Price to Market metrics shows the metrics at 30-day inventory intervals. As managers begin to adopt and follow velocity principles for managing their used vehicle inventories, many choose to set their pricing on even shorter time-frames, typically in 15-day buckets.

"My turn has increased by changing to 15-day buckets," Creran says. The reason: He's even more dialed in to his market and can make more frequent and more precise pricing adjustments to sell vehicles faster.

"When I look at the buckets, I ask 'how come this car hasn't moved?'" he says. "If I know customers touched the car, and there's nothing wrong with it, I've got to address the price."

Used vehicle consultant Tommy Gibbs has long advocated this kind of market-focused attention to inventory pricing. He advocates a pricing model that offers buckets to appeal to buyer interest and budgets. When coupled with paint-based metrics like Price to Market, this approach produces winning results—provided there's the kind of proper attention dealers like Creran and others apply.

"To maximize profits, pricing has to be done in a disciplined and controlled manner," Gibbs says. "It's not just something you do when you get around to it."

"PAINT" METRIC 3: COST TO MARKET

When I discuss the three key paint metrics to drive velocity-minded used vehicle management, dealers and used vehicle managers quickly see the benefits of the Market Days Supply and Price to Market metrics.

It's a no-brainer to understand that competitively priced vehicles with high demand and low supply will be winners for any store. Any retailer of any product should recognize that.

But many dealers and used vehicle managers get stuck when they ponder the bigger, operational outcome of adopting these metrics at their

stores: How in the world am I going to make any
money by pricing vehicles aggressively to beat the
competition?

The answer to this question comes with the third
critical paint metric, Cost to Market. This metric
did not exist when I was a dealer when I, too, managed cost to wholesale or water versus managing
against the more significant and relevant value, the
current market price.

Cost to Market allows dealers and used vehicle
managers to base their wholesale acquisition cost
thresholds on what a customer is likely to pay at
retail, rather than what dealers are willing to pay
at wholesale. It goes to the heart of a dysfunction
that occurs today when dealers and used vehicle
managers acquire vehicles with no consideration for
whether the market will bear the wholesale costs
they've paid.

"You have to adopt the mentality that it's worth
what I can sell it for—not how much I have or
might put in it," says Tom Kelley. "Sometimes you
luck out and get a car cheap. So, do you sell the
car cheap? No, you sell it for what it's worth. How
much you put in a vehicle is immaterial. It's worth
what a customer will pay."

Ironically, dealers understand the principles behind
the Cost to Market metric when they acquire and

price new vehicles. As we discussed earlier, they typically do not add in a mark-up from the invoice price they paid to their factory partners. They set the price based on what the market will bear.

The Cost to Market metric offers a way to take the same astute, market-based approach to determining what a used vehicle is worth when considering whether to acquire one at auction or trade-in.

The metric is the cost of a vehicle divided by the average retail selling price of identically equipped, competing vehicles in a dealership's market area. As noted, today's leading technology allows these market comparisons for identical, competing vehicles in a given market.

> **Cost to Market**
>
> DEFINITION:
> A vehicle's cost divided by the average retail asking price of identically equipped competing vehicles in your market

So, if the cost of a vehicle is $7,500 and the average retail asking price is $10,000, the Cost to Market for that unit is 75 percent.

The upshot: If a dealership makes this acquisition, the store has a 25 percent margin to factor in costs for reconditioning and a gross profit target for that unit—based on real-time market data indicating what a consumer's likely to pay.

Given that our business typically operates on single-digit net profit margins, it seems that an initial 25 percent margin would be a good place to start a used vehicle's life cycle at a dealership.

Velocity dealers and used vehicle managers pay close attention to this metric because it offers a data-driven approach to establish buy lists and determine the right amount to pay for a vehicle by reverse-engineering the acquisition cost off the prevailing retail prices in the market.

The composite on the next page shows how the Cost to Market metric, when combined with the other two paint metrics of Market Days Supply and Price to Market, can create significant competitive advantages for the dealers and used vehicle managers who adopt these metrics as guides for a velocity-based approach to managing their used vehicle operations.

When I share this composite with dealers and used vehicle managers, some are quick to spot why the velocity-minded dealer is performing much better than its traditional-minded competitors.

In each of the inventory buckets, the velocity dealer is able to acquire their vehicles at Cost to Market ratios that are significantly lower than their traditional counterparts. Any retailer worth his or her salt should be able to make a good living selling a

Days in Inventory	Key Metric	Velocity Dealer	Traditional Dealer #1	Traditional Dealer #2
1-30	Market Days Supply	32	67	114
	Price to Market	90%	108%	105%
	Cost to Market	70%	85%	90%
31-60	Market Days Supply	34	73	104
	Price to Market	85%	105%	107%
	Cost to Market	75%	90%	98%
61-90	Market Days Supply	–	76	87
	Price to Market	–	105%	110%
	Cost to Market	–	95%	104%

product that they can acquire for 15 percent to 20 percent less than the competition.

But then comes incredulity and even doubt: How are the velocity-based stores able to achieve these margins? It's impossible to find some vehicles at wholesale prices less than what we typically charge at retail, given the increased competition and wholesale pressure in today's used vehicle marketplace. How is a 5 percent, let alone a 15 percent, margin even possible?

The answers to these questions lie in the way that velocity dealerships go about sourcing and acquiring vehicles. Let's examine the elemental components:

Establishing a baseline wholesale acquisition cost. As many dealers and used vehicle managers know, this is an increasingly tricky proposition, whether it's at an auction or trade-in appraisal.

The reason this can be tricky is because today's more volatile used vehicle marketplace can trigger dramatic wholesale values swings in a heartbeat. Anyone who was around dealerships in the latter part of 2008 should know this.

Gas price swings and a troubled economy combined to effectively crush wholesale values on large trucks and SUVs, and it spurred a spike in wholesale values for more fuel-efficient vehicles.

Most dealers and used vehicle managers did their best to keep up. They consulted the wholesale price guides from Kelley, Black Book, NADA, and other sources. But they still found themselves facing problems with aging vehicles and wholesale losses.

This was due, in part, to the wholesale guides having trouble keeping up with the rapid price changes. In fact, it's this very breed of volatility that has spurred wholesale guide providers to step up the frequency of publishing used vehicle values in the past 12 to 18 months. In some cases, these wholesale guides are now offered daily or weekly, but they still may not accurately catch the in-the-moment swings in wholesale values that can and do occur, particularly at crowded auction lanes.

These are the reasons why velocity dealers and used vehicle managers switch to using the Cost to Market metric to determine how much a vehicle is worth at wholesale. They know the metric offers a constant, real-time read of a non-debatable data point: The average retail asking price of a vehicle in a given marketplace.

From there, these velocity dealers and used vehicle managers can reverse engineer what they'll pay to acquire a vehicle.

For example, let's say a dealer and used vehicle manager are considering whether they should acquire a '07 Honda Accord that has an average retail asking price of $15,767 for a vehicle with similar mileage. This figure is the starting point for calculating an acquisition price that's right for the store.

The dealer and used vehicle manager would first decide how aggressively they need to price this car based on its physical qualities, appeal, and, importantly, its Market Days Supply. For example let's say they decide they need to be in the top 10 cars in their market for similarly equipped '07 Honda Accords and that this requires that they need to price it at 95% of average market price. First, they would subtract the amount they expect to pay for reconditioning (say, $800) and the $2,000 gross profit from the asking price to arrive at an acquisition price of $12,179 (a 77% Cost to Market ratio).

If it's a trade-in, they'd send that figure to the desk. If it's an auction purchase, the dealer and used vehicle manager may go a step further, and set the ceiling on the acquisition price at $12,979 (determined by adjusting the gross profit expectation to roughly $1,200 and weighing the benefit of bringing a fast-moving unit into their inventory).

Exit Strategy

Avg. Market Price	$	15,767
Adj % of Market X		95%
Asking Price	$	14,979
Reconditioning	$ -	800
Profit Objective	$ -	2,000
Appraised Value	**$**	**12,179**

Now, let's contrast this market-attuned approach to establishing the right wholesale acquisition with what traditional dealers and used vehicle managers are likely to do.

As noted above, they'd potentially consult the wholesale value guides, but there's also a chance they might neglect the guides and go with their guts. Likewise, they might get caught up in the irrational exuberance at auction and pay more than they should—even if they knew the acquisition cost outpaced a wholesale value guide.

"I pity the poor guy who's only got a Black Book or other guide," says dealer Joe Kirby of Edd Kirby Adventure Chevrolet, Dalton, Georgia. "He's not going to know everything he needs to make a good decision."

In early fall 2009, Kirby and his buyer are walking out of auctions without buying any vehicles, a rare move that comes from knowing his Cost to Market thresholds on the units he might acquire for his store. "We've seen eight months of appreciating values," Kirby says. "That has not happened in the history of mankind."

Given these factors, the reverse engineer approach that velocity-minded dealers and used vehicle managers follow, based on the Cost to Market metric, is a far more reasonable, measured, and data-supported way to determine what wholesale price the store should pay for a given vehicle than traditional practices.

This approach to establishing what to pay is a key reason why the velocity dealer in the composite example is able to achieve a Cost to Market for its inventory that's far lower than the traditional-minded competition.

Sourcing vehicles. The traditional stores in our composite are likely to rely on one or two local auctions to source their vehicles. What's more, the used vehicle manager or buyer is probably accustomed to going to an auction only occasionally, perhaps once every two weeks—potentially more frequently at larger stores. (Remember, these stores have historically relied more on trade-ins than auctions to drive the bulk of their used vehicle inventories.)

Let's contrast this auction expertise with that of the buyers and used vehicle managers at velocity stores where, by definition, they need to continually feed their fast-turning inventories:

- It's not uncommon for these stores to have inventory specialists who spend 80 percent of their time scouring auction run lists to find vehicles that fit their Market Days Supply parameters.

- They fly two to three days a week to the auctions (sometimes with airfare and hotel expenses paid by the auctions themselves, thanks to their volume of business) with up-front knowledge of the specific auction lanes and run times for the vehicles they want. Likewise, they take full advantage of the online sales offered by Manheim, ADESA, Openlane, and factory sales.

- They know when they can pay all day long and when to let a vehicle go because the bidding goes well beyond the Cost to Market metric they calculated before they left the store.

- They know which auctions offer better acquisition price points based on specific vehicle segments. Example: Southeast auctions appear better for high-lines than other locations.

- They know the auctions that typically offer vehicles in the best condition and offer the best prospect for a low reconditioning expense. Example: It's not at Midwest auctions like those in Detroit and Chicago where winter driving conditions almost guarantee paint and bodywork in the recon line.

- They've arranged transports for the vehicles they plan to purchase in advance, or they've invested in their own transports, thereby shortening the time and expense required to get the vehicles back to their stores.

- They have additional opportunities to bid on vehicle batches that sell outside the auctions.

I've analyzed the cumulative effect of these more efficient sourcing tactics and believe they account for a full 5 percent of the Cost to Market differential noted in the three-store composite.

Our industry has long believed that someone who holds the title of used vehicle manager necessarily makes a good buyer. The examples I've shared here, which reflect the real-life experiences that occur every day at velocity dealerships, underscore that this belief needs revisiting.

Reconditioning Expenses. Two blessings that flow from a velocity-minded approach to managing used vehicle operations are the efficiencies and economes of scale that result from moving a higher number of vehicles through the used vehicle department. This plays out in a profound way when it comes to reconditioning vehicles.

Velocity-minded dealers have established processes that shorten the time it takes to move a vehicle from the transport to the reconditioning/detailing department and to the front line in just two or three days. It's not uncommon for more traditional stores to see a week or more pass before a vehicle is ready for retail.

With volatile wholesale values and holding costs increasing, these delays can be costly for stores that fail to speed up their reconditioning turn times.

Likewise, velocity dealers pay less for oil filters, fenders, belts, fluids, windshields, and the cleaning products they use to get vehicles reconditioned and ready for retail. Or they pay less on a per-vehicle basis to the vendors that do this work for them. No dealer or used vehicle manager would argue that it costs less per vehicle to recondition 200 vehicles than 20.

Such economies of scale are another key reason why the Cost to Market metric in the three-store composite is lower for the velocity store than its traditional-minded competitors.

Taken together, the kinds of efficiencies that velocity dealerships are able to achieve—from setting a reliable benchmark on what they should pay to acquire a vehicle to achieving economies of scale in reconditioning—account for the margin advantage these stores retain over their competition.

When I share this overview of the Cost to Market metric, and explain why velocity dealerships are able to achieve a cost advantage compared to their competitors, dealers and used vehicle managers begin to get the picture.

In essence, it reflects one of life's key blessings and truths: The more you do something, the better you'll get at it.

FINE-TUNING THE COST TO MARKET METRIC

Similar to the Price to Market metric, the Cost to Market metric is only a benchmark. There are definitely occasions when velocity dealers and used vehicle managers may want to hedge their bets to suit other business purposes.

For example, Tom Kelley shares an example of a loyal customer who traded in a '06 Cadillac STS with 11,000 miles. The vehicle was in like-new condition—a well-maintained unit with a 70-year-old single owner. The store's target Cost to Market (80 percent) pegged the trade-in value at $17,500.

But Kelley paid $19,500 to own the unit. Why? It helped him book a new car deal for a loyal customer and his examination of the competitive data on the vAuto system showed the vehicle was a true-blue creampuff.

"I know I can get more than $20,000 for the car," says Kelley, who acknowledges the front-end gross of the retail deal may be thinner than he'd get if he'd been stricter about sticking to the Cost to Market metric. But, in this instance, he's taking the gamble.

"I'm less concerned about going outside the metric parameters on this car. You can't get killed on a car like that with 11,000 miles," he says.

Sometimes, as Kelley relates, it may make sense to put the Cost to Market metric aside. The key, however, is making sure such a decision follows a careful assessment of the potential risks and rewards of doing so—which one can only truly assess by evaluating the Market Days Supply and Price to Market metrics on a vehicle in tandem with the Cost to Market metric.

I would say Kelley made the right call. He checked the market, assessed the good will he'd get from a loyal customer, the benefit of a new car deal, and his ability to retail the STS, even with a thinner margin. Given that his stores turn their inventory nearly 18 times a year, it's a fair bet that STS won't be around very long on his lot.

How might this deal have gone at another, more traditional dealership?

They probably would have paid the $19,500, given the seller is a loyal customer. Then, the dealer and used vehicle manager would likely have reflexively placed a $4,000 mark-up on the unit—putting it on the market at $23,500.

The store *may* find a buyer at that price, but I would be willing to bet good money that this store will spend more time waiting for this buyer than the one who's likely to hop online, see the unit priced more competitively at Kelley's store, and snap it up.

In the end, who's made the more profitable deal?

I would suggest it's Kelley, who's already bought and sold at least one other vehicle with the money he initially invested in the '06 STS in the time it took the traditional store to turn its initial investment.

VELOCITY METRICS AND THE ROAD AHEAD

There's an axiom in business that one should always put a positive spin on things—even if something is undeniably negative.

There's no sense mincing words here: Adopting a velocity-based philosophy and effectively using the "paint" metrics described in these chapters—Market Days Supply, Price to Market and Cost to Market—to manage used vehicle operations won't work for every dealership.

I'm not saying they *can't* work, because I believe wholeheartedly that they do. I'm just saying that the transition to a velocity-based philosophy and metrics-minded management approach is not easy. This stuff's new. It runs counter to what most dealers and used vehicle managers consider the right thing to do.

We'll see more of that in the next chapter.

I'll share why an increasing number of dealers are giving up their long-held obsession with uber per vehicle gross on used cars, and focusing more on total gross, storewide net profits, and more efficient operations. We'll learn how these stores are changing job descriptions and creating new ones to get the jobs of online merchandising, sourcing, and selling vehicles done with more effectiveness and proficiency. We'll also examine how difficult it is to make this critical transition, and why some dealers and used vehicle managers don't make the cut.

It's an exciting story. I can't wait to tell it.

"PAINT-BASED" PROCESSES AND PRESSURE POINTS

I want to be clear about something—I didn't invent velocity-based management principles.

The last thing I want or need is an "Al Gore[8]"-like rap against me. I may be one of the first in our industry to openly and publicly advocate for using market-based velocity principles for managing used vehicle departments. But these management principles are as old as the financial hills. They've been in use for years in stock and commodity markets as well as in a host of other retail-focused industries.

---

[8]http://www.snopes.com/quotes/internet.asp

Even so, these concepts are new and different for most traditional dealers and used vehicle managers. Interestingly, I'm not the only person in automotive retailing who thinks this is a far better way to run a used vehicle business in today's more volatile, efficient, and Internet-enabled used vehicle marketplace than traditional best practices.

Take a peek at how the 30-something founders of online auto retailing powerhouse Texas Direct think about their business—culled from their book, *0 to 60:*

> *"The Internet market is different than what most dealers are used to. The books are of little use; the only index that matters is the global market. The only way to know the market is to be buying and selling in it, day in and day out. Will the market bear a profit on a certain vehicle at a given purchase price? If so, then buy. If not, then don't buy.*[9]*"*

> *"By being as fast as possible, you protect yourself from market fluctuations. It's one thing to buy something and sell it for a profit. It's another to use that same money twice in one month and make a profit twice. We turn our inventory of 400 vehicles more than once a month.*[10]*"*

---

[9] *0 to 60*, p. 36.
[10] *Ibid*, p. 69..

I share this excerpt for a couple of key reasons:

> First, the guys at Texas Direct are eating the lunches of many franchised dealers and used vehicle managers—and not just in Texas. The outfit's success comes from buying and selling vehicles across the country. Customers fly in from all corners to take delivery of vehicles they've purchased. They are keen competitors.

> Secondly, the fact that two young guys, with no prior experience in auto retailing and a comparatively scant brick-and-mortar investment, have crafted a 400-plus-per-month sales success based on velocity-like principles should be a significant wake-up call for traditional dealerships.

It's clear that technology and data-driven insights about the market, as well as a need for inventory turn speed, serve as the underlying foundation of the Texas Direct business model. That's velocity, baby, and it's working wonders for their operation. The young entrepreneurs at Texas Direct created and crafted their velocity-minded operation sans any regard for traditional used vehicle management best practices. In fact, judging from their book, they basically assessed those best practices and decided on a different direction. To them, the way we've long managed used vehicle operations is too inefficient and dealer-centric to work in today's marketplace.

That's bad news for traditional dealers and used vehicle managers. Why? Because it underscores how much work it takes to transform long-standing culture and processes into the velocity-based practices we discussed in the past three chapters.

This chapter seeks to ease this important transition. It focuses on some of the most critical flashpoints that occur as dealers and used vehicle managers adopt velocity-based paint metrics and management principles. These pressure points crop up in every department that touches a used vehicle during its life cycle, and they create ongoing "out with the old, and in with the new" struggles at every store that walks this bold new path.

In some ways, the cultural clashes that occur between velocity-based and traditional used vehicle best practices are essentially battles for greater efficiencies. With velocity-based management principles, speed and turn are key elements of this highly time-sensitive approach. With traditional best practices, speed and turn play little, if any, role, and time is an ally, not an enemy.

So with the backdrop of industry newbies capitalizing on the benefits that velocity-based management offers in today's more volatile and efficient used vehicle marketplace, let's examine the areas that give dealerships that have adopted this new mindset the most trouble.

Get Off the Gross and Go with 'Net'

The controller and accounting team of a South Carolina-based dealer group were at a loss as to why one of its stores consistently grew net profits while front-end gross profits were softer than they'd been in years past.

"It's because of an old school mentality that focuses on gross," says the store's GM, who, since adopting a velocity-based approach to management has doubled the store's used vehicle sales volume to 200-plus in six months. "They couldn't understand how I was making so much net profit when my grosses were lower."

The store's front-end gross profit average on used vehicles hovers around $1,200. But as the GM is quick to note, that's only a part of the profit picture at his store. The following are examples of improvements experienced since implementing velocity-based management principles:

- Service revenues from reconditioning work have tripled to more than $600,000 in the first three months. The increase owes to the greater number of used vehicles that now need reconditioning work. "We're running 300 units a month through service to sell 200," the GM says.

- F&I penetration has increased to 150 percent, up from 125 percent. The store is looking to hire additional F&I managers.

- The store's new vehicle sales volume is increasing, albeit at a slower clip than usual due to high unemployment in the region. Still, the GM says, "we're doing more deals because we can pony up at the pump on trades."

Such is the total profit picture at dealerships that adopt a velocity-based management philosophy and paint metrics to run used vehicle operations. It's more about net profit across multiple dealership departments than average gross profit on a retailed unit (PVR).

"I'm all about running my dealership based on net, not gross," says Bill Pearson. "Net profit matters most."

"You absolutely have to let go of gross as part of your decision-making," echoes John Malishenko. "It must shift to turn and net profits. It's a leap of faith because it's totally contrary."

Indeed, it is. This velocity-based mentality is not easy to achieve at stores where traditional dealers and used vehicle managers have long focused on PVR as an elemental read on whether a used vehicle department is healthy or not.

Even velocity dealers and used vehicle managers who have achieved improvements in net profits across multiple departments still have to contend with owners, partners, and parents who believe they'd make even more money if they just ratcheted up gross profits a bit more.

"It's difficult for my dad and partner," says dealer Dan Sunderland at Sun Motor Cars, Mechanicsburg, Pa. "If we're making $2,400 front-end gross on a car, and we used to make $3,500, he thinks we're leaving $1,100 on the table. I can't look him straight in the eye and say that's not sometimes the case.

"But if you add the additional gross in fixed operations, the grosses from buying and selling more vehicles from manufacturer programs, and the reduction in wholesales losses, we are making more money. But the money's in different pockets," Sunderland says.

The challenge for velocity dealerships like Sun Motor Cars is balancing the gross profit expectations against the need to turn inventory. This ever-important balancing act is typically achieved by vectoring the Market Days Supply, Price to Market and Cost to Market metrics to get the best shot at a gross profit while a vehicle is freshest in inventory.

Remember Chris Irwin's strategy of being in the middle, price-wise, when a vehicle hits his lot for retail? He aims for his best gross profit out of the gate, and dials back expectations as vehicles age. Sometimes, given market metric data, he may come out as a price leader because it's necessary to move the vehicle fast, given a weaker initial profit position.

Even then he's focused on turn and overall gross for the used vehicle department, not PVR.

Some traditional dealers and used vehicle managers simply can't get off the PVR juice. They'll hear that gross profits on individual deals don't matter as much as they used to and they'll hit a mental wall.

It's understandable because it's very difficult to let go of practices and beliefs that have served us all well for years.

But the dismissal of velocity metrics and management principles misses some key benefits that may not be readily apparent. These benefits are a natural bi-product of the application of a velocity-based philosophy and gain momentum as they are utilized.

Together with the storewide efficiencies and net profit gains that flow from adopting velocity principles, these benefits demonstrate that once dealers and used vehicle managers put the efficiency-fueled velocity train on its tracks, it can become an express line to used vehicle success.

Benefit 1: Inventory that's innately ready to move. Velocity dealers and used vehicle managers are more likely to stock vehicles with favorable Market Days Supply metrics. So, in some ways, by implementing the velocity management strategies the pressure to move inventory is already reduced because these store buy the right vehicles.

What's more, because these vehicles are in demand, customers seek out the dealers who sell them. This translates to velocity dealers and used vehicle managers dumping traditional advertising costs altogether—a cost reduction that goes straight to the bottom line. Of course, this savings won't show up on a PVR report, but it'll fatten up the department's net profit picture.

Benefit 2: Less pressure on gross at point of sale. We all know what happens with hot new vehicles that command prices above MSRP. Customers know they're paying a premium to get a vehicle ahead of their neighbors. They may inquire about a discount, but a little push-back from salespeople generally results in customers ponying up to pay the premium. The same dynamic is true at velocity stores where they use the Market Days Supply and Price to Market metrics effectively. Customers have done their shopping online; they arrived on a unit because it represents a good value compared to identically equipped, competing vehicles. In most cases, their efforts to negotiate for a discount really amount to testing a dealership only to check if it is strong and transparent enough to stand behind its market-based pricing. "You don't have to be the cheapest to sell today's price-savvy customers," is a comment I hear all the time. And it's true. Velocity dealers know when vehicles can command big grosses, and they know when leaner margins are more appropriate, given market dynamics. All they're doing is linking their pricing decisions to match what customers already know. The end result is a greater number of deals with less negotiation and fewer discounts to arrive at a selling price in which both sides walk away winners.

"When customers come to us, they're ready," says Steve Barnes, used vehicle manager at Sun. "It's amazing. They know the car. They know the price. If we give up any money during negotiations, it's only a few hundred dollars from our price. It's rare to have a long, grinding negotiation on a deal."

When the Market Days Supply and Price to Market metrics are properly aligned, the phones ring at velocity stores. As previously stated, the advertising savings these stores achieve goes straight to the bottom line—and they'll go unnoticed by traditional dealers and used vehicle managers who focus solely on PVR.

Benefit 3: The ability to dial in for dollars. It'd be an interesting exercise to see how much time and productivity is lost at traditional dealerships as they wait for customers to show up and land on a used vehicle that's been priced to achieve a fantasy mark-up. In these environments, it's not uncommon for a salesperson who achieves 10 to 15 sales a month to be regarded as a good seller.

At some velocity dealerships, however, 10 units a month is the price of entry for salespeople. As we'll discuss shortly, pay plans at velocity stores are structured for salespeople to average 15 to 20 units a month—with good sellers hitting 25-plus deals.

The velocity-based metrics and management principles support this level of proficiency and productivity because dealers and used vehicle managers are able to adjust their prices when needed to bring in customers. The expertise they develop for this move the market technique is uncanny. Some even know the time and day of the week that will result in more phone calls and foot traffic as a result of pinpoint price changes.

Craig Belowski says Thursday price changes make for a profitable weekend. He adds that his attention to market-based pricing gives him a competitive edge.

"I'm checking our pricing every day. Nobody else around here is doing that," says Belowski, whose store averages 140 units a month and consistently ranks as a top regional Toyota certified pre-owned retailer.

I would urge traditional dealers and used vehicle managers to "get off the gross and go with 'net.'" It's a significant change, for sure, but the benefits strike me as far better than those that result from retaining traditional best practices in today's more efficient and volatile used vehicle marketplace.

IT'S A SOURCING PROBLEM, NOT A SHORTAGE

I've had dozens of conversations about what some dealers and used vehicle managers believe is a shortage of used vehicles.

> *"We can't find the vehicles we need at prices we can afford to pay."*

> *"We have to pay the same at wholesale as we charge at retail."*

When we peel back the layers of this onion, it becomes clear to me that these dealers and used

A Volume-based Velocity Payplan

It's not uncommon for velocity-minded dealerships to see sales volumes increases create problems with commission-based compensation plans for salespeople.

It's to be expected as salespeople do more deals and traditional, 25 percent commission-based pay plans start eating away at profitability for a department that's focused on turn and net rather than PVR.

Here's how one velocity-minded dealer solved the problem—a pay plan that keeps his compensation costs at a respectable 22 percent and his salespeople earning a good living.

The plan gives a $2,000/month base, with the following bonuses:

    6 units sold by the 15th: $200
    10 units a month: $500
    15 units a month: $500
    @ 5 add'l units: $500

In addition, the store pays up to 4 percent commission on total F&I dollars that flow from a salesperson's deals, based on $10,000 increments (*e.g.*, $0-$10,000 = 1 percent).

The dealer expects salespeople to do at least 10 deals a month or they'll be looking for another job.

The keys here are the initial spiff to spur front-of-month sales and the incentive to ensure salespeople set up potential F&I penetrations. It's important to underscore the F&I office's value early on with today's customers, whose online shopping exposes them to a variety of do-it-yourself financing and warranty options.

vehicle managers are running up against a problem other than a shortage of vehicles. The vehicles with low Market Days Supply are out there—but they're not necessarily available at the local auctions traditional dealers and used vehicle managers have relied on in the past.

The real problem is that many dealers and used vehicle managers, including some that have adopted velocity-based management principles, now have to work harder to find the vehicles they need to feed their inventories.

"The cars are out there, but they're not at the traditional places we've gone to in the past," says velocity-minded dealer Keith Kocourek of Kocourek Chevrolet, Wausau, Wis. "They're also not the traditional cars we've had in the past."

Another problem arrives when velocity dealers and used vehicle managers find the vehicles that fit their Market Days Supply metric: they aren't the only ones who want to buy them, translating to purchase prices that often go north of the desired acquisition prices.

The GM for the South Carolina store says he's seen his Cost to Market climb from 72 percent to 80 percent in 2009 as a result of greater pressure and demand for auction vehicles. "It hurts the margin and gross, but I think it will get better," he says.

Adam Simms, dealer/owner of Toyota Sunnyvale (Calif.), takes a similar view. "It's ridiculous to say there's a shortage when at any given time, there are nearly 3 million used vehicles in some stage of preparation or sale," says Simms, noting the nation's $40 million annual used vehicle sales tally. "You can always buy the cars, but you have to adjust your expectations for your margin. I still buy the cars because I want to maintain velocity and be the only guy who has them."

This breed of confidence comes from the fact that Simms knows his acquisition, stocking, and pricing strategy is more market-attuned than his traditional-minded competitors. His store currently sells about 220 used units a month and he's planning for additional growth.

Simms concedes that the market in 2009 marks "a period of time when margins may well be thinner" and every store must work harder to proficiently acquire vehicles—and know when to hold, fold, or buy the units they seek.

Here's a look at how some velocity dealers address the challenge of sourcing the vehicles they need at the price that's right for their stores:

Designate an inventory specialist(s). "Hey, Hoss. What can you do for me on that '07 Escalade?"

That's Kyle Cornwell on the horn with an auction rep, trying to resolve a problem with a vehicle that got damaged in transport. So it goes at the centralized appraisal and buying office at Sam Swope Auto Group, Louisville, Ky.

"I call Kyle 'The Hammer,'" says Burnell King, Cornwell's partner in the centralized appraisal and buying office at the dealer group. "I just give him a phone number and the problem gets taken care of."

Arbitrations are a part of life here, where a majority of the vehicles that fuel Swope's 700-unit monthly used vehicle sales volume get purchased online. King estimates he and Cornwell average about 25 vehicle buys a day, plus they handle appraisals for group stores.

King and Cornwell are grinders. They work from 9 a.m. to 9 p.m. five days a week and a half-day on Saturdays, using a host of technology and tools to buy and appraise vehicles. An open box of Raisin Bran cereal on the top of a small refrigerator serves as testimony that these guys are glued to their computers and telephones, making deals and moving metal.

"We don't really have time for lunch," King explains. "That's when auctions are at their peak. And, we're also trying to slim down a bit."

Each morning this tandem reviews buy lists pre-pared the night before from reviews of auction run sheets and velocity metrics. For the next seven hours, King and Cornwell are monitoring auction sales, making bids, checking proxy bids, and scour-ing for vehicles.

They tend to buy in small batches versus truckloads to ensure they're getting vehicles that match up squarely with the Market Days Supply, Price to Market, and Cost to Market metrics for the stores they serve. "We do the same amount of up-front work to purchase 3 vehicles as we do 30," King says. "If we need 3 vehicles, and an auction has 300, we have to review them all."

The smaller-batch purchases also help speed up the time it takes to transport vehicles back to Swope—a critical aspect of the efficiency-focused sourcing. "The challenging thing is that these vehicles hit the DMS as soon as we buy them," King says. "That's when the clock starts ticking."

In my travels around the country, the centralized appraisal and buying operation at Swope is one of the most efficient sourcing operations I've had the pleasure to visit. It's this kind of sourcing profi-ciency and efficiency that's necessary for dealerships to thrive in today's used vehicle marketplace.

The work King and Cornwell do looks nothing like the auction fishing trips that many traditional dealers and used vehicle managers still rely on to source vehicles. King and Cornwell remind me of snipers: Armed with buy sheets derived from calibrating auction run lists and their velocity metrics, they know exactly when to pull the trigger and when to hold their fire.

"We source vehicles the same way we sell—with a lot of information about our market," says Cary Donovan, who set up the centralized office as a way to streamline sourcing and create a more cost-efficient and aggressive method for feeding his velocity-focused used vehicle operation. "Their job boils down to one thing—putting the right price on every car. They both know their stuff and do it extremely well."

From my observations, I would have to agree. It's pretty easy to tell, after a short visit to King and Cornwell's shared office, that they're the right guys for the job.

King, who spent about six years on the road buying vehicles for CarMax before joining Swope, says the market-driven metrics and methods they follow at Swope gives him more latitude to exercise his paint skills.

"You get to think a little more and put your own spin on things," King says. "CarMax is more robotic. You work with what's put in front of you."

Get creative. In addition to bringing on inventory specialists and going beyond local and familiar auctions, dealers like the Swope Auto Group are making house calls to acquire vehicles. In 2009, Donovan launched a "We Pay Cash For Cars" effort that now brings in 20 to 25 units a month from customers the store probably would not have seen without the program. Cornwell and King's office runs the program and "it creates a natural flow of traffic," King says. "People who have a car to sell generally need a car, too."

The program does mean Swope pays for rough cars that go immediately to wholesale. But, with the market-based metrics to set the right purchase price, "it's a profit center if it goes wholesale or retail," King says.

The West Herr Automotive Group has also found that purchasing cars from customers can be a helpful way to source and sell vehicles, says Jack Anderson. In spring 2009, the group began offering a program to help customers sell their vehicles online. The store would help prep descriptions and photos and offer an appraisal.

In most cases, the customers simply took the appraisal offer and the dealership sourced another vehicle. "It's not high pressure and most customers appreciate the fact that we offer fair appraisals," says Anderson, who estimates about half of these customers wound up purchasing a used vehicle to replace the one they sold. In the fall of 2009, the company plans to market and launch the program more aggressively.

"You can't put all your eggs in one basket when it comes to sourcing," Anderson adds.

Dealership consultant Steve Nickelson agrees. He believes such creative sourcing approaches are critical, given greater demand at wholesale for vehicles.

"The dealerships that don't re-think sourcing and stick to the traditional mode of sending somebody to the auction to raise their hand, are going to be at a significant disadvantage," he says. "Having a variety of sourcing options will be critical going forward."

Avoid the appraisal games on trades. Dealer Jon Whitman says today's technology allows him to show customers why the store can only pay a certain dollar amount for a vehicle, rather than a figure that either over-allows or under-allows on a given trade. "We knew a vehicle was worth $10,000 and we'd allow $11,000 for some customers all the time," he says.

This traditional practice may be an occasional necessity to satisfy loyal customers or close a new vehicle deal. He notes it must be a decision that's informed with an honest assessment of Cost to Market and Price to Market metrics to ensure the vehicle doesn't end up priced too high for the market to accommodate the over-allowance.

"We make sure the person who appraises the car doesn't price the car," says John Malishenko. "You have to take any biases and ego out of the decision-making and still use common sense."

The upshot of today's sourcing game is that it's more difficult and challenging than ever before. It requires an investment of time, money and resources to do the job proficiently and to set the stage for a positive return on investment for every vehicle a store acquires.

This is a far cry from the gut-based buying decisions and wasted time that's typical of the way most traditional dealers and used vehicle mangers sought out used vehicle inventory—if they did it at all.

TURNING WRENCHES, TURNING CARS

Another key challenge that velocity-minded dealers and used vehicle managers confront early on in their journey to create a fast-turning inventory is ensuring that all used vehicles get attention and priority in their service departments.

Make no mistake: This shift amounts to a cultural change at most dealerships and it requires up-front effort to ensure service directors, advisors, and technicians all understand that every vehicle slated for reconditioning represents an investment of the dealership's money, and that any delay—no matter the cause—crimps the store's ability to generate the maximum return on investment on any given unit.

For example, if a store's average days-in-inventory runs 17-25 days, a benchmark that's fairly common at velocity-minded stores, a 5-, 6- or 7-day lag in service hampers profitability. Such lags can cut as much as 50 percent of the time a vehicle lives in the 15-day buckets many velocity-minded stores use for their retail pricing strategies. If that occurs, it absolutely undermines the dealership's potential to garner a maximum level of profit.

From my conversations with velocity dealers, a "carrot and carrot" approach to achieving a shared understanding that time is of the essence in service seems to work best. That is, it's more effective to foster a culture of collaboration and shared goals than one that relies on the "stick" of penalties and charges to the service department for delays.

One of the key factors in achieving buy-in in service is the straight-up fact that everyone in the shop stands to benefit from a velocity-based approach. Paychecks will get fatter for service teams that accommodate the incremental influx of work.

The next step is a process that ensures the prioritization and turn for vehicles.

The GM at the South Carolina store aims for a three-day timeframe to complete all reconditioning work (the third day goes to paint/body work if it's needed). He tracks the progress "like crazy" using a status board posted in the service department. He also discusses vehicle status daily with the service manager to address any issues, such as delays for parts, costs that run north of preliminary estimates, etc., that inevitably come up.

"It's very collaborative," he says. "Everybody has to play their position."

Bill Pearson sets an even more aggressive expectation for his reconditioning turn: Within 48 to 72 hours, his vehicles are detailed, reconditioned, and loaded up to his online listings. His detailing manager handles the photos and gets paid based on meeting Pearson's goals for getting the vehicle ready for sale.

"It's all about being efficient and making sure everybody understands that," Pearson says.

Malishenko says he found success at building service department buy-in by empowering his team members to devise the best ways to ensure speedy through-put of used vehicles. The buy-in flowed from an education and training process that came without mandates. In effect, it let GMs at stores work with their service departments to devise the best ways to ensure vehicles didn't suffer from time delays.

"We wanted this change to be their idea," he says. "We took our time, and had hours and hours of dialogue. To be successful, it has to be a holistic thing that everybody understands—the service manager, the detail manager, the reconditioning technicians, the salespeople, and the new and used car managers."

The key take-away is that a velocity-minded approach requires astute management of expectations in service and other departments to ensure a storewide focus on efficient movement of used vehicles through their lifecycle.

Along the path of this important, time-is-critical cultural shift for reconditioning work, it's not uncommon for velocity stores to encounter another issue: Just how much is the correct amount to pay to get a vehicle ready for sale?

The answer to this question varies, depending on the vehicle. Velocity dealers and used vehicle managers share a wide range of average reconditioning costs, from $400 to $2,000.

The disparity flows from their business models: Are they trying to be price leaders in the market? If so, the average reconditioning will likely run closer to the $400 average. Are they aiming to be competitive while providing a vehicle that may command a higher mark-up? If so, the store will likely fall closer to the $2,000 average.

Such considerations have given rise to what West Herr Automotive Group calls its value vehicles. These are units—denoted by a green-colored sticker—that may have some cosmetic flaws, but offer a good buy for customers. Anderson says the approach helps mitigate situations where the "money we spend to make a car look good" may not be best for positioning the vehicle competitively in the market.

Of course, factory certification programs add another layer of complexity to the reconditioning equation. By their nature, the reconditioning costs for these vehicles will be higher. The question for dealers and used vehicle managers is how much higher should these reconditioning costs be? And, if they invest this money, will it attract customers willing to pay the premium?

At Acton Toyota, Craig Belowski says the difference in reconditioning costs between certified and non-certified vehicles runs between $300 and $400. The trick, he says, is studying the market to know what vehicles will command a better premium than others with the CPO badge.

For example, he says a loaded Sienna AWD van might command a $2,000 premium, while a less well-equipped Camry LE might only add $500. Likewise, certification on a '09 Camry program car might not matter as much as on an older vehicle.

Here are some key notes on CPO:

1. One shouldn't arbitrarily assume that it makes sense to certify every vehicle. Market Days Supply and Price to Market offer good gauges on the hot spots where the cost of certification meets the perceived value in the eyes of consumers.

2. It's essential to brand CPO vehicles effectively in online merchandising to distinguish their value proposition. Belowski makes sure the main photos for certified vehicles carry the Toyota CPO logo, and his descriptions note the certification right up front. "You have to differentiate," he says. Overall, Belowski believes such branding helps draw customers to vehicles, but adds that the person-to-person rundown of the CPO benefits typically seals customers on the value of the program.

3. It's more challenging to market non-certified used vehicles against CPO units at franchised stores. "I have that problem with Honda," Belowski says. "I can sell one

An "As-Is" Option for Recon Work

Check out this menu approach for reconditioning work: Do the used vehicle inspection, complete the RO and then offer customers the option of buying the unit with or without the work completed at the dealership.

Dealer John Schenden of Pro Chrysler Jeep, Denver, says he stumbled on the idea but finds it works.

He estimates about 20 incremental sales a month flow from the program—with most taking the "as-is" option.

Schenden separates these factory program units from other stock. Salespeople offer them up when they can't make another deal work. "We'll say, 'follow me, I've got an idea,'" Schenden says.

I think it's a brilliant stroke. Why not give the customer the option? At worst, the store misses some service revenue, but there's still a shot at F&I if the customer buys the vehicle without the recon work.

Perhaps most intriguing, though, is the credibility-building it offers by extending the choice and being transparent about reconditioning costs.

Some say the idea's ripe for come-back trouble. Schenden says the program's been fine so far—in part, I suspect, because the deals firmly place responsibility for any problems with the customer.

"We've found a segment of the market that we were missing," he says. I think he's on to something.

if I'm a price leader, but if I'm positioned at number five, that vehicle will be around a while." (It should be noted that this certified vs. non-certified dynamic plays out more pointedly for CPO programs under brands with strong customer loyalty, such as Toyota, Mercedes, BMW, and Honda.)

PAINT PROCESS PROFICIENCY IS NOT ENOUGH

As much as I'd like to say that addressing the paint-based pressure points that occur when dealers and used vehicle managers adopt velocity-based metrics and management processes is all it takes for used vehicle success, I cannot.

The fact is, there's a whole separate degree of proficiency that's required in today's more efficient, volatile, and Internet-driven marketplace. This proficiency lies in what's become the pixel side of our business.

In today's marketplace, the vast majority of used vehicle customers begin their shopping process online, typically through online listing sites like *AutoTrader.com* and *Cars.com*. They also scout individual dealer websites, and check out online car shopping portals like *KBB.com*.

The upshot: If a dealer or a used vehicle manager neglects the pixel side of the business, they might as well keep the lights off and doors locked at their stores. Success in this Internet-driven retail environment requires the know-how to manage and massage online merchandising with the same care and attention many traditional dealers and used vehicle managers apply to their physical front line.

The next chapter details what this new breed of pixel proficiency is all about. It will also disclose and dissect what I believe are the critical, velocity-based pixel metrics that are essential for today's used vehicle success.

A SINFUL "PIXEL" PROBLEM

There's a disturbing disconnect—call it a sin even—that exists at most dealerships.

While the Internet is undoubtedly the single most important way of connecting dealerships with their potential customers, few have much, if any, knowledge of how well they leverage this medium to drive sales.

To be sure, many dealers and used vehicle managers know their inventories get posted to sites like *AutoTrader.com* and *Cars.com*. Some will also have a sense of how well these sites are working for their stores.

But that's about as deep as the knowledge typically goes.

I say this based on the hundreds of conversations I've had in the past year or two with dealers and used vehicle managers about what I call the pixel side of our business—the online merchandising that's necessary in today's Internet-driven used vehicle marketplace to get on a customer's shopping list for a specific vehicle.

It's not uncommon for these conversations to follow this track:

> *Dealer/used vehicle manager: "I'm paying way too much money to my third-party site for the results I'm getting. We're spending $4,000 a month to sell only a half-dozen vehicles. That's nearly $700 a car. We're thinking of firing them."*
>
> *Me: "Hold on a minute. Let me ask a couple questions before you do anything rash. How many Search Results Pages are you seeing on a monthly basis (SRPs)[11] ?"*
>
> *Dealer/used vehicle manager: "I don't know."*

---

[11]The Search Results Page metric is from *AutoTrader.com*, which I'm using solely for the sake of the example. *Cars.com, Carsdirect,* and other third-party classified sites offer similar benchmarks with different names to show dealers and used vehicle managers how online shoppers interact with their inventory listings.

Me: "OK. How about your detailed page views (VDPs)?"

Dealer/used vehicle manager: "I don't know that either."

Me: "OK. I'm asking about these metrics because they provide insight into what might be happening with potential customers on the third-party site. Let's try something different. Go to the vendor's site and plug in a vehicle you've got for sale. How about that '07 Toyota Camry?"

Dealer/used vehicle manager: "Hang on. OK. I'm in. I'm typing in '07 Camry."

Me: "Great. Now, when the results show up, they'll be from highest to lowest price. Most customers will probably re-sort the listings to see the lowest price, so do the re-sort and tell me where your vehicle shows up."

Dealer/used vehicle manager: "Got it. Hmmm...I'm not seeing my car on the first page, or the second. Hang on. Let me check a couple more. Oh, there it is. It's on the eighth page."

Me: "I see. How many total pages of '07 Camrys are there?"

Dealer/used vehicle manager: "Uhhh, 10 total pages."

Me: "OK. You're on the eighth page and it took you a couple of minutes to find it. Do you think a customer is likely to find your vehicle?"

Dealer/used vehicle manager: "Probably not."

Me: "What this tells me right away is that your price is near the top of the pack. That may or may not be OK. It depends on the vehicle. But it's fair to say the positioning isn't helping you connect with customers. The eighth page probably isn't in most customers' shopping sweet spot. How many photos are there, compared to the next vehicle?

Dealer/used vehicle manager: "Let's see... mine has 9, the next one has 27 and a video."

Me: "That may be another reason customers aren't clicking on your vehicle first. It's not as compelling. By the way, have you ever done this exercise before?"

Dealer/used vehicle manager: "No."

To me this kind of exchange is disturbing. How is it that any dealer or used vehicle manager who claims to be in the used vehicle business does not know the fundamentals of the online game?

Yet these conversations are all too frequent and familiar, and they suggest that many dealers and used vehicle managers have a boatload of catching up to do.

Automotive Internet retailing experts like Jared Hamilton of *DrivingSales.com* agree that many dealers misunderstand the role the Internet plays in the marketing and merchandising of their vehicles. To him, the third-party sites like *AutoTrader.com* and *Cars.com* are the point-of-entry for most stores.

Hamilton also agrees that many dealers and used vehicle managers "have a pile of data and don't realize the gold it contains."

I like Hamilton's explanation for why this disconnect occurs. As a third-generation dealer, he recognizes that stores often use imperfect systems to count showroom traffic.

"I talk to my dad and he is super-lucky if he has a good grasp on how many walk-ins, demos, and write-ups the store gets," he says. "You're counting on an imperfect system to collect data, hoping it can it can give you accurate data. With the Internet, it's almost unfathomable that we can have this kind of really articulated data. It's like we've been trained not to look for it."

Hamilton's take is spot-on. At most stores, the dealer and used vehicle manager know, in a heartbeat, what their average foot traffic should look like on any given day of the week. They'd probably also know the traffic averages on a monthly basis, too. That's true for almost every dealer and used vehicle manager I've ever encountered. Foot traffic is a key barometer/predictor of sales; hence dealers and used vehicle managers pay attention to it, as they should.

But there's little attention to the metrics like Search Results Pages and Detailed Page Views –the equivalent of online drive-by and foot traffic—at most stores.

Dealers and used vehicle managers are too often like the ones in my hypothetical conversation. They simply aren't aware of the essential building blocks of what makes a solid-performing pixel strategy.

In addition, I've found there's very little attention paid to the kind of online presentation tactics that truly resonate with today's online consumers, including pictures, consistent pricing, videos, descriptions, and the like.

So the time has come for dealers and used vehicle managers to shed the pixel sins of the past and gain a better understanding of pixel proficiency and how to leverage it effectively for their used vehicle operations.

The knee-jerk reaction of many dealers and used vehicle managers when they're dissatisfied with the expense and results of their online merchandising vendors is to blame them for the perceived shortcomings.

The ultimate responsibility for understanding the fundamentals of online merchandising and pixel proficiency rests squarely on the shoulders of dealers and used vehicle managers who are generally unaware.

I am hopeful that our discussion here will spur more conversations and to-do action lists at stores across the country as dealers and used vehicle managers recognize what they should be doing to enhance their own online merchandising.

But this discussion is only the proverbial tip of the iceberg. The next chapters will further emphasize why I believe pixels are just as important as paint for success in today's Internet-driven used vehicle marketplace.

Why "Pixel Proficiency" Is Critical

Flashback: Remember the initial discussions surrounding the impact the Internet would have on car dealerships?

Along with it came predictions and concerns such as those listed below:

- Factories would sell vehicles directly to consumers (a perception that execs like Jacque Nasser at Ford only helped fuel);

- Emotional debates about posting vehicle prices and inventories online;

- Scrambles to be the "exclusive first" to sign up for the hottest new lead generation provider;

- Scads of factory and third-party "build your website" options;

- Bitter disputes between Internet and showroom salespeople over who qualifies to be an Internet customer and who gets paid for those deals;

- Scores of Internet consultants who would turn dealerships into Internet stores;

- Fears of the demise of automotive retailing.

Thankfully, the "sky is falling" mentality has settled down. It's fair to say most dealers and used vehicle managers understand that the Internet plays such an essential role in today's business that they need to be online to have a shot at selling used vehicles.

The challenge now, however, is that just being online isn't good enough, particularly in used vehicles. This is true for several reasons:

1. Factories don't provide the same degree of online help for used vehicle departments as they do for new vehicle departments. Indeed, there are factory-sponsored online marketing and lead generation programs to support certified pre-owned programs, but beyond

that? Dealers and used vehicle managers are largely on their own when it comes to pixel support for their used vehicles.

2. Online customers are increasingly smarter about finding the sites they need to aid their shopping and product comparisons. Research from the Pew Internet and American Life Projects show that 80 percent of U.S. households have an Internet connection and they aren't just checking email.[12]

The upshot: Consumers know a good online experience when they encounter one. They know how to navigate websites to find what they need and they get annoyed when an online process is cumbersome or deliberately obtuse.

3. More dealerships are getting smarter about finding, targeting, and selling to today's online used vehicle buyers. These dealers and used vehicle managers know their SRPs and VDPs. They've nailed down processes to post pictures quickly, write compelling vehicle descriptions, price vehicles competitively and provide a customer-centric experience.

Some of these same stores are also heavily into advanced pixel proficiency that involves

---

[12] Pew Internet and American Life Project, http://www.pewinternet.org/Trend-Data/Online-Activities-20002009.aspx.

online marketing campaigns, search engine optimization (SEO), search engine marketing (SEM), social media engagement, and other outreach intended to enhance their store brands and sell more customers.

Among the stores that focus on search-related marketing, those who strike first will have a long-standing advantage. Search engines give credit to the longevity of web-sites and the traffic they capture—a factor that means "first to market is everything," notes Brian Benstock, the velocity- and pixel-savvy GM and Vice President for Queens, N.Y.-based Paragon Honda.

This should inject some degree of urgency into ratcheting up the pixel proficiency at dealerships, particularly those where deal-ers and used vehicle managers still rely on traditional paint-based ways of managing their used vehicle operations and have yet to fully leverage their presence on third-party sites like *AutoTrader.com* and *Cars.com*.

4. Pixel proficiency is a key stage toward a successful, velocity-based approach to managing used vehicle operations. It's one thing for a store to get all of its paint-based metrics—Market Days Supply, Price to Mar-ket and Cost to Market—in line with the market. It's quite another when a dealership

takes that foundation and builds upon it an efficient, velocity-minded online marketing and merchandising platform that positions inventory in places and at price points consumers will find appealing.

THE BUILDING BLOCKS OF "PIXEL PROFICIENCY"

I've been tracking the pixel proficiency of a composite of over 100 velocity-minded dealerships to gain a better understanding of what matters most when it comes to the online merchandising of used vehicles.

From a broad perspective, the dynamics around the placement, pricing, and positioning of used vehicle inventory can be divided into two main buckets— how consumers shop for used vehicles online and how dealerships can best capture the interests of online used vehicle shoppers.

Bucket 1: How consumers shop for used vehicles online and what they see. Industry statistics suggest that the majority of used vehicle shoppers like to see comparisons of vehicles when they shop. This explains the popularity of sites such as *AutoTrader.com*, *Cars.com*, *KBB.com*, and others. In a study conducted in late 2008, J.D. Power and Associates affirms these sites are the dominant players for online used vehicle shoppers and notes that shoppers are spending an increasing amount of time (about nine hours on average) researching, reviewing, and comparing vehicles they might purchase.[13]

"Consumers are going deeper in their searches," affirms Mitch Golub. "They're looking at more vehicles."

Consumers typically start their shopping queries at search engines, but the online listing sites offer the best unit-to-unit comparison functionality. In addition, these sites spend lots of money on advertising to brand themselves as go-to destinations for consumers.

And what about dealers' own websites? The importance of these sites should not be underestimated. But, for the most part, these sites currently play a secondary role to third-party sites when it comes to used vehicle shoppers. This dynamic is changing a bit but for our discussion of pixel proficiency, I'm going to limit the focus to the external sites that a) are utilized by a wider array of used vehicle shoppers with regularity and frequency and b) represent the best initial investment of time, money, and attention for dealers and used vehicle managers who seek to enhance their pixel proficiency.

---

[13] J.D. Power & Associates 2008 Used Vehicle Market Report, Dec. 2008, http://www.jdpower.com/corporate/news/releases/pressrelease.aspx?ID=2008267

These third-party sites typically break into two camps:

1. **Information-oriented sites, such as** *KBB.com,* **that provide a wealth of resources and car-buying pointers for consumers, as well as links to inventory listings.** From these listings, sites like *KBB.com* sell leads to dealers and used vehicle managers. Comparatively speaking, the leads these sites generate are less vehicle-specific than emails, queries, and calls that result from used vehicle shoppers landing on a dealer's used vehicle listings from sites like *AutoTrader.com* and *Cars.com.*

2. **Online classified sites.** These are the *AutoTrader.com* and *Cars.com* sites that host dealers' inventories and allow consumers the ability to search and sort listings in a variety of ways (by price, year/make/model, zip codes, etc.). These sites, which are really the online equivalent of the newspaper classified ads that dealerships purchased to advertise used vehicles in the past, typically do not let consumers drill into specific features and equipment in the initial search stages. Instead, online buyers narrow their choices and must-have options the deeper they explore inventory listings.

There are some important fundamental considerations dealers and used vehicle managers should
understand about these third-party sites:

Pay-to-play nature: Dealers can list their inventories for free on these sites, but they have
monetized the e-real estate in a way that pushes
dealerships to spend more money to achieve
maximum presence and merchandising flexibility. This is not necessarily a bad thing but
the lack of in-depth knowledge I've discerned at
most traditional dealerships suggests that some
dealers and used vehicle managers are paying
for functionality and e-real estate they're not
using as effectively as they could or should.

Size matters: Few dealers and used vehicle
managers understand that while sites like *Auto-
Trader.com* and *Cars.com* are ubiquitous, they
don't carry the same weight and potential for
every store. This occurs for two reasons:

1. The number of active shoppers varies from
    market to market. I've seen velocity dealer-
    ships in my 100-store sample with active
    shopper tallies that range from 25,000 to
    400,000 and above. The average active
    shopper tally in my sample on one of these
    third-party sites is 120,000. Most dealers
    and used vehicle managers are unaware of
    the active shopper statistic for their respec-

tive markets—a foundational data point for pixel proficiency and for evaluating why one site may work better than another.

It's absolutely true that many dealers and used vehicle managers have a sense that one site works better for them than another. But when I hear this comment and drill down, I rarely hear anyone mention active shopper stats to draw this conclusion.

2. The number of inventory listings, and their relevance to a given market, play a key role in capturing a consumer's eye online. In my 100-store sample, there's no question that velocity dealers with 200 units listed online get more SRPs and VDPs than dealers with only 40 units. This is true even when both stores have properly aligned their inventories to the Market Days Supply metric to assure they have the most in-demand vehicles.

As consumers are exploring these initial search listings pages, and then clicking to see a specific vehicle, they like to view photos, videos, and other features. This is also where price sensitivity and preference for one dealer's vehicle versus another's comes into play. It is also the point, for some consumers, where their online shopping stops.

Here's what I mean: Assume that two vehicles from competing dealers are comparable, they are both priced competitively, and they both tout the features and value that resonate with a buyer. This consumer might call or email the stores. He/she might also print out a map or print a copy of the individual vehicle listings.

The third-party sites track these behaviors and they can be useful drill-downs to show the degree to which consumers are interacting with a dealership's inventory listings. But the usefulness of this data only goes so far.

This is because an estimated 60 percent (some velocity dealers and used vehicle managers think it might be as high as 85 percent) of the shoppers who visit these sites will never call or email the store they intend to visit. They just show up. And when they do, they expect to find the vehicle they spotted available at the online advertised price. This dynamic speaks to a comment noted in the prior chapter that customers who call a dealership are ready to buy. So are many of the customers that just show up.

"You can't just be looking at emails and phone calls," says Chip Perry at *AutoTrader.com*. He notes an *AutoTrader.com*/Northwood University study from early 2009 that reports 60 percent of online shoppers do not raise their hands prior to visiting a dealership[14]. "Stores that only focus on chasing

---

[14] http://autotrader.mediaroom.com/index.php?s=43&item=148

leads are likely missing 60 percent of the closing opportunities."

Perry suggests this propensity for online shoppers to just show up signals a need for traditional dealerships to ensure their showroom sales team understands they are often dealing with well-informed customers. He recommends initial upfront qualifiers that identify these shoppers and respect what they likely already know about a vehicle and its price.

"Dealers need to take off their dealer glasses and put on their consumer glasses," Perry adds. When they do, they'll likely arrive at showroom sales processes that are better suited to work effectively with today's Internet-enabled buyers.

Bucket 2: How dealerships can best capture online shopper interest. One of the blessings of the third-party sites is that they are structured in a way that enables dealers and used vehicle managers to zero in on what matters most to capture customers. That is, each of the sites has specific elements that dealerships can leverage and light up to showcase their vehicle listings, depending on how much they decide to pay.

In essence, they are aiming to capture online shoppers' pick and click behaviors that occur when third-party sites serve up vehicle listings for consumers to review.

For example, when the sites list the equivalent of a Search Result Page that shows a series of vehicles from the sorts customers choose, they only see a top-line view: A photo, a brief description, and a few clues about what's in store for them if they click on the listing. Let's call this the bait for buyers.

From my 100-store sample, the velocity-minded dealerships that are more effective at baiting their top-line listings see more action than those that don't. This means playing up vehicle descriptions and having ample photos and video. For example, it seems more likely that a consumer would pick and click on a top-line listing that baits them with 27 photos and video, versus one that offers only nine photos and no video.

Perry agrees with this conclusion and notes that many dealers and used vehicle managers still take shortcuts on these important elements.

Of course, there are a myriad of variables that affect these consumer pick and click behaviors: the quality of photos/videos, the degree to which descriptions are compelling, the price of a vehicle, the unit itself, the premium placements dealerships might purchase, and more.

As Bill Pearson says, "you've got to do them all well, because they all play a part."

Other factors that affect the ability of dealers and used vehicle managers to capture online shopper interest are:

Inventory the market craves. I mentioned earlier that size matters in terms of inventory quantities dealerships post on third-party sites. More inventory means more chances for online consumers to review a store's inventory and follow the pick and click behaviors.

But it's more than just adding more vehicles to a store's inventory listings. The vehicles need to reflect the high-demand, low-supply characteristics measured by the Market Days Supply metric. The vehicles need to be right for a market, something traditional dealers and used vehicle managers with franchise first and gut-based biases will often miss.

Think of it this way: If a store stocked 1,000 Yugos and posted them online, would it see much consumer interest?

The answer is obviously no. But it's a hypothetical question that underscores how imperative it is to stock in-demand vehicles that the market deems worthy of the investment.

I would guess that many of the dealers and used vehicle managers who have beaten up their third-party site reps over poor results may not have recognized the role their own inventory mix played in driving outcomes that did not meet expectations.

Consistent, market-based prices. This is where velocity-minded dealers who use metrics like Price to Market have an edge on their traditional counterparts. Consumers are price-sensitive, and they understand when a dealer's asking price reflects the market. Likewise, they can spot when a vehicle's priced too high for a market.

This does not mean that every dealer and used vehicle manager needs to have the lowest price to attract shoppers—but it certainly doesn't hurt. Velocity dealers and used vehicle managers know that if they set a vehicle to be a price leader in its segment compared to other competing vehicles, they will see spikes in consumer interest. This is a valuable insight that helps them move out aging inventory to make way for fresher units with greater profit potential.

Mitch says he's seeing a sizable increase in the number of dealers in the past year who are actively making price changes on their vehicles. "It's increased precipitously," he says. "The best-performing dealers are those who are changing prices as much as four to five times a day."

This sensitivity to price reflects the fact that a wider number of dealers and used vehicle managers recognize that price is important and competitive prices are paramount.

Golub and I share a laugh when we discuss pricing and how it has come full circle from the early days of the Internet when dealers and used vehicle managers resisted showing any prices at all online. As it happens, the fears that consumers would take posted prices and beat up salespeople on every deal have been replaced with the reality that consumers expect to see prices online and, if they don't, quite often move past the un-priced vehicle to shop vehicles that show a price.

A cautionary point about pricing: It's not uncommon for consumers, after they review a dealership's vehicle listing on a third-party site, to check out the store's website to confirm that a vehicle is available and to find out more about how the store conducts business.

This is a critical part of the shopping funnel that creates a few challenges for dealers and used vehicle managers:

1. **Pricing parity:** Between the third-party sites and dealers' own websites, there are often multiple back-end feeds that handle the updates of prices, photos, and other bait elements to individual vehicle listings. It's

not uncommon for snags to occur that result in the same vehicle being priced differently across these multiple platforms. Consumers can spot these inconsistencies, and they are potential interest-killers as it suggests a dealership is less transparent about pricing than others. It suggests old school pricing and sales practices that can be a turn-off for today's buyers.

The good news: Today's technology allows audits of pricing across the third-party platforms and dealer websites to ensure customers see the consistency they seek when they shop online.

2. **Showroom parity.** At some velocity dealerships, dealers and used vehicle managers capitalize on the fact that they're using the Price to Market metric to set their used vehicle prices. They tell consumers they mine the Internet for prices, and set theirs accordingly.

At Sam Swope Auto Group in Louisville, Kentucky, they call this Internet Value Pricing. "We address this right up front," says Cary Donovan. "We'll even go online and say, 'Let's make sure this is the correct price.'" The approach builds credibility with customers and eases anxiety they might have had about the store sticking to the price they saw online.

Donovan adds that it's not uncommon, given the dealer group's daily attention to the Price to Market metric, for customers to get an even lower price than the one that they saw online. "We go with the price that's posted on a given day—which is often more favorable for customers," he says.

"PIXEL PROFICIENCY" PITFALLS

There are a lot of spots along the path to pixel proficiency where things can run amuck.

One of the key trouble spots is properly allocating the work that's necessary to be effective with online merchandising and marketing.

At many stores, these responsibilities often fall to the used vehicle managers. In some cases, this translates to a savvy paint-minded manager being charged with pixel proficiency when he or she lacks the time and/or skills to do so effectively. I've compiled a list of what I call the "murky water" of the daily tasks associated with "pixel proficiency."

The upshot: It's unreasonable to expect any one person, particularly those who have long been paint-minded experts, to do this job. It takes a coordinated effort across a dealership organization to effectively execute a winning pixel strategy for today's used vehicle marketplace.

A second pitfall results from the distrust and disinterest many dealers and used vehicle managers hold toward the third-party site reps that make monthly visits to their stores.

This pitfall became crystal-clear to me during a recent lunch when I was discussing the relationships two dealers had with their third-party reps.

> **Dealer #1:** "I can't stand my rep. Every time he's here, he's always asking me to spend more money. I don't even make time for him anymore. I let my used vehicle manager handle that."

> **Dealer #2:** "That's a big mistake, Don. You need to hug that guy. You need to love the guy you hate. You spend a lot of money with them and they hold the key to a lot of information that you need to excel."

This disparity is both striking and profound. It certainly explains why some dealers and used vehicle managers lack any real understanding of SRPs and VDPs or their equivalents and other fundamentals that drive success on third-party sites.

From my conversations with *Cars.com* and *AutoTrader.com*, the view of Dealer #2 is gaining ground. "We're seeing higher-level people in dealerships showing up at our training," says Golub at *Cars.com*.

Peek into the murky water

% of vehicles in the shop for more than 72 business hours?

% of vehicles on your lot that don't have a window sticker matching current price?

% of vehicles that have multiple prices?

% of vehicles with unacceptable time to Internet?

% of vehicles on your physical lot not yet on the Internet?

% of vehicles with no online price?

% of vehicles with incorrect prices?

% of vehicles that are not being published to all designated sites?

AutoTrader.com's notes that the company is investing heavily in training its reps to play a more active, consulting role with their dealership clients to help them gain a better understanding of the existing metrics to improve their pixel proficiency.

"PIXEL PROFICIENCY" 101 : NEW BENCHMARKS TO GUIDE SUCCESS

It's impossible for anyone to perform at their best if they lack an understanding of what defines best.

In business, achievement or success is often defined by clear benchmarks and goals. In used vehicles, our historic benchmarks have been gross profit per vehicle retailed (PVR) and sales volumes.

It should be clear from this book that these metrics remain useful in today's more efficient and volatile used vehicle marketplace, but they are crude barometers compared to the more market-attuned and data-rich management insights that come from guiding used vehicle operations with paint-based metrics such as Market Days Supply, Price to Market, and Cost to Market.

When it comes to online merchandising of used vehicles, or pixel proficiency, our industry has not yet clearly defined the benchmarks that offer a clear path for where time and effort should be focused to most efficiently and effectively drive success.

In the previous chapter, we noted how dealers and used vehicle managers often fail to pay attention to the basic metrics that flow from the third-party vendors that provide the shopping portals most used vehicle buyers pass through as they shop for the car that's right for them.

But even with these metrics, such as Search Results Pages (SRPs) and Vehicle Detail Pages (VDPs) and their equivalents, there's little understanding of what constitutes a good job. For example, 25,000 search results pages or 10,000 detailed page views sound like big numbers, but what do they mean? Should these numbers be 200,000 and 12,000, respectively? What kind of conversion ratio might dealers and used vehicle managers expect from their SRPs? What is the relationship between these metrics and sales?

From my study of 100 velocity dealerships, I've come up with benchmarks to help dealers and used vehicle managers gain a clearer understanding of the baseline performance they should expect from their efforts to merchandise and sell used vehicles online.

These benchmarks offer insights to help dealers and managers enhance their pixel proficiency. The benchmarks offer clues on any hiccups that might occur in the shopping funnel. For example, if a store has a high number of SRPs, and few VDPs, it suggests something's wrong with the initial bait that's meant to entice a click-through, or it may signal a problem with pricing.

Similarly, if a store has a low number of SRPs and a high conversion rate to VDPs, it suggests the bait is working fine but something is off in the initial positioning, quantity of inventory, pricing, or vehicle mix.

It's my hope that the pixel benchmarks I've developed from my 100-store sample will help answer these important questions. The ultimate goal for dealers and managers is to become more astute about their pixel proficiency and enjoy the rewards of the additional used vehicle sales volumes and profits that await those who properly leverage this proficiency.

Before sharing these new benchmarks, however, I'd like to address a few problems with the benchmarks many dealers and used vehicle managers currently use to evaluate ROI from third-party listing sites and demonstrate why the new pixel benchmarks offer a better way forward.

Problems With "Pick and Click" Benchmarks

Before reading this next section, I might suggest that dealers and used vehicle managers remove any untethered items from their immediate reach. What I'm about to share may raise the blood pressure for some readers.

In my discussions with dealers and used vehicle managers about the ROI they get from third-party sites, and the often-reflexive dissatisfaction with results, I've come to realize that these ROI benchmarks are flawed.

These benchmarks are typically the cost-per-lead and cost-per-vehicle sold. Each of these flows from the pick and click behaviors that result when consumers drill down to a specific vehicle listing (a VDP or its equivalent).

That is, once an online shopper takes an interest in a vehicle, he/she may make a phone call, send an email, or print out directions to a store or the vehicle listing itself.

Let's examine both of these calculations and why they don't show a true picture of the two-way nature of a third-party site's performance for a dealership:

Cost per lead. For this benchmark, dealers and used vehicle managers take the number of phone calls or emails they receive from a third-party site, and divide that figure into the total cost they pay on a monthly basis for the site's listing services.

So if a dealership receives 100 phone calls from a third-party site, and pays $5,000 a month to list its inventory, the cost per lead is $50. Most dealers and used vehicle managers believe that this is an accurate read on the traction they receive from the third-party site and the effectiveness of the site's ability to draw in customers.

I believe this calculation is problematic. For example:

Reason 1: The 100 phone calls represent only a portion of the customers who viewed the inventory. Remember the *AutoTrader.com*/Northwood University data I referenced earlier? For every 100 shoppers who visit and view used vehicle listings, an estimated 60 percent will show up at a store without making a call or sending an email.

By some estimates, phone calls and leads represent hand-raisers who account for about 20 percent of all the shoppers who may view a dealership's inventory listings. So, the cost per lead calculation is only counting a portion of the site's ability to attract customers.

Reason 2: Most dealers and used vehicle managers understand that the costs for individual third-party sites vary. *AutoTrader.com*, for example, offers more advertising options and functionality for dealers and used vehicle managers who sign up and pay for their Partner and Alpha programs.

By definition, the leads that flow from this site will cost more than others. So a strict, cost-per-lead analysis would suggest *AutoTrader.com* may not be worth the money compared to another vendor.

This is a misguided conclusion. In addition to not accounting for *all* of the shoppers who may become customers via a third-party site, the cost-per-lead calculation doesn't capture the value that leads from one site might offer compared to another. What if the phone calls from one third-party site resulted in more F&I income? What if one site proves to be a better outlet for price leaders, high-line vehicles, and/ or early model vehicles?

The cost-per-lead calculation does not capture these nuances. A store that strictly follows cost-per-lead calculations to determine ROI could be missing out on some key opportunities.

Reason 3: The simple cost-per-lead calculation fails to account for other critical details, such as the number of unique vehicles receiving leads. For example, what if 20 of the 100 monthly leads came from a single vehicle? While it's true that a lead is a lead, this additional information might affect the way the dealership values these leads and assess their online listing costs.

Reason 4: What if a dealership's own listings lack the quality and depth of photos, descriptions, and value proposition on its vehicles compared to competitors? How does a cost-per-lead calculation account for these pixel deficiencies? Is it fair to hold a third-party site accountable for a store's own pixel execution shortcomings?

My point here is that the cost-per-lead calculation has value, but it does not definitively offer any make-or-break ROI conclusions about a third-party site's performance nor does it deliver any solid, practical insight on how to fix shortcomings in a store's online merchandising and pixel presentation.

Cost-Per-Vehicle Sold: This calculation, which divides the monthly cost for a third-party site by the number of vehicles a store gives it credit for delivering, falls victim to some of the same shortcomings that render the cost-per-lead calculations ineffective as a barometer of a third-party site's performance.

In addition to the fact that this calculation does not account for online shoppers who visit a site and view listings but do not call or email before showing up at a dealership, the cost-per-vehicle sold calculation incorrectly saddles the third-party vendor with accountability for a store's sales processes.

For example, let's say the store in our example above that spent $5,000 a month sells 20 vehicles from the 100 calls it received from its third-party partner (a 20 percent conversion rate). That translates to a cost-per-vehicle sold of $250.

The problem? The third-party site has nothing to do with the ability of a store to convert leads into sold customers. What if the store was able to close 35 percent of the 100 leads it received? If it did, that would put the cost-per-vehicle at $143. In this instance, dealers and used vehicle managers would likely view that as a positive, and credit themselves for a high close ratio. I doubt they'd turn to their third-party vendor and say, "You did a great job helping us close our leads."

Likewise, the cost-per-vehicle sold metric also fails to account for a dealership's own shortcomings with its online merchandising and pixel presentation. It does not assess how many customers got away because they didn't like what they saw on the detailed vehicle listing.

Now, I suspect some readers are poking holes in my assessment of the value of these pick and click-based ROI calculations.

The most obvious hole might come from dealers and used vehicle managers who have great faith in their showroom traffic assessment tools that capture and detail how an "up" arrived at their stores.

These dealers and used vehicle managers will say their salespeople and BDC teams are well trained and know how to properly and respectfully ask customers to detail the specific third-party sites they visited and where they saw the vehicle that brought them to the store.

To them, I tip my hat. They have apparently solved one of the most persistent and problematic issues that have plagued dealerships from the beginning of time. In addition, they must have figured out a way to ensure that every customer remembers their online shopping and shares it truthfully.

Most dealerships lack the kind of traffic-tracking sophistication that would make the cost-per-lead and cost-per-sale metrics truly reliable gauges of a third-party site's performance. For them I would suggest that new pixel metrics are more reliable ways to assess the blend of the third-party site's platform and a dealership's ability to effectively execute its pixel proficiency within the platform.

As the old saying goes, "it takes two to tango," and this is especially true with the third-party sites.

NEW BENCHMARKS TO GAUGE PIXEL PROFICIENCY

As noted earlier, dealers and used vehicle managers need to better understand the equivalent of SRPs and VDPs, and how they relate to each other, to get the best read possible on their pixel proficiency on third-party sites.

It's through understanding these data points and related benchmarks that dealers and used vehicle managers can begin to see where they may be falling short with their online merchandising and pixel presentation of used vehicles.

The new benchmark metrics I'm about to share flow from my study of 100 velocity-minded dealerships across the country. Each of these stores retails at least 100 used vehicles a month, they hail from markets of different sizes, and their respective inventories possess similar paint metric characteristics—Market Days Supply, Price to Market and Cost to Market.

This pool was selected to normalize the study: By meeting the benchmark averages for the paint metrics, these stores all carry inventory their markets crave at price points that are compelling to potential buyers. This normalization is necessary because, as noted in the last chapter, the type of inventory and prices for specific units play a key role in whether an online shopper will click on a dealership's vehicle listing or go to another one.

So with this normalization, we can begin to examine the relationships between SRPs and VDPs or their equivalents.

A quick refresher: SRPs are merely opportunities. The statistic represents the number of times online shoppers viewed a search results page that included a specific dealership's inventory listing. VDPs represent the next, more valuable step: The number of consumers who actually clicked on a dealership's inventory listing to more closely examine a vehicle.

So, given the interplay between SRPs and VDPs, here are the baseline benchmarks that matter most:

SRP Baseline Benchmark: On average, the velocity-minded stores in the sample group generate 250,000 SRPs each month. Some see as many as 1.5 million, some as few as 25,000. The best I can tell, the difference owes mostly to three factors:

1. The number of active shoppers in a dealer's market area. The dealership that sees 1.5 million often has a larger shopper base than the store with 25,000 SRPs.

2. The amount and position of screen real estate the velocity dealerships leverage on the third-party sites. The dealer that buys up every advertising option available has positioned himself to realize a higher number of SRPs than a dealer that has a more limited investment. It is an inescapable fact that screen real estate matters a lot in getting your vehicles noticed. Dealers often balk at online sales reps that propose additional expenditures while the truth is these incremental investments pale in comparison to the price of purchasing less effective conventional media such as newspaper, radio, or television.

3. The size of each dealer's inventory. The dealer with higher SRPs has 400 units in inventory, while the second dealer carries about 50 units.

Now here's where this example gets interesting: The second dealer decided he wanted to increase sales volumes. He bought up all the advertising options available on the third-party site and increased his inventory. His SRP count now runs nearly 400,000. It's still less than the dealer with 1.5 million SRPs, but the example shows that inventory size and screen real estate are critical drivers for SRP counts.

VDP Conversion Benchmark: Given the variability in market size noted in the above SRP discussion, the number of VDPs is less important for benchmark purposes than the ratio of conversions from SRPs to VDPs. From my study, dealers and used vehicle managers should aim for a conversion rate benchmark of 3 to 4 percent to be considered pixel proficient. So, if a store has 100,000 SRPs, they should expect a minimum of 3,000 VDPs.

If the VDP conversion rate is lower, it suggests a problem with the pixel bait that appears with a vehicle listing on a search result page: Is there a photo? Does it look good? Is the price correct? Is the description fresh and snappy? Or does its VIN decode text read like Ben Stein's monotone: "Bueller...Bueller?[15]"

Likewise, if the VDP tally is higher, it suggests a store understands the SRP sweet spots that entice customers to click deeper.

In my study, velocity stores that consistently hit this conversion ratio each month sustained their sales

---

[15] http://en.wikipedia.org/wiki/Ferris_Bueller%27s_Day_Off

volumes while stores that fell below the ratio did not. It's worth noting that when the ratio dropped, the dealers and used vehicle managers report some aspect of their pixel processes fell short.

For example, the dealer who bought up all the advertising options to increase his SRP tally saw an unexpected two-point drop in his VDP conversions. The dip caused him to look harder at his pixel presentation and processes. His conclusion: The additional volume was not being well managed—photos and prices were missing online. After correcting these errors, his VDP conversions returned to a pixel proficient level. It should therefore be noted that it is not prudent to purchase additional screen real estate and/or increase inventory size until and unless the dealership is able to convert SVPs into VDPs efficiently. To do so would be the equivalent of spending additional money to drive more traffic to the showroom without adequate sales personnel to handle the incremental "ups."

Such is the nature of pixel proficiency. It takes a mix of investment and trial and error to find the sweet spot of inventory mix, pixel bait, and price to consistently connect with online shoppers. This type of hands-on attention is critical for dealerships who aspire to do a better job with their used vehicle operations.

Dealers and used vehicle managers who pay greater attention to SRP and VDP benchmarks, and understand the paint and pixel elements that drive them, will be better positioned to capture consumer attention and will see more opportunities to sell vehicles.

As noted earlier, the reps from third-party sites recognize that dealers and used vehicle managers need to develop a better understanding of what matters most to drive consumer interest in a store's used vehicle listings.

Here's a two-part agenda I would recommend every dealer and used vehicle manager follow for the next monthly visit from third-party site reps:

1. **A review of SRP and VDP benchmarks.** The discussion should address expectations, given the number of active shoppers in a market and comparable stats from competitors.

2. **Deeper discussions of any differences/variations in a store's pixel performance.** Prior to the meeting, dealers and used vehicle managers should do their own review to see what they think might be falling short—whether it's photos, price, inventory mix, descriptions, etc. These insights will drive a more fruitful and telling discussion with the third-party site reps.

Every dealer and used vehicle manager has heard the old management phrase: You have to inspect what you expect. The benchmarks in this chapter lay the groundwork for what dealerships should expect from their online listings on third-party sites. Now, the time has come for pixel inspections to begin in earnest.

A REAL-TIME AUDIT OF "PIXEL PROFICIENCY"

It's pretty telling what one sees by taking off the "dealer glasses" and putting on the "consumer glasses."

For a little fun, I decided to jump on the *Auto-Trader.com* website and do a couple vehicle searches. My thinking: Let's see how dealers in a 25-mile range of my Chicago-area zip code are doing with their "pixel proficiency." I settled on two different searches for vehicles, and opted to solely view the listings pages.

Here's what I found:

> **Search 1: The "Family Car" Search.** I figured I'd look for what might be a typical second car, and entered a broad query for a 2004-2009 four-door sedan, priced between $12,000 and $15,000. There were 25 pages of results, so I set a low to high price sort and looked closely at the vehicles on the first page.

"Family Car" Search Stats

Total # of dealers: 19 (one independent)
   # of dealers with multiple listings: 5
Total # of private sellers: 1
Average # of photos/listing: 16
   # of listings without photos: 1
   # of listings with 27 photos*: 3
   # of listings with videos: 6
      (4 from two dealers, 2 from individual stores)
   # of listings with Carfax reports: 8

*27 is the maximum number of photos AutoTrader.com allows.

The findings are eye-opening:

- **Inconsistencies across listings from the same stores and dealer groups.** Of the five stores that had multiple listings, four offered vehicles with different numbers of photos on each listed unit; one offered a video on one listing but not another.

- **Inconsistent descriptions and/or pricing:** To me, a one-word change (One Owner! to 1 OWNER!), doesn't count as a compelling or unique vehicle description but this is how a Nissan store differentiated two '06 Nissan Altimas (one blue, one gold). Another potential problem: Despite the exact same equipment and an 11,100-mile odometer difference, the store listed both vehicles at $12,490. These strike me as signs of an inattentive hand.

- **Varying degrees of snap in vehicle descriptions.** Of the three descriptions below, which one comes from the keyboard of the sole private seller on my listing page?

  (A.) Power Steering, Power Brakes, Power Door Locks, Power Windows, Alloy Wheels, Trip Odometer, Tachometer, Air Conditioning, Tilt Steering Wheel, Cruise Control, Interval Wipers, Rear Defroster, Console, Front Bucket Seats, Cloth Upholstery, Center Arm Rest, Drive

  (B.) All scheduled maintenance, Always garaged, Fully loaded, Ice cold A/C, Looks & runs great, Must see, New tires, No accidents, Non-smoker, One owner, Power everything, Perfect first car,

Runs & drives great, Satellite radio, Very clean...

*(C.) *CONSTRUCTION SALE NOW IN PROGRESS******CALL NOW TO MAKE AN OFFER***, Tilt Wheel, Dual Front Air Bags, Power Windows, Air Conditioning, Power Door Locks, MP3 (Single CD), Power Steering, Cruise Control, AM/FM Stereo, PWR FRONT DISC/REAR DRUM BRAK.*

The answer: B. There's no question the text reads and feels better than the other two.

While we're on the subject of vehicle descriptions and having a little fun, check out these descriptions from the listing page and my commentary[16]:

From the "cluttered cliché" file: *This searing-hot 2007 Chevrolet Impala is the high-performance car you've been aching to get your hands on. All good things must come to an end, but don't worry...it'll be there in your driveway next morning, waiting for another adrenaline...*

My take: Did you drink too much Red Bull?

---

[16]My apologies to anyone who recognizes a description here. My aim is to educate, not humiliate. I hope you view the feedback as valuable

From the "kill 'em with ALL CAPS" file:
LOADED LACROSSE HERE!! FUEL EFFICIENT V6 ENGINE KEEPS THIS LUXURY SEDAN GOING WITHOUT KILLING YOU AT THE PUMP!! WHAT LUXURY YOU ASK?? HOW ABOUT A SUNROOF!! FULL POWER TILT AND SLIDE!! COMFORTABLE LEATHER SEATS ARE FULL POWER AND HEATED!! AM/FM/CD

My take: Aside from the ALL CAPS, I like how this description plays up fuel economy and value-add features like a sunroof.

From the "honesty" file: *Stop by to Experience the (dealer name removed) Difference !!! - This vehicle shows no sign of paint work. This vehicle was tastefully optioned. With just 38,946 miles, this car is barely broken in. This vehicle has been inspected. Very clean interior!*

My take: Honesty is never a bad policy. I like the language. But I wonder what happened to the tasteful options? Did somebody steal them?

From the "folksy" file: *"THIS LIKE NEW GALANT IS PRICED TO SELL! (NAME REMOVED) OUR USED CAR MGR SAYS THERE'S OVER 42K MILES OF FULL FACTORY WARRANTY LEFT!! THIS*

*GALANT QUALIFIES FOR EXTRA LOW-
LOW-LOW PAYMENTS!!! YOU BETTER
HURRY IN AND GET THIS GREAT DEAL
WHILE IT S...*

My take: Nice personal touch to include the manager's name. FYI: The "caps lock" key is located at the left of most computer keyboards, just above the "shift" key.

From the "Bueller Bueller" file: *Driver Air Bag, Passenger Air Bag, A/C, AM/FM Stereo, CD Player, Front Disc/Rear Drum Brakes, Rear Defrost, Child Safety Locks, Front Wheel Drive, Auto-On Headlights, Daytime Running Lights, Power Driver Mirror, Pass-Through Rear Seat, Cloth Seats.*

My take: Thank God! This car has rear drum brakes. I was looking for a set of those.

Search 2: The "Hot Seller" Search. My goal here was to see how listings might look for a hot-selling used vehicle. Would they showcase a greater degree of pixel proficiency, given the hot-model status?

I searched for a used 2005-2009 Prius entering the same zip code as for the Family Car Search above. I didn't set any price parameters, or specify a certified vehicle. I sorted by low-to-high price, and looked closely at the first 25 listings (see stats box, this page).

Again, the listings were revealing:

- **Consistent use of videos.** Three stores used videos consistently across their listings, though the number of photos they offered across listings varied by two or three photos.

- **Fewer "Bueller Bueller" descriptions.** By my count, 17 of the listings showed some sign of a human touch. Theme-wise, "Go Green" played prominently in descriptions from two dealerships, a wise nod to the hybrid's appeal.

- **Favoring photos/videos over descriptions.** One of the stores that offered a full complement of photos and video included the same vehicle description for three of its four units.

"Hot Seller" Search Stats

Total # of dealers: 11
   (no independent or non-Toyota dealers)
   # of dealers with multiple listings: 6
Total # of private sellers: 0
Average # of photos/listing: 16
   # of listings without photos: 3 (all "newly listed")
   # of listings with 27 photos: 7
   # of listings with videos: 10 (all from three dealers)
   # of listings with Carfax reports: 18

- **One "Alpha" dealer.** This dealer has invested additional money to have a logo/listing appear on *AutoTrader.com's* "search-in-progress" screen and a prominent listing on the listing page.

- **Expired financing options.** Vehicle descriptions from two separate dealers noted reduced-rate financing deals with expired "act now" dates.

- **ALL CAPs continues.** Nine of the 25 listings were in ALL CAPs. I'm blind, so this doesn't really bother me. But I'm told with conviction from my wife, family, and colleagues that it's ANNOYING and it is considered shouting. That's enough for me to suggest dealers and used vehicle managers discontinue the practice.

All in all, it's safe to say that pixel proficiency remains spotty across the results of my two random searches. Some dealers and used vehicle managers do a better job, others do a not-so-good job. The fact that I found so many pixel trouble spots after reviewing only 50 listings suggests a larger problem for our industry. Namely, that we are missing opportunities.

Technology Improves Pixel Consistency, Pizzazz

A first step to correcting the pixel problems in this chapter is a self-assessment. I would encourage every dealer and used vehicle manager to take the time to see how their inventory listings on third-party sites stack up against other dealers in their markets.

In suggesting this, I recognize why this exercise has gone undone at many stores. It's a flat-out pain to get vehicle photos and descriptions online in the first place—let alone tweak the finer points of pixel proficiency.

A lack of time is not a good enough excuse to let such process and execution shortcomings undermine a store's profit potential because, make no mistake, these efforts will directly affect online traffic, showroom "ups," and, ultimately the bottom line.

Velocity dealerships use technology to audit their pixel proficiency and figure out why they may see drops in their SRPs and VDPs or their equivalents. This technology can spot inconsistencies in pricing and missing photos/videos/vehicle descriptions and offer alerts when these issues occur.

Joe Pistell, marketing director for *UsedCarKing.com,* which has three locations in upstate New York, noticed a lead-count drop from *Cars.com*. His lead averages were fine from *AutoTrader.com*, so he suspected a potential problem on the former site.

Using the tracking technology, Pistell found a 20 percent discrepancy between the number of photos on *Cars.com* compared with *AutoTrader.com* (184 units without photos). Technology allowed him to create and send a list of the vehicles and stock numbers to his Web team. It took him 30 minutes to create the list, and his team fixed the problem by the following day. His lead tallies subsequently picked up.

"Like every good manager, I make my rounds walking the online inventory," Pistell says. "I look around and see a missing picture here and there, but I'd *never* connect this to a larger problem. By far, that was the best 30 minutes I've spent in a long time. This technology saved me time and money."

In addition to audit technology, some velocity dealers and used vehicle managers also use technology to automate vehicle description-writing—another key time-saver.

"This changes the whole game of getting good descriptions," says a West Coast dealer who uses the tool.

The intent of this chapter is to underscore the importance of putting the time, energy, and effort into ensuring that all aspects of the pixel bait that consumers see on third-party sites bear the same kind of consistency and pristine look and feel that dealers and used vehicle managers work hard to achieve with their physical inventories every day.

If I was the dealer or used vehicle manager at the stores I spotted in my used vehicle searches, I would have a sizable to-do list for my pixel team.

Simply stated, it is no longer acceptable to allow inconsistencies and holes to erode the impact of online inventory listings. Photos and descriptions are far too important, and the screen real estate here is far too expensive and valuable, to publish what amounts to bush league pixel bait.

From what I can tell, virtually every dealer and used vehicle manager can and should do a better job on this front. It's really a choice of conviction to change or complacency.

Let's move into some examples of pixel proficiency done right.

Dialing Up "Pixel Proficiency"

Here's another chapter that needs a bit of explanation. While there is a lot of buzz about more sophisticated Internet marketing tactics that will be described below, I believe that dealers should defer taking action until they have mastered the basic pixel proficiencies outlined to this point.

Therefore, don't get too spun up on some of the heavy detail, just take what you need when needed.

For more than a decade, a soundproof booth played a key role in the advertising and marketing strategy for the Sam Swope Auto Group.

"We did testimonial advertising exclusively for 14 years," says Sam Swope, the 83-year-old first generation dealer who's built a powerhouse of 15 stores from the humble beginnings of a Dodge/Plymouth store he opened in 1952 in Elizabethtown, Ky.

"We had a soundproof booth upstairs from the showroom. We'd always ask our customers, 'How much did you save?'" Swope explains. "We gave the customer $1 and they dutifully stated the amount of their saving. The salesman's reward was that we put his name in the ad."

These days, however, it's a different kind of booth that plays a critical role in the advertising and marketing strategy for the Swope operation. This booth occupies the corner of a warehouse that houses the used vehicle detailing and touch-up shop, located about a quarter-mile from Swope's campus-like collection of stores.

It's an open-air space, with movable backdrops and light diffusers, and a 16'-diameter revolving platform in the center. The platform shows the tire tracks of vehicles that make their way up to sit for the 27 photos that will become a critical part of the pixel presentation for Swope's online used vehicle inventory.

Swope's director of used vehicle operations, Cary Donovan, says he's not done tweaking the booth's lighting, camera placements, and other technical specs. "I'm still working on the concept," he says. "There's no template for this."

And he's right. Across the country, dealerships are figuring out how best to showcase their used vehicles online and to do so in a manner that allows speed and control of the process. It's the desire for speed and control—and the efficiencies that come from both—that push some dealers and used vehicle managers to take a do-it-yourself (DIY) approach to handling the pixel processes of their online used vehicle merchandising and sales.

Craig Belowski also favors a DIY approach. He has cross-trained his Internet manager and salespeople to handle the photo-taking for when his part-time student photographer isn't available. They also know how to do touch-up work in Photoshop, an editing program. The store dedicates a delivery bay for photo-taking and seeks a unified look and feel for all of its used vehicles, with an average of 18 photos per vehicle.

"The photos are done consistently," Belowski says. 'They're an important part of our process."

In many instances, trial and error plays a key role in the learning curve. The playbook for pixel proficiency is still being written and, as every dealer and used vehicle manager knows, advances in new technologies and online destinations seem to keep pushing the finish line further away.

A better way to think of pixel proficiency is to realize that there is no finish line. By its nature, online merchandising and marketing of used vehicles is evolutionary. What works today may be outdated by tomorrow. Such is the nature of today's technology-driven business environment, and the role the Internet plays in retailing used vehicles.

That's why a metrics-minded approach to managing and monitoring pixel proficiency is critical. Technology can change, but the metrics remain constant beacons for what works and what doesn't. It's like a boat on storm-whipped waters at night. The captain may not be able to see exactly what's coming, or even know for certain that all is well, but his compass provides the course for a safe return to port.

With that backdrop, let's take a closer look at the pixel-based processes that some velocity-minded dealers and used vehicle managers use to do a better job of online merchandising and marketing their used vehicle inventories.

Pixel-Based Best Practices for Online Merchandising

As noted, photos of used vehicles are key elements of the pixel bait that can attract potential buyers to a dealership's online inventory. In addition to the DIY approaches that Donovan and Belowski use for taking photos, they also ensure this part of the pixel process doesn't delay their potential to make maximum gross profit.

Donovan strives for a 48- to 72-hour turnaround from the time a vehicle arrives at Swope to the time it is reconditioned, photographed, and posted online. This is a far faster turnaround rate than what occurs at many traditional dealerships.

In fact, at many of these stores, dealers and used vehicle managers aim for a 3-to-5-day turnaround, but the reality is closer to 7 to 10 days. At velocity stores where the average time in inventory is typically less than 25 days, a 10-day lag is an unacceptable delay that translates to lost profit potential.

At Finish Line Ford in Peoria, Ill., this kind of delay is unacceptable. Thanks to technology, Bill Pearson has at least one photo posted online within minutes of his acquisition of any used vehicle at auctions. He relies on back-end data transfers (including the stock photos from auctions and other sources) to post the unit to his DMS and get it online quickly.

"We can have the car online and for sale the same day or within 24 hours, even if it hasn't been through service," says Pearson, whose detailers and touch-up crews get paid for fast work as soon as a vehicle arrives on a transport. "If your car isn't online, it's not for sale."

Here are a few other pixel process nuggets to consider for photos:

Brand your store. This may be an obvious point, but some dealers and used vehicle managers overlook the branding opportunities that exist for their stores via store-logoed frames, backdrops, and license plate holders. In fact, there is new technology available that allows dealers to put a watermark on each and every photo.

Highlight the finer features. If the Market Days Supply reflects that a unit's sunroof, GPS, entertainment system, leather seats, or other features

---

A Personalized Pixel Approach

Here's a quick look at how one store does a little extra pixel work with customers.

Once a customer lead arrives, an Internet sales person calls and typically leaves a message. Next step: Send a biography on the vehicle that includes photos, Carfax report and directions to the dealership and a quote. They also send a custom, from-the-desk video that explains how the salesperson will handle his/her role in guiding and completing a deal.

After an appointment is set, salespeople then use flip phones they've purchased themselves to send a 60-second walk-around of the vehicle the customer likes.

The upshot: "Customers recognize that we're going out of our way to help," the store's e-commerce director says. "That's been the big difference for us."

add to its value, it's important for photos to showcase these gems. Some dealers and used vehicle managers tweak the order of the photos they serve up on vehicles to give more prominence to these value-building add-ons.

Show your team. Few stores do this, but it strikes me as a nice touch. The photos show sales team members and speak to a store's "we'll take care of you" message.

Beyond photos, videos and descriptions play a key role in effective, pixel-smart online merchandising. Here's a brief look at both topics:

Vehicle videos: These are all the rage as consumers pay more attention to vehicles that include videos than those that only offer up pictures. It adds one more piece of pixel bait to the initial search listing pages online shoppers see when they hunt third-party sites for vehicles.

Typically, dealers and used vehicle managers include vehicle-focused videos that may be a collection of still photos, with an audio track. Other stores go a step further and create walk-around videos of the vehicle with audio from a member of the Internet or sales team.

Howard Polirer, director of industry relations for *AutoTrader.com* says video testimonials offer another credibility-building component to a dealer's pixel bait. The goal, he notes, is "why buy from me?" differentiation. "A lot of the obstacles with videos have been removed," says Polirer, referring to difficulties with uploads and customer load times.

It's important to note that videos also feed the online marketing aspects of a dealership's pixel proficiency. A growing number of dealers are using *YouTube* as the repository for storing their videos and providing link connections to and from their third-party site listings and dealership websites.

The purpose: To expand a store's online screen real estate and leverage the lift these online spaces can provide for a dealership's content when consumers use search engines to look for used vehicles and dealerships online.

"The key here," says automotive Internet marketing consultant Sean Bradley, "is the proper optimization and back-end keyword coding to make sure search engines see each video as different."

Vehicle descriptions: The biggest challenge for dealers and used vehicle managers, as noted in the last chapter, is creating a process that drives compelling vehicle descriptions that highlight the most valuable features of a vehicle in a time-efficient manner.

The time crunch is the main reason many dealers and used vehicle managers rely on the VIN decode/

explosion option that populates the vehicle descriptions with the usual fare of equipment and features. The problem here is two-fold:

1. Many of the descriptions result in rote recitations of power steering, power brakes, and other features/equipment that many of today's buyers deem a given. Why use this valuable screen real estate and pixel bait on bland items such as these?

2. The descriptions do not play up the most salient and valuable features of a specific vehicle.

A point of efficiency: I've heard some stores charge the person who takes photos with writing descriptions, assuming the individual's got a solid knack for writing. Likewise, managers say it's helpful to keep a library of descriptions to feed creative comments on specific units.

John Creran sums up the coaching he provides to a part-time, college student who writes descriptions: "I don't want to hear this is a low mileage, clean, no-smoker car. Give it some life. Be funny. Be creative. There are no boundaries. Stay away from all the gray areas. Have fun with it."

There's a final take-away from the approaches Creran and other velocity-minded stores have adopted: The job of writing vehicle descriptions likely falls below the pay grade for most used vehicle managers. This will become increasingly true as today's efficient used vehicle marketplace continues to put margin pressure on dealerships that fail to adopt more efficient and less costly pixel-based processes.

PIXEL-BASED BEST PRACTICES FOR ONLINE MARKETING

When Auction Direct USA, an independent used vehicle retailer with three stores in New York, North Carolina, and Florida, opened for business they crafted a compelling mission statement[17]:

> *"Auction Direct USA is committed to revolutionizing and legitimizing the used car business, guided by the principles of trust and open information exchange, to provide a truly unique and satisfying automotive purchase experience for every guest, in every way."*

The founders had a vision of building a brand around this mission statement and using both brick and mortar and online platforms to convey it.

On the brick and mortar side, the company's stores lack any offices. Showrooms have only one vehicle. A bar-style horseshoe serves as the focal point where customers and salespeople work out deals. Customers have access to computers to research

---

[17]http://www.auctiondirectusa.com/dsp_about.cfm

or browse the Internet, whether they're buying a vehicle or not.

"If you weren't paying attention, you might not think you're in a car dealership," says Eric Miltsch, IT director and partner for the company, which retails about 700 vehicles per month across its three current locations. "It's a unique experience."

The company's pixel presence is similarly compelling. It conveys the company's core mission statement and underscores its "no hassle, no haggle" transparent style of retailing vehicles. It touts a three-day, 500-mile guarantee and clean-conscience certification on all vehicles.

More than that, though, Auction Direct is everywhere online: In *Google* search listings for used vehicles in its markets, in social media spaces such as *Facebook, Twitter,* and *YouTube*, and on third-party sites. Each of these online spaces links to the others, creating a spider web-like platform that supports itself and, through careful day-to-day management of the individual anchors, grows bigger over time.

I have always believed that consumers *prefer* to view a variety of listings from multiple dealers to shop for a vehicle that fits their budget and needs and, therefore, third-party sites like *AutoTrader. com* and *Cars.com* would be where dealers and used vehicle managers would connect best with shoppers.

At the same time, however, I recognize that many online shoppers get to these sites from search engines. My problem has been clearly understanding how dealerships can or should connect to this initial stage of the online shopping funnel and the value it may bring.

Miltsch and other velocity-minded dealers and used vehicle managers have helped educate me about how this works. It's not all about trying to position specific vehicles or deals within the organic listings that appear when consumers use a search engine. Instead, it's about demonstrating that a) a store has the vehicles and b) it understands consumers want selection and resources to guide their decisions.

For example, Miltsch optimizes his dealership's website to appear when someone types in "used vehicles NY." He's done the research to know the term is relevant and frequently used by shoppers. To optimize the page he wants to appear in search results, he makes sure the "used vehicles NY" appears in the page title and content on the page so search engine spiders view it as relevant to the online consumer's initial query.

The Auction Direct listing on this term that appears in search results (No. 5, when I checked) contains the keyword term and talks about the company's best used cars. A click-through goes to the home page that offers a search function that's similar to what a third-party site offers consumers.

Micro-sites also aid the efforts in gaining consumer attention in the search. Brian Benstock, Paragon Honda, has a host of sites—including a blog based on his name—that work together to drive traffic to his store's website. "We have a saying, 'go viral or go home,'" he says.

This summer his store joined an effort to follow the federal Cash for Clunkers program with a dealer-run plan that includes used vehicles. The effort ties Paragon and other dealers to a website, *www.autostimulusplan.com*, that seeks to capture customer interest in the federal program and offer up used vehicles it did not include.

"Cash for Clunkers applied to 10 percent of the population," Benstock says. "We think if we can tap into the 90 percent of the market that's out there, we think we can do monster business over the next 90 days."

OK. So this is starting to make sense. These guys are creating and optimizing content that appeals to a customer's interests based on keywords. At this stage, it's less about merchandising a specific vehicle and more about merchandising the dealership—making sure customers can see their stores as a viable choice to help them accomplish what they need—whether it's a vehicle purchase or resources to give them additional information around their search query.

"It's about understanding how search engines work," Miltsch says. "They reward you when you provide a site that has some type of valuable and relevant content that is linked to just as many valuable and highly authoritative, highly relevant content-related sites."

I had to ask the question: What about SEO and SEM for specific vehicles or deals?

In this case, Miltsch zeroes in on makes/models that are hot sellers, rather than trying to position specific vehicles in search listings. For example, if he knows "used Ford Explorer" is a common term, he'll optimize a search results page for Ford Explorers from his site to appear high in search listings. The idea: He knows shoppers will want to compare, so he serves up a page that offers immediate comparisons.

Miltsch and other velocity-minded stores also sprinkle their pixel-based online marketing with pay-per-click and display advertising to address more deal-specific messaging. Typically, these will complement other organic optimization efforts that seek to position dealership website pages in search engine results. The idea: the paid and organic listings complement each other and serve up messaging that's relevant to the potential customer's search query.

But Miltsch and others note this kind of optimization work isn't possible at all dealerships due to the frame-based website structures they use that are search-unfriendly.

The problem: The frame architecture that some dealer website developers use create pages within pages that search engine spiders have trouble reading and indexing for search results listings[18].

Likewise, these sites offer less flexibility to create/change search-friendly URLs for specific pages or to embed keywords in page content so that search engine spiders deem them relevant and rank them higher in search results listings.

'We did away with that framed-in solution and did our own to control our URL structure and create a canonical design to help our optimization efforts," Miltsch says.

Chris Fousek, e-commerce director at Village Auto Group, Boston, agrees frame-based sites are problematic. "Framed inventory detracts from your whole site," he says. "We're focused on text-based sites to help us in search."

Dean Evans, chief marketing officer for *Dealer.com*, says the problem of frame-based sites is one that

---

[18] http://www.seonotepad.com/seo/seo-and-html-frames/

stems from dealers and site developers aiming for flashy presentations over search-friendly functionality. The pendulum is shifting but Evans notes some dealers still opt for sites and SEO programs based on a good sales pitch rather than a clear track record of improving search results listings and traffic gains for dealerships.

A key take-away: Dealers and used vehicle managers who are unfamiliar with the ins and outs of SEO and SEM should make sure their websites are at least set up to allow this kind of marketing to support their pixel proficiency.

In addition to optimizing their own sites, some dealers and used vehicle managers are embracing other online marketing tactics to build and manage their online presence:

Reputation management. A growing number of dealers and used vehicle managers are investing time and energy to encourage customer reviews on sites that rate dealerships—these include *Dealer Rater, Google Local, Yelp,* and *Citysearch* sites. Joe Orr, GM for Dick Hannah Dealerships, Portland, Ore., says salespeople encourage customers to make comments on these sites. After a year-long concerted effort, the dealership has tracked more than 460 "ups" for sales, service, and parts—incremental business that flowed directly from the listings (more than 700 in '08) on the review sites.

These are free calls compared to leads from other sites, Orr says. In addition, because the store is more aware of managing customers' online feedback, salespeople are more focused on their satisfaction. CSI ratings have climbed about 2 points higher in the past year as Dick Hannah stores have made online reputation management a higher priority.

"People read this stuff. It works," echoes John Creran. He's focused on positive listings on *Dealer Rater.*

Of course, these online reviews carry risks of negative comments from customers. The best practice here: Do everything possible to contact customers and resolve complaints, and address those outcomes in responses to online complaints. This provides balance to any mis-information or misconceptions conveyed in the complaints.

One benefit of a concerted focus on positive listings: The sites typically post comments from most recent to older reviews. So, in time, negative comments get pushed down and coun-ter-balanced by more favorable reviews.

"We're confident we can get past a couple of bad reviews," says Belowski at Acton Toyota.

Social Media Spaces: More dealers and used vehicle managers are engaging social media spaces like *YouTube, Facebook,* and *Twitter* to further connect their stores with the online spaces where past and potential customers congregate.

"That's where people are, so our strategy is to go there and not try to pull them away," Miltsch says.

Auction Direct's messaging and discussion in these spaces is not about selling cars. Rather, they skew toward topics that automotive enthusiasts might find compelling—whether it's tips on purchasing a car, discussions about new models, or warnings about the dangers of using cell phones while driving.

"After two or three years' worth of effort, we have actually sold vehicles from those channels," Miltsch says. "It's helped maintain relationships, drive traffic, and build the brand."

DrivingSales.com founder Jared Hamilton says social media spaces should not be any big mystery to dealers. Participation in these spaces is much like the memberships in the Rotary Club and chamber of commerce and sponsorship of Little League teams. They generate good will and, occasionally, they may make a connection that leads to a deal.

These spaces can also be channels for fun stuff, like customer-generated videos. Auction Direct invited customers to create their own commercial for the company, offering a $5,000 award for the best one.

"We got 25 goofy videos. We keep them there. They keep getting views," says Miltsch, who notes *YouTube* also holds the active TV commercials the store runs in its markets.

Automotive Internet consultant Sean Bradley notes that spaces like *YouTube* are increasingly becoming go-to places where online consumers search for information, much like they do on *Google* or *Yahoo*.

The upshot: Online videos should be optimized to connect with the keywords that consumers might use when they look for videos. Bradley notes this includes knowing the keyword terms that matter most and embedding those terms in video titles, descriptions, and tags—the elements of optimization.

A Moment of Internet Marketing Levity

We could go on and on about the potential opportunities that exist for dealers and used vehicle managers when it comes to building their brands and screen real estate.

As I'm writing, real-time chats and mobile phone technologies appear as two emerging areas of online marketing that dealers and used vehicle managers will likely need to address in the near future.

It's potentially overwhelming and is a far cry from the way our business has been for much of the past century.

The key here is setting priorities. It would be a mistake to chase all these online marketing opportunities without a clear strategy and a sustained degree of pixel proficiency across the online spaces where, for the most part, the bulk of the current action occurs—namely, the third-party sites and dealers' own websites.

As Mitch Golub says, there's a danger of "stepping over $20 bills to pick up dimes" for dealers and used vehicle managers who skip past the fundamentals of pixel proficiency and beat a fast path to cash in on the buzz that surrounds social media spaces and other online marketing channels.

Hamilton at *DrivingSales.com* agrees. "The easiest starting place is the online classifieds. There is no primary skill that's needed for your sales staff to take advantage of those leads, unlike the specialized skills for search optimization and marketing," he says. "You've got to have someone that knows how to price and take the pictures and knows how to write descriptions."

Perfecting this degree of pixel proficiency is the critical point of entry that leads to more robust e-endeavors that seek to make a dealership's website the primary catch-point for all online marketing activities.

"The dealership website is an extension of their store," Hamilton says. "If you want your website to be a marketing arm for you, you have to get into search engine marketing, search engine optimization, and other things to drive traffic to your site. Then, the way you manage your website is through conversion rates. Its job is to convert traffic to leads."

How Velocity Principles Boost Profitability

Brian Benstock of Paragon Honda took a big gamble in 2007.

The store had been spending $100,000 a month on newspaper advertising to spur used vehicle sales. But Benstock had seen floor traffic diminish and, when the contract with one of the city's top papers came up for renewal, he sought a reduced rate.

"The ad rep, who has since been fired, wasn't being flexible," Benstock says. "So, I called his bluff and cancelled our contract."

That decision triggered a new focus at the dealership: using the Internet as its chief marketing channel to build used vehicles sales.

At the same time, Benstock knew he had a problem. The store was land-locked, which meant his desire to grow used vehicle volumes could not come on the back of a larger investment in inventory. He simply didn't have the room.

His solution came with the adoption of velocity-minded management principles and technology and a more efficiency-focused strategy.

"Our focus went from dollars per unit to dollars per day per space," Benstock says. "The dollars per unit focus meant we were trying to make $3,000 a car no matter how long it took. We might take up that real estate for 90 days to get that $3,000.

"When we started looking at dollars per day per space, we said, 'Perhaps in that 90 days if we made $1,000 on the car and could turn that space four times or more in 90 days, we'd be better off,'" he says.

"It didn't take a genius to figure out that four turns of $1,000 was better than one turn of $3,000. And when you add in all the components—the service, F&I, and aftermarket opportunities—the $1,000 actually ends up being more like $2,500."

Paragon stats suggest Benstock's gamble has paid off. "Our used business has doubled and doubled again to 300 units a month. We turn our inventory 15 to 16 times a year," he says. Meanwhile, the store's average advertising cost-per-vehicle has dropped about 50 percent to $240. Much of that spend goes to ongoing costs to seed and feed the store's formidable Web presence.

These gains come on top of a reduced, front-end gross profit average on the sale of each vehicle—something that might have once rubbed Benstock the wrong way.

"I used to be the highest average grossing used car dealer," he says. "Now I just make the most money. It's a complete paradigm shift and it's one that will make you rich."

So go the benefits of a used vehicle management strategy that focuses on velocity and efficiency. In today's used vehicle marketplace, where the enhanced knowledge of Internet buyers and the rising costs of running a business create new margin pressures, it's essential for dealerships to focus on ways to reduce costs, improve turn rates, and build profitability.

For some traditional dealers and used vehicle managers, Benstock's success is a head-scratcher. They intuitively understand that a faster rate of turn can yield greater ROI, but they question whether velocity- and efficiency-minded processes can actually result in store- and lifestyle-sustaining profits.

The difficulty in seeing the profit potential is understandable. Since its inception, our business has focused on gross profits per vehicle retailed (PVR). This affects everything dealers and used vehicle managers do—they price vehicles (e.g., the $4,000 to $5,000 mark-up-from-cost) and sell vehicles (e.g., four-square, shell game-like processes) to achieve maximum PVR on every unit.

By contrast, Benstock and other velocity dealers go a different route. They strive for efficiency in pricing vehicles to their markets and selling vehicles in a transparent manner that consistently reflects the information their customers have already seen on the Internet. This approach leaves PVR by the wayside. For traditional dealers who struggle to see the value in efficiency- and velocity-minded management, let's take a closer look at some of the reasons why velocity dealers like Benstock can still achieve respectable PVRs and why the overall gains in net profits for their stores typically outpace those of the competition.

The "Race to the Bottom" Myth

Traditional dealers and managers often express their concern about the profitability that can flow from a velocity approach to used vehicle management with the following question:

"If everybody started doing this, wouldn't it create a 'race to the bottom' where dealerships sell more vehicles but nobody's making any money because everyone's selling at the lowest price possible?"

The question's completely fair, but it misses the mechanics of how efficient markets work, and the innate opportunities these markets create for astute players who look for them.

As noted in earlier chapters, today's used vehicle marketplace meets the definition of an efficient market—one where there's equal knowledge of choices and alternatives between buyers and sellers, and the dynamics of supply and demand determine the selling prices of products.

Traditional commodities markets, such as grain, oil, cattle, etc., meet this definition. These markets create winners and losers every day, and sometimes they're the same individual(s).

Investors in these markets carefully attune their buying and selling to account for supply and demand dynamics and the return they can expect from commodity prices on a given day. So, if the market for corn softens because of high supply and low demand, these investors will likely shift their focus to another market where the prospect for a return on their investment is brighter. As these investors exit the corn market, its dynamics shift. In time, the supply and demand swings level off and re-attract investors who opted out previously.

These are the kinds of market dynamics that velocity dealerships dial into every day. If the market softens for SUVs, the savvy market-attuned velocity-minded stores will shift their attention to vehicle segments where Market Days Supply, Price to Market and Cost to Market metrics offer a more favorable potential ROI for their respective stores.

Just like hot-and-cold commodities markets, today's more volatile used vehicle business offers up market segments that can be winners one day and losers the next. It's through seeing such market shifts that velocity dealers adjust their inventories to capture the profit sweet spots across vehicle segments, and reduce their exposure to risk by eliminating vehicles that have turned into losers. It's not uncommon for velocity stores that have long considered themselves truck or SUV specialists to broaden their inventories and give more attention to other vehicle types their markets crave.

"If you're on a 15-day turn, you can get out of the pain much quicker than somebody who's on a slower turn," Benstock says. "You react quicker to the market."

When it comes to pricing, these market sweet spots typically offer higher PVR potential. Velocity dealers leverage this knowledge to achieve the maximum gross profit the market will bear from the moment they acquire these units. (Note: Some velocity dealers may "skinny up" their PVR expectations to turn a vehicle faster, and sell a second or third unit that falls in the sweet spot.)

In any case, these velocity stores will avoid a mark-up-from-cost approach to setting their retail asking prices. Their goal is to meet rather than make the market. To do so, they'll tune into the paint metrics to determine the appropriate price point that will yield the best PVR and their store's business goals, based on the vehicle's condition, mileage, and trim/equipment configuration.

So the race isn't toward the bottom, it's a race to:

- Understand the efficient market's equilibrium points—those moments that occur in vehicle segments when the market is ripe for acquiring and retailing specific types of units, given high demand or low supply;

- Find these vehicles more quickly and more efficiently than the competition;

- Identify the moments when the market starts to rot on a given vehicle, given shifts in supply and demand dynamics;

- Make stocking and pricing decisions that accurately reflect ripe and rot stages of individual vehicles in a market.

STORE-WIDE PROFIT AND SAVINGS POTENTIAL

As I've studied the successes of velocity dealers like Benstock, it's amazing to see the trickle-down benefits that come to dealerships that adopt velocity management principles.

The focus on more cost-effective and efficient operations translates to bottom line benefits that outperform those seen at traditional stores—even if they are fortunate enough to have a steady stream of buyers who lay down on deals with sizable PVRs.

These benefits flow directly from faster turns and lower operating costs in the used vehicle departments, and they reflect the profit-positive outcomes that well-managed and well-executed paint and pixel processes generate.

In prior chapters, we've noted how faster turn rates on used vehicles increase revenue and profit opportunities in service and F&I. I would consider these direct rather than trickle-down benefits, as they flow in kind from a greater degree of activity in the used vehicle department.

The trickle-down benefits are those that are less easy to spot. They come in the form of reduced operating costs and greater efficiencies velocity stores achieve when they focus on and perfect their paint and pixel processes.

The following chart highlights the cost savings that trickle down to used vehicle departments at velocity stores—on top of the direct gains they enjoy from increased sales volumes. The chart compares typical expenses at tradition dealerships and velocity-minded stores.

Financial Benefits	Traditional	Superstore	Savings
Comp Dollars per Retail	$627	$474	$153
Total Comp as a % of Retail Gross	25.5%	22.5%	3.0%
Advertising Dollars per Retail	$322	$189	$133
Advertising as % of Retail Gross	17.9%	12.2%	5.7%
Floor Plan	$53	$23	$30
As a % of Used Vehicle Gross	2.9%	1.5%	1.4%
Total Used Selling Expense per Retail	$1,083	$765	$318
Total Used Selling Expense % of Gross	44.2%	36.7%	7.5%

All of these benefits—savings on floor plan, advertising, and compensation—result from the fact that velocity stores focus on finding the market's sweet spots that ensure fast inventory turn and maximum ROI. This approach reduces exposure to the costs of holding on to inventory, spiffing sales teams, and advertising spending that traditional dealerships typically pay as they wait for willing buyers.

When I share these financial benefits with skeptical dealers and used vehicle managers, they start to understand why a velocity approach to used vehicle management is much, much more than a race to the bottom. It is, in fact, a race to a more profit-favorable bottom line.

Dealers like Jon Whitman say the adoption of a velocity-based management philosophy has helped his store thrive, rather than just survive.

Whitman's dealership is located in southeast Michigan where the unemployment rate runs 20 percent and new jobs are not likely to appear anytime soon given the region's dependence on automotive manufacturers.

"If I had to depend on my town to survive, I wouldn't be here," Whitman says. "I'm not complaining. It is what it is. I just have to deal with it, be more efficient, and do the best I can with the tools and technology I have at my disposal."

Implementing a combination of paint-based metrics and pixel proficiency has helped Whitman expand his dealership's market area and sell a greater number of used vehicles than ever before.

"The guy who buys my vehicle is sitting three hours away. He's coming to me from towns with names I can't even spell, because I've never heard of them," he says.

As Whitman and other dealers and used vehicle managers adopt and deploy velocity-based processes, I'm absolutely convinced that they will succeed at the expense of traditional dealerships.

I like Benstock's "broken record" take on this: "The more turn you have, the fresher your inventory; the fresher your inventory the more turn; and the more turn, the fresher your inventory," he says. "It gets crazy. All of a sudden you start realizing I don't want to make a lot of money on this car. I don't want to marry it. I don't want to date it long. I want to have it come here, get a reasonable ROI as quickly as possible, and move on to the next one."

One final point about the trickle-down, profit-driving benefits of velocity-based principles: The figures shared here are based on the early experiences of velocity-minded stores. As noted in prior chapters, many are currently tweaking their paint and pixel processes to achieve an even greater degree of efficiency and profitability.

In evaluating the moves these velocity dealers and used vehicle managers are making, it's become clear that a new structure for variable operations at dealerships may well deliver an even greater degree of efficiency and profitability.

A Case for "Efficient," Profitable Variable Operations

It's striking to see the variations in approach and process that dealerships have taken as they embrace the Internet's role in retailing new and used vehicles.

Here are three common models:

The BDC: Some stores rely on business development centers (BDCs) as the hub to receive and tracks calls and emails that flow from online used vehicle listings. In many cases, the BDC teams set appointments on behalf of salespeople. Sometimes, dealerships put salespeople in BDC areas for mandatory, rotating shifts.[19] It's not uncommon for BDCs to handle all incoming communications, including sales, service, and parts.

Stand-alone Internet Departments: These departments are the designated hitters for incoming leads (calls, emails, and other queries) that flow from third-party listing and lead generation sites. Typically, these teams include salespeople who have little traditional showroom-selling experience. On occasion, these teams also include salespeople who have proven their showroom skills, and earn the chance to take fresh "ups" from online sources.

Integrated Internet Selling: This model is often born from unsuccessful attempts by dealers and used vehicle managers to make the previous models work. The idea is that every salesperson should be able and equipped to handle any customer, whether they come from Internet sources or more traditional channels. These salespeople handle all leads, appointment-setting, and other work needed to capture and close customers.

Out of these three, it's difficult to call one a clear winner in terms of effectiveness. In my travels and

---

[19] The inclusion of salespeople at BDCs has given rise to derogatory terms like "Business Detention Centers," which makes this approach one of the more difficult to run successfully.

speaking at industry conferences on the Internet and automotive retailing, each of the three is or has been described as the best approach for today's dealerships.

In addition, there are probably a half-dozen other hybrid approaches that flow from these basic models—sometimes incorporating tasks necessary for effective online merchandising and sometimes relegating those duties to managers who also handle desking and inventory management responsibilities.

What's going on here? It's nothing short of today's franchised automotive retailers trying to figure out the best way to address the role the Internet plays as a chief conduit for their sales operations.

There isn't a job today in the variable operations at dealerships that isn't somehow connected to the Internet—whether it's the branding and marketing of a store, the online merchandising of new and used vehicles, the tracking and management of new/used sales leads, or the sourcing of new/used vehicle inventories. Put another way, there's a darn good reason why there's a computer on every desk.

But our industry's quest to find a solution is hampered by our past.

As I see it, dealers are either:

1. Bolting Internet-related tasks and responsibilities onto existing new and used vehicle departments, a shift that can place responsibility for pixel proficiency in the hands of people who are more paint-savvy; or

2. Creating separate layers of people and processes to manage Internet-driven business because existing managers and salespeople aren't up to the task.

We don't have TV departments

I should come clean on one of my biases: I've never thought that a stand-alone Internet department made sense from a managing the overall business perspective.

In effect, stand-alone departments splinter a customer base that, for all intents and purposes, is the same. All buyers use the Internet.

The Internet is a marketing channel similar to other mediums, such as radio, cable and broadcast TV.

In the past, dealerships never created stand-alone TV, radio or newspaper departments to manage leads or "ups" from these channels.

I understand why stand-alone Internet departments came into being. I firmly believe, however, their time has come and, in the not-so-distant future, they will be relics.

This invites dysfunction and cost inefficiencies—neither of which any store can afford in today's more fast-moving, efficient and volatile marketplace.

This is the backdrop that has led me to ruminate on a key question: What's the best way to most efficiently and profitably serve today's Internet-enabled customers and effectively manage the paint and pixel proficiency that's a necessity for every dealership?

As I've studied the ways velocity-minded dealers and used vehicle managers are working to answer it for themselves, I've arrived at a structure for the variable operations of dealerships that appears to be best suited to addressing the critical needs for paint and pixel proficiency, as well as profitability, that today's more efficient market requires.

At its core, this new structure recognizes that the Internet is the single most important driver for all vehicles sales—not just used—and puts the all-important pixel-related tasks in the hands of people who are innately wired to effectively and efficiently do them well. Put another way, it's time for the old structure variable operations to be replaced by one that is more functional and tailored to the times.

THE SALES DEPARTMENT

For 57 years, every Monday morning sales meeting at the Sam Swope Auto Group starts with a discussion of used vehicles.

"We are not a new car dealer with a used car department," says Sam Swope, the 83-year-old founder of the 15-store group. "We are used car dealers who, in most cases, happen to have a new car franchise."

Swope's stores consistently average a 2-plus:1 ratio of used to new vehicle sales. It's a track record born of the recognition that he, as the dealer, controls his destiny in used vehicles—from picking what to sell to setting the price. Swope understands that the opportunities in used vehicles are rich, and they merit a more primary degree of attention than most dealerships give them.

"If you're trying to make it only on new cars and sell the trade-ins as they come in, the used vehicle department is a stepchild," he says.

Can I just say how much I love this business? Where else could a blind guy get a chance to talk to an auto retailing master like Swope? This guy isn't ahead of the curve; he helped create it!

Forgive me. I'm just struck by Sam Swope's philosophy. He didn't go the route of many of his first generation peers, who put a greater emphasis on new vehicles at the expense of used. Here we are, 60 years later, and the consequences of this backseat status for used vehicles are coming home to roost for too many dealerships.

Meantime, Sam Swope is out riding his motorcycle across the country. He's got guys like Dick Swope and Cary Donovan carrying on the used vehicle tradition. "The secret is to surround yourself with guys who are a lot smarter than you are," Swope says. "I don't have much trouble doing that."

See what I mean about a master? The pearls of wisdom fall like rain. Thank you, Mr. Swope.

A Single Sales Team

Given the costs in people and processes to run separate new and used sales departments in addition to stand-alone Internet departments at some stores, it makes sense for dealerships to combine the new and used car departments.

After all, new and used customers shop online with equal energy and aplomb and, in today's credit-challenged environment, the best deal for a customer may well be a used vehicle, or vice versa, regardless of what vehicle the customer thought they might buy when they contacted the dealership.

Also, today's new and used vehicles are not as different from one another as they were in the past. Basically, selling a car, new or used, requires the same skills of meeting, greeting, qualifying, demoing, presenting price, and asking for the order. Moreover, today's used car is likely to be a highly reconditioned, possibly certified vehicle with some manufacturer's warranty that requires little if any creative and artful apologies to get it out the door. While there are still differences between selling new and used cars, the gap is simply not large enough to justify the overhead and expense of separate new and used car sales forces and management staffs.

As I've discussed the idea of a single sales department with velocity dealers and managers, they immediately see the potential cost savings and efficiencies a single team of Internet- and customer-savvy salespeople would deliver for a store.

But implementation of the idea is another matter, particularly as velocity dealers and managers assess their current sales teams and their ability to adjust to the new processes and roles that would be essential under a single sales department.

This is especially true in used vehicles, where the "hold 'em and fold 'em" style of selling has long been deemed a best practice and the Internet has leveled the playing field between dealers and customers. Many used vehicle departments at traditional stores still pay good negotiator salespeople top commissions for their ability to close customers.

By contrast, velocity dealers are sensing that negotiation skills are less essential when they tune their inventory and pricing to market metrics and move away from sales models that aim solely for maximum gross profits on every deal.

As we've noted, holding gross is still important, but it's on equal footing with a transparent, open-book type of transaction that uses market data to justify pricing and value. Put another way, salespeople at these stores have nothing to apologize for with the vehicles and pricing they're selling to customers.

The type of salesperson who fits best in this new process—call him "Salesman Sam"—is one who has a people-focused personality and a knack for keeping up with updates to CRM systems and ongoing contact with customers. It's also true, as we've noted in earlier chapters, that these individuals work well under pay plans that are based more on salary/volume rather than commission.

As I'm writing, the Dick Hannah Dealerships have taken what it hopes will be an initial step toward a single sales department that serves all customers, regardless of the sales channel that landed them on a vehicle or whether they are shopping for new or used.

GM Joe Orr says this transition has two key components:

1. An hourly wage-based pay plan. The plan offers $15/hour for 10 vehicles in a month and climbs to $25/hour for 20 or more vehicles.

2. A different breed of salesperson. Orr says the pay plan's intended to attract a more responsible and educated salesperson who has been socially conditioned to seek out hourly wages and follow processes that are critical to the success of any organization.

This initial step toward a unified sales department comes as Orr's four stores still retain separate Internet sales teams. He plans to offer a transition period to sales team members and it's entirely possible some salespeople will leave. Orr notes that the online posting of the initial help wanted ad drew 16 applicants in less than two hours.

"We're tired of pushing and pulling salespeople to do the processes that ensure success and let them enjoy ongoing business from loyal customers," Orr says. "Many salespeople think they get paid for getting a 'yes' and the job requires more than that.

"Our commitment to transferring our dealership group to a full Internet dealership that doesn't separate brick and mortar and digital will take a while," he continues.

Orr is not the only one who sees dealerships evolving toward a single sales department that place all customers—Internet and otherwise—in the hands of a sales team that's qualified to serve them. The prediction: Stand-alone Internet departments will go by the wayside.

"It's just a question of how fast it will happen," says Jared Hamilton, CEO and founder of *DrivingSales. com*. "The good dealers will get there faster than others, and some are already there. The fact is, you have 90 percent of customers starting online and you have 10 percent of your sales staff handling that medium. That just doesn't make any sense."

I would be remiss in this section if I didn't include a contrary view. At Toyota Sunnyvale, Adam Simms purposely has a direct sales team that handles all incoming Internet leads and a showroom team to handle walk-ins. His thinking: Today's customers use email, phone calls, text messages, and other ways to contact stores—a variety of channels that requires a level of time and attention that makes it impossible to charge a single team with these responsibilities and handling walk-in traffic.

Simms takes great pains to ensure his showroom team recognizes, respects, and responds to the online shopping customers have conducted before they arrive at the store. "Most customers transition to the physical, walk-in pathway," he says. "To collapse these two teams into one doesn't make sense to me."

I respect his viewpoint and see its merits. However, Simms' approach is still more nuanced than the Internet/traditional sales structures at most dealerships—particularly in his sweat-the-details approach to ensuring that his showroom team is technically savvy.

NEW ROLES FOR MANAGERS

One of the consequences of the back-seat status of the used vehicle departments at many dealerships is that while the business has grown more varied, complex, and volatile, its management has largely remained static. The traditional best practices for management often remain in place, and the to-do list keeps lengthening.

The "Used Car Joes" of our business have a whole lot more to worry about than they ever did. What's more, as many used vehicle managers like Joe struggle to keep up, they end up being less effective at everything they do.

There's an inherent mismatch. Joe is sometimes a talented negotiator and/or closer. Joe is sometimes a paint specialist. Joe is sometimes good with computers. Joe is sometimes good at managing sales teams. Joe is sometimes good at handling inventory and pricing decisions. Joe is sometimes good at managing reconditioning and detailing processes. Joe sometimes understands all the elements of pixel proficiency.

"To Do List"

Check storefront · Lot maintenance · **Website management**
Certification responsibility · Window sticker management · **Respond to internet leads**
Log internet leads · Hiring · **Appraisals** · Online pricing
Validate URLs · **Manage inbound calls** · Training · TOs · SEM, SEO, PPC
Website navigation · Scheduling · Desk management · Vendor
relationships · Online advertising · Wholesale acquisition · **Classified promotions** · Daily
work plans · Cost per lead · Wholesale disposition · **Manage
photos** · CRM management · Compensation · F&I · **Counting ups**
Working deals · **Counting calls** · Reconditioning · **Manage descriptions**
Lot pricing · Publish prices · Background checks

When one considers the complexity of today's used vehicle manager's roles and responsibilities, particularly in light of the Internet's role in used vehicle retailing, is it possible that a single person has the skills and temerity to do all this well? The answer is obviously "no."

This realization leads me to two conclusions:

> First, it is longer feasible to simply hire a great used car manager like Joe and say, "Okay Tiger, go get the job done."

> Second, the job of the used vehicle manager needs an overhaul. Under this new sales department structure, Joe would be slotted in a role that suits his/her skill set and interests the best.

At some stores, Joe might best function as a kind of operations manager who oversees the processes that ensure paint and pixel proficiency and profitability. At other stores, Joe might work best as a desk manager who handles deals and customers, or he/she might handle sales team management functions, assuming there's an innate ability to provide the kind of nurturing management that individuals like Salesman Sam need to perform at their peak.

Suffice it to say, this single sales department would require significant up-front effort by dealers and managers to define the processes and tasks that are critical for success and match these to individuals who are best suited to perform them well.

Brian Benstock recently made the move to a single sales department where each salesperson handles any deal or customer, and he's divvied up the role of used car manager.

"At my Acura store, I no longer have a used car manager," Benstock says. "I no longer have a used car staff. I have product specialists. They can do what's best for our customer. At the end of the day, what's best for the customer is best for the dealership."

THE INVENTORY AND PRICING DEPARTMENT

I hesitate to even refer to this second new department as a department because, for many dealerships, it might involve a single or even part-time employee that stocks and prices for both new and used vehicles. This person might even be Joe, whose job changed under the new sales department structure detailed in the last chapter.

Why does placing the responsibility for stocking and pricing vehicles in the hands of specialists make sense? It's because the used car market is as efficient as the new vehicle market and the funda-mentals behind stocking and pricing for new and used are essentially the same.

The goals of this department (or individual) are to stock new and used vehicles that have the highest demand and least supply, and to price and appraise these vehicles based on their individual physical qualities and respective price sensitivities based on real-time market dynamics. While the tools needed for performing these tasks may differ somewhat for new and used vehicles, the guiding principles for stocking, pricing, and appraising are identical.

Currently, most traditional dealerships split the management of new and used vehicle inventories between their respective department managers. This split used to make sense—used vehicles were different than new vehicles, and they required someone with traditional paint skills to manage them.

This split does not hold as much weight as it once did, given the shared efficiencies in new and used markets, and the identical skills needed to follow assessments of supply and demand data and dynamics in a dealer's market area.

The idea for this department is also supported by the steps many velocity dealers and used vehicle managers are already taking to address the more time-intensive needs of acquiring, stocking, and pricing the right vehicles for their used vehicle inventories.

Enter "Duane the Stocking and Pricing Guy." He would be the workhorse in this new, inventory and pricing department. He's got a gift for understanding technology and interpreting market data to make informed decisions on what to stock and sell in a dealership's market. He would work closely with the manager of the single sales department, as well as Used Car Joe to find, acquire, and price the inventories that are right for a store.

As noted, some velocity dealerships have already moved toward a centralized inventory management operation. They've appointed inventory specialists like Duane to work in conjunction with Joe and other managers to right-size both new and used inventories for their dealerships.

This single inventory and pricing department would likely have its most profound impact on used vehicle operations—where Joe often lacks the time and/or interest to aggressively hunt online to source vehicles and mine market-based paint metric data to determine the best vehicles to stock.

Duane would also help eliminate other inventory management dysfunctions that are all too common at many of today's traditional dealerships such as the following:

- **Reliance on past history.** Many stores look to what they've sold in the past to guide their stocking decisions. The problem: This is only useful as a starting point. Notions of core inventory often miss opportunities that dealerships have not tested, due in part to biases Joe brings to the table about what works at a store. Duane would challenge those biases and let market-based metrics determine the inventory that's truly right for a store.

Today's used vehicle market moves so fast, "what happened eight, nine, or ten months ago might not matter," observes George Gabriel, head of Gabriel & Associates, a dealership consultant who specializes in used vehicle department and sales process training. "Dealers need to reach out beyond what they call their 'core' and maximize their opportunities based on market data."

- **A "franchise-first" mentality.** We've already discussed how velocity-minded dealers and used vehicle managers are adjusting their inventory mixes to a roughly 50/50 split between franchise and off-brand vehicles. The market-based data Duane uses to guide inventory management would help a store achieve its optimal inventory mix and alleviate the biases that lead to inventory that's often too heavy in a single brand.

- **Emotional bonds to vehicles.** At many traditional stores, it's not uncommon for Joe to hold on to an aging vehicle because he made the initial decision to stock it and believes he'll find a buyer who's willing to pay up to meet the gross profit expectations he set on the vehicle. In reality, this practice delays the recognition that Joe might have made a mistake. What's more, the decision to keep a vehicle prevents the store from replacing the aging unit with one that may deliver a faster turn on the store's investment and offer better ROI potential. Duane would take such emotional bonds out of the initial stocking decisions by setting market-based parameters for what to purchase and how much to pay for auction and trade-in vehicles. Likewise, Duane would make it easier for managers to let go of aging units that have lost their ROI potential. He'd be the guy responsible for monitoring the point at which a vehicle's inventory age saps its ROI potential and signals it's time to move on.

- **"Reflexive" pricing.** Duane would be wired into technology-driven metrics like Market Days Supply, Price to Market and Cost to Market. Through this data, he'd be able to ID the correct acquisition prices for vehicles and know, up front, what retail asking prices are competitive for a dealership's market. Of course, a manager would need to approve these pricing recommendations but this process would eliminate the "mark-up-from-cost" approach currently in use—a method that often results in vehicles being priced above the market for competing vehicles or, even worse, way too low for a vehicle that we stole.

- Appraisal tension. At many traditional dealerships, it's not uncommon for used vehicle departments to play second fiddle to new vehicle departments on appraisals. With a single inventory department, the market-based values that Duane provides would offer a more objective trade-in value that's fair to both the customer and the dealership.

With an Inventory and Pricing department, staffed with an individual such as Duane, I am confident of better stocking and pricing decisions that will be rendered with lower costs as well as greater speed and efficiencies.

THE MARKETING DEPARTMENT

With the Internet playing a more centralized role in the marketing of new and used vehicles, as well as service, parts, and the dealership as a whole, it makes sense to structure a marketing department around this paradigm-shifting medium.

A single marketing department would eliminate many of the inefficiencies at dealerships where new and used vehicle managers, and service and parts managers, often handle marketing and promotions for their respective departments. At the same time, a GM or dealer typically manages marketing of the store as a whole. In some instances, dealerships hire an outside agency to assist with overall marketing, often working in conjunction with dealers, GMs and individual department managers.

In all this, the oversight of online merchandising and marketing is more diffuse: New vehicle managers might handle online merchandising of new vehicle inventories, and used vehicle managers might handle the pixel proficiency for their inventories. Meanwhile, an Internet department or an e-commerce director might be responsible for managing online merchandising of new/used vehicles, as well as maintaining the store's online presence and marketing campaigns through its websites and emerging social media spaces.

To me, a single department, overseen by a GM or e-commerce-type director, offers a more effective approach to leveraging the power of the Internet as a critical branding and marketing channel for dealerships.

The department workhorse would be someone like "Digital Debbie," who has the aptitude and interest to juggle the multiple tasks associated with a store's pixel proficiency and guide the ever-growing online presence and engagement with today's customers through a dealership's website, social media channels, and online marketing campaigns.

Debbie would be the centralized hub for the pixel proficiency, overseeing the effectiveness of processes for creating and uploading vehicle descriptions, photos, and videos on third-party inventory sites. She'd track pixel metrics and feed her "what's working/not working" insights to managers in sales, inventory management, and other departments. She'd be responsible for assessing the ROI for online marketing campaigns and relationships with lead providers and third-party inventory listing sites.

Debbie would also have a keen understanding of SEM and SEO. She'd handle the job of lacing relevant keywords into website pages and online advertising campaigns to ensure greater visibility for her dealership. She'd know how to oversee the build-out of new web pages and sites, if not the ability to do this creative work herself.

Because Debbie lives for this kind of work, I suspect she would be far more efficient at these tasks than the people who hold these responsibilities today. In many cases, a store's pixel proficiency and online marketing efforts fall to the manager who may lack the fundamental understandings of pixel metrics and how-to execution for SEO and SEM efforts.

With a person like Debbie at the helm, I suspect stores would more quickly gain proficiency and results in these critical pixel-driven efforts; and they'd likely lose less investment to trial and error, as well as losses due to lack of sufficient supervision and tracking of online and other marketing activities.

A single marketing department would offer other benefits such as the following:

- **More efficient allocation of resources.** It's not uncommon for used vehicle managers, Internet managers, and e-commerce directors to lament about the evenings they lose at home playing catch-up on tasks that Debbie might be better able to handle. I realize ours is a business where whiners are deemed losers, but some of the workloads and responsibilities strike me as unsustainable over the long haul. I think Debbie's help on such tasks would make for more clear-headed and satisfied managers at many stores. Their time and attention could be focused on helping Salesman Sam and Duane the Stocking and Pricing Guy become specialized experts at what they do. In turn, stores would see gains in CSI and repeat business as managers focus on improving and refining the processes that yield these benefits.

- **Consistent execution of marketing campaigns.** Much of the online marketing and pixel proficiency success that's been achieved at dealerships today has resulted from trial and error. This is not a bad thing, but Debbie would help stores build on what they've learned and establish more consistent processes, checklists, and performance standards to ensure more ROI-friendly tests of what works and doesn't.

- **Improved vendor ROI.** Debbie's knowledge of pixel proficiency and online marketing would help dealerships do a better job of evaluating the solutions the myriad of online marketing, SEO, and other pixel-minded vendors offer to stores. Today, many of the managers who make these decisions lack a fundamental understanding of how best to leverage their vendor relationships—a task that Debbie is more innately wired to do well.

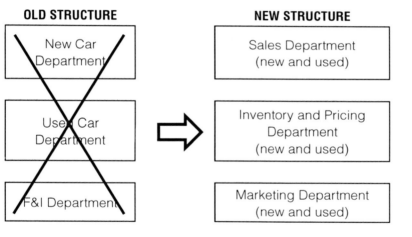

OLD STRUCTURE

New Car Department

Used Car Department

F&I Department

NEW STRUCTURE

Sales Department
(new and used)

Inventory and Pricing
Department
(new and used)

Marketing Department
(new and used)

ONLY THE FITTEST WILL SURVIVE

I've shared this three-department structure because I believe it offers a way to address the inefficiencies and dysfunction that exist in many stores as they try to transition their operations to meet the interests and needs of today's Internet-driven marketplace.

The fact that our industry has spent much of the past decade struggling to figure out how best to fit Internet-focused sales, inventory management, and marketing/merchandising into existing dealership department structures suggests a bolder, out-with-the-old/in-with-the-new approach may be in order.

This new structure may be a difficult pill for many dealers and used vehicle managers to swallow. I'll also concede that it may not work at some stores, where the current investment in Internet-driven processes has been a flat-out loser.

But even at these stores, I suspect the net profit returns on dealership operations still hover in the 1.5 to 2 percent range.

As expenses for people, facilities, and equipment continue to rise, the pressure on these margins will only grow. To me, the best way to mitigate these future profit pressures is to seek out the most efficient approaches to managing the processes and tasks necessary for success in today's more volatile, Internet-driven marketplace.

If nothing else, the three-department structure outlined here should at least spur conversations at dealerships to seek out the best way to position their people and processes for profitable, future-focused success.

A Peek into Dale's "Crystal Ball"

Anyone jumped into the car and made the trip to Blockbuster Video lately?

I can't remember the last time that happened in my family.

The fact is, we digitally record the movies we want to watch with TiVo, or Netflix sends them to us, or we go to *Hulu.com* to watch them. Nothing much has changed about our love for a good movie, but we sure have changed how we rent them.

I'm thinking of Blockbuster as I ponder the future of automotive retailing. To be sure, the business of renting videos is a far cry from selling cars.

But a closer examination of Blockbuster's current financial trouble and its struggle to adapt to the profound disruption the Internet has caused for the movie rental business reveals four telling similarities:

- **Significant overhead.** Blockbuster stores seemed to sprout in every bustling shopping center and strip mall across America. That was a foundational element of the company's early success: It knew how to pick its places.

  Now, Blockbuster is dismantling its empire. Against competitors who had considerably less invested in bricks and mortar, Blockbuster's retail footprint became a liability.

Dealers can't ditch their capital investments, but they can drive more performance and production from what they've built. This is the essence of velocity-minded management in used vehicles—doing more with less.

The dealers who remain in business as of this writing will shift from survive mode to thrive mode as they become more cost effective, efficient, and profitable in all they do.

- **An outdated business model.** Blockbuster
failed to adapt quickly enough to the TiVos,
Netflix, and Redboxes of the world. These
more efficient and technology-enabled competitors found a way to offer the same movies
cheaper, with more convenience and without
late fees. They dialed into changing consumer
preferences while Blockbuster maintained the
status quo.

Traditional-minded dealerships now confront a
similar quandary. They face more efficient and
technology-powered competitors—including Texas
Direct, CarMax, Auction Direct, and a growing
number of velocity-minded dealers—who leverage
these advantages to acquire and sell vehicles at a
faster rate for less money and earn better returns on
investment along the way.

- **Changing consumer loyalties.** Blockbuster
saw huge success because it was largely the
only game in town for many years. Its in-store
movie selections were a big draw, and in-store
customer associates were often knowledgeable
and friendly. Late fees were a black eye for the
company, but most customers accepted them
as a consequence of their own inattention.

Of course, these customers bolted in droves
when offered the more convenient option of
getting the same movies at home for less cost,
without the hassle of late fees.

Just like Blockbuster, franchised dealers enjoyed being the only game in town for their brands. That's still somewhat true for new vehicles, and far less true for used, with the exception of a handful of makes.

Today's vehicle buyers are like Blockbuster's former customers: They are quick to bail on a dealership that offers a less friendly process—from online to the showroom—when they find the vehicle they want to purchase. Inventory selection and price are top considerations, too, but it's the convenience, ease, and transparency of process that will turn a shopper into a buyer and repeat customer.

- **Pride of management.** Some studies of Blockbuster suggest that the company's 10-year management team failed to see, and respond to, the threats that emerged from competitors like Netflix in as early as 1999. In 2007, the company brought in a new C-level team, but as recent reports indicate, the effort may turn out to be too little, too late[20].

A similar problem exists at many dealerships today. It's striking to visit dealers and used vehicle managers who at one time were Kings of the Hill in their markets: They are often the most reluctant to hear, let alone accept, that their declining sales volumes

---

[20] http://www.scribd.com/doc/2621921/Blockbuster-Crisis-Management

and deeper wholesale losses are a direct result of their *best* efforts to fix them.

It's difficult to tell guys who have been successful that the methods that drove their prior successes no longer fit a changed marketplace and, in fact, may be resulting in losing *future* business because they rub today's buyers the wrong way.

Unlike Blockbuster, however, today's dealers have an opportunity to catch the fall before it becomes fatal. They can start to have the conversations that eluded Blockbuster management for too long. They can begin to chart the transition to more customer-centric, efficient, and velocity-minded approaches to managing dealership operations.

I've intended this book to be part of this important transition. It's a bridge between dealers and used vehicle managers who have already come to terms with the realities of today's market and the more traditional stores that are struggling to understand what's hit them.

Velocity dealerships are the transition trailblazers. The stories they've kindly shared in this book offer important insights to guide all dealers and used vehicle managers toward more efficient and profitable Internet-focused organizations.

Not surprisingly, the Internet will continue to be the key change driver—starting with how car deals will go down in the not-so-distant future. The Internet will be a key cause of and solution to some of the challenges I see when I look into "Dale's Crystal Ball:"

Real Deal-Making. I have a saying—"documentation is the new negotiation." It conveys the idea that absolute transparency in deal-making, transforming it into real deal-making, will be paramount for sustained success at dealerships.

Think about the current flight of Carfax TV commercials. These commercials essentially tell today's dealer to "show me the Carfax."

Such are the expectations of today's buyers. They don't want to play deal-making games. In fact, most buyers despise them.

That's the opinion of Mark Rikess, CEO of The Rikess Group. He believes the preponderance of women and a younger generation of buyers, who want a fair deal without a hassle, indicates a shrinking percentage of buyers (30 percent, overall) with a thirst to negotiate a deal.

Interestingly, some velocity-minded managers are finding that a greater degree of transparency in their pricing and desking of deals results in customers *negotiating for less, if at all* when they buy.

This observation agrees with a study of deal-making transparency at Sam Swope Auto Group where salespeople shared real-time pricing information with consumers when they sat down to desk a deal. The test: How would customers react if salespeople addressed the group's Internet Value Pricing on a vehicle right up front?

Donovan says nearly 70 percent of customers at the test Cadillac store negotiated for less than $300 when salespeople explained the pricing approach up front, and shared a real-time view of online pricing and competitor comparisons to show supportive stats.

"We do it right up front in a proactive, not a defensive, way," Donovan says. "We have a lot more credibility and transparency."

The test results aren't surprising to Rikess, a pioneer in one-price selling who's developing sales models for limited negotiation-style deal-making.

"The interest in one-price and limited negotiation selling is growing," Rikess says. "It's a reflection of what today's customers are looking for."

To me, real deal-making isn't about one-price, but, rather, it's about transparency and showing the goods on a vehicle in ways many dealers have resisted for years. That's what private sellers do on

Craigslist—they're wide open about the benefits
and flaws of the vehicles they sell.

Adjusting to this more transparent way of doing
business, and adopting tools for in-store and online
processes to address it, will be key challenges for
all dealerships in the coming months and years. I
predict some dealers like Swope will do even more
to brand the real deal-style of doing business—akin
to how labor groups implored consumers to "look
for the union label[21]."

Dealership consultant George Gabriel offers
another salient point on transparent sales processes
and negotiation: The less transparency, the more a
dealership is asking for negotiation. "The way dealers price cars, the way prices appear, and the way
dealers present prices to customers are all designed
to go for the big grosses," he says. "The way to get
gross today is by not trying to get it."

Adam Simms of Toyota Sunnyvale agrees. His
sales teams do not negotiate on used vehicle
prices. Rather, they explain the store's market-
based approach to pricing and use it to build
value around a specific vehicle and its asking price.
"Offering our car at the very best price up front
seems to be a winner for the consumer and me,"
Simms says.

---

[21]http://unionsong.com/u103.html

This breed of transparency also offers a variation on what Simms calls the old "take-away close."

"We'll do a consultation and show them the other vehicles they may want to consider if they don't buy our car," Simms says. "We'll note, of course, that our car might not be here when they come back."

Fierce competition from former franchised dealers. I received a note from a top-performing dealer who got the factory boot. He'd played by the rules, and leveraged his success with GM to buy a Chrysler store. His CSI, effective sales, and absorption rates were top tier. Yet, both factories pulled the rug out from under him. The investment he thought had built effectively went up in smoke. It pains me to relay his story. So what's he going to do?

Take a look and tell me this velocity dealer isn't going to grab some market share in both sales and service:

> "I have a passion for used cars and since I adopted velocity principles I have tremendous confidence in turning them. I will set a business plan for a used vehicle dealership that can offer maintenance service, tires, wheels, and details. I can use the service and detail area to feed the used business at a $20 less effective labor rate! I will take the best parts of both dealerships I lost, combine them into one tightly-run dealership, and start to enjoy life again. All this with

no flooring, no control from manufacturer, no
expense attributed to new vehicle sales, and
best of all no more selling cars for little or no
margin."

More Credit-Challenged Customers. Despite recent
increases in the personal savings rate, the financial fundamentals for most consumer households
remain weak. This will likely create a train wreck
as dealers and used vehicle managers work with
lenders who are reluctant to craft deals for customers with poor credit ratings and little cash to make
down payments.

Of course, this will also create opportunities, particularly in the sub-prime arena. But even this
business will prove more difficult to retain and
keep.

Joe Orr at the Dick Hannah Dealerships says his
group launched its own sub-prime financing company to address the virtual shutdown of lending to
this sector of business.

Orr says the number of customers is almost too
plentiful to handle. In addition, he calls the business
challenging because the conditions the company
uses to mitigate risk—like absolutely requiring job
histories without lapses—are difficult for some
customers to provide. "We don't sway from the
guidelines at all," he says.

A related point: I should note that the velocity principles I've outlined in the book are not well suited for the sub-prime marketplace. The reason? Lenders have undue influence shaping the market. They control who qualifies for deals and the vehicles they can buy—effectively making the market. The lenders' role in sub-prime makes obtaining statistically valid reads on supply and demand metrics and trends nearly impossible.

The sub-prime lending marketplace appears to be loosening up, and I suspect the risk managers at finance companies will find a way to feed the marketplace's need for financing options that fit troubled household budgets.

I also wonder, however, if the credit-challenged nature of so many consumers may give rise to a completely different type of transaction—a hybrid that blends sub-prime financing with the time share-like vehicle use of Chicago's I-GO car-sharing program[22] or Zipcar. It's a far-out idea, but the seeds have been planted for this type of transportation purchase alternative to take shape.

Less Traditional Advertising. A shift is already happening at velocity dealerships where dealers and used vehicle managers have all but eliminated newspaper, radio, and TV advertising. Indeed, traditional advertising is often now focused on building

---

[22] http://www.igocars.org/   http://www.zipcar.com/

the dealership brand and directing customers to check out convenient online shopping experiences.

Meanwhile, spending for online advertising—including investments in search-related marketing—will be a key focus for dealerships in the coming year. At Dick Hannah, Orr says the dealership's emphasis is on building positive online customer reviews and optimizing its web presence to capture consumers.

"Dealers need to take control of their own websites and online marketing," he says. "It's amazing to see what happens when you focus on this."

Ralph Paglia, head of digital marketing for ADP, agrees that dealers will increase their self-directed online marketing to attract customers, using browser cookie-based tactics like behavioral advertising that serves up ads when online shoppers visit non-automotive sites.

"We've flipped 180 degrees with online advertising and marketing," Paglia says. "Previously, dealers would buy leads and then advertise. Now they're advertising to drive more online consumers to their own inventories and websites, and then buying leads if they need them."

Shake-up in Third-Party Listing Sites. I'm told that *Google* is working on automotive pages that it hopes will rival those of *Cars.com* and *AutoTrader.com*. Dean Evans, chief marketing officer for Dealer.com, doesn't think *Google* will get in the business of listings, but it will continue to perfect its mission of serving up the most relevant content its algorithms believe consumers want to see. This offers opportunity for dealers, and it will put pressure on lead vendors to perform.

Google want to bring their customers as close to the final product as possible, and not the middle man," Evans says.

Such discussions suggest that we'll see new opportunities for inventory listings and marketing that haven't existed to date.

Some evidence: In July 2009, *KBB.com* and *Vast.com, Inc.*, announced a partnership to deliver what they call The Trusted Marketplace for vehicle shoppers and dealerships. The companies believe dealers and used vehicle managers will respond to an inventory listing and lead generating platform that lets them set bids for the frequency and prominence of their vehicle listings that appear when consumers shop/search on *KBB.com*.

Vast's Benjamin Cohen says the pay-for-performance platform works similar to pay-per-click advertising on *Google* and other search engines. Advertisers bid for the frequency and placement of their ads to appear—thereby letting the market, rather than vendors, set the expense thresholds, he says.

So, dealers could dial up or dial down the advertising expenditures on a per-vehicle basis. The more they allocate, the more frequently and prominently their specific listings would appear. Cohen says the approach allows flexibility for dealers to address the needs of specific vehicles to drive leads and it gives them tools to monitor ROI on their spends.

"We see dealers increasing bids on older-age vehicles, just like they would spiff those cars on the physical lot," Cohen says.

To me, this signals that the world of online merchandising and marketing vendors for dealers is headed for what will likely to be another level of pixel proficiency.

A Rise of Regional Mega-Dealers. There's an axiom in our business, "volume cures a lot of ills." Actually, the saying is more factually sound when restated as, "volume masks a lot of ills and leaves them for another day."

For many of the larger urban and suburban dealers, that day has arrived.

New vehicle sales at these stores are down, and used vehicle departments are not picking up enough of the slack—a struggle due to inefficient and traditional-minded processes for managing this side of the business.

Faced with revenue declines, these stores are struggling under the weight of expenses for buildings, land, inventory, people, and equipment that continue to rise. In some ways, these overhead costs are similar to the albatross of high health care and labor costs that squashed the ability of domestic automakers to refashion their businesses to meet a changing market. These large urban and suburban dealers also face more limited access to capital to re-shape their financial position. Such factors, coupled with resistance to adopt more efficient, velocity-minded processes and principles, are making it more difficult for these stores to survive, let alone thrive in today's more efficient and volatile marketplace.

While these stores grapple with problems akin to those at Blockbuster, a new breed of efficient and velocity dealers and used vehicle managers are rising up and claiming market share from the communities these larger dealers formerly served. These new regionally focused stores have innate cost and operational efficiencies that allow them to acquire market share and sell vehicles at margins that make no sense at the larger stores, given their innate inefficiencies and overhead.

These new regional players don't face the same cost pressures for buildings, land, equipment, and people that confront larger urban and suburban stores. What's more, they've become aggressive Internet retailers, allowing them to expand their target market areas and shift the historic balance of power that once favored larger competitors.

If I were an aspiring dealer today, I'd do what many manufacturing businesses have done: Search out the regions where population trends suggest growth and operational costs are far lower than the urban and suburban areas that once appeared as no-brainers for locating a new point.

More Creative Vehicle Sourcing. I've noted in previous chapters that I take issue with claims that there's a shortage of used vehicles. At the moment, the vehicles are available, but they're harder to find and acquire at prices that are right for a dealership, even for stores that adopt velocity management principles.

Used vehicle consultant Tommy Gibbs of Tommy Gibbs and Associates agrees. "The first thing dealers need to do is to quit listening to the propaganda that says they can't find used cars," he says. "The used cars are out there but dealers need an all-out assault on the marketplace in order to find them. More important is finding the ones that are going to turn the fastest."

That said, the past two years have seen far fewer new vehicles in factory production pipelines, and the outlook for the next two years is roughly similar to what we've already seen. New vehicle sales are not likely to surpass 14 million in the coming years. In addition, there are fewer leased vehicles in the current pipeline and rental fleets are holding their vehicles longer—although there are signs that leasing is picking up some steam.

These realities have led some dealers and used vehicle managers to predict a future shortage of used vehicles, potentially as early as 2011.

Will we see a used vehicle supply "shortage?"

The answer is yes in some price-sensitive segments of used vehicles. In the summer of 2009, the federal Cash for Clunkers program has removed tens of thousands of older gas-guzzlers from used vehicle supplies—a trend that will add to sourcing pressures for dealers and used vehicle managers with low price lots that feature vehicles in the $3,000-$6,000 price range.

More broadly, market dynamics will make it more difficult for dealers and used vehicle managers to find and acquire prime late model vehicles. This may *feel* like a shortage but I predict dealers and used vehicle managers will devise creative solutions to feed their inventories. Programs like We Pay Cash for Your Car and buy-out offers in service lanes will gain in popularity as dealers and used vehicle managers hunt more diligently for viable inventory. At the same time, I expect velocity dealerships to hire inventory specialists like Duane the Stocking and Pricing Guy to help mine online sources more effectively for acquisitions.

The fact is, there will always be used vehicle buyers—and economic conditions suggest demand will only grow. The key for dealers and used vehicle managers will be establishing the processes that efficiently feed a science-like approach to inventory engineering to drive success in the coming years.

Technology-powered Pixel Oversight and Accountability. Most dealers and used vehicle managers rely on a variety of vendors to assist them with the tasks associated with pixel proficiency—from taking/uploading photos to handling the online marketing campaigns and SEO and SEM efforts. I expect more dealerships to hire people like Digital Debbie to bring these skills in-house, or to at least increase their own proficiency at overseeing these third-party efforts. It won't be long before technology gives Debbie and others more tools to do so.

Already, technology vendors are offering dashboards that distill, track, and audit the presentation of their vehicles on third-party and dealer-owned websites. This will go a step further, I believe, as technology allows one-stop audits of pixel processes and metrics—potentially even pixel proficiency scores to guide effective online merchandising and marketing.

With this technology, Debbie and other managers will be able to see where delays may occur in uploads of vehicles online or updates to key websites. Likewise, they'll see real-time feeds of online conversions and cost-per-lead data to better manage a store's pixel proficiency and online marketing efforts.

Overall, this is a good thing. It signals that pixel proficiency will gain greater attention and focus as dealers and used vehicle managers recognize their long-term success will be directly tied to how well they can execute efficiency-minded and technology-driven processes that enable them to truly become Internet Retailers.

A Critical Choice Awaits

My Crystal Ball predicts that the road ahead won't be an easy one, and, it's got plenty of potholes to throw the wheels of a dealership's operation out of alignment.

I do believe, however, that dealers and used vehicle managers who adopt velocity principles and shore up their paint and pixel proficiency will be the best positioned to see the potholes and avoid the bumpy ride that less market-attuned stores are likely to encounter.

It's not easy for dealers and used vehicle managers to adopt a velocity-minded approach for managing used vehicle operations. It takes guts, commitment, and fortitude to make what amounts to a dramatic departure from the traditional ways of doing business.

But given the road ahead, and the margin pressures that come with today's more efficient and volatile marketplace, dealerships face a make-or-break choice: Do we adopt newer, more efficient, profit-minded, and market-attuned ways of doing business or do we stick with tradition and hope for the best?

In the words of Bob Dylan, "The times they are a-changin'" and I say there's no time to waste. What path will you choose?

INDEX

The Author, Dale Pollak

Dale Pollak is the Founder and Chairman of vAuto, Inc., named by *Inc. Magazine* as the second fastest growing software company in America. vAuto was established to help auto dealers improve the performance and profitability of their used vehicle departments. Through its state of the art technology, vAuto empowers dealers to appraise, stock, price and merchandise their used vehicles using real-time knowledge of marketplace supply, demand and price sensitivity trends. More than 2,500 franchised and independent dealerships, including five out of the six largest franchises of their respective brands, rely on the market-based metrics Pollak's innovative system provides to drive and fine tune their used vehicle operations.

For more information on vAuto and its product suite, visit www.vauto.com.

CPSIA information can be obtained at www.ICGtesting.com
Printed in the USA
BVOW02s1058230915

419332BV00025B/293/P

SUSTAINABILITY FOOTPRINTS IN SMEs

Strategy and Case Studies for Entrepreneurs and Small Business

LOWELLYNE JAMES

Published by John Wiley & Sons, Inc., Hoboken, New Jersey
Published simultaneously in Canada

For general information on our other products and services or for technical support, please contact our
Customer Care Department within the United States at (800) 762-2974, outside the United States at
(317) 572-3993 or fax (317) 572-4002.

Wiley also publishes its books in a variety of electronic formats. Some content that appears in print may
not be available in electronic formats. For more information about Wiley products, visit our web site at
www.wiley.com.

Library of Congress Cataloging-in-Publication Data:

James, Lowellyne.
Sustainability footprints in SMEs : strategy and case studies for entrepreneurs and small
business / Lowellyne James.
      pages   cm
   Includes index.
   ISBN 978-1-118-77943-9 (cloth)
1. Small business–Environmental aspects.   2. Sustainable development–Environmental aspects.
3. Social responsibility of business.   I. Title.
   HD2341.J36 2014
   658.4′083–dc23

                                                                              2014018625

Cover Artwork by Ade Adesina

Printed in the United States of America

10   9   8   7   6   5   4   3   2   1

To my son Cameron and the hope of
a more sustainable future

CONTENTS

FOREWORD

Sustainability is the single most important issue facing business and society today. In the 1980s and 1990s, the hot topic for discussion was sustainable competitive advantage. Today, the focus is on creating businesses that are both sustainably competitive and sustainable in an environmental context.

Most organizations have recognized that the two concepts are not, as many assumed, incompatible. The customer is increasingly environmentally aware and is signaling to producers that they would prefer to consume goods and services that are produced and supplied by means that protect the environment. In other words, it is becoming simply good business to produce in a way that is environmentally sustainable.

If we add to this the increasing number of government policies and pieces of legislation that are forcing businesses to behave in a way that is environmentally friendly so as to stem the tide of global warming, which is now scientifically undeniable, then the pressure to operate in an environmentally friendly manner is unstoppable.

In these circumstances, the main question becomes not one of *should* we operate our business in an environmentally friendly way but *how* do we develop environmentally friendly business practices? This book, grounded in extensive research, seeks to provide some of the answers to the question of "*how*."

The research underpinning the book sought to identify best practice among SMEs, which could be regarded as environmental champions, and then produce practical tools to aid businesses in achieving environmental and business sustainability. The book is among the leaders in its field in identifying practical actions that can be taken by business to achieve these twin goals, which for many years were seen as dichotomous. I would strongly recommend the book to business leaders in organizations of any size or in any sector that are seeking to achieve these twin goals. I would also recommend the book to academics who are interested in sustainability from both the business and the environmental perspective.

Dean of the Business School,   PROFESSOR GEORGE STONEHOUSE
Edinburgh Napier University,
Scotland

ACKNOWLEDGMENTS

As a quality, safety, and environmental practitioner implementing management systems within a small and medium sized enterprise (SME) operational context, I was unable to source case studies that presented the business case for carbon footprint measurement. Existing case studies and research literature focused on success stories in large multinationals with access to considerable human resources and financial capital. Undeterred, I began measuring and managing the carbon footprint for Capital Cooling utilizing a free software tool from Best Footprint Forward as part of an ISO 14001 Environmental Management Certification project that indicated results that, to my delight, not only reduced carbon emissions but also generated income from waste streams such as plastic. The ability to receive payment for materials that were previously destined for landfill for a minimal investment cost, for example, the purchase of a baling machine, inspired management to embrace other sustainability initiatives such as facilitating with stakeholder engagement through support for employee volunteer activities. Although participation in voluntary schemes assisted with greenhouse gas performance benchmarking, there was limited feedback on best practices and tools required to improve sustainable performance.

Therefore, I conducted research into SMEs that were recognized environmental champions and had implemented carbon footprint measurement to understand the critical success factors necessary for sustainable growth. First initially as a benchmarking exercise and second to observe if there were similarities in the methods by which these SMEs embed sustainability within their organization from which a practical model can be developed that will assist entrepreneurs, managers, and employees. As businesses react to external stimuli, it was essential that I also examine the policymaking context of which the United Kingdom was an ideal crucible being influenced by EU policy and as a global leader in the fight against climate change through its enactment of groundbreaking climate change legislation.

Creative endeavors have no prescribed format, so I started writing these acknowledgments during the latter phases of the book project. Firstly, I thank God for giving me the opportunity to realize a boyhood dream of writing a book.

This book would not have been possible without the guidance of unsung heroes, my teachers Marva Marcano, Eldon Braithwaite, and Juliana Alexander, who inspired me to love learning and strive for excellence. The patience of mentors like Dennis Nurse, who provided me with an in-depth understanding of the application of management systems as a young professional, and the encouragement of friends, family, and colleagues such as Professor Mike Bonaventura, CEO of Crichton Carbon Centre, and Lisa Gibson, who were both invaluable in soliciting support from the Log House People Ltd and Moffat Golf Club.

So on one rainy Edinburgh evening at the Edinburgh Napier Business School, I began my interviews with our first SME Director Hugh Gourlay of the Log House People, a sustainability enthusiast and keen entrepreneur. In my journey to capture best practice, I traveled from Edinburgh to Dumfries and Galloway seeking to identify if sustainability can be implemented even within the traditional Scottish pastime of golf and was pleasantly surprised by the approaches adopted by Ken Humphreys, Dick Ibbotson, and Michael Wilson at the Moffat Golf Club. I am forever thankful to Matthew Aitken of Underwood Consultants for sharing their midday meal and the prayer of blessing from Minister Norman Hutcheson of Dalbeattie Church, all those many months ago at the Aitken's family farm.

As a sustainability practitioner, I was indeed envious of the numerous environmental awards and sterling commitment of Hazel Rickett and her team at Rabbie's Trail Burners, so I was quite pleased that she accepted my offer to participate in our research. The insight into the operations of Rabbie's Trail Burners provided useful techniques that can be adopted by SMEs to reduce the environmental impact of their operations and contribute to social causes.

This book project may never have materialized without the direct encouragement and guidance from Alister McLean, Chief Executive Officer of Capital Cooling Ltd, whose vision to pursue ISO 14001 certification influenced my search for sustainable development best practice among SMEs. In particular, I am thankful to Stephen Ayr, Technical Manager at Capital Cooling Ltd, for taking a chance in hiring an armed forces veteran and also my colleagues at Capital Cooling Ltd, Pamela Murray, Ian McGill, Nick McCracken, Brian Duncan, Craig Kerr, Darren Henderson, Frank Little, Graham Frew, Fraser Scotcher, and Rob McLennan, who sacrificed time from their busy schedules to document their contributions and were instrumental in my quest to develop the *Sustainable Strategic Growth Model*.

Instrumental to the success of the ISO 14001 implementation program at Capital Cooling was the technical support provided by Allan and Roseanne Tye in the design and initial development of the environmental management system as well as the timely advice provided by John Bathgate, Quality, Health and Safety, Environmental Manager, Mainetti (UK) Ltd, and Thomas Neilson, Occupational Health and Safety Advisor, National Health Service, UK.

I am grateful for the support of the Scottish Government and one of its key institutions the Scottish Environmental Protection Agency in providing access to information on Scotland's environmental performance. It would be amiss if special mention is not given to Jane Wood, CEO, Scottish Business in the Community, and Andrew Millson, Chief Development Officer at Social Development Scotland, for their candid views on sustainability and the application of carbon footprint methodologies.

I am thankful to Dr Sajjad Haider and Dr Maneesh Kumar for their career advice and guidance by identifying sustainability as a research area without whom this book may not have been possible; Dr Eleni Theodoraki for her critique of my writing style, although at times I know I exhausted her patience; and Professor George Stonehouse, Dean of Edinburgh Napier Business School, for his encouragement and kindness in contributing the foreword that sets the tone for the book. Heartfelt gratitude is also extended to Professor Alex Scott for supporting a Heriot-Watt MBA alumnus career aspirations.

Despite his reservations regarding the development of this book project, I would also like to thank Professor Alex Russell, Head of the School of Management, Aberdeen Business School, for providing the space to develop my research.

A special thank you is offered to all of the staff of Edinburgh Napier University and Robert Gordon University who provided administrative support that allowed me to pursue my writing, as well as the financial support provided by the Soldiers, Sailors, Airmen and Families Association, Royal Naval Benevolent Trust, Poppyscotland, and the Institute of Chartered Accountants of Scotland is also acknowledged.

It would be amiss if I did not extend my warmest appreciation to Pauline for taking care of our son to whom this book is dedicated, which is a responsibility we both share. I am thankful always for the continued love provided by my parents Winston and Annabella as well as my sisters Avanella and Annesia whose timely advice focused my decision making during the many months of reflection and writing.

Course Leader, MSc Quality Management,   LOWELLYNE JAMES
Aberdeen Business School, Robert Gordon University
Chair of the Chartered Quality Institute, North of Scotland

email: lowellynej@hotmail.com
website: www.lowellynejames.com
www.sustainabilityfootprints.com

GLOSSARY OF ABBREVIATED TERMS

AA1000	Accountability 1000
AAU	Assigned Amount Unit
ASQ	American Society for Quality
BRE	Building Research Establishment
BREEAM	Building Research Establishment Environmental Assessment Method
BS	British Standard
CCS	Carbon Capture and Storage
CCX	Chicago Climate Exchange
CDP	Carbon Disclosure Project
CERES	Coalition of Environmentally Responsible Economies
CH$_4$	Methane
CO$_2$	carbon dioxide
CO$_2$e	carbon dioxide equivalent
CQI	Chartered Quality Institute
CRC	Carbon Reduction Commitment
CSR	Corporate Social Responsibility
DECs	Display Energy Certificates
DEFRA	Department for Environment, Food and Rural Affairs
EFA	Ecological Footprint Analysis
EMAS	Eco-Management and Audit Scheme
EPCs	Energy Efficiency Certificates
ESA	European Space Agency
ESG	Environmental and Social Governance
EU ETS	European Union Emissions Trading Scheme

GCC	Global Climate Coalition
FAO	Food and Agriculture Organization
FSSD	Framework for Strategic Sustainable Development
FTSE	Financial Times Stock
GRI	Global Reporting Initiative
GTC	Giga Tons of Carbon
GVA	Gross Value Added
GWP	Global Warming Potential
HFCs	Hydrofluorocarbons
ICAEW	Institute of Chartered Accountants in England and Wales
ICUN	International Union for Conservation of Nature
ILO	International Labor Organisation
IMF	International Monetary Fund
INCR	Investor Network on Climate Risk
ISO	International Organisation for Standardization
JUSE	Japanese Union of Scientists and Engineers
PBE	Probiodiversity Enterprise
IST	Integrative Sustainability Triangle
$kgCO_2$	kilogram of carbon dioxide
$kg\ CO_2/m^2/year$	kilogram carbon dioxide emissions per square meter per year
KPI	Key Performance Indicator
$kWh/m^2/year$	kilowatt hours per square meter per year
LCA	Life Cycle Analysis
LCEGS	Low-carbon and environmental goods and services sector
LCI	Life Cycle Inventory
LCIA	Life Cycle Inventory Assessment
lm/W	Lumens per Watt
$m^3/person/year$	Cubic meters per Person per Year
MOSO	Model of Sustainable Organisation (MoSO)
N_2O	Nitrous Oxide
NASA	National Aeronautical Space Agency
NRBV	Natural Resource-Based View of the Firm
OECD	Organisation for Economic Cooperation and Development
PFCs	perfluorocarbons
QOL	Quality of Life
RBV	Resource-Based View
RGGI	Regional Greenhouse Gas Initiative
RSA	Royal Society for the Arts
SA8000	Social Accountability 8000
SAP	Standard Assessment Procedures
SEPA	Scottish Environmental Protection Agency
SF_6	Sulfur hexafluoride

SME	Small and medium-sized enterprise
t C/ha/year	Tons of Carbon per Hectare Annually
tCO₂e	Carbon Dioxide Equivalent per Ton
TEEB	The Economics of Ecosystems and Biodiversity
TNS	The Natural Step Framework
UNFCC	UN Framework Convention on Climate Change

1

INTRODUCTION

Reflecting on the major stories of the past few years—floods in Australia and Brazil, Typhoon Haiyan, BP Deepwater Horizon incident, poor working conditions of garment factory workers in Bangladesh, food riots that led to the overthrow of a dictatorship in Tunisia—common themes emerge such as the *environment, climate change, ethics,* and *human rights,* which all fall under the vast umbrella of *sustainability*. Increasingly, governments are implementing policies and enacting legislation designed to reduce unabated carbon emissions through market mechanisms such as cap and trade schemes [1].

The BP Deepwater Horizon incident crystallizes the centrality of sustainability to business strategic success. Costs to BP arising from the absence of a quality culture that incorporates "minimal loss" to the society has been a $91 billion reduction of market value between April and June 2010, over 350 lawsuits from the general public, damage to its brand image, loss of support from environmental groups with the U.S. Audubon Society who consider the oil spill to be the "largest uncontrolled science experiment" in U.S. history, shareholder dissatisfaction, and the demise of BP's industry leadership [2].

This absence of a quality culture gave rise to the following quality failures leading to the explosion aboard Deepwater Horizon [3]:

1. **Incorrect parts**: Centralizers, key equipment used in drilling operations, were received from supplier not to specification.

Sustainability Footprints in SMEs: Strategy and Case Studies for Entrepreneurs and Small Business, First Edition. Lowellyne James.

2. **Breach of existing well design**: The centralizers used in operations totaled to 6 instead of 21, a casualty of the misdirected focus on reducing the cost and not reducing the cost of quality.

3. **No product verification**: Incoming inspection tests were not conducted on the cement foam upon receipt from the supplier Halliburton.

4. **Poor supplier management**: The cement supplied by Halliburton failed in-house tests. The need to develop *mutually beneficial supplier relationships* is a corner stone of total quality management and quality management standards such as ISO 9001. BP's relationship with its supply chain Transocean and Halliburton, as events have revealed, can be described as combative at best.

5. **Poor process management**: "Negative Pressure Test" was not dictated on the oil platform's work plan. There was no procedure for conducting the "Negative Pressure Test."

6. **No management of change procedure**: "Negative Pressure Test" was added to the work plan at the "eleventh hour." This confusion led to the acceptance of one positive test result despite three failed negative pressure tests, a decision that sealed the fate of the crew of Deepwater Horizon.

These six *quality failures* resulted in the catastrophic loss of life and environmental disaster—the *safety consequence*—a cost that is unquantifiable.

Safety is not the issue but a consequence of the absence of an understanding of quality and its impact on the triple bottom-line, that is, economic, social, and environmental. It is time for business and regulators to adopt an industry-wide approach that embraces continuous improvement that goes "*beyond quality.*"

Humanity's insatiable appetite for knowledge and space exploration has also impacted negatively on the environment of earth's orbital atmosphere. Most of us with our feet firmly planted on the ground may find it incredible that to date it is estimated that there are more than 21,000 man-made objects measuring more than 4 inches in earth's orbit with millions of other objects measuring a centimeter or less. These man-made objects, benignly described as space debris, can range from spent booster stages, nuts, batteries, and nuclear waste to derelict satellites, all moving faster than 20 times the speed of sound, reaching speeds of up to 18,000 miles per hour just to remain in orbit. The management or lack of management of waste extends to the more distasteful issue of human waste matter, which in some instances is launched into the vastness of space [4].

Environmental concerns placed aside the existence of space debris is a hazard that increases the risks inherent with space travel. Large companies such as Virgin Galactic, who are in the forefront in the race to commercialize space flight and colonize space, the existence of these hazards are being either ignored or muted in favor of economic or financial expedience [5]. The risks of these hazards, however, are so acute that the U.S. Space Surveillance Network, an arm of the U.S. Department of Defense, daily tracks all space debris larger than 10 cm.

The National Aeronautical Space Agency (NASA) has taken the lead in embracing a more sustainable approach to space flight in earth's orbit by developing mitigation standards aimed at reducing orbital debris. Similar plans have been developed by other countries such as Japan and institutions such as the European Space Agency [6]. Although commendable, these efforts fall short of a cleanup of the earth's orbital space, whose costs may prove prohibitive with the hope of incentives such as government subsidies to spur entrepreneurial activity in this sector, which may seem but a pipe dream in an age of government cutbacks and financial austerity. Despite the enormous challenge of removing space debris, two Japanese firms are engaged in a joint venture to develop space debris removal systems [7].

Modern human activity on our planet, both terrestrial and atmospheric, is inherently carbon intensive [8]. Armed with an understanding that the sustainability issues facing our planet are not only earth bound and that waste has gone orbital, I attended the Edinburgh Napier Business School for a meeting with the sustainability program course leader. During our conversation, I noticed four origami swans on his desk. Upon enquiring further, my colleague intimated that the items were found at the end of one of his lectures on the seat vacated by an anonymous student, jokingly suggesting it is symbolic of the quality of the lecture during which one of the students found origami more interesting!

Swans in mythology have helped Greek gods move across the sky and are considered by many ancient and indigenous people to symbolize transformation, balance, and elegance depending on their color. For example, black swans symbolize mystery or uncertainty.

My own research into the phenomenon of sustainability footprints (i.e., the use of carbon footprint, water footprint, ecological footprint, and the emerging concept of social footprint to evaluate present nonfinancial consequences and future risk implications of strategic decisions) indicates that sustainability footprint methodology is at the nexus of three management concepts (Fig. 1.1), which are as follows:

Risk—sustainability footprint risk must incorporate environmental, social impact and its effect on cost structure and revenue streams [9, 10].
Natural Resource-Based View—sustainability footprint measurement contributes to strategy through pollution prevention, product stewardship, and sustainable development [11–15].
Shared Value—as indicators, sustainability footprint assists firms in the mitigation of environmental impacts arising from value chain activities [16, 17].

These theories reveal four key areas within which sustainability footprints can contribute to the success of the firm in terms of *cost impact, innovation impact, environmental impact,* and *stakeholder impact*—the four swans of sustainability. The research study also categorized perceptions of the impact of sustainability footprints among small and medium-sized enterprise (SME) managers and personnel along a qualitative scale consisting of *sustainability positive, sustainability passive,* and *sustainability negative*.

Results of this research indicate that sustainability footprints can transform stakeholder perceptions of waste from being a cost center to a profit center, reduce carbon emissions by diverting waste from landfill, and stimulate innovation through the search for potential energy savings.

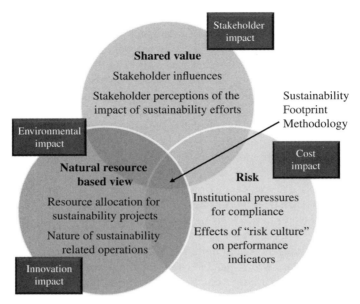

FIGURE 1.1   Philosophical position of sustainability footprint methodology within existing management theory. Source: Author.

Firms that do not measure their sustainability footprints, for example, carbon, social, and water footprint, expose themselves to uncertainty and risk especially within the context of climate change as they fail to adopt behaviors or make decisions that are expressly sustainable.

This book utilizes the results of this study to provide strategic options for SMEs to embed sustainability and highlights the role of quality management in sustainable development.

Firstly, it is essential to briefly define the role of quality in sustainable development. As a quality practitioner, I reviewed the responses from practitioner bodies to the U.K. government's consultation on a long-term focus for corporate Britain with some disappointment. I felt it did not define the centrality of the role of quality management and quality practitioners, managers, and entrepreneurs in assisting UK plc in maintaining a long-term focus.

Critically, in my opinion, the response from practitioner bodies was not as incisive regarding the following three issues [18]:

1.1   THE CONCEPT OF CUSTOMER SATISFACTION

A search on the Chartered Quality Institute (CQI) website for the word "customer" reveals a concept linked to the traditional process model interpretation of the definition as "a generic term for the person who buys goods or services from a supplier" [19].

The traditional process model of input–process–output intuitively recognizes waste as a result of economic activity but interprets waste as an unavoidable externality.

The quality profession has led the way in waste reduction by developing techniques and tools such as lean manufacturing and Six Sigma. However, these innovations were never designed to account for the effects of externalities such as carbon emissions resulting from global industrialization and fossil fuel consumption. From this perspective, the concept of the customer should be redefined to include all stakeholders affected by the activity of the organization. Extending the concept clearly redefines quality beyond the boundaries of mere product and service conformity to include its role in sustainable development.

1.2 THE DECOUPLING OF QUALITY FROM SUSTAINABLE DEVELOPMENT

The Brundtland Commission's seminal definition of sustainable development as *"development that meets the needs of the present without compromising the ability of future generations to meet their own needs"* has influenced all approaches to sustainability over the past two decades [20]. Inherent in this definition is the concept of satisfaction of the "needs" of humanity, both present and future.

The quality profession is perfectly placed to assist businesses in reinterpreting their approach to sustainable development and investment by focusing efforts on the development of a sustainable culture based on the use of quality principles and techniques. The messaging of the importance and applicability of basic techniques, such as the plan–do–check–act cycle in implementing sustainable solutions to business functions, is steadily being usurped by a recent emphasis on the use of triple bottom-line reporting by organizations.

This has led, in some instances, to a distinct focus on economic, environmental, and social indicators to the detriment of quality and safety indicators. The result of this focus by corporations has contributed to product failures at Toyota [21] and unfortunate but avoidable disasters such as the BP oil spill in the Gulf of Mexico.

1.3 THE INABILITY TO RESPOND TO THE DILEMMA INHERENT IN THE PRINCIPAL–AGENT RELATIONSHIP

The recent financial crisis identified with terrific clarity the inherent failings of the principal–agent relationship. This is clearly demonstrated by the bankruptcy of Lehman Brothers in autumn 2008, when a lack of definition of the term "customer," or a focus on customer satisfaction and the needs of the customer from the perspective of sustainable development, was at fault [22]. The entire focus of the company was on short-term profits to the detriment of the principals; that is, shareholders, investors, and society. Lehman's customer or principal in this context was global society, due to its size and reach. The board failed to understand their duty to society, and this translated into unsustainable practices, such as bonuses linked to purely financial indicators and investment decisions that resulted in the death of this 158-year-old institution.

It is imperative that the quality profession broadens its unique selling proposition beyond the traditional roles of quality assurance and ISO 9000 and extend its remit. The Japanese Union of Scientists and Engineers, American Society for Quality, and CQI should take the lead in disseminating knowledge on management systems in general including business continuity, risk management, and social responsibility, as these are evolving as major parts of the quality professional's role and are expressed in ISO 26000, the new social responsibility standard.

This expansion is necessary if quality management is to continue to attract the individuals who can contribute to the development of the profession. I subscribe to the view that not only UK plc but also global economy can regain its competitiveness, but this can only happen if quality is placed right at the heart of sustainable development by focusing not on the management of quality but on the quality of management.

Secondly, regarding the strategic options for SMEs to embed sustainability, tools such as carbon footprint reporting are voluntary initiatives of which implementation costs are considered prohibitive except for those firms with near-monopolistic profits [23]. Research studies also infer that sustainability footprints, for example, carbon footprint, by nature record historical impact and do not incorporate the views of future generations [24]. The lack of utility of sustainability indices such as the Global Reporting Index as an indicator of an organization's state of sustainability or absence sustainability and *the difficulty in quantifying the benefits of sustainability footprints* have seen its limited adoption by SMEs [25, 26]. Significantly, research into sustainability footprint tools has focused on larger organizations with limited research into sustainability footprint reporting in SMEs [27, 28]. Contemporary research reveals that the success of best practice initiatives, for example, carbon footprint measurement, seems to benefit from the organization having prior 'built-in' capability [29]. SMEs are also faced with a conundrum of short- versus long-term aims within the constraints of limited resources when adopting best practice initiatives, the value of which must be judged by the achievement, deployment, and overall sustainability of the capability generated by the initiative with implementation decisions being affected by the ability of management to apply sustainability models that have been *"over engineered"* precluding their suitability to the operational SME context [29, 30]. This has contributed to an emphasis on "quick wins" when the long-term success of best practice initiatives requires ongoing support [29]. Performance measurement tools such as carbon footprint reporting are voluntary activities as small businesses are not required to participate in carbon trading schemes such as the European Union Emissions Trading Scheme (EUETS) or unduly influenced by pressure from institutional investors [30]. In the absence of direct grants or legal pressures to pursue sustainability initiatives, SMEs can be encouraged by the increased spending on energy, environmental, and sustainability initiatives by large customers despite recent global economic challenges and as such may be influenced to adopt sustainable business practices [31, 32].

This book explores the key challenges facing businesses striving to embed sustainability, that is, *philosophical, cultural,* and *social.* The *Sustainable Strategic*

Growth Model is provided as an option to overcome the key challenges regarding the incorporation of sustainability within strategy with four case studies outlining practical approaches in deploying strategic intent within the resource constraints of the SME operational context. Through the implementation of the *Sustainable Strategic Growth Model,* organizations evolve from small businesses to *Sustainably Managed Enterprises,* the new SMEs.

In the race to exploit earth's resources, commercialize space, and colonize future planets, we must aim to incorporate sustainability principles in our technological innovations. The choices are clear; our species *Homo sapiens*, which when translated from the original Latin means "wise man" must achieve sustainable development.

REFERENCES

[1] Unknown. British Safety Council World heading for irreversible climate change, IEA warns. Feature Article; Dec 15, 2011.

[2] Audubon. Audubon scientists find gulf birds & oil too close for comfort; 2010. Available at http://gulfoilspill.audubon.org/oil-and-birds-too-close-comfort. Accessed on Dec 2, 2013.

[3] James L. BP's deepwater horizon: a quality issue or a safety issue? Available at http://lowellynejames.blogspot.co.uk/ Accessed on Dec 5, 2013.

[4] Moon and Back. JAXA and fishing net maker team up to catch space junk; 2011. Available at http://moonandback.com/2011/02/07/jaxa-and-fishing-net-maker-team-up-to-catch-space-junk/. Accessed on Dec 2, 2013.

[5] Unknown. Safety. The North Star. Available at http://www.virgingalactic.com/overview/safety/. Accessed on Dec 2, 2013.

[6] Unknown. Orbital Debris Mitigation. Available at http://orbitaldebris.jsc.nasa.gov/mitigate/mitigation.html. Accessed on Dec 2, 2013.

[7] Nitto Seimo. Space debris removable. Available at http://english.nittoseimo.co.jp/13/9/. Accessed on Dec 2, 2013.

[8] Unknown. World heading for irreversible climate change, IEA warns—British Safety Council. Feature Article, December 15, 2011.

[9] Krysiak F. Risk management as a tool for sustainability. J Bus Ethics 2009;85:483–492.

[10] Lash J, Wellington F. Competitive advantage on a warming planet. Harvard Bus Rev 2007;85(3):94–102.

[11] Winter S. Knowledge and competence as strategic assets. In Teece D, editor. *The Competitive Challenge*. Cambridge: Ballinger; 1987. p. 159–184.

[12] Hart S. A natural resource based view of the firm. Acad Manage Rev 1995;20(4): 986–1014.

[13] Teece D, editor. Profiting from technological innovation: implications for integration, collaboration, licensing, and public policy. In *The Competitive Challenge* Cambridge: Ballinger; 1987. p. 185–220.

[14] Porter M. *Competitive Strategy*. New York: Free Press; 1980.

[15] Porter M. *Competitive Advantage*. New York: Free Press; 1985.

[16] Porter M. The big idea: creating shared value. Harvard Bus Rev; January 2011; 89(1/2):62–77.

[17] Porter M, Kramer M. Strategy & society: the link between competitive advantage and corporate social responsibility. Harvard Bus Rev December 2006;84(12):78–93.

[18] James L. The CQI must expand its role. Available at http://www.thecqi.org/Knowledge-Hub/Qualityworld/Qualityworld-archive/Columns/Soapbox-March-2011/. Accessed on Dec 5, 2013.

[19] Unknown. Customers. Available at http://www.thecqi.org/Knowledge-Hub/Knowledge-portal/Customers-and-stake-holders/Customers-/. Accessed on Dec 5, 2013.

[20] Brundtland Commission. *Our Common Future*. Oxford: United Nations World Commission on Environment and Development; 1987.

[21] Timeline Toyota's recall woes. Available at http://www.theguardian.com/business/2010/jan/29/timeline-toyota-recall-accelerator-pedal. Accessed on Dec5, 2013.

[22] Elliot L, Treanor J. Lehman Brothers collapse, five years on: 'We had almost no control'. Available at http://www.theguardian.com/business/2013/sep/13/lehman-brothers-collapse-five-years-later-shiver-spine. Accessed Dec 5, 2013.

[23] Hicks M. BP: social responsibility and the easy life of the monopolist. Am J Bus 2010;25(2):9–10.

[24] Holland L. Can the principle of the ecological footprint be applied to measure the environmental sustainability of business. Corp Social Responsib Environ Manage 2003; 10:224–232.

[25] Demos T. Beyond the bottom line: our second annual ranking of global 500 companies. Fortune 2006; October 23.

[26] Gray R, Bebbington J. *Corporate Sustainability, Accountability and the Pursuit of the Impossible Dream*. Available at CSEAR Website: http://www.st-andrews.ac.uk/~csearweb/researchresources/dps-sustain-handcorp.html. Accessed on Mar 20, 2012.

[27] Price Waterhouse Coopers. Financial Times Stock Exchange Carbon Disclosure Project Strategy Index series 2010. http://www.ftse.com/Indices/FTSE_CDP_Carbon_Strategy_Index_Series/index.jsp. Accessed on Mar 20, 2012.

[28] CDP 2010. Global 500 report. Available at https://www.cdproject.net/CDPResults/CDP-2010-G500.pdf. Accessed on January 1, 2014.

[29] Done A, Voss C, Rytter NG. Best practice interventions: short-term impact and long-term outcomes. J Opera Manage 2011;29(5):500–513.

[30] Hendrichs H, Busch T. Carbon management as a strategic challenge for SMEs. Greenhouse Gas Measure Manage 2012;2(1):61–72.

[31] Unknown. Sustainable investment by large firms set to grow—British Safety Council Feature Article, March 8, 2012.

[32] Unknown. Climate change report highlights need for business resilience—British Safety Council Feature Article March 22, 2012.

2

SUSTAINABILITY AND CORPORATE SOCIAL RESPONSIBILITY—CONTEXT AND DEFINITION

2.1 INTRODUCTION

The evolution of the use of sustainability footprint tools is firmly rooted in the adoption of corporate social responsibility (CSR) and wider sustainability theory by business. Although some commentators may perceive sustainability as autonomous management theory, this sentiment is not yet universal among business leaders and academics. Therefore, it is useful to explore sustainability footprint methodology within the context of contemporary management theory models and existing knowledge involving sustainability and CSR.

The risk of irreversible climate change arising from greenhouse gas emissions generated by economic activities of organizations is a growing concern to governments globally [1]. This has led to the enactment of various environmental regulations among major western economies [2] and the inclusion of emissions data [3] in CSR/ sustainability reports [4]. CSR and sustainability are on the agenda in boardrooms across the world and increasingly are considered as a yardstick by investors in determining the effectiveness of a firm's environmental and social governance (ESG) [5]. The use of carbon footprints and other methodologies to measure ecological and social impact is part of a long continuum of human attempts to understand or measure the effects of rapid industrialization within what is now being defined as the *Anthropocene* era on the well-being of our species and our impact on the natural world within which we live [6].

Sustainability Footprints in SMEs: Strategy and Case Studies for Entrepreneurs and Small Business, First Edition. Lowellyne James.
© 2015 John Wiley & Sons, Inc. Published 2015 by John Wiley & Sons, Inc.

The scepter of irreversible climate change and human ability to adapt has led to the use of sustainability indicators such as the carbon footprint as benchmarks of an organization's commitment to good ESG [7]. The increasing use of carbon footprint methodology by businesses has spawned a number of certification schemes and organizations offering consultancy services designed to measure or "footprint" carbon, water, and social impact. With considerable investment by organizations in terms of both financial resources and nonfinancial resources such as management time in carbon footprint and social footprint measurement, there is a need to explore the impact of using such nonfinancial tools on corporate performance.

This trend in corporate spending on environmental and sustainability initiatives such as the carbon footprint is set to grow in the United Kingdom by 16% a year between 2012 and 2016 [8], propelled by the legislative ratification of mandatory greenhouse gas reporting for companies listed on the London Stock Exchange [9].

The prevalence of carbon footprint data in CSR/sustainability reports may create the impression that businesses voluntarily accepted CSR principles; however, the history of CSR/sustainability and the use of techniques such as carbon footprints to measure ecological impact present an alternative version of historical events.

2.2 DEFINITIONS AND HISTORICAL CONTEXT

To understand the emergence of carbon footprint and other metrics as key performance indicators, we must explore their role within the historical context of CSR and sustainability.

Sustainability theories can be viewed from different perspectives in that sustainability refers to *artifacts* that may be entities as in the case of tangible products or *constructs* as in the case of processes. Sustainability is also goal orientated when viewed from the lens of *absolute* success based on a comparison between polar extremes, what is sustainable or nonsustainable, and *relative* success, which uses an incremental approach to improvement targeting [10]. The interaction of the *artifact* with its ecological and social environment forms the *static* perspective, where the environment itself is static, or a *dynamic* perspective, whereby the *artifact* adapts to environmental changes [10].

Sustainability/CSR academic research mirrors the development and application of sustainability/CSR best practices by practitioners as illustrated by the *Sustainability/CSR Best Practice Timeline* (Fig. 2.1).

Based on this trend, the development of sustainability/CSR definitions and research can be grouped into four main evolutionary transitions as illustrated in the *Sustainability/CSR Evolutionary Model* (Fig. 2.2):

1. **Sustainability/CSR Awareness**—fundamental research and definitions that have influenced or defined sustainability and CSR. A key milestone in this period is the development of environmental reporting by practitioners.

2. **Sustainability/CSR Aspect Management**—definitions and research reviewed sustainability in terms of its components, namely, the social, economic, and

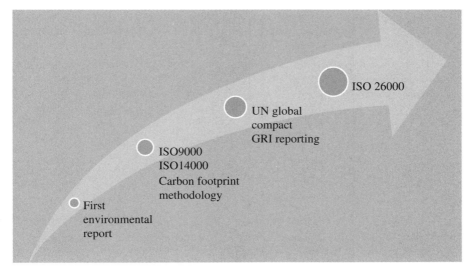

FIGURE 2.1 Sustainability/CSR best practice timeline. Source: Author.

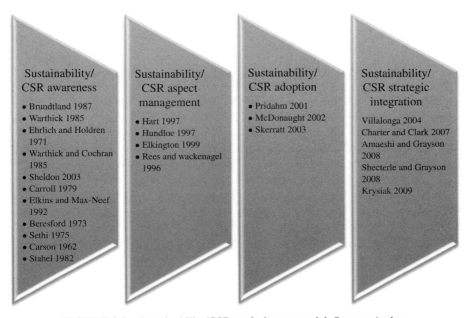

FIGURE 2.2 Sustainability/CSR evolutionary model. Source: Author.

environmental. Reflecting practitioner emphasis on ISO 9001 Quality Management Systems, ISO 14001 Environmental Management System certification, and the use of carbon footprint methodology.

3. **Sustainability/CSR Adoption**—research and definitions explored implementation initiatives encapsulated in the context of ESG. Within this period, businesses began focusing their efforts on using voluntary reporting schemes to confirm their commitment to ESG principles among their various stakeholder groups.

4. **Sustainability/CSR Strategic Integration**—research and definitions focus on the integration of economic, finance, and risk management theories to name a few in order to provide a strategic view as sustainability/CSR concept moves from the periphery of best practice to the realm of corporate strategy. This period is benchmarked by the introduction of the ISO 26000 standard.

Using this model as a conceptual framework, the historical context within which sustainability/CSR definitions and initiatives were conceptualized can be understood.

2.3   DEFINING SUSTAINABILITY…

The most widely quoted definition of sustainability is *"Development that meets the needs of the present generation without compromising the ability of future generations to meet their own needs"* [11]. It must be emphasized that this definition focused on a specific context being sustainable development but has since been used as a catch-all definition for sustainability in general. The Brundtland Commission's definition has formed the core philosophy underpinning all sustainability and CSR approaches within the past 20 years. Although it is an intuitively flexible definition that may be useful in a broad macroeconomic context but generally is incongruous with the profit maximization imperative imposed by financial markets and institutions.

The groundbreaking Brundtland Commission's definition of sustainability development mirrors the views expounded by Dave Packard, cofounder of Hewlett Packard, *"Many people assume, wrongly, that a company exists simply to make money. While this is an important result of a company's existence… people get together…so that they are able to accomplish something collectively that they could not accomplish separately—they make a contribution to society, a phrase which sounds trite but is fundamental"* [12]. A similar sentiment stated by Packard was expressed more than 50 years later by Hundloe *"It is important to note that the separation of economics from the environment and from ethics is no longer appropriate"* [13]. John R. Ehrenfeld, a prominent environmentalist, proposed a new definition of sustainability *"as the possibility that human and other life will flourish on the planet forever"* [14].

Other contributions to defining sustainability considered the total environmental impact or environmental burden of humanity on the planet, which they expressed mathematically by the following formula:

$$I(\text{Impact}) = P(\text{Population}) \times A(\text{Affluence}) \times T(\text{Technology}) [15,16].$$

The shortcoming of this formulaic analysis is a narrow view of the potential of technology to assist humanity in reducing or eliminating the effects of harmful emissions either through efficient energy consumption or through carbon sequestration. Enlightened commentators such as Porritt organically extended the definition of sustainability by defining it as the capacity to continue in the future with sustainable development as the process whereby we move from the present to a more sustainable future [17]. The danger of adopting this philosophical approach to sustainability is that it assumes that there is an endpoint to sustainability and negates the need for continuous improvement and technological innovation to efficiently use earth's finite resources to the benefit of global society. Elkington [18], Savitz, and Weber [19] explored the value of the information provided by nonfinancial indicators as part of a "triple bottom-line" encompassing environmental, economic, and social issues. The *"triple bottom*-line" has formed the template upon which many reporting schemes such as the Global Reporting Initiative (GRI) are based; however, its broad categorizations present too wide a scope for value-added interpretation that will provide tangible strategic outcomes, for example, increased market share. The drive to integrate existing management systems such as the ISO 9000, ISO 14001, and OHSAS 18001 with sustainability ethos has led to the extension of the triple bottom-line to a six-point approach that consists of the *economic*, *ecology, social*, *quality*, *ethics*, and *long-term perspective* [20]. Another conceptual leap in sustainability and CSR management is the "Cradle to Cradle" approach coined by Walter Stahel [21] and later further developed by McDonough and Braungart [22]. Stahel conceptualized the circular or closed-loop economy whereby business should seek to extend raw material use through *reuse, repair,* and *reconditioning* with *recycling* as the last resort when the previous three options have been exhausted and only as *"a locally available raw material"* input into the production process [21]. As restrictive as Stahel's definition of recycling may imply, it prevents the incurrence of carbon emissions that arise from the transport of recyclable material for further processing at another site [21].

These researchers focused on gearing product life cycles and supply chains towards continuous recycling of natural and biological nutrients [22]. However, the link between "Cradle to Cradle" approaches and profitability is yet to be proved.

In a recent extension of sustainability philosophy, Krysiak [23] defines sustainability as *"a framework for assessing the impact of present decisions on the situation of future individuals"* thereby acknowledging that future impacts cannot be predicted with absolute certainty. Krysiak [23] argues for the incorporation of risk management principles into sustainability modeling in which the probability of harm is limited by a constant α with the ideal state being $\alpha = 0\%$. Krysiak's [23] interpretation succumbs to the "silver bullet" paradigm in that there is a specific strategy that will generate an ideal state or equilibrium in which a business satisfies all its commitments in environmental, social, and economic areas, resolving any issues it has with incorporating the potential concerns of future generations. Taking inspiration from earlier theories, management researchers McElroy et al. [24] developed the Binary Theory of Sustainability in which a firm's sustainability is determined by scores on sustainability performance as either nonsustainable or sustainable. The use of this scalar dimension may lead to subjectivity in practical applications; the absolute nature of the rankings may fail to identify incremental successes of the firms and falls into the fallacy that sustainability is a static goal.

2.4   EMBEDDING SUSTAINABILITY...

Florida [25] described the tactical approaches to meet the challenge of sustainability among manufacturing firms as being total quality environmental management—incremental environmental improvements are made using traditional total quality management techniques and worker improvement in pollution prevention. The concept of total quality environmental management is an extension of earlier work conducted by Ōno [26], the father of Toyota Production System (TPS) who defined eight wastes referred to in Japanese as *muda*:

- Waste in overproduction
- Waste of time on hand (waiting)
- Waste in transportation
- Waste of processing
- Waste of stock on hand (inventory)
- Waste of movement
- Waste of making defective products [26]

The focus of *TPS* is a relentless drive to eliminate waste and maximize value thereby reducing financial loss [26]. The Chartered Quality Institute definition of quality management stretches the boundary of loss:

> Quality Management is an organisation-wide approach to understanding precisely what customers need and consistently delivering accurate solutions within budget, on time and with the minimum loss to society [27].

The Chartered Quality Institute's *"minimum loss"* imperative does not externalize environmental and social factors arising from business operations but incorporates these elements as part of organizational product/service innovation to meet customer requirements [27]. However, recent research by Charter and Clark [28] reveals that there is little sustainable innovation being conducted by business even though resource use in terms of ecological, capital, and labor inputs is critical to continued economic activity [29].

Schecterle and Senxian [30], in a study into sustainability initiatives in supply chains of best-in-class companies, identified three reasons for organizational pursuit of "green" initiatives as firstly *"desire to be a thought leader for green/sustainabil*ity," secondly *"rising cost of energy/fuel,"* and thirdly *"competitive advantage/differentiator."*

Supply chain risks aside, the exposure of firms to regulatory, litigation, and reputational risks is the operational factor that must also be taken into account by business investors such as pension funds, as detailed in the Pension Act 1995. Pridahm [31] states the adoption of socially responsible investment approaches is gaining importance in investment management decisions. Later research conducted by Jayne and Skerratt [32] confirms the ideas postulated by Pridahm [31] in that environmental consideration is critical to investment decision making among fund managers. As identified by Lash and Wellington [33], regulatory risks abound as manifested in the likelihood of mandatory greenhouse gas reporting currently a statutory aspiration of the Climate Change Act 2008. A recent study conducted by Amaeshi and Grayson [34] found that information provided in sustainability and CSR reports are yet to capture the confidence of institutional investors and that tools/metrics to measure ESG issues pertinent to investment decision making require development.

In an attempt to develop a practical performance measurement system for sustainability, McElroy [35] stated *"The sustainable performance (S) of an organisation is a measure of either its social or ecological impacts (I) relative to its proportionate share of the supply of, or demand for, carrying capacity of related capitals (or C)."* Even more controversial to environmental practitioners is the separation of the environmental concerns from the business case in that Villalonga [36] infers that *"sustainability is measured the persistence of firm specific profits"* and is influenced by *intangibles* such as reputation, corporate culture, brand image, and technology, with the strength of competitive positions being determined by the level of investment in *intangibles*. Embodied within this view is the concept of *resource-based view of the firm*, which states that long-run sustainability of competitive advantage is inextricably linked to the level of its *"intangible"* resources. Villalonga's [36] highly empirical study concluded that investments in innovation such as research and development, for example, green tech, is a high-risk–high-return strategy, a premise that subscribes to the view that green initiatives and branding are *intangibles* and is limited to its applicability as no comparisons were made with other investment options. Fortunately, a recent report compiled by the Massachusetts Institute of Technology and the Boston Consulting Group [38] has identified top performing companies *Embracers* aligning their corporate strategy with sustainability principles as opposed to *Cautious Adopters*—firms who view sustainability in terms of reduced costs, that is, eco-efficiency, material efficiency, and risk mitigation. *Embracers* are evolving into *Harvesters*—organizations that affirm materialization of financial rewards from the sustainable adaptation of organizational structure, business model, and operations [38].

2.5 CSR DEFINITIONS...

Although a parallel concept, CSR can be traced in its early manifestations through the work of Oliver Sheldon in his book *The Philosophy of Management* in which he surmised that management should extend its objectives to include the welfare of labor, ethics, and prosperity sharing with society to which it has a *"communal responsibility"* [39]. Carroll [40] later distils these early concepts into a defining statement *"the social responsibility of business encompasses the economic, legal, ethical and discretionary expectations society has of organizations at a given point in time."*

An organization's social obligation transcends mere compliance but is bordered by the ethical belief of the society within which it functions. The measurement and understanding of an organizational social performance caught the attention of the accounting profession through a study of Fortune 500 companies in the early 1970s which identified some dimensions of CSR as environment, equal opportunity, society, product, shareholders, and information disclosure [41].

Warthick and Cochran [42] in their search to measure corporate social performance viewed its outcome as the result of the timely interaction of the principles of social responsibility, the process of social responsiveness, and policies aimed at ameliorating a social issue. Warthick and Cochran [42] defined the factors that contributed to corporate social performance; however, their analysis does not provide a workable model to measure social impact. Foreseeing shifts in societal views as to the role of business, Sethi [43] expounded that business responsibility *"will soon elevate corporate behavior to a level consistent with currently popular social norms, values and objective."* The incorporation or "normalization" of CSR is thus far unrealized if viewed from the context of recent high-profile environmental disasters such as the BP oil spill in the Gulf of Mexico.

The use of CSR and sustainability as part of everyday business lexicon is not attributable to any one particular aspect of popular social movements in the twentieth century. The labor and civil rights movements of the 1950s and 1960s converged with the women's liberation movements in the 1970s as the negative effects created by the rise of multinationals and globalization began to take root. Activists began voicing concern for the pay and working conditions of individuals in developing countries who were subcontracted to manufacture products on behalf of multinationals. Influential at this time was the publishing of the book *Silent Spring* [44], which inspired a generation of environmental activists. Under pressure from environmentalists in the 1970s, firms in North America began generating corporate environmental reports with Monsanto [45], being the first company to report on its toxic emissions. This concern for ethics, defining acceptable corporate behavior, and the concept of the legitimacy of business within the context of international trade and global society are themes that are routinely reflected in contemporary CSR initiatives. Criticism of CSR as a management concept came also from within the academic community. One of the first to express his views was Theodore Leavitt [46] in a seminal Harvard Business Review article entitled "The *dangers of social responsibility,"* in which he critiqued that rational economic arguments of cost will always outweigh social concerns, therefore removing any pretext for ethical considerations by the organisation when faced with purchasing or investment decisions. This insensitivity for social concerns precipitated the development of nongovernmental organizations (NGOs) that exerted pressure on major businesses to accept responsibility for the negative effects arising from globalization and industrialization then identified as pollution, "sweat shops," and inner city smog. NGOs consisting mainly of community leaders, clergy, activists, and ordinary citizens reacted to the visible consequences of the pursuit of economic returns without acceptance of the true cost of "externalities" by businesses as in the case of tobacco companies and the link between its use and lung cancer.

At their inception, NGOs and other activist groups were male dominated and mainly based in developed Organisation for Economic Cooperation and Development countries; despite these biases, they have evolved to include women in the decision-making process and women's issues in the sustainability debate, thereby ushering the conceptual shift of CSR from being "good practice" by transnational corporations to explicit international standards such as the ISO 26000, an important contribution that cannot be readily dismissed [47].

The emergence of Green politics on the political landscape was another seismic shift in the debate on the environment especially in the European context [48]. Within this sociopolitical landscape, business leaders began to adopt an enlightened view to changing public values as to their role to which they responded by developing advocacy organizations such as the Business in the Community in the 1980s and International Business Leaders Forum in the 1990s. Achieving a high-water mark with the launch of voluntary reporting schemes focused on disclosing business climate–related activities such as the GRI in 1997 established by the Coalition of Environmentally Responsible Economies (CERES), a U.S.-based NGO, the Carbon Disclosure Project in 2000, and the Investor Network on Climate Risk (INCR) in 2003, both driven by the financial investor community [49]. The emergence of voluntary sustainability reporting schemes created an informal regulatory system that generated compliance without the need for direct legislative action mainly due to the fear of reputational damage arising from nondisclosure or poor performance [49].

This shift in societal mood to improve working conditions was not readily sensed by every major transnational corporation as in the case of the targeting of Nike, the global sportswear brand, and their subcontracted manufacturing sites mainly in Asia and the lobbying of DeBeers by Global Witness to stop trading in conflict diamonds. Sectors connected to fossil fuel consumption established special interests groups to lobby lawmakers against the enactment of greenhouse gas regulations notably the Global Climate Coalition and the Climate Council, whose activities were instrumental in derailing the development of carbon trading in the United States as well as American ratification of the Kyoto Protocol [49, 50].

The development of the Eco-Management and Audit Scheme and ISO 14001 Environmental Management System in 1996 transformed the business imperatives from pollution prevention to the continuous improvement of environmental performance. Arising from the adoption of environmental management systems was the generation of environmental reports by various organizations, which included the use of a then-new metric of ecological and/or carbon footprint data. The effects of climate change such as drought, famine, and deforestation and the identification of greenhouse gases have made carbon footprint performance a regularly used nonfinancial performance indicator. The possibility of a commitment by world leaders to specific greenhouse gas emission targets was met with the disappointment of United Nations accord arising from the Copenhagen Climate Summit 2009 [51]. However, the sustainability issues surrounding the consumption of fossil fuels returned to the global spotlight due to the environmental and human tragedy that was precipitated by the BP oil spill in the Gulf of Mexico [52]. This unfortunate event has seen major industrialized nations make tangible progress to support initiatives to achieve global agreement to emissions reduction at the Cancun Climate Summit [53]. Action on climate change tethers on the brink and subsequent climate negotiations in Durban, Rio de Janeiro, and Warsaw indicate a waning of momentum with lack of consensus regarding carbon emission reduction targets among leading economic powers [54]. However, researchers such as Segerlund [47] too eagerly assume that the normalization of CSR is complete among transnational corporations and that this apparent normalization translates across the wider economy. This view of the normalization of CSR has also been promulgated by academics working for business advocacy organizations such as the World Business Council for Sustainable Development (WBCSD) who prefer reliance on the efficiency of markets [55].

Increased emissions as a result of global consumption have impacted less-affluent nations adversely due to the shifting of manufacturing industries from the developed world to emerging economies, increasing support at the macroeconomic level for a sustainable global economy [16]. If globalization and growth in emerging economies are to continue, business must commit to reduce carbon emissions and meet implied social obligations.

REFERENCES

[1] Unknown. *World Energy Outlook 2011, IEA 2011*. Available at http://www.iea.org/Textbase/npsum/weo2011sum.pdf. Accessed May 8, 2012.

[2] United States Environmental Protection Agency. *Greenhouse Gases Threaten Public Health and the Environment*; 2009. Available at http://yosemite.epa.gov/opa/admpress.nsf/0/08D11A451131BCA585257685005BF252. Accessed June 28, 2014.

[3] United Kingdom Department. Fluorinated Greenhouse Gas Regulations 2009. Available at http://www.legislation.gov.uk/uksi/2009/261/contents/made. Accessed Nov 3, 2012.

[4] Securities and Exchange Commission 2010. 17 CFR Parts 211, 231 and 241, Commission Regarding Disclosure Related to Climate Change. Available at http://www.sec.gov/rules/interp/2010/33-9106.pdf Accessed June 29, 2014.

[5] Bonini S, Brun N, Rosenthal M, McKinsey. McKinsey Global Survey Results: Valuing Corporate Social Responsibility 2009, Available at: http://www.mckinsey.com/insights/corporate_finance/valuing_corporate_social_responsibility_mckinsey_global_survey_results. Accessed Jun 30, 2014.

[6] Unknown, Welcome to the Anthropocene. Economist. Available at http://www.economist.com/node/18744401. Accessed May 29, 2011.

[7] Potts J, van der Meer J, Daitchman J. International Institute for Sustainable Development. The State of Sustainability Initiatives Review 2010: Sustainability and Transparency 2010;12–14:47.

[8] Unknown, *UK Sustainable Business Spending 2010–15*, Verdantix; 2011. Available at http://www.verdantix.com/index.cfm/papers/Products.Details/product_id/322/uk-sustainable-business-spending-2010-2015/-. Accessed July 21, 2012.

[9] Jowitt J. New emissions policy will force biggest UK firms to reveal CO_2 figures. Guardian, June 19, 2012. Available at http://gu.com/p/38e6f/em. Accessed Sept 13, 2012.

[10] Faber N, Jorna R, van Engelen J. The sustainability of 'sustainability' - a study into the conceptual foundations of the notion of "Sustainability". J Environ Assess Policy Manage 2005;7(1):1–33.

[11] Brundtland Commission. *Our Common Future.* Oxford: United Nations World Commission on Environment and Development; 1987.

[12] Williams D. A New Capitalist Manifesto: Balancing Profits, Forbes 2012 with purpose. Available at http://www.forbes.com/sites/davidkwilliams/2012/08/01/a-new-capitalist-manifesto-revisited-balancing-profits-with-purpose/. Accessed Jun 29, 2014.

[13] Hundloe T. Green and blue trade policy in context of sustainable development. Int J Social Econ 1997;24(7–9):771–784.

[14] MIT 2009. An interview with John Ehrenfeld—Flourishing Forever. MIT Sloan Manage Rev July 14, 2009. Available at http://sloanreview.mit.edu/article/flourishing-forever/. Accessed Jun 29. 2014.

[15] Ehrlich P, Holdren J. Impact of population growth. Science 1971. Available at http://people.reed.edu/~ahm/Courses/Reed-POL-372-2011-S3_IEP/Syllabus/EReadings/07.1/07.1.EhrlichHoldren1971-03-26Impact.pdf. Accessed Jun 29 2014.

[16] Hart S. Beyond greening: strategies for a sustainable world. Harvard Bus Rev January–February 1997; 25(1):66–76.

[17] Porritt J. *Capitalism: As If the World Matters.* London: Earthscan; 2005.

[18] Elkington J. *Cannibals with Forks: The Triple Bottom Line of 21st Century Business.* Capstone: Oxford; 1999.

[19] Savitz A, Weber K. *The Triple Bottom line, How Today's Best-Run Companies Are Achieving Economic, Social and Environmental Success and How You Can Too.* San Francisco: John, Wiley & Sons; 2006.

[20] Oskarsson K, Von Malmborg F. Integrated management systems as a corporate response to sustainable development. Corp Social Responsib Environ Manage 2005;12:121–128.

[21] Stahel WR. The product life factor. In: Orr SG, editor. *An Inquiry into the Nature of Sustainable Societies: The Role of the Private Sector (Series: 1982 Mitchell Prize Papers).* The Woodlands: HARC; 1984.

[22] McDonough W, Braungart M. *Cradle to Cradle: Remaking the Way We Make Things.* New York: North Point Press; 2002.

[23] Krysiak F. Risk management as a tool for sustainability. J Bus Ethics 2009;85: 483–492.

[24] McElroy M, Jorna R, van Englen J. Sustainability quotients and the social footprint. Corp Social Responsib Environ Manage 2008;15:223–234.

[25] Florida R. Lean and green: the move to environmentally conscious manufacturing. California Manage Rev 1996;39(1):80–105.

[26] Ōno T. *Toyota Production System: Beyond Large-Scale Production.* Portland: Productivity Press; 1988.

[27] Unknown. *What Is Quality?* Chartered Quality Institute. Available at http://www.thecqi.org/The-CQI/What-is-quality/. Accessed Aug 14, 2013.

[28] Charter M, Clark T. *Sustainable innovation.* Available at http://www.cfsd.org.uk/Sustainable%20Innovation/Sustainable_Innovation_report.pdf. Accessed Nov 17, 2012.

[29] Elkins P, Max-Neef M. *Real Life Economics.* London: Routledge; 1992.

[30] Schecterle R, Senxian J. *Building a Green Supply Chain: Social Responsibility for Fun and Profit.* Boston: Aberdeen Group; 2008.

[31] Pridahm H. Better returns from adopting higher principles. Guardian Unlimited; January 25, 2001.

[32] Jayne M, Skerratt G. Socially responsible investment in the UK—criteria that are used to evaluate suitability. Corp Social Responsib Environ Manage 2003;(10):1–11.

[33] Lash J, Wellington F. Competitive advantage on a warming planet. Harvard Bus Rev 2007;85(3):94–102.

[34] Amaeshi K, Grayson D. *The Challenges to Mainstreaming Environmental, Social and Governance (ESG) Issues in Investment Decisions EABIS 2008 Colloquium.* Cranfield: Corporate Responsibility & Sustainability.

[35] McElroy MW. Leaving social footprints. Business & The Environment With ISO 14000 Updates 2006;17(6):1–3, Business Source Complete, EBSCO*host,* viewed January 16, 2013.

[36] Villalonga B. Intangible resources, Tobin's q, and sustainability of performance differences. J Econ Behavior Organ 2004; 54(2):205–230.

[37] Haanes K, Arthur D, Balagopal B, Kong MT, Reeves M, Velken I, Hopkins MS, Kruschwitz N. Sustainability: the Embracers seize advantage. MIT Sloan Manage Rev and The Boston Consulting Group, Winter 2011. Available at http://sloanreview.mit. edu/reports/sustainability-advantage/. Accessed on Jun 29, 2014.

[38] Haanaes K, Reeves M, Von Streng Velken I, Audretsch M, Kiron D, Kruschwitz N. Sustainability nears a Tipping point; 2012. Available at http://sloanreview.mit.edu/reports/sustainability-strategy/introduction/. Accessed Dec 31, 2013.

[39] Sheldon O, Thompson K. *The Philosophy of Management.* New York: Routledge; 2003.

[40] Carroll A. A three-dimensional conceptual model of corporate performance. Acad Manage Rev 1979;4(4):497–505.

[41] Beresford D. *Compilation of Social Measurement Disclosures in Fortune 500 Annual Reports.* Cleveland: Ernst and Ernst; 1973; Beresford D. How companies are reporting social performance. Manage Account 1974;56(2):41–44; Beresford D. *Social Responsibility Disclosure in 1974 Fortune 500 Annual Reports.* Cleveland: Ernst and Ernst; 1975; Beresford D. *Social Responsibility Disclosure—1976 Survey of Fortune 500 Annual Reports.* Cleveland: Ernst and Ernst; 1976.

[42] Warthick S, Cochran P. The evolution of the corporate social performance model. Acad Manage Rev 1985;10(4):758–769.

[43] Sethi P. Dimensions of corporate social responsibility. California Manage Rev 1975;17(3):58–64.

[44] Carson R. *Silent Spring.* Boston: Houghton Mifflin; 1962.

[45] Cerin P. Communication in corporate environmental reports. Corp Social Responsib Environ Manage 2002;9:46–66.

[46] Levitt T. The dangers of social responsibility. Harvard Bus Rev 1958;36(5):41–50.

[47] Segerlund L. *Making Corporate Social Responsibility a Global Concern: Norm Construction in a Globalizing World.* UK: Ashgate Publishing Limited; 2010.

[48] Porritt J, Winner D. *The Coming of the Greens Fontana.* London: Collins; 1988.

[49] Kolk A. Sustainability, accountability and corporate governance: exploring multinationals reporting practices. Bus Strat Environ 2008;18:1–15.

[50]   Levy DL, Egan D. A neo-Gramscian approach to corporate political strategy: conflict and accommodation in the climate change negotiations. J Manage Stud 2003;40(4):803–830.

[51]   UNFCCC. Copenhagen Climate Change Conference—December 2009. Available at https:// unfccc.int/meetings/copenhagen_dec_2009/meeting/6295.php. Accessed Oct 17, 2013.

[52]   James. BP's deepwater horizon: a quality issue or a safety issue?. Sustainability and CSR Insights (Blog), Oct 21, 2012. Available at http://ow.ly/nQVjf. Accessed Jan 18, 2014.

[53]   UNFCCC. Cancun Climate Change Conference—November 2010. Available at http:// unfccc.int/meetings/cancun_nov_2010/meeting/6266.php. Accessed Oct 17, 2013.

[54]   Bernstein L. Washington Post Warsaw Climate Conference Produces Little Agreement. Available at http://www.washingtonpost.com/national/health-science/warsaw-climate-conference-produces-little-agreement/2013/11/22/705a06d0-538f-11e3-a7f0-b790929232e1_story.html. Accessed Dec 31, 2013.

[55]   Schmidheiny S, Zorraquin F. *World Business Council for Sustainable Development (WBCSD), Financing Change: The Financial Community, Eco-Efficiency and Sustainable Development*. Cambridge: MIT Press; 1996.

3

THE DILEMMA OF SUSTAINABILITY AND CORPORATE SOCIAL RESPONSIBILITY

3.1 INTRODUCTION

As humanity finally comes to terms with its symbiotic role within our planet's ecosystem, we are faced with the dilemma of economic growth, but at what cost? And is there a point at which sustainable development becomes unsustainable [1]? Such questions are inherent to the continued interpretation of sustainability, corporate social responsibility (CSR), and its relevance to the changing business environment. Utilizing contemporary research, it can be surmised that sustainability and CSR adoption are influenced by three interoperable factors as illustrated in the *sustainability/ CSR conceptualization diagram* (Fig. 3.1):

The *philosophical challenge*—ethical frameworks within which humans justify sustainable action or inaction

The *cultural challenge*—norms and values that are either nurtured or assimilated, which manifests itself in the public sphere as societal norms or within businesses as the organizational culture

The *strategic challenge*—a holistic expression of organizational goals that assimilates philosophical/cultural values contributing sustainable outcomes for the business entity and society within the prevailing economic context

The pursuit of sustainability and CSR involves a balancing act between business goals of profitability and stakeholder expectations for the organization to contribute

Sustainability Footprints in SMEs: Strategy and Case Studies for Entrepreneurs and Small Business, First Edition. Lowellyne James.
© 2015 John Wiley & Sons, Inc. Published 2015 by John Wiley & Sons, Inc.

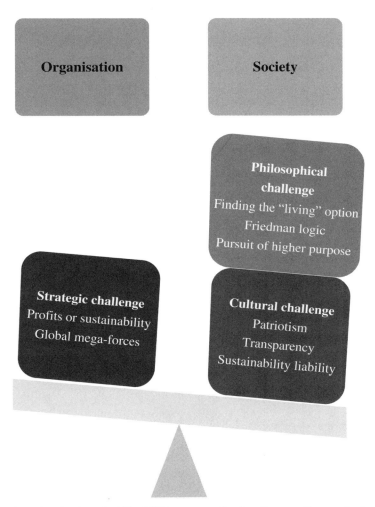

FIGURE 3.1 Sustainability/CSR conceptualization diagram. Source: Author.

to wider societal aims that go beyond employment, legal compliance, and good governance. The dynamic of this balancing act for an organization involves the integration of each challenge, namely, *philosophical*, *cultural*, and *strategic*, and is changing the way we view the role of the organization and the role of management and staff as actors within this context.

3.2 THE PHILOSOPHICAL CHALLENGE

Managers are routinely faced with decisions that impact on the environment on a daily basis. This dilemma of profits or the environment is influenced by the ethical and social reference of the decision maker [2].

From a purely Western perspective, the realization of this dilemma emerged with societal sensitivity to the degradation of the environment in the 1960s. This ascription of rights on nonhuman species by animal liberation activists however finds its early beginnings in Bentham's [3] musings: "The question is not, can they reason? Nor can they talk? But can they suffer?" Kant [4], a contemporary of Bentham, argued for the treatment of humanity as the ends as opposed to the means. The difficulty that managers face is that they themselves are disconnected from the environment by the trappings of modernity. This disconnection of postmodern Western society from nature affects not only views on the natural environment but also solutions to environmental issues such as carbon emissions and personal environmental impact, that is, individual carbon footprints. The malaise has contributed to the potential environmental consequence of irreversible climate change even though there is an immediate cessation of carbon emissions [5].

The present management utilitarian paradigm is focused on consequences, mainly financial, that is, profit maximization being the main purpose of management. Aristotle [6] postulated that an individual is a sum of his or her habits; the pattern of actions over time reveals *telos* or purpose. The Roman Empire gave new meaning to *telos* or purpose: by redefining the role of the individual and organizations as *civilitas*, a combination of graciousness, courteousness, politeness, and the art of good governance. Traditionally, governance has been reserved for the institutions of the state to define rights and values of the society, but this role has been usurped by multinational corporations who today are in some instances economically more powerful and influential than sovereign governments. As with individuals, organizations reveal their purpose to society at large via a series of actions or signals. These actions are in the form of product catalogues, annual financial reports, and sustainability and CSR reports that send signals of intent in terms of price, target market, and socioeconomic and environmental objectives. Each stakeholder group interprets each message and performs economic actions that may be to the advantage or disadvantage of the firm, for example, consumer boycotts of Nike merchandise in the 1990s.

In as much that businesses have a life of their own, that is, having an ethical construct that may lead to actions that may or may not be in the interest of stakeholders creating a unique phenomenon—a "personality" with organizations developing set values and identity [7, 8]. These actions or signals are interpreted by stakeholders whose expectation of business behavior includes positive actions by businesses to improve society [9, 10] such as taking action for the greater good or when exercising corporate citizenship due to an implied sense of moral duty and fairness that goes beyond the tax contributions of corporate entities [11]. Therefore, the corporation is more than a legal entity but a social institution seeking the interests of a myriad of stakeholders both internal and external to the organization seamlessly surmounting or traversing any boundaries should they exist [12]. The environment—"the atmosphere, hydrosphere, lithosphere, ecosystem processes and all human and non-human life forms" [13]—is usually the overlooked "silent" stakeholder, as it is affected by the actions of corporate entities; due consideration must be given to ensure its rejuvenation and renewal [14–16].

The definition of *telos* or purpose is critical to strategic planning; therefore, if the maxim of sustainable development is expressed as development that meets the needs of the present without compromising the ability of future generations to meet their own needs, herein lies the *sustainability and CSR dilemma* in the mind of the strategic planner, that is, profit maximization or sustainability. In the pursuit of purpose, individuals and business entities legitimize their status with society by accepting the values of the society; the absence of this alignment may cause the destruction of the firm [17].

Societal norms in themselves are not homogeneous within societies and across societies. Strategists are not devolved from the strategic choice of using sustainability as a strategic option but are prisoners to embedded social norms, societal values, background, and the culture of the firm. The influence of these societal norms and values creates blocks of opinions [18] that stimulate the adoption of a particular course of action either through supply chain pressures, benchmarking, or customer demands [19–21]. A factor of customer demand is their perception of the product or service social and environmental sustainability in relation to their environmental expectations or viewpoints [22].

Accepting that human perception is not static but dynamic changing dependent on stimuli received from the environment or context and utilizing Department for Environment, Food and Rural Affairs (DEFRA) [23] segmentation Model of individual attitudes/behaviors toward the environment. It can be inferred that individual behavior traverses a three-dimensional format ranging from overtly *sustainability positive* to *sustainability negative* and *sustainability passive* depending on their proximity to the sustainability issue (Fig. 3.2). This state of ambivalence has

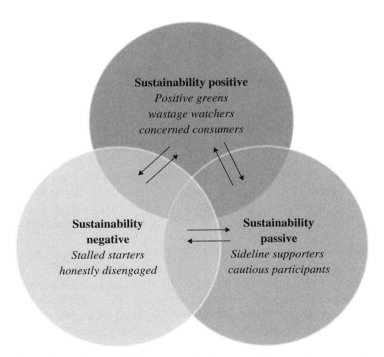

FIGURE 3.2 Sustainability perceptual orientation diagram. Source: Author.

been observed in scenarios where individuals are faced with an ethical dilemma, for example, trust, and there are simultaneous conflicting emotions such love and hate [24]. A recent Royal Society for the Arts (RSA) study identified that 63.9% (about two thirds) of the British population are in *stealth denial*, an acceptance of the reality of anthropogenic climate change yet internalizing personal attitudinal contentment in three areas: *emotional denial* ("I don't feel uneasy about climate change"), *personal denial* ("My daily actions are not part of the climate change problem"), and *practical denial* ("There is nothing I can do personally that will have any significant effect on limiting climate change") [25, 26].

The philosophical challenge therefore is to explore the range of *"living"* options [27] that would optimize resource use, reduce harmful greenhouse gas emissions, benefit society, and contribute to profit maximization. In practical terms, each option must propel the firm to a "desirable future state" for all stakeholders [28].

When viewed from the lens of benefit to society, value creation can be seen to also encompass carbon footprint, corporate reputation, technological innovation, employee and customer satisfaction [29]. This can be achieved through a combination of traditional financial metrics and other key performance indicators that now must reflect the environmental/ecological truths and externalities. Due to the universal acceptance of financial performance, some commentators argue that the impact of sustainability and CSR initiatives should be expressed in terms of accounting measures to determine the profitability of these activities [30]. The adoption of this approach will only capture financial risk without any incorporation of nonfinancial risks such as carbon emissions, safety and customer satisfaction which corporations such as BP have to their detriment incurred spiraling financial costs and reputational damage arising from the oil spill in the Gulf of Mexico.

Sustainability indicators by nature should be pertinent, understandable, and measurable reflecting the environmental impact of the product/service during its value creation process [31]. As such, indicators are waymarks [32] with sustainability as an endpoint that is achieved by a thorough understanding of the economic, social, and environmental operational context when viewed in the form of three secrets that are as follows: **understand the business case** (*the environment is an opportunity*), **what to do** (*think solar, cyclic, safe, and ecoefficient*), and **how to do it** (*build a corporate culture that rewards continuous improvement and innovation*).

Kane's philosophy confines sustainability for organizations as defined target; my alternative view proposes that sustainability is an ever-changing goal that evolves with changes in technology as businesses decarbonize and dematerialize products and processes.

The sustainability/CSR dilemma necessitates the converting the skeptics and creating sustainable action if we are to avoid the potential dangers of environmental collapse as resource consumption continues unabated [33]. Individuals and businesses making daily decisions to reduce their environmental impact via recycling, going beyond green, that is, reduce, recycle, reuse to "blue sky thinking"—rethinking the way businesses can inspire and motivate their *People* to efficiently use the resources of the *Planet* to deliver sustainable *Profit* to shareholders while reducing the externalities of resource use, namely, carbon emissions [34]. Although inspirational, Fisk does not provide a practical framework for action that is a major shortcoming of his analysis of the strategic options for global business.

The concept of People, Planet, Profit [34] sustainability is aligned with achieving a higher purpose whereby the role of business is not simply profit maximization but making a difference to the lives of all its stakeholders.

3.3 CORPORATE CITIZEN OR FRIEDMAN LOGIC

This vision of a higher purpose must be clearly defined and communicated by the leadership of the organization with the Chief Executive Officer (CEO) and board of directors acting as catalysts for change. Leadership must consciously make courageous strategic decisions to build sustainability into the core of their business. Matten and Crane [35] conceptualize the higher purpose as the firm's corporate citizenship obligation due to the cross-border nature of global business. It is readily accepted that the corporate entity has a social function but it may be delusionary to transcribe concepts of citizenship and rights to corporate entities that are transnational or transient through the subcontracting of operations across borders; the most appropriate term would be *global corporate citizenship* [35] especially when environmental aspects such as carbon emissions and "embodied carbon" are considered. The firm as corporate citizen is not congruent with prevailing financial systems that focus on organizational profitability as the primary determinant of success with aspects such as carbon emissions or social impacts considered as unavoidable externalities and not direct product or service costs. Until these costs are fully understood and reflected in the pricing of goods and services, then business may be able to appreciate and address its impact on the environment and its commitment to society. Even though this lack of congruency persists between corporate citizenship and the capitalist model due to the externalizing of environmental and social costs, this does not indemnify the firm from financial loss due to ineffective social and environmental polices [36].

Porter and Kramer [36] contend that CSR can only be incorporated into the boardroom agenda if social issues are understood in three main areas: *generic social issues* (i.e., social issues that are not affected by the firm's operations), *value chain societal impacts* (i.e., social issues that can be affected by a firm's operations), and the *social dimensions of competitive context* (i.e., social issues that affect the dynamics of the environment within which the firm operates). Porter and Kramer have redefined the traditional perception of the firm's role as economic engine from which it can be inferred that due to the increasing size and influence of corporations creates a unique capability to affect the lives of individuals globally. The effects of the recent financial crisis confirm that the firm cannot divorce itself from its social responsibilities to its wider stakeholder audience in terms of providing social inclusion and stability as well as economic security. Paramount of these social issues is poverty especially when caused by greenhouse gas emissions generated as a result of increased industrialization and globalization such as the effects of climate change, for example, floods, deforestation, and desertification.

The continued influence of Judeo-Christian religious philosophy on the economies in the EU and United States in terms of the approach, language, and tone of business courses and MBA programs cannot be readily discounted. This concern for the key role that business school education contributes to the development of future management leaders has led Sir Michael Rake [37] to comment: *"Business Schools need to teach sustainability as an integral part of practical business and leadership skills. These things are critically important because the next generation of business leaders will really need to understand both the moral cases, as well as the business opportunity. There is enormous potential for the business schools to create a properly integrated fully rounded approach and develop the research that underpins it."*

Another philosophical challenge to sustainability is the "Friedman condition" [38] that persists among senior management where many are not advocates of business being involved in poverty relief and agree with the prevailing philosophy of our global economy; the *protestant work ethic* in that poverty is linked with laziness. Similar sentiments are also expounded by the "Incompatibility Thesis Mindset" [16] that suggests an incompatibility between market capitalism and concern for the environment. Beliefs such as "For ye have the poor always with you" [39] still resonate in the European and North American societies and have contributed to apathy in business circles to the plight of the poor especially in metropolitan areas. There is a tendency "to look the other way" due to the complicated issues surrounding poverty and the apparent inability to accurately measure poverty reduction initiatives [40]. In parallel with the issue of poverty is gender equality with women and their young offspring that are usually victims of the economic and social collapse of societies; an example is the recent civil war in Rwanda and political disturbance in Kenya [41, 42]. In developing economies, women are disproportionately affected by climate change due to their key role in food and livestock production. Developed economies perform no better in this issue in that there is continued underrepresentation of women in boardrooms, trade unions, and transnational organizations such as the IMF and World Bank [43]. The existence of gender inequality is one of the persistent inefficiencies of the current capitalist model; the failure of the society to leverage the full potential of its human resource provides business with another opportunity to release value.

Factor Five [44] explores the value creation potential of sustainability initiatives and builds on the legacy of the previous book *Factor Four* published some 15 years earlier. In visionary language, it points business leaders to the potential of 80% reduction in environmental impact per unit of output. In their view, the sustainability of business must be aligned with timely government intervention through incentives and taxes, thus stimulating the adoption of technological innovations and sustainable best practices. Enthusiastically advocating the view that the visible hand of government is needed if the capitalist model is to incorporate the ecological truth in prices of goods and services, this price reflection will act as a catalyst to a new green wave of innovation. Unfortunately, the belief in the divine hand of benign political structures enacting environmental and social regulation for the greater good may be misguided and is dependent on the actors, that is, the politicians themselves not being influenced by corporate lobbyist as in the United States or personal self-interest such as the "cash for honors" scandal in the United Kingdom [45, 46].

3.4 THE TRANSITION

It is argued that the transition to a resource-efficient low-carbon economy must be supported by a societal shift away from consumption to sufficiency and stewardship [16]. This concept of sufficiency concedes that resources are not infinite—therefore, there must be limits to greed, growth, and consumption; importantly, the latter three are not determinants of societal happiness [47]. The sufficiency principle appeals to an innate rationality for self-preservation but ignores opportunities for humanity to develop clean technology systems, for example, artificial trees and *carbon sequestration* to combat the effects of global emissions, thereby aiding the transition to a low-carbon future.

The low-*carbon* transition will involve dialogue among stakeholders that is a cornerstone of CSR initiatives. There are four main approaches to engaging stakeholder opinions and support, namely, *proactive dialogue* involving the soliciting of new ideas engaging stakeholders through a collaborative learning process, *stakeholder relationship management* as part of a wider business resilience strategy, *engaging stakeholders as part of risk management planning*, and *gaining competitive advantage by developing stakeholder dialogue channels and communication programs* [48]. In practice, firms subsume stakeholder dialogue on sustainability issues as part of strategic management framework. Although experts [49] agree that dialogue can be facilitated by the use of consultants, it may construct another communication barrier for stakeholders with any subsequent sustainability messages being perceived as corporate "spin" or a "green washing" exercise.

3.5 THE CULTURAL CHALLENGE

Cultural and societal influences play an important part in the interpretation and adoption of CSR and sustainability practices with indications that CSR principles are not homogeneous across borders [50]. A supporting survey of the European, North American, and Asian organizations identified differences in the interpretation of CSR as being due to social, cultural, and institutional factors [51]. An interesting example is China whose ideas of CSR and sustainability are heavily influenced by Western academia. A study into the indigenous characteristics of Chinese corporate responsibility found that it is similar to Western approaches but emphasizes the following dimensions: (1) *employment* (increasing job opportunities, easing national employment burden, and employing disabled individuals), (2) *good faith* (sound business ethics and honoring contractual obligations), and (3) *social stability and progress* (patriotism, service to society, and promotion of social progress) [52].

It is apparent that Chinese approaches to CSR and sustainability are influenced by its communist sociopolitical culture through values that the society considers important, that is, patriotism and employment, although unofficially Chinese folk wisdom provides the underlying ethical framework within which business decisions are evaluated [53]. However, it would be prejudicial to infer that a sense of *communitarianism* is isolated only to China, but other countries such as Germany and Japan have adopted this consensus-based approach that has shaped their CSR reporting as opposed to individualistic business systems relying on self-regulation that are more prevalent in the United States and the United Kingdom [54].

Cultural differences also affect consumer perceptions of sustainable products; in U.S. markets, sustainable products are associated with gentleness as opposed to strength creating a *"sustainability liability"* that can be improved by emphasizing the product strengths [55]—similar sentiments were also expressed by consumers in U.K. study who also view sustainable products to be inherently inferior to unsustainable alternatives [56]. Some academics suggest that defining CSR may in itself yield little utility as the concept of corporate responsibility differs between countries and may form part of the research question [57].

Transparency and the use of external verification are key issues in CSR and sustainability reporting in Japanese and European firms who traditionally have been more explicit of their sustainability performance as compared to their American counterparts with the provision of complaint mechanisms forming part of Japanese sustainability culture but are less prevalent in the European context [58]. Not surprisingly, 58% of FTSE 250 companies were willing to disclose their emission performance to the Carbon Disclosure Project in 2008 [59]. In May 2001, France became the first country in the world to enact legislation requiring mandatory CSR reporting, confirming the European attitude to corporate disclosure [60]. Australia's carbon tax was an attempt by its political class to align the country's development along a sustainable path as Australia is one of the world's highest greenhouse gas emitters due to the continued reliance on coal for energy generation [61]. The United Kingdom not to be left outdone has enacted mandatory greenhouse gas emission reporting for companies listed on the London Stock Exchange [57]. The impact of these legal obligations on the supply chains of multinationals especially small- and medium-sized enterprise (SME) suppliers within these supply chains is yet to be determined.

Interestingly, European firms also lead the way in seeking external verification of sustainability reports, and a quarter of Japanese firms also seek external assurance of their reports with U.S. companies being less likely to adopt such initiatives [62]. Environmental policies and environmental reporting, although regularly featured as part of corporate communications, are not weighted as heavily as labor-related concerns such as pay and working conditions but are gaining ascendency as a priority among decision makers largely fuelled by external communication in relation to climate change to which environmental issues such as greenhouse gas emissions are inextricably linked [63].

3.6   THE STRATEGIC CHALLENGE

Strategic choices adopted by firms are influenced by their perceived value or trade-off between pursuits of purely economic or social objectives. Critical to this argument is not that sustainability and social responsibility is good for business but who pays for it; Edgar Blanco, Research Director at the Massachusetts Institute of Technology, Center for Transportation and Logistics, expresses this conundrum eloquently when he states:

> This is where you say, Who pays for it? And this is the question and that's why it's hard. But it's what needs to happen. You have at some point decide how committed you are to the process. [63]

Based on this perceived trade-off, firms adopt varied positional orientations from being *skeptical*, *pragmatic*, *engaged*, and *idealistic*; each form of orientation is not mutually exclusive as firms may adopt a combination of approaches in response to external stimuli [64]. There is an imperative for organizations to pursue sustainable development as a strategic option; however, pragmatic approaches should be adopted that will lead to decision making that incorporates environmental issues into the decision-making process [65]. Pragmatic strategic planning involves the acceptance of facts as truths to validate decision making. By extension, strategists must acknowledge ecological truths and pursue strategies that mitigate against adverse impacts. The absence of acknowledgment of environmental impacts and constraints will only lead to decreasing competitive advantage [66]. This echoes earlier sentiments that societal norms and values are embedded in its institutions and they form the nature of things [64, 67]. In recent developments such as businesses optimizing the carbon efficiency of their commercial assets and products, building new low-carbon businesses, and increasing environmental regulation, strategists may be left with very few options for long-term growth apart from sustainability [68]. The use of sustainability in business strategy may be the "default" option with the continued rise of "10 mega-forces," that is, *climate change, energy and fuel, material resource scarcity, water scarcity, population growth, urbanization, wealth, food security, ecosystem decline,* and *deforestation* [69].

Societal influences pervade both the evolution and adoption of sustainability and CSR. Firms generally react to stakeholder pressure by developing "green" approaches, for example, green marketing and environmental management to their business model to either solicit more business, improve customer satisfaction, or gain the approval of influential stakeholders such as financial markets [70]. Research into the factors that influence customers of MRI scanners indicates that sustainability as a selling proposition differentiates the product offering in the minds of target customers [71]. In most cases, reactive responses by firms to environmental concerns to stakeholders may leave the organization at a disadvantage when compared to more proactive competitors. A recent investigation into investing in sustainability initiatives suggests that it can create long-term value [72].

In the case of CSR reports, globalization has changed the strategic tone of CEO letters appearing in annual reports of Swedish companies [73] initially from a national communitarian view of CSR to a more international self-regulating view of CSR. Surprisingly, it was identified that CSR initiatives outlined in CEO letters usually predate their popularity as a concept [73]. Therefore, the role of CEO/strategist cannot be underestimated; as leaders, they provide the impetus for sustainability and CSR initiatives by making the case for change, translating this vision for sustainability into tangible actions, and nurturing sustainable growth by expanding boundaries envisioning possible futures within the confines of present market understanding [74]. Building the case of corporate sustainability must not only be the right thing to do morally ethical case but also deliver financial and economic returns for the business, that is, the business case. The challenge for the CEO is to fully understand the implications that poor social performance has on the firm's long-term success and to communicate the importance of CSR and sustainability to functional managers [75]. The effectiveness of the articulation of the sustainability imperative will be determined by the ability of frontline managers to interpret and commit to sustainability and CSR goals in their operational decision-making capacity. The clarity of articulation however is constrained by the longtime horizons associated with sustainability and CSR initiatives, which is plagued by difficulties in measuring the success or lack of success as a result of selecting a particular strategic option for investment [75].

The social screening of investments can benefit from the sustainability reporting guidelines such as the Global Reporting Initiative (GRI). The GRI is a voluntary reporting initiative that examines the environmental and social aspects of a firm's performance facilitating comparisons in performance within and across sectors [76]. However, it was observed that due to the diverse stakeholder groups and information requirements, it is imperative that managers of Socially Responsible Investments (SRI) use information found in GRI compliant reports to supplement information collected from traditional media, online media sources, market reports, questionnaires, and interviews [76]. The continued insistence by shareholders, customers, the public, and employees for companies to grow sustainably has propelled managers to pursue sustainability improvements through assimilating those factors that drive sustainability performance and develop the operations and structures to enhance corporate social performance [77–79].

3.7   STRATEGIC FRAMEWORKS

To guide the understanding of the impact of sustainability and CSR initiatives on performance, researchers argue for a framework incorporating five components— *corporate and business unit strategy, sustainability actions, sustainability performance, stakeholder reactions,* and *corporate financial performance*—so that each component can be defined and their interrelationships between each component understood [75].

At an international level, discussions on climate change and biodiversity created the impetus for the development of new methods such as The Economics of Ecosystems and Biodiversity (TEEB) established by the United Nations Environmental Protection Program to demonstrate the application of economic theory to the conservation of ecosystems and biodiversity [80]. A task of the TEEB project was to explore the relationship between business and biodiversity that has been championed by TEEB for Business Coalition and partner organizations such as the Institute of Chartered

Accountants in England and Wales (ICAEW), the HRH The Prince of Wales's Accounting for Sustainability Project, the World Business Council for Sustainable Development (WBCSD), the International Union for Conservation of Nature (IUCN), the World Wildlife Fund of the United Kingdom (WWF-UK), and the GRI [80]. The TEEB for Business Coalition advocates the use of market-based approaches to the deployment of sustainability within economies identifying eight principal mechanisms that drive change not only within a business context but also influence behavioral change.

These eight mechanisms—*corporate strategies, supply chain pressure, stakeholder engagement, voluntary codes, rating* and *benchmarking, taxes* and *subsidies, tradable permits, requirements and permissions*—are seen as promoting sustainability outcomes with the support of assurance processes, information, and reporting [80].

Alternatively, some commentators suggest that firms view sustainability strategy from the lens of environmental strategy that is considered to comprise of three stages, *pollution prevention, product stewardship*, and *clean technology* [81], which is articulated with the addition of one more criterion, the *sustainability vision*. Although useful for developing solutions to environmental aspects, Hart's proposed stages do not fully satisfy the economic and social dimensions of sustainability nor develop a framework for sustainability strategy development.

A supporting strategic framework, *ecoinnovation*, advocates the assimilation of sustainability and competitiveness by understanding the connections between economic activity and its effect on the sustainability of our planet. As a concept, ecoinnovation can only flourish in an environment conditioned for change; that is, the focus of the market economy should be to achieve sustainability, reward ecoinnovators, and account for negative externalities arising from the inefficient use of resources [47]. Secondly, political solutions in the form of government policy, taxes, and regulation aimed at the moving barriers to ecoinnovation are seen as an enabling factor critical to the adoption and acceptance of ecoinnovations [47].

Within these conditions, the benefits of each dimension of ecoinnovation such as *design, user, product/service*, and *governance* can be leveraged. At an organizational level, the stimulus for the adoption of ecoinnovations was identified as top-level management commitment to environmental performance. Directors and CEOs of organizations provide leadership and resourcing to implement innovative strategic options that range from life cycle analysis and ISO 14001 to scorecards that increase competiveness (*efficiency principle*) but are also good for the environment (*effectiveness principle*) [82]. There is however a perceived bias toward the use of political instruments such as government policy to change the external business environment and not enough focus on practical models that can be applied to the strategic operations of business. Some researchers advocate a policy-oriented approach to their application of ecoinnovation as a tool in sustainability strategy, which may alienate SMEs who may wish to initiate sustainability programs as SMEs have different overarching strategic issues such as *survival, staff motivation* and *retention*, and *community relations* [83].

The implementation of sustainability and CSR in the service sector produces its own unique challenges. Services are defined "as economic activities that replace the customer's own labor with activities conducted by the service provider, either personally, automatically or in advance through planning and design"; using this definition, they categorized service ecoefficiency based upon their level of dematerialization into four main groups: *ecodesign with service (functional) approach, product-based services, result-oriented services*, and *nonmaterial services* [83]. Dematerialization is an easily quantifiable goal for business but is shortsighted if not combined with the decarbonization of global business of which evidence seems to suggest that modest ecoefficiency gains are accrued by service innovations and that these efficiency gains do not generate immediate reductions in material consumption; value can be accrued by focusing upon making existing service offerings sustainable [83].

However, research that explored significant differences in performance between the Dow Jones Sustainability Index and the Dow Jones Global Index infers that the link between performance indicators and CSR/sustainability initiatives is negative with implementation expenses in the short-term positioning firms at an economic disadvantage to other late adopter firms [84]. Positive internal and external outcomes from investments in CSR are also affected by marketing strategy, industry sector (e.g., tobacco), existing reputation, demographics, competitor CSR initiatives, segment characteristics, and size [85]. Consumers in their view incorporate both product quality and CSR initiatives in the purchasing decision with heightened sensitivities toward negative CSR information [85].

Not all researchers advocate the use of indices as an indicator of a company's performance in regarding CSR due to the methodologies used in some indices; the pursuit of rankings in itself diverts from strategic objectives and denigrates CSR to a public relations exercise with little societal value. Instead, the integration of business with society through understanding of the firm's *inside-out linkages*, that is, its impact on the wider society, and *outside-in linkages*, —the influence of existing social norms and conditions with the objective of CSR being the creation of shared value for both the business and society by utilizing value chain analysis and Porter's Five Forces model [36].

Overall, the strategic approach to CSR by organizations is seen to evolve along a continuum from *responsive CSR* ("good corporate citizenship") to *strategic CSR* using CSR to consolidate or leverage its competitive position [36]. Van der Ven [8] identifies three strategic approaches to CSR—the *strategy of reputation protection and improvement, the strategy of building a virtuous brand*, and *ethical product differentiation*, advocating subtle approaches to the communication of CSR initiatives such as the "silence speaks a thousand words" policy of the Dutch logistics company TNT. However, their indifference to the usefulness of indices and stakeholder satisfaction measurement as useful benchmarks may leave organizations without any yardstick upon which to measure their progress and the benefits of their investment in CSR.

3.7.1   Sustainability Partnerships

Sustainability partnerships (SP) are a recommended option for embedding sustainability both within the internal value chain and business supply chains that arose from the UNEP Agenda 21 plan [86], consisting of three main categories: *government–community partnerships* (GCP) (these are institutional frameworks to promote sustainability within national boundaries), *business–business partnerships* (BBP)—the formation of green alliances and value chains that support *enviropreneurship*, i.e., *the formulation and implementation of ecologically beneficial corporate policies that protect the market position* while *creating revenue* and basic *learning partnerships* (LP) [86]. Values are at the heart of SP as society and businesses are sensitized to the importance of environmental regulation; however, the institution of corporate policy is in no way a substitute for a value-driven decision-making conscience regarding the ecological issues that will allow business to benefit from goodwill and trust of its stakeholders. The development of a value-centered business ecostrategy is influenced by various organizational drivers [86]:

Stewardship to natural capitalism—optimization of productive effort aimed at efficient use of the earth's natural capital. The concept of natural capitalism is based on four principles:

- Radical resource efficiency
- Strategic shift to pursue waste avoidance
- The use of leasing in preference to ownership
- Ecological restoration

Efficiency to ecoefficiency—the transition from total quality-focused initiatives to also include environmental impact reduction through the implementation of four stages of ecoefficient development:

- Increasing process efficiency
- Cooperative ventures to revalorize by-products while striving for zero waste
- Ecoefficient product design
- Reducing material flow by changing consumer preferences for material intensive products

Business image to environmental champion—a commitment to SP that is manifested by organizational policies and procedures aimed at implementing environmental best practice.

The development of a value-driven culture aided by organizational drivers that strengthens the four elements of ecostrategy [86]:

Learning—complements efforts within the organization to build capability in areas such as quality, ethics, information, sustainable efficiency, and strategy.

Legal compliance and beyond—regulations establish the boundaries within which businesses operate by instituting explicit benchmarks for minimum performance regarding environmental aspects. Herein lies the predicament: mere compliance does not necessarily remove legal or environmental risk; therefore, senior management must always manage from a standpoint of due diligence—a duty to care for the environment that transcends compliance. *SP* between business and regulatory agencies necessitate the replacement of adversarial conditions with cooperation and collaboration to leverage synergies and develop opportunities for self-regulation thereby improving quality and profitability.

Leadership—making sustainable leadership part of organizational strategy by encouraging others to pursue sustainability goals within the organization and externally through "greening" of the supply chain, the attainment of sustainable goals, recognizing stakeholder achievements in support of sustainable development, and being a best practice model for sustainability. Participation in award schemes such as the Vision in Business for the Environment of Scotland (VIBES) demonstrates commitment to environmental leadership.

Leverage—using network influence within supply chains through collaboration with sustainability partners such as nongovernmental organizations (NGOs) and government institutions to create environmentally beneficial legal, social, and cultural change.

To assist in the implementation of sustainability initiatives, Jenkins [82] proposes a "business opportunity" model of CSR for SMEs, which consists of a five-step process involving *value setting*, *scoping*, *seeking corporate social opportunities*, *strategy development*, and *benchmarking*. The "business opportunity" model is very prescriptive and may mislead strategists into developing organizational values and vision in isolation without stakeholder engagement.

3.7.2 Integrative Sustainability Triangle

Kleine and Hauff [87] have proposed the *integrative sustainability triangle (IST)* as a useful sustainability model based on the triple-bottom-line approach to sustainability; this model has been successfully implemented by organizations in the German state of Rhineland-Palatinate (Fig. 3.3). The three corners of the model represent *strong association* with the *ecology*, *social*, and *economic* dimensions of sustainability, *partial association* being denoted by adjacent fields, and *weak association* that is ascribed to fields furthest away with the center field exhibiting the equilibrium of all sustainability dimensions (Fig. 3.3). The *IST* involves the implementation of four stages consisting of:

- *Identification of issues* through the use of stakeholder analysis
- *Selection of focal topics* by exploring legal, cultural context and an understanding of stakeholder expectations
- *Implementation* of management systems and policies with the visible participation of senior management
- *Reporting and communication* of CSR performance

The IST is highly theoretical that may lead to misinterpretation by business leaders who are not sustainability practitioners; this characteristic of the model makes it readily applicable to large organizations who may have the resources and in itself creates an implementation barrier for its adoption by SMEs.

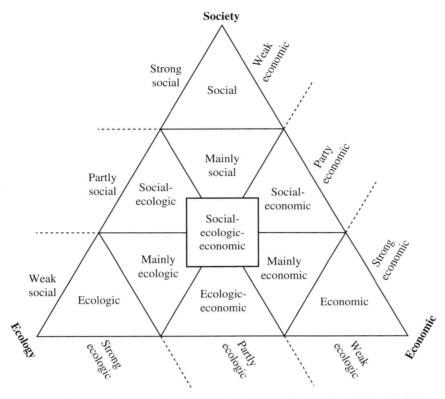

FIGURE 3.3   Integrative sustainability triangle. Source: Kleine and Hauff [87]. © Springer.

3.7.3   Model of Sustainable Organisation

The Model of Sustainable Organisation (MoSO) [88] was developed by the Deming Special Interest Group of the Chartered Quality Institute as an attempt to reconcile quality management approaches with the sustainable development goals. Although the MoSO model does not define a sustainable organization, it recommends that organizations pursue sustainable development utilizing eight guiding principles, namely, *customer focus, systems thinking, daily work of the organization, wisdom from numbers, leadership, innovation, protection of the natural environment*, and *respect for people*. The main elements of the MoSO model are:

- Customers
- Operating systems
- People, culture, leadership, and management
- Societal influences/learning
- Environment
- Plan, Do, Study, Act (PDSA)

- Voice of the customer, voice of the people, and voice of the system
- Essential interactions and communications

These elements are interpreted as part of a holistic view of an organization's role within the context of the society, environment, leadership style, and culture. In its application, businesses should review the relationship among elements to adapt the model that best suits the organizational objectives. The PDSA cycle is at the core of the MoSO model and allows its integration with existing management system standards such as ISO 9001, ISO 14001, and OHSAS 18001 by fostering continuous improvement.

3.7.4   Sustainable Value Model

Laszlo et al. [89] recommend the adoption of a new slant to sustainability strategy by categorizing shareholders as a separate group from stakeholders and as a consequence identifying a potential growth option for the firm through *sustainable value* creation to reduce the risks of *customer deselection, regulation, loss of market share* and *reputation damage, legal fines* and *penalties* arising from unsustainable business strategies (Fig. 3.4). To create *sustainable value*, organizations must pursue a disciplined three-phased program involving:

Diagnosis—the identification and analysis of organizational activities that create or destroy value for stakeholders for the development of strategies that anticipate future stakeholder expectations and market opportunities while seeking to reduce business risks associated with current activities

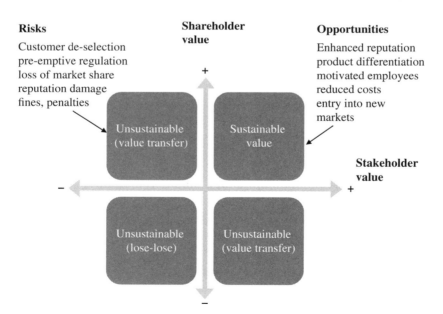

FIGURE 3.4   Sustainable value framework. Source: Laszlo et al. [89]. © Greenleaf Publishing.

Value creation—the adoption of strategic choices that create both shareholder and stakeholder value or reduce value destruction through the acquisition of resources to leverage strategic partnerships with key stakeholders

Value Capture—the implementation, measurement, and validation of actions taken to enhance shareholder and stakeholder value [89]

Laugel and Laszlo [90] suggest a symmetry between *sustainability* and *sustainable value* defining both within the business context as "*a dynamic state that occurs when a company creates ongoing value for its shareholders and stakeholders*" with the quest for shareholder value at the expense of stakeholders or vice versa leading to value transfer and exposure to competitive risk.

The prevarication of value destruction activities entails that organizations must create processes that embed business value along value chains and across six levels of value creation:

Risk—compliance-oriented management of risks and protecting license to operate

Efficiency/Process—reducing energy, waste, or other process costs

Product—creating product differentiation based on technical and environmental/social features

Market—addressing new markets driven by consumer and societal needs

Brand/culture—gaining stakeholder recognition and preference

Business context—changing the "rules of the game" to create advantage for sustainable strategies [89, 91] (Fig. 3.5)

The *value creation* phase provides opportunities for management to create value along the six levels of strategic value creation. However, the approach to sustainability

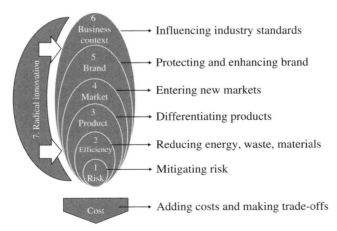

FIGURE 3.5 Six levels of value creation. Source: Laugel and Laszlo [90]. © Greenleaf Publishing.

strategy adopted by Laugel and Laszlo [90], although intuitively attractive within the context of large corporate entities, is of limited applicability to SMEs constrained by lack of both human and financial resources where the entrepreneur/shareholder is also an employee/stakeholder.

3.7.5   Carbon-Informed Complexity Management Model

As businesses operate in an increasingly complex, carbon-constrained, and cost-competitive environment, researchers such as Gell [92] advocate the adoption of carbon cost reduction measures such as:

- High-efficiency heating, ventilation, and cooling systems
- Use of energy-efficient office equipment
- Replacement of inefficient equipment with energy-saving models (e.g., high-efficiency electric motors and variable-speed pumping and airflow systems)
- Water conservation projects that capture and use storm water runoff
- Maintaining the water quality in HVAC towers to allow reduction in the number of cycles that boilers operate
- Energy audits and retro-commissioning (ensuring that existing equipment is optimized for maximum efficiency)
- Heat recovery on exhaust systems
- Maximizing natural light and use of energy-efficient and motion-sensor lighting
- Low-flow plumbing fixtures
- Right-sizing building chiller systems
- Increased employee awareness
- Use of recycled materials (e.g., in flooring and ceiling coverings)
- Use of ecopaints and varnishes
- Changes in waste management for paper recycling, turning disposal expenses into sources of revenue as materials such as concrete, brick, block, asphalt, and copper (other reusable materials are recycled)
- Equipment refurbishment to minimize the purchase of new equipment
- Teleconferencing and virtual workspaces to reduce travel

Carbon reduction strategy within this framework is assessed in three components: *internal* (exploration of opportunities to conserve energy and utilize renewable energy), *vertical* (identification of waste streams), and *horizontal* (implementation of activities to reduce supply chain impacts).

Within this carbon-constrained environment, carbon reduction strategy is deployed within organizations using detailed *ecoplan* that addresses the organizational *structure*, *conduct*, and *performance* (SCP). Ecoplans operate not in isolation but as part of an organization's integrated enterprise architecture that consists of *data management architecture* (DMA), *information management architecture* (IMA), *knowledge*

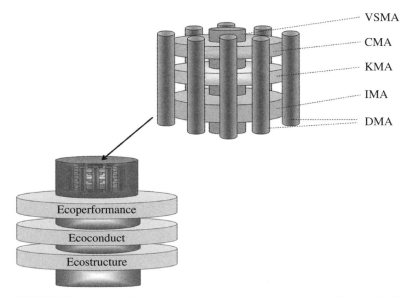

FIGURE 3.6   Carbon-informed complexity management model. Source: Gell.

management architecture (KMA), and *complexity management architecture* (CMA). These systems combine to feed into and support the *value systems management architecture* (VSMA) providing information that will manage the organizational ecoperformance, monitor ecoconduct, and improve business ecostructure (Fig. 3.6). Within larger organizations, VSMA supports reporting and compliance initiatives such as the GRI.

The business continuity risk (BCR) created by unabated carbon emissions is forcing enterprises to integrate into *carbon-constrained networks*, which in itself has created a global step change in operational environments. Enterprises are driven to identify opportunities to reduce cost and carbon emissions (A), as further opportunities to decrease BCR are exploited ("*the cusp*") (B) and supply chain pressures stimulate the development of *carbon-constrained networks* (C). Gell [92] describes firstly a five-stage progression within which enterprises move from carbon reduction to zero waste:

- *Stage 1*—the carbon-reducing enterprise signals to its supply base that it requires suppliers to reduce carbon and save costs.
- *Stage 2*—the enterprise then moves deep within the supply chain to monitor and drive changes.
- *Stage 3*—under performing suppliers are required to improve or are ejected, and high-scoring suppliers are introduced.
- *Stage 4*—the supply chain is undergoing significant morphing, and a competitive form of low-cost, low-carbon enterprise network emerges in preparation for the step change.

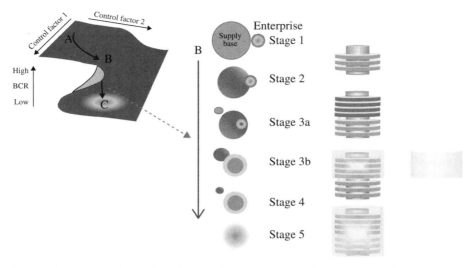

FIGURE 3.7   Transformation of enterprise systems on entry to a low-carbon economy. Source: Gell.

- *Stage 5*—striving for zero waste, preservation of resources, and maximized environmental sensitivity, giving them powerful cost, carbon and performance advantages, and market leaders (Fig. 3.7).

However, enterprises within the new low-carbon economy can achieve environmental restoration through innovation creating new business niches (Stage 6), which can translate into the development of new enterprise systems and kick-start the green economy (Stage 7).

3.7.6   Carbon Management Framework

The carbon management framework was developed for SMEs whilst most contemporary climate strategies and carbon management models were developed for large enterprises and is derived from Plan, Do, Check, Act (PDCA) model postulated by Deming [93]. Essentially, the carbon management framework consists of a seven-stage process involving *project framing, status quo analysis, scenario outlook, identification and reduction measures, target setting, implementation*, and *reporting and communication* [93] (Fig. 3.8):

Project framing—is the process of identifying environmental aspects and defining carbon emission reporting boundaries within business value chain(s). Allied to these activities is the selection of sustainability leaders to champion the project as an activity ensuring the coordination of administrative and organizational resources.

Status quo analysis—the calculation of the organizational carbon footprint.

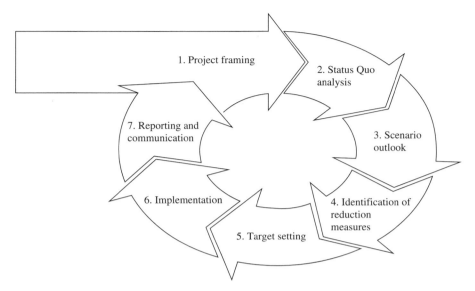

FIGURE 3.8   Seven steps of the SME carbon management framework. Source: Hendrichs and Busch [93]; www.tandfonline.com. © Taylor & Francis.

Scenario outlook—sensitivity analysis of the firm's exposure to carbon-related risks from energy, fuel price volatility, and legislative or legal risks.

Identification of reduction measures—an examination of all potential opportunities for greenhouse gas reduction that is ameliorated by the level of organizational control and the location of potential "hotspots" or environmental aspects that produce high emissions.

Target setting—researchers advocate a three-tiered approach to target setting involving:

- *An absolute target expressed as the percentage of total emissions compared to a baseline year*
- *A relative target based on an improvement of the firm's carbon intensity over a given time frame (e.g., total emissions over sales)*
- *A qualitative target describing the intended reduction measures and timeline for implementation*

Carbon offsetting must only be considered when all feasible reduction measures have been exhausted.

Implementation—is the stage during which organizational carbon emission reduction targets are articulated to a strategic business unit (SBU) or departmental level. Leaders are appointed to monitor performance and promote sustainable behavior among staff with the explicit commitment of senior management of the organization.

Reporting and communication—transparency in the reporting of carbon management to all stakeholder groups to position the company as a low-carbon enterprise among its customers and especially rewarding employees for their contribution to carbon emission reduction.

3.7.7   Ecoenterprise Strategy

Ecoenterprise strategy is an alternative approach that can be utilized by organizations to resolve the sustainability/CSR dilemma. Philosophically, *ecoenterprise strategy* framework is based on the three analytical components of *enterprise strategy*, namely, *value analysis* (identification of the organization's *core* values and *instrumental* values activities or mechanisms that bolster ethical approaches), *issues analysis* (awareness of the societal context), and *stakeholder analysis* (understanding the power relationship between the firm and its various stakeholders) [94]. *Ecoenterprise strategy* subscribes to the premise that organizations appreciate the risks arising from environmental degradation, social injustice, and war derived as a result of industrialization and globalization (Fig. 3.9), therefore opting for approaches that place sustainability as a *core* of business value supported by *instrumental* values, for example, wholeness, diversity, posterity, smallness, quality, community, dialogue, and human spiritual fulfillment—a *sustainability-centered values network* (Fig. 3.9). The model acknowledges population, affluence to be increasing contributory issues that are ameliorated by the ability of technology to reduce the stress arising from human activity—the *ecological issue system* as well as the primacy of earth as the primary stakeholder whose position is championed by a range of stakeholder groups

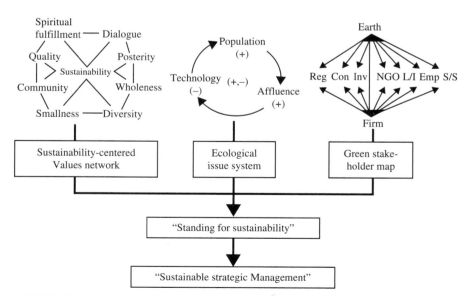

FIGURE 3.9   Ecoenterprise strategy model. Source: Stead and Stead [94]. © Springer.

such as regulators, employees, legislators, green consumers, and environmental groups (Fig. 3.9). A *green stakeholder map* can assist organizations with developing an understanding of the types and influence of stakeholders (Fig. 3.9).

Armed with clear values, a comprehension of societal issues, and the relative influence of stakeholders on its strategy, senior management must align corporate strategy with development goals that emphasize growth that focuses on both the economic and environmental with assured social benefits in essence—"*Standing for Sustainability*" (Fig. 3.9).

This conceptual shift to place sustainability at the core of corporate strategy is the goal of *sustainable strategic management* by reducing resource use, pollution prevention, and product stewardship utilizing frameworks such as total quality environmental management as a platform to achieve zero environmental impact and improve the quality of life (QoL) on the planet [94].

3.7.8 Sustainability Footprint Model

The *sustainability footprint model* is a decision-making tool that resolves the issues that arise in the determination of the sustainability of an activity or strategic option [95]. Comprised of two key elements: the *ecological footprint* (a methodology that determines the land and water area that is required to support the consumption and waste generation needs of a given population within existing economic and technological constraints) and QoL or value-added standard living derived from the consumption of resources. This implies that projects, organizations, and countries that have a low ecological footprint but a high QoL can be considered sustainable.

Within this interpretation, a *sustainability footprint* is defined *as the rate of change of some measure of system performance, as it pertains to the well-being of the system users (e.g., QoL), as a function of environmental costs associated with attaining that system performance (e.g., the consumption of natural resources and generation of wastes)* and is mathematically expressed as [95]

$$Sustainability\ footprint\ (\text{SF}) = \frac{quality\ of\ life\ (\text{QoL})\ change}{resource\ usage} \times waste\ generation$$

The use of the *sustainability footprint* model provides a number of advantages such as:

- Quantitative measures that can help decision makers ascertain the rate of change of QoL as a function of the ecological footprint.
- Supports comparative analysis of countries, regions, or companies by focusing on the environmental cost of improvements in QoL.
- Minimum standards can be set for sustainable performance when QoL is expressed as a function of the ecological footprint per capita.

- Conversely, ceilings or limits to growth or development can be established that does not exceed the ability for natural replenishment (*strong sustainability*) or substitution by technical innovation (*weak sustainability*).
- It addresses the sustainability/CSR dilemma by indicating options for sustainable growth.
- A dual-purpose tool that measures both "*well-being*" and environmental impact.

Arguably, the *sustainability footprint model* is macroeconomic in approach and as such maintains the status quo by preserving growth as being a desirable objective as long as the standard of living achieved is not at the expense of the environment. However, the use of the *sustainability footprint model* provides a formative basis for the development of performance standards for sustainable development, maintenance of sustainability standards through the effective planning and monitoring—*Sustainability Standards Management*, the development of *Sustainability Footprint Trading* (SFT) and as a potential indicator of social progress for disadvantaged groups by identifying the minimum standards for QoL [95].

3.7.9   Balanced Scorecard-Based Sustainability Frameworks

The balanced scorecard was developed to assist organizations in embracing a uniformed approach to investment decisions reconciling issues of a focus on short payback period expectations and past orientation of modern management accounting practices [96]. Fundamental to understanding the balanced scorecard approach is the recognition of the connection between *leading indicators* and *lagging indicators*. *Leading indicators* are organizational-specific performance measures that impact on the achievement of overall objectives [96]. *Lagging indicators* are measurements that reflect the organizational or business unit performance in relation to the achievement of strategic objectives. Figure 3.10 illustrates potential indicators or measures that can support the deployment of sustainability principles within business strategy.

As required, these potential measures can be disseminated from a corporate strategic level to SBU level using a cascaded balanced scorecard [97].

The balanced scorecard supports the alignment of *leading* and *lagging* indicators that may be nonfinancial or financial, with the organizations' overall strategy using four dimensions or perspectives, namely [96, 97]:

Financial perspective—highlights the relationship between other perspectives of the balanced scorecard approach, shareholders' interests, and financial performance and strategy on business economic success

Customer perspective—identifies the key customer/segments, measures, and product/service value propositions required to achieve competitive advantage in chosen target markets

Internal process perspective—focuses on the implementation of business processes that enables the firm to delight both internal and external customers

Financial		Customer	
Environmental	**Social**	**Environmental**	**Social**

environmental $ saved
$ fines/penalties
EH&S costs (% of sales)
% proactive vs. reactive expenditures
increase in relative % of proactive expenditures
% environmental costs direct-traced
$ capital investments
Energy costs
Disposal costs
Recycling revenues
Revenues from green products
$ operating expenditures
Reduction in cost of debt
Cost avoidance from environmental actions
	philanthropic $ contributed
	$ workers compensation costs
	# employee lawsuits
	$ employee benefits
	legal actions / costs
	training budgets
	reduction in hiring costs
	revenue from socially positioned products
		$ cause-related marketing
		# "green" products
		products safety
		# recalls
		customer returns
		unfavourable press coverage
		% products reclaimed after use
		# stakeholder communications
		product life
		functional product eco-efficiency
		(e.g., energy costs of a washing machine)
			customer perceptions
			# of cause-related events supported (e.g., breast cancer AIDS)
			$ Community support (parks, safety, recreation, etc.)
			# community meetings
			Customer satisfaction
			social report requests
			# product recalls
			customer group demographics

Internal Business Processes		**Learning and Growth**	
Environmental	**Social**	**Environmental**	**Social**

# LCAs performed 	
% materials recycled
% waste to landfill
# certified suppliers 	
# accidents/spills 	
# audits/year 	
# truck miles 	
% office supplies recycled
internal audit scores
energy consumption
% facilities certified
% of product remanufactured
packaging vlume
non-product output
# supplier audits/year 	
fresh water consumption
greenhouse gas emissions
air emissions
water emissions
hazardous material output
vehicle fuel use
habitat changes due to operations
	# employee accidents
	# lost workdays
	# days work stoppages
	average work week hours
	$ warranty claims
	$ minority business purchases
	# plant tours/visitors
	# non-employee accidents
	Certifications
	# suppliers certified
	# supplier violations
	environmental quality of facilities
	observance of international labour standards
	# safety improvement projects
		% of employess trained
		# training programs/hours
		reputation per surveys
		inclusion in "green" funds
		# employee complaints
		# community complaints
		# shareholder complaints
		unfavourable press coverage
		# violations reported by employees
		# of employees with incentives linked to environmental goals
		# of functions with environmental responsibilities
		management attention to environmental issues
		% of employees using car pools
			workforce diversity (age, gender race)
			management diversity
			# internal promotions
			employee volunteer hours
			average length of employment
			# involuntary discharges
			employee education $
			# family leave days
			$ employee benefits
			salary gaps between genders/races
			employee satisfaction
			$ "quality of life" programs
			% of employees owning company stock
			# applicants/job openings
			# employees with disabilities
			# employees grievances
			workforce equity

FIGURE 3.10 Examples of balanced scorecard measures of sustainability. Source: Epstein and Wisner [97]. © Wiley.

Learning and growth perspective—are the capabilities and resources required to achieve organizational excellence both within existing and future competitive scenarios

As sustainability is a multidimensional concept comprising economic, social, and environmental aspects, researchers argue that the balanced scorecard framework can assist with the embedding of sustainability values within business strategy. This is due mainly to the hierarchical, top-down approach of the balanced scorecard model that assists in the development of business objectives and performance measures from strategic goals for the *financial perspective*, *customer perspective*, *internal process perspective*, and the *learning and growth perspective*, thereby potentially resolving any philosophical conflicts that emerge among the economic, social, and environmental spheres of sustainability.

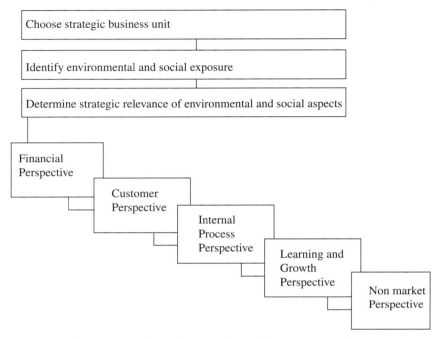

FIGURE 3.11   Process of formulating an SBSC. Source: Figge et al. [96]. © Wiley.

The nonprescriptive nature of the balanced scorecard model affords the exploration of three alternative options for deployment of sustainability:

- *Integration of environmental and social aspects in the four balanced scorecard perspectives*
- *Introduction of an additional nonmarket perspective into the balanced scorecard*
- *Deduction of a derived environmental and social scorecard*

The latter option, the generation of the derived environmental and social scorecard, can only be achieved if the previous options have been implemented. The inclusion of an additional dimension to the balanced scorecard approach, that is, nonmarket perspective, is preceded by two important preconditions:

(a) Environmental and social factors must be pertinent to the strategic context either as core aspects or performance drivers.

(b) Identified environmental and social factors cannot be readily assimilated within the standardized balanced scorecard framework.

The satisfaction of these preconditions provides the bedrock for the development of the sustainability balanced scorecard (SBSC) [96] (Fig. 3.11).

| | | Environmental exposure | | | | | | | Social exposure | | | | | | | |
| | | | | | | | | | Direct stakeholders | | | | Indirect stakeholders | | | |
		Emission	Waste	Material input/intensity	Energy intensity	Noise and vibrations	Waste heat	Radiation	Land use	Internal	Along the value chain	In the local community	Societal	Internal	Along the value chain	In the local community	Societal
Strategic core issues	#1																
	#2																
	...																
Performance drivers	#1																
	#2																
	...																

FIGURE 3.12 Matrix to determine the strategic relevance of environmental and social aspects. Source: Figge et al. [96]. © Wiley.

SBSC development consists of three fundamental stages:

- **Choose the SBU**—the enterprise must choose an SBU or group within which sustainable methods can be adopted but does not preclude the pursuit of the development of sound business strategy by senior management.
- **Identify environmental and social exposure**—develop an environmental profile of the business. Similar analytical techniques are prescribed to assist firms in identifying stakeholder groups and potential social claims or issues arising from business activities.
- **Determine the strategic relevance of environmental and social aspects**—through the development sustainability objectives and indicators that are linked to organizational strategy and as such may be *strategic core issues* for which lagging indicators are to be outlined, *performance drivers* or *hygienic factors* essential for business success. Figure 3.12 provides a useful matrix within which the strategic importance of social and environmental issues can be identified to decide whether they represent *strategic core issues*, *performance drivers*, or *hygiene factors* being triangulated against *leading and lagging* indicators.

The use of the SBSC allows enterprises to address the potential disconnect between the profit objectives and sustainable development goals. This flexible approach grants firms the ability to incorporate environmental and social aspects into conventional approaches to corporate strategy without being prescriptive (Fig. 3.12).

Figge et al. suggest a useful extension of the SBSC concept in its use in developing strategy maps for the firm that illustrate both the competitive opportunities and risks created by sustainability/CSR (Fig. 3.13).

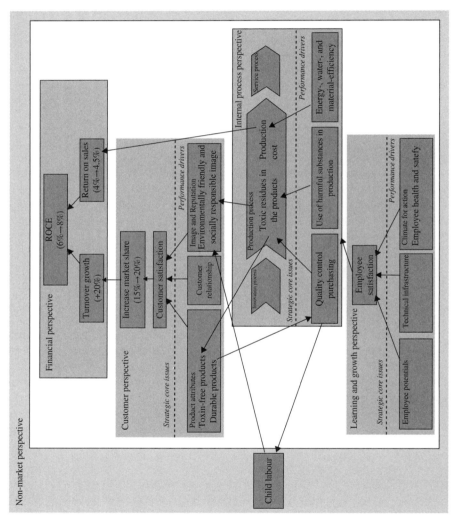

FIGURE 3.13 SBSC as a strategy map for a sample company. Source: Figge et al. [96]. © Wiley.

3.7.10   The Natural Step Framework or Framework for Strategic Sustainable Development

The Natural Step (TNS) framework was developed by a Swedish scientist, Karl-Henrik Robert, from his observation of the community-oriented spirit generated during the care of a juvenile cancer patient [98]. Robert surmised that this innate collective concern can be harnessed to promote the human life on the planet and build a consensus among stakeholders for sustainability. At the core of the TNS framework is an understanding of the symbiotic relationship and dependency of human existence with planetary natural cycles.

TNS framework is buttressed by four sustainability principles that state that in order *to become a sustainable society, we must eliminate our contributions to*:

1. *The systematic increase of concentrations of substances extracted from the earth's crust*
2. *The systematic increase of concentrations of substances produced by society*
3. *The systematic physical degradation of nature and natural processes*
4. *Conditions that systematically undermine people's capacity to meet their basic human needs*

These principles are used to guide organizational *"backcasting"* or the preparation for successful future outcomes based on sustainability principles through the implementation of key objectives within the present.

TNS framework comprises a 5-level framework (5LF) consisting of a *systems level, success level, strategic level, actions level,* and *tools level* [99].

At the *systems level*, the organization is required to develop a holistic understanding of the interdependency between ecology systems, the economy, and the society. The *success level* encourages organizations to espouse a sustainability-biased interpretation of success that involves the outlining of the characteristics of success that are inimitable, for example, products/services or organizational culture, an irrevocable commitment to sustainability principles and an all-inclusive view which emphasizes the organization as operating within a socioecological system. Enterprises prioritize activities using *backcasting* techniques that will enable the achievement of sustainable goals at the *strategic level. Backcasting* assists enterprises in aligning their goals with societal aspirations, allocates resources to sustain success, and identifies ineffective methods. The *actions level* necessitates the implementation of both tangible steps, for example, energy-saving devices, and intangible steps, such as training and monitoring. Various methods can be adopted to embed sustainability within the organization at the *tools level* for example Environmental Management Systems, ISO 14001, and Zero Emissions.

This concept of *backcasting* forms a key element of TNS's ABCD methodology to planning that involves [98]:

Awareness and visioning—a holistic approach is applied that combines the TNS's four sustainability principles and basic science to align business strategy with nature. To achieve sustainable strategic outcomes, the organization must build a consensus regarding sustainability and envision itself in a future sustainable scenario.

Baseline mapping—a review of organizational performance in relation to sustainability principles by identifying any gaps in performance in terms of culture, products, and processes that reveal opportunities for improvement.

Creative solutions—individuals are encouraged to brainstorm and provide solutions to gaps in performance that will assist the organization in achieving a future sustainable state. This technique prevents the planning and implementation of "quick wins" that will only satisfy short-term objectives in relation to sustainability.

Decide on priorities—the goal being to propel the organization on the path to its future vision, initially through the execution of options that are "low-hanging" fruit with the performance of subsequent continuous reviews to ensure the organization is on track to achieve stated future sustainability goals.

3.7.11 ISO 26000: An International Guide to Sustainability/CSR Strategy

Historically, the International Organization for Standardization efforts have been focused on issues surrounding quality, product specification, and information technology management. Therefore, it was late in understanding the shift in the debate as to the role of business in society from being catalyst of economic growth to also enablers in the development of the society as a whole. In 2002, sensing the growing need for comprehensive guidance on social responsibility, the International Organization for Standardization began to work on developing the ISO 26000 standard [100]. To ensure that all stakeholder views and concerns were included in the developmental stages of the ISO 26000 standard, its working group included well-known NGOs such as the Consumers International and the International Organisation of Employers [100]. Support was also enlisted from other sustainability initiatives such as the International Labor Organization (ILO), the Organisation for Economic Cooperation and Development (OECD), and the UN Global Compact whose sustainability framework established a decade earlier has been adopted by over 8700 participating organizations [100]. Well-known NGOs such as the Amnesty International and the World Wild Life Fund (WWF) International also contributed to the development of the ISO 26000 standard; however, both organizations have since refocused their attention to other initiatives [100].

The ISO 26000 standard builds on the Brundtland Commission's definition of sustainable development by defining *social responsibility* as the responsibility of an organization for the impacts of its decisions and activities on society and the environment, through transparent and ethical behavior that contributes to sustainable development, including health and the welfare of the society taking into account the expectations of stakeholders. Ensuring compliance with applicable law, consistent with international norms of behavior; and is integrated throughout the organization and practiced in its relationships [101].

This definition confirms the interconnectedness of social responsibility and sustainability as core operational concepts with the ISO 26000 standard. To incorporate social responsibility and sustainability within business operation, organizations are required to define their priorities in respect of the following core subjects:

- *Organizational governance*—the systems, structures, and processes whether formal or informal by which an organization makes decisions in regard to social responsibility and sustainability.
- *Human rights*—are accepted norms regarding the sanctity of life such as civil, political, economic, and social rights in which it is implied that an organization should actively support and respect these.
- *Labor practices*—are policies and procedures regarding the selection, recruitment, and retention of labor including subcontractors and their ability to solicit the assistance of external bargaining or develop their own bargaining mechanism within the organization.
- *The environment*—the ISO 26000 standard encourages organizations to review their impact on the environment from a global perspective by improving their environmental performance using the precautionary approach, sustainable procurement techniques, environmental risk management, climate change adaptation, adoption of clean technology, and ecoefficiency programs.
- *Fair operating practices*—this core subject encompasses the ethical values of the organization in respect of its dealings with other organizations, for example, competitors, suppliers, and government authorities in areas such as anticorruption and fair competition.
- *Consumer issues*—are all activities that communicate and reduce risk, improve product performance and longevity, and increase sustainable consumption of products and services during all stages of its life cycle from material extraction, manufacturing, marketing, distribution, and recycling or disposal.
- *Community involvement and development*—are activities in which the organization participates that strengthens the civic institutions from which the organization gains its wealth but also builds a bond between the organization's *internal stakeholders*, that is, owners, shareholders, employees, suppliers, and subcontractors, and its external stakeholders in the community and the wider society [101].

The ISO 26000 standard does not provide a prescription for implementing social responsibility within organizational strategy but highlights key areas that define CSR excellence. Organizations should adapt the standard to suit its size, mission, values, and cultural and regulatory environment. This tailored approach ensures that stakeholders are engaged for their opinions using communicative means that are beyond simple consultation on issues regarding the centrality of social responsibility to the organizational strategy but importantly the role of stakeholders in implementing sustainability and social responsibility within the organization.

The interdependence of each core subject is embodied in the holistic approach to social responsibility and sustainability espoused by the ISO 26000. The holistic approach to sustainability also implies that any organization embarking on implementing the core subjects of the ISO 26000 must conduct a gap analysis of its existing performance regarding social responsibility and the requirements of the standard to determine the relevance of each core subject to the stakeholders within its competitive environment, therefore also ensuring that the relative emphasis placed by the organization on each core subject will vary regionally; for example, businesses that operate in Bangladesh and India that are implementing social responsibility may place greater emphasis on issues surrounding labor practices, community involvement, and development due to the socioeconomic environment that exists on the Indian subcontinent.

The organization having understood which core subjects are relevant to its stakeholders then proceeds to integrate social responsibility into the fabric of the organization through policy development, the establishment of sustainability targets, sustainability awareness raising campaigns, and transparent reporting of the organizational performance in a manner that is timely and balanced.

The use of social responsibility reporting as a tool for benchmarking and communicating sustainability performance is another key requirement of the ISO 26000 standard. The ISO 26000 standard has cross-referenced its framework across existing CSR initiatives such as the GRI, thereby potentially ensuring its applicability to all organizations irrespective of reporting requirements.

Strategists and frontline managers already burdened with the management of ISO 14001 Environmental Management Systems, ISO 9001 Quality Management Systems, and OHSAS 18001 Safety Management Systems may view the ISO 26000 standard as an unwelcomed distraction from other operational issues. As with any organizational change initiative, senior management commitment and support is paramount as the implementation of social responsibility policies may be in direct competition for resources with other business initiatives at a time where budgets are constrained. Therefore, the business case for sustainability and social responsibility must be developed; however, despite these challenges, using the ISO 26000 standard as a template for implementing sustainability and social responsibility strategy can provide organizations with the following benefits:

- No certification costs—the ISO 26000 standard is not yet a certifiable standard.
- Easy integration with existing standards, for example, ISO 14001 and OHSAS 18001, using the holistic approach to sustainability social responsibility.
- Reduced reputational risk arising from poor labor practices and unethical conduct.
- Enhanced brand and product image.
- Incorporates the criteria of existing CSR schemes such as the GRI and UN Global Compact.
- Facilitates good corporate governance ensuring that senior management adopts a long-term outlook to decision making.
- Develops and improves stakeholder engagement and building trust with the organizations' immediate community.
- Improves environmental efficiency and resource use within the organizations' supply chain.

- Improves organizational safety and builds employee morale.
- Facilitates organizational innovation.

The parallel concepts of sustainability and social responsibility are evolving areas of management taught and practice; this is reflected in the rather broad approach of the ISO 26000 standard. The ushering of the ISO 26000 on the global stage has not been without its controversy with some nations viewing the new standard as a potential barrier to free trade or a threat to their national sovereignty in terms of its support for human rights [100]. Organizations that do not subscribe to such myopic views will use the framework of the ISO 26000 standard to create new competitive models and produce products and services that not only sustain corporate growth but contribute to the development of the society. For all the alluded to benefits the ISO 26000 it is encyclopedic in nature and is not conducive to its assimilation into the strategy of SMEs.

3.7.12 BS 8900 Standard: Guidance for Managing Sustainable Development

This standard predates the ISO 26000 and provides a more intuitive approach for a business to implement sustainable development strategies. The BS 8900 standard, although adhering to the Brundtland Commission's definition of sustainable development, expresses sustainable development as *"Sustainable development is about integrating the goals of a high quality of life, health and prosperity with social justice and maintaining the earth's capacity to support life in all its diversity. These social, economic and environmental goals are interdependent and mutually reinforcing. Sustainable development can be treated as a way of expressing the broader expectations of society as a whole"* [102]. The standard was developed with a purpose of enabling businesses to achieve key outcomes such as strengthening relationships with key stakeholders, enhancing internal cohesion within the organization, developing trust and confidence by promoting transparency and good governance, and stimulating stakeholder involvement through engagement and the management of risks and opportunities. Stakeholder identification is considered a critical activity that identifies relationships between the organization and the society, the organization and its stakeholders, as well as stakeholders and the society. The BS 8900 standard states that sustainable development incorporates the following:

- **Inclusivity**—the capability to benefit from all stakeholder views
- **Integrity**—an operational ethos that promotes good corporate governance
- **Stewardship**—the pursuit of sustainable resource management
- **Transparency**—disclosure and communication of organizational operational practices

Organizations are encouraged to include additional principles that align with sustainability objectives but emphasize the need for senior management commitment and leadership [102].

The BS 8900 standard provides a *Sustainable Development Maturity Matrix* to support the understanding of the evolutionary process of sustainable development within organizations illustrating a linear progression from minimal organizational involvement to full engagement on sustainable development issues [102].

REFERENCES

[1]   Eccles RG, Serafeim G. The impact of a corporate culture of sustainability on corporate behavior and performance. Working Paper 12-035. May 2012. p. 1–57.

[2]   Porter M, Van der Linde C. Toward a new conception of the environment—competitiveness relationship. J Econ Perspect 1995;9(4):97–118.

[3]   Bentham J. *An Introduction to the Principles of Morals and Legislation.* New York: Oxford University Press; 1789, 1982.

[4]   Kant I. *Groundwork of the Metaphysics of Morals.* Cambridge: Cambridge University Press; 1785, 1985, 1997.

[5]   *Insights into Climate Change Adaptation by UK Companies.* CDP Project. Production Studios; 2012.

[6]   Aristotle C. *Nicomachean Ethics.* 2nd ed. Indianapolis: Hackett Publishing Company; 1999.

[7]   Kay J. The stakeholder corporation. In: Kelly G, Kelly D, Gamble A, editors. *Stakeholder Capitalism.* Basingstoke, Hampshire: MacMillan Press Ltd; 1997. p. 125–141.

[8]   Ven B. An ethical framework for the marketing of corporate social responsibility. J Bus Ethics 2008;82(2):339–352. DOI: 10.1007/s10551-008-9890-1.

[9]   Cumming J, Bettridge N, Toyne P. Responding to global business critical issues: a source of innovation and transformation for FTSE 350. Corp Gov—Int J Bus Soc 2005;5(3):42–51.

[10] Wilkes VD. Dealing with a global issue: contributing to poverty alleviation. Corp Gov—Int J Bus Soc 2005;5(3):61–69.

[11] Bowie N. *Business Ethics: A Kantian Perspective.* Malden and Oxford: Blackwell; 1999.

[12] O'Higgins E. Corporations, civil society and stakeholders: an organizational conceptualization. J Bus Ethics 2010;94:157–176.

[13] Driscoll C, Starik M. The primordial stakeholder: advancing the conceptual consideration of stakeholder status for the natural environment. J Bus Ethics 2004;49(1):55–73.

[14] Kolk A, Pinkse J. Towards strategic stakeholder management? Integrating perspectives on sustainability challenges such as corporate responses to climate change. Corp Gov—Int J Bus Soc 2007;7(4):370–378.

[15] Bendheim CL, Waddock S, Graves S. Determining best practice in corporate-stakeholder relations using data envelopment analysis: an industry level study. Bus Soc 1998; 37(3):306–338.

[16] Gibson K. Stakeholders and sustainability: an evolving theory. J Bus Ethics 2012;109(1):15–25. DOI: 10.1007/s10551-012-1376-5.

[17] Lindblom C. *The implications of organizational legitimacy for Corporate Social Performance and Disclosure Critical Perspectives on Accounting Conference,* New York; 1994.

[18] Bendell J, Kearins K. World review: heading for divorce. J Corp Citizenship 200414:6–12.

[19] Adams C, Zutshi A. Corporate social responsibility: why business should act responsibly and be accountable. Aust Account Rev 2004;14(3):31–39.

[20] Bond S. The global challenge of sustainable consumption. Consumer Policy Rev 2005;15(2), 38–44.

[21] Ogrizek M. The effect of corporate social responsibility on the branding of financial services. J Financ Serv Mark 2002;6(3):215–228.

[22] Isaksson R, Garvare, R. Measuring sustainable development using process models. Manag Audit J 2003;18(8):649–656.

[23] DEFRA. A framework for pro environmental behaviors. Available at https://www.gov. uk/government/uploads/system/uploads/attachment_data/file/69277/pb13574-behaviours-report-080110.pdf. Accessed Dec 17, 2013.

[24] Lewicki R, McAllister D, Bies R. Trust and distrust: new relationships and realities. Acad Manage Rev 1998;23(3):438–458.

[25] Royal society for the encouragement of arts. A new agenda on climate change: facing up to stealth denial and winding down on fossil fuels. Available at: http://www.thersa. org/__data/assets/pdf_file/0004/1536844/J1530_RSA_climate_change_report_16.12_ V51.pdf. Accessed Dec 17, 2013.

[26] Rowson J. Turning the volume up on climate change is not changing behavior. Available athttp://www.theguardian.com/sustainable-business/behavioural-insights/climate-change-denial-behaviour-change. Accessed Dec 18, 2013.

[27] James W. *The Will to Believe and Other Essays in Popular Philosophy*. Volume 6. New York: Longman Green & Co; 1897.

[28] Funk K. Sustainability and performance. MIT Sloan Manage Rev 2003;44(2):65–70.

[29] Hart S, Milstein M. Global sustainability and the creative destruction of industries, MIT Sloan Manage Rev 1999;41:23–33.

[30] Gladwin T, Kennelly J, Krause T. Shifting paradigms for sustainable development: implications for management theory and research. Acad Manage Rev 1995;20(4):874–907.

[31] Fiksel J, Mc Daniel J, Spitzley D. Measuring product sustainability. J Sustain Product Design July 1998; 6:1–15.

[32] Kane G. *The Three Secrets of Green Business—Unlocking Competitive Advantage in a Low Carbon Economy*. Oxford: Earthscan; 2010.

[33] Fisk P. *People, Planet, Profit: How to Embrace Sustainability for Innovation and Business Growth*. London: Kogan Page; 2010.

[34] Matten D, Crane, A. Corporate citizenship: toward an extended theoretical conceptualization. Acad Manage Rev 2005;30(1):186–179.

[35] Pies I, Beckmann M, Hielscher S. Value creation, management competencies, and global corporate citizenship: an ordonomic approach to business ethics in the age of globalization. J Business Ethics 2010;94:265–278.

[36] Porter M, Kramer, M. Strategy & society: the link between competitive advantage and corporate social responsibility. Harvard Bus Rev. 2006;84(12):78–92.

[37] Rake M, Grayson D. Embedding corporate responsibility and sustainability–everybody's business. Corp Gov—Int J Bus Soc 2009;9(4):399.

[38] Marsden C. The new corporate citizenship of big business: part of the solution to sustainability? Bus Soc Rev 2000;105:19–25.

[39] The Gospel of Matthew, Holy Bible, King James Version Chapter 26 verse 11.

[40] Boyle M, Boguslaw J. Business poverty and corporate citizenship: naming the issues and framing the solutions. J Corp Citizenship Summer 2007;26:101–120.

[41] Collier P, Hoeffler A. On economic causes of civil war. Oxford Econ Pap 1998;50(4):563–573.

[42] BBC Viewpoint: Can Kenya avoid election bloodshed? Available at: http://www.bbc.co.uk/news/world-africa-19948429. Accessed Jan 2, 2014.

[43] Lister R. *Citizenship: Feminist Perspectives*. 2nd ed. London: Palgrave; 2003.

[44] Weizsacker von E, Hargroves K, Smith M, Desha C, Stasinopoulos P. *Factor Five: Transforming the Global Economy Through 80% Improvements in Resource Productivity*. Oxford: Earthscan; 2010.

[45] Guardian. Cash for honors. Available at: http://www.theguardian.com/politics/cashforhonours. Accessed Jan 2, 2014.

[46] Its business that rules us now. Available at: http://www.theguardian.com/commentisfree/2013/nov/11/business-rules-lobbying-corporate-interests. Accessed Jan 2, 2014.

[47] Hermosilla J, Gonzalez P, Konnola T. *Eco-Innovation—When Sustainability and Competitiveness Shake Hands*. New York: Palgrave Macmillan; 2009.

[48] Van Hijstee M, Glasbergen P. The practice of stakeholder dialogue between multinationals and NGOs. Corp Soc Responsib Environ Mgmt 2008;15:298–310.

[49] Maignan I, Ralston, D. Corporate social responsibility in Europe and the US: insights from businesses self-presentations. J Int Bus Stud 2002;33(3):497–514.

[50] Welford R. Corporate social responsibility in Europe, North America and Asia: 2004 survey results. J Corp Citizenship 2005;17:33–52.

[51] Xu S, Yang R. Indigenous characteristics of Chinese corporate social responsibility conceptual paradigm. J Bus Ethics 2010;93:321–333.

[52] Szeto RWF. Sustainability of conventional sagacity among Chinese managers. Chinese Econ 2011;44(3):5–21. DOI: 10.2753/CES1097-1475440301.

[53] Haake S. National business systems and industry specific competitiveness. Organ Stud 2002;23(5):720–727.

[54] Luchs M, Nayleor R, Irwin J, Raghunathan R. The sustainability liability: potential negative effects of ethicality on product preference. J Marketing 2010; 74:18–31.

[55] Department for Environment, Food and Rural Affairs. A Framework for Pro-Environmental Behaviors (p. Annexes H); 2008. Available at: https://www.gov.uk/government/uploads/system/uploads/attachment_data/file/69277/pb13574-behaviours-report-080110.pdf. Accessed Jun 30, 2014.

[56] Matten D, Moon, J. Implicit and explicit CSR: a conceptual framework for a comparative understanding of corporate social responsibility. Acad Manage Rev 2008;33(2):404–424.

[57] Kolk A. Sustainability, accountability and corporate governance: exploring multinationals reporting practices. Bus Strat Environ 2008;18:1–15.

[58] FTSE 250 Companies keep their Carbon Footprints hidden. The Environmentalist Issue 66. IEMA; October 2008.

[59] Tschopp D. Corporate social responsibility: a comparison between the United States and the European Union. Corp Soc Responsib Environ Mgmt 2005;12:55–59.

[60] Reuters. Australian Senate passes carbon tax. Available at http://gu.com/p/337yc/em. Accessed Nov 10, 2013.

[61] Jowit J. New emissions policy will force biggest UK firms to reveal CO_2 figures. Available at http://gu.com/p/38e6f/em. Accessed Jan 10, 2014.

[62] Naeem M, Welford R. A comparative study of corporate social responsibility in Bangladesh and Pakistan. Corp Soc Responsib Environ Mgmt 2009;16:108–122.

[63] Hopkins M. The four-point supply chain checklist: how sustainability creates new opportunity. MIT Sloan Manage Rev 2010;51(4):65–69.

[64] York J. Pragmatic sustainability: translating environmental ethics into competitive. Advan—J Bus Ethics 2009;85:97–109.

[65] Freeman RE, Reichart J. Toward a life centered ethic for business. Ruffin Ser Soc Bus Ethics 2010;2:143–158.

[66] Dewey J. *The Essential Dewey: Pragmatism, Education and Democracy.* Volume 1. Bloomington: Indiana University Press; 1998; p. 391–400.

[67] Enkvist P, Nauclér T, Oppenheim J. Business strategies for climate change. McKinsey Quart 2008;(2):24–33.

[68] Lacy P, Arnott J, Lowitt E. The challenge of integrating sustainability into talent and organization strategies: investing in the knowledge, skills and attitudes to high performance. Corp Gov—Int J Bus Soc 2009;9(4):484–494.

[69] *Expect the Unexpected: Building Business Value in a Changing World.* KPMG International; 2012. Available at http://www.kpmg.com/global/en/issuesandinsights/articlespublications/pages/building-business-value.aspx. Accessed Jun 30, 2014.

[70] Saha M, Darnton, G. Green companies or green Companies: are companies really green, or are they pretending to be? Bus Soc 2005;110(2):117–157.

[71] Lindgreen A, Antioco M, Harness D, Van der Sloot R. Purchasing and marketing of social and environmental sustainability for high tech medical equipment. J Bus Ethics 2009;85:445–462.

[72] Bebbington J. Sustainable development: a review of international development business and accounting literature. Accounting Forum 2001;25(2):128–157.

[73] Tengblad S, Ohlsson C. The framing of corporate social responsibility and the globalization of national business systems: a longitudinal case study. J Bus Ethics 2010;93:653–669.

[74] Goleman D, Lueneburger C. The change leadership sustainability demands. MIT Sloan Manage Rev 2010;51(4):49–55.

[75] Epstein M, Roy M. Sustainability in action: identifying and measuring the key performance drivers. Long Range Planning 2001;34:585–604.

[76] Willis A. The role of the global reporting initiative's sustainability reporting guidelines in the social screening of investments. J Business Ethics 2003;43(3):233–237.

[77] Christman P. Effect of best practices of environmental management on cost advantage: the role of complementary assets. Acad Manage J 2000;43(4):663–680.

[78] James Jr H. Reinforcing ethical decision making through organizational structure. J Bus Ethics 2000;28:43–58.

[79] Wood D. Corporate social performance revisited. Acad Manage Rev 1991;16(4):691–718.

[80] DEFRA. TEEB for Business Coalition. Available at: http://www.teebforbusiness.org/js/plugins/filemanager/files/TEEB-for-Business-Coalition.pdf. Accessed Dec 2, 2013.

[81] Hart S. Beyond greening: strategies for a sustainable world. Harvard Business Rev January–February 1997; 75(1):66–76.

[82] Jenkins H. A 'business opportunity' model of corporate social responsibility for small and medium sized enterprises. Bus Ethics Eur Rev. 2009;16(1):21–36.

[83] Heiskanen E, Jalas M. Can services lead to radical eco-efficiency improvements?—a review of the debate and evidence. Corp Soc Responsib Environ Mgmt 2003;10:186–198.

[84] Lopez Perez M, Garcia Santana A, Rodriguez Ariza L. Sustainable development and corporate performance: a study based on the Dow Jones sustainability index. J Bus Ethics 2007;75:285–300.

[85] Bhattacharya C, Sen S. Doing better at doing good: when why and how consumers respond to social initiatives. California Manage Rev 2004;47(1):9–24.

[86] Ryan P. Sustainability partnerships: eco-strategy theory in practice? Manage Environ Qual Int J 2003;14(2):256–278.

[87] Kleine A, Von Hauff, M. Sustainability-driven implementation of corporate social responsibility: application of the integrative sustainability triangle. J Bus Ethics 2009;85(3):517–533.

[88] CQI. Model of Sustainable Organisation. Available at: http://www.thecqi.org/Community/Special-Interest-Groups-SIGs/Deming-SIG/The-Sustainable-Organisation/. Accessed Dec 18, 2014.

[89] Laszlo C, Sherman D, Whalen J, Ellison, J. Expanding the value horizon. J Corp Citizenship 2005;20:65–76.

[90] Laugel JF, Laszlo C. Turning point. Financial crisis: the opportunity for sustainable value creation in banking and insurance. J Corp Citizenship Fall 2009;(35):24–38.

[91] Unknown. Sustainability Value Partners. Available at: http://www.sustainablevaluepartners.com/. Accessed Sep 9, 2013.

[92] Gell M. Business transformations in carbon constrained markets. The Environmentalist, IEMA 2008;(66):14–18.

[93] Hendrichs H, Busch T. Carbon management as a strategic challenge for SMEs. Greenhouse Gas Measure Manage 2012;2(1):61–72.

[94] Stead JG, Stead E. Eco-enterprise strategy: standing for sustainability. J Bus Ethics 2000;24(4):313–329.

[95] Amekudzi AA, Khisty JC, Khayesi M. Using the sustainability footprint model to assess development impacts of transportation systems. Transport Res Part A Policy Pract 2009;43(4):339–348.

[96] Figge F, Hahn T, Schaltegger S, Wagner M. The sustainability balanced scorecard–linking sustainability management to business strategy. Bus Strat Environ 2002;11(5):269–284.

[97] Epstein MJ, Wisner PS. Using a balanced scorecard to implement sustainability. Environ Qual Manage 2001;11(2):1–10.

[98] Unknown. The Natural Step. Available at http://www.naturalstep.org/. Accessed Dec 4, 2013.

[99] Waldron D, Henrik Robèrt K, Leung P, McKay M, Dyer G, Blume R, Khaleeli R, Connell T. *Guide to the Framework for Sustainable Strategic Development, Strategic Leadership towards Sustainability*. Sweden: Blekinge Institute of Technology; 2008.

[100] Henriques A. ISO 26000: a new kind of standard, IRCA INform e-zine; 2010(28). Available at: http://www.irca.org/en-gb/resources/INform/archive/issue28/Features/Management-systems-the-missing-competence111/. Accessed Jun 23, 2012.

[101] ISO. ISO 26000: 2010 Guidance on Social Responsibility, Geneva; 2010.

[102] BSI. Managing Sustainable Development of Organizations. London: British Standards Institute; 2013.

4

SUSTAINABILITY FOOTPRINTS: TOOLS FOR GROWTH

4.1 INTRODUCTION

For more than a three decades, businesses have been producing environmental reports, in some cases being gently coerced by national legislation [1, 2]. Environmental reports usually include indicators such as carbon footprint, which is chosen because of its link to greenhouse gas (GHG) emission reduction performance and climate change risks.

For clarity, **sustainability footprints** are alternatively defined *as methodologies for assessing the social and environmental impact of the economic investment in a specific strategic option in relation to other strategic alternatives and the potential risk to the survival of future generations.*

Sustainability footprints comprise the use of carbon footprint, water footprint, ecological footprint, and the emerging concept of social footprints to evaluate the present nonfinancial consequences and future risk implications of strategic decisions. Previous attempts to define sustainability footprints [3] imply the assimilation of ecological footprint methodology with *quality of life (QOL)*, an all-encompassing concept that factors in issues such as air quality, water quality, and soil quality. The scope embodied in the concept of *QOL* makes its adoption by business firms quite challenging.

Sustainability footprints utilize a full LCA approach in determining environmental impact of projects, products, and processes. Adopting a life cycle approach focuses efforts on material, water, and carbon efficiency and prevents the reallocation of GHG emission increases to other parts of the value chain [4].

Sustainability Footprints in SMEs: Strategy and Case Studies for Entrepreneurs and Small Business, First Edition. Lowellyne James.
© 2015 John Wiley & Sons, Inc. Published 2015 by John Wiley & Sons, Inc.

4.2 CONCEPTUAL FRAMEWORK

At a glance, due to the origin of sustainability footprint concepts such as the carbon footprint that were originally postulated by environmental scientists using positivist research approaches, conceptualizing a strategic fit with contemporary management theory may be a case of comparing "apples with eggs."

However, from an ontological perspective, the increasing use of sustainability footprint tools by business is indicative of the need of organizations to measure value creation. Porter [5] introduced the concept of value chains; the emergence of sustainability as a new management paradigm has seen a [6] revisit of the value chain model and mapping of the social and environmental impact of business. Porter et al. [6, 7] argue for the adoption of responsive corporate social responsibility (CSR) that incorporates good corporate citizenship and shared values by mitigating the harm arising from value chain activities. This conversion of Porter's view from a narrow emphasis of shareholder value to a search for shared values is supported by other leading management thinkers and consultants [8].

This extension of value chain philosophy to assist firms in developing CSR strategy places sustainability footprint tools such as carbon footprint, social footprint, and water footprint as key indicators for measuring a diverse range of impacts, from emissions and waste, water usage, packaging usage, and employment policies. Although satisfying the core principles of sustainability, that is, accounting for the needs of future generations, the limitations of value chain analysis confine its use to the operational context of the firm; however, when combined with the competitiveness model, the firm can then select CSR initiatives that create shared value for both the firm and society. When viewed from this perspective, the use of sustainability footprint tools to measure and drive corporate performance meets business and society's needs for shared value.

Inherent in the creation of shared value is the need from a perspective of business to reduce risk, that is, preventing the loss of its perceived legitimacy among its stakeholders. Krysiak [9] illustrated the potential of using risk management approaches to sustainability but cautioned against the sole use of risk management that may limit our ability to improve the fate of future generations.

It can be argued that sustainability footprint tools are in themselves risk indicators of a firm's ability to ably manage its environmental and social responsibility. The challenge that society faces is the determination of what is acceptable risk in respect to the environmental and social impact on future generations. Intrinsic to the debate in the determining what is acceptable risk is the recognition of an element of uncertainty as future predictions are not consistently accurate.

Sustainability indicators provide benchmarks that although do not predict the future, enlighten the path toward sustainable process improvements. However, Krysiak [9] expresses doubts in the ability of risk management techniques to define "acceptable" risk with regard to protecting the ability of future generations to flourish. Lash and Wellington [10] adopted a more intuitive approach to risk management by categorizing sustainability footprint risk, specifically carbon footprint risk, into six main groups: *regulatory*, *supply chain*, *product and technology*, *litigation*, *reputation*, and *physical*. This categorization of sustainability footprint risk must be viewed from the context of not only environmental impact but from the impact on the firm's revenue stream and cost structure.

Porter [5, 11] identified the strategic connection between cost structure and revenue stream for business. He surmised that to gain competitive advantage, a firm can choose a *low-cost* approach or alternatively *differentiation* through investing in brand development and niche marketing. Although simplistic, Porter's strategies for competitive advantage have formed one of the pillars of the resource-based view (RBV) in that effective competitive advantage leverages the firm's *capabilities*, that is, technology, production, design, distribution, procurement, and service, to create a rare, valuable, nonsubstitutable product or service. Sustainability footprint methodologies were developed so that techniques are replicable by firms; however, strategies to improve an organization's carbon, water, or social footprint are both tacit and socially complex [12, 13], requiring coordinated effort by varied personnel within an organization. Hart [14] postulated that infinite global economic growth is not feasible within the resource constraints of a finite planet. To aid firms to survive in the long run, he proposed three strategies—*pollution prevention*, *product stewardship*, and *sustainable development*—which he defined as the *natural resource-based view* (NRBV) *of the firm*. The use of sustainability footprint methodology by business fits within the framework of the NRBV not only as an indicator of level of emissions to the environment but also as the firm's contribution to the development of society that extends beyond profit-making imperative. In order for sustainability footprint measurement to be a success, it must be integrated and embedded in the firm's culture in so creating a unique competitive position for the firm.

It must be noted that Hart's postulations of the NRBV precede Rees and Wackernagel [15] seminal work on environmental footprints, which has spawned the use and development of sustainability footprints as reporting indices. Therefore, Hart [16] interprets pollution prevention from the perspective of total quality environmental management in that firms that have already embraced total quality management can exploit the opportunities that accrue from pollution prevention strategies as opposed to the costly pollution control strategies.

Hart cautions that organizations may be focused on maintaining these unique capabilities that in so doing they are chained to procedure adherence even though the competitive environment has evolved. This *embeddedness* is considered the downside of *interconnectedness* derived from the strategic progression from pollution prevention to sustainable development.

4.3 KYOTO PROTOCOL AND GHG

The effect of the consumption of fossil fuels and its potential impact on the global atmospheric carbon cycle was first identified by Arvid Högbom, a Swedish geologist, in 1895 [17]. His postulations were later expanded by his fellow compatriot Svante Arrhenius [18]; based on awareness of only two GHG—carbon dioxide and water vapor—he forecasted that continued combustion of fossil fuels may cause the warming of the earth's atmosphere as well as the increase in global temperatures by 5.7 °C arising from the doubling of GHG concentrations, however falsely believing that such effects would not occur for a few millennia. The ramifications of these early scientific predictions were not fully comprehended but ignored until research in the 1960s using modern test instruments calculated that existing GHG emissions exceed preindustrial levels [17]. With the burgeoning scientific evidence came an increased interest from international policymakers initially through the introduction of UN General Assembly Resolution 43/53 in 1988 identifying that climate change is a "common concern for mankind" and Resolution 45/212 in 1990 that led to the creation of the UN Framework Convention on Climate Change (UNFCC) [19–21]. Instrumental to the now politicized climate change awareness debate is the theorizing of *global warming potential (GWP)*, a comparative index that highlights the global warming impact of individual GHG to enable cost-effective mitigation strategies to be implemented [17].

The concept of GHG emissions gained prominence with the ratification of the Kyoto Convention in 1992; this document encourages international governments to accept their responsibility to combat the effects of climate change by acknowledging "common but differentiated responsibilities" between developed and developing economies [19]. Government policymaking actions will involve development of climate change policies, dissemination of information regarding GHG measurement mitigation, and adaptation of best practice [19]. The Kyoto Protocol differs from the Kyoto Convention by committing 37 key industrialized nations and the EC to binding GHG emissions targets [22]. The burden however for climate change reduction is borne by developed economies arising from 150 years of industrialization. Specifically, the Kyoto Protocol targets emission reductions for *carbon dioxide* (CO_2), *methane* (CH_4), *nitrous oxide* (N_2O), *hydrofluorocarbons* (HFCs), *perfluorocarbons* (PFCs), and *sulfur hexafluoride* (SF_6)—now collectively known as GHG [23]. Emission targets on average amount to 5% on 1990 levels over a 5-year reporting period, for example, 2008–2012 [22]. Signatory nations to the Kyoto Protocol are required to develop their own approaches to climate change and emission abatement, which may consist of climate change adaptation strategies as well as the provision of financial and technical support to developing economies [22, 24]. However, the agreement provides three specific mechanisms to assist nation-states with GHG reduction: *emission trading, clean development mechanism (CDM)*, and *joint implementation (JI)* [22].

4.4   EMISSION TRADING

A market mechanism was constructed by the Kyoto Protocol to regulate emissions by giving each country a stipulated level of allowable emissions or *assigned amounts*. The *assigned amounts* are then bundled into *assigned amount units* (AAUs) [25].

Countries with excess AAUs are allowed to sell to signatory countries that have exceeded their stipulated emission targets or *offset* emissions, thereby creating a mechanism for claiming a reduction in GHG emissions [25, 26]. This process is commonly described as a *carbon trade* in reference to the most pervasive GHG, carbon dioxide (CO_2), and involves the transfer of *carbon credits* equivalent to one ton of CO_2 at a defined currency value [25].

The EU has taken the lead by developing the EU emission trading scheme (EU ETS) in 2005, which commoditized GHG emissions; it is now the largest emission trading scheme in the world [23].

In the absence of mandatory carbon trading, similar voluntary schemes such as the Western Climate Action Initiative, Regional Greenhouse Gas Initiative (RGGI),and Chicago Climate Exchange (CCX) have been established to serve North American businesses [27, 28].

4.5 CDM

CDM is a scheme that acknowledges investments in emission reduction projects in developing nations by countries with emission restrictions [29]. For a project to qualify, it must be verified that emissions incurred are below conventional expectations [29]. Qualifying projects are awarded tradable *certified emission reduction* (CER) credits, each equivalent to one ton of carbon dioxide (CO_2) [29].

4.6 JI

Emission reduction project investments among signatory nations with emission restrictions or limitations are afforded similar concessions as under the CDM. These tradable market instruments are described as *emission reduction units* (ERUs) and are equivalent to one ton of carbon dioxide (CO_2) [30].

The measurement of carbon impact has increased in the years following the Kyoto Protocol, a legally binding agreement ratified in 1997 committing industrialized nations to reduce GHG by 5% on 1990 levels. There is now a growing consensus in industry that measuring emissions leads to good management [31].

The carbon trading mechanisms created by the Kyoto Protocol highlighted the need for standardized approaches to GHG quantification, which is challenging when climate science is evolving and there are revisions to the GWP of individual GHG [17]. As the Kyoto Protocol is aimed at nation-states, governments have sought to infer similar responsibilities for GHG emissions on corporate entities that produce high GHG emissions such as power stations and industrial facilities [17].

4.7 CARBON FOOTPRINT REPORTING AND GHG ACCOUNTING

Globally, there has been an emphasis on carbon footprints with most CSR and sustainability reports including footprint data or GHG reports as they are criteria in most sustainability/CSR indices. GHG reports are more commonly known as carbon footprints; a "corporate carbon footprint" represents the total direct and indirect emissions that a company is responsible for as a result of its business activities. It is essential to understand the differences between "accounting for" carbon emissions, which is concerned with compilation of GHG data relative to the operations of a company, and the "reporting of" carbon emissions, that is, the formatting of GHG information to suit the needs of stakeholder groups [32].

4.8   TYPES OF CARBON FOOTPRINTS

Carbon footprints or GHG footprints within a commercial context consists of two types:

Organizational carbon footprint—measures carbon emissions that arise from the operational activities of a business [33]. The measurement of an organizational carbon footprint can be achieved by implementing the following six steps [33]:

1. *Decide on the method to be followed*—Consistently use a standardized approach to GHG emission calculation.
2. *Define organizational and operational boundaries*—Identify all emissions within an organization's operations that will be included and excluded from the report, giving due consideration as to the ease of availability in acquiring the data.
3. *Collate the Data*—Manage data arising from the organizations operational activities, for example, fuel consumption.
4. *Apply emission factors*—Use emission factors provided by government sources to determine carbon impact.
5. *Verify the results*—Verification may be achieved through review from an approved verifier or reporting to voluntary third-party schemes.
6. *Verify your emission reduction*—Although optional, organizations can seek third-party verification of their carbon emission reduction, thereby providing independent confirmation of an organizational carbon reduction claims to its various stakeholders.

Product carbon footprint—is a life cycle view of GHG emissions generated by a product from raw material extraction to disposal, incorporating emissions arising during production forming part of the organizational carbon footprint [33, 34].

Carbon footprint is considered a hybrid of earlier environmental concepts such as the *ecological footprint*, which is defined as the productive land area required to sustain a human population; the carbon footprint can also be described as the productive land area required to absorb CO_2 produced by a human population during the life as a chemical compound [35]. Originally an environmental science concept, the carbon footprint began life as a GWP indicator [35]. The term carbon footprint is used interchangeably with terms such as *embodied carbon, carbon content, embedded carbon, carbon flows, virtual carbon, climate footprint,* and *GHG footprint* [35]. *Carbon accounting* is not without its own contradictions as its definition depends on the

Estimation calculation measurement monitoring reporting validation verification auditing	of	Carbon carbon dioxide greenhouse gas	Emissions to the atmosphere removals from the atmosphere emission rights emission obligations emission reductions Legal or financial instruments linked to the above trades/transactions of any of the above Impacts on climate change impacts from climate change	at	Global national sub-national regional civic organizational corporate project installation event product supply chain	level for	mandatory voluntary	Research compliance reporting disclosure benchmarking auditing information marketing or other	purposes

FIGURE 4.1 Carbon accounting definition. Source: Ascui and Lovell [17]. © Emerald.

technical orientation of the user group—as a technique for verifying carbon emissions for scientists, guidelines for comparing emissions when defined by diplomats, an account of emission obligations or rights that can be assessed under various trading schemes with carbon finance practitioners considering carbon accounting as the quantification of emissions in relation to a baseline, enabling the sale or purchase of carbon credits within carbon trading schemes [17, 36–39]—in essence the colonizing of carbon accounting to suit commonly shared beliefs and specialist expertise [17, 27].

These various interpretations contributed to carbon accounting being identified as in Fig. 4.1.

This definition highlights disconnect between the quantification of GHG emissions and the monetization of GHG emissions, which differentiates carbon accounting from traditional forms of accounting methods [27].

This multivariate interpretation of "carbon" has contributed to an atmosphere of technical exclusivity, misinterpretation leading to fraud within carbon and GHG accounts in carbon markets undermining climate change initiatives [17, 27].

Despite terminological issues, carbon trading and taxation have transformed carbon footprint into a "spatial indicator" of impact; hence, some scholars have argued for the use of the term *carbon mass* or *carbon weight* [35, 40, 41]. The quantitative nature of carbon footprint makes it a useful tool for identifying emission sources, enabling operational improvements to be implemented; this can be achieved through the application of LCA of product/service carbon impacts from raw material extraction to disposal [35].

4.9 CARBON FOOTPRINT STANDARDS

The hybrid nature of GHG reporting contributed to the creation of various approaches to its measurement and calculation. The first published international GHG measurement standard—the *GHG Protocol Initiative*—was established in 1998 by the World Resources Institute (WRI) and the World Business Council for Sustainable Development (WBCSD) [42]. The GHG Protocol consists of two distinct but compatible documents: the *GHG Protocol Corporate and Accounting Standard* that provides guidance for enterprises to report GHG emissions and the *GHG Protocol Project Quantification Standard* that assists organizations in the measurement of GHG mitigation projects [42]. Although a voluntary standard, it has gained international acceptance by governments, NGOs, and influential bodies such as the Organisation for Economic Cooperation and Economic Development (OECD), which has recommended the implementation of the GHG Protocol developed by the WRI and the WBCSD [31]. The GHG Protocol has formed the basis of the subsequent GHG measurement standards such as the U.K. Department for Environment Food, and Rural Affairs (DEFRA) reporting guidance and the International Organization for Standardization (ISO) 14064 standard [35].

Publicly Available Specification (PAS) 2050—PAS 2050 provides guidance on measuring the embodied carbon emissions from goods and services. PAS 2050 incorporates existing life cycle assessments standards such as ISO 14040 by focusing specifically on carbon impact measurement [43]. This British standard may be superseded by ISO 14067, which is due to be ratified by the ISO [35]. To support organizational compliance with PAS 2050, the Carbon Trust developed an accompanying document—**Code of Good Practice for Product GHG Emissions and Reduction Claims**—that aids organizations in assessing the carbon footprint of their products with guidance for determining reductions in the GHG emissions of products over time and communicating product carbon footprint assessment and reductions [44].

PAS 2050 outlines the following steps in determining a product carbon footprint:

1. *Build a process map*—Detail all the materials, activities, and processes that could contribute to each stage of the chosen product's life cycle.
2. *Check boundaries and determine priorities*—Identify emissions that will be included and excluded.
3. *Collect data*—Collect data from operational activities, for example, actual electricity meter readings, and select appropriate emission conversion factors, for example, $KgCO_2$/liter of fuel (kilograms of carbon dioxide per liter of fuel).
4. *Calculate footprint*—Calculate the GHG emissions ($kgCO_2e$ per product unit) from each source.
5. *Verify your carbon footprint*—Provide an assessment of the margin of error for calculations. This can be a statistical analysis or a simple assessment of data quality [44].

A recent development in sustainable footprint methodology is the market segregation of products by using a "carbon label" that indicates to consumers the carbon intensity of a product [45]. Leading brands such as Walker Crisps are guiding the way for other consumer products by measuring and reducing the carbon intensity of their product [46]

    ISO 14040—This standard is an international standard that specifies the requirements for measuring the impacts of the inputs and outputs of a product or production system during its life cycle—also known as life cycle analysis or

LCA—and for performing, interpreting, and reporting a life cycle inventory (LCI) analysis and life cycle inventory assessment (LCIA) [43, 47].

PAS 2060—Arising from the adoption of carbon footprint methodology, some organizations have claimed *carbon neutrality* or no net increase in the carbon emissions to the atmosphere arising from an entity's operation [26]. PAS 2060 outlines the requirements to be met by any entity wanting to achieve and demonstrate carbon neutrality [26].

ISO 14064, Part 1—This standard details the requirements for an organization to actively develop, design, manage, and report GHG emissions [48]. The standard assists organizations to establish the *boundaries* within which GHG emissions occur or GHG *sinks are* present. A GHG *sink* is any mechanism that removes GHG from the atmosphere; it may manifest itself as a physical unit or process [48]. GHG impacts are categorized by the standard in three areas [48]: *Direct GHG emissions and removals*—Organizations are required to calculate GHG emissions arising from operational activities that it owns or is within its control.

Indirect GHG emissions—Quantification of GHG emissions arising from the use of energy that was not produced within the operational boundaries of the business, for example, purchased electricity.

Other indirect GHG emissions—These are GHG emissions that are incidental to the activities of the organization, for example, emissions from waste and employee travel.

As with accounting, GHG measurement must paint a true and fair view of carbon impacts by adhering to the following principles [32, 48]:

Relevance—Defining the boundaries within which the organization's GHG emissions occur

Completeness—Quantification of all GHG emissions within the specified organizational and operational boundaries with the disclosure of any omissions

Consistency—The use of standardized techniques, methodologies, and measurements to allow comparative analysis of GHG emissions over time with the documentation and disclosure of any factors or material changes

Accuracy—Prevention of the overestimation or underestimation of reported emissions through the identification of any uncertainties and the provision of assurance to stakeholders as to the integrity of the GHG measurement

Transparency—Presentation of GHG emission data to facilitate audit and review

ISO 14064, Part 2—This standard is primarily focused on GHG projects or projects designed to mitigate carbon emissions, outlining the requirements for managing, monitoring, and reporting these activities. This standard espouses GHG measurement principles of the ISO 14064 standard such as *relevance, completeness, consistency, accuracy, and transparency* but includes *conservativeness,* thereby preventing overestimation of the benefits of a proposed project.

The overall aim of the ISO 14064 standard is to provide an internationally recognized framework that improves the consistency and transparency of GHG reports that will help organizations to manage GHG impacts and where possible allow the development of suitable schemes that assists organizations to mitigate against carbon impacts through the trade of emission credits [49].

4.10   DEFRA GUIDELINES

The DEFRA guidelines of the United Kingdom establish that a standard GHG report illustrates an organization's environmental impact in terms of carbon dioxide equivalent (tCO_2e) per ton (a universal measurement used to indicate the GWP of a GHG expressed in terms of the GWP of one unit of carbon dioxide). Carbon dioxide equivalents (CO_2e) are also defined as a unit to compare the radiative forcing of a GHG when compared to carbon dioxide [43]. DEFRA guidelines utilize the GHG Protocol's reporting structure, which categorizes GHG emissions in three main areas or scopes:

Scope 1—Direct emissions arising from activities that are owned or controlled by the business. An example of this are the emissions from company cars and vehicles to the atmosphere.

Scope 2—Indirect emissions arising from activities that are not under the exclusive control of the business [42, 50, 51].

Scope 3—Emissions arising from activities of third parties who contribute inputs to the organization's various processes or consume its outputs, that is, products/service.

When viewed using a process-based approach it is possible to identify a symbiotic relationship between carbon inputs derived from the use of fossil fuels and by-products such as plastics—*ecosphere*, human activities—*anthroposphere* and GHG emissions into the *atmosphere* [52, 53]. DEFRA's GHG reporting methodology is one of the nine leading carbon emission schemes of which there exist 30 such schemes globally [31].

In 2010, a survey of Financial Times Stock Exchange (FTSE) 350 companies conducted by the Carbon Disclosure Project, a quasi-nongovernmental organization consisting of institutional investors, indicated that 59% of respondents are measuring Scope 1 and Scope 2 emissions [54]. Examples of these types of emissions include the use of electricity and heating and cooling systems. The Institute of Environmental Management and Assessment postulates that there are synergistic dividends from pursuing GHG reporting initiatives, for example, cost savings, competitiveness, and reputation [55].

Sustainability footprints are useful indicators for CSR reporting purposes due to its flexibility in measuring the efficiency of carbon management and social performance programs at both the corporate and project levels. As a communication tool, sustainability footprints can express both carbon management and social performance to various stakeholder audiences.

Recent research by Hoggart [56] identified the emergent use of GHG reporting as differentiating criteria in the contractor selection process. The use of GHG reports as a differentiating factor in supplier selection has stimulated the creation of "business constellations" [57] involving businesses that examine each other's carbon footprint and make competitive decisions accordingly. Gell [57], in spite of his candid insights, did not postulate a strategic model as a launch pad for sustainable corporate growth. Lash and Wellington [10] made the first attempt to describe the main risks posed to business arising from GHG emission-induced climate change as consisting of risks mainly from *regulatory*, *supply chain*, *product and technology*, *litigation*, *reputation*, and *physical factors*. In their view, businesses must seek to measure their carbon footprint, understand their carbon-related risks, build new competitive strategies to decarbonize their processes [10], and implement carbon-related abatement initiatives better than competitors by benchmarking carbon management performance as is emerging in the U.K. supermarket sector [58].

4.11   U.K. POLICY LANDSCAPE

In the United Kingdom, compliance is a main driver for carbon emission reporting with 54% of publicly traded companies who reported to schemes such as the Carbon Disclosure Project [54] including emission data on annual reports. However, 73% of the respondents in the Carbon Disclosure Project Global 500 [59] survey reported emissions in their annual report, with 65% of respondents making public disclosures. The continued interest in emission reporting in the United Kingdom is influenced by the following regulatory policies and legislation.

Climate Change Act of 2008, the first legislative commitment by any nation to reduce GHG, commits the United Kingdom to developing a low-carbon resource-efficient economy. The act binds the United Kingdom to an 80% reduction in GHG emissions by 2050 below 1990 levels with an interim target of 34% in GHG emission reductions by 2020. In addition to these ambitious targets are enacted provisions for a carbon budgeting system and mandatory reporting of GHG emissions by business enterprises [55]. Scotland's devolved government is pursuing even more ambitious plans: 80% reduction in GHG emissions by 2020 but with an interim target of 42% in GHG emissions by 2020 under the Climate Change Act (Scotland) of 2009. The U.K. government policy measures are a response to the unabated increase in carbon emissions, which although decreasing is 20% higher when compared to the 1990 levels, and a doubling of GHG emissions arising from consumption of imports [60]. Although Her Majesty's Treasury has the ability to offset any shortfall in achieving these mandatory reductions by purchasing carbon offsets, the U.K. Committee on Climate Change advises that carbon budgets are achieved through the implementation of domestic reductions in resource use in the economy [55]. This "political" accounting of carbon emissions is considered to influence "market enabled" carbon emission reporting [17].

Carbon Reduction Commitment (CRC) requires companies consuming more than 6000 megawatt hours (MWh) to participate in mandatory reporting with the purchase of carbon credits on the open market to offset any emission increases.

Climate Change Levy is a voluntary agreement that enables energy-intensive sectors to lower their emissions between 2-year reporting periods in return for levy reductions.

EU Emission Trading System (EU ETS) is a European-wide trading scheme involving energy suppliers, heavy industry, and aviation companies that provides limits on carbon emissions and a tradable market value for CO_2.

EU Directive on the Energy Performance of Buildings is targeted to improve energy efficiency in the built environment through the issue of mandatory Energy Performance Certificates (EPCs). Display Energy Certificates (DECs) provide information on energy usage and are required to be displayed in public buildings such as large restaurants and hotels.

Building Regulations, Part L, 2011, are regulations that govern the energy efficiency of new buildings, renovations of existing buildings, and extensions such as conservatories, reducing the gap between theoretical energy performance calculated at the design stage and the actual performance during use and ensuring a 25% reduction in CO_2 emissions relative to 2006 standards.

Therefore, it can be deduced that U.K. regulators are biased toward pursuing policies targeted at energy efficiencies [61]. The usefulness of this policy approach is validated from research that reveals that energy consumption reduction savings can contribute economic benefits, which are equivalent to a 5% increase in sales [62]. However, the drawback with this approach is that it excludes emissions arising from other economic activities in the supply chain such as the transport sector, which accounts for 21% of U.K. overall GHG emissions [63]. Recent U.K. GHG policy initiatives are specifically targeted at large organizations and do not provide the institutional support required to assist SME's in GHG emission reporting. Bradford and Fraser [61] recommend three policy options: *mandatory free energy audits of SMEs, free energy assistance from local authority* or *regional SME support organizations,* and *energy pricing schemes to encourage energy efficiency measures.* Implementation of these policy options may alleviate the effects of *firm size, competitive position,* and *energy intensity* that influence the adoption and perceptions of environmental policy [64]. These recommendations are supported by a DEFRA report indicating that there is an indirect relationship between emission reporting and emission reduction—*a unique combination of other factors such as investor pressure, transparency, compliance with regulations, senior management commitment, target setting, efficiency-saving opportunities, brand management,* and *ethical considerations influences emission reporting* [31].

4.12   WATER FOOTPRINT AND WATER ACCOUNTING

Water is an essential component of life and is a critical business resource due to its use in agricultural systems, which accounts for 86% of freshwater consumption [65]. Therefore, the effective management of water resources is integral to both the sustainability of business and the survival of life on the planet. A failure to understand water consumption impacts can expose businesses to potential operational risks arising from a "failure to manage the fresh water issue: damage to the corporate image, the threat of increased regulatory control, financial risks caused by pollution and insufficient freshwater availability for business operations" [66]. Business sensitivity to water impacts traditionally varied depending on factors such as availability, seasonal variability, industry sector, and geographic location; however, globalization has created a virtual trade in embedded water arising from the purchase of raw materials and goods from countries with water resource constraints [67]. Water footprint assessment and water accounting are tools that can assist businesses in determining the environmental impact of their operations in regard to water consumption.

Water footprint is defined as "an indicator of freshwater use that looks not only at direct water use of a consumer or producer, but also at indirect water use" [68]. This method adopts a full life cycle approach to the calculation of water impacts in manufacturing a product incorporating the volume of freshwater consumed by the supply chain. Methodologically, the water footprint is comprised of three main areas [68]:

- **Green water footprint**—Generally the consumption of all rainwater except run-off
- **Blue water footprint**—Consumption of surface and groundwater within the supply chain
- **Grey water footprint**—*"the volume of fresh water required to absorb a load of specified pollutants given natural background concentrations and existing ambient water quality standards"*

Water footprint assessment is an analytically rigorous activity that quantifies and locates the water footprint of a process, product, producer or consumer, or geographic area to determine the sustainability of water consumption and formulate strategies to mitigate against any impacts.

Water footprint assessment consists of four distinct phases [68] (Fig. 4.2):

- **Setting goals and scope**.
- **Water footprint accounting**—The collation of water footprint data within a previously defined scope.
- **Water footprint and sustainability assessment**—The determination of the sustainability of a specific water footprint from a social, environmental, and economic perspective.

FIGURE 4.2 Four distinct phases in water footprint assessment. Source: Hoekstra et al. [65]. © Earthscan.

• **Water footprint response formulation**—The development of strategies to reduce water impacts through water efficiency techniques and reduced pollution. *Water footprint offsetting* helps to ameliorate the negative impacts of unavoidable water consumption, which can be achieved through direct contribution by the business in the development of sustainable and equitable use of water within the local area of the water footprint impact.

The concept of being *water neutral* does not imply that water impacts are reduced to zero but confirms that all practicable steps have been taken to reduce the water footprint of a process, product, community, or business and ensure that all negative impacts have been offset [68].

4.13   SOCIAL FOOTPRINT

The *social footprint* method is a unique sustainability indicator that seeks to incorporate nonfinancial capital to quantify the impact of an organization on society or the social contribution of an organization's activities to climate change mitigation [69, 70]. This methodology is based on the WRE350 scenario—a scientific assumption that global CO_2 emissions will rise steadily and plateau at 350 parts per million by 2050 down from current levels of 385 parts per million with the implementation of climate change mitigation efforts [70, 71]. Social footprint methodology classifies nonfinancial capital into four main types:

Natural (or ecological) capital—Quality of land, air, and water.
Human capital—Health and human ingenuity.
Social capital—Social networks or government institutions; when framed from an economic perspective social capital, it is defined as "the capacity to generate social values like, friendship, collegiality, trust, respect and responsibility" [72].
Constructed capital—Man-made systems, for example, technology and transportation.

The later three groups are described as *anthro* capitals or human-produced capital [69, 73]. The social footprint method seeks to determine an organizational sustainability based upon its contribution or stewardship of *anthro* capitals essential for human well-being [71]. These nonfinancial "capitals" are allocated by the social footprint process using a new unit of measure, *people feet (PF)*, which is calculated as the number of employees multiplied by the proportion of time they spend working [73]. The *social footprint* is based on the principle of individual responsibility for personal choices as well as the actions of societal leaders. As such, an organization's or an individual's *social footprint* is expressed as a societal quotient—"*total social imprint" (social contributions by individuals/organizations) divided by "own share of supply gaps in related capital*" [73] *(the identified social need)*; therefore, a social footprint ≥ 1 is considered sustainable. Critics of social footprint methods argue its idealistic approach to the valuation in that individual concepts of responsibility are influenced by the cultural context and may not adequately reflect the overall societal impact of activities such as religion except only in financial terms [73].

4.14 SOCIAL STANDARDS, SOCIAL ACCOUNTING, AND THE SOCIAL FINGERPRINT

Increasing concern regarding business activities that produce negative social outcomes such as poor working conditions, wage exploitation, child labor, and environmental degradation has contributed to the adoption of voluntary stakeholder engagement standards [74]. There are over 100 social standards ranging from sector-specific standards, for example, Responsible Care in the chemical industry to internationally recognized standards such as Social Accountability 8000 (SA8000), Accountability 1000 (AA 1000), and Global Reporting Initiative (GRI) [74]. Social standards establish a framework for the implementation of management systems that provide information that enables the quantification of social performance through the identification of social costs, that is, "*the costs involved in actions that went beyond those normally required for competitive business reasons*," and the measurement of the "*economic costs of socially relevant actions*" forming the cornerstone of social accounting [75]. Early studies into social accounting theory were bounded by arguments for and against business as a social agent within society, thus highlighting the nefarious nature of social accounting as "*Social Responsibility is a moving target, socially relevant activities are small and ancillary to the main activities of the corporation*" and the *recency* of CSR as a management issue [75]. These dynamics have contributed to the regular updating of social standards such as the SA 8000 that led to the evolution of a complimentary approach—the *Social Fingerprint*, defined as "*a program of ratings, training and tools designed to help companies measure and improve social performance*" [76]. The *Social Fingerprint* adopts a proactive approach consisting of two tracks: the development of company social performance measurement and the assessment of supply chain social performance [76].

4.15 ECOLOGICAL FOOTPRINT ANALYSIS

The use of even more exotic techniques, for example, the ecological footprint "measured as the amount of productive land and/or water supporting human activities and required to sustain human life" [77] or "standardized estimate of the Earth's biological carrying capacity required to support humanity's resource use and waste production" [78], is not yet mainstream among businesses even though ecological footprint measurement was empirically tested as being applicable to business use more than a decade ago [15]. The adoption of ecological footprint methodology by business has been stalled by a failure in the development of international ecological footprint standards as well as *the abundance of modified footprint methods that cloud the distinction between ecological footprint analysis (EFA) and other kinds of sustainability analyses*, creating a need for further research into the application of EFA in policy, business, and lifestyle analysis [78].

Methodological issues also affect the implementation of ecological footprints within industry as it is underpinned by a reliance on the Food and Agriculture Organization's (FAO) global agriculture ecological zone (GAEZ) indices that value biocapacity in terms of human needs, thereby discounting the contribution of mountains, deserts, and oceans to human survival except in terms of carbon sequestration—the process of storing carbon dioxide in the soil ocean or underground [78, 79].

4.16   CRITICISMS OF FOOTPRINT METHODOLOGIES

The use of sustainability footprints, namely, carbon footprint, as an impact indicator for large companies can also be reasonably extended to measure the impacts of international trade, individual establishments, and planning applications [80]. Consumers may even begin to utilize carbon labels on consumable items such as food as a guide in purchasing, discriminating against products with high carbon intensity [81]. The impact on such value judgments on the international trade cannot be underestimated even though initial research indicates that carbon labeling has negligible effect; however, Edwards-Jones et al. [81] state, "*Conversely, given the growing political and commercial importance of the climate change agenda it could be argued that carbon footprints will become the predominant factor influencing choice between alternative goods.*"

Potentially, investors are capable of using existing carbon emission data disclosed in company reports to understand the environmental impact and climate change risks, taking action to "*carbon optimizing*" portfolios by benchmarking and the use of techniques such as "*carbon overlay*" to balance a portfolio's emission performance [31, 82]. The emergence of share market indices, for example, FTSE Carbon Disclosure Project Carbon Strategy Index, which highlights the carbon risks of publicly listed companies underlining increasing investor incorporation of risk arising from unabated GHG emissions [54]. The development of the FTSE Carbon Disclosure Project Carbon Strategy Index is a response to investor search for α, that is, new window(s) of potential value in companies, looking beyond emission data to other factors such as the likelihood of emission regulation and the cost of emission offsetting [83]. However, critics of carbon footprint reporting suggest that there is limited evidence to infer that investors incorporate carbon risk in the decision-making process [28, 84].

Stipulated sustainability footprint data is not weighted heavily by reporting schemes in relation to other CSR/sustainability index criteria as revealed in the following statement: "*the rankings don't measure performance outcomes such as CO_2 emissions. Instead, they look at management practices: Does a company have procedures for listening to critics? Are its executives and board members accountable? Has it hired an external verifier?*" [84]. Contemporary management researchers support these arguments, suggesting that limited value can be derived from the pursuit of carbon footprint measurement as part of CSR/sustainability reporting, which is a voluntary exercise whose costs are prohibitive except for those firms with near-monopolistic profits [85]. Critics of sustainability indices such as the GRI fail to see its utility in providing clear indications as to an organization's sustainability or unsustainable position [86]. The inability of scientists to give definitive advice on noncarbon impacts such as the inclusion of new chemicals to GHG inventories or methodologies to measure emissions from land as well as the various approaches to calculate GWP has prevented consensus on carbon footprint reporting [17, 27, 87]. These uncertainties will be reduced and accuracy improved as scientific advancement continues; however, the attitudes to sustainability of future generations will always be an unknown quantity [27]. Scientific arguments aside, critics state that footprints, which by nature record historical impact, do not aid in the SWOT analysis of the risk faced by firms arising from climate change or incorporate the views of future generations; that the application of tools such as LCA in carbon footprint measurement requires expertise, which may be unavailable within SME organizations; and that voluntary carbon reporting presents challenges in terms of interpretation and consistency of information [17, 28, 77].

Although a valid criticism of sustainability footprint methodology, it is quite a limited perception of the process of footprint measurement, which although cannot claim to speak for future generations, reveals opportunities for organizations to reduce immediate impact either through resource optimization, reduction, or substitution with less harmful alternatives. Firms face no alternative but to participate in the experiment of carbon markets by developing carbon accounting systems mainly due to the NGO pressure to disclose sustainability performance, the emergence of carbon trading, legal requirements such as the EU ETS, potential of future carbon regulation, and increasing opportunities to offset carbon emissions [17, 27, 28].

The use of markets on its own will be unable to address the main issues facing business in the twenty-first century, *the legitimization of the capitalist model, the decarbonization of the global economy, the accounting of environmental externalities as a result of resource use or misuse, the free movement of labor,* and *the global alignment of pay and working conditions.* This view is supported by Cerin [88] who suggests a role for regulation as stimuli to produce radical change in environmental conditions and the standards of business conduct in relation to profit maximization. Business must account for profitability by acknowledging its interrelationship with environmental impact and climate change, which can be measured using the currency of greenhouse emissions—CO_2e and other sustainability footprint indicators.

The use of sustainability footprints by business will improve the accuracy of macroeconomic data regarding the true scale of GHG emissions so that effective measures can be designed to combat against environmental impact arising from economic growth.

However, the *proliferation of various reporting schemes* and *the lack of external verification of GHG data* have stifled the adoption of sustainability footprints. Verification of sustainability reports is a controversial issue that must be addressed if sustainability reports are to have any credence with the markets or society at large; some researchers have observed that existing verification use consultancy approaches and without any interest to promote transparency [89].

Therefore, there is a need for regulation in sphere of sustainability reporting that is critical if we are to appreciate the true costs of investment decisions from the perspective of sustainability footprint measurements and make the quantum leap from viewing environmental impacts as risks but strategic opportunity. A recent development to improve the transparency of sustainability reporting is the establishment of the *International Integrated Reporting Framework* [90].

The *International Integrated Reporting Framework* is the brainchild of the International Integrated Reporting Council (IIRC): "*a global coalition of regulators, investors, companies, standard setters, the accounting profession and NGOs*" that aims to promote integrated thinking in the generation of corporate reports, thereby improving the quality of information, accountability, stewardship of resources, and enhance decision making [90]. The *International Integrated Reporting Framework* adopts a value-centered approach that extends the traditional process model to move beyond outputs to include outcomes both for the business and society.

Businesses create value through transformative activities converting capitals, that is, *financial*; *manufactured,* for example, buildings; *intellectual,* for example, patents; *human*; and *natural* through *social interactions and relationships,* in order to create value-added services and products for others, that is, stakeholders, however taking into account the extent of the externalization of its impacts.

The extent of the externalization of negative impacts, for example, carbon emissions, will require organizations to change their business model to ensure sustainable outcomes. This entails placing sustainability at the heart of the organization's mission and vision, establishing governance structures that support sustainability initiatives through risk and opportunity identification, developing sustainability strategy, resourcing to ensure that strategy is effectively implemented, monitoring of the achievement of performance targets, and an overall strategic orientation toward sustainability supported by top management review and commitment.

Based on this philosophical approach, firms generate balanced reports of the process of harnessing existing valuable *capitals* and transformation to create new valuable *capitals* using eight principles [90]:

- **Strategic focus and future orientation**—Provide a review of the organization's strategic approach in creating value in the short, medium, and long term.
- **Connectivity of information**—Highlight the interrelatedness of factors that influence the creation of value over time.
- **Stakeholder relationships**—Examine business critical relationships and organizational response to their needs and concerns.
- **Materiality**—Disclosure of issues that are integral to the realization of value by the organization.
- **Conciseness**
- **Reliability and completeness**—Use of rigorous measures to ensure accuracy and balance in reporting both positive and negative occurrences.
- **Consistency and comparability**—Uniformity in reporting performance that affords comparative analysis with similar organizations.

Despite overwhelming evidence as to the benefits of sustainability footprint tools such as carbon footprints as indicators, very few companies set emission targets [91].

Martin Baxter, Executive Director—Policy, Institute of Environmental Management and Assessment, states that *"The reality for many is that carbon and GHG emissions are a low or non-existent priority; the subject doesn't feature as an issue in their business—even though reducing energy consumption is good for the bottom line and improves environmental performance. There is a significant challenge—to overcome the barriers that prevent these companies from minimizing their impact and maximizing the opportunity"* [55].

REFERENCES

[1]   Kolk A. Social and environmental accounting. In: Clubb C, editor. *The Blackwell Encyclopaedia of Management Accounting*. 2nd ed. Blackwell: Malden; 2005. p. 393–398.

[2]   Kolk A. Environmental reporting by multinationals from the Triad: convergence or divergence? Manage Int Rev 2005;45(1, special issue): 145–166.

[3]   Amekudzi A, Jotin Khisty C, Khayesi M. Using the sustainability footprint model to assess development impacts of transportation systems. Trans Res Part A 2009;43:339–348.

[4]   Balkau F, Sonnerman G. Managing sustainability performance through the value chain. Corp Gov 2009;1(1):46–58.

[5]   Porter M. *Competitive Advantage*. New York: Free Press; 1985.

[6]   Porter M. Kramer M. Strategy & society: the link between competitive advantage and corporate social responsibility. Harvard Bus Rev December 2006;84: 78–93.

[7]   Porter, M. The big idea: creating shared value. Harvard Bus Rev January 2011;89:62–77.

[8]   Caulkin S. Swap the management-speak for plain English. Financial Times 2011,p. 9.

[9]   Krysiak F. Risk management as a tool for sustainability. J Bus Ethics 2009;85:483–492.

[10] Lash J, Wellington F. Competitive advantage on a warming planet. Harvard Bus Rev 2007;85(3):94–102.

[11] Porter M. *Competitive Strategy*. New York: Free Press; 1980.

[12] Teece D, editor. Profiting from technological innovation: implications for integration, collaboration, licensing, and public policy. In *The Competitive Challenge*. Cambridge: Ballinger; 1987. p. 185–220.

[13] Winter S. Knowledge and competence as strategic assets. In: Teece D, editor. *The Competitive Challenge*. Cambridge: Ballinger; 1987. p. 159–184.

[14] Hart S. A natural resource based view of the firm. Acad Manage Rev 1995; 20(4): 986–1014.

[15] Rees W, Wackernagel M. *Our Ecological Footprint—Reducing Human Impact on Earth*. Gabriola Island: New Society Publishers; 1996.

[16] Hart S, Milstein M. Global sustainability and the creative destruction of industries. MIT Sloan Manage Rev Fall 1999;41:23–33.

[17] Ascui F, Lovell, H. As frames collide: making sense of carbon accounting. Account Audit Accountability J 2011;24(8):978–999. DOI: 10.1108/09513571111184724.

[18] Arrhenius S. On the influence of carbonic acid in the air upon the temperature of the ground. The London, Edinburgh and Dublin Philos Magazine J Sci 1896;41:237–276.

[19] United Nations Framework Convention on Climate Change (UNFCCC). Available at http://unfccc.int/essential_background/convention/items/2627.php. Accessed Jan 8, 2012.

[20] United Nations General Assembly Resolution 43/53. Protection of global climate for present and future generations of mankind. Available at http://daccess-dds-ny.un.org/doc/RESOLUTION/GEN/NR0/530/32/IMG/NR053032.pdf?OpenElement. Accessed Jan 15, 2013.

[21] United Nations General Assembly Resolution 45/212. Protection of global climate for present and future generations of mankind. Available at http://daccess-dds-ny.un.org/doc/RESOLUTION/GEN/NR0/566/01/IMG/NR056601.pdf?OpenElement. Accessed Jan 15, 2013.

[22] United Nations Framework Convention on Climate Change. Kyoto protocol. Available at http://unfccc.int/kyoto_protocol/items/2830.php. Accessed Jan 8, 2012.

[23] Reilly J, Mayer M, Harnisch J. The Kyoto protocol and non-CO_2 greenhouse gases and carbon sinks. Environ Model Assess 2002;7:217–229.

[24] Cirman A, Domadenik P, Koman M, Redek T. The Kyoto protocol in a global perspective. Econ Bus Rev 2009;11(1):29–54.

[25] United Nations Framework Convention on Climate Change. International emissions trading. Available at http://unfccc.int/kyoto_protocol/mechanisms/emissions_trading/items/2731.php. Accessed Jan 8, 2012.

[26] Publicly Available Specification 2060. Specification for demonstrating carbon neutrality. York: British Standards Institute; 2010.

[27] Bowen F, Wittneben B. Carbon accounting: negotiating accuracy, consistency and certainty across organizational fields. Account Audit Accountability J 2011;24(8), 1022–1036.

[28] Kolk A. Sustainability, accountability and corporate governance: exploring multinationals reporting practices. Bus Strat Environ 2008;18:1–15.

[29] United Nations Framework Convention on Climate Change (UNFCCC). Clean development mechanisms. Available at http://unfccc.int/kyoto_protocol/mechanisms/clean_development_mechanism/items/2718.php. Accessed Jan 8, 2012.

[30] United Nations Framework Convention on Climate Change (UNFCCC). Joint Implementation. Available at http://unfccc.int/kyoto_protocol/mechanisms/joint_implementation/items/1674.php. Accessed Jan 8, 2012.

[31] Department of Environment Food and Rural Affairs. The contribution that reporting of greenhouse gas emissions makes to the UK meeting its climate change objectives: a review of the current evidence. Available at http://archive.defra.gov.uk/environment/business/reporting/pdf/corporate-reporting101130.pdf. Accessed Jan 7, 2013.

[32] Ritter K, Nordrum S, Shires T. Ensuring consistent greenhouse gas emissions estimates. Chem Eng Progr 2005;101(9):30–37.

[33] Carbon Trust Carbon Footprinting. The next step to reducing your carbon emissions. Available at http://www.carbontrust.com/media/44869/j7912_ctv043_carbon_footprinting_aw_interactive.pdf. Accessed Jan 10, 2013.

[34] Christoph JM, Scott MK, Ramesh S, Klaus SL. Fast carbon footprinting for large product portfolios. J Indus Ecol 2012;16(5):669–679.

[35] Pandey D, Agrawal M, Pandey JS. Carbon footprint: current methods of estimation. Environ Monit Assess 2011;178(1–4), 135–160. DOI: 10.1007/s10661-010-1678-y.

[36] Watson C. Forest carbon accounting: overview and principles. United Nations; 2009. Available at http://www.undp.org/content/dam/aplaws/publication/en/publications/environment-energy/www-ee-library/climate-change/forest-carbon-accounting-overview---principles/Forest_Carbon_Accounting_Overview_Principles. Accessed on Jun 30, 2014.

[37] Ministry of the Environment, Japan (MOE). *CDM/JI Manual for Project Developers and Policy Makers*. Tokyo: Ministry of the Environment; 2009.

[38] IPCC. Intergovernmental Panel on Climate Change IPCC special report on carbon dioxide capture and storage. Available at https://www.ipcc.ch/pdf/special-reports/srccs/srccs_wholereport.pdf. Accessed Feb 25, 2014.

[39] International Accounting Standards Board (IASB), International Accounting Standards Board (IASB) – information for observers: emissions trading schemes; board meeting May 20, 2008. Available at http://www.ifrs.org/Current-Projects/IASB-Projects/Emission-Trading-Schemes/Meeting-Summaries/Documents/ETS0805b03obs.pdf. Accessed Jan 14, 2013.

[40] Hammond G. Time to give due weight to the 'carbon footprint' issue. Nature 2007; 445(7125):256.

[41] Jarvis P. Never mind the footprints, get the mass right. Nature 2007;446:24.

[42] WBCSD/WRI. *The Greenhouse Gas Protocol: A Corporate Accounting and Reporting Standard*. Revised ed. Geneva: World Business Council for Sustainable Development and World Resource Institute; 2004.

[43] Publicly Available Specification 2050. Specification for the assessment of the life cycle greenhouse gas emissions of goods and services. York: British Standards Institute; 2011.

[44] Code of Good Practice for Product GHG Emissions and Reduction Claims. *Guidance to support the robust communication of product carbon footprints*. UK: Carbon Trust; 2008.

[45] Carbon Trust. The carbon reduction label explained; 2010. Available at http://business.carbon-label.com/business/label.htm. Accessed Mar 12, 2012.

[46] Walker crisps taking steps to reduce our carbon footprint. Available at http://www.walkerscarbonfootprint.co.uk/. Accessed Mar 12, 2012.

[47] ISO 14040.2006. Environmental management—life cycle assessment—principles and framework. Geneva: International Organisation for Standardization; 2006.

[48] ISO 14064-1.2006. Greenhouse gases Part 1: SPECIFICATION with guidance at the organization level for quantification and reporting of greenhouse gas emissions and removals. Geneva: International Organisation for Standardization; 2006.

[49] Weng CK, Boehmer K. Launching of ISO 14064 for greenhouse gas accounting and verification. Geneva: ISO Management Systems; 2006;206: 15.

[50] James L. Embedding the environment into company DNA. Environmentalist 2010; (97):20–21.

[51] Department of Environment Food and Rural Affairs. Guidance on how to measure and report your greenhouse gas emissions. Available at http://www.defra.gov.uk/environment/business/reporting/pdf/ghg-guidance.pdf. Accessed Mar 12, 2012.

[52] Hoffmann VH, Busch T. Corporate carbon performance indicators: carbon intensity, dependency, exposure, and risk. J Ind Ecol 2008;12(4):505–520.

[53] Hendrich H, Busch T. Carbon management as a strategic challenge for SMEs. Greenhouse Gas Measure Manage 2012;2(1):61–72.

[54] CDP. Carbon Disclosure Project FTSE 350 Report. Available at https://www.cdproject.net/CDPResults/CDP-2010-FTSE350.pdf. Accessed May 21, 2013.

[55] Institute of Environmental Management and Assessment. Special Report on GHG Management 2010. Available at http://www.iema.net/iema-special-reports. Accessed on Jun 30 2014.

[56] Hoggart C. A giant step for industry. WET News 2008;14(5):17.

[57] Gell M. Business transformations in carbon constrained markets. Environmentalist 2008;(66):14–18.

[58] Mackenzie C, Hikisch D, Ivory S. UK supermarkets 2009 Carbon Benchmark Report. London: ENDS Carbon.

[59] CDP. Carbon Disclosure Project, Global 500 Report. Available at https://www.cdproject. net/CDPResults/CDP-2010-G500.pdf. Accessed May 21, 2013.

[60] United Kingdom Government. UK Carbon Footprint 1990–2009. Available at http://data. gov.uk/dataset/ghg-emissions-relating-to-uk-consumption-1990-to-2008. Accessed Aug 16, 2011.

[61] Bradford J, Fraser E. Local authorities, climate change and small and medium enterprises: identifying effective policy instruments to reduce energy use and carbon emissions. Corp Soc Responsib Environ Mgmt 2008;15:156–172.

[62] Carbon Trust. Good practice guide 367-better business guide to energy saving. London: Her Majesty's Stationery Office; 2005.

[63] Department of Environment Food and Rural Affairs. Car product roadmaps. Available at http://www.defra.gov.uk/environment/business/products/roadmaps/cars.htm. Accessed Jan 7, 2013.

[64] de Groot HLF, Verhoef ET, Nijkamp P. Energy savings by firms: decision-making, barriers and policies. Energy Econ 2001;23:717–740.

[65] Hoekstra AY, Chapagain AK. Water footprints of nations: water use by people as a function of their consumption pattern. Water Resour Manage 2007;21(1):35–48.

[66] Ercin AE, Hoekstra YA, Chapagain KA, Aldaya MM, Mekonen MM. Corporate water footprint accounting and impact assessment: the case of the water footprint of a sugar-containing carbonated beverage. Water Resour Manage 2011;25:721–741.

[67] SAB Miller WWF Water Footprint Report 2009. Available at: http://www.waterfootprint. org/Reports/SABMiller-GTZ-WWF-2010-WaterFutures.pdf. Accessed on Jun 30, 2014.

[68] Hoekstra YA, Chapagain KA, Aldaya MM, Mekonen MM. *The Water Footprint Assessment Manual, Setting Global Standards*. London: Earthscan; 2011. p. 2.

[69] McElroy M, Jorna R, van Englen J. Sustainability quotients and the social footprint. Corp Soc Responsib Environ Mgmt 200;15:223–234.

[70] Report Your Corporate Social Bottom Line for Global Warming. Business & The Environment with ISO 14000 Updates; 2007;18(4):7.

[71] U.S. Environmental Protection Agency. Model for the Assessment of Greenhouse Gas Induced Climate Change. A Regional Climate Scenario Generator MAGIC/SCENGEN. Available at http://www.cgd.ucar.edu/cas/wigley/magicc/. Accessed on Jan 15, 2013.

[72] Klamer A. Accounting for social and cultural values. De Economist 2002;150(4): 453–473.

[73] McElroy M. Leaving social footprints. Business & The Environment with ISO 14000 Updates 2006;17(6):1–3.

[74] Beschorner T, Müller M. Social standards: toward an active ethical involvement of businesses in developing countries. J Bus Ethics 2007;73:11–20.

[75] Churchill N. Toward a theory for social accounting. Sloan Manage Rev 1974;Spring:1–16.

[76] Social Fingerprint. What is the Your Social Fingerprint. Available at http://www.social fingerprint.org/newUser.html. Accessed Apr 10, 2013.

[77] Holland L. Can the principle of the ecological footprint be applied to measure the environ-
      mental sustainability of business. Corp Soc Responsib Environ Mgmt 2003;10:224–232.

[78] Venetoulis R, Talbert J. Refining the ecological footprint. Environ Dev Sustain
      2008;10:441–469.

[79] Qian Y. Can Turfgrass sequester atmospheric carbon? Assessment using long-term soil
      testing data. TPI Turf News, Mar/Apr 2003, p. 23.

[80] Simmons C, Chambers N. Footprinting UK households—how big your garden. Local
      Environ 1998;3(3):355–362.

[81] Edwards-Jones G, Plassmann K, York E, Hounsome B, Jones D, Canals L. Vulnerability
      of exporting nations to the development of a carbon label in the United Kingdom.
      Environ Sci Policy 2009;12(4):479–490.

[82] Thomas S. Measuring carbon intensity and risk. In: Oulton W, editor. *Investment
      Opportunities for a Low Carbon World*. London: GMB Publishing Ltd; 2009.

[83] Sullivan R, Kozak J. Investor case studies—climate change: just one more investment
      issue. In: Oulton W, editor. *Investment Opportunities for a Low Carbon World*. London:
      GMB Publishing Ltd; 2009.

[84] Demos T. Beyond the bottom line: our second annual ranking of global 500 companies.
      Fortune; October 23, 2006. Available at: http://archive.fortune.com/magazines/fortune/
      fortune_archive/2006/10/30/8391850/index.htm. Accessed on Jun 30, 2014.

[85] Hicks M. BP: social responsibility and the easy life of the monopolist. Am J Bus 2010;
      25(2):9–10.

[86] Gray R, Bebbington J. Corporate sustainability, accountability and the pursuit of the
      impossible dream. CSEAR Website. Available at http://www.st-andrews.ac.uk/~csearweb/
      researchresources/dps-sustain-handcorp.html. Accessed Sep 25, 2011.

[87] Shine K, Fugelsvedt J, Hailemariam K, Stuber N. Comparing climate impacts of emis-
      sions of greenhouse gases. Climate Change 2005;68:281–302.

[88] Cerrin P. Creating environmental change by reassigning property rights: diminishing
      the adversities of information asymmetries in the value chain. Working Paper the
      Department of Industrial Economics and Management. Stockholm: Royal Institute of
      Technology; 2002.

[89] Ball A, Owen D, Gray R. External transparency of internal capture, the role of third-party
      statements in adding value to corporate environmental reports. Bus Strat Environ 2000;9:
      1–23.

[90] International Integrated Reporting Council. The International Framework. Available at
      http://www.theiirc.org/international-ir-framework/. Accessed Dec 20, 2013.

[91] Bonini S, Brun N, Rosenthal M. McKinsey Global Survey Results: Valuing Corporate
      Social Responsibility 2009, 1–9. Available at: http://www.mckinsey.com/insights/
      corporate_finance/valuing_corporate_social_responsibility_mckinsey_global_survey_
      results. Accessed on Jun 30, 2014.

5

SUSTAINABLE STRATEGIC GROWTH MODEL: A SOLUTION TO THE SUSTAINABILITY/CSR DILEMMA

5.1 INTRODUCTION

To aid business in developing and measuring sustainability objectives that are pertinent to their specific organizational context and to define the relevance of philosophical, cultural, and strategic challenges on an organization's transition to becoming a *sustainably managed enterprise (SME)* led to the creation of the **Sustainable Strategic Growth Model**, which is based on the following principles:

- *Do no harm [1], and engage and listen to all stakeholders [2].*
- *There are no barriers or limits [3] to sustainable growth, only challenges [4].*
- *Sustainability is an ever changing goal [5].*
- *There is no "silver bullet"—sustainability strategy is ever evolving to meet society's present and future expectations [1, 6].*
- *Sustainability is measurable—**use both sustainability footprints [7] and traditional financial indicators to benchmark sustainable growth and performance [8].***

Sustainability Footprints in SMEs: Strategy and Case Studies for Entrepreneurs and Small Business, First Edition. Lowellyne James.
© 2015 John Wiley & Sons, Inc. Published 2015 by John Wiley & Sons, Inc.

Using these principles, a practical model for sustainability strategy development to improve business performance will be demonstrated by reference to four United Kingdom-based organizations:

- Capital Cooling Ltd.
- The Log House People
- Moffat Golf Club
- Rabbie's Trail Burners

Figure 5.1 is a diagrammatic illustration of the **Sustainable Strategic Growth Model** that describes the possibilities of the application of technology, research, and development to develop products and services that increase resource efficiency

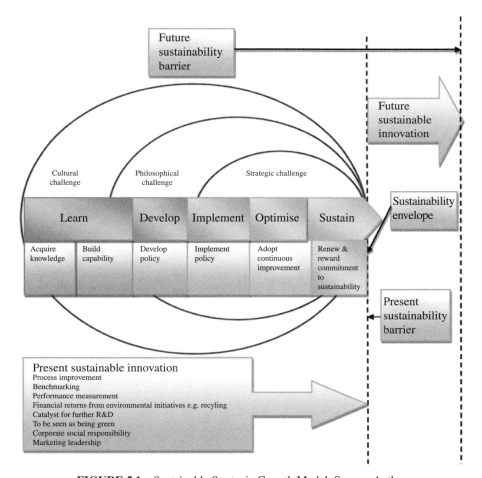

FIGURE 5.1   Sustainable Strategic Growth Model. Source: Author.

and improve carbon productivity [9]. Developing concepts expounded by commentators such as Enkvist et al. [9], the **Sustainable Strategic Growth Model** aims to guide firms along the process of decoupling strategic growth from greenhouse gas emissions while fostering the implementation of social objectives that yield value to the business and its stakeholders through the implementation of five steps: *learn, develop, implement, optimize,* and *sustain* (Fig. 5.1).

5.2   SUSTAINABLE STRATEGIC GROWTH MODEL

Using the **Sustainable Strategic Growth Model** in essence defines **sustainability** *as the effective utilization of assets and information by an organization to develop strategic solutions that provide benefits to society of reduced environmental impact, socioeconomic value creation ensuring the continued profitability of the organization, and prosperity for future generations.* This definition of sustainability extends the Brundtland Commission's earlier postulation as well as the Integrative Sustainability Triangle model by including information—an anthropogenic resource as a new dimension, the impact of which is now being fully understood with the emergence of social media. Our dependence on information systems has transformed the nature of sustainability to a pyramidal construct consisting of four elements, namely, *information, economic, environmental,* and *social* (Fig. 5.2).

This *information footprint* has three dimensions: *length,* the extent to which information has been diffused outside organizational boundaries that when interpreted from an organizational context manifests itself as efficiency, that is, faster inventory cycle time and improved customer satisfaction [10]; *depth,* the extent to

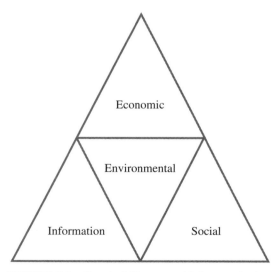

FIGURE 5.2   Sustainability pyramid. Source: Author.

which information is diffused within the organization to improve effectiveness of decision making; *breadth*, the exploitation of information to identify opportunities to enter into new markets or develop new products and services, thereby promoting entrepreneurship [10].

The three dimensions of *length*, *depth*, and *breadth* increasingly place the management and control of information as a strategic concern for major global economies with increasing cyber attacks, proliferation of electronic surveillance, and inequality of access to information [11]. In 2007, the nightmare scenario of cyber attacks capable of crippling vital services, for example, hospitals and civil aviation, moved from science fiction to reality in Estonia where communication and banking systems were subjected to a denial-of-service (DOS) attack [11]. Cyber attacks can disproportionately affect small nation-states who can ill afford the economic and societal disruption resulting from such events. The role of *information* as a strategic resource is potentially creating a global underclass of individuals and nation-states comprising of information "haves" and "have not's" despite the seeming transparency of the Internet an emerging new form of poverty surfaces "resource rich but cash and information poor" unable to benefit from access to information relegated to economic activities based on subsistence entrepreneurship.

The continued reliance of international financial and banking systems on information technology infrastructure creates an acute risk to the sustainability of business particularly SMEs as customers opt for electronic financial transactions [12]. Businesses will prefer to reduce risk and transfer resources to countries with reliable and secure access to information, thereby stifling innovation and stagnating development. A related impact of our insatiable thirst for real-time information is the increasing growth of waste electrical and electronic equipment (WEEE) such as "obsolete" mobile phones and computer monitors, presently the fastest growing waste stream in the United Kingdom, accounting for approximately 1 million tonnes annually [13]. Exposure to both direct and indirect risks arising from the need for *information* by nation-states and firms either through limited access, loss, inaccuracy, or WEEE affects not only competiveness but also safety and security. Sustainable organizations and nations must combine the goals of *zero errors* and *zero emissions* into the pursuit of the strategic goal of *absolute zero, the point at which no more adverse risk can be removed from a system*, which is a benchmark upon which sustained customer satisfaction can be achieved.

This new definition of sustainability is given operational expression at each stage of the **Sustainable Strategic Growth Model**, for example:

Learn consists of two key constructs—*acquire knowledge* and *build capability*:
 Acquire knowledge—A review of all potential risks and opportunities arising from actions or demands from strategic groups such as customers, governments, nongovernmental organizations, competitors, companies in other industrial sectors, industry groups, and business support organizations, which can affect the present and future sustainable growth of the business.
 Build capability—The process of assimilating information gathered from both internal and external sources to generate organizational goals, structure, and

responsibilities in regard to sustainability pertinent to an organization and its competitive landscape. In practice, involving strategic review of all products, processes, human resources, and infrastructure within the direct control of the firm, for example, human resource and information technology systems, determine the competences, capability, and suitability of both tangible and intangible assets to sustain growth [14]. This necessitates examination of all existing best practice, standards, and legislation in sustainability and corporate social responsibility (CSR), for example, ISO 14001 Environmental Standards, ISO 26000 Guide to Social Responsibility, AA1000 Assurance Standard, SA8000 standard, Global Reporting Initiative (GRI) standard, and BS8900 Guidance for Managing Sustainable Development. Benchmarking analysis of existing organizational arrangements against current best practice will highlight performance gaps and assists the organization in developing business models specific to its competitive situation. This internalization and assimilation aspect is critical to the success of the program as it defines the strategic boundaries in which the organization seeks to compete effectively either through the development of new products, services, and processes modification of existing products, services, and processes; divestment of existing product portfolios; or entering new markets.

Develop company policy that aligns sustainable business practices with strategic goals:

Develop policy—A consultative process of translating strategic vision into policy statements seeking to identify key sustainability goals that are relevant to the organization in relation to its size and competitive environment. Consultation may be initiated by *passive* stakeholder engagement in the form of employee surveys and customer satisfaction surveys or *active* stakeholder engagement by the inclusion of customer representatives on decision-making teams.

Implement involves the commitment of senior management to engage stakeholders in embedding sustainability policy. Organizations should seek to:

Implement policy—A process of disseminating sustainability policy across all operations within the organization, utilizing tools such as training, instruction, supervision, review, and reporting to engage stakeholder's emotional commitment to the organizational sustainability policy. The emotional commitment of stakeholders is critical to the success of sustainability policy implementation as it aligns individual stakeholder motivations with the sustainable goals of the organization. *Sustainability policy implementation* may involve the development of departmental or site-specific procedures that are aligned to an organization's sustainability policy.

Systematic reporting of financial and nonfinancial data such as greenhouse gas reports (carbon footprints) are used at this stage to evaluate the effectiveness sustainability strategy in relation to overall policy goals. A study completed by Price Waterhouse Cooper on behalf of the Department for Environment, Food and Rural Affairs confirms that the discipline of measuring and reporting emission data identifies opportunities for ecoefficiency and cost savings [15, 16]. Recent surveys suggest that 34% of companies choose to publicly disclose greenhouse gas emission data in CSR reports, with 27% providing greenhouse gas data in sustainability reports as it affords an opportunity for firms to showcase their sustainability achievements and progress in this area [17].

Optimize the use of resources by the implementation of sustainable business practices; businesses should:

Adopt continuous improvement—There are immediate measurable benefits to the company and society from sustainability initiatives like improved reputation; environmental impact reduction, for example, reduced greenhouse gas emissions due to energy purchases from renewable suppliers; safety/employee well-being programs; integrated management systems [18]; and resource efficiencies, for example, waste recycling and cost savings that accrue from sustainability initiatives. Value creation at this stage is generated from "greening" strategies with the focus on current products, processes, and stakeholders [18, 19].

Sustain value creation through rewarding sustainable behavior by the use of two main approaches:

Renew and reward commitment to sustainability—As the maximum economic, social, and environmental returns achievable by the organization and society from a given strategy using existing technology and resources, the firm approaches a *sustainability barrier*, beyond which further sustainable growth can be achieved by reinvigorating stakeholders to participate in new low-carbon initiatives, supported by investment in training and new technology (e.g. wind turbine and solar power), processes, and systems (e.g., IT video conferencing facilities, research and development (R&D)). At this stage, creative destruction must occur as management and stakeholders review and implement each stage of the **Sustainable Strategic Growth Model**, with decision making focused on emerging opportunities to exploit new low-carbon technology, enter new markets, and engage stakeholders [20]. Therefore, *telos* or purpose of management is the development of sustainability strategy that continually moves organizations beyond the *sustainability barrier* to realize the benefits of future growth, ensuring the survival of the organization by maintaining both its economic and social value.

The *Sustainable Strategic Growth Model* illustrates an incremental increase in sustainable performance as a result of the assimilation and implementation of sustainability practices, which will enhance organizational knowledge and build sustainability competencies. Basically, as the organization implements the framework, and develops and implements procedures, its sustainability knowledge and competencies increase.

Each stage of the framework is influenced by the outputs of previous stages; process synergy is achieved where each stage intersects, that is, the firm moves through the five stages, *learn, develop implement, optimize*, and *sustain*, a new low-carbon state is created primed for further investment to generate future sustainable growth. Stakeholders from SME case study firms perceive the adoption of sustainability initiatives such as carbon footprint measurement as leading to innovation in process improvement, benchmarking, performance measurement, and financial returns from environmental initiatives (e.g., recycling and catalyst for further R&D), to be seen as being green as well as demonstrating CSR and marketing leadership.

The role of technology investment in generating future sustainable growth is critical if organizations are to succeed in the emerging new global green economy and in the ever-growing contribution of university research centers in enhancing long-term energy security and prosperity. Authors such as Jolly [20] emphasize that the independent yet complimentary roles of domestic policy in terms of tax incentives must be matched by investor commitment to clean tech solutions and innovations as the change to a low-carbon economy cannot be sustained without financial funding and sufficient economic stimuli. These innovations such as modern wind turbines, biomass/combined heat power (CHP) generators, wave technology, carbon capture and storage (CCS), geoengineering, and controversial nuclear energy reveal the possibilities that can be explored to assist the United Kingdom and the world in not only meeting its energy security needs but also achieving its climate change targets [20]. New approaches such as geothermal engineering appeal on a cognitive level as a useful tool, but the prospect of "artificial trees" that capture carbon dioxide may generate some apprehension [20]. However, the consequences of not abating carbon emissions outweigh any concerns of utilizing man-made engineering solutions to answer the questions and deal with the threats posed by climate change.

The philosophical underpinning of the **Sustainable Strategic Growth Model** also builds on views expressed in a Business of Sustainability Survey conducted by the Massachusetts Institute of Technology, which recommends that organizations adopt a systems thinking approach, form alliances with stakeholders, add scenario planning capabilities, measure capabilities, practice transparency, invest in sales, retool marketing and R&D, and critically determine when to partner to develop new models and management practices [21].

The model has influenced a new conceptual definition for **CSR** *as voluntary strategic initiatives that add value to the organization and society involving the pursuit of policies that promote good governance, prevent environmental degradation, and enhance the human spirit.*

The Sustainable Strategic Growth Model and definitions will be used to explore the implementation of sustainability footprints within four case studies of SMEs and the policymaking context that influences business strategy.

REFERENCES

[1]   White P. Building a sustainability strategy into the business. Corp Gov 2009;9(4):391, 393.

[2]   Lacy P, Arnott J, Lowitt E. The challenge of integrating sustainability into talent and organization strategies: investing in the knowledge, skills and attitudes to high performance. Corp Gov 2009;9(4):484–494.

[3] McDonough W, Braungart M. *Cradle to cradle: remaking the way we make things.* New York: North Point Press; 2002.

[4] Stahel WR. The product life factor. In: Orr SG, editor. *An Inquiry into the Nature of Sustainable Societies: The Role of the Private Sector* (Series: 1982 Mitchell Prize Papers). The Woodlands: HARC; 1984.

[5] Weizsacker von E, Hargroves K, Smith M, Desha C, Stasinopoulos P. *Factor Five: Transforming the Global Economy Through 80% Improvements in Resource Productivity.* Oxford: Earthscan; 2010.

[6] Flower J. Knowledge review: sustainable goes strategic. Strat Bus 2009;(54). Available at http://www.strategy-business.com/article/09110?pg=all. Accessed on Jun 30, 2014.

[7] Holland L. Can the principle of the ecological footprint be applied to measure the environmental sustainability of business. Corp Soc Responsib Environ Manage 2003;10:224–232.

[8] Villalonga B. Intangible resources, Tobin's q, and sustainability of performance differences. J Econ Behav Organ 2004;54(2):205–230.

[9] Enkvist P, Nauclér T, Oppenheim J. Business strategies for climate change. McKinsey Quart 2008;(2):24–33.

[10] Sampler J, Earl M. What's your information footprint? Sloan Manage Rev. Available at http://sloanreview.mit.edu/article/whats-your-information-footprint/?social_token=4c0 12ea4f371c8c49b702a810bf3f2d5&utm_source=twitter&utm_medium=social&utm_ campaign=sm-direct. Accessed on Dec 31, 2013.

[11] North Atlantic Treaty Organisation. The history of cyber attacks a timeline. Available at http://www.nato.int/docu/review/2013/Cyber/timeline/EN/index.htm. Accessed on Dec 29, 2013.

[12] Reuters. JPMorgan warns 450,000 card users on data loss after cyber attack. Available at http://www.reuters.com/article/2013/12/05/us-jpmorgan-dataexposed-idUSBRE9B405R20131205. Accessed on Dec 29, 2013.

[13] Scottish Environmental Protection Agency. Waste Electronic and Electrical Equipment. Available at http://www.sepa.org.uk/waste/waste_regulation/producer_responsibility/weee. aspx. Accessed on Dec 29, 2013.

[14] Finn M, Rahl G, Rowe Jr W. Unrecognized assets. Strat Bus Autumn 2006. Available at http://www.strategy-business.com/article/06301?pg=all. Accessed on Jun 30, 2014.

[15] Department of Environment Food and Rural Affairs (DEFRA). Car product roadmaps. Available at http://www.defra.gov.uk/environment/business/products/roadmaps/cars.htm. Accessed on Jan 7, 2013.

[16] Institute of Environmental Management and Assessment, Special Report on GHG Management 2010. Available at http://www.iema.net/iema-special-reports. Accessed on Jun 30, 2014.

[17] Tibbs H. How green is my value chain. Strat Bus October 2007. Available at http://www. strategy-business.com/article/li00048?gko=42bf7. Accessed on Jun 30 2014.

[18] Oskarsson K, Von Malmborg F. Integrated management systems as a corporate response to sustainable development. Corp Soc Responsib Environ Manage 2005;12: 121–128.

[19] Hart S, Milstein M. Global sustainability and the creative destruction of industries. MIT Sloan Manage Rev 1999;41:23–33.

[20] Jolly A, editor. *Clean Tech, Clean Profits.* London: Kogan Page; 2010.

[21] Hopkins M. Long-viewed, see through, collaborative and retooled. MIT Sloan Manage Rev 2009;51(1):46.

[22] Department of Environment Food and Rural Affairs (DEFRA). The contribution that reporting of greenhouse gas emissions makes to the UK meeting its climate change objectives: a review of the current evidence [online]. Available at http://archive.defra.gov.uk/environment/business/reporting/pdf/corporate-reporting101130.pdf. Accessed on Jan 7, 2013.

6

THE POLITICS OF SUSTAINABILITY

6.1 INTRODUCTION

This chapter describes the policymaking climate under which each case study organization operates. Background information on each policymaking institution is provided as well as statements from key policymakers or advisors, which provide insight into the philosophical, cultural, and strategic context of sustainability footprint implementation within Scotland.

Scotland, the cradle of capitalist thinking as espoused by intellectual giants such as Adam Smith, now stands at the crest of a new wave of ecoinnovations such as wind energy, wave energy, tidal energy, and carbon capture and storage (CCS). This hive of scientific and industrial endeavor is supported by robust government statutory initiatives [1] such as the Climate Change (Scotland) Act 2009, which aims to cut Scotland's greenhouse gas (GHG) emissions by setting an interim 42% reduction target for 2020, with the legislative power for this to be adjusted based on expert advice, and an 80% reduction target for 2050. The act requires that the Scottish Government set annual targets for the period 2010–2050 with the stipulation that continued reductions are 3% lower than the previous year from 2020 onward [2]. The Scottish Government is leading this transition to a low-carbon economy by enshrining the requirement for regular reporting of GHG emission performance by public bodies. The Environmental Economic Analysis Unit provides environmental data such as GHG emissions to allow Scottish ministers to make informed decisions as to

Sustainability Footprints in SMEs: Strategy and Case Studies for Entrepreneurs and Small Business, First Edition. Lowellyne James.

their achievement of emission reduction targets. The collection and analysis of Scotland's GHG emissions have become part of the Environmental Economic Analysis Unit's remit since 2008. As an adviser to the Scottish Government, the Head of the Environmental Economic Analysis Unit was interviewed, and responses were analyzed to provide insight as to the policymaking perception within the Scottish Government regarding the use of sustainability footprint tools within industry.

The policymaking landscape is also influenced by two other organizations: the Scottish Environmental Protection Agency (SEPA) and Scottish Business in the Community (SBC).

6.1.1   SEPA

The SEPA is an environmental body established by the Environment Act 1995 to regulate and monitor activities relating to Scotland's environment. Philosophically, the SEPA as an organization views itself as part of a long history of attempts to protect the environment that began with the 1388 Act of the realm in the reign of King Richard II [3]. Since its inception, the organization has assumed the mantle for promoting environmental best practices by publishing an environmental report [4]. Unsurprisingly, the SEPA [4] has actively measured its carbon emissions since 1997.

To gain insight into SEPA's policymaking approach to carbon footprint measurement, an interview was conducted with the Head of Environmental Strategy. The Head of Environmental Strategy oversees a team that provides a "horizon scanning service" that assists the SEPA with developing strategy to combat future challenges such as sustainability, human health, climate change, energy consumption, and renewable energy.

6.1.2   SBC

The SBC [5] views itself as Scotland's champion for better business practices. Established in 1982, this Prince's Trust organization has as its mission *Building better business for a better Scotland* by creating consensus within the business community for the adoption of sustainable business practices. One of the organization's key initiatives is the Mayday Network—a collection of businesses engaged in taking action on climate change. Since 2007, the Mayday Network has encouraged voluntary annual reporting of GHG emissions by its 3800+ member organizations.

The Chief Executive Officer and the Head of the Environment of SBC were both interviewed to ascertain the organizational policy regarding carbon footprint measurement.

Interviews were conducted with key policymakers from the Scottish Government, SEPA, and SBC and later transcribed with perceptual views detailed in the narrative of this chapter. The interviewees are policymakers with practical experience in the collection and analysis of carbon footprint data and are therefore able to express relevant views regarding the challenges and critical success factors involved in carbon footprint measurement. This practical element of their experience as policymakers bolsters the validity of their statements:

As Chief Executive… Well I just facilitate and encourage the internal team allow them the time to focus on it and encourage good results.

(CEO [11])

I am kind of I guess responsible for putting it all together.

(Head of Environment [6])

We do the carbon footprint of the budget internally so we collect all the information ourselves on emissions and the input–output tables. When we commission it is mainly provision of consumption data that is required for the contractor to do their work.

(Head of the Economic Analysis Unit [7])

It is through the externally validated route so we will gather together the various pieces of information we need and send all that into our report and I guess another way which we contribute is that we feedback to people like DEFRA and others what we think of their standardized approaches.

(Head of Environmental Strategy [8])

6.2 BACKGROUND

Uniquely, Scotland is pioneering the use of "consumption-based" emission methodology [9]. Consumption-based emission methodology involves the calculation of emissions arising from the consumption of goods and services from Scottish nationals wherever they occur in the world as opposed to only "production" emissions, which are generated within Scottish territory [9]. The use of the consumption-based emissions is enshrined within the Climate Change (Scotland) Act [10] 2009 and is the main methodology employed to calculate Scotland's carbon emissions. In practice, it involves the application of the environmentally extended input–output analysis method that takes into account not only trade volumes and full life cycle impacts but also the embodied energy impacts of raw materials within supply chains [10]. Both Scotland's carbon footprint and ecological footprint are used as national indicators [10].

Official figures indicate that Scottish GHG emissions for 2009 were 52 million ton CO_2e—a reduction of 27.6% using 1990 as a base year [1]. The business sector accounted for 13.2% of Scotland's GHG emissions [2]. Significantly, the business sector accounts for all sulfur hexafluoride (SF_6) emissions, 68.5% of hydrofluorocarbon (HFC) emissions, and 98.3% of perfluorocarbon (PFC) emissions [2]. Despite these pioneering efforts, there is a perception articulated by the government that Scotland's carbon footprint is a separate variable that does not impact on Scotland's economic growth, while the majority of policymakers view the carbon footprint measurement as essential to encourage business to adopt best practice:

We are very conscious of trying to manage our own emissions because it is very important to the scheme of things to try and show what can be done, to show leadership and to explore and show real approaches.

(Head of Environmental Strategy [8])

> I do not see quite the connection between the carbon footprint and Scotland's economic
> future. I think they are quite independent of one another.
>
> (Head of the Environmental Economic Analysis Unit [7])

Policymakers agree on the overall importance of carbon footprint measurement, yet experiences among policymaking institutions in the measurement, management, and reporting of carbon emissions vary with the SEPA [4] being a pioneer initiating carbon emission reporting in 1997. The Scottish Government began actively measuring and reporting carbon emissions in 2008 closely followed by the SBC whose carbon emission reporting program was initiated a year later in 2009:

> We did this in 2008 for the first time. Yes, it's fairly new.
>
> (Head of the Environmental Economic Analysis Unit [7])

Although fundamentally *sustainability positive* in regard to the impact of carbon emissions on Scotland's economic future, there is some uncertainty expressed regarding the importance of carbon footprint measurement to SMEs:

> Hard to tell I don't know how far people will become or will make their decisions... their
> consumption decisions on the carbon friendliness of the products, it's still up in the air.
>
> (Head of the Environmental Economic Analysis Unit [7])

> It is critical it is not up for question anymore it is not a nice to do, it is a must happen but
> it is something that has still got a way to go in terms of the SMEs understanding and
> I still think we have got work to do in Scotland in positioning it as a bottom line asset.
>
> (Chief Executive Officer [11])

Similar opinions are expressed by interviewees when considering the contribution of SME emission reduction programs to Scottish Government GHG emission targets. Public sector policymakers disagree, with some preferring tailored approaches to suit the SME sector, while other government representatives suggesting methodological issues as barriers to implementation. Nongovernmental policymakers are in favor of SME emission reporting due to their influence in the economy accounting for 99% of all businesses, thereby making SMEs the norm rather than the exception when viewed from an economic perspective:

> To Scotland's carbon footprint measurement exercise... Well SMEs are 60% of the
> workforce or 40% one or the other and 99% of businesses so in terms of business emis-
> sions there is a huge role that SMEs can play in reducing business emissions.
>
> (Head of Environment [6])

> I think by SMEs using these systems it would help the assessors and people who pro-
> duce these systems come up with better suited more proportionate approaches for
> smaller companies. That is what it is all about, no point is it to take something that
> works for IBM and give it to a local printing company you have got to tailor it.
>
> (Head of Environmental Strategy [8])

The perceived centrality of importance of carbon footprint measurement to the success of the Scottish economy has led to the adoption of carbon footprint and ecological footprint methodology to the exclusion of other techniques such as water footprint and social footprint among policymaking institutions. In respect to nongovernmental organizations (NGOs), there is expressed concern as to the difficulty in determining the boundaries of their social footprint because it forms the foundations of their organization's business:

> Well we did also measure the ecological footprint in the same round as we had the carbon footprint calculated.
> (Head of the Environmental Economic Analysis Unit [7])

> We don't measure our water footprint at all.
> (Head of Environment [6])

The pursuit of carbon footprint measurement within policymaking institutions is influenced by legal requirements, senior management commitment, stakeholder expectations, and best practice leadership. There is apprehension among government policymakers that the reductions in domestic carbon emissions may detract from efforts to tackle the export of carbon emissions as a result of manufacturing being transferred to emerging economies and importation of water through the consumption of imported agricultural and forestry products:

> For all those reasons we were saying earlier because we had a commitment to reduce because other people expect us to…senior managers wanted us to… our staff expect us to and because we want to show leadership for all these different reasons.
> (Head of Environmental Strategy [8])

> It is in the law and because it is clear that reducing the production footprint alone may not be the be all and end all on reducing our impact on climate change.
> (Head of the Environmental Economic Analysis Unit [7])

Interviewees suggest SMEs are motivated to pursue carbon footprint measurement for mainly commercial reasons to show corporate responsibility and help customers make better informed decisions and for resource efficiency, cost reduction, supply chain pressure, and commitment to climate change:

> To allow its customers to make better informed decisions and to show corporate responsibility and to manage its resources or its resource use better.
> (Head of the Environmental Economic Analysis Unit [7])

> Either because they are committed to climate change the whole agenda and or they want to save money.
> (CEO [11])

The long-term Scottish Government strategy is the development of a low-carbon economy; this policy shift was defined by Ian Marchant, Chair of the 20:20 Climate Group, as *"Low carbon is a way of thinking, behaving and operating that minimizes carbon emissions while enabling sustainable use of resources, economic growth and quality of life improvements"* [12]. Global economies are still reeling from the effects of sluggish economic growth as a result of the recent financial crisis. Public sector policymakers are convinced that there is a derived positive impact on the carbon footprint of their organization as a result of existing economic conditions. Interviewees at the SBC, an NGO, however consider economic conditions as having negligible impact on the carbon footprint of their operations:

> I would have expected it to have gone down simply by reducing production both at home and consumption of imported goods.
>
> (Head of the Environmental Economic Analysis Unit [7])

> I don't think you can actually say the economic environment has affected our own internal carbon footprint.
>
> (CEO [11])

There is however consensus among interviewees that prevailing economic conditions have impacted on the carbon footprint of SMEs either through reduced productive activity, climate change, increased recycling cost, or linkages between high-carbon emissions and resource consumption. This *"sustainability positive"* outlook is tempered by awareness that management of some SMEs may consider carbon footprint measurement a luxury or an unnecessary activity outside of their core business:

> Again my impression would be that there are two tensions the sort of risk as market conditions decline and everything gets tighter companies jettison everything that are not core so presumably there are companies out there who are cutting back on sustainability and carbon footprints because they think it's a luxury."
>
> (Head of Environmental Strategy [8])

The challenging financial constraints created by stringent government economic policies within the new "Age of Austerity" [13] have imposed hardships on public sector bodies both directly and indirectly. The effect of government policies on charitable funding to NGOs such as the SBC has made cost reduction a critical management issue among policymakers [13]. These factors have not deterred policymaking institutions from pursuing carbon footprint measurement as part of their organizational strategy. Interviewees state that carbon footprint measurement costs can range in some instances from £20,000–£200,000 for public sector organizations to less than £1,000 for NGOs:

> Cost SBC. That's a good question we probably spend... we have had three of us at least working through it ....under a thousand pounds.
>
> (Head of the Environment [6])

> We commissioned the carbon footprint from 1996–2006 and that cost about £15000 and added to that would be... I am not sure just thinking about that how we do it and who does it will cost between ten to twenty thousand pounds per year.
>
> (Head of the Environmental Economic Analysis Unit [7])

In the case of public sector interviewees, the need for verification and validation of carbon footprint data may have ameliorated concerns of cost, reducing any apprehensions regarding the use of consultancy support and assistance. The SBC as an NGO however captures environmental data and analyzes carbon footprint performance using internal resources within the organization:

> No, it is verified in so far as it is an independent institute doing it for us so we have not done it ourselves and the Stockholm Environmental Institute is a well-respected academic institution.
>
> (Head of the Environmental Economic Analysis Unit [7])

> There is this ISO 14001 Audit as I mentioned they would require us if they so choose to go into the books and say "so show me" and they have done that sometimes the main route is this annual report called "Greening SEPA" so we have our targets and then we report against them and we always have that externally validated. We appoint an independent company every year we usually tender for the work. It may be a different company but they have to be qualified auditors of some kind they will have some certification behind them and it is there job to basically make us justify every statement and we pay £5000 or more a year to get that done.
>
> (Head of Environmental Strategy [8])

The ability of public sector policy advisers to communicate reliable data to stakeholder groups such as government ministers and NGOs necessitates the need to rely on assistance from external consultants due to the lack of specialist technical expertise in GHG assurance and validation:

> Well could do it ourselves but the quality would have been slightly lower… that is because this Input–Output analysis is very specialized and we can do it for Scotland but we don't have the information for the emissions that arise abroad or the Input—Output tables of our trade partners which you need in order to do a comprehensive analysis so we could have done a footprint based on UK & Scottish Input—Output tables which would have given us a footprint similar to the one we got from SEI the Stockholm Environment Institute who did the work for us but we opted for an independent body to do it for us and to rely on their expertise and the information they have got at hand about foreign emissions and foreign Input—Output tables.
>
> (Head of the Environmental Economic Analysis Unit [7])

However, third-party assistance is considered essential to assist SMEs in collating information on energy consumption, determining the level of Scope 3 emissions, and developing capability to conduct carbon footprint measurements in-house. This structured "*quality assurance*" approach is not universally accepted as the only solution; a "*light-touch*" intuitive approach using online calculators with support from the government using incentives; technical support from organizations such as the Carbon Trust, Business Gateway, and Zero Waste Scotland; and the knowledge of environmental students is postulated as an alternative mechanism for building GHG measurement capability among SMEs:

I think they should, I am not totally convinced it should be a quality assurance route all the time or if it is it has to be a light touch one but certainly having simple tool and having the assistance of the Carbon Trust or Zero Waste Scotland or whoever it is a very good idea... it should be embedded within Business Gateway, the local authorities and enterprise companies.

(Head of Environmental Strategy [8])

I think they probably need too until they understand all the issues that relate to this... Well actually there are three phases the first phase is for SMEs to start collecting properly their information on energy consumption.....The second phase is about including scope 3 emissions and that is where I think they need more support..... The third stage if they understand how that works they can do that themselves and in conjunction with everyone else doing it the information becomes available on scope three through product footprints much more easily... they would be able to do the whole footprint in-house.

(Head of the Environmental Economic Analysis Unit [7])

6.3   CHALLENGES: TRANSITIONING TO A LOW-CARBON ECONOMY

The transition to a low-carbon economy presents Scotland with the opportunity to gain competiveness in the newly emerging global green economy but also assists in the development of effective mitigation measures against its exposure to climate change and energy costs in a carbon-constrained world [12]. If unabated, the risks arising from climate change and increased energy costs may create a scenario involving [12]:

- The loss of public access to clean, safe water either through the flooding of infrastructure or drought
- Damage and disruption to communication and transport systems as a result of flooding or adverse weather events
- Inability to provide services during adverse weather conditions that will become more frequent due to climate change
- Increased cost of raw materials and instability in global financial markets

To manage these potential risks, public sector organizations have instituted carbon management policies aligned to achieving the carbon reduction targets stipulated in the Climate Change (Scotland) Act 2009. The SBC has not developed a formal policy regarding carbon footprint measurement but has enshrined a commitment to operate sustainably as part of the Prince's Trust:

CSR Group who look at all our internal sustainability policies we do not have a formal policy we have a commitment to work as sustainable as we can.

(CEO [11])

Yes, absolutely it is direct emissions at the minute but you can go on our website and you will see our policy. It is written into our standard approaches, it is written into our values and one of our values is the environment obviously. It is written into our staff objectives our training program and our core competencies for staff. It is externally validated and reported monthly and quarterly to the corporate management team and board. I would say it is pretty much now embedded in terms of carbon with the one caveat that it is not the full picture... it is the direct emissions part.

(Head of Environmental Strategy [8])

SBC's carbon footprint policy approach may be due to the lack of stakeholder interest in carbon footprint measurement despite attempts to foster stakeholder engagement. The SEPA due to its role as Scotland's environmental regulator has its carbon performance subjected to regular media scrutiny, while the Scottish Government's key policymaker perceives a lack of awareness among its stakeholder base:

I don't think I have ever been asked once about our own internal sustainability policies and our footprint.

(CEO [11])

Policymakers hold divergent views on the value of formal carbon footprint policies with SBC and Scottish Government advisers not only advocating universal adoption by all SMEs supported by suitable advice but also considering carbon footprint policy development as a desirable activity with SEPA's policymaker preferring a targeted sector-specific approach:

I don't know if they perceive a need for it but I think from a policy perspective it would be desirable to simply foster more awareness of the carbon consequences both for the producer as well as the consumer.

(Head of the Environmental Economic Analysis Unit [7])

I would like to say 'Yes' that would be a bit disproportionate maybe it should be more targeted. The government should be more involved or maybe SEPA should be giving a lot more advice to the companies that should have and then for everybody else it should be an option.

(Head of Environmental Strategy [8])

The deployment of carbon footprint policy to the supply chain varies among policy-making institutions with the SBC requiring membership of their Mayday Network, a voluntary emission reporting scheme as a contractual prerequisite. Public sector policymakers however adopt a flexible approach requiring evidence of environmental policy statements and commitment to future implementation of carbon footprint measurement as part of the prequalification questionnaire:

We do not have that many suppliers, to be honest and it has not been that huge focus. In terms of our cleaners MITIE they are a member company so I am well aware of their CSR agenda because we helped them with it.... any of our suppliers if they are big enough we would ask if they want to work with us we are not big enough really to have a policy but obviously but in terms of office supplies cleaning it's good to have member companies that we know who are committed to CSR.

(Head of Environment [6])

That is a live issue for us, we certainly require them to show us their environmental policy for what they are doing but at the minute we do not require that but it is certainly on our list. I think what we will do as part of our future targets is an assessment of our buying goods and services and then from that the major ones that cause impact and ask them to provide some data to us some would anyway because they have the data but it is not systematic at the minute.

(Head of Environmental Strategy [8])

At a macroeconomic level, carbon emission reduction is perceived as a key factor that is supported by behavioral change in terms of consumption and resource efficiency [12]. This is also reflected at an institutional level whereby carbon footprint reduction is also a key issue that is discussed at management meetings by both SBC and SEPA policy advisers; however, the government key policy adviser contends that the use of carbon footprints is only a tool that provides the context within which product-based emissions can be understood:

The key issue is to reduce our production based emissions the carbon footprint puts that into context and makes us realize that we have not been successful in driving down our global emissions impact.

(Head of the Environmental Economic Analysis Unit [7])

Policymakers agree that carbon footprint reduction should be on the management agenda of SMEs along with other sustainability indicators. Using this balanced approach, SMEs can fully contribute to the Scottish Government's targets for carbon reduction and transitioning to a low-carbon economy:

Ideally yes I think that would be very helpful to support the government's aims to meet its emissions reduction targets.

(Head of the Environmental Economic Analysis Unit [6, 7])

Would we like it too absolutely, but not just carbon it is quite narrow I do not think it should be carbon necessarily it could be on the environment more generally also the social impact of what the business is doing should be on the agenda. So we are looking at real triple bottom-line reporting on the agenda.

(Head of the Environment [8])

However, the environmental and climate change movement in the view of some policymakers has not engendered itself to business by the use of terminology and jargon such as *"carbon footprint"* and *"low carbon"* are concepts that are inherently alien to traditional business lexicon of *"pounds, pence, and shillings"* or *"dollars and cents."* Language itself is perceived as a barrier that creates a veil of exclusivity to an altogether invisible subject. This may necessitate a cultural shift within the business community in general and SMEs in particular as well as overcoming traditional barriers such as cost, lack of information, time pressure, and resource constraints:

> I think it is similar to our barriers part of it is knowing the opportunities, part of it is having the tools, the information available to decide how to proceed, I think the biggest one though is the issue that faces all SMEs... is time pressure.
>
> (Head of Environmental Strategy [8])

> I think one of the barriers we have not talked about is language. I think another one of the barriers is that your normal SME your average business will see climate change or whatever element within climate change whether its environmental or carbon or whatever is shared as an area that is owned by policy makers scientists, eco-warriors and economists.
>
> (CEO [11])

The view from within policymaking institutions is diverse with the government key policy adviser perceiving limited barriers to carbon footprint measurement except for the conundrum of dealing with consumption-based emissions over which there is little influence. Consumption-based emissions are the equivalent of Scope 3 emissions within DEFRA's GHG emission guidance. The reporting of Scope 3 emissions by SMEs is perceived by the key government policy adviser as challenging but only really useful if measured by a vast majority of SMEs. Interviewees from the SEPA and the SBC infer that internal barriers mirror that of SMEs in terms of resource constraints, cost, lack of information, and time pressure but uniquely differ in areas such as target setting and "initiative overload" of employee schedules:

> Another barrier is initiative overload so even for an environmental agency there is only so much change and new initiative someone can take there is so much resistance initially "Oh there is another thing that I have got to do". So this is in a nutshell understanding what our contribution should be, finding the most cost effective solutions putting in place data and systems to support people to change, then constant reinforcement of the message that this was not going to go away and to engage with them.
>
> (Head of Environmental Strategy [8])

6.4   CONTRIBUTIONS TO GROWTH

Scotland's low-carbon and environmental goods and services (LCEGS) sector estimated at £8.8 billion in 2007–2008 is expected to grow to 12 billion by 2014–2016 or 10% of the Scottish GDP [9]. An estimated 50% of LCEGS sales are expected to occur in subsectors such as sustainable buildings with opportunities for sales in green tourism and timber construction [12]. The ability of carbon footprint measurement to stimulate innovation and contribute to the development of new products and services is universally accepted among interviewees, and these benefits are not only perceived as accruing exclusively to policymaking institutions but also SMEs:

> I think understanding of the barriers and obstacles to carbon footprint and environmental engagement. We are certainly developing mechanisms and tools so for us it has

enabled us to understand what mechanisms we can produce for our members we doing some quite exciting and innovative work in that area.

(CEO [11])

Well we are assessing our budget in the same way as the carbon footprint is being calculated so we can use input–output analysis and emission intensities for all industries in order to estimate basically the carbon footprint of our spending proposals to give parliament an understanding of the emissions consequences of public spending.

(Head of the Environmental Economic Analysis Unit [7])

I would expect that carbon footprint would lead to improved decision making and greater awareness about different options to reduce emissions within the company by changing processes or changing suppliers.

(Head of the Environment [6])

Distilleries again used to take the waste and had to pay for it to go to land fill or pay for it to go to a farmer's field and then the carbon pressure comes along and they say why can't we use this as a fuel? Can we use this as a renewable resource? Can we turn this into bio-butanol? Definitely a new service and there are other examples where the things that were wasted are an actual resource that we can sell.

(Head of Environmental Strategy [8])

Interviewees from public sector policymaking institutions indicate that their stakeholders have expressed an interest in their carbon footprint. This experience differs in regard to the SBC whose stakeholders are passively indifferent:

Yes they are very keen on us producing this type of footprint information mainly the carbon footprint.

(Head of the Environmental Economic Analysis Unit [7])

No, absolutely not.

(CEO [11])

There is unanimity of perception regarding the generation of interest for the goods and services produced by SMEs through the participation in environmental award schemes such as the Vision in Business for the Environment of Scotland (VIBES) by enhancing customer ability to influence management decision making by purchasing low-carbon or environmentally friendly products and services, supply chain pressure from large customers to adopt carbon reduction policies, a differentiating factor in purchasing decisions, a proxy for good management performance, unique selling proposition (USP) for products and services, improve SME competiveness and reduced risk of environmental noncompliance. These benefits of carbon footprint measurement are perceived as also accruing naturally to SME firms although varying by sector:

Yes I think can it can be very well become an USP for an SME if its products are very low carbon and it is produced sustainably. Yes in the first instance it might be something for them to raise their competiveness in the market.

(Head of Environmental Economic Analysis Unit [7])

> I think it is quite sector specific I think some sectors naturally there will be more of a divide as with the likes of Marks and Spencer, ASDAs.... what the retailers are doing for their suppliers and really pushing their suppliers in terms of sustainability so if you want to get on to the supply chain of those suppliers it is essential. In some other industries mainly in the professional services industries it is still important but maybe less important again depending your client base.
>
> (Head of Environment [8])

The drive to reduce GHG emissions embodied in the products and services consumed by the public has influenced the development of the Waste (Scotland) [14] Regulations 2012. Despite recovering from the effects of the global financial crisis, Scotland's devolved government launched an ambitious Zero Waste Plan on June 9, 2010. Scotland's Zero Waste Plan [15] hopes to achieve waste recycling rates of 70%, with 5% of waste going to a municipal landfill by 2025. The recent enactment of the Waste Information (Scotland) Regulations 2010 provides a clear indication of the intention of its lawmakers to influence business to efficiently manage the consumption of resources. Parallel to the ratification of environmental legislation are a rise in carbon emission reporting by organizations and the proliferation of voluntary carbon reporting schemes. The SEPA participates in two major voluntary reporting programs: the Local Authority Management program and the World Wildlife Fund (WWF) One in Five Challenge [3, 4]. Through participation in the One in Five Challenge, the SEPA has reduced business flights by 48% and emissions by more than 90 tons, saving £100,000 in travel costs during 2009–2010, which is equivalent to a 50% reduction in travel expenditure. The SBC discloses carbon performance through its Mayday Network reporting scheme, while the Scottish Government conveys GHG emission performance as part of the United Kingdom's overall carbon emission report. Although benefits such as best practice leadership and stakeholder awareness are derived from participating in carbon footprint reporting schemes, these are not perceived by some policymakers as being substantial:

> Often we are doing it from a leadership point of view to try and encourage others with often not huge benefits to ourselves because we understand our mission quite well by showing others what we've done it and showing others it can be done.
>
> (Head of Environmental Strategy [6])
>
> Just through the Mayday Network.
>
> (Head of Environment [8])

Policymakers however agree that reporting schemes are beneficial to SMEs but their perceptions differ regarding the approach, that is, mandatory or voluntary. Nongovernmental policymakers contend that SMEs are confused due to the proliferation of reporting schemes with an accompanying bureaucracy of varying reporting requirements that has a potential of creating an administrative burden. Policy advisers within the Scottish Government are biased toward SME participation in reporting schemes as the process of reporting may improve the quality of their carbon footprint analysis:

> Should a business of ten have to go through a reporting scheme I am not convinced... I am not sure it depends what the reporting scheme is I think in CSR and sustainability overall there is a lot of reporting schemes.
>
> (Head of Environment [6])

> In so far as these reporting schemes improve the quality of the analysis.
>
> (Head of Environmental Economic Analysis Unit [7])

Divergent views are expressed by interviewees regarding the benefits of participating in reporting schemes, yet their representative policymaking institutions routinely produce carbon footprint reports. Scottish Government agencies consider carbon footprint reports as directed to external stakeholders differing from SBC policymakers who regard carbon footprint reporting as directed mainly at internal stakeholders:

> Well it is for external reporting really it's to allow anyone the public the NGOs to understand where we're at... We have produced the carbon footprint as well as the ecological footprint. It's part of a performance information framework.
>
> (Head of the Environmental Economic Analysis Unit [7])

> Our own reports are primarily internal as I said we've never been asked externally before but we need to be accountable as a Princes Charity we represent a brand we need to be accountable for it... We would not push it out there probably we like it better that way as we still got work to do we're still developing it and I think it's important we are keen to share with SMEs because we understand the challenges ourselves and that's the most important thing that you can share your own challenges which sometimes creates a safe environment for a good conversation.
>
> (CEO [11])

Disagreement exists as to the approaches SMEs should adopt regarding carbon footprint reporting with the Scottish Government policy adviser preferring a phased approach initially targeting carbon footprint reports to internal stakeholders to enable them to improve resource efficiency and optionally reporting their progress in areas such as product carbon footprints to external stakeholders. Alternatively, the SEPA advocates external reporting utilizing a sector-specific approach to create competitive advantage and to satisfy supplier expectation with the aspiration that all Scottish SMEs should measure their carbon footprint. Policymakers at the SBC recommend carbon reporting for SMEs especially for procurement and contract bidding purposes if the methodologies used are honest and robust, thereby acting as an employee engagement tool supporting sustainable behaviors and best practices:

> That as a minimum there should be certain sectors where there is a competitive advantage or a supplier expectation that they report so those ones as a minimum should

report externally… Hotels and Tourism businesses and those businesses which sell to Tesco and other major retailers or those industries that are a major source of carbon.

(Head of Environmental Strategy [8])

It depends how good it is as I mean we've said they should use it for procurement and contract bidding if it's sound and honest and measurable but they should also use it to engage their employees around those behaviors that create good practice about carbon measurement.

(CEO [11])

Despite enthusiasm for carbon footprint reporting only, the SBC requires suppliers and subcontractors to participate in its Mayday Network as part of their supplier/ subcontractor prequalification process. The SEPA requires both their suppliers and subcontractors to provide environmental policy statements, while the Scottish Government is considering the use of carbon assessments as part of their supplier/ subcontractor prequalification process:

Well we are looking at options of doing that we are including some kind of carbon assessment into our procurement decisions but it has to be done in a fair manner not all of our contractors have the capability with providing us that sort of information we have to find ways of enabling them to provide information.

(Head of the Environmental Economic Analysis Unit [7])

Public sector policymakers are acutely aware that supply chain pressures to meet the demands of large retail customers such as Tesco, Marks & Spencer, and B&Q are forcing SMEs to report carbon emissions with the Scottish Government adopting a practical view as to the feasibility of SMEs to influence companies within their supply chain to report their carbon footprint emissions. Nongovernmental policy-makers advocate that SMEs adopt a flexible approach factoring in price concerns, which may involve a balancing act between cost, social and environmental issues:

Again I think it would be desirable but I do not think it is feasible.

(Head of the Economic Analysis Unit [7])

Yes, again certainly in the major industries and I think it is already happening at Marks & Spencer suppliers, B&Q, Tesco… I think absolutely a way to drive change if the people you supply require it. It makes you do it. I think it is really important.

(Head of Environmental Strategy [8])

Cost considerations and resource constraints do not deter interviewees from consid-ering carbon footprint measurement as a useful tool. Policymakers perceive carbon footprint measurement as a process management tool and performance indicator for providing a holistic view of carbon emissions and identifying areas of global impact and a useful mechanism for comparative analysis of carbon emissions:

We would certainly say so because if you cannot measure it you cannot manage it's simple… Yes absolutely.

(Head of Environmental Strategy [8])

I do think it's useful as it does remind us no matter how much we are able to reduce or no matter how successful we are at reducing our own footprint. We still have to be mindful that other countries have to do the same in order for us to be able reduce our global impact and it includes the impact we have through the imports we consume.

(Head of the Environmental Economic Analysis Unit [7])

There is also a shared understanding among policymakers that carbon footprint measurement is a useful tool for SMEs as a performance indicator, an evolutionary mechanism for SMEs to measure Scope 3 carbon emissions, and a tool for SMEs to reduce Scopes 1 and 2 carbon emissions. Policymakers from the SBC suggest that the SMEs that do not pursue carbon footprint measurement may not realize benefits such cost savings, innovation, and supply chain efficiency:

I think carbon footprint measurement is very useful for SMEs because if they are not measuring it they are not going to reduce it. Simple as that if you are not measuring it you are not reducing it you are not reporting it then you lose all the benefits surrounding having sound environmental policies and action. Whether that is pure cost savings, innovation or whether it is up the supply chain.

(CEO [11])

6.5   CRITICAL SUCCESS FACTORS

The Scottish Government is keen to apply carbon measurement techniques to identify opportunities to reduce the adverse impact of waste on the environment and its contribution to climate change in addition to using traditional quantitative measures, for example, weight in the analysis of its waste management performance [14].

A key to achieving this societal step change is a policymaking shift in viewing waste not as cost but as revenue. Policymakers lack unison regarding their adoption of carbon footprint measurement as a key performance indicator (KPI):

No, but it is one piece of information it's not a performance indicator as such.

(Head of Environmental Economic Analysis Unit [7])

Interviewees agree that the carbon footprint is a useful KPI for SMEs who require support from the U.K. Government and trade bodies regarding the setting of emission targets intimating that carbon footprint measurement can also improve the management of energy use and be a motivating influence for the adoption of sustainable practices when included in job descriptions:

I think that they should have targets it is always useful. I think when you are managing employees you got to assume they are not part of this they don't get it, let's assume that most employees don't get it you will have targets are good. I think it's good to make a KPI part of the senior manager or middle manager's KPIs because that will feed down the line.

(CEO [11])

Yes, certainly as a minimum for those sectors that is important for Carbon Emissions. Ideally for everybody but certainly for those sectors where it is a key priority.

(Head of Environmental Strategy [8])

Due to this view of carbon footprint reduction being a useful KPI, it necessitates the setting of achievable emission reduction targets. However, target setting has not been explicitly adopted by the Scottish Government and SBC for their emissions, but the SEPA has established formal emission reduction targets aligned to the Climate Change Act. As an NGO, the SBC is challenged to decouple its growth as a membership body from its carbon emissions, a large proportion of which arise from business travel:

No that has been our target... that's been informal as being part of the Mayday Network and everything else. That was our target there... where we are we have got a number of challenges without going into too much detail about our carbon footprint there are a number of challenges specifically about how they are made up and obviously our location of where we are so there are limited things that we can do. Our carbon footprint is quite small it's minimal in the grand scheme of things and yes we can reduce it by two or three tons and we have been reducing it by two or three tons. People still need to go to meetings in respect to the challenge that we have got is that the more members we have the higher our carbon footprint will probably become like as with any small business you need to start looking at absolute reduction or are you looking at decoupling your emissions basically from your business growth or not and that obviously is quite a challenge because from where we are... we encourage people to take the trains.

(Head of Environment [6])

SME carbon emission reduction targets are considered challenging due to a large proportion of SME carbon footprint being comprised of Scope 3 emissions, which are outside the control of individual SMEs. Carbon emission targets for Scope 1 and Scope 2 emissions or production-based emissions are considered by government policymakers as achievable. Nongovernmental policymakers consider employee "buy-in" and support, the review of the carbon impact of core processes, and the adoption of sustainable behaviors as prerequisites for the establishment of carbon footprint targets. These prerequisites in conjunction with government support in the determination of sector- or company-specific emission reduction targets are perceived as being adequate for SMEs:

Yes, I think it is a good thing to do to get all the staff bought into it but I think businesses if they set targets have to support their own employees.

(CEO [11])

It is very difficult to set targets because it is very difficult to set what is achievable. So you can set targets but they are relatively meaningless I think because we do not know what is actually achievable I think it is much more useful to put targets on what is within your control and much of the carbon footprint is outside your control and the Scottish

government. Scotland I think has put a target of what is in our control which is the production based emissions.

(Head of the Environmental Economic Analysis Unit [7])

Policymakers also agree that carbon footprint measurement and target setting help to
identify carbon emission sources and carbon impacts clarifying the link between
production- and consumption-based emissions:

Yes, absolutely because again it has forced us to just do more analysis on where the
impacts are. So five years ago I could not tell you the major components of our carbon
footprint now I can tell you whether you want to know what our impacts are, where they
are coming from and what we are doing about them.

(Head of Environmental Strategy [8])

The ability to measure and set GHG emission targets within a policymaking institutional context has contributed to an air of confidence that similar benefits that were
accrued by their organizations were also realizable within the SME operational environment inferring carbon footprint measurement can act as a catalyst for GHG
emission reduction, providing insight into harmful emission-producing activity or
processes, contributing to organizational effectiveness through the discipline of
reporting and target setting which are tools that identify emission sources and impacts:

I think it is an important piece of information especially in an environment where our
production based emissions are going down but somehow our consumption based emissions remain stubbornly constant. So we do have to realize that we are perhaps not as
performing as well as we think we are partly because more energy intensive industries
have relocated abroad or shut down shop here but we still demand their products so we
have to import them and it is partly to do with the fact that we are getting richer and
consuming more things.

(Head of the Economic Analysis Unit [7])

Although the focus of most footprint measurement initiatives has been on
identifying carbon-related impacts, policymakers are aware of other areas of
environmental impact. As organizational entities, policymaking institutions have
no plans to measure their water footprint and fail to understand the carbon
intensity of providing a fresh and clean water supply requiring a total of 450
gigawatt-hours of electricity annually accounting for 1.5% of Scotland's electricity
consumption [16]:

No, not at the minute it is something I would be interested in as we go forward. Certainly
there is the possibility but no firm plans at the minute in my mind.

(Head of Environmental Strategy [8])

For the core of Scottish Government you will find information on our water consumption. No … not at the moment, the problem is the data that you need to do something

similar to the carbon footprint is not really available so you need water use by industry and that is not collected.

(Head of Environmental Analysis Unit [7])

The Scottish Government policy adviser considers water footprint measurement to be a low priority on the policymaking agenda for the SME sector as Scotland has an abundance of water resources. While the SEPA policymakers prefer a sector-specific approach based on water consumption intensity, the SBC policymakers advocate an opportunistic approach based on the availability of resources such as finance, time, and labor to conduct water footprint measurement:

I think you can if you have the resources to do it… I think the only thing we did is that we removed the water cooler... we use tap water.

(CEO [11])

I do not think it is very high up on our policy agenda for SMEs but for the water footprint to be collected by SMEs is desirable. Simply because we have got plenty of water… yes it is a non-issue.

(Head of the Economic Analysis Unit [7])

The effective evaluation of social impact of sustainability footprint reporting is evolving. This is acknowledged by government policymakers who consider the methodologies for social footprint measurement to be multidimensional in comparison to carbon footprint methodologies. The multidimensional nature of social footprints and social impact analysis has made such measurement tools a lower priority on the policymaking agenda. As an NGO, the SBC policymakers perceive difficulty in separating social impacts from the operational aspects of the business due to its mission as a charity:

In terms of our social footprint that is interesting actually we measure the number of days but we have policies around how much staff volunteering is allowed and encouraged. We monitor how many people are taking up volunteering opportunities and getting into the community it is quite a challenge for us in many respects because it is what we do. So some days I do not know whether I am volunteering and do not report it or whether I am helping out on a program I was doing mentor training now that is having a big impact on the community, it is what we do. So defining what we do away from CSR is sometimes a challenge so it should be what we do which is a good thing.

(Head of Environment [6])

Social footprint has not been demanded to my knowledge either. I think carbon footprint lends itself to being calculated relatively easily using IO (input–output) Social footprint I am not entirely sure I will agree that there is a simpler way of doing that there are many more dimensions on the social side of things. Carbon is just one measure it is just one unit on the social side I think you can find that the issues are many fold and reducing that to a single number or to a single footprint does not do justice to the problem.

(Head of the Environmental Analysis Unit [7])

Public sector policymakers however recommend that SMEs measure their social impact using social footprint methodology conceding however that social footprint methodology is less well developed. SEPA policymakers are biased toward the implementation of water footprint measurement among SMEs because of the ethical and macroeconomic risk created by the importation of goods and services from emerging economies with limited water resource:

> I think the water one is very interesting I am not too sure about the social one. I do not know enough about it to comment maybe but the water one really does interest me in the sense. If we are exporting our carbon then we are certainly importing our water now that bothers me from an ethical point. So we are not only exporting the pollution but importing our water in the products and services we buy from countries that cannot afford it and I think that is an issue coming certainly for food. In Scotland it is certainly an issue in some of the products presumably some of the wood paneled products there must be an awful lot of embodied water coming from countries that could barely afford it. It is something that starts with the bigger companies again with the smaller ones too if we know about climate change it is going to drive water scarcity. It just does not seem right to have no understanding of that but policy in government is quite at an early stage.
>
> (Head of Environmental Strategy [8])

> Social Footprint possibly… I think that methodology for that might be less well developed than for carbon and water footprint and therefore less reliable but they should also think about the wider resource use, non-renewable materials they use in their production and how that is included in the material cycle.
>
> (Head of the Environmental Economic Analysis Unit [7])

The philosophical leaning of policymakers toward the promotion of carbon footprint measurement as the preferred tool for measuring environmental impact is their perceptual connection between carbon footprint reduction and combating climate change:

> Yes, clearly the higher your carbon footprint worst it is for climate change the less you have done about reducing your impact. If SMEs were mindful of their carbon footprint and were aiming to reduce it that would clearly feed through to the national footprint.
>
> (Head of the Environmental Economic Analysis Unit [7])

> Yes in the sense that we need to get the emissions down which means we need everybody to play their part which means we need to understand what is happening in each sector and the individual parts of each sector.
>
> (Head of Environmental Strategy [8])

This desire among policymakers to combat the effects of climate change has dictated their overall preference for carbon footprint measurement as an indicator. In a sense, they have developed a *"carbon myopic"* view to answering the challenges created by unabated climate change. Policymakers perceive carbon footprint measurement as a KPI that helps in the understanding of the impact of carbon emissions on a sector or country basis and a tool for reducing the impact of carbon emissions, providing benefits of reduced costs and resource efficiency:

Yes, although I do not know whether that is the primary motivation or whether it's rather the reduction costs that you get if you manage your resources in a more efficient manner with a beneficial effect on emissions.

(Head of the Environmental Economic Analysis Unit [7])

Yes because I think again if you don't measure it you don't manage it… if it is not one of your own key performance indicators it is one of those things that is always nice to have. Well if you understand your contribution to the bigger picture your sector, country surely that is going to help us all.

(Head of Environmental Strategy [8])

This *"carbon myopia"* is borne by a limited interpretation of sustainability in the policymaking arena and by extension of sustainability footprints, which has led to varying perspectives of sustainability footprints. Public sector policymakers' perceptions range from being unaware to interpretations that separate the concept of sustainability from the methodology or action of measurement in essence separating the qualitative philosophical elements from the quantitative techniques:

To me these are if you are saying sustainability you are trying to understand not just the environmental but the social and economic consequences of your activities. There is usually a dimension of ethics and fairness in it as well so thinking about our global to local impacts through time that this should be about decisions that affect the future as well as the present. Footprint implies to me quite a defined and measurable metric the difference to me between "footprint" and sustainability approaches is that I might have an approach which is quite high level and quite qualitative. When somebody says "footprint" to me it triggers into my mind standard methodologies as to approaches which deal with boundary issues, reporting and are usually quantified. So when I hear sustainability footprint it takes me down that route quantification measurement, metrics analysis rigor. In a way if I say sustainability approaches it could be a bit more qualitative.

(Head of Environmental Strategy [8])

Although policymaking institutions regularly focus on emission reduction and carbon footprint measurement as a tool in combating climate change, there is lack of consensus as to the feasibility of carbon footprint measurement as a good investment of organizations' resources mainly due to the inability to calculate a return on investment however nonfinancial benefits such as the ability to analyze carbon emission impacts, best practice leadership, adoption of sustainable behavior, employee retention, employee motivation and engagement:

Yes, I do think it is a good idea to have that information at hand and be able to analyze the impact of Scotland's consumption.

(Head of the Environmental Economic Analysis Unit [7])

I think it is important from pure cost investment but overall in terms of the other benefits employee motivation, retention, engagement.

(Head of Environment [8])

Policymakers within the public sector advise that firms tailor their carbon footprint methodology according to the firms' size and overall environmental impact with a "lighter"-touch approach for SMEs. Specifically measuring Scope 1 and Scope 2 emissions to identify potential efficiencies and gain value from the investment. Nongovernmental policymakers contend that value to SMEs is realizable depending on the efficiency and effectiveness of the implementation actions to reduce carbon emissions:

> I do not know it depends on how expensive it would turn out for them... I think doing scope one and two is a good investment probably because it does help you identify scope for efficiencies.
>
> (Head of the Environmental Economic Analysis Unit [7])

> I think for the smaller companies you can take a much lighter touch approach but you still got to take an approach.
>
> (Head of Environmental Strategy [8])

Public sector policymakers differ in terms of their view of the value of carbon footprint measurement to SMEs ranging from environmental awareness, carbon emission data that will inform decision making, increased market share, and innovation in goods and services to perceptions of carbon footprint measurement as a low-value-added activity when viewed in isolation in the macroeconomic context in relation to Scotland's GHG emissions. Nongovernmental policymakers adopt a pragmatic view as to the value of carbon footprint measurement to SMEs, which they contended must contribute to the bottom line and reduce carbon emissions and environmental impact:

> As we said the value it has got to give them is bottom line value and reducing their impact on carbon emissions and the environment.
>
> (CEO [8])

> I think it's what we talked about earlier again it is understanding, it is data to inform priorities, it is potentially market share, it is potentially innovative goods and services. All those things that can come from understanding.
>
> (Head of Environmental Strategy [11])

Although views regarding the value of sustainability footprint measurement vary among policymaking institutions, it is perceived that institutions are driven by the pursuit of sustainability footprint measurement tools such as the carbon footprint in order to receive the benefits of cost reduction; to meet customer requirements, carbon emission reduction, stakeholder expectations, and senior management commitment; and to encourage the adoption of sustainable behavior and teamwork, employee engagement, and best practice leadership:

> Well it is legislation and there is a policy interest simply to know and understand the wider context to the emissions reduction that we achieve within Scotland.
>
> (Head of the Environmental Economic Analysis Unit [7])

Policymakers perceive that SMEs are driven to measure their carbon footprint for similar reasons such as cost reduction, energy management, corporate social responsibility, procurement, employee engagement, brand leadership, marketing, customer requirements, senior management directive, staff morale, innovation, and graduate recruit expectations:

> Well again better management of energy, to bring about some cost savings and to demonstrate to their customers that they act sustainably.
>
> (Head of the Environmental Economic Analysis Unit [7])

> I think we have answered it cost, procurement and employee engagement.
>
> (CEO [11])

These drivers alone are ineffective to ensure that SMEs adopt carbon footprint measurement, a growing realization that has contributed to divergent views among public sector policymakers with the SEPA proposing a competitive landscape where policymaking institutions play an integral part in promoting best practices, inspection, advice, and guidance in establishing carbon emission targets and clarifying expectations. Although Scottish Government advisors infer the possibility of further carbon emission regulation, they imply that it is in the best interest of the SME sector to understand carbon footprint guidance and where necessary seek consultancy support suggesting SMEs should not expect government support as their focus is on reducing public sector emissions. The SBC as an NGO views their role as to represent its membership and when required provide support to SMEs by the secondment of university graduates to assist with carbon footprint measurement, critique government policy, and provide feedback to government regarding SME concerns and expectations:

> Primarily carbon footprint is voluntary and should be in the SMEs interest to undertake… There is plenty of guidance available if you want to do it. There are plenty of contractors available to do it we are supporting the rest of the public sector to account for their carbon but ultimately the responsibility of the private sector is to do what they need to do but what they find most important for them....
>
> (Head of the Environmental Economic Analysis Unit [7])

> On a more practical level... a more operational level we run programs for university students we put them through training then let them go in and measure SME carbon footprints so we do a lot in that field.
>
> (Head of Environment [6])

Carbon emission reduction is viewed by policymakers as a critical success factor for business in the future. Public sector policymakers perceive an indirect relationship between organizational success and carbon footprint measurement as the process of carbon emission reporting may lead to greater awareness of the need to collect and use performance information with the benefit of competitive advantage for Scotland as an economy through the efficient use of resources as commodity prices increase. The SBC advocates a focus on wider sustainability issues such as social impacts with carbon footprint measurement as one indicator of the sustainability performance. Although NGO policymakers imply that the benefits of improved organizational performance identified in FTSE 350 companies can be accrued by SMEs, full materialization of these benefits may be dependent on the industrial sector:

> Well I don't know. There might be an indirect relationship in that SMEs that look at their carbon emissions will or perhaps be more conscious of the need to collect the right management information and therefore be more successful. They might have a greater awareness of the need to collect and use performance information in managing a business so I could imagine the SMEs that collect this information now are generally better run.
>
> (Head of the Environmental Economic Analysis Unit [7])

6.6 SUMMARY

6.6.1 Cost Impact

Perceptions of cost impact and its effect on SMEs vary with the functional or strategic orientation of the policymaking unit or institution. Government policymaking frames *cost impact* within a macroeconomic shroud stating a disconnect between carbon footprint and Scotland's economic future but acknowledging a direct relationship between carbon footprint measurement and Scotland's economic growth due mainly to the perception of higher economic growth contributing to high GHG emissions. The extent to which SMEs can benefit from carbon footprint measurement in terms of *cost impact* is determined by the overall value customers place on the carbon friendliness of products and services as purchasing criteria.

As Scotland's environmental champions, SEPA policymakers consider carbon footprint measurement as providing business with an understanding of the relationship between costs and carbon impacts. The link between carbon pressures and cost pressures is apparent especially as it is understood that SMEs reallocate resources to core activities during declining economic conditions.

Membership of the Prince's Trust has relieved Scottish Business in the Community of the burden arising from cost pressures as a result of implementing carbon footprint measurement within the organization due to senior management commitment. However, from an operational perspective, they contend that SMEs must consider carbon footprint reporting as a resource but more specifically a bottom-line asset that contributes to growth and provides cost savings.

6.6.2 Innovation Impact

The Scottish Government through its program to measure Scotland's carbon emissions adapted the extended input–output analysis to carbon footprint measurement. Through the implementation of this *innovation*, the government gained a better understanding of the global impact of Scotland's economy in terms of the carbon emissions of Scotland's consumption activities. This enhanced understanding has contributed to the development of carbon performance benchmarks and the development of legally binding carbon reduction targets. Life cycle analysis and DEFRA methodology for carbon footprint measurement are perceived as useful tools that will engender innovation within SMEs. *Innovation impact* of carbon footprint measurement is viewed as yielding positive benefits for SMEs such as effective carbon policy through understanding the consequences of carbon decisions, measurement of product carbon footprint to inform customers, and recording and management of emissions and carbon footprint in itself creating a USP for SMEs. Government advisers postulate that carbon measurement is a useful management tool for SMEs that builds awareness of environmental impacts, helps its customers make better decisions, and promotes competiveness, good resource management, and corporate responsibility.

At the SEPA, there has been a strategic focus on carbon emission reduction since 1997. Carbon footprint measurement is pursued within the SEPA because of senior management directive, to meet or exceed stakeholder expectations for environmental governance and to provide best practice leadership. The organization's carbon policy is devolved to all levels of the organization and has led to *innovation* in the use of information systems, building management, journey planning, and field operations management. The policymaking view of the SEPA contends that carbon management can lead to better understanding of resource flows, recommending a sector-specific approach to carbon policy adoption among SMEs. Carbon emission reporting by SMEs in voluntary schemes such as the Mayday Network is considered to drive *innovation* with further opportunities in the area of water footprint to understand the ethical issues surrounding the water impacts of exports/imports of goods and the development of new products/services or processes to combat these new challenges.

Within the SBC, carbon footprint measurement is philosophically considered a component of corporate social responsibility with carbon management policy being articulated by an internal CSR group. The organization's ethos to promote not only carbon footprint measurement as a tool but the entire CSR agenda contributed to *innovation* in voluntary carbon reporting through the online Mayday Network scheme, which helps SMEs monitor carbon emissions and environmental impact through an annual reporting cycle. Policymakers at the SBC perceive that SME adoption of sustainability footprint tools such as the carbon footprint is driven by customer expectations for sustainable behavior. They recommended that SMEs produce a simple policy or statement of intent regarding carbon footprint measurement and use a carbon calculator to assist with carbon footprint reporting. The implementation of these measures is perceived to contribute to the development of carbon management best practice within SMEs with innovation seen as a natural outcome of carbon footprint measurement, the ultimate goal being for SMEs to utilize triple-bottom-line reporting.

6.6.3 Environmental Impact

Due to the macroeconomic orientation within the government policymaking context, there is limited understanding of the *environmental impact* of carbon emissions as a result of water consumption and sewage treatment within Scotland. The policymaking focus on carbon emission reduction has contributed to "*carbon myopia*" with concern regarding the reliability of information derived from using social footprint methodology. Critically, SMEs are considered to have an important but not a quantitatively significant influence in reducing Scotland's emissions due to target setting challenges as a great proportion of SME carbon emissions are outside their sphere of control but fails to consider the behavioral change contribution that can arise by SME pursuit of sustainability initiatives. However, carbon footprint measurement is perceived as helping SMEs understand their *environmental impact* through identifying source emissions and developing mechanisms to reduce emissions.

As an environmental regulatory body, SEPA's use of carbon footprint measurement techniques has furthered an improved understanding of its *environmental impact*. This enhanced understanding has contributed to effective target setting for reducing carbon footprint. Policymakers at the SEPA however advocate a sector-specific approach to the use of carbon footprint as a KPI for SMEs and also to the use of water footprint measurement by SMEs.

Policymakers at the SBC are convinced of the link between GHG emissions and climate change by extension of carbon footprint reduction and SME success—a conceptual leap that is unique among policymakers within the Scottish context. In their view, the objective of carbon management strategy is to either make an absolute reduction in GHG emissions or decouple GHG emissions from growth. SBC policymakers recommend carbon footprint reduction as a useful KPI for SMEs with reduction targets being set after meaningful stakeholder consultation. The promotion of CSR and triple-bottom-line reporting is a key aim of the SBC policymakers suggesting the water footprint reduction is a useful strategic objective for SMEs if resources can be allocated to the measurement of the organization's water footprint.

6.6.4 Stakeholder Impact

The adoption of carbon footprint measurement is perceived by government advisers as a proxy for good management providing value through *stakeholder* engagement, commitment to climate change, as well as a tool for evaluating overall impact and maintaining competitive advantage. Despite this, Scottish Government policymaking orientation postulates that the challenges with using social footprint methodology to measure social performance are multidimensional and cannot be expressed by a single calculation. Carbon footprint is a good investment for SMEs depending on cost and opportunities for efficiency, thereby contributing to positive *stakeholder impact* because of potential cost savings resulting from effective carbon management and a general overall commitment to sustainability.

SEPA policymaking orientation considers carbon footprint measurement as improving *stakeholder impact* because carbon emission calculations are based on present notions of the future climate change that imposes social and ethical obligations on individuals and businesses to improve resource use. A tailored approach to carbon footprint measurement is preferred for SMEs that is aligned to their existing capabilities with a long-term objective being the reduction of carbon impact in SME supply chains. However, the success of carbon emission reduction must overcome the challenges of managing "initiative" overload when other organizational projects are also an imperative.

As a key policymaking institution, the SBC views its role as creating a safe space for sustainable debate as well as providing technical support with carbon footprint measurement for SMEs through the Carbon Master's Program. Policymakers at the SBC contend that carbon footprint measurement contributes to the adoption of sustainable behaviors and better employee motivation and retention. Carbon footprint measurement is perceived as a good investment for SMEs by creating value through reduced carbon emissions and reduced environmental impact.

REFERENCES

[1] Scottish Government Statistics. High level summary of statistics—environment; 2011. Available at: http://www.scotland.gov.uk/Topics/Statistics/Browse/Environment. Accessed on Jun 30, 2014.

[2] AEA Group. Greenhouse gas inventories for England, Scotland, Wales and Northern Ireland; 2011. p. 1990–2009. Available at: http://uk-air.defra.gov.uk/assets/documents/reports/cat07/1306070907_DA_GHGI_report_2011_Issue1.pdf. Accessed on Jun 30, 2014.

[3] Scottish Environmental Protection Agency. Protecting Scotland's environment—a 10 year perspective; 2010. Available at: http://www.sepa.org.uk/about_us/publications/10_year_perspective.aspx. Accessed on Jun 30, 2014.

[4] Scottish Environmental Protection Agency.Annual environmental report 1999/2000 for SEPA's own activities; 2000. Available at: http://www.sepa.org.uk/about_us/publications/greening_sepa.aspx. Accessed on Jun 30, 2014.

[5] Scottish Business in the Community. Available at http://www.sbcscot.com/. Accessed Nov 7, 2013.

[6] Head of the Environment. Interview by author. Edinburgh; Oct 24, 2011.

[7] Head of the Environmental Economic Analysis Unit. Interview by author. Edinburgh; Nov 21, 2011.

[8] Head of Environmental Strategy. Interview by author. Edinburgh; Nov 11, 2011.

[9] Scottish Government. Scotland's action to attack climate change; 2012 [online]. Available at http://www.scotland.gov.uk/Topics/Environment/climatechange/scotlands-action. Accessed Jan 7, 2013.

[10] Scottish Enterprise. Baselining and research into the Scottish Construction Sector—a final report to Scottish Enterprise; March 2012. Available at http://www.scottish-enterprise.com/~/media/SE/Resources/Documents/Sectors/Construction/Baseline%20report.pdf. Accessed Jan 22, 2013.

[11] Chief Executive Officer. Interview by author. Edinburgh; Oct 24, 2011.

[12] Scottish Government. A low carbon economic strategy for Scotland: Scotland—a low carbon society 2010. Available at: http://www.scotland.gov.uk/Resource/Doc/331364/0107855.pdf. Accessed on Jun 30, 2014.

[13] Cameron D. Conservative Party Spring Forum Speech, April 26, 2009. Available at http://www.conservatives.com/Video/Webcameron.aspx?id=b3b3d2c1-353a-4d53-bef2-c5ab79fbae5d. Accessed Jun 23, 2013.

[14] United Kingdom, Waste (Scotland) Regulations 2012. Available at http://www.legislation.gov.uk/sdsi/2012/9780111016657/contents. Accessed Jan 3, 2014.

[15] The Scottish Government. Scotland's Zero Waste Plan 2010. Edinburgh. Available at http://www.scotland.gov.uk/Resource/Doc/314168/0099749.pdf. Accessed Jan 3, 2014.

[16] McConnell I. Scottish water chief sets ambitious green targets. Scottish Herald. Available at http://www.heraldscotland.com/business/company-news/scottish-water-chief-sets-ambitious-green-targets.14616656. Accessed Dec 17, 2013.

7

CAPITAL COOLING: SUSTAINABLE REFRIGERATION AND AIR-CONDITIONING ENGINEERING

7.1 INTRODUCTION

Capital Cooling Ltd is an awarding company specializing in the manufacture, supply, and maintenance of stationary refrigeration and air-conditioning equipment. Although a family-owned enterprise, it has grown from very humble beginnings to achieve a turnover of over £22m in 2009 and was ranked 63rd on the Heating, Ventilation, Air Conditioning, and Refrigeration Index [1] 2012. The company's founder Alister McLean having a passion for refrigeration established the company in 1996, reflecting on his motivations for establishing the company:

> What led me to establish Capital Cooling... basically having a passion for refrigeration once I completed my apprenticeship, once I learnt the industry. Just having a passion for the commercial refrigeration industry.
>
> (CEO [2])

This passion for refrigeration has extended to his offspring who assist him in managing the business. His son, a qualified refrigeration and air-conditioning engineer who completed his apprenticeship within the company, is involved in the expansion of the product development department. His daughter, an actuarial science major, is spearheading the company's human resource management

Sustainability Footprints in SMEs: Strategy and Case Studies for Entrepreneurs and Small Business, First Edition. Lowellyne James.
© 2015 John Wiley & Sons, Inc. Published 2015 by John Wiley & Sons, Inc.

121

function—a role that was once executed by her mother who has been appointed to an advisory role within the operations of the business. All four members of the family form the nexus of the decision making within the organization, supported operationally by the Finance Director and Managing Director who ensure that budgetary controls are maintained within the enterprise and are the only senior members of the management that are not relatives. Instrumental to the company's success has been its management team, of which some have been with the company since its inception, being ably supported by an administrative and engineering staff. The staff members consider the company's carbon footprint as a key topic for deliberation at management meetings; viewpoints of managers concerning importance of the carbon footprint on the company agenda vary from a nonpriority to emerging priority that is included within the sustainability of the business. Overall, staff and managers alike perceive carbon footprint reduction as a key issue for the company, thereby exhibiting a *sustainability positive* bias. However, this is not unanimous as carbon footprint reduction is not perceived to be a consideration at management meetings:

> I would like to think it does feature somewhere on any management meeting but everyone can see that we are obviously recycling and whatever money we get back for it is looked upon as a bonus for recycling and getting everybody involved in it.
>
> (Sales Coordinator [3])

> Are we talking at Capital Cooling? Not at a management meeting.
>
> (Installation Manager [4])

> I think it will be again its where it fits in … it is all got priority I don't know it's always there if something is quite bad for the environment we know we are not going to do it I don't know if it takes a lead in the decision making process but at this moment in time probably not but it always will be considered in some shape or form.
>
> (Marketing Coordinator [5])

As an employer that recruits from the local community within the vicinity of its operational sites, the company has been rewarded in return with high staff loyalty levels [6] with 32% of employees having been with the organization for more than 5 years. A demographically diverse [6] organization comprised of 47% of the staff under age 40, 5% of the staff being from ethnic minority backgrounds and 9% being female managers. This unique mixture of youth and experience has enabled the organization to readily embrace information technology such as handheld personal digital assistants (PDAs) for field engineers and delivery drivers.

From its inception, Capital Cooling has attracted blue-chip clientele, initially winning a bid to supply integral refrigeration cabinets to John Menzies plc in the first year of operation. This success with listed companies continued in 1998 with the securing of a contract to supply refrigeration equipment to Co-operative Group plc, a partnership that has continued to the present day. In that same year, the firm commissioned its first environmental report that originally was drafted as part of a student research project. The student in question later became an employee who still works at the company's main offices to this present day. Concerns for the environment and sustainability have been part of the founder's ethos:

> What created the environmental route? Obviously we all listen to the daily news, the current legislation out there we all have got to be aware of what is happening around us. So being environmentally aware and friendly ... there are long term benefits.
>
> (CEO [7])

In 2002, the company began developing its own range of refrigeration and air-conditioning equipment and launched its first integral refrigeration unit the *Perge* [7]. From these explorative beginnings in product development emerged the company's *Capital* range of environmentally friendly refrigeration and air-conditioning equipment.

With an evolving product strategy, senior management then proceeded to align operational processes to benefit from synergy and generate growth. In early 2009, the management of the organization adopted a strategic approach of aligning the company's environmentally friendly product strategy with its process strategy [8]. Central to this strategic approach was the implementation of an ISO 14001 Environmental Management System (EMS), which laid the foundations for the development of the firm's sustainability/corporate social responsibility (CSR) policy. Embodied in the DNA of the organization is the concept of *Do no harm*; this strand of thought drives the approach of management, employees to the business, and its role in the society and the planet. As dictated by its sustainability/CSR policy [6], Capital Cooling endeavors to meet this obligation by:

- *Building sustainable value-added relationships with our employees, suppliers, and customers*
- *Striving to ensure that our actions as a corporate entity have no or minimal impact on our planet*
- *Contributing to economic growth by maximizing the resources of our society and planet*
- *Incorporating sustainability in the design and manufacture of our refrigeration and air-conditioning equipment*
- *Reducing the carbon footprint of our operations, products, and services*
- *Communicating our CSR and sustainability performance to all stakeholders*

To fulfill this social contract, Capital Cooling continuously engages with its stakeholders using all available communication channels and platforms. The nature of each obligation requires the organization to be honest in evaluating its current state of sustainability, maintaining openness in discussing the validity of actions taken to mitigate its impact, and being ready to innovate and continuously improve its people/ products and processes.

The carbon footprint forms a key part of the company's sustainability ethos, and its importance to the business is fully appreciated by staff at all levels of the organization:

> At this stage I think it is very important going forward we want to be seen as a proactive company with all the requirements of not just the government legislation but our own customer requirements. We have to be seen and doing in line with their requirements.
>
> Installation Manager [4])

> Very important for the environment going forward.
>
> (PPM Administrator [9])

Staff members perceive a link between carbon footprints the future survival of the business and the planet, risk management, legal compliance, cost savings, satisfying customer requirements, and market leadership.

The preemptive decision to reduce the firm's exposure to risks from legislation such as the Climate Change Act [10] 2009, the Fluorinated Greenhouse Gas Regulations [11] 2009, and the possible EC-wide ban on the use of virgin hydrofluorocarbons (HFCs) and the enactment of Zero Waste Regulations [12] in Scotland has been supported by the strategic intent that since 2010 has seen investments made in expanding the organization's operational sites, which now comprise its head offices and warehousing facilities in Scotland complemented by sales offices, warehousing facilities, and an industry first "technology center" located in England.

7.2   CONTEXT

An analysis of the industry using Michael Porter's Five Forces model identified a competitive scenario within which the market is dominated by brands from larger organizations offering similar products and services [13] (Fig. 7.1).

Within this intense competitive environment, Capital Cooling as a sustainably managed enterprise (SME) is constrained in terms of financial, infrastructure, and personnel resources. The prevailing economic climate naturally dictates that buyers are price sensitive however with high expectations of exceptional service and product performance. This sensitivity to the prevailing economic conditions is echoed in the sentiments of staff with interviewees generally having a *sustainability positive* outlook. This was not a general consensus among management as there were alternative perceptions that economic conditions have no impact on the carbon footprint with nontechnical staff unsure of the impact of economic conditions:

> Again I don't really have access to figures I would assume that there is always going to be some form of impact money is going to be more focused on other aspects not as freely sometimes it will be treated as a kind of luxury but again I can't comment officially without any figures.
>
> (Marketing Coordinator [5])

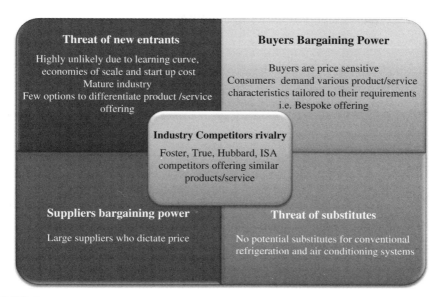

FIGURE 7.1 Competitive analysis of the U.K. commercial refrigeration sector. Source: © Capital Cooling Ltd.

The continued increase in fuel costs and economic pressures has transformed opinions about the relationship between the waste and profitability, thereby extending the concept of the bottom line. Financial contributions to operating cost from the waste recycling program have cemented the link between financial performance and carbon performance. Carbon footprint measurement is valued as a vital element of the company's cost reduction initiatives. However, despite this consensus, carbon footprint measurement is not considered cost neutral, and sustainability initiatives are considered by some employees as a luxury in a credit-constrained environment:

> The answer to that is probably Yes … we are trying to reduce our footprint first and foremost because of the footprint and secondly because of the economic climate. Whatever downturn in business you have as a net result in less running about … fewer calls to do … fewer deliveries to make etcetera and also as the margins get strangled a lot by everything that is affecting it we have got to try and reduce our costs which has a knock on effect of reducing our carbon footprint. Primarily it is reducing costs but alternatively it is about reducing carbon. We don't want to run about effectively to cause damage to the environment we don't want to run about to cause damage to the company financial wise so it is very much both hand in hand to try and reduce the costs which reduces the carbon footprint.
>
> (Logistics Manager [14])

Within this competitive landscape, potential entrants into the industry incur economies of scale and learning curve challenges in a constrained lending environment. Suppliers of components dominate the bargaining process forcing buyers to

TABLE 7.1 Comparative analysis of Capital Cooling with a leading brand

Foster	Capital Cooling
Corporate carbon footprint using Carbon Trust guidelines	Corporate carbon footprint using DEFRA guidelines
Corporate Social Responsibility Reporting	Corporate social responsibility reporting
ISO 14001	ISO 14001
ECA Product approval	ECA product approval
Green and blue papers	
Green achievements	

Source: © Capital Cooling Ltd.

continually search further afield, creating extended supply chains with resultant carbon impacts [13].

Comparative analysis of the sustainability initiatives of Capital Cooling and one of its competitors suggests similar strategic approaches to addressing sustainability issues such as carbon emissions in terms of ISO 14001 certification, CSR/sustainability, and carbon footprint measurement (Table. 7.1). A performance gap however existed in the communication of Capital Cooling's green achievements and eco-friendly product features.

7.3 ENVIRONMENTAL AND LEGAL CHALLENGES

The refrigeration and air-conditioning industry's main environmental impacts emanate from the following:

- Pollution to land and water from end-of-life equipment
- Refrigerant emissions

Conventional refrigeration and air-conditioning uses refrigerant, normally a gas, as a cooling agent and is still the prevailing means for temperature control within the air-conditioning and refrigeration industry. Refrigerants are also key criteria for categorizing refrigeration and air-conditioning equipment as hazardous or special waste within the United Kingdom. This is due to the prevalent use of fluorinated greenhouse gases (F-gas) such as HFC refrigerants. HFCs were originally invented as replacements for ozone-depleting chlorofluorocarbon (CFC) and hydrochloro-fluorocarbon (HCFC) refrigerants that were used earlier in the development of the refrigeration and air-conditioning industry. When viewed from a climate perspective, HFCs are considered to be a main contributor to climate change. It is estimated that globally emissions of HFCs [15] are approximately 560 million tons of CO_2e.

Fluorinated greenhouse gases now account for 2% of all global greenhouse gas emissions and are set to grow due to burgeoning demand from the emerging economies. Industry analysts have classified HFCs as "super greenhouse gases" due to its high global warming potential (GWP). There are two types of greenhouse effects:

Natural—This occurs when the sun's rays are reflected from the earth's surface; this radiated heat is then trapped between clouds in much the same way as a greenhouse.

Anthropogenic—A phenomenon that results when the sun's radiated heat is trapped by various industrial emissions such as HFCs. For example, a commonly used refrigerant HFC 134a has GWP that is 1400 times that of CO_2; therefore, a domestic refrigerator may contain refrigerant that has an environmental impact that is the equivalent to driving a car from London to Berlin and back again [15].

Early research estimated that the recovery of HFCs can reduce emissions by 20% with transition to hydrocarbon gas technology contributing an additional 50% to reducing the sector's emissions if the technology was adopted early enough [16]. Existing measures such as refrigerant gas recovery [16] can reduce the refrigeration and air-conditioning sector's emissions by 20%.

The European Union has banned the use of HCFCs as refrigerants since 2009 and has introduced legislation to control the use of HCFCs through F-gas directives, which comply with existing international protocols [16]. The United Kingdom has adopted these measures and enacted the Fluorinated Greenhouse Gas Regulations [9] 2009 requiring engineering personnel to be trained in the safe handling of refrigerants.

This legislative landscape is further exacerbated with the introduction of the Climate Change Act [4] 2009, which aims to cut Scotland's greenhouse gas emissions by *setting an interim 42% reduction target for 2020, with the power for this to be varied based on expert advice, and an 80% reduction target for 2050*. Potentially looming over the business is a future characterized by increased emission regulation and punitive taxation, a likely scenario that has not gone amiss by its employees. Despite this, all employees regardless of their status have a *sustainability positive* orientation to the adoption of carbon measurement:

> Because of the size of the company by law we have to do it, I think we will choose to do it anyway. If you have a certain amount of employees within a company you would have to consider your carbon footprint.
>
> (Engineering Manager [17])

> I think legislation is in place because of the EC and the British Government to reduce carbon footprint that's why it should be our primary reason to comply with legislation both from the EU and the British government.
>
> (Installation Manager [4])

Employees are sensitized to the impact of carbon emissions and potential legal implications of unabated carbon emissions on the future of the company. Carbon footprint measurement is considered a voluntary act that confirms the company's compliance with existing legislation, and it is an extension of its commitment to the wider community. Internally, the company's carbon footprint policy is perceived as part of the wider CSR/sustainability policy along with recycling initiatives. Among the firm's employees, there is a *sustainability positive* outlook toward the establishment of a formal policy for carbon footprint measurement with some managers and nontechnical staff having *sustainability passive* orientations ranging from being unaware to being observed but not read in depth:

> Yes, we have recycle bins throughout the company, which get emptied on a daily business. There are cans, plastic, paper, glass and also from the warehouse side of things we have got a bundle for cardboard, plastic, wood scrap. We also recycle all of our redundant refrigeration equipment which we get paid for in weight, it leaves here on a weekly basis which in the past we paid for most of these services to be done now we get companies to pay us.
>
> (Sales Coordinator [3])

> There is a formal environmental policy which encompasses all aspects of the business from energy usage to the actual carbon footprint.
>
> (Marketing Coordinator [5])

Though legal, environmental, and competitive pressures abound, employees of Capital Cooling view cost, customer requirements, manpower, time, financial constraints, and lack of knowledge as conspiring factors forming significant barriers to the implementation of the carbon footprint policy:

> I would think the financial predominantly … I would think with the economic climate it would be financial at the moment
>
> (Installation Manager [4])

> I think education is still quite a big problem not everybody understands the effects of their action it will be probably the main barrier not everybody knows about it. To be honest not everybody cares people have to be educated to understand it. Other barriers are obviously tough financial times and there is a significant financial aspect involved then that will always be taken into consideration. It is not a case of money no object the way business is at the moment.
>
> (Marketing Coordinator [18])

7.4   CONTRIBUTIONS TO GROWTH

Building on the earlier efforts to develop environmental awareness within the organization in the second financial quarter of 2009, the company's Quality, Safety, and Environmental (QSE) Manager approached the CEO with a comprehensive proposal to implement an EMS compliant with the ISO 14001 standard and also a Safety Management System compliant with the OHSAS 18001 standard. An executive decision was then made to pursue the development of EMS that would complement the environmentally friendly approach to product design [8].

Acknowledging the potential business risks that may result from the poor management of environmental aspects and the anticipated introduction of mandatory greenhouse gas reporting, the CEO instructed the QSE Manager to participate in the Institute of Environmental Management and Assessment (IEMA)/Department for Environment, Food and Rural Affairs (DEFRA)-sponsored consultation on guidance for greenhouse gas reporting held on July 29, 2009, in Edinburgh, Scotland. At an operational level, the CEO also authorized the institution of a cross-functional management committee to systematically monitor environmental performance [8].

With this mandate, an Environmental Management Committee was established comprising key managers selected from specialisms such as sales and account management, quality, warehousing, and transport [8]. The main criterion for selection was the individual's ability to influence change and their interest in environmental management. Focused on continuous improvement, the committee convenes regularly to monitor the development and implementation of the Environmental Management utilizing simple agenda to improve environmental performance [8]:

1. Review of environmental management implementation plans
2. Agree actions
3. Review of environmental legislation and compliance
4. Review of environmental aspects

In September 2009, the Environmental Management Committee reviewed information provided by the Finance Department on the organization's environmental aspects, which are:

- Paper
- Ink and toner cartridges
- Electricity
- Gas
- Fuel
- Water
- Waste
- End-of-life waste electrical and electronic equipment (WEEE)

Senior management then adopted a strategic view toward environmental aspect analysis in terms of its impact on the commercial marketability of products and services:

> In terms of its environmental aspects we are driving towards most of our products using hydrocarbon refrigerant and getting ECA approval. The introduction of the test chamber to ensure that we are using the most energy efficient components all of these things and the quality of our engineering development staff to create an exceptional product … what we give our customer is great value for money equipment.
>
> (CEO [7])

This review and analysis provided a few surprises such as a gap in their reporting system, specifically the absence of pertinent quantitative data regarding the tonnage of waste produced, the tonnage of end-of-life "Capital Cooling"-branded refrigeration equipment, and the level of inadvertent refrigerant gas emissions resulting from leaks arising from both installation and maintenance activity. The operational managers also acknowledged that the organization was not prepared for business risks arising from poor carbon management and the introduction of mandatory greenhouse gas reporting [8].

At the initial meetings of the Environmental Management Committee, fluorinated greenhouse gases were an issue that was deliberated by the management in terms of regulatory compliance and refrigerant leakage reduction albeit with limited appreciation of the carbon impacts of inadvertent refrigerant leakages [19]. The prevailing use of financial indicators—mainly direct cost—was considered the only, if not preferred, yardstick for interpreting the impacts to the business from energy consumption, stationery usage, and waste disposal.

To improve awareness of the carbon impact of environmental aspects, the QSE Manager calculated the organization's carbon footprint and generated the company's benchmark DEFRA—compliant greenhouse gas report 2008–2009 covering Scope 1 and Scope 2 activities [20]. *Environmental aspects are any part of an organization's processes, products, and services that have an impact on the natural environment.*

Although employees are aware of the carbon footprint, the methodology used to calculate the impact was generally unknown. Employees internalized their contribution in terms of recycling processes and environmental mitigation techniques:

> I don't know the exact methods but I know about the work done by the Quality and Environmental team to do it. I don't know the physical methods
>
> (Marketing Coordinator [5])
>
> Energy consumption is the only way you can calculate it.
>
> (Product Development Manager [21])

For the reporting period August 2008–August 2009 Scope 1 activities of the business accounted for 1145.786 CO_2e tons and Scope 2 activities accounted for 126.961 CO_2e tons of emissions resulting in combined total emissions of 1272.746 CO_2e tons (Figs. 7.2 and 7.3).

The firm has since measured and monitored its carbon impacts documenting these efforts in the Capital Cooling Ltd. Greenhouse Gas Report 2009–2010 [22] and Capital Cooling Ltd. Greenhouse Gas Report 2010–2011 [2].

Personnel have differing views as to when the company adopted greenhouse gas reporting as a performance measurement tool. This variation is due to individual association or knowledge of carbon footprint as a concept or methodology. Although most managers interviewed are aware of the firm's active engagement in carbon footprint measurement, some are unaware of the length of

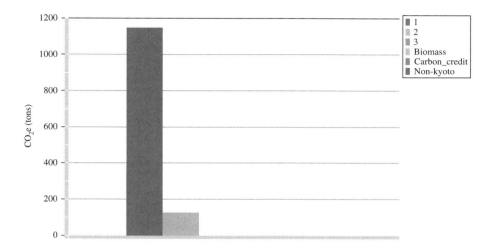

FIGURE 7.2 Capital Cooling greenhouse gas analysis by DEFRA scope 2008–2009. Source: © Capital Cooling Ltd.

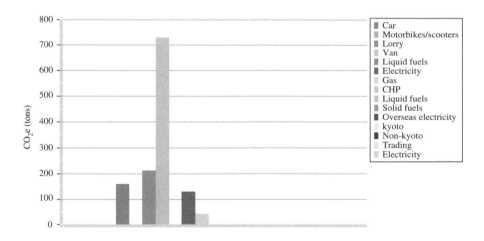

FIGURE 7.3 Capital Cooling greenhouse gas analysis by type 2008–2009. Source: © Capital Cooling Ltd.

time of this involvement with technical personnel perceiving carbon footprint measurement as a recent initiative:

> We have being doing it at some level for about two and a half years probably slightly over that albeit in a small starting process but more intense now as we now reap some of the reported benefits that we are actually getting. We are able to use measurement tools

and actually able to now go back and formulate a reduction policy .... So the initial set up was to understand what our carbon footprint was to enable us to go forward to try and put some reduction processes in place and that was a year and a half in the making but all through that year and a half ... it was then showing us what we needed to do and how we needed to go forward so much so that I don't think we will ever come to an end of that and we will continue to look at new ways of measuring, looking and reducing

(Logistics Manager [14])

Seriously probably within the last ten ... five to seven years .... maybe in the last four ... three to four years. We have really taken it seriously we have measured it within the last five years but I would say within the last three years we have really taken it seriously.

(Technical Manager [23])

Employees consider greenhouse gas emissions to be a key performance indicator that focuses organizational efforts on carbon footprint reduction, business growth, and market leadership. However, within management, there is skepticism as to the benefits of carbon footprint measurement, which is perceived as being time consuming:

If I am willing and required to give time many other people within the company are doing exactly the same thing so it is very important and it does form part of our KPI it is a table of measurement of all that we are trying to do and we can only do that based on the information we have actually gleaned. The services we have actually put in place so from fuel, the waste that we actually have disposed ... returned and the wood. We have always recycled the wood that comes in old pallets ....even that now is going to a different source and a different way of recycling so everything is measurable and will continue to be done and it does form part of the KPIs. Next year we will be looking to reduce even more and we will be reducing to make bigger savings and we can only do that if we actually know what we are doing at present.

(Logistics Manager [24])

Yes it does... I think the company does looking at the way we can be a market leader in the design and manufacture of our cases. It then goes hand in hand with being the market leader in carbon footprint.

(Technical Manager [23])

Management and staff of the company are also convinced of the dual purpose of sustainability footprint reports such as the carbon footprint as a communicative tool targeted at both internal and external audiences:

I think it is definitely an external thing it can be used as a marketing too, not in any detail but a simple proof of a reduction again going back to the methods rather than figures. These are things we are doing to improve the business it is something that I looked at on our offering on our website is the chance for people to purchase and offset the carbon produced from the product they are buying. So if they are buying a bottle cooler and we know to get the bottle cooler manufactured delivered to them and operated for five years costs X amount in tons of carbon. They can purchase it which we then offset with a partner.

(Marketing Coordinator [5])

Both … its internal use to make sure you get the smallest carbon footprint possible but external use to make sure that the carbon footprint meets the ECA certification.

(Product Development Manager [21])

Capital Cooling embarked on the implementation of an EMS compliant to ISO 14001 system requirements. This strategic approach was disseminated through the development of a sustainability culture, which is driven by environmental policy and procedures. As a result, the program has necessitated the implementation of environmental awareness training for all staff and subcontractors that covered the relationship between environmental aspects and the carbon footprint. This had the immediate effect of adding the word "carbon footprint" to the operational lexicon of the company. However, some managers and nontechnical staff interviewed are unaware of the different types of sustainability footprints; this may have arisen from either poor communication or lack of training. However, initially, personnel were concerned about the relevance of the carbon footprint to Capital Cooling as an SME as expressed by one manager's comments:

I can only answer from what I was involved in which is from the direct carbon footprint from vehicles, from the rubbish that we actually create. I have also alluded to the fact that I think that has rubbed off to the home life but the measurement tool I think it is entirely down to the QSE Manager in the way that he presents that to us at the end of the time as he is are aware he comes under exceeding pressure to verify some of the things that he actually does so the report that he puts together in the way of presenting the carbon footprint tables that we have within site are very much queried until such times as we can then accept it. So it is entirely down to QSE Manager and all the individual people within the company to provide the information from their own departments for QSE Manager to then create the table or the carbon footprint or the policy going forward as the whole group or company.

(Logistics Manager [14])

The role of the quality, safety, and environmental management professional is pivotal to the successful embedding of sustainability principles within an organization as well as influencing lifestyle choices among work colleagues.

To embed sustainability values within Capital Cooling's overall management strategy to deal with nonfinancial risks, for example, environmental aspects such as waste, a company-wide recycling program was initiated for the following waste streams:

- Cardboard
- Polystyrene
- Plastic
- Paper

In particular, the recycling of polystyrene and cardboard required investment in compacting equipment (Figs. 7.4, 7.5, and 7.6).

This investment achieved a dual purpose by assisting with the measurement and management of the environmental impact of polystyrene and cardboard packaging waste through the preparation of these materials for onward recycling, thereby expanding on an already existing wood and end-of-life refrigeration recycling program [25].

FIGURE 7.4   Polystyrene compactor. Source: © Capital Cooling Ltd.

FIGURE 7.5   Polystyrene briquette. © Source: Capital Cooling Ltd.

FIGURE 7.6   Polystyrene briquettes ready for recycling. Source: © Capital Cooling Ltd.

The information generated from the recycling program contributed to the assessment of waste in terms of its carbon impacts. Waste cardboard and polystyrene destined for the local landfill sites were now attributed an economic value. The policy shift from waste from being a cost center to a profit center led to a reassessment of individual concepts of the value of sustainability management to the business and its relationship to resource constraints within the economy:

> I am not so sure … we are getting paid for our waste I don't think that is something that we done years ago we just dispose of the thing and we would have paid to dispose of it but now I think it is different where people are actually paying for your waste whether it is metal, wood … So I am not so sure … people are actually paying for your waste now I think it has more to do with the economy rather than your carbon footprint.
>
> (Sales Coordinator [3])

Measurement of the organization's carbon footprint is a voluntary exercise whose costs are not evaluated. Employees' views of the cost of carbon footprint measurement range from the sheer impossibility of the calculation to general unawareness of costs or an evaluation of carbon footprint measurement costs in terms of nonfinancial criteria such as man-hours. Managers and technical personnel within the firm perceptions are oriented toward being *sustainability negative* with perceptions of technical personnel being *sustainability positive*. Nontechnical personnel and some managers are unaware of the costs; this is a legacy of limited environmental cost evaluation:

> It's impossible to calculate … how long is a piece of string? It comes from so many elements there is R&D cost on reducing the carbon footprint it is something you can't actually measure
>
> (Product Development Manager [21])

It cost quite a lot of time man hours that is sometimes quite difficult to quantify nevertheless it is an important part without a starting figure and an end figure it is difficult to quantify where you are so it is really all man hours. We have started this some maybe about two years ago monitoring measuring to try and reduce the impact and I think we have successfully done that so it is really time now the basics have been done which sets us up to be able to do the measurement. It's only man hours that is put into place it is quite substantial at times it is not something to be looked at as a two minute job there isn't a two minute job it is not a two minute fix it is an on-going job it is quite an involved job but it is quite a lot of hours but without that we can't get what we are looking for which is either the carbon footprint reduction or the financial reduction that goes along with it you can't get one without the other.

(Logistics Manager [14])

Delivering refrigeration and air-conditioning equipment and responding to planned and reactive engineering calls from customers 24 hours a day, 365 days a year, are critical to the survival of the company. Fuel consumption is a two-edged sword creating both economic risks as result of fuel price fluctuations and environmental risks from vehicle exhaust emissions. Arising from the Greenhouse Gas Report 2009–2010, the company partnered with the Energy Saving Trust to conduct a comprehensive review of the transport fleet management, which comprised 67 commercial vehicles and 25 company cars [26]. The company's vehicle fleet consumes 439,436 liters of transport fuel, which accounts for 86% of the company's carbon footprint [26]. The report specifically recommended the pursuit of a number of actions to reduce the environmental impact of our fleet such as:

- Fleet Management Review
  - *Procurement policies biased toward low-emission vehicles*
  - *Introduction of a driver handbook*
- Adopting cleaner vehicles and fuels
  - *Vehicle specification*—environmental performance key criterion in the purchasing decision
  - *Whole-life costs*—comparative analysis of procurement costs including fuel in relation to vehicles that are lower in price
  - *The environment*—a focus on vehicle efficiency and emissions
- Reducing fuel consumption
- Reducing number of miles traveled

To reduce the carbon impact of the transport fleet, the Logistics Department is committed to the specification and selection of articulated lorries with aerodynamic features [27], which reduce drag and wind resistance on the vehicle [6] (Figs. 7.7 and 7.8). This *"teardrop"* design has been validated by independent tests [27] to improve fuel consumption by 11%, highlighting further potential fuel savings of up to 15.7%.

In combination the use of selective catalytic reduction equipped engines, AdBlue, a fuel additive, greatly improves performance and reduces harmful emissions arising

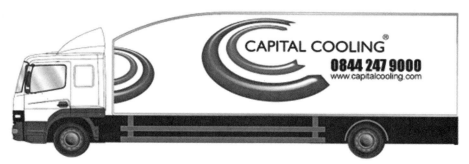

FIGURE 7.7 Diagram of "teardrop" design delivery vehicle with aerodynamic features. Source: © Capital Cooling Ltd.

FIGURE 7.8 New design vehicles as part of Capital Cooling's green fleet. Source: © Capital Cooling Ltd.

from diesel exhausts [6]. Historically, the senior management of Capital Cooling tacitly supported the purchase of fuel-efficient vehicles; this has now evolved into an established policy of actively procuring low-emission service vehicles and company cars with emission levels of 99g/km CO_2e.

We manufacture our products in Poland, Italy, and Turkey and in China. Let's take for example Turkey we don't bring the product by road. In fact we use a mixture of sea, rail and road. We find that it is the most cost effective method to bring the product here and caring for the environment there are pressures to drive every business to produce at a cost. So we believe we can deliver a quality product with the least impact to the environment using these methods … likewise with China it all comes by sea very little on the road because we are quite fortunate the factories we are using are quite near the port it is coming by container to the nearest port which is here. We recently introduced our new truck for example … incorporated some aerodynamics to make it environmentally friendly as possible so the body of the truck actually shapes reducing the drag so we get more miles per gallon out of the vehicle. We recently ordered some new service vehicles with the lowest emissions possible on these service vehicles so again the impact on the environment. We are looking at company cars was 99g/km CO_2 emissions so again that is reducing it to where we were years ago. So every part of the transport whether it is equipment coming in to us, service engineers going out doing reactive and planned calls on equipment or sales and technical people visiting customers, the cars every part of it we are looking at the impact on the environment.

(CEO [28])

The aforementioned improvements in addition to better journey planning using an integrated transport system that generates a real-time computerized route planning system for delivery drivers and field engineering staff that could potentially reduce CO_2 emissions by 20%, a total of 232 tons of CO_2e, which is equivalent to £108,000 in savings over a 3-year period [26]:

We have various methods that we are actually using we have the cost per mile in the vehicles to see if we are effectively monitoring each and every drivers response and that's important as we can have some "heavy footed" drivers. Overall they are doing the same mileage but they are doing it the expensive and heavy carbon way of getting their foot to the floor high revving of the gears not correct to the efficiency of:

(a) the vehicle and
(b) the output of the carbon

It is monitored on our green fleet through IT system which is a full tracking and vehicle analysis system that we have monitoring on a daily, weekly and monthly basis. We have some high users some of the engineers do some substantial mileage and we have to make sure that is done in an effective way. We also have to measure vehicle against vehicle and not just driver against driver we've got vehicle against vehicle to see what's the most cost effective and carbon effective vehicle in the road. We have three or four different manufacturers of vehicles with the comparisons being done manufacturer against manufacturer, vehicle against vehicle also within their own vehicle group and within their own driver group to give us a comparison.

(Logistics Manager [14])

Continuously searching for opportunities to grow and meet the expectations of its customer base, the company acquired the site of its head offices in Scotland in 2003. The company's U.K. head office is situated on 4895 m^2 of floor space comprising offices, warehouse facilities, and engineering workshop. Although financially aware of the energy cost of operating their Broxburn head offices, the true environmental impact of these facilities was not apparent until the firm's benchmark carbon footprint report triggered an initiative to measure and understand the carbon footprint of the organization's infrastructure and incorporate these externalities along with cost. Thereby enhancing the overall picture of risk and cost within the organization, now armed with kilowatt-hour consumption data and cost, senior management converted energy consumption data to generate carbon footprint of the building—an essential first step in determining the full scale of carbon impact of energy use within their head office. During the period 2010–2011, Capital Cooling head office building consumed 249,820 kWh of electricity, which is equivalent to 136 CO_2e tons at a cost of £20,573, and 210,951 kWh of gas, which is equivalent to 39 CO_2e tons at a cost of £6,139 (Fig. 7.9). Electricity accounted for 77% of the carbon footprint of the buildings with the remaining 23% being due to gas consumption [2, 29] (Fig. 7.9).

kWh/m²	Utility	Consumption		Cost		CO_2e	Production units per year	N/A
		kWh/year	%	£/year	%	tons		
51	Electric	249,820	54%	£20,573	77%	136	**Electricity** average. cost p/kWh	**8.24**
43	Gas	210,951	46%	£6,139	23%	39	**Gas** average. cost p/kWh	**2.91**
94	**Total**	**460,771**	**100%**	**£26,712**	**100%**	**175**		

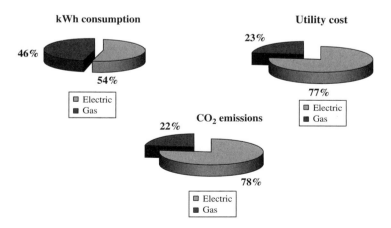

FIGURE 7.9 Greenhouse gas emissions and utility consumption in Broxburn. Source: © Capital Cooling Ltd.

TABLE 7.2   Greenhouse gas emissions and utility consumption Quinton

kWh/m²	Utility	Consumption		Cost		CO$_2$		
		kWh/year	%	£/year	%	tons	Production units per year	N/A
12	Electric	25,047	100%	£3,507	100%	14	**Electricity** average. cost p/kWh	**14.00**
0	Gas	0	0%	£0	0%	0	**Gas** average. cost p/kWh	**0**
12	**Total**	**25,047**	**100%**	**£3,507**	**100%**	**14**		

Source: © Capital Cooling Ltd.

A similar assessment was conducted for the company's distribution center located in Quinton, England. The Quinton site [30] consumed 25,047 kWh of energy, which is equivalent to 14 CO$_2$e tons at an annual cost of £3,507 (Table. 7.2).

A campaign directed at behavioral change included the use of various communication devices such as posters and emails; environmental awareness training and one-to-one talks were conducted with staff members to sensitize staff regarding energy consumption. At a strategic level, the use of renewable energy sources, for example, solar PV, was considered as an option in an effort to reduce the overall carbon impact and along with the use of a biomass boiler fueled by damaged wooden pallets. The Energy Saving Trust was also invited to conduct an energy audit of the premises [31] and reported the potential for carbon reduction and energy savings if their recommendations were deployed (Table. 7.3).

Although most of the recommendations for energy tariff management, staff awareness, and behavioral change in terms of energy monitoring were readily adopted by the company, however the nomination of Energy Champions to assist in the monitoring of energy use and to encourage others to help reduce energy consumption was a recommendation that was considered by the Environmental Management Committee for future implementation [31, 32]. The upgrade of lighting and boiler equipment proved prohibitive within existing financial restraints; however, the use of free cooling from fresh air using a "push–pull" ventilation system was deemed feasible in reducing the electricity consumption arising from air-conditioning use during warmer periods.

TABLE 7.3 Potential Savings From the Adoption of Various Carbon Reduction initiatives

No cost action	Annual savings	kWh savings	CO_2e savings	Payback years
Staff awareness	830	13,497	4.3	0.0
Temperature control	2343	26,411	11.3	0.0
Low cost action				
Free cooling from fresh air	2343	26,411	11.3	1.0
Photocell control of lighting	1556	17,550	7.5	1.0
Fit low energy lamps	439	4,950	2.1	1.0
Capital cost action				
Replace boilers	1419	50,143	9.5	2.8
Total	8930	138,962	46.0	—

Source: © Capital Cooling Ltd.

Sustainability has been at the heart of the business from its inception [28]. Within the first 2 years of operations in 1998, senior management commissioned the organization's very first environmental report covering the impacts of the business on the environment. This report laid the foundations for future development of sustainability management within the company. Utilizing in-house expertise in the maintenance, servicing, and refurbishment of refrigeration and air-conditioning equipment, Capital Cooling designed its first product, the **Perge** integral multideck cabinet. This conceptual design was the catalyst for the launch of a pantheon of eco-friendly and energy-efficient refrigeration and air-conditioning equipment models such as the **Mars**, **Apollo,** and the **Troy** integral multideck—the first refrigeration product from a U.K. manufacturer to be accepted on the Carbon Trust Energy Technology List (ETL) [33, 34]. Presently, Capital Cooling has registered over 29 models of refrigeration equipment on the Carbon Trust ETL scheme [35]. As a result, product developers at Capital Cooling consider the eco-friendly and energy-efficient product strategy as enhancing the organization's carbon footprint:

> It is very important because we are then seen to be a company that is following the green impact for our equipment on the rest of the business.
>
> (Product Development Manager [21])

> The Carbon footprint is very important to Capital Cooling we pride ourselves on being energy efficient whether it be in our cases or whether it be in every department in our building. We want to be green … We want to be seen as being green as possible to be a market leader within these processes.
>
> (Technical Manager [23])

Unique in its industry, refrigeration products marketed under the Capital brand are designed by engineers with practical experience in the maintenance of refrigeration and air-conditioning equipment [36]. Design features include the positioning of components at the front of the equipment for ease of servicing and maintenance, energy-efficient scroll compressors, light-emitting diode (LED) lights, and antifrost fan motors that reduce corrosion extending the useful life of the equipment [37] (Fig. 7.10). Unlike conventional refrigeration equipment, the energy consumed in regulating the temperature that is transferred as heat in the form of warm air is used to evaporate condensate moisture collected on a natural fiber wicking system, which is more energy efficient than electrically powered condensate heating trays used on conventional refrigeration and air-conditioning equipment (Fig. 7.10). The company's flagship Troy range of refrigeration equipment that utilizes hydrocarbon refrigerant

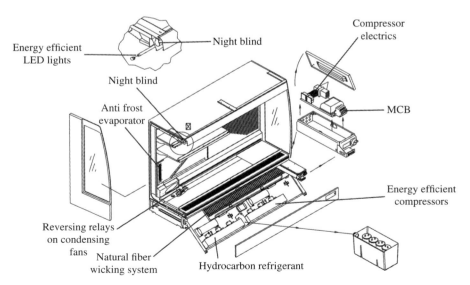

FIGURE 7.10 Schematic of Troy 26 integral multideck refrigerator. Source: © Capital Cooling Ltd.

can achieve daily energy savings 26 kWh or 14 kg/CO_2e; as a bonus, the use of night blinds [38] can contribute an additional 20–30% energy savings (Fig. 7.10).

As an entrepreneur, the CEO of the company has an intimate knowledge of his products and their energy-efficient features:

> A Resource Data Management type controller is a clever device which can control the lights, rather than relying on a member of staff in the retail outlet to put the lights out. It can also control the defrosting; it can control the door frame heaters. There are many features and benefits … such as the design of our evaporator condensers we can actually get 15% more efficiency out of an evaporator by the type of technology we have used and developed over the years now that is a great saving. We are developing a new fan motor that is going to deliver better quality for us. We are continually looking at every-thing we are doing and question ourselves … let's try and make it better all the time.
>
> (CEO [28])

Employees of the company express similar sentiments regarding the catalytic effect of carbon footprint measurement on the development of new products and ser-vices. There is a perception of a general link between carbon emission reduction and the company's pioneering eco-friendly refrigeration and air-conditioning products and services. Managers and nontechnical interviewees agree that carbon footprint measurement is either a direct contributing factor or an indirect influencing factor on product development:

> Chicken & egg … It is chicken and egg as much as 'Yes' the carbon footprint we have had to develop products that have a low carbon footprint to meet the ECA legislation so 'Yes' it is.
>
> (Product Development Manager [21])

> Product wise with our hydrocarbons, the design of certain components on cabinets as we have discussed … Yes.
>
> (Area Manager 2 [39])

> Yes, it has very much, then again over the last two or three years the development of our own product has gone down the line of the carbon footprint moving away from refrigerant that is harmful to the atmosphere to other types of refrigerant which are a. less refrigerant within the case itself and b. non-hazardous refrigerant to the envi-ronment and yes the development has been huge and will continue to be huge and then again our main clients are demanding that but they are demanding that on the back of our own development. We had seen the light three or four years ago and have taken that forward with a full understanding that some of the CFCs and gases we are using were
>
> a. being banned and
> b. should be banned and we took a very bold step…. to go on a different route.

> We are still exploring different avenues as we speak different types of refrigerant that can be used which are either zero harm to the environment or less harm to the environment than the ones that are used at present so yes very much so our development process.
>
> (Logistics Manager [14])

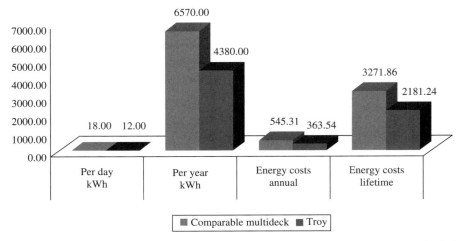

FIGURE 7.11 Energy and cost comparison between comparable multideck and Capital Cooling Troy 26. Source: © Capital Cooling Ltd.

Capital Cooling's design thrust has been focused on the use of environmentally friendly, zero ozone-depleting refrigerants such as hydrocarbon-based refrigerants. Hydrocarbon refrigerants have been used by the refrigeration industry since the 1800s; its current renaissance is due to low GWP and excellent thermodynamic properties of hydrocarbons. These characteristics of natural refrigerants have led to improved component compatibility and overall energy efficiency.

The organizations' refrigerant of choice is R1270, which is 97.5% pure containing low levels of saturated hydrocarbons and sulfur. This level of purity reduces corrosion and improves compressor performance at lower refrigerant charge level. Independent tests by Unilever have found that the use of hydrocarbon refrigerants such as R1270 improves component efficiency by 10% [15, 40]. Internal comparability tests between their flagship Troy 26 range of multideck integral refrigerated equipment and a similar model manufactured by a leading competitor revealed energy cost savings of at least £1090.81 or between 21% and 34% savings over the useful life of the equipment [7] (Fig. 7.11).

The decision to pursue a low-carbon product strategy was initiated by senior management who exploited a gap in the market for commercial refrigeration and air-conditioning:

What lead us to invest in hydrocarbon equipment basically energy would be one driver. The equipment is more energy efficient it is suggested 10–20 % more savings can be achieved by the introduction of hydrocarbon refrigerant as compared with traditional refrigerants. Of course the actual operating charge in each system that contains hydrocarbon as against traditional refrigerants is a lot less for example you might have a 1.4 meter multi-deck cabinet might hold 2kgs of R404 refrigerant and equally you might have a 2.5 meter cabinet with R1270 with 850 grams. So you have smaller pipe work. You know we are really ticking the right boxes there with a lot of our equipment being approved for the Enhanced Capital Allowance (ECA) scheme and the reduced impact on the environment.

(CEO [28])

7.5   SUSTAINABLE PERFORMANCE

The company began in 2010 still reeling from the effects of the credit crunch and uncertain as to the developments on the horizon during a U.K. election year. To counteract these economic challenges, senior management launched a catalogue of new environmentally friendly products under the *Capital* brand targeted to the commercial refrigeration and air-conditioning market [33]. This expansion saw the acquisition of a site at Quinton, which is located at the outskirts of Northampton, and sales offices in Dorset and Bracknell [7]. Opportunities to expand the company's product portfolio were also sought through the introduction of bespoke cold-room design and installation services.

As a result, the company has achieved increasing operating profit; however, the development of our sustainable approach to growth has changed our attitude toward corporate performance not solely from the lens of financial success with a shift interpreting environmental impacts in terms of its carbon emissions. The conversion of waste data to CO_2e emissions initially began in 2010 with the collation of data from waste produced and recycled by the organization, being analyzed using DEFRA carbon emission factors that reflected a carbon impact, which in most cases is greater than the physical weight [28] (Fig. 7.12).

The investment of time and resources in the company's waste recycling program has yielded dividends for Capital Cooling in three main areas:

- Carbon reduction
- Diversion of waste from landfill
- Financial revenue

Waste recycling has decreased the firms' overall carbon emissions by approximately 28.5% when compared to the pursuit of the status quo diverting 540.591 tons of CO_2e from landfill [28] (Fig. 7.13).

Commercially, the diversion of cardboard, plastic, polystyrene, and WEEE from landfill directly contributed over £1815 in the first 12 months of the recycling program, August 2010–August 2011. Overall, the company's sustainability program contributed over £52,945 in revenue during the same reporting period [41] (Fig. 7.14).

Yet the mere fact that the organization has voluntarily measured its carbon footprint consistently since 2009 conveys a perceived legitimacy that the carbon footprint report has been verified by a third-party organization such as the Carbon Trust,

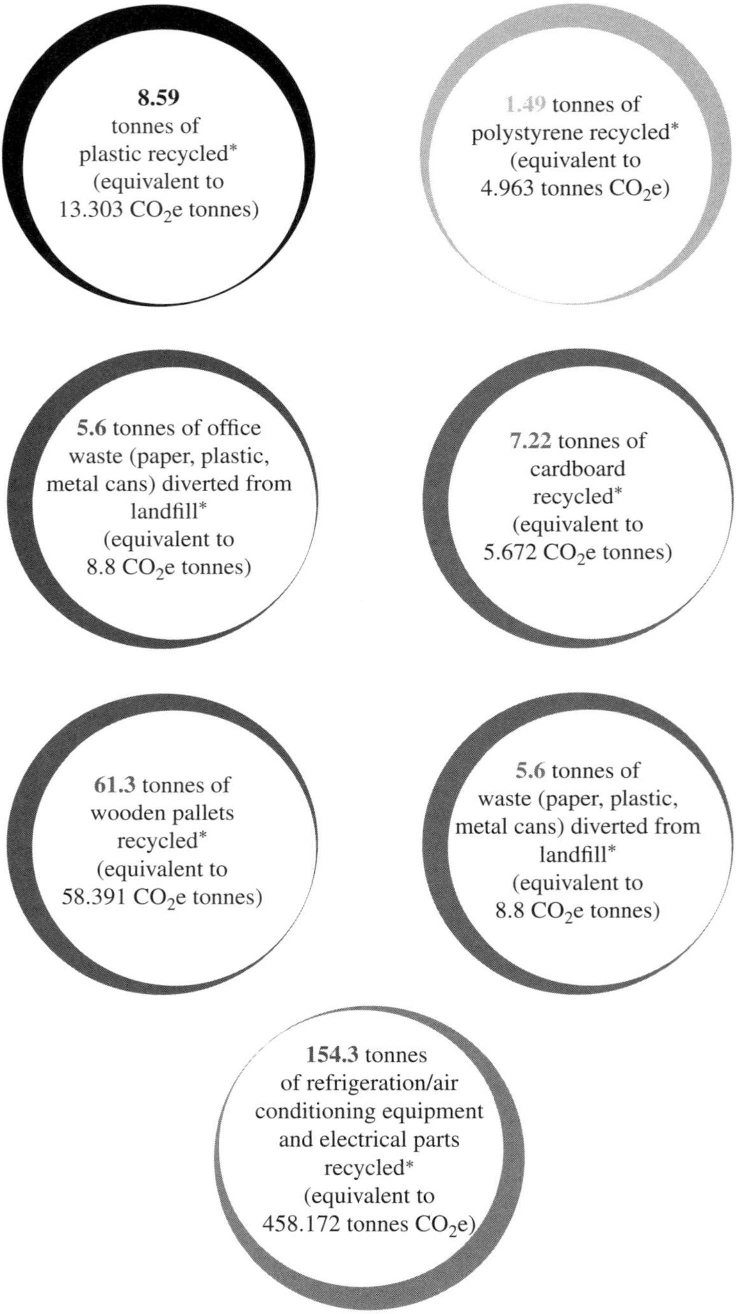

8.59
tonnes of
plastic recycled*
(equivalent to
13.303 CO_2e tonnes)

1.49 tonnes of
polystyrene recycled*
(equivalent to
4.963 tonnes CO_2e)

5.6 tonnes of office
waste (paper, plastic,
metal cans) diverted from
landfill*
(equivalent to
8.8 CO_2e tonnes)

7.22 tonnes of
cardboard
recycled*
(equivalent to
5.672 CO_2e tonnes)

61.3 tonnes of
wooden pallets
recycled*
(equivalent to
58.391 CO_2e tonnes)

5.6 tonnes of
waste (paper, plastic,
metal cans) diverted from
landfill*
(equivalent to
8.8 CO_2e tonnes)

154.3 tonnes
of refrigeration/air
conditioning equipment
and electrical parts
recycled*
(equivalent to
458.172 tonnes CO_2e)

FIGURE 7.12 Capital Cooling waste recycling and carbon reduction data. Source: © Capital Cooling Ltd.

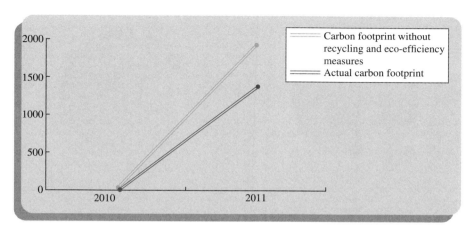

FIGURE 7.13 Carbon emission reduction as a result of recycling and ecoefficiency measures. Source: © Capital Cooling Ltd.

a view that was shared by some employees even though their sentiments were not borne by the reality:

> Yes, the exact details of which I am not sure of it is a Quality, Safety and Environmental area not so much the marketing but I am sure to the best of my knowledge there is reporting on it all also under the ISO.
>
> (Marketing Coordinator [5])

> Apart from the ECA … No …. not from the cabinet development side I don't know other sides of the business but from cabinet development … No.
>
> (Product Development Manager [21])

Similarly, the act of reporting also creates a veneer expertise in so much that there is a belief among employees that the company contracted consultants or other third-party organizations to measure its carbon footprint:

> Unsure about the answer to that question I would think that this is the type of thing that (the consultant) is involved in but is he not?
>
> (Engineering Manager [17])

> As far as I am aware of yes who with I can't remember off the top of my head but I do remember we had a meeting with the guy who came into to do it didn't we?
>
> (Marketing Coordinator [5])

> Yes, everything was independently tested with an independent certificate.
>
> (Product Development Manager [21])

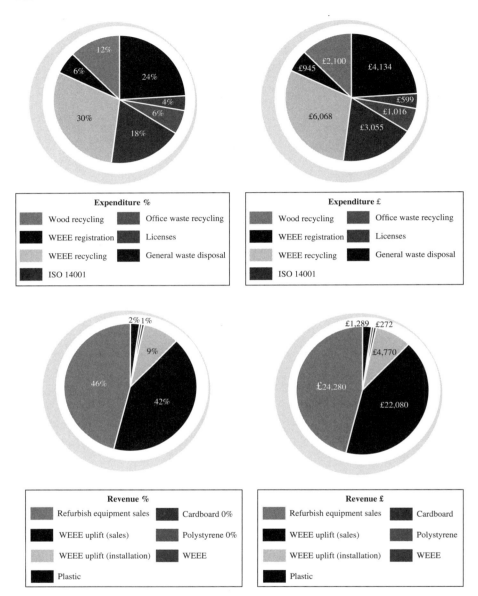

FIGURE 7.14   Capital Cooling environmental cost and revenue 2011. Source: © Capital Cooling Ltd.

Overall, employees share the sentiment that carbon footprint reporting has improved the understanding of environmental impacts and their role in the process of emission reduction:

Everyone is much more aware of carbon footprint actually means and of the importance of the carbon footprint as well.

(Engineering Manager [17])

Yes, it has broadened my understanding of the carbon footprint impact on the environment.

(Installation Engineer [42])

Yes I think you don't before you actually look the figures the impact that certain things have you don't realize how many tons of paper the company consumes until you actually see it then you can realize its 6 tons or whatever quite a hefty amount obviously you are quite aware a lot of our business expenses and lot of our footprint is from the transportation of our products to us and from us to our clients. I would assume that is main generator of carbon from us how we get around that I don't rightly know we have obviously gone for more aerodynamic vehicles when it comes to the trucks, company cars are going to the more CO_2 friendly business blue efficiency or efficient dynamic models wherever possible so there are obviously changes that way that have come about because people are getting a better understanding.

(Marketing Coordinator [5])

The measurement of the company's water and social footprints although not on the agenda of the company is a potential source of innovation that can, as perceived by some interviewees, contribute to the future prosperity of the organization and the planet:

I wouldn't have an answer to that but I would suggest that when we are dealing with the design and our input in the design of ice machines. We are aware of the water consumption in relation to the ice produced because we now seem to be moving into the larger market of ice machines. The more ice the more aware we have to become the more machines we sell the more aware we have to become if we can save a liter a day from each machine that we sell by this time next year that can make a big difference.

(Engineering Manager [17])

Yes, I think is something that we need to do and we are not a high user of water in the first instance … it would not fall into the top twenty of items that we really need to do. If we were in an industry that used of a lot of water then it would trickle up the list but we are not a high user of water. We only use water in the normal domestic situations i.e. toilet water, wash hand basins we don't use water for any other domestic issues. We do wash vehicles … to maintain our presentation of the vehicles to our clients and to our own personnel but there is not a huge amounting of water used within that process it is something that would get measured but I don't see it being a high priority certainly not as much as say the refrigerant issue or the recyclable issue on materials and used waste products etcetera.

(Logistics Manager [4])

7.6   CRITICAL SUCCESS FACTORS

Capital Cooling has made enormous strides to engage stakeholders through its online presence and charitable work in aid of local communities. The benchmark customer satisfaction survey [43] in 2010 outlined customer perceptions of Capital Cooling's products and services (Fig. 7.15).

A subsequent customer satisfaction survey [44] conducted in 2011 mirrors overall customer sentiment for the organization but outlines opportunities for communicating the Capital Cooling's sustainability performance (Fig. 7.15).

Although the company consistently achieves high levels of customer satisfaction, interviewees are not convinced of customer interest in the carbon footprint and its effect on purchasing decisions as it forms part of the tendering process especially for stock exchange-listed customers. Although staff members perceive that customers are interested in the organization's carbon emissions, its primacy in relation to other criteria in purchasing decisions is not universally accepted:

It has not created any interest it has been part of the tender selection process without it you don't pass the first post.

(Product Development Manager [21])

Yes, from major clients not necessarily independent clients corporate clients like the COOP, Sainsbury's, Morrison's … certainly independents.

(Area Manager 1 [45])

Existing customers definitely, CoOp and any other large companies that come on board will be asking.

(PPM Administrator [11])

Yes as I have already said it is part of the required tendering and factors now I think as some of the big "multiple" clients request your carbon footprint knowledge before you can actually go and tender a lot of these issues are getting played out by many of the major organizations now the individuals are going to follow suit but it is going to take them a little bit longer. However because 98% of the business comes from multiples … hopefully we can satisfy 98% of our customers by what we are doing in the way of Carbon Reduction and we only have got the 2 percent of individual clients then that is what we need to work on next.

(Logistics Manager [14])

Trade associations such as the Scottish Federation of Meat Traders have come to rely on Capital Cooling's expertise as a leader in quality refrigeration and air-conditioning equipment by hosting one of their key membership training events at company's head office. In 2011, the opportunity arose for the firm to participate in the EuroShop Global Trade Fair to showcase their environmentally friendly product range of energy-efficient refrigeration and air-conditioning equipment. The feedback and ideas received from this visit contributed to the relaunch of the firm's online presence for Capital Cooling and Capital Products. This was closely followed later

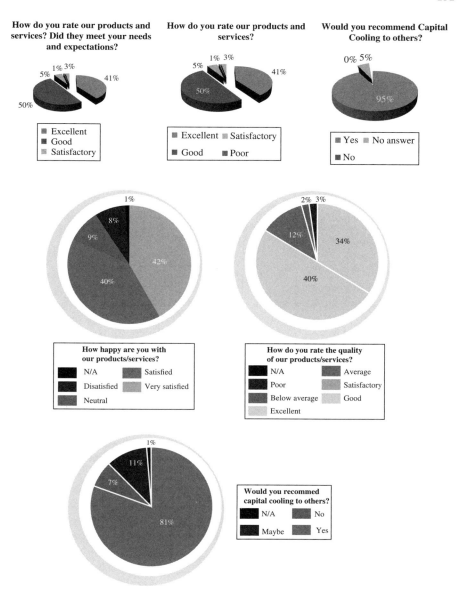

FIGURE 7.15 Capital Cooling customer satisfaction key indicators 2010 and 2011. Source: © Capital Cooling Ltd.

that year by the publication of their second product catalogue that introduced to their stakeholders to an expanded range of new and exciting refrigeration and air-conditioning products and services.

Capital Cooling initiated a program of employee engagement by conducting their benchmark engineer satisfaction survey to look at issues affecting our frontline staff.

Feedback from this initiative led to the development of the "Tell Alister Program" whereby staff and engineers directly communicated their ideas, concepts, and projects to the CEO.

In 2011, the organization increased their staffing complement by 10%, thereby also contributing to the economy of the local community. Capital Cooling's stakeholder engagement in sustainability/CSR has boosted staff morale, employee sense of worth and well-being, which in turn has helped the company attract, retain, and motivate the best talent. This expansion created its own challenges in terms of impact on the carbon footprint but also operational synergy across multiple sites, which required the induction and training of new personnel into the organizational culture.

7.7 SUSTAINABILITY/CSR CHARTER: SETTING THE COURSE WITH SUBCONTRACTORS AND SUPPLIERS

Sustainably managing the organization's supply chain is critical to Capital Cooling's continued success in the refrigeration sector. With subcontractors and suppliers located in Poland, Turkey, Italy, and China, strategic approaches were adopted to ensure their commitment through a robust vetting process. This review required subcontractors to disclose their readiness to pursue or maintain ISO 14001 certification and compliance with European directives on the restriction of the use of certain hazardous substances (RoHS) such as lead and cadmium. At the company's World Quality Day 2009 seminar for subcontractors entitled *"Capital Cooling Ltd in partnership with our contractors—Providing high quality, environmentally friendly Refrigeration & Air Conditioning products and services to our customers safely,"* subcontractors received environmental awareness training. The success of this initiative was published as best practice article in *Safety Management* [46], the official journal of the British Safety Council.

Organically evolving from this success, the firm developed their *Sustainability/ CSR Charter* [47], *which is an extension of the organization's sustainability/CSR policy* that forms a key requirement of their supplier/subcontractor assessment process. The Sustainability/CSR Charter seeks supplier and subcontractor commitment to achieve four main aims:

- To develop and provide refrigeration products and services, which have no negative impact on the planet
- To operate in a sustainable manner at all times by reducing waste and energy usage
- To support and contribute to the success of the local community and the country as a whole
- To improve the working lives of employees by offering training, support, and rewards

There is however uncertainty as to the need to require suppliers and subcontractors to provide the sustainability footprint data and the extent to which small suppliers and subcontractors can be expected to comply with a largely voluntary initiative with some interviewees emphasizing the importance of quality, safety, and environmental practitioners in sustainability management:

> Yes, because it's all part of our carbon footprint.
>
> (Installation Engineer [42])

> Suppliers we would expect.... sub-contractors it may be slightly beyond them at the moment. Again I would imagine that if they are a sub-contractor for us they are a lot smaller their focus is more on the business side rather than the operational side of things and having the capability to provide that type of information not all our sub-contractors could have a QSE Manger to provide that type of information.
>
> (Area Manager 2 [39])

> Yes, every one of them is tasked on that before they are employed by Capital Cooling they are vetted and verified.
>
> (Technical Manager [23])

Although the company's *Sustainability/CSR Charter* is not specifically requiring their suppliers and subcontractors to measure and manage their carbon footprint, it is implied through their commitment to reduce waste and energy usage, thereby charting a new course for long-term growth within the business.

The organization's interaction with its stakeholders extends beyond the contractual obligations and pursuit of profit. The organization is involved with various charitable fundraising events such as the Wear It Pink Day and the MacMillan Cancer Trust Big Coffee Morning and its perennial support for Help for Heroes fundraising drives. In 2012, the firm contributed to the Scottish Business in the Community (SBC)—a member of His Royal Highness Prince of Wales Trust community outreach program by introducing refrigeration engineering and environmental management as potential career opportunities. The owner of the business understands the benefits of local community outreach and engagement:

> The business contribution to the wider community is something that we could have done much smarter in the past certainly it is going to be on the agenda for the future to actually look at how we can actually help others about us who are not so fortunate as us so that may be down as a work in progress for us watch this space.
>
> (CEO [28])

Keen to make good on a promise, the CEO authorized the company's participation in the SBC Think Ahead to Work program, which provides an introduction to the world of work to primary school students. Capital Cooling also voluntarily reports its carbon performance to the Mayday Network scheme managed by the SBC earning a reputation as an SME:

> Scotland's transition to a low carbon economy presents a real opportunity to provide thousands of jobs to a future workforce. By working with companies like Capital Cooling, we are able to bring real life examples of a career in environmental sustainability to life. Capital Cooling is seen by many as a great example of how best to reduce carbon emissions, now, through its school engagement program, it is taking these learning's to the future workforce by engaging with local schools in an innovative and proactive manner. This represents a win-win for both the business and the school pupils. At high school most students are already thinking about careers and we are keen to get students educated and enthused about the wide range of opportunities available. There has been great interest in the transition programs throughout Scotland and we have a number of projects lined up throughout the year.
>
> (Head of the Environment [28])

Communicating carbon performance to external stakeholders has been a key thrust of the sustainability communication campaign, yet messaging of the company's participation in voluntary schemes such as the Mayday Network has not been effectively disseminated despite the company achieving substantial emission reduction with some managers and nontechnical personnel being unaware of the company's achievements in this area:

> I am not aware of it.
>
> (Installation Manager [4])

> Yes, the exact details of which I am not sure of it is a Quality, Safety and Environmental area not so much the marketing but I am sure to the best of my knowledge there is reporting on it all also under the ISO.
>
> (Marketing Coordinator [5])

> Apart from the ECA … No … not from the cabinet development side I don't know other sides of the business but from cabinet development … No.
>
> (Product Development Manager [21])

> I would say yes but I don't know them off the top of my head I have seen them their names but I can't remember I have seen their names on the website on the PC.
>
> (Area Manager 1 [45])

Although engaged in social issues, employees are unaware of social footprint methodology perceiving it as the domain of senior management with an underlying feeling that the firm is unable to influence the social environment as it is beyond the control of the organization:

> It's a hard one I think there is … as in the water side of things the water usage with the company we are trying our best to limit the amount of water we are using, I think we

have always looked at that in the way of waste … we want to try to limit the amount of waste as we possibly can. Social it is a harder one to try and evaluate the social footprint because it is out with the work. So socially what do you do? You can't legislate for what happens outside … out with your work. As long as we focus on the footprint of employees within the organisation within their working time I think we will be doing all we can.

(Technical Manager [23])

Not as far as I am aware of but that is something that (Quality, Safety & Environmental Manager) is dealing with at the far end of the chain.

(Installation Engineer [42])

The firm's major challenge in implementing its carbon footprint program is the perceived cost, management perceptions of sustainability, and resource allocation in terms of personnel and time.

To fully exploit the strategic opportunity presented by CSR/sustainability footprint, the management of the firm found it necessary to review and update the existing structure. The following changes were proposed by the QSE Manager [13] (Fig. 7.16):

1. A change in the title of the QSE Manager to **Sustainability/CSR Manager** reflecting the strategic nature of the role that aligns with the mission of the organization: "reducing the environmental impact of standard business practices and the development of cutting edge environmentally friendly products"

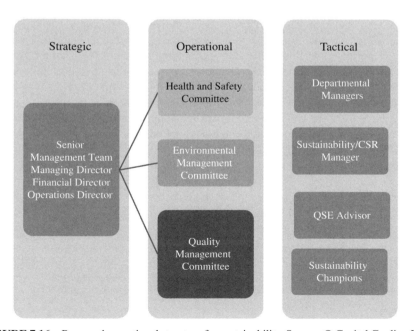

FIGURE 7.16   Proposed operational structure for sustainability. Source: © Capital Cooling Ltd.

2. The inclusion of a **QSE Advisor** to provide operational support at the Quinton site and to assist departmental managers with the delivery of sustainability toolbox talks and monitoring

3. The nomination of **Sustainability Champion(s)** who will provide leadership on quality/safety and environmental issues

As pictorially illustrated in Figure 42, the glue that holds the structure together is the effectiveness of the key functional committees such as:

Environmental Management Committee—The sole remit of this committee originally focused on the operational management of the *ISO 14001 EMS*. The responsibility of this committee was extended to include energy management, fuel management, and sustainability/CSR.

An effective sustainability/CSR program also involves implementing sustainable environmental practices such as the carbon footprint and management systems across all aspects of our operations such as *BS 8900 Standard for Sustainable Development* and incorporating best practice approaches outlined in the *ISO 26000 Guidance on Social Responsibility.*

Through the strengthening of the existing operational structure, the organization can then exploit opportunities to measure its DEFRA Scope 3 impacts. Presently, the focus has been to measure and manage Scope 1 and 2 emissions leaving supply chain emissions largely unchecked; a proposal to measure the carbon footprint of its product range, reduce emissions where possible, and offset emissions that cannot be reduced was presented to management in 2010. Although product development is engaged in producing energy-efficient products, the carbon-neutral aspects of the product offering and its potential as a marketing tool are yet to be fully realized. Although a wide variety of organizations are involved with the measuring, certifying, and communicating the carbon footprint associated with their products or services. The Carbon Trust, an independent certification body responsible for carbon labeling products and services, reports that "carbon labeling is not actively explored by any other refrigeration and air conditioning company" competing in the firm's target markets.

Quantifying the greenhouse gas emissions of the company's products/service is not only a useful indicator of environmental performance, but when combined with carbon offsetting, it provides customers with a carbon-neutral purchase. Carbon offsets range from conservation projects, for example, tree planting in Scotland, to charitable programs in the developing world, which can be purchased along with the product or included in the product/price/promotion mix.

A project feasibility study was conducted by Scottish Enterprise [13] later that year to determine the eligibility of the proposal for government funding of product carbon footprint measurement initiatives. An initial analysis of the competitive benefits of adopting product carbon footprint suggests the potential for an *eco-friendly/energy-efficient* and *carbon-neutral strategy* to create competitive advantage that is not easily replicable by competitors, and this benefit outweighs any other short-term strategic option as graphically illustrated in Figure 7.17 [13].

Implementation of CSR and sustainability management systems can have a long-term positive impact on Capital Cooling as a business. Increasing global competition among businesses for raw materials and resources means that in the

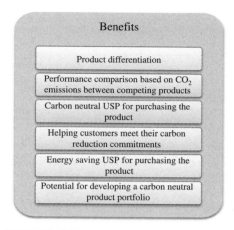

FIGURE 7.17   Benefits and challenges of product carbon labeling. Source: © Capital Cooling Ltd.

future, all organizations will be required to contribute to building a sustainable society through better use of resources and raw materials evolving into *Sustainably Managed Enterprises* (SMEs). Organizations that fail to embrace the sustainability agenda now may therefore be putting their future prosperity and long-term survival at risk.

Sustainability footprints are an emerging concept that has been embraced by the organization. The employees of the organization define sustainability as comprising recycling, carbon emission reduction, and continuous improvement:

> Well I would say continual improvement unless I am misinterpreting it … Sustainable … it has got to be continuously trying to seek continual improvement I think.
>
> (Engineering Manager [17])

> Is making something with the lowest possible CO_2 footprint which means it is using less energy which means it more sustainable.
>
> (Product Development Manager [21])

> To maintain what you have at the moment or a better footprint … To maintain it.
>
> (Area Manager 1 [45])

> Is it keeping a constant level of the processes we are doing … Sustaining that.
>
> (Area Manager 2 [39])

As a management tool, the firm's employees suggest that sustainability footprints act as a useful performance benchmark, marketing, or sales tool for contract bidding, which can lead to positive customer feedback:

> Very much so for probably all the reasons I have just mentioned previously for getting contracts for being considered for contracts for opening the doors to contracts we don't have yet and as Capital Cooling grows as a company the carbon footprint has to be treated the same it is just as important.
>
> (Engineering Manager [17])

Massively useful it gives everybody an idea of the level where we are and the level where we want to be... it is always something that pushes people the extra mile. I know it is something that sounds pretty clichéd by saying we are green company but we always want to be a green company and we want to be seen as a green company and as I said previously we want to be a market leader and a market leader in everything we do and that includes the carbon footprint having the best carbon footprint that we possibly can and then not stopping there making it better.

(Technical Manager [23])

Remarkably, employees have modified their disposal patterns at work, which has extended to their domestic environment yielding positive environmental dividends in terms of adopting more sustainable lifestyles.

By extension, employees of the firm construe a positive link between their recycling program and efforts to reduce the company's carbon footprint and tackling climate change. This expressed concern is confirmed by their own observations of changing weather patterns and details of the social impact of climate change on their daily life. However, this perceived link between carbon footprint and climate change is not accepted by all of the company's management:

Yes, but I also see all options available I look at both the positives and the negatives ... individuals that say it relate to it and individuals that say it do not but I share my own opinions on that but I will always strive to think and be aware of the carbon footprint and the reductions that will be required.

(Engineering Manager [17])

Yes, you are saving the environment ... your emissions.... going into the atmosphere if you are reducing that you are helping the environment. Waste as recycling wood.... Cabinets.... Polystyrene ... cardboard everything gets recycled its good for the environment.

(Area Manager 1 [45])

Yes, obviously if you are conscious of your carbon footprint and you do take measures to reduce it. It's going to have a positive effect on the environment.

(Area Manager 2 [39])

Yes the more we do to help it the less we are going to get the effects of the weather changes or the damage that we have been causing all these years.

(PPM Administrator [11])

Support for carbon footprint methodology abounds, but the need to set targets seems to elude the management of the firm. By nature, SMEs are embryonic corporations or transnational organizations of the future, making target setting a challenging exercise. However, employees assume there are explicit targets for carbon reduction; however, they are unaware of the exact details. Their conceptualization of carbon footprint target setting is influenced by their direct contribution in areas such as recycling and process improvements:

Continually trying to reduce it in any way can be done whether it is operational, design, transport every department should always be seeking to reduce their carbon footprint.

(Engineering Manager [17])

I think just as a company every year we want to improve on the recycling we are doing whether that is measured by weights ... disposing of wood, plastic cardboard or whatever I am not sure but I would like to think that there is a target that has been set.

(Sales Coordinator [3])

Not that I personally know of but I must say that there must be targets that we have to meet to help lower the carbon footprint.

(Installation Engineer [42])

The underlying rationale for the adoption of carbon footprint methodology is to measure a firm's level of greenhouse gas emissions, reduce costs and consumption to combat against climate change. When challenged as to the usefulness of carbon footprint measurement as a tool for SMEs to combat climate change, employees generally indicate a genuine benefit from the exercise despite the "*sustainability liability*" associated with the costs of the environmentally friendly features of the product:

Yes and no. Yes because it is useful for us personally to be seen to be going down the right route. No because it makes our products somewhat expensive because we would not win that piece of business or we would not quote for that piece of equipment.

(Product Development Manager [21])

Yes it is a useful tool we always need to be improving on it which can only be a positive. As time goes on I see it constantly evolving into something else then you have the improvements that even we have made. It is an important tool for SMEs.

(Area Manager 2 [39])

Yes definitely without that you would not know you would just be guessing it's a definite yardstick.

(Technical Manager [23])

Carbon footprint as an investment although handicapped by long payback period and time-consuming data collection techniques is considered by employees as a valued investment that aids in carbon reduction and the economical use of financial resources:

Managed sensibly ... and being financially aware in that investment.

(Engineering Manager [17])

Yes, you may not get your money back right away as investment but over a long period of time it will start to pay dividends.... but in the long term you will get your money back just for example your cardboard, polystyrene, plastics before that it probably got (disposed) now it gets recycled. Now you have paid money for all these machines to do this you won't get that back right away but through a period of time. It does take time to start to get back your money again. You are not paying for dump trucks to come in here and pick up the rubbish.... If they are coming to pick up they are coming to give you money.

(Area Manager 1 [46])

As I said going forward everybody is going to have to do it and everybody should be doing it we are trying to prepare and protect what for the future for others and if we don't start now when do we start.

(PPM Administrator [11])

As a result of the success of this program, the firm achieved ISO 14001 EMS certification and the Scottish Green Award for Best Green SME and is presently considered an example of organizational best practice [6]. Employees however consider the value of carbon footprint methodology to SMEs as comprising competitive differentiation, marketing/public relations leverage, a response to supply chain pressure, energy savings, increased market share, market leadership and contributing to the development of a "caring organization":

There is obviously a financial implication if you are talking water footprint we can reduce the amount of water we are using, reduce the amount of fuel we are burning. It's going to be positive to us on the flip side it would generate revenue as well by attracting more business going forward.

(Area Manager 1 [45])

The point is twofold as I have already said the point is to satisfy Capital Cooling and Capital Cooling's employees that we are doing our part to the environment. The return that comes back from that is additional but I think we didn't start out to actually to gain financial reward immediately from that... to be at the top of somebody's list because we are doing something. We did it because we care I think that is the important part we can't forget that we are doing it because we care and that is the important part.

(Logistics Manager [14])

Despite of the organizations' pioneering achievements, employees view a role for policymaking institutions in supporting the uptake of carbon footprint measurement by creating a fair competitive marketplace and providing incentives such as grants, tax relief, training, guidance, and enforcement:

They can provide information on the best ways to go about reducing your carbon footprint and obviously the way forward in the future to try and keep it low.

(Installation Engineer [42])

Better grants, more grants, wider grants ... That's the only way you are going to get people to buy into it... financial tax reductions.

(Installations Manager [4])

I think it would be nice to see rewards, grants tax relief similar to the ECA Scheme for people that are making the effort similar and doing their best for the environment. Obviously we have the ECA scheme for our products that's if a retailer buys a cabinet they can claim back their corporation tax in the first year. If there was something for that based on reducing your carbon footprint then I am sure more people would do it but obviously there is the cynical side that says people are doing it to save money, the environmental aspect will certainly be a healthy by-product.

(Marketing Coordinator [5])

Despite the absence of incentives, it is perceived that the firm is driven by the following factors to measure its carbon footprint: legislation, waste reduction, senior management commitment, operational requirements, and cost reduction:

> Legislation but I believe we have a CEO that strives to be at the top of the field in everything that we enter and this is part of it and he wants to be the best at it.
>
> (Engineering Manager [17])

> To reduce waste in general to make sure we are not paying to dispose of waste and we are necessarily getting paid to dispose of waste instead to try and reduce our carbon footprint we are putting out there compared to what we might have been a few years ago.
>
> (Sales Coordinator [3])

> Is there not a charge from the government for the higher your footprint? The lower your carbon footprint the better it is for the company and for everyone else.
>
> (Installations Engineer [42])

7.8 SUMMARY

Without any clear indication of its contribution and impact on growth of the company, the management of Capital Cooling Ltd. implemented carbon footprint measurement as a strategic tool and in so doing changed perceptions of the waste produced by the company, which is now viewed as a profit center and quantified based on carbon emission impact. In addition to senior management commitment, employee engagement using all available communication channels and platforms was critical to the success of this strategy. Using this approach requires the organization to be honest in evaluating its current state of sustainability and maintaining openness in discussing the validity of actions taken to mitigate its environmental impact; it has seen the organization ready to innovate and continuously improve its people/products and processes. This preemptive decision to reduce the firm's exposure to risks from legislation such as the Climate Change Act 2009 has not only generated financial returns but has influenced employees to adopt sustainable behaviors and purchasing decisions. Capital Cooling's commitment to sustainability and CSR has contributed to the development of its benchmark CSR/Sustainability Report—a first for any SME in the refrigeration and air-conditioning industry.

However, despite this consensus, carbon footprint measurement is not considered cost neutral, and sustainability initiatives are considered by some employees as a luxury in a credit-constrained environment.

Importantly, employees perceive similar benefits of sustainability footprint methodology identified in larger organizations such as reduced risk, reduced energy consumption, and market segregation; environmental impact indicator and value indicator also accrue to the company.

Although this is an in-depth analysis of perceptions of carbon footprints, critically, it highlights opportunities for policymaking institutions to influence and change views within SMEs of sustainability footprint methodology as being a luxury, questionable expense or perceived "sustainability liability" of eco-friendly products and services through the provision of grants, training, and tax relief.

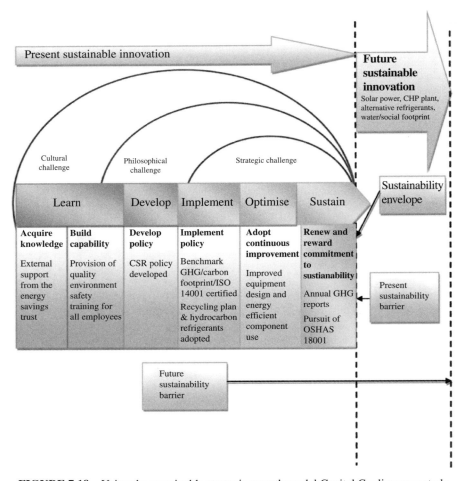

FIGURE 7.18   Using the sustainable strategic growth model Capital Cooling case study.

Adopting the use of sustainability footprint strategy as outlined in this case study could potentially yield cost savings in terms of reduced compliance costs and efficiency but can also create new niche markets, which can contribute to future growth in the short to medium term. When connected with wider business initiatives in a coherent, seamless strategy, linking other programs such as product development, that is, environmentally friendly products, and process improvements such as ISO 14001 EMS can contribute to long-term survival of the business.

At a glance, the Sustainable Strategic Growth Model illustrates (Fig. 7.18) initiatives undertaken by the firm in implementing carbon footprint methodology and deploying sustainability throughout the organization by overcoming the cultural challenge, the philosophical challenge, and the strategic challenge using the *learn, develop, implement, optimize,* and *sustain* approach.

The organization initially developed a culture of continuous learning acquiring knowledge on carbon footprint measurement from organizations such as the Energy Saving Trust, British Safety Council, Chartered Management Institute, and IEMA. This knowledge was not retained among senior management but disseminated throughout the organization by a series of workshops, thereby building consensus concerning the importance of sustainability initiatives and capability to implement sustainable change within the organization. Environmental awareness training was a key component in overcoming both the cultural challenge and philosophical challenge.

The management of the organization ratified organizational policies that extended the boundaries of its quality ethos defining its principles regarding safety, environment, and CSR. Specifically, this case study illustrates that ISO 14001 company certification and carbon footprint measurement are natural complementary outcomes that emerged from senior management comment to sustainability/CSR policy with the dissemination of the benchmark CSR/Sustainability Report providing the business case that capitalizes on conventional views encapsulated in the strategic challenge. The use of ozone-friendly hydrocarbon refrigerants and recycling plans not only reduced the organizations environmental impact but also provide new revenue streams and a unique selling proposition (USP) to market the business and its products.

This willingness to exploit opportunities contributed to the development of new equipment utilizing energy-efficient components that aligned the emergent sustainability culture with its preexisting continuous improvement ethos. The pursuit of OHSAS 18001 demonstrates senior management commitment to sustainability by ensuring that employees work in a safe operating environment with an appropriate reward system for the achievement of safe and sustainable behaviors. The strategic continuum of *learn, develop, implement, optimize,* and *sustain* can only assist the firm to transition the present sustainability barrier and generate future sustainable growth by investing in research and development into the use of alternative refrigerants and renewable energy such as solar power and generating energy from wood waste by utilizing a combined heat power plant (CHP) and the implementation of water footprint and social footprint techniques.

REFERENCES

[1] HVAC Index. RAC News. Available at http://data.racplus.com/hvacrindex. Accessed on Apr 4, 2012.

[2] Capital Cooling Greenhouse Gas Report 2010–2011.

[3] Sales Coordinator. Interview by author, Edinburgh; Oct 26, 2011.

[4] Installation Manager. Interview by author, Edinburgh; Oct 31, 2011.

[5] Marketing Coordinator. Interview by author, Edinburgh; Oct 31, 2011.

[6] Capital Cooling CSR/Sustainability Report 2010.

[7] Capital Cooling Company Overview 2012.

[8] James L. Embedding the environment into company DNA. Environmentalist May 2010 (97).

[9] PPM Administrator. Interview by author, Edinburgh; Nov 18, 2011.

[10] United Kingdom Government, Climate Change (Scotland) Act 2009. Available at http://www.legislation.gov.uk/asp/2009/12/contents. Accessed on Jan 3, 2014.

[11] United Kingdom Government, Fluorinated Greenhouse Gas Regulations 2009. Available at: http://www.legislation.gov.uk/uksi/2009/261/contents/made. Accessed on Jan 3, 2014.

[12] Waste (Scotland) Regulations. 2012. Available at http://www.legislation.gov.uk/sdsi/2012/9780111016657/contents. Accessed on Jan 3, 2014.

[13] Capital Cooling Carbon Neutral Proposal 2010.

[14] Logistics Manager. Interview by author, Edinburgh; Nov 29, 2011.

[15] Reducing emissions of F-gases as a means of avoiding dangerous climate change—a background briefing. Environmental Investigation Agency, Sep 2011.

[16] Reilly J, Mayer M, Harnisch J. The Kyoto protocol and non-CO_2 greenhouse gases and carbon sinks. *Environ Modeling Assess* 2002;7:217–229.

[17] Engineering Manager. Interview by author, Edinburgh; Nov 11, 2011.

[18] Marketing Coordinator. Interview by author, Edinburgh; Oct 31, 2011.

[19] Capital Cooling Environmental Management Committee Minutes.

[20] Capital Cooling Greenhouse Gas Report 2008–2009.

[21] Product Development Manager. Interview by author, Edinburgh; Dec 1, 2011.

[22] Capital Cooling Greenhouse Gas Report 2009–2010.

[23] Technical Manager. Interview by author, Edinburgh; Oct 26, 2011.

[24] Logistics Manager. Interview by author, Edinburgh; Nov 29, 2011.

[25] Capital Cooling CSR/Sustainability Report 2012 (draft).

[26] Capital Cooling Green Fleet Review 2011.

[27] Banner S. Rigids can be smooth. *Commercial Motor*; Jun **26**, 2010, p. 32–35.

[28] Capital Cooling Ltd CSR/Sustainability Report 2012 (draft).

[29] Capital Cooling Ltd—Broxburn Utility Costs Data 2010–2011.

[30] Capital Cooling Ltd—Quinton Utility Costs Data 2010–2011.

[31] Capital Cooling Energy Efficiency Report 2011.

[32] Capital Cooling EMS Committee Minutes.

[33] Capital Products Catalogue 2010.

[34] Capital Products Catalogue 2011.

[35] DECC. Energy Technology List. Available at: http://etl.decc.gov.uk/etl/find/_QuickSearch. Accessed on Jul 8, 2011.

[36] ACR. Passionate about quality. ACR Today; November 2011, p. 10.

[37] ACR. Different by design. ACR News Today; November 2011, p. 26.

[38] Unknown. Help Save the Planet, Technical Bulletin, Use of night blinds on multideck chiller cabinets, Potential Energy Savings, 2011.

[39] Area Manager 2. Interview by author, Edinburgh; Nov 17, 2011.

[40] EIA. Chilling Facts III—Supermarkets are reducing their climate change impact. Environmental Investigation Agency, 2011.

[41] Capital Cooling Environmental Cost & Revenue 2010–2011.

[42] Installation Engineer. Interview by author, Edinburgh; Oct 24, 2011.

[43] Capital Cooling Customer Satisfaction Survey 2010.

[44] Capital Cooling Customer Satisfaction Survey 2011.

[45] Area Manager 1. Interview by author, Edinburgh; Nov 15, 2011.

[46] British Safety Council. Capital keeps its cool with Level 1 course. Safety Management; 2010, p. 26.

[47] Capital Cooling Sustainability/CSR Charter.

8

THE LOG HOUSE PEOPLE: LOW-CARBON CONSTRUCTION

8.1 INTRODUCTION

The Log House People Ltd. is a British civil engineering company specializing in the supply and construction of log houses for personal or commercial purposes [1]. Established in 2008 by Hugh Gourlay and his father, Frank Gourlay, a former Chairman of the Dumfries and Galloway Tourist Board, The Log House People combines a family interest in the building of log homes with a concern for the environment [1, 2]. The company is managed from a rented office in Edinburgh and a home office located in Sandyhills, Dumfriesshire, that is staffed by two full-time employees with additional staff being hired on a project basis [3]. The seeds of this interest in log home construction began with Frank Gourlay who has constructed log homes since 1970 such as the holiday chalets at the Barend Holiday Village, which consists of 78 log homes, as well as 8 log homes in Riverview, Dumfriesshire, with subsequent investments in a Ski company, expanding his knowledge in the building of log homes [1]. Leveraging his understanding of the local tourist sector, he identified that there was a need for larger holiday homes and so, in partnership with his son, began importing log homes from North America [1].

Hugh Gourlay has spent most of his formative years living in log homes and was a witness to the development of the Barend Holiday Village [1]. Although educated

Sustainability Footprints in SMEs: Strategy and Case Studies for Entrepreneurs and Small Business,
First Edition. Lowellyne James.

as a product designer, Hugh Gourlay wanted to combine his interest for the environment with his familiarity with log houses [1]:

> The Log House People was started in 2008 by me and my father. My Father has actually been building log homes since 1970 and has built a holiday village in Dumfries and Galloway. I got involved with him in business in 2008 and we started the Log House People to import log homes from America which we build for clients and we have been doing it since 2008.
>
> (Director [4])

Initially, the first 7 log homes were built using Scottish pinewood; as supply became unavailable, Douglas fir from Aberdeenshire was then procured to construct an additional 53 dwellings. Scandinavian pine from Finland was later used as a construction material but was found not to be suitable for the Scottish weather conditions [3]. The importation of timber, mainly American pine from the United States and western red cedar [1] from Canada, was due mainly to the inability to procure within the United Kingdom timber log dimensions measuring $0.15\,m \times 0.2\,m \times 6\,m$.

The company prides itself in purchasing timber harvested from mature forests located in the Blue Ridge Mountains of North Carolina using sustainable techniques such as the selection of only mature trees for felling and the planting of two new trees for each tree that has been harvested [1].

As a senior director of The Log House People, Hugh Gourlay was interviewed to ascertain his perceptions regarding the benefits of sustainability footprint methodology to his business as an SME.

8.2   CONTEXT

Domestic buildings contribute 27% of the United Kingdom's greenhouse gas emissions with the built environment accounting for 40% of Scotland's emissions [5]. Recent studies suggest that the construction sector, which is largely dominated by SMEs, has a significant role to play not only in the provision of energy-efficient housing and "zero-carbon" homes but also in the creation of green jobs thereby supporting the U.K. Government's low-carbon strategy [4, 6, 7].

As an SME within the construction sector, The Log House People began measuring their carbon footprint as a member of the Crichton Carbon Centre's Carbon Smart Project in 2009. Management of the company considers carbon footprint measurement to be important to the company because of its usefulness as a measure of the organization's output in terms of carbon emissions and a performance indicator of environmental impact:

> I did it last year because I was working on a project within the Crichton Carbon Centre and that was my first introduction to carbon footprints. I think it is important and it is a good measure of your company's output in terms of carbon emissions. It's a useful way to measure what you are doing and your impact on the planet … it is a very useful thing to do.
>
> (Director [4])

The Crichton Carbon Centre's Carbon Smart Program requires participating organizations to nominate a Carbon Champion and develop a carbon management policy, which were both implemented by the company. Surprisingly, of The Log House People's Directors, Hugh Gourlay is the only one that is actively engaged in the reduction of the environmental impacts arising from operational activities in his role as a "Carbon Champion" perceiving generational issues in the recognition of the climate change impacts of business operations. This denial of climate change impacts in itself affects the nature of the type of management decisions taken in regard to environmental mitigation efforts:

> Because he is older is less interested in that kind of thing … but he would be retiring soon and it is something that I would probably have more of an impact upon.
>
> (Director [4])

The divergent views held between the organization's key decision makers create a communication barrier that negates against the effective implementation of sustainability initiatives with the deferral of proposals until the retirement of the senior director or an agreed succession:

> Just my father's not lack of interest but failure to recognize the benefits of it and I suppose a dinosaur but the dinosaurs became extinct.
>
> (Director [4])

Generational issues aside the organization's main operations are based in Dumfries and Galloway, a region of Scotland whose economic growth lags behind both Scottish and U.K. levels [8]. In terms of the economic outlook for the Scottish construction sector, there has been a decline [6] in the sector's GVA contribution to the Scottish economy from £11.1 billion in 2008 to £8.7 billion in 2009. The decline in revenue is as a result of low demand for housing, which contributed to increasing business insolvency within the construction sector with SME firms reducing investment in training, skills, and innovation [6]. Operational challenges also arose from government policies to improve the energy efficiency and sustainability of the construction sector without provision of practical solutions to achieve policy aims [6]. Despite these difficulties, the Scottish construction sector is projected to grow by 2.4% annually and provides employment for 6% of the workforce in Dumfries and Galloway [6]. The seasonal nature of the rural workforce [8] complements the organization's strategy to hire on a project basis [3]. Activities to market the business products and services are considered contributing factors that can increase the firm's carbon footprint:

> Last year obviously we did a base line footprint so I am taking it from there this year in terms of trying to get more marketing I probably actually increased my footprint instead of decreasing it because it was a very quiet year…. I am doing more to try and bring in more business and this year is going to be a busier year so my carbon footprint will have probably increased purely through being busier that is why I think the measurement of the carbon footprint is interesting because you could think that a business is doing

nothing can have a smaller footprint than a business that is doing a lot even if the business is the same size. I think my footprint would be bigger this year.

(Director [4])

Carbon footprint measurement is considered cost neutral by the management of the firm as it was one of the many derived benefits of participating in the Carbon Smart Program, which included carbon management training of senior management and an additional member of the staff [3]:

> Last year it didn't cost anything because I was doing the project with the Carbon Centre and they taught me how to do it as part of the project so it was a case of using their smart meters to measure electricity and taking various readings from the office building I was in and that sort of thing so no it does not cost anything.

(Director [4])

This perception of cost neutrality is fuelled by the "hands-on" approach adopted by the firm's Carbon Champion in collaboration with the Crichton Carbon Centre to determine the boundaries of the organization's baseline carbon footprint [3], ensuring senior management support for the Crichton Carbon Centre recommendations for reducing the firm's carbon footprint report were implemented, a task from which some personal satisfaction is derived in so much that in reflection the director responsible for greenhouse gas implementation comments "*I do the whole lot*" [3].

Apprehensions of cost did not factor into management's decision to pursue greenhouse gas measurement as an organizational objective, but marketing considerations and synergies to exploit assets from existing businesses such as the Barend Holiday Village under an ecotourism banner formed the business case to adopt carbon footprint methodology. The business case is bolstered by senior management's personal belief in the care for the environment and social responsibility:

> Well it was part of the Carbon Smart project which I got involved with because I felt that it was apart from anything else a useful marketing tool utilizing some sort of eco-tourism banner or that you do care about the environment and equally because I have a belief that we should be taking responsibility for our carbon footprint and our actions.

(Director [4])

This personal concern for the environment contributed to the articulation of the company's environmental policy and carbon management policy [1]. The organization's policy stance is based on two premises: firstly, that pressures to decarbonize the construction sector will lead to "greenwashing" as competitors seek to raise the profile of their offerings and, secondly, resistance to change to adopt low-carbon technology [1]. The company is keen to emphasize the sustainability of its building techniques that combine traditional approaches such as the use of logs precluding the need for the consumption of cement or cement products in the building process [1]. Cement production [9] is an important contributor to global carbon emissions accounting for 1.8 Gt CO_2 in 2005. Therefore, its use in the construction sector is a contributory factor to the continuing environmental impact of cement production. Recent studies confirm that the carbon sequestrated in American hardwood timber during its growth as a tree exceeds the emissions that arise as a result of the harvesting and transportation to Europe [10–12]. Timber as a building material compares well against other building materials in terms of embodied carbon emissions even if the carbon sequestration benefits are negated [12]:

Fully aware of both the thermal and carbon sequestration properties of timber, The Log House People recently extended its corporate policies to include a carbon management policy that is pursuing GHG reduction in the business operations, construction, and development of carbon-neutral log homes [1]:

> We have an environmental policy but in terms of carbon footprinting we do not.
>
> (Director [4])

As well as organizational policy, the company is driven to measure its carbon footprint by a number of factors including entrepreneurial interest in environmental issues, participation in the Carbon Smart scheme, corporate responsibility, an inherent belief in personal responsibility for the environment, and continuous learning:

> Well obviously it was part of my Carbon Smart project with the Carbon Centre that was the key thing that instigated me to do it and taught me about it but my awareness of the world and the environment and what we are doing to the planet and my interest in environmental issues is a driver. On a personal level it has always been something that I have always been interested in … I think their needs to be an onus on individuals and companies to accept responsibility. We have too much and there is too little responsibility accepted whether it be on an individual level or a company/corporate level … people need to be aware of what they do, this is from an environmental perspective … a good avenue and a good way to do that … So I guess my key driver was learning about it that gave me an interest in doing it … It is something that I want to do on a yearly basis so it is changing how we are performing.
>
> (Director [4])

8.3 CONTRIBUTION TO GROWTH

Motivated to understand the full extent of carbon impacts the firm began measuring the greenhouse gas emissions [3] over which it has direct control (*Scope 1*), indirect control (*Scope 2*), and limited or no influence (*Scope 3*). The organization's Carbon Champion in collaboration with Crichton Carbon Centre ensured that the carbon footprint measurement was compliant with the DEFRA guidance and included emissions from the following aspects [3]:

Scope 1—Fleet fuel consumption and gas
Scope 2—Electricity use at both offices
Scope 3—Staff commuting, procurement, water consumption, and waste disposal

Though The Log House People perceives limited influence over emissions generated by staff commuting, water consumption, and waste disposal, these aspects were considered within the *boundaries* of the carbon footprint [3]. However, the following *Scope 3* emissions were excluded: customer travel and supplier travel [3]. A baseline greenhouse gas report for a 12-month period was generated within which the carbon impact of the organization's identified key environmental aspects was calculated using DEFRA's emission conversion factors [3]. The greenhouse gas emission data from the process contributed to actions targeted at reducing fuel consumption; however, management is unaware or unconcerned of the measurement methodology but interested in its practical applications:

> Methods in terms of what using smart meters to measure electricity … I don't know the answer to that I basically used whatever the carbon centre told me to use what they taught me to use.

> (Director [4])

Management has recently adopted carbon reduction as an organizational objective; the novelty of carbon footprint measurement may be a determining factor in the limited awareness of the methodology and concepts.

For the reporting period April 1, 2009,–March 31, 2010, Scope 1 activities of the business accounted for 4.044 CO_2e tons of emissions, Scope 2 activities accounted for 2.855 CO_2e tons of emissions, and Scope 3 activities accounted for 1.587 CO_2e tons of emissions, resulting in combined total emissions of 8.486 CO_2e tons [3]. Fleet fuel consumption accounts for 46.5% of the carbon footprint and gas consumption accounts for 1.2%; both are the main components of Scope 1 of the organization's greenhouse gas emissions. Electricity consumption accounts for 33.6% of carbon footprint and is the main source of emissions arising from Scope 2 of The Log House People greenhouse gas emissions, while procurement accounts for 9% of carbon emissions, office waste for 0.9%, and water consumption for 0.5% of the organization's greenhouse gas emissions (Table 8.1).

The management of the organization considers the carbon footprint to be a key performance indicator that is used to measure the impact of the firm's output. Careful consideration is given to the implementation of carbon reduction initiatives during periods of reduced organizational activity as it may yield no added benefit to the firm. However, comparative analysis of annual carbon footprint reports is proposed to ensure that greenhouse gas emissions are being managed:

> Because we are so small and it's been a slow year last year. I think if we were to try to reduce our carbon footprint on last year will end up achieving nothing. So it is important in the scope of keeping it in line as business increases and we do get busier to keep an eye on it. Doing obviously a carbon footprint year on year and comparing it to output and getting it in proportion it is important to bring it in line and to keep it in check.

> (Director [4])

Understandably as a key performance indicator, carbon footprint data is used primarily for internal analysis of the organizational performance, but there is a

TABLE 8.1 The Log House People carbon emission data.

Emission source	Activity data		Emissions	
	Amount	**Unit**	**kgCO$_2$e/year**	**% total**
Scope 1			**4044**	**47.7**
Fleet fuel consumption	9509	miles/year	3942	46.5
Gas consumption	498	kWh/year	102	1.2
Scope 2				
Electricity consumption	5247	kWh/year	**2855**	**33.6**
Scope 3			**1587**	**18.7**
Procurement	1412	£/year	1468	9
Office waste	260	kg/year	75	0.9
Water use	31943	Liters/year	43	0.5
Staff commuting	0	Miles/year	0	0
Total			**8,486 kgCO$_2$e/year** **8.486 tCO$_2$e/year**	

Source: © Log House People.

willingness on the part of the management of the firm to provide access to stake-holders and the public to carbon emission data:

> The last year it was used for external purposes for the sake of the Carbon Centre. I would say it would probably be used mainly internally but I am happy to publish results so others could see.
>
> (Director [4])

This focus on carbon footprint methodology as a sustainability indicator is at the expense of other sustainability footprint measurements such as the water footprint, and social footprint can be described as "*carbon myopic.*" The firm's consumption impacts such as water are being expressed in terms of carbon emissions without measures or analysis being conducted on the avoidance, reduction, or recycling of water:

> Water obviously was taken into account but no direct footprint.
>
> (Director [4])

By extension, the use of social footprint calculations is also negated as a performance indicator.

Although the company is seeking to deploy water conservation techniques such as "water hippos" to reduce domestic water consumption, the pervasiveness of carbon footprints within both the macroeconomic and microeconomic spheres may have contributed to the management of The Log House People opting not to pursue water footprint measurement as confirmed by the brief comment of *"Not at the moment"* stated by the firm's director [4].

A unique selling proposition of log homes is there energy efficiency and carbon friendliness when compared with traditional or contemporary building structures. To ensure the comparative analysis of the energy efficiency for the diverse mixture of the U.K. housing stock, the former Department of Environment commissioned the Building Research Establishment (BRE) [13], a charity that promotes innovation, education, and research in the built environment, to develop Standard Assessment Procedures (SAP) in 1992.

Since 1992, various versions of the SAP have been produced—1993, 1996, 1997, 1998, 2001, 2005, 2009, and 2012—the current version with underpinning in law for its use being given in Part L of U.K. Building Regulations [13]. As an extension of the carbon footprint measurement initiative and to comply with building regulations, the management of the organization commissioned an initial assessment of a proposed building design "No.2 Riverview Park" to SAP standards specifically looking at the HVAC systems, dimension, volume, fabric performance, and location [3] (Fig. 8.1).

Energy assessment results were itemized in two categories: **energy efficiency** rating calculated in kilowatt-hours per square meter per year and **environmental impact** rating calculated in carbon dioxide emissions per square meter per year with performance being expressed into performance bands along a descending scale from **A** (highest) to **G** (lowest) [3]. The results of this assessment indicated that using the proposed "No.2 Riverview Park" design configuration yielded an energy efficiency rating of **C**-80 (95 kWh/m^2/year) and an environmental impact rating of **C**-78 (22.05 kg CO_2/m^2/year), which was below the performance level of an identical dwelling using Scottish Building Standards 2009 data [3]. To enhance the energy performance [3] of the design specification, the building insulation was improved, and energy-efficient lighting use was increased from 50 to 100%. A subsequent SAP assessment based on the on the new design configuration indicated improved performance with energy efficiency rating of **B**-82 (89 kWh/m^2/year) and an environmental impact rating of **C**-80 (18.13 kg CO_2/m^2/year). Management insists that these improvements in building design do not radically alter their product offering but have contributed to ensuring that future log homes meet or exceed mandatory energy efficiency performance requirements [4].

The organization's Carbon Champion although aware of the environmental impacts of business operations considers carbon footprint as an effective measurement and assessment tool that can be used in the comparative analysis of carbon management performance with other businesses:

I have always been aware of environmental impacts and carbon emissions from when I was at university. I don't think it has improved it … It has helped understanding of how

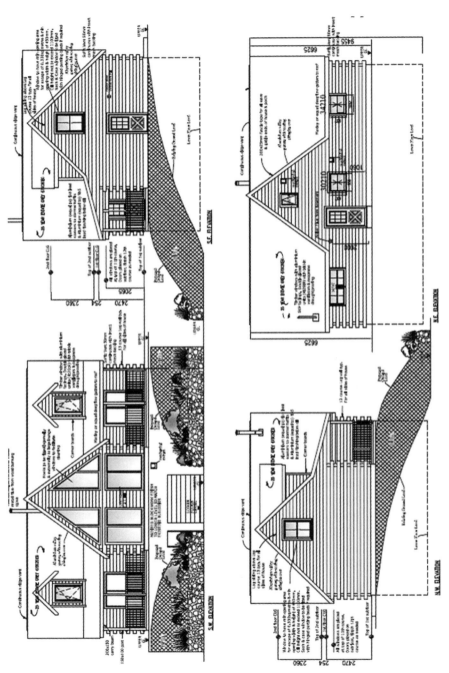

FIGURE 8.1 "No. 2 River Park" design extracted from a carbon footprint assessment for The Log House People. Source: © The Log House People.

one can measure it and assess it and actually give yourself a figure that you can compare to other businesses but I would not say it has affected my understanding of the environment and the impact of carbon but what I would say it's made me more aware of for example when you see a pint of milk in the supermarket when Tesco's put on their carbon footprint per a pint of milk and it makes you think that is a lot of carbon used in the production of that bottle of milk.

(Director [4])

Environmental impacts arising from the firm's operations are a concern for the business that influenced the adoption of carbon footprint measurement but has not contributed to disclosure of carbon footprint reports to any carbon reporting scheme [4].

Nonparticipation regarding external verification of the organizations' carbon footprint by independent third-party organizations such as the Carbon Trust persists as measurement by the Crichton Carbon Centre provides a veneer of reliability regarding the accuracy of the carbon footprint report:

I guess … Yes from the Crichton Carbon Centre.

(Director [4])

Initially, The Log House People accepted professional assistance from the Crichton Carbon Trust in the determination of the organizational boundaries and scope of its carbon emissions. Subsequent incorporation and assimilation of carbon footprint methodology into the company's business processes has precluded the need for continued third-party assistance, which was confirmed by the firm's Carbon Champion statement of "*No*" during a brief reflection [4].

8.4   CRITICAL SUCCESS FACTORS

The continuing global financial crisis is a contributing factor to insolvencies among firms in the construction sector [6]. A casualty of this high-level economic uncertainty has been innovation within the construction sector, which is considered by some of its stakeholders as being traditionally slow to innovate with notable exceptions; larger organizations consider innovation as necessary to business survival [6]. The adoption of innovation within the sector is influenced by government low-carbon policies; however, business priorities are firmly entrenched with cost cutting in a financially constrained environment and limited investment in innovation or research and development, firms are unable to capitalize from potential low-carbon growth opportunities [6]. Innovations such as carbon footprint measurement are perceived to be useful yet at times ambiguous tools due to the ability of firms to omit operational aspects or lack of control over operational aspects, for example, suppliers, when determining GHG measurement boundaries:

I think it can be certainly from a bigger company's perspective it can be weighted perhaps unfairly in terms of what they bring into the scope of their carbon footprint.

It has to be this way otherwise it is very difficult to measure sometimes but you can take out one of the things that you don't like let's say external supply for example can be ambiguous and sometimes unfairly weighted. For example our shipping of log homes because that is a supplier not something directly emitted by my company I cannot of course leave it out it is not kind of factored in a way it should be.

(Director [4])

Overall, management views the carbon footprint measurement as not useful unless sustainable change is implemented and included in the organization's accounting process with transparency being provided through public access to the firm's carbon footprint information. Measurement of the carbon footprint builds awareness and interest by encouraging other members of the organization to contribute to the development of carbon policy. The usefulness of carbon footprint as a measurement tool for SMEs to combat climate change can be enhanced by the development of a national monitoring scheme or database to compare performance:

Just measuring it on its own is not useful it depends on what people do with the data once its measured if its compiled you can almost put into a league table … become part of the accounting process for Companies House so you can publicly see how companies were performing then it can be useful tool. Just by measuring it is useful to other people in the organisation brings their awareness to the subject. I think national monitoring or some kind of database … would be more useful.

(Director [4])

This conviction that carbon footprint measurement is a useful tool does not translate into customer enthusiasm or interest in the use of the sustainability footprint tools such as the carbon footprint by the company.

There is a perceived apathy regarding the organization's carbon footprint regardless if they are existing customers or new customers. This presents an opportunity to use ecolabeling to create interest in the company's low-carbon achievements through an application for Building Research Establishment Environmental Assessment Method [14] (BREEAM) accreditation for the sustainability and environmental performance of its buildings [3].

In attitudes reflective of their customer base, the company does not require their suppliers to provide sustainability footprint data such as the carbon footprint. A proposed green procurement initiative seeks to address this shortfall in sustainability by committing the organization to pursue an eco-friendly strategy in selecting suppliers [3].

Pursuit of ecolabeling and green procurement policies augurs well for the success of The Log House People as a *probiodiversity enterprise* [15] *(PBE)*. However, disputes as to the importance of sustainability footprint measures such as the carbon footprint among senior management and the focus on carbon footprint measurement as the sole sustainability indicator are transitional hurdles in the assimilation of sustainability within the organization:

Until I read your research statement I did not know of the term except for as in the context of carbon footprint.

(Director [4])

The owner of the business is convinced that individual and organizational carbon footprint measurements are vital to reducing carbon impacts and acknowledging anthropogenic contributions to climate change. A personal conviction fostered by an academic interest in environmentally sensitive design as a young and impressionable university student:

> Absolutely well ... every company has the carbon emissions ... there is as a result an increase in carbon. I do recognize that by measuring everyone's carbon footprint one can reduce one's carbon impact on the world. I certainly believe that affects climate change. That said also when I was in university one of the subjects I studied was environmentally sensitive design one of my professors did argue the case that if you look back in history there is an ice age every x number of thousands or millions of years and that we were actually due an Ice Age his argument the climate will warm up.... the climate could change in order to bring about another Ice Age. So I do believe it is carbon related whether or not it is to do with us ... I do believe it is to do with us we are certainly increasing emissions there is no doubt that we are increasing the amount of carbon in the world.
>
> (Director [4])

Reduction targets for both individual and organizational carbon footprints are affected by the operational realities such as the "*just in time*" nature of the organization's supply chain reliant on obtaining building materials from North American suppliers. The dependence on North American suppliers for quality building materials contributes to perceptions of difficulty in setting carbon reduction targets. Research has shown that transportation emissions are offset by the carbon sequestration properties of wood as a building material [12]. However, mitigation efforts such as environmentally friendly heating and sustainable building materials are being trialed by the firm to reduce the carbon impact of log homes during their life cycle:

> In terms of the things we could do to reduce emissions ... in terms of figure percentages ... That is very difficult to say at the moment there are things we could do to reduce it. At the moment we have been getting this is out of our direct carbon output but shipping from America, one house at a time because the orders have always been that way but if we were building let's say two at a time instead of using three containers we might get it into two containers so that could be smaller otherwise other than that I am looking at environmentally sound heating options to put into houses and more sustainable technologies in that field.
>
> (Director [4])

The challenges of target setting however have not prevented senior management of the company from realizing the inherent value of carbon footprint measurement in aiding the business as an SME to recognize its carbon impacts, mitigate carbon emissions, and accept as a corporate body its responsibility to combat climate change:

> If it promotes or helps small and medium sized enterprises recognize the impact of carbon, the effects it has on climate change and helps them accept responsibility and deal with their carbon output. It has a lot of value but if it is something that people churn

out at the end of a tax year because it is something they have to do then I think it does not have very much (value). I think it is something that has to be understood in much the same way as Health & Safety policies and things like that are … If it is done in that way I think people kind of embrace it and deal with it on a personal level which then obviously adds to each level if it is dealt with by one person it has a big change … changing one person obviously does not make a huge difference.

(Director [4])

The perceived value of carbon footprint measurement is further enhanced by the low-cost threshold that was afforded through participation in the Carbon Smart Program. Benefits arising from participation in the Carbon Smart Program have encouraged senior management to continue to invest the organization's resources into carbon footprint measurement:

Absolutely at the time it did not cost me anything this year my situation has changed a bit I am no longer in the same office but I would potentially buy some smart meters this year to measure to kind of work it out the same way we did it last year. Yes I think it is a worthwhile thing to do and worthwhile use of the resources.

(Director [4])

Policymaking institutions have an influencing role to play in the adoption of sustainability footprint tools such as the carbon footprint by SMEs. The firm's management suggests that SMEs can be encouraged to implement carbon footprint measurement if it were included as a legal requirement as part of the annual auditing process and a carbon performance league table created to encourage benchmarking with penalties such as fines to ensure reporting compliance:

I think in terms of making it voluntary or compulsory potentially it could do as I mentioned earlier make it part of the company's auditing process at the end of the year put on to Companies House on their website with everything else along with their financial turnover and carbon turnover, that would be the most sensible thing to do otherwise I guess they could impose fines and a league table. The measurement has to be relational to the output I don't know how it would be done of course obviously a smaller company will have a much smaller output carbon footprint than a bigger company. Maybe it's something that is divided by its turnover or number of employees. By making it compulsory as part of their annual audits that would be helpful.

(Director [4])

8.5   SUMMARY

The Log House People is competing in a market dominated by conventional building methods utilizing materials with high embodied carbon content, for example, cement and steel, while promoting a product that may be perceived as a luxury. The existence of generational differences regarding sustainability initiatives has made implementation challenging for the Carbon Champion who is also the offspring of the Managing Director. This scenario highlights the philosophical challenge emerging from differences in opinion among senior management on the impact of climate change on business operations. The Sustainable Strategic Growth Model illustrates the initiatives undertaken by the firm and opportunities for improvement to move the firm beyond the sustainability barrier.

The organization gleaned useful knowledge of greenhouse gas measurement techniques and carbon management from its participation in the Carbon Smart Program. Despite being a small business, a director has been allocated as a "Carbon Champion" ensuring that sustainability is on the agenda at senior management meetings.

This senior management commitment to sustainability is affirmed by the establishment of environmental and carbon management policies with actions taken to measure and manage greenhouse gas emissions as a result of business operations (Fig. 8.2).

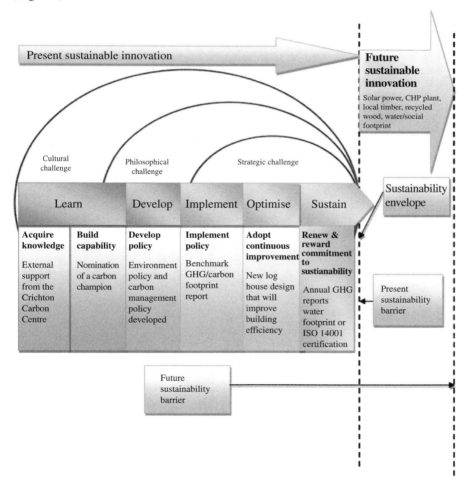

FIGURE 8.2 Using the sustainable strategic growth model—The Log House People Case Study.

However, to *sustain* growth, the organization must exploit opportunities to improve performance and reduce environmental impact by using water footprint and social footprint techniques.

Future sustainable growth can be achieved when all potential opportunities to reduce environmental impact and minimize loss to society have been exhausted, necessitating investments in low-carbon building materials; microgeneration, for example, solar panels; CHP utilizing waste timber; and improved building techniques.

The essential few building blocks of sustainable strategic growth *learn, develop, implement,* and *optimize* have been explored by senior management. To prevent inertia and overcome the sustainability barrier, senior management can *sustain* strategic growth by implementing initiatives such as ISO 14001 or OHSAS 18001 to improve business performance.

REFERENCES

[1]   Log House People. Available at http://www.theloghousepeople.com/Home.html. Accessed Jan 21, 2013.

[2]   Herald Scotland. Tourist chief dies. Available at http://www.heraldscotland.com/sport/spl/aberdeen/tourist-chief-dies-1.386450. Accessed Jan 21, 2013.

[3]   CCC. Carbon Footprint Assessment—The Log House People. Dumfries: Crichton Carbon Centre; 2011.

[4]   Director. Interview by author. Edinburgh; January 10, 2012.

[5]   CEER. Centre for Enterprise and Economic Research. Final Report for BERR Enterprise Directorate: SMEs in a Low Carbon Economy. London: CEER; 2009.

[6]   Scottish Enterprise. Baselining and Research into the Scottish Construction Sector—A Final Report to Scottish Enterprise; March 2012. Available at http://www.scottish-enterprise.com/~/media/SE/Resources/Documents/Sectors/Construction/Baseline%20report.pdf. Accessed Jan 22, 2013.

[7]   Scottish Government. A low carbon economic strategy for Scotland: Scotland—A Low Carbon Society; 2010.

[8]   Dumfries and Galloway Local Economic Council. Dumfries and Galloway Economic Development Strategy; 2008. p. 1–40.

[9]   Organisation Economic Cooperation Development/International Energy Agency. Tracking industrial energy efficiency and CO_2 emissions; 2007.

[10] Bergman R, Bowe S. Environmental impact of producing hardwood Lumber using a life-cycle inventory. Proceedings of the 10th International IUFRO Division 5, Wood Drying Conference; Aug 26–30, 2007; Orono, Maine. p. 180–185. Available at http://www.corrim.org/reports/pdfs/woodfiberscience_bergman_bowe_2008.pdf. Accessed Mar 4, 2014.

[11] Johnson LR, Lippke B, Marshall JD, Comnick J. CORRIM: Phase I Final Report, Module A, Forest Resources Pacific Northwest and Southeast—Review Draft of June 1, 2004. Available at http://www.corrim.org/reports/final_report_2004/Module%20A%20-%20For_Resources_June%2017_2004_FINAL.pdf. Accessed Mar 4, 2014.

[12] Oliver R. A preliminary assessment of the carbon footprint of American Hardwood Kiln dried lumber supplied to distributors in the European Union. American Hardwood

Export Council. Available at http://www.americanhardwood.org/fileadmin/docs/ sustainability/US_hardwood_carbon_footprint_01.pdf. Accessed Jan 23, 2013.

(a) All figures for timber exclude carbon sequestered during forest growth. If carbon sequestration is included, timber products have a negative carbon balance (i.e. they store more carbon than they consume during manufacture).

(b) Source for products other than American hardwoods: University of Bath, UK, "Inventory of Carbon Emissions" (ICE, Version 1.6a, 2008). Available at: http:// people.bath.ac.uk/cj219/

[13] DECC. Department of Energy and Climate Change Standard Assessment Procedure. Available at https://www.gov.uk/standard-assessment-procedure. Accessed Jan 24, 2013.

[14] BREEAM. Building Research Establishment Environmental Assessment Method (BREEAM); 2012. Available at http://www.breeam.org/about.jsp?id=66. Accessed Feb 2, 2013.

[15] Dickson B, Watkins D, Foxall J. The working partnership: SMEs and biodiversity. Cambridge: Fauna & Flora International; 2007.

9

MOFFAT GOLF CLUB: GREENER GOLF

9.1 INTRODUCTION

The tourism and leisure sector has been earmarked as a key area for low-carbon growth by the Scottish Government [1]. Within the tourism sector, golf tourism contributes £220 M to the Scottish economy; this represents £120M gross value added (GVA) [2]. Among the approximately 550 golf courses in Scotland [3], the Moffat Golf Club is considered "the Jewel in the South" [4]. The Moffat Golf Club was established in 1884 during the heyday of its local town Moffat [4], a Victorian tourist spa destination due to the presence of mineral springs in the area and the construction of a bath (now the site of the town hall) that was built to satisfy the needs of its visitors [5]. Work on the existing golf course began in 1904 based upon designs from Ben Sayers of North Berwick, a renowned golf practitioner [4]. Situated 670 feet above sea level on Coats Hill, this 18-hole golf course [4] is within the vicinity of an ancient Roman signal fort [6] overlooking the market town of Moffat in Dumfriesshire [7]. The design of the course incorporates all the natural undulations with expansive views of the countryside and is a great example of a traditional Scottish moorland course [4]. Infrastructure on the site consists of a clubhouse, which is a composite of an older wooden building and conservatory with a flat-roofed extension of brick construction to provide improved amenities. The amenities within the clubhouse include a bar, dining room area, club offices, pool table, dartboard, table tennis, and male and female changing facilities and are operated by

Sustainability Footprints in SMEs: Strategy and Case Studies for Entrepreneurs and Small Business, First Edition. Lowellyne James.
© 2015 John Wiley & Sons, Inc. Published 2015 by John Wiley & Sons, Inc.

a full-time staff of two individuals. Investments in three electric golf carts were made to enhance the appeal of its existing golfing facilities [7]. The Moffat Golf Club also promotes a weekly snooker tournament in addition to its established golf tournament schedule [8].

As a keen operator in the tourism sector, the Moffat Golf Club pursued carbon footprint measurement in 2009 as a strategy to sustain the organization now in its second century of existence. Interviews were conducted with the Greens Convenor and Greenkeeper to provide insight into challenges and critical success factors in the adoption of sustainability footprints within the business.

9.2 CONTEXT

The Moffat Golf Club as a membership-driven organization faced in 2009 operating challenges arising from increasing energy costs and a stagnating economic environment due to the effects of the global financial crisis [8]. The organization has since opted to become members of the Crichton Carbon Centre's Carbon Smart Project in an effort to reduce energy costs and provide information on carbon off-setting of its emissions.

9.2.1 Crichton Carbon Centre

The Crichton Carbon Centre is a Scottish charity that assists individuals, communities, and organizations such as businesses, schools, and universities with transitioning to a low-carbon economy. The Carbon Smart Project was a 2-year program that assisted 24 rural organizations with implementing carbon management policies [8]. Participant organizations of the Carbon Smart Project were required to adopt the following steps [8]:

- Appoint a "Carbon Champion" and provide carbon management training for key staff
- Understand the organization—conduct a baseline carbon footprint assessment
- Conduct a carbon opportunities workshop
- Plan for change—develop a carbon management policy and action plan
- Implement the carbon management action plan and monitor progress

The Moffat Golf Club management appointed its Greens Convenor and another senior committee member as "Carbon Champions." The Greens Convenor being a retired senior fire officer was eager to reduce the impact of the organization on the environment and to explore opportunities to sell carbon credits derived from existing forest surrounding the golf course. Although a senior management-led initiative, carbon footprint measurement is not perceived by staff members as being a key issue for discussion at management meetings. At a tactical level, the Greens Convenor as "Carbon Champion" monitors fuel and electricity consumption of both the building and plant equipment, being ably supported by the Greenkeeper who monitors rainfall patterns to assist in the efficient use of fertilizer and pipe-borne water supplies:

> I am only involved in the green side and if it is my convenor will be doing that job for us.
>
> Greenkeeper [9]

In addition to the golf club, Moffat is also the home of two community-based organizations, Moffat Carbon Neutral (Moffat CAN) and Let's Live Local, that actively promote sustainable development.

9.2.2   Moffat CAN

Moffat CAN is an award-winning community-based organization established in 2009 that initially focused on the promotion of domestic energy efficiency through the implementation of energy audits and the installation of building insulation. This energy efficiency campaign also incorporated an energy use and energy efficiency awareness training targeted at Moffat primary school students [10]. As a social enterprise, Moffat CAN has extended the scope of its projects to include other sustainability initiatives such as [10]:

- *Renewable energy*—community renewable energy project
- *Food and household waste recycling*—composting of food waste from the homes and restaurants within the town
- *Reuse*—restoration of the town's Old Free Church erected in 1834 through the installation solar panels that provide energy to the building and the replacement of derelict fixtures and fittings
- *Local food production*
- *Aquaponics*—a combination of aquaculture and hydroponics whereby the nutrient-enriched water from the aquaculture tanks is used to grow vegetable crops
- *Cycle hire*

9.2.3   Let's Live Local

Let's Live Local is a community interest company established in Moffat in 2009, which aims to support the "localization" of jobs, skills, and investment within the community [11]. The organization believes this can be achieved by sustainably reengineering the community's consumption patterns in four key areas [11]:

- *Food*—Encouraging the purchase of locally grown food produce.
- *Economy*—Through the establishment of a local currency the "ram," a local credit union, bartering system that provides credit "time" for the supply of free services that can then be exchanged for needed services at a later date and recycling of preowned items through "Moffat Freeshare" or online sales portal "Moffat Car Boot."

- *Homes*—The promotion of homeworking and the development of a community design code to maintain the historic fabric of Moffat.
- *Community*—In support of these aims, Let's Live Local established a social networking site "Moffat Online," which provides details of events, restaurants, and other social activities of interest to the local community.

Moffat CAN and Let's Live Local have created the awareness of climate change and energy efficiency within the local community, thereby acting as external stimuli for energy reduction initiatives at the Moffat Golf Club. The importance of energy reduction initiatives such as the carbon footprint is appreciated by both management and employees despite adaptation issues arising due to an aging population. The management representative of the organization expresses a pragmatic approach as carbon footprint is perceived to improve operational efficiency and "bottom-line" financial stability. Alternatively, technical personnel consider carbon footprint measurement as an enabling factor in the reduction of chemicals and the alignment of good environmental management practices with sound financial management:

> We just do not have any spare money to be nice that is the cruelty about this, that is the bottom-line and if you were to ballot our members and ask them if they would pay £10 more subscription so that we could be more responsible regarding the carbon footprint they would not pay it, they just would not that is the truth of the matter.
>
> (Greens Convenor [12])

Economically, Dumfries and Galloway was not a high-growth region prior to the global financial crisis with overall economic growth and well-being considerably below Scottish and U.K. levels [13]. Employment prospects remain weak, dominated by seasonal, self-employment, and part-time jobs with increasing migration of individuals in the 18–45-year-old age group, a scenario symptomatic of a rural economy [13]. The effects of present economic conditions and declining visitors have led decision makers to seek opportunities to reduce cost through staff reduction and efficient fuel consumption and chemical use:

> Yes, in some ways ... in a positive way as we have less people coming so there are less road miles coming here so there is less diesel, petrol used to get here. As we economize, we use less fossil fuel ... for example we had a member of staff on Mondays, Wednesdays and Fridays for four hours during the day. It is cheaper for us to tell that member of staff to stay at home than it is for us to heat this place. We are using hundreds of liters less gas because we are not heating the place so the recession in a perverse way has reduced our carbon footprint.
>
> (Greens Convenor [12])

As the home of golf, Scotland has the highest number of golf courses per population, one course for every 9,300 persons [2]. The Moffat Golf Club is located in the southwest region of Scotland, which boasts 124 golf courses including the famous Prestwick and Turnberry golf courses and 32 link courses, the largest number in any of the Scottish regions [2]. There is intense competitive rivalry within the Scottish golf tourism market with 70 golf courses accounting for over 75% of the revenue [2]. Potential entrants into the Scottish golf tourism industry require substantial capital investment to compete, yet this has not deterred investors [14].

The range of scenery, flora, and fauna is a unique selling proposition for golf courses with 46% of golf tourists indicating that the golf courses were the most positive aspect of their visit to Scotland [15]. This interaction and dependence with nature further defines organizations such as Moffat Golf Club as *probiodiversity enterprises (PBEs)* [16]. PBEs face challenges around the human resource retention, management of knowledge, networking, and the acquisition of technical expertise [17]. Within this competitive environment, the management and technical staff consider cost reduction and senior management commitment as the main factors that encouraged the company to pursue carbon footprint measurement:

> Finance that was the point.
>
> (Greens Convenor [12])

> People like the (Greens Convenor) who are on the committee who actually are quite passionate about it and people like that can push people forward.
>
> (Greenkeeper [9])

The strategic decision to adopt carbon footprint measurement by Moffat Golf Club is mainly financially driven, motivated by senior management's desire to reduce cost and preempt climate change legislation.

To achieve energy cost reduction necessitated changes to the lighting system of its buildings, adjustments to the water system, and alterations to the building fabric. A practical but altogether informal approach to carbon footprint policy and carbon management was implemented; this deployment of organization's policy was understood by management but not its technical staff:

> I suppose in a way we do but it is financially driven not carbon footprint driven but we have changed the lighting system of the clubhouse we have changed the water system up at the Greenkeeper's hut and have actually altered the building to reduce the amount of energy that we use but in truth it was not done to reduce the carbon footprint it was done as a result of somebody auditing our carbon footprint so the outcome was directly from that audit that is what drove it in the first place but in truth we are much more driven by finance.
>
> (Green Convenor [12])

> No not at the moment.
>
> (Greenkeeper [9])

Golf courses present a potential carbon sink due to the presence of trees, shrubs, and grass while providing a natural haven for wildlife. Recent studies indicate that putting greens can provide not only leisure benefits but also *carbon sequestration* services to society [18, 19]. *Carbon sequestration* is a process of storing carbon dioxide in natural carbon pools or through the use of potentially man-made mechanisms, for example, *carbon capture and storage* (CCS). Natural carbon pools include oceans, which are estimated to store 38,000 gigatons of carbon (GtC); the geosphere amassing just under 3700 GtC; and atmospheric carbon storage accounting for approximately 760 GtC with the biosphere, that is, soil, vegetation storing almost 2300 GtC. Specifically putting greens capable of storing approximately 0.33 tons CO_2 per acre annually through the process of natural carbon sequestration [19]. The management of the Moffat Golf Club is eager to realize the potential financial value that may arise from the sale of carbon credits that may accrue if government policies acknowledge the carbon sequestration value of the golf course and its surrounding woodland. To build its case, the organization has developed working relationships with Moffat CAN and Let's Live Local, which are perceived as *carbon footprint driven* when compared to the Moffat Golf Club's *financially driven* approach. The use of carbon footprint as a tool by senior management to secure potentially lucrative financial outcomes such as the acquisition of carbon credits for resale ensures that carbon footprint reduction is on the management committee's agenda. However, the technical staff representative considers cost and the availability of equipment as barriers despite measures adopted by the organization that will reduce its carbon impact:

> No there would be no barriers if I said we need to include carbon footprint on the agenda of the next meeting nobody would say we are not they would say okay we would wait and see what that is about. We have had a guy from Let's Live local at an open day in actual fact a full afternoon where we threw the golf course open to the public to come and have a look at what we are doing but this was in terms of the possibility to harvest this timber and recycling and a lot of people came to see what we are about. We have a loose connection with Moffat CAN in truth there is not a lot of common ground between the two of us there is a lot of common ground between us and Let's Live local with that statement both Moffat CAN and Let's Live Local are carbon footprint driven where as we are definitely financially driven.... My frustration is nobody has done an audit of all this forestry to actually see what we are doing to reduce our own carbon impact you see the government lets you down initially they said if you large areas of forestry then we would give you carbon credits for that and then you can trade those now along with Wishaw Golf Club we were looking very hard and saying we have all this grass and all these trees all of which are converting carbon can we go to BP and sell our carbon credits.
>
> (Greens Convenor [12])

9.3   CONTRIBUTIONS TO GROWTH

Building on the existing awareness of carbon-related impacts within the wider Moffat community, the golf club began the process of measuring its carbon footprint with the help of experts from the Crichton Carbon Centre. The Crichton Carbon Centre in agreement with the golf club's Greens Convenor established the boundaries of the carbon footprint measurement exercise. These boundaries were defined using DEFRA's carbon footprint measurement framework guidance [8]. Using information received from the golf club's accountant, the team of assessors from the Crichton Carbon Centre identified the organization's reporting boundaries as follows:

Scope 1—Propane gas
Scope 2—Electricity use in the clubhouse and the electric golf carts/buggies
Scope 3—Electricity used by catering companies

Scope 3 assessment did not include water, fuel, or food and beverage consumption by staff and visitors mainly due to the challenges of the collection of data [8]. A baseline annual report period was selected within which the key environmental impacts on the organization—propane gas and electricity consumption—were calculated using DEFRA's emission conversion factors [8]. The carbon emission data derived from this analytical process contributed to the implementation of measures to reduce fuel consumption; however, decision makers are yet to be comfortable with the process of carbon footprint measurement and the use of carbon dioxide equivalents (tCO_2e) preferring to discuss carbon reductions in financial terms. Technical personnel perceive carbon footprint methodology to be within the remit of senior management:

> I am not entirely sure you can accurately measure it we do not consciously measure it we would not say we have used 500 liters less gas therefore our carbon footprint has been reduced by at least x kilograms of CO2 we don't do that what we do is say we have used 500 liters less of gas which has saved us £800.
>
> (Greens Convenor [12])

For the reporting period June 1, 2009–May 31, 2010, Scope 1 activities of the business accounted for 33.222 tCO_2e, Scope 2 activities accounted for 19.974 tCO_2e, and Scope 3 emissions accounted for 5.331 tCO_2e, resulting in combined total emissions of 58.528 tCO_2e of emissions [8] (Table 9.1). Propane gas use accounts for 57% of the carbon footprint and is the main component of Scope 1 of the organization's greenhouse gas emissions (Fig. 9.1). Electricity consumption accounts for

TABLE 9.1   Moffat Golf Club Carbon Emissions

Emission Source	Activity Data		Emissions	
	Amount	Unit	$kgCO_2e$/year	% total
Scope 1				
Propane gas consumption	22,195	Liters/year	33,222	57
Scope 2				
Electricity consumption	36,706	KWh/year	19,974	34
Scope 3				
Staff commuting	9,797	KWh/year	5,331	9
Total			**58,528 $kgCO_2e$/year**	
			58.5 tCO_2e/year	

Source: © Moffat Golf Club.

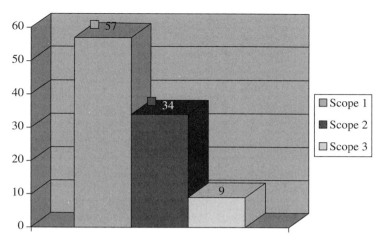

FIGURE 9.1 Moffat Golf Club carbon emissions by DEFRA scope. Source: © Moffat Golf Club.

34% of carbon footprint and is the main component of Scope 2 of the Moffat Golf Club's greenhouse gas emissions, while staff commuting accounts for 9% of the carbon footprint and is the main component of the golf club's Scope 3 greenhouse gas emissions (Fig. 9.1).

The reluctance of senior management to use carbon footprint terminology may be due to the novelty of its use as a measurement indicator within the golf club even though the organization has monitored components of its carbon footprint prior to its benchmark report (Fig. 9.1).

Although carbon footprint measurement was a novel concept within the organization, both senior management and staff consider the organization's carbon footprint to be a key performance indicator (KPI). The golf club's management representative is keen to clarify that motivations for carbon footprint measurement are financially driven with carbon footprint reduction being a secondary outcome:

> I would be misleading you if I said it did unless it was financially driven but then it would be a secondary outcome in truth.
>
> (Greens Convenor [9])

> My convenor certainly does ... Yes.
>
> (Greenkeeper [12])

The Moffat Golf Club have provided open access to carbon footprint performance information to staff, external organizations, and the general public. However, technical staff seem unaware of this flexible approach to information sharing and disclosure of carbon footprint performance:

> Depends what you mean by external reporting purposes it was made available to every member of the golf club and we are completely free with it ... for any other organisation

to look at it, there are no secrets. We are more than happy to share it and of course it would have been used for research at the Crichton Centre. I guess the answer is it is both externally available as well as internally available.

(Greens Convenor [9])

No idea.

(Greenkeeper [12])

As well as a KPI, carbon footprints are considered by management as a useful indicator that supports grant applications as it demonstrates the organization's commitment to environmental best practices. Water footprint and social footprint methodology is not fully understood by management, but practices such as water management and community engagement through the provision of student access to the golf course and assistance with the management of the community rugby and football fields indicate that sustainable principles are being implemented in these areas. Technical personnel are unaware of the use of water or social footprints and consider this activity as the role of management:

Yes, we do ... that is actually quite important and would be in our business plan ... our carbon footprint reports from the Crichton Carbon Centre and all the rest of it will definitely go into that grant application because the council or the government or sports organizations would most certainly want to see some sort of responsibility towards the environment within an application so it would figure very much in grant applications just the same as demonstrating that we are inclusive with the community.

(Greens Convenor [20])

Operationally, climate change is a key issue for the golf club due to the unpredictability of seasonal weather at its west of Scotland's location as revealed by overall seasonal weather patterns from 1961 to 2002, which indicate the following [21]:

- Increase in average temperature by over 1° C from 7.8° C to 8.7° C
- Increase in annual rainfall by 23%
- Increase in the growing season by 36 days

The organization has a very well-developed water management program that includes the monitoring of rainfall patterns over 2–3-year periods. This allows for the planning of golf course irrigation to match rainfall patterns. The impact of climate change arising from increasing annual precipitation in the region was confirmed by the recording of 7½ feet (90 inches) of rainfall in 2011; this negated the use of irrigation systems at the site during the year. Early plans to harness the water from nearby streams or "burns" through the establishment of a small dam hydropower scheme were shelved due to a levy imposed by the Scottish Environmental Protection Agency to the dismay of the golf club's senior management who considered their proposal as contributing to carbon emission reduction. Microgeneration initiatives such power schemes can reduce demand for energy from power stations. Carbon emissions from the energy sector accounted for 38% of the U.K. emissions with conventional power generation systems losing 65% of primary energy input via heat loss [12]:

> We have quite a number of burns running around the place ... we had seven foot six of water running last year and must be able to harvest this water so we looked at where it runs that along the road to build a dam in there and harvest the water Scottish Environmental Protection Agency implied that is all very well but we will be charging you so many pence per liter for harvesting your own rain water.
>
> (Greens Convenor [22])

This philosophical positioning toward the use of water resources for both domestic water consumption and energy generation, that is, hydro schemes, is part of an underlining distrust of wind power among the management of golf club, which is viewed as a politically driven short-term solution to achieve the United Kingdom's Kyoto obligations as well as its perceived negative impact on the golf course scenery. The issue of the building of onshore wind farms in idyllic settings in the U.K. countryside has been met with resistance by rural communities [12]:

> I think the answer to the UK's energy requirements absolutely and utterly lies in water not in wind ... wave energy I believe is possible both below surface and above surface whichever way they choose to use it—water capture with barriers I think it's absolutely and utterly a possibility ... let the water in imprison it and let the water out. All of that works, wind energy is just a complete waste of time but the reason we are doing it is very simple we went to Kyoto and we signed an agreement and then for 15 years we did nothing not a single thing none of the western world bothered themselves then all of a sudden we find ourselves seriously embarrassed because the rest of the world comes to us and says right okay we having another meeting how much progress you have made ... none. How could we convince the world politically we have responded? I know we can stick these turbines up because we can put them up in 12 months and the credit for that will fall to our party before the next election quick fix, short term ... politically driven.... I am here because I believe in the place and I would defend it to the hilt so any attempt to spoil the environment that this golf club sits in is really going to find some opposition from me we are facing a situation where the pylons are going to come right in front of here from the wind farms and the wind farms are going to go just top of those hills over there ... so that's who I am and why I am doing the job.
>
> (Greens Convenor [12])

In its search to increase its water supply from sustainable sources, the organization located and repaired a natural spring from which it receives 1200 gallons of water daily, which is filtered and used for drinking and domestic purposes with a potential saving of £15,000–£20,000 annually. Alternative uses for the supply of spring water such as the golf club's grey water system and the application of environmentally friendly techniques such as UV water treatment to improve water quality are also being explored:

> We found the original water supply; a spring found it to be running we cleaned it all up and we are now harvesting 1200 gallons a day of what in actual fact is drinking

water. It is drinking water quality we filter it and feed it back the work is still to be completed but everything is laid in place to filter it and put it into our storage area ready for use this year. They cannot charge us for that because it has been there so many years it is not new ... that will save us £15000–£20000 per year on our water bill. This is what is driving us many people are saying lovely they have got the old spring working gain it is all pink and fluffy and nice but in the end its that ... what we are also looking at is to take that same water re-plumb our grey water system in the club house so that toilets will be flushed with all that water ... we even looked at the possibility of putting in a UV system so that we can sterilize the water and actually use it as drinking water because it was used that way for 70 odd years so anything like that we are very alert to and are constantly looking for different ways to go about our business.

(Greens Convenor [12])

Rainfall and water consumption measurement is routinely monitored by the organization without the application of water footprint methodology to support the analysis. Technical personnel are convinced that the application of water footprint techniques is within the remit of the management but continue to maintain records of annual rainfall statistics:

We do measure it all the time ... we need to.

(Greens Convenor [12])

There probably is but that is again down to Greens Convenor they will take care of that if they need any input from me I keep records of rainfall which has an effect on our irrigation use any way it gives me an idea if I look back into records over the last 2–3 years I could see if there are patterns for rainfall at the time so I don't put irrigation on and we just leave it at that and 9 times out of 10 it does work. If we do get a dry spell we keep it to an absolute minimum as far as that is concerned we don't really have much use for irrigation these days we have had 7½ feet of rain last year.

(Greenkeeper [9])

The Moffat Golf Club historically has had cultural ties with the local communities that have been strengthened through initiatives such as providing opportunities for children to learn to play golf, and ground maintenance support to the local bowling club is testimony to the organization's community engagement. Critically, these activities are part of the organization's business plan despite lack of awareness of social footprint techniques:

One thing Moffat Golf Club has done since it opened is the local schools initially the private schools of course and when the communities and councils started to provide education, schools in the area had free access to bring students up to learn to play golf ... We have a lot of expensive technical equipment so we go and maintain the local football field and rugby field, aerate or roll it for them on an annual basis we look after the bowling green so on that end we are quite involved with the community the local schools and sports organizations.

(Greens Convenor [12])

The cost of undertaking carbon footprint measurement is not actively considered due mainly to the low-cost threshold barriers created by its participation in the Crichton Carbon Centre's Carbon Smart Project. The management of the club calculate that £1000 of consultancy effort was allocated by the Crichton Carbon Centre to measure the organization's carbon footprint. Although financially driven, the management of the golf club do not consider the calculation of carbon footprint costs as a business critical activity:

> No, we could not afford a consultant to do that the Crichton did it free of charge so I guess its value is a minimum of a £1000 worth of effort was put into it by the Crichton Carbon Centre to come and measure for us but we do not consciously measure.
>
> (Greens Convenor [12])

Critical to golf as a sport is its direct interface with the environment through land use and ground maintenance. The Moffat golf course inherited sustainable solutions that were incorporated into its design during the late Victorian period using traditional methods, manual labor, horse, and cart to create a surface to play golf that complemented the natural contours of the golf club's hilly location. The course designer Ben Sayers who was fully aware of seasonal weather patterns constructed the course along the *dual pond principle*. The *dual pond principle* involved the creation of an artificial basin, which was then layered with soil. The effect being in spring as the winter snow melts and early rain showers fall, water will be captured in the basin, the grass will grow and naturally extend its roots deep into the soil both to retrieve both moisture and nutrients. The use of this design that complemented natural cycles helped reduce the golf club's water dependence, solving both the cost and logistical challenges of supplying water to a location 670 feet above sea level with limited access to mechanized transport and industrial equipment. As a result of the use of natural processes created a straw-colored playing surface in summer of basically dead or dying grass that would be considered unacceptable to modern golf enthusiasts who have become cultured to lush green playing surfaces:

> That was built with horses, carts, picks, shovels & laborers and they literally pulled ground out of the hill to make a level place upon which to play golf that's how they created the greens but they were clever people. The greens were created on the dual pond principle so they scooped out a big saucer of land and the filled it back in again and the idea was that the winter snow melts and the rain will soak through the greens and then rest in this saucer and summer the grass will be forced to produce long roots that will go down to the water which means the grass had a massive long root over the length they would gather nutrients and water. Those greens in summer over 100 years ago and to all intents and purposes were dead and everybody accepted that's how it was; now if our Greenkeeper's were to present those greens in summer as straw colored dead grass nobody will play golf on it.
>
> (Greens Convenor [12])

This prevailing customer perception has led to the use of fertilizers especially high nitrogen applications on the golf course. The use of fertilizers has a short-term benefit providing golf patrons with picturesque green playing surface. However, the long-term climate change impacts of fertilizer use are mainly due to the high-energy-intensity fertilizer production accounting for 1.2% of global energy consumption and 1.2% of global greenhouse gas emissions [23]. An unexpected consequence of fertilizer use was that it created an additional layer of "thatch" composed of rotting grass clippings and fertilizer residue that acted as an impermeable membrane that prevents water drainage, thereby reducing the benefits of the "dual pond principle." To counteract this, the management of the golf club adopted environmentally friendly approaches to land management by aerating the soil, an action that made the layer of "thatch" permeable and compostable and allowed the grass to utilize both its nutrients and access water. Financially, the golf club benefited through reduced costs and fertilizer consumption:

> What we have been doing is driven by the bottom-line because fertilizer is very expensive and because we were putting this fertilizer on and these greens that were never designed to be that way then actually nature rebelled against us as it often does we got this layer of what you call thatch underneath the playing surface of the green and this is actually rotting material it is rotting grass cuttings it's the residue of the fertilizer and the whole thing is going desperately wrong this presented itself as a water barrier so the greens were not draining they were holding water. If you then bring mother nature back into the equation you can cut back on the fertilizer … saving money because all the greens needed was air they just need oxygen nothing more complicated than that you then take a piece of machinery across it and you then push tens of thousands of holes into it to let in the oxygen… what happens then very interestingly is that this layer of rotting material that is there as you have applied chemicals to it dries turns into compost and the grass that the thatch was killing now feeds off that because it is compost and you get these healthy greens with much reduced applications of fertilizer as it feeds off the compost ultimately the green would consume that layer of thatch and then it would be interesting to see whether we have to increase the feed again but as it stands at the minute we can logically reduce the amount of feed by working much more closer with nature and I think that there needs to be more focus on using nature as an alternative to some of the quick fixes that we are currently using.
>
> (Greens Convenor [12])

The search for natural solutions is a contributory factor in the adoption of carbon footprint measurement by the organization. Strategically, senior management viewed carbon footprint measurement as driving change in the processes by which the golf club delivers the golf leisure experience by aiding in reduction of fertilizer consumption and a redesign of the building to achieve energy efficiencies. There is however a critique of the carbon assessment process as being narrowly focused on energy efficiency but not on the wider carbon impact of operations. The business critical nature of fertilizer consumption in terms of cost led the organization to seek advice from agronomists to provide natural low-cost solutions. The rate of adoption of new technological developments in greenkeeping by the golf course is only restricted by affordability:

> It has led to a change in the way we go about our business in the way we have arranged our premises and so in terms of products and services nothing ongoing … it has changed us on the side of the fertilizers and so we have cut down on what we use … partly

financially driven because the Crichton never looked at the green bit they only looked at this building but many of our suppliers were suggesting different ways of going about things a good organisation to talk to might be agronomists because the majority of the agronomists who would advise us on the technical aspects of our courses are definitely steering people away from the heavy nitrogen applications.

(Greens Convenor [12])

In the green keeping industry there is stuff going about that we can all use, then again you are restricted by what you can afford and what you cannot. There are always new developments coming through and eventually there is going to be a reduction in the use of chemicals that we are going to have to find a way around.

(Greenkeeper [9])

Energy consumption such as annual heating costs of £12,000 remains a key issue on the organization's agenda with proposals to leverage both the renewable energy value and carbon credit value of its Sitka spruce woodland. Sitka spruce is a conifer native to North America and was introduced to Britain in 1831 because of its incredibly fast growth of up to 80 m in 40–60 years; it has increased the popularity of its use in commercial timber plantations in upland areas [24]. A recent study has highlighted this fact that Sitka spruce biomass growth increases in conditions of high atmospheric CO_2 concentration under fertile soil conditions [25]. This evergreen conifer provides an additional benefit as a haven for wildlife such as deer, foxes, and birds as well as its vital role in carbon sequestration with annual net uptake of carbon ranging from 7.30 to 11.44 t C/ha/yr (tons of carbon per hectare annually) through absorption of carbon in the soil, wood, bark, and foliage [24, 26]. Sitka spruce in particular is known for its versatility as a timber source in shipbuilding, pallets, and paper making due to the white color of the wood and its long cellulose fibers [24]. Besides carbon sequestration and traditional role as timber, Sitka spruce has an ascribed "*social value*," which is defined as "the benefit in savings from damage avoidance" in relation to the effects of climate change when expressed in economic terms—per-hectare mean net present value (NPV) of sequestered carbon for Sitka spruce was calculated at £2311 annually [27].

Sitka spruce was planted on the site of the Moffat Golf Club during the 1980s to be eventually sold as construction material for mining pits. The matured trees in the absence of felling now shade the course and are a safety hazard due to the likelihood of trees falling during strong wind conditions. The intended market for the timber no longer exists as a result of the closure of many coal mining operations in the United Kingdom in the late twentieth century. Therefore, collaboration was sought with the local sustainability charity Let's Live Local to review the possibility of harvesting the woodland for fuel through the establishment of a firewood processing plant in the town. Firewood would be sold locally and provide jobs to the unemployed in the community with the added benefits of minimal disruption to the golf course scenery and reduced heating bills through the use of biomass energy:

It cost us 12000 a year to heat this building we have got thousands of those Sitka spruce trees out there all of which are five years off from being ready to harvest that's a crop that's not the environment that's a crop if those were oak trees then that is the environment the Sitka spruce they are a crop they are no different from pulling the carrots up at the end of the year from your garden. Those need to come out because if they don't they will fall down the wind will blow them down so what do we do with them well in the past when they were planted 30 years ago we were going to sell them for pit props ... guess what no pits. They are rubbish every one of them there is no use for those trees other than possibly firewood. We are talking with Moffat Let's live Local with a view to them setting up a firewood processing unit in the town sounds very grand it would be a yard with a fire wood machine. We would harvest (the spruce) and they will be processed into firewood and sold to people in the town. So worst it will travel one and half miles down that hill be processed and travel half mile on average to the households who will use them as fuel I am happy if that works we have a return they have a return we then go to wood burning here (on site) and they then process our firewood.

(Greens Convenor [12])

The management of the golf club extended its search for solutions to harvest this woodland resource by inviting a specialist company who proposed an industrial approach at no upfront costs involving the processing of the timber and the conversion of less profitable bark into wood fuel to be sold to the golf club for biomass energy use. This option was rejected due to minimal perceived benefit to the organization:

They were going to come in and cut our trees.... thousands at a time as we have thousands of trees, bringing heavy machinery across the golf course taking the trees away ... they remove the usable timber from the middle and then process the waste and sell it back to you at £80 per ton its nonsense of course we did not go for it.

(Greens Convenor [12, 28])

With inability to source an acceptable solution to releasing embodied energy and financial benefits from its woodland assets, the organization then focused on opportunities in carbon trading, which is defined as *the buying and selling of carbon credits* [28]. These *carbon credits* also known as *carbon offsets* are *quantities of sequestered carbon claimed against CO_2 emissions* [24]. The U.K. Government policymaking is presently focused on providing credits and incentives for new forestry initiatives under the Forestry Commission's Woodland Carbon Code, a voluntary scheme that assesses a forestry project for its contribution to *biodiversity*, *ecological impact*, and *additionality*—the need for financing to ensure success, risk management, and carbon capture measurement [12]. This policy stance excludes the carbon sequestration benefits provided by existing forest and woodland in the United Kingdom, thereby disadvantaging the golf club as the organization that can neither sell carbon credits nor offset its operational carbon emissions against its extensive woodland asset:

My frustration is nobody has done an audit of all this forestry to actually see what we are doing to reduce our own carbon impact. The government lets you down initially they said if you have large areas of forestry then we would give you carbon credits which you can trade. Now along with Wishaw Golf Club we were looking very hard and saying we have all this grass and all these trees all of which are converting carbon can we go to BP and sell our carbon credits? No and the reason being we cannot if we had said if we planted 20000 trees can we have those as carbon credits? Yes … I cannot see the sense in that, the 20000 trees today would not be converting as much carbon as these trees for 30 years but we cannot have any credit for what we have got it is for new initiatives. Why is it for new initiatives? … because the politicians who are hoping to be re-elected … and we have had 6 million new trees planted to combat carbon emissions it's all about them sticking badges on than it is about the environment.

(Greens Convenor [9])

The search for cost savings triggered an interest in energy savings and carbon emission reduction, enhancing the organization's understanding of its environmental impacts. Although this sentiment is accepted by both management and employees, technical staff suggest that knowledge of environmental impacts is predetermined by individual motivation, interests, and ability:

It probably would, had I put a bit more time and effort into it … I am a lazy sod and I think I am going to have to look into all these things and to just make myself learn and it is pretty difficult to do this it's like painting the Forth Road Bridge because when you paint one end you have to go back and start again.

(Greenkeeper [12])

Apart from these initiatives, the management and staff at the club have considered investing in innovative soil fertilization techniques that preclude the need for fertilizers also opting for zero-emission electric-powered golf carts as the preferred means of visitor transport on the golf course:

We are constantly looking for different ways to go about our business we spoke with a senior agronomist and he came up with a method … sounds bizarre … you take a large amount of soil 3 tons from your golf course and you put it into a water vat and you leave it to settle and almost ferment and then you feed it back on to your land. You produce a mixture and instead of using fertilizer you apply this mixture back to the land again it is a fertilizer free way of keeping your green surfaces, he wanted £1000 for a plant to set up to make your own mixture we did not go for it because we did not have a spare £1000 but I was very impressed … I would not dream of ever having petrol golf carts on here we have battery operated golf buggies. We do get people occasionally saying that's good, that's better for the environment … No it isn't there is still a power station churning away making the electricity that charges them at night … what we are actually saying is that we are doing good things.

(Greens Convenor [9])

Although proud of having taken the strategic step of measuring its carbon footprint, the organization does not participate in any voluntary reporting schemes due mainly to the financially driven focus of senior management. However, the Greenkeeper views reporting issues to be a consideration at senior management meetings:

Again not that I am aware of … but the Greens Convenor deals with that kind of things at management meetings.

(Greenkeeper [29])

Similar attitudes persist regarding external verification of the golf club's carbon footprint by independent third-party organizations such as the Carbon Trust. Analysis by the Crichton Carbon Centre is seen as sufficient to inspire confidence in the integrity of performance claims outlined in carbon footprint report.

9.4 CRITICAL SUCCESS FACTORS

Golf is a membership-driven sport with popular golf courses exacting a premium fee for membership; however, the golf tourism industry is plagued by overcapacity [29], a hangover from the boom period of the 1990s that witnessed a 20% increase in golf courses while membership increased by only 5%. Tailored packages and payment plans are being used by golf clubs to retain and increase membership in an operating scenario that has seen golf membership decrease [29] by 2.6% in 2008 and 1.9% in 2009. Climate change impacts such as increasingly wet summers have not only affected domestic membership but are also considered a decision-making factor in choosing Scotland as a golf tourist destination [15]. Unsurprisingly, the Moffat Golf Club's customers are not concerned with the organization's carbon emission performance but rather on affordability and the pursuit of self-interest:

> The current membership all vote the way things will suit them because it is a selfish environment on golf courses it is very difficult to get people together as you would find everything is based on how much we can afford as far as the membership is concerned.
>
> (Greenkeeper [9])

Factors such as customer apathy toward sustainability issues and financial constraints have influenced purchasing policy, which does not require suppliers to provide sustainability footprint data. Price sensitivity is an overriding factor in purchasing decisions despite awareness of environmental consequences:

> No, if someone has to haul the sand an extra 30 miles for us to save £5 a ton then that would be fine by us.
>
> (Greens Convenor [12])

The sustainability/CSR dilemma facing the organization is based on the practicalities of operating budgets and its commitment to the environment as a *PBE* [16]. At the heart of this dilemma is limited understanding of the role of sustainability footprints within the organization, which is viewed by senior management as being mainly concerned with emission and fuel reduction:

> It is that reduction in carbon footprint that you can sustain year on year rather than just a short term fix to reduce something so if you reduce your fuel consumption by X this year it is x +1 next year and so on to keep the thing going and not do what they do with the wind farms pretend.
>
> (Greens Convenor [12])

Management and staff view carbon footprint measurement as a useful tool for any organization regardless of its size by identifying opportunities to reduce cost and aid to strategic planning, providing the SMEs with "green credentials" that support marketing and business strategy. However, "green credentials" are not perceived as a lucrative differentiating factor in the golf tourism sector:

> A good question really … it is a useful tool because small to medium sized businesses are interested in reducing their cost so it is a useful tool from that point of view … For those that are in a luxurious position not having to worry too much about the bottom line it is a useful tool to know where you are going and there might just be an element in certain industries not this one where your green credentials could be very good business marketing strategy.
>
> (Greens Convenor [12])

> I think it should be useful to everyone small or big.
>
> (Greenkeeper [9])

Climate change science is considered as a complex subject that has been tarnished by allegations of deception and lack of credibility among its supporters. A clear understanding of the concept has been clouded by the introduction into the debate of additional terminology such as global warming. The validity of carbon footprint measurement however is not being questioned but being perceived as "real" or tangible, requiring teamwork in order to overcome the impact of carbon emissions on the climate, which threatens the survival of the business:

> The climate is definitely seen a huge change in climate so I am hoping we can all work together and try and do something about it because it is certainly not any good for our business.
>
> (Greenkeeper [9])

> It is a very good question carbon footprint is real … climate change is such a woolly concept that I have not signed up to it at all. I think the whole thing needs reviewing … I think it needs to present itself through more credible people than it has done and I think it has got to stop the emotional blackmail of climate change and get into some facts that we could stand and say absolutely right. I can see that the deception that has gone on along with the climate change industry is almost as bad as the MPs expenses. They have got to clean up their act so I totally believe the carbon footprint is measurable there is no argument about that it is scientific you can measure it. The climate change stuff there has always been climate change in one way I have to be careful what I say here the thing that is deceptive is the global warming bit.
>
> (Greens Convenor [12])

The acceptance of the tangible nature of carbon footprint measurement has not translated into the establishment of explicit emission reduction targets. Financial outcomes are considered absolute with all other nonfinancial objectives such as water or carbon footprints as secondary to financial objectives. The Greenkeeper demarcates "greenkeeping" emission targets, which are expressed in operational terms such as reduced consumption of water and chemicals as differing from "general" organization-wide emission targets, which are within the remit of senior management:

> In general again you have to ask Greens Convenor because that goes into management meetings because they will be looking at that. On the golf course side we will be looking to reduce our wastage, to cut back on chemical use of water on the surfaces and keep it to a minimum if we can and maybe in the future look to buy machines that are going to be a lot more friendly to the environment etc. that's something we keep biting away a bit at a time and hopefully we can get their one day.
>
> (Greenkeeper [9])

> If it saves us money ... that's how the targets would be set is if it saves us money ... Carbon reduction would be a secondary outcome.
>
> (Greens Convenor [12])

As a consequence of the absence of emission targets, carbon footprint data is not considered in isolation by the management of the firm but is linked to cost savings that may accrue by the adoption of sustainable alternatives, financial survival not planetary survival, while technical staff suggest carbon management activities to be inherently beneficial:

> Not unless it is linked to financial return. If you don't keep your eye on financial return the organisation ceases to exist and then it contributes nothing ... It has to be survival ... Survival comes first.
>
> (Greens Convenor [12])

> Yes, anything that is going to help in that way is good for any business.
>
> (Greenkeeper [9])

Both management and employees agree that carbon footprint measurement is a value-added exercise that enhances the golf club's reputation and credibility and is an indication of strategic thinking in areas such as reduced chemical use:

> Reputation, credibility and an indication of forward thinking.
>
> (Greens Convenor [12])

Policymaking institutions such as the government and regulating agencies can actively support the value-added initiatives such as carbon footprint measurement by providing grants and requiring carbon footprint measurement as an awarding criterion:

> By making it a condition of giving grants that's their big stick you have got to prove your carbon credentials in order to get a grant. It is as simple as that if you really want to force organizations to do it that's the route.
>
> (Greens Convenor [12])

There is no doubt … if you even go down the road of grants so we can actually get into it properly without the business struggling … we have very little money anyway at the end of the course you have to prioritize things unfortunately if we have a machine that cuts grass and has to be replaced it gets priority over everything else. I think if there were grants available to help people go down that road well … Yes, coming from a small business point of view that would be huge.

(Greenkeeper [9])

9.5 SUMMARY

The organization is financially driven to measure its carbon footprint, macroeconomic issues such as financial crisis, and competitive pressures within the golf industry, invariably influencing decisions to adopt carbon footprint measurement. The cost impact of carbon footprint measurement contributed to a reduction in energy consumption and material and chemical use. Despite these achievements, carbon footprint measurement is considered impossible to fully measure with carbon emission reduction a useful secondary outcome.

Through its efforts to reduce its chemical and fertilizer consumption, the organization has developed an understanding of the symbiotic relationship between the organization and its natural environment. This has led to innovation in golf course land management and water conservation, thus remaining true to the original intent of the golf course designers. A key characteristic of the organization's culture is a curiosity to explore untested ideas in soil management and a willingness to share best practice knowledge through the publication of technical papers. Overshadowing the innovation impact of the golf club are financial constraints that restrict the adoption of new techniques in greenkeeping.

Climate change is viewed as a complex concept mired with credibility issues, while greenhouse gas measurement is considered scientific leading to environmental impact benefits such as cost reduction and improving the organization's green image. Yet environmental impact indicators, for example, carbon emission targets, are not explicit as financial considerations that supersede any nonfinancial concerns.

The Moffat Golf Club's stakeholder impact is evident by the support it provides to the local community and its links with organizations that champion sustainability such as Moffat CAN. Carbon footprint is inextricably linked to financial return as management although championing carbon footprint measurement is price sensitive and may defer carbon emission considerations in favor of lower material prices. The challenging operating environment within the Scottish golf tourism sector and the overall global economic conditions have intensified the sustainability/CSR dilemma of "profits or the environment" for managers of this historic golf club.

Using the lens of the Sustainable Strategic Growth Model (Fig. 9.2), the approach adopted by the management of the Moffat Golf Club follows the path of *learn, develop, implement, optimize,* and *sustain.* Technical expertise in greenhouse gas measurement was sourced from the Crichton Carbon Centre with land management advice sourced from local agronomists. Internal organizational carbon management capability was fostered in the role of Carbon Champion, which was entrusted on the Greens Convenor showing the commitment of senior management to sustainable growth. In spite of this commitment, the *philosophical challenge* (Fig. 9.2) emerges when purchasing decisions are dictated by lowest costs rather than lowest environmental impact. Opportunities were explored to leverage internal capabilities and resources through partnerships with local sustainability-focused charities such as Moffat CAN and Let's Live Local.

The presence of these charities created an operating environment that ameliorated decision-making dilemmas caused by the *cultural challenge* (Fig. 9.1) as employees who are also community members were already sensitized to sustainability issues. Senior management initiated implicit policies that engendered the implementation of a benchmark greenhouse gas report. The greenhouse gas report revealed opportunities to improve efficiency in areas such as energy efficiency and water conservation.

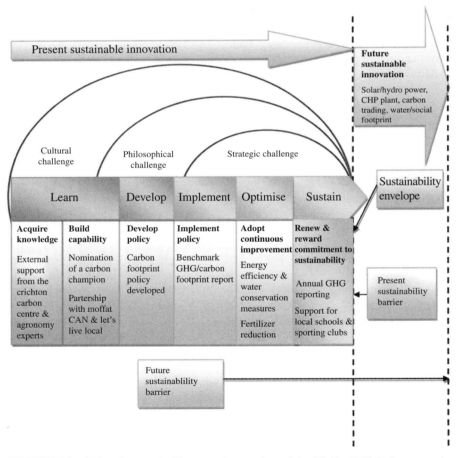

FIGURE 9.2   Using the sustainable strategic growth model—Moffat Golf Club case study.

Moffat Golf Club by improving fertilizer use through better soil management techniques, simultaneously also reduced operating cost. The organization demonstrates its commitment to sustainable growth by annual greenhouse gas measurement and reporting its performance to all stakeholders along with volunteer activities with local charities providing an opportunity to promote the organization to the wider community and foster goodwill among stakeholders.

Early efforts to pursue opportunities to innovate in through developing, for example, hydropower, carbon trading can move the organization beyond the present sustainability barrier but require capital investment and favorable government policy changes. The Moffat Golf Club's present success is a combination of being designed with sustainability in mind by its founders and foresight by present management to return to its roots—sustainability.

REFERENCES

[1] Scottish Government. A low carbon economic strategy for Scotland: Scotland—A low Carbon Society; 2010.

[2] Scottish Golf Tourism Market Analysis Report. Scottish Enterprise; 2009.

[3] Tourism Scotland 2020. The future, in our hands, Scottish Enterprise. Available at http://www.scottish-enterprise.com/~/media/SE/Resources/Documents/STUV/New%20Tourism%20Industry%20Strategy.pdf. Accessed Feb 27, 2013.

[4] Moffat Golf Club Brochure 2011.

[5] Turnbull WR. *The History of Moffat: With Frequent Notices of Moffatdale and Annandale.* Glasgow: William Gilchrist; 1871.

[6] Royal Commission. On ancient and historical monuments in Scotland; 2012. Available at http://canmore.rcahms.gov.uk/en/site/48397/details/coats+hill/. Accessed Nov 13, 2012.

[7] Unknown. Moffat Website. Available at http://www.moffatgolfclub.co.uk/. Accessed Nov 13, 2012.

[8] Crichton Carbon Centre. *Carbon Footprint Assessment for Moffat Golf Club.* Volume 038915; 2010.

[9] Greens Keeper. Interview by author. Edinburgh; Jan 30, 2012.

[10] Unknown. Moffat CAN Website. Available at http://moffatcan.org/index.php?page=home. Accessed Nov 14, 2012.

[11] Unknown. Moffat Online Website. Available at http://www.moffatonline.co.uk/. Accessed Nov 14, 2012.

[12] Greens Convenor. Interview by author, Edinburgh; Jan 30, 2012.

[13] Dumfries and Galloway Council. Dumfries and Galloway Local Economic Forum. Dumfries and Galloway Economic Development Strategy; 2008. p. 1–40.

[14] Trump Golf Scotland. Available at http://www.trumpgolfscotland.com/. Accessed Nov 15, 2012.

[15] Scottish Enterprise. Scottish Golf Tourism Market Analysis Report; 2009.

[16] Dickson B, Watkins D, Foxall J. The working partnership: SMEs and biodiversity. Cambridge: Fauna & Flora International; 2007.

[17]   CEER. Centre for Enterprise and Economic Research. Final Report for BERR Enterprise Directorate: SMEs in a Low Carbon Economy 2009.

[18]   Qian Y. Can Turfgrass sequester atmospheric carbon? Assessment using long-term soil testing data. *TPI Turf News* March/April 2003, p. 23.

[19]   Sahu R. Technical assessment of the carbon sequestration potential of managed turf-grass in the United States. Research Report. Available at http://opei.org/new-study-shows-responsibly-managed-lawns-reduce-carbon-footprint/. Accessed Dec 12, 2012.

[20]   Unknown. Moffat CAN Climate Webpage. Available at http://moffatcan.org/index.php?page=climate. Accessed Nov 28, 2012.

[21]   Allen SR, Hammond GP, McManus MC. Prospects for and barriers to domestic micro-generation: a United Kingdom perspective. Appl Energy 2008;85:528–544.

[22]   Strachan PA, Lal D. Wind energy policy, planning and management practice in the UK: hot air or a gathering storm? Regional Stud 2004;38(5):549–569. DOI: 10.1080/0143116042000229311.

[23]   Wood S, Cowie A. A review of greenhouse gas emission factors for fertilizer production. IEA Bioenergy Task 38, 2004;1(1):1–20.

[24]   Forestry Commission, Sitka Spruce webpage. Available at http://www.forestry.gov.uk/forestry/INFD-5NLEJ6. Accessed Nov 29, 2012.

[25]   Murray MB, Smith RI, Friend A, Jarvis PG. Effect of elevated [CO2] and varying nutrient application rates on physiology and biomass accumulation of Sitka spruce (Picea sitchensis). *Tree Physiol* 2000;20:421–434.

[26]   Black K, Bolger T, Davis P, Nieuwenhuis M, Reidy B, Saiz G, Tobin B, Osborne B. Inventory and eddy covariance-based estimates of annual carbon sequestration in a Sitka spruce (Picea sitchensis (Bong.) Carr.) forest ecosystem. Eur J Forest Res 2005;126(2):167–178. DOI: 10.1007/s10342-005-0092-4.

[27]   Brainard J, Lovett A, Bateman I. Social & Environmental Benefits of Forestry Phase 2: Carbon Sequestration Benefits of Woodland Report. Edinburgh: Forestry Commission; 2003.

[28]   Broadmeadow M, Matthews R. Forests, carbon and climate change: the UK contribution. UK: Forestry Commission; 2003. p. 1–12.

[29]   Scottish Golf Union. SG Update Winter 2011, p. 5–7.

10

RABBIE'S TRAIL BURNERS: CARBON-FRIENDLY SIGHTSEEING AND TOURS

10.1 INTRODUCTION

Rabbie's Trail Burners Ltd is an award-winning SME in the Scottish tourism sector achieving the Vision in Business for the Environment of Scotland (VIBES) Award in 2011 Scotland's highest environmental accolade. The company has been operating small tours initially for elderly visitors since 1993 with a maximum of 16 individuals for each coach trip. Since then, the organization has rapidly expanded to 13 full-time staff and a vehicle fleet consisting of 16 modern Mercedes minicoaches and 1 people carrier [1, 2]. This focus on small tour groups and personalized service has yielded dividends helping the company achieve £3.4 million turnover in 2011 with 40,000 satisfied customers choosing the company to provide unique holiday experience [3]. However, this strategy was a result of necessity rather than planning as the company's founder and Managing Director Robin Worsnop explains [3]: *"It was a trying time because I didn't have any money—I made about £4000 profit that was what I lived on."*

As Chairman of the Edinburgh Tourism Action Group (ETAG), a tourism industry body, the firm's Managing Director actively champions innovation in the Scottish tourism sector recently contributing to the development of a 3-year strategy to maintain Edinburgh's position at the forefront of the United Kingdom's tourism industry. In his own business, he has pursued a similar 5-year growth strategy through the development of pilot operations first in Ireland and then the rest of the United Kingdom [3].

Sustainability Footprints in SMEs: Strategy and Case Studies for Entrepreneurs and Small Business,
First Edition. Lowellyne James.
© 2015 John Wiley & Sons, Inc. Published 2015 by John Wiley & Sons, Inc.

Philosophically, the firm's approach to sustainability is grounded in the concept of "small is beautiful" first postulated by E.F. Schumacher but operationally applied within the business through the use of small coaches and local tour guides that provide visitors with access to remote and exciting places such as the Scottish Highlands [1, 2]. In an attempt to lure visitors away from using their own cars, the firm provides an accommodation booking service that caters for individual tastes ranging from local hotels to hostels [3]:

> Effectively what it does is put that money directly into that community, traditional tours have a hotel owned by the operator and the profits are extracted out of the community. This allows our customers to stay in small places and meet the local people.
>
> (Managing Director [3])

This concern for the impact of the business on its wider community has formed part of the organization's ethos since the establishment of its first office near Edinburgh Castle, which provided an outlet for local artisans [3]. Unsurprisingly, the management of the organization opted to pursue carbon footprint measurement in 2010 in an effort to demonstrate its continued commitment to environmental best practice. From the company's staffing complement of 13 individuals, the Sales Manager is entrusted with the role of "Carbon Champion." Within the remit as Sales Manager is the responsibility for the measurement of the carbon footprint of office activities.

> I measure the office Carbon footprint.
>
> (Sales Manager [4])

Therefore, Sales Manager is aptly placed to provide insight into the contribution of sustainability footprint measurement to the success of the business and highlight the factors critical to successful implementation.

10.2 CONTEXT

In 2011, revenues generated from tourism-related activities contributed £11bn to the Scottish economy including creating over 200,000 jobs [5]. Despite good performance, the tourism sector hopes to increase visitor spend by £5.5–£6.5 billion through the promotion of Scotland's natural scenery, heritage, and activities such as hill walking, castle visits, and mountain climbing, which are key assets to be developed to enhance visitor experience [5]. The Scottish tourism sector is renowned for the quality of its customer experience however seeking to deliver this capability by growing sustainably [5]:

> In tandem with shaping a better quality visitor experience, we will also be building a more sustainable industry. Because this is not a strategy for growth at any cost, this is a strategy for sustainable growth—economic, environmental and social. [5]

The company has adopted sustainability footprint methodologies such as the carbon footprint for altogether altruistic reasons involving considerations regarding the economic, social, and environmental impact of its operations on its various stakeholder communities with the aim being *"To measure how sustainably we were operating"* [4]. As a result, unsurprisingly, the firm's carbon footprint regularly features on the agenda at management meetings.

Carbon footprint measurement is seen as an extension of the firm's environmental policies articulating their commitment not within the narrow definition of contemporary notions of the environment but as *responsible policies* [6] highlighting the synergistic role of the environment, community, and visitors to the business as a *probiodiversity enterprise (PBE)* [7].

The importance of visitors to the business cannot be underestimated as statistics of the coach tourism segment indicate average visitor annual spend of £96m for the period 2008–2011 mainly due to an expansion of the "staycation" market consisting of British-based tourists [8]. However, this sense of stability does not reflect the overall decreasing spending levels by visitors [8]. The reduction of visitor spends within the coach tour segment of the Scottish tourism sector is considered to have affected the organization's carbon footprint due to the reduced operational activity and hence lower emissions.

In the face of static overall growth within the coach tour segment, senior management of the organization have not quantified the costs of conducting greenhouse gas (GHG) measurement to the business as it is perceived as a routine exercise:

Unsure—the time taken to do it has not been calculated—we do this on a regular basis.

(Sales Manager [4])

Even though GHG measurement is routinely conducted by the organization, the initiative is not specifically stated in the organization's policies but is captured within statements that reflect practical steps undertaken by the organization to reduce its GHG emissions such as efficient tour scheduling to avoid traffic congestion and recycling [1]. The firm's *responsible policies* are drafted in customer-friendly language with the absence of environmental jargon; a similar approach has also been used to communicate their commitment to sustainable best practice to customers through a bespoke visitor's guide [2].

Despite this user-friendly approach adopted by the organization's management in communicating their commitment to reducing carbon emissions, there is a perceived barrier in placing carbon footprint reduction on the agenda due to varying interpretations of the concept and purpose of carbon footprints that influenced sentiments such as *"Everyone's understanding of carbon footprint"* as stated by their Sales Manager [4].

10.3   CONTRIBUTIONS TO GROWTH

Aligned to the owner's passion for sustainable growth, the company initiated carbon reduction policies in 2007, firstly by creating a new key performance indicator (KPI) expressed as liters of fuel used per passenger for 100 km traveled. This initiative was extended to include the calculation of the firm's carbon footprint; these early calculations were later refined by students participating in the Carbon Master's Program, a joint project between the University of Edinburgh and Scottish Business in the Community (SBC) to provide businesses with postgraduate student interns who conduct short-term projects in areas of carbon management [1]. Using the technical support provided, the carbon footprint reporting boundaries were defined using DEFRA's carbon footprint measurement framework guidance [1]. The data received from the firm's information management systems was subsequently categorized within organization's carbon reporting boundaries that were defined as follows [1]:

Scope 1—Fuel consumption for vehicles
Scope 2—Electricity consumption
Scope 3—Water consumption and waste disposal

However, these carbon reporting boundaries are expressed by practitioners within the organization in operational terms: *"Measuring fuel, miles, passenger numbers, electricity, water, waste, recycling"* [4].

For the reporting period March 2009–February 2010 [1], Scope 1 activities of the business accounted for 433 CO_2e tons of emissions, Scope 2 activities accounted for 8.8 CO_2e tons of emissions, and Scope 3 emissions accounted for 0.6 CO_2e tons of emissions resulting in combined total emissions of 442.4 CO_2e tons of emissions (Fig. 10.1). Vehicle fuel consumption accounts for 97.9% of the carbon footprint and is the main component of the organization's GHG emissions due to the key operational activities of the business being concentrated on minicoach tours (Fig. 10.1). Electricity consumption accounts for 2% of carbon footprint and is the main component of Scope 2 GHG emissions, while Scope 3 emissions account for 0.1% of the carbon footprint (Fig. 10.1).

Although the Rabbie's Trail Burners has been monitoring and measuring various components of its carbon footprint since 2007, the company began using DEFRA's guidelines in 2010 to generate its carbon footprint reports.

The company has pursued a two-pronged KPI strategy firstly in terms of monitoring the liters of fuel used per passenger for 100 km traveled, a consumption-based indicator that serves a dual purpose aimed at reducing fuel consumption and carbon emissions per passenger, and secondly by ensuring that each travel tour bus operates at full capacity, thereby helping to reduce overall carbon emissions per passenger.

Disclosure of the firm's carbon management performance through carbon footprint reporting is considered to have a dual purpose both internally as part of the quality management process to verify the achievement of KPIs and externally to communicate the firm's green credentials to its stakeholder base.

Sustainability reporting within the company is biased toward carbon footprint measurement with water consumption being converted to a common reporting language of CO_2e within which water consumption data and social impact value of its business activities are expressed. This use of CO_2e as an all-embracing sustainability measurement in the absence of the use of water footprint and social footprint methodology is borne from a focus on fuel reduction that comprises the majority of the firm's environmental impacts [1].

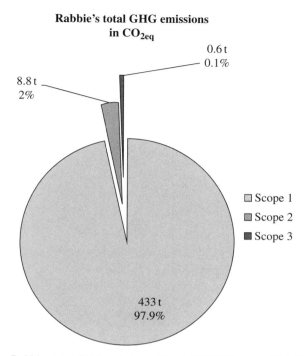

FIGURE 10.1   Rabbies total GHG emissions, March 2009–February 2010. Source: Rabbie's Trail Burners.

Among the organization's environmental impacts [1], water usage arising from the operational activities of the firm consumed 103 m^3 of water accounting for 108 kg CO_2e emissions during the period 2009–2010. The expression of water consumption in CO_2e and the common understanding of carbon impacts within the firm spurred the implementation of water conservation techniques by the organization such as *mixer tap water saving adaptors* that provide a 70% reduction of water usage when compared to conventional water faucets improving both water consumption and reducing the organization's carbon footprint. This initiative has helped reduce water consumption at the company's head offices [9] from 7.9 to 3.8 m^3/person/year, which is nearly half of the Environment Agency's best practice guideline of 6.4 m^3/person/ year. However, despite these phenomenal gains the firm does not actively calculate the impact of its water consumption using water footprint methodology but may factor as a future sustainability initiative as suggested by the firm's management representative: *"We measure our water so could potentially look in to this"* [4].

Similarly, the organization's social impacts are viewed from a carbon emission perspective with the alignment of carbon reduction goals to social programs through the imposition of a self-imposed *carbon tax* donating £10 to local and national charities for every ton of carbon emissions generated from business operations [2]. An innovative strategy that combines carbon management objectives with the sustainability aims of the business and provides an alternative to carbon emission offsetting.

(a)

Total distance travelled	1,312,403 km
Total fuel used	162,271 l
Total passengers	5,098
Total absolute GHG emissions	434 tons CO_2eq
GHG emissions per passenger	85 kg CO_2eq

(b)

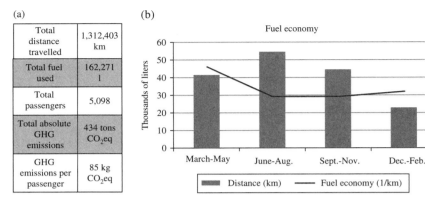

FIGURE 10.2   Rabbie's Trail Burners fuel economy, March 2009–February 2010. Source: Rabbie's Trail Burners.

Carbon footprint measurement as a tool is not considered by the management in itself to have led to the development of new products and services but has improved journey planning and influenced implementation of green fleet policies such as fuel efficiency and better driving practices [2].

The organization's carbon footprint report provides a framework within which the true impact of its main environmental aspects—diesel, water, electricity consumption, inert waste plastic, metal cans, and glass—can be fully understood. As vehicle fuel consumption accounts for 97.9% of the firm's carbon footprint, the management of the organization has instituted green fleet policies such as fleet upgrades every 5 years being fully aware of the possible trade-off between the weight of new diesel mini-coaches and overall fuel economy [2]. Included in this eco-friendly approach to fleet management is a robust vehicle maintenance program supported by behavioral change initiatives such as the provision of ecodriver training to improve fuel efficiency [2, p. 13]. Further analysis of the organization's fuel consumption led to a review of vehicle fuel economy during the period March 2009–February 2010 (Fig. 10.2).

The analysis identified that fuel economy varied on a quarterly basis reflective of the decline in tourists seeking to go on sightseeing trips during the winter months [1]. Seasonal variation in visitor numbers was an additional factor that affected fuel economy including difficult road conditions, engine idling, and low tire pressure due to ambient temperatures [1] whereby a 12 °C drop in temperature can create a 0.4 decline in fuel economy, increased rolling resistance, and aerodynamic drag by 2%. To ensure that the firm fully exploits all potential efficiency savings identified from the process of carbon footprint measurement, the following actions were recommended [4]:

1. *Green Fleet Review from the Energy Saving Trust*—Recommendations from this initiative are projected to reduce the firm's annual carbon emissions by a maximum of 29.3 tons of CO_2e and yield annual cost savings of £14,390 from essentially a free service provided by the Energy Saving Trust, a United Kingdom-based social enterprise organization that helps individuals and businesses reduce their carbon emissions.

2. *Tire assessment*—Tire pressure monitoring can reduce annual emissions by 8.4–21.3 tons of CO_2e with annual savings of £4220–£10,550 at a modest initial investment cost of £3363 for tire pressure equipment.

3. *Purchase of fuel tracking software*—The use of software to manage fuel consumption is estimated to reduce carbon emissions by 8.4–16.9 tons of CO_2e, providing annual savings of £4220–£8440 for an initial investment of £10,837.

Although electricity consumption accounts for only 2% of carbon emissions, the company has continued to actively monitor this environmental aspect of their business activities since 2005. The measurement of the firm's carbon footprint provided an opportunity to analyze electricity consumption patterns over a 3-year period, March 2007–February 2010 (Fig. 10.3).

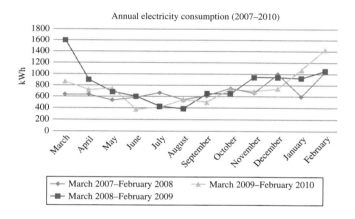

Month	Electricity use (kWh)
March-09	1,597
April-09	1,330
May-09	1,380
June-09	691
July-09	758
August-09	1,014
September-09	926
October-09	1,343
November-09	1,279
December-09	1,353
January-10	1,977
February-10	2,633
Total	**16,281**

FIGURE 10.3 Annual electricity consumption, 2007–2010. Source: Rabbie's Trail Burners.

Figure 10.3 illustrates expected seasonal increases in electricity consumption during winter months except for March 2008 during which there was an abnormal increase in consumption that differed from expected trends. To improve the organization's energy performance, the management of the firm searched for opportunities to improve the thermal properties of the building, but these were limited including potential improvements in the building's infrastructure in areas such as lighting where T5 fluorescent lighting is used affording improved luminal efficiency of 84 lm/W and a 25% reduction in energy consumption when compared with T8 fluorescent lighting. The possibilities of applying engineering solutions being fully explored management then embarked on a behavioral change campaign that focused on empowering employees to actively participate in the energy reduction through the shutting down of heating appliances, computers, and electrical equipment using creative but subtle communicative devices such as "reminder" stickers.

Senior management affirms the support for carbon performance disclosure by stating a resounding "*Yes Mayday/GTBS*" [8], highlighting their active participation in two voluntary carbon reporting schemes: the Mayday Network established by the SBC, a Prince's Trust charity, and the Green Tourism Business Scheme developed in 2001 in conjunction with Visit Scotland and a consortium of private sector partners. Voluntary carbon reporting is considered by senior management of the organization as a form of external verification and provides an opportunity to showcase the firm's environmental initiatives to its customers and other key stakeholders.

10.4 CRITICAL SUCCESS FACTORS

The organized coach tour market has remained relatively stable despite the operating challenges created by the global financial crisis generating an average of 362,000 trips during the period 2008–2011 and the preferred form of travel used by 33% of international visitors [8] yet witnessing reductions in visitor spend during the same period [8]. Despite its popularity, organized coach tours face increased competition from alternative forms of transport such as car hire and public transport, while fuel costs have been steadily increasing [8]. The sector's aging customer base consists mainly of over 55's who regard "meeting people" and "value for money" as key reasons for choosing organized coach travel [4]. Initially, the firm's pursuit of carbon footprint measurement was to identify opportunities to reduce operating costs such as fuel and energy use and not a reactive response to customer requirements who are seeking value from their travel expenditure. Information from a subsequent customer satisfaction survey conducted by the company seems to suggest that customers' views are shifting and organizational environmental credentials are an influencing factor when selecting coach tour hire.

Conversely, the provision of sustainability footprint data is not a requirement of the Rabbie's Trail Burners subcontractor selection process. This may have arisen from a limited interpretation of the concept underpinning sustainability footprints to the exclusion of supply chain emissions although sustainability footprints are perceived by management as being aligned to sustainable development [8].

Carbon footprint measurement as a tool has provided direct benefits to the firm in three areas:

- *Carbon emission reduction* through coach tour journey planning and the use of public transportation by staff.
- *Energy savings*—Engine remapping, ecodriver training, and the purchase of fuel-efficient vehicles have contributed to £28,165 reduction in fuel consumption in 2010.
- *Marketing* through the enhancement of the firm's green credentials.

The realization of these benefits is due to the continued commitment by the management of the organization to sustainable development and stewardship of natural resources, fostered by a benign understanding of the connection between organizational environmental impacts and climate change [4].

This commitment to sustainable growth is evidenced by the institution of "stretch" targets for carbon management performance. The company aims to maintain its fuel consumption, *"Keeping below 0.99 liters of fuel per customer 100km travelled"* [8].

The success of the implementation of Rabbie's Trail Burners sustainability initiatives has ensured that fuel consumption in 2010 was 0.905 liters of fuel per customer for 100 km traveled, an accomplishment that is even more spectacular when compared to the fuel efficiency of 6 liters per 100 km for a contemporary automobile [4]. Financial benefits arising from energy savings and carbon emission reduction are influencing factors that have led senior management to perceive carbon footprint measurement as a good investment of the firm's resources.

10.5 SUMMARY

Carbon footprint measurement specifically is considered a critical value to Rabbie's Trail Burners operations helping the firm to differentiate its product/service offering as a green tourism provider. The organization's eco-friendly approach to coach tour operations has not gone unnoticed by its external stakeholders such as the tourism industry and the Scottish Government achieving numerous accolades for sustainability and environmental management such as:

- Green Tourism Business Scheme—Gold Award
- VIBES Award 2011
- 2011 VESTAS European "Outstanding example" of Sustainable and Responsible Tour Operator
- 2011 Winner Big Tick—Climate Change Award—Business in the Community
- Scottish Thistle Awards 2010—Winner of the Award for Innovation
- VIBES Award 2009
- Keep Edinburgh Clean—Gold Award since 2007

These awards have not only raised the profile of the organization but confirm the value of sustainability footprint measurement in enhancing the marketability of its services as a coach tour operator:

> For us fuel efficiency, to measure the company's success/costs etcetera.
>
> (Sales Manager [4])

As an SME, the firm is driven to measure its carbon footprint mainly to improve fuel efficiency and reduce costs but also as a yardstick of the company's overall success. However, the management of the firm is keen to highlight opportunities for policymaking institutions to contribute to the adoption of sustainability footprint measurement tools such as the carbon footprint through the provision of consultancy services that can assist SMEs with the understanding and measurement of carbon

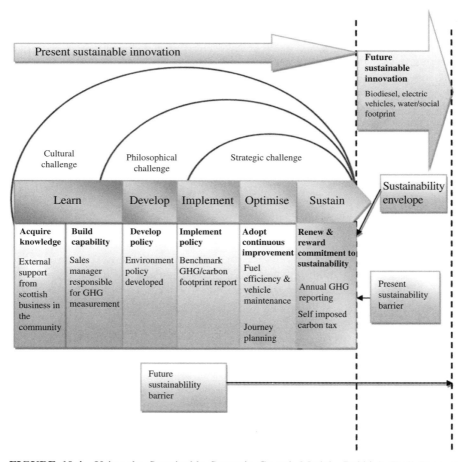

FIGURE 10.4   Using the Sustainable Strategic Growth Model—Rabbie's Trail Burners case study.

emissions advising: *"Make it easier—offer a service to help companies understand it or a service to measure it for the company"* [4].

Recent U.K. policy shift to mandatory carbon emission reporting for listed companies' signaling intent within the policymaking landscape is yet to be conveyed to decision makers within SMEs. Clarity of policymaking expectations and intent is crucial to enable entrepreneurs to incorporate carbon-related risks within business strategic planning.

The Sustainable Strategic Growth Model (Fig. 10.4) provides a framework within sustainability risks, for example, GHG emissions can be easily understood. Driven by an entrepreneurial commitment to sustainability, the *philosophical challenge* was inconsequential; however, management faced a *cultural challenge* to build a sustainability culture within the organization and a *strategic challenge* making profits realizable from the pursuit of sustainable goals (Fig. 10.4). Senior management sourced external support from the SBC mainly for methodological verification of in-house calculations of the organization's carbon footprint. The appointment of the Sales Manager as Carbon Champion facilitates the *learn* aspects of the model.

Sustainability is at the heart of the Rabbie's Trail Burners approach to tour guide operations with environmental policies in place that direct senior management decision making. The implementation of carbon footprint measurement revealed opportunities to improve performance through reduced fuel and energy consumption. Organizational focus on annual GHG reports and the imposition of a voluntary carbon tax on emissions assists in embedding their commitment to sustainable growth.

The *sustainability barrier* (Fig. 10.4) can only be transitioned by investment initiatives, for example, use of alternative low-carbon emission fuel such as biodiesel, deployment of electric vehicles within the organization's fleet, and transition to solar energy, thereby requiring the organization to *learn, develop, implement, optimize,* and *sustain* performance to overcome a *future sustainability barrier.*

REFERENCES

[1]   Carbon Footprint and Audit Report for Rabbie's Trail Burners 2011.

[2]   Green Transport Case Study—Rabbies Travel Tours 2011.

[3]   Bain S. Rabbie's tours founder sets sights on expansion, Herald Scotland. Available at http://www.heraldscotland.com/business/company-news/rabbies-tours-founder-sets-sights-on-expansion.16504949. Accessed Feb 27, 2013.

[4]   Sales Manager. Rabbie's Trail Burners, email, 2011 Nov 30.

[5]   Tourism Scotland 2020. The future, in our hands. Scottish Enterprise. Available at http://www.scottish-enterprise.com/~/media/SE/Resources/Documents/STUV/New%20Tourism%20Industry%20Strategy.pdf. Accessed Feb 27, 2013.

[6]   Rabbies. How do you protect the environment and communities we visit; 2013a. Available at http://www.rabbies.com/tours_vacations_faqs/protect_environment.asp?lng. Accessed Feb 27, 2013.

[7]   Dickson B, Watkins D, Foxall J. The working partnership: SMEs and biodiversity. Cambridge: Fauna & Flora International; 2007.

[8]   Coach Tourism in Scotland Market Size & Profile. Visit Scotland. Available at http://www.visitscotland.org/pdf/Coach%20Tourism%20in%20Scotland%20-%20Market%20Size%20and%20Profile%20%282%29.pdf. Accessed Feb 27, 2013.

[9]   Environment Agency. How much water we should be using? Environment Agency; 2013. Available at http://www.environment-agency.gov.uk/business/topics/water/34866.aspx. Accessed Mar 10, 2013.

11

CONCLUSION

The evolution of the concept of corporate social responsibility and sustainability from sustainability/CSR awareness to sustainability/CSR integration reflects global society's concern over increasing dependence on fossil fuels to generate the energy that powers our homes and businesses, the effects of which have contributed to climate change. Fossil fuel consumption is the unfortunate by-product of our fascination and fixation on the internal combustion engine, a contributing factor to increasing carbon emissions. Growing industrialization of the global society has created both a social and an agricultural phenomenon, and as such, we now live further from our natural resources such as food, water, and fuel through suburbanization. This distancing of human beings from the resources upon which our lives are dependent has led to the desensitizing of individuals regarding the impact of their lifestyles and businesses on our planet. Within this mix, there has emerged the social inequities between the affluent nations and less-affluent nations whose attitudes to sustainability are influenced by cultural factors leading to the exacerbation of poverty despite the availability of resources and access to information. Humanity is slowly coming to terms with the fact that all we have is our little blue planet; there is no "backup" planet. This growing acceptance has created a proliferation of definitions of sustainability and methodologies for achieving sustainable development.

To address the issue of measuring the impact of business (and indirectly our lifestyles) on the planet, practitioners and academics have devised the carbon footprint, social footprint, and water footprint concepts. Each footprint methodology yields its

Sustainability Footprints in SMEs: Strategy and Case Studies for Entrepreneurs and Small Business,
First Edition. Lowellyne James.
© 2015 John Wiley & Sons, Inc. Published 2015 by John Wiley & Sons, Inc.

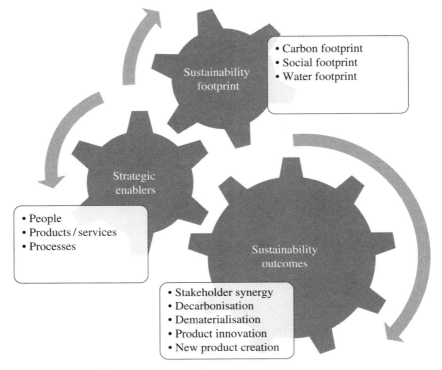

FIGURE 11.1   Sustainability footprint cycle. Source Author.

own benefits but when amalgamated—the **sustainability footprint**—and applied to **strategic enablers**—*people, products/services, and processes*—can lead to *stakeholder synergy, decarbonization, dematerialization, product/service innovation, and new product/service creation*, the new **metrics** of sustainable strategic growth (Fig. 11.1).

The use of carbon footprint methodology among large organizations has been the subject of recent surveys and reports from both governmental and nongovernmental sources. However, the use of alternative sustainability footprint tools, for example, water footprint and social footprint methodologies, has been less well documented. The SMEs profiled are focused on carbon footprint measurement due to either direct or implied supply chain or stakeholder pressure.

The key issue with the use of sustainability indicators such as the carbon footprint is the inability of such tools to confirm whether an organization is sustainable; specifically SMEs are unable to quantify benefits and justify the costs of carbon footprints [1, 2]. Cost differences vary depending on the size of the organization, pay scales of personnel involved in sustainable footprint measurement, reporting scope, organizational policy, the use of external verification, the influence of senior management, and the level of integration. Fundamental to the mainstreaming of sustainability footprints is the verification of sustainability reports to instill confidence of financial markets and society at large, regarding environmental claims and ascribed social benefits [3, 4].

The *Sustainable Strategic Growth Model* supports the adoption of sustainability initiatives within organizations through the identification of the *philosophical challenge, cultural challenge,* and *strategic challenge.* The use of the five steps of *learn, develop, implement, optimize,* and *sustain* helps organizations resolve these challenges and address the four elements of sustainability, namely, *economic, social, environment,* and *information.*

These case studies highlight that individuals demonstrate ambivalent [5] "love/ hate" relationship in regards to sustainability that is dynamic and changes depending on their proximity to the issue, for example, wind farms or sensitivity to environmental issues, which is influenced by their level of awareness of sustainability, socioeconomic group, age, and gender. Demographics aside, sustainability in itself is a concept that is multidimensional of which we have now only awaken to the environmental reality of our inefficient consumption of earth's resources. This multidimensional nature makes it difficult to arrive at a consensus of what sustainability is; however, like quality we know when sustainability is absent. The nature of this ambivalence impacts on the adoption of sustainability initiatives by senior management and the buy-in into sustainability strategy by employees/stakeholders. Therefore, the pursuit of sustainable strategy or the adoption of strategic alternatives may not be based on sustainability-driven business case but is influenced by the perceptual orientation [6] of the strategist, that is, *sustainability positive, sustainability passive,* or *sustainability negative.* Likewise, stakeholder support may not be forthcoming depending on perceptual orientation. Managers should seek to encourage stakeholders, for example, to remain *sustainability positive* in orientation through appropriate training, instruction, supervision, and the promotion of proactive learning [7].

Critically, firms appear unable to quantify the financial benefits of sustainable footprint reporting preferring to draw attention to the nonfinancial benefits, for example, "to be seen as being green." The use of the Sustainable Strategic Growth Model will assist managers in promoting *sustainability positive* attitudes and behaviors thereby realizing the financial benefits that accrue from embedding sustainability strategy in the DNA of the business.

The implementation of sustainability as a core value of the business can build upon existing approaches to quality management. Sustainability/CSR professionals and managers can adopt approaches such as the plan, do, check, and act (*PDCA*) methodology as a framework for finding solutions to the three sustainability/CSR challenges *philosophical, cultural,* and *strategic* [8]. Quality management within its modern reincarnation during the past century has dealt with the same challenges faced by sustainability/CSR professionals in areas such as waste, supplier engagement, safety, identifying the "hidden costs" of poor management, culture change within organizations, and empowerment of staff to achieve customer satisfaction. Sustainability/CSR professionals can benefit from an arsenal of quality models and tools such as cause and effect diagrams, Pareto charts, check sheets, control charts, histograms, scatter diagrams, and flowcharts and Six Sigma [9]. Arguably quality in itself can be considered as having achieved a state of normalization within the modern business context as evidenced by the reduced number of board members specifically dedicated to quality tasks. The quality movement can learn from sustainability/CSR by extending the concept of the "customer" to include global society, intuitively aligning environmental and social concerns with the brand image. Lifecycle analysis may not be a recent approach but the understanding of the symbiotic dependence of man on the planetary ecosystem yields added value to quality management as a philosophical concept, that is, waste is not just a cost to the enterprise but a cost to our global society.

Leading sustainability pioneers such as John Elkington consider sustainability to be the new quality envisaging a convergence between sustainability and quality propelled by a desire to produce "zero defects" as well as "zero emissions" [9, 10]. The materialization of this vision will lead to the development of efficient and effective products/services that not only meet present human needs but will protect the planet for future generations. Sustainability is not "free"; there is cost to the environment although presently socialized but will be borne by future generations if businesses do not adopt a balanced view that incorporates the needs of "economic growth," "ecological balance," and "social responsibility" [11].

REFERENCES

[1] Hicks M. BP: social responsibility and the easy life of the monopolist. Am J Bus 2010;25(2):9–10.

[2] Demos T. Beyond the bottom line: our second annual ranking of global 500 companies. Fortune; October 23, 2006. Available at: http://archive.fortune.com/magazines/fortune/fortune_archive/2006/10/30/8391850/index.htm. Accessed on Jun 29, 2014.

[3] Ball A, Owen D, Gray R. External transparency of internal capture: the role of third-party statements in adding value to corporate environmental reports. Bus Strat Environ 2000;9:1–23.

[4] CEER. Centre for Enterprise and Economic Research. Final Report for BERR Enterprise Directorate: SMEs in a Low Carbon Economy; 2009.

[5] Lewicki R, McAllister D, Bies R. Trust and distrust: new relationships and realities. Acad Manage Rev 1998;23(3):438–458.

[6] DEFRA. A framework for Pro environmental behaviors. Available at https://www.gov.uk/government/uploads/system/uploads/attachment_data/file/69277/pb13574-behaviours-report-080110.pdf. Accessed on Dec 17, 2013.

[7] Van Hijstee M, Glasbergen P. The practice of stakeholder dialogue between multinationals and NGOs. Corp Social Responsib Environ Manage 2008;15:298–310.

[8] Sapru R, Schuchard R. CSR and quality: a powerful and untapped connection. Available at http://www.bsr.org/reports/BSR_ASQ_CSR_and_Quality.final.pdf. Accessed on Mar 4, 2014.

[9] Corporate Sustainability Initiatives. The Next TQM, Korn Ferry. Available at http://www.kornferryinstitute.com/sites/all/files//documents/briefings-magazine-download/Corporate%20Sustainability%20Initiatives%20-%20The%20Next%20TQM%3F%20.pdf. Accessed on Feb 18, 2014.

[10]   Guardian. Is Sustainability the New Quality? Available at http://www.theguardian.com/
       sustainable-business/sustainability-with-john-elkington/sustainability-new-total-
       quality-management. Accessed on Feb 18, 2014.

[11]   Zink K. From total quality management to corporate sustainability based on stakeholder
       management. J Manage History 2007;13(4):394–401.

INDEX

Sustainability Footprints in SMEs: Strategy and Case Studies for Entrepreneurs and Small Business,
First Edition. Lowellyne James.
© 2015 John Wiley & Sons, Inc. Published 2015 by John Wiley & Sons, Inc.